RAGNAROK

'They took everything they wanted by fire and sword,' Caius told her grimly, 'because we'd grown timid from years of civilised living under the protection of Mother Rome! And out of that time of darkness, of chaos, one man came with such a hold over the minds of men that the land mourns him still. Arturius! With his stupendous victory at Badon he did what no other man could do. He took the sword from the Saxon and saved us all!'

She shook her head, her eyes on his dark face. 'Could I –' she hesitated – 'be part of the Fellowship?'

For my husband
Charles Robert
with
love and gratitude

RAGNAROK

Anne Thackery

BANTAM BOOKS
TORONTO · NEW YORK · LONDON · SYDNEY · AUCKLAND

RAGNAROK
A BANTAM BOOK   0 553 17658 7

First publication in Great Britain

PRINTING HISTORY
Bantam edition published 1989

This book is set in 10/11 Erhardt

Bantam Books are published by Transworld Publishers Ltd.,
61-63 Uxbridge Road, Ealing, London W5 5SA, in Australia
by Transworld Publishers (Australia) Pty. Ltd., 15-23 Helles
Avenue, Moorebank, NSW 2170, and in New Zealand by
Transworld Publishers (N.Z.) Ltd., Cnr. Moselle and
Waipareira Avenues, Henderson, Auckland.

Made and printed in Great Britain by
The Guernsey Press Co. Ltd.,
Guernsey, Channel Islands

CHAPTER 1

It was a time of snow and ice-winds that froze the land into stillness and covered the pale green glass of windowpanes with patterns of sharp and delicate beauty, which her grandmother called the flowers of Rhiannon.

The lamps stayed lit, though it was well past noon. In their light Grandmother looked small, old, remote, dozing uneasily amongst the cushions of her wicker chair. Rhianneth sat at her feet, shivering in the warm glow of the brazier with its sweet smell of burning applewood, remembering cold and darkness, and the terror in the night.

A farmhouse, like theirs, had burned. She had seen the blackness of the sky turn red across the meadow, beyond the trees; sparks had fallen like stars, and the moon was swallowed up in smoke. The air had trembled with the crash of falling timbers and glass that shattered into fragments.

But the family had gone, Rhianneth's father had reminded her in his gentle way as he carried her back to bed. There was no danger. The house had stood empty since the Beltain celebrations at the beginning of the summer. He had sent Giff to settle down beside her, but even with her fingers tangled deep into the dog's rough warm coat Rhianneth trembled with cold and fright.

When it grew light enough, she had watched her father and Lovan the bailiff ride out across the meadow towards the burnt-out farm, their horses snorting and tossing their heads at the smoke-tinged air. Geraint and Mostyn from the hill had stayed behind.

Now Rhianneth could hear their voices, coming clear from the kitchen, though the words were muffled by the walls between. She guessed that Olwen had gone to make yet another offering for safety to the powerful god Cernunnos, the Horned One, Lord of the Wild; in her mind she followed her across the frozen stones of the yard, and in her heart she added her fervent prayers to Olwen's. And yet, she reminded herself, her father had gone riding out into the dark winter day, armed with his long hunting knife, and only Lovan was with him. She would not have them know that she was still afraid.

She crouched lower at her grandmother's feet, watching the flicker of light from the pale tallow lamps send masking shadows over the cracked and broken mosaics of the floor. Long, long ago, when the house was young, the picture-floor had been polished by soft Roman house-slippers. Now rough nailed boots scarred it, though she could still trace the delicately coloured figures with her finger. Thick curtains of scarlet merged with the old dark red of the faded wall panels, to create a small world which shut out the winter day. But an east wind had risen sharply since dawn, and now it banged against the wooden shutters and whistled through the cracks until the fire flared and the lamplight wavered.

Her grandmother stirred, turning her head to look at Rhianneth tensed like some small wild thing in cover listening to the howling of wolves outside. She gave her one of her rare smiles, and the child bent her head, trying to shut out of her mind the jagged fears that stalked this quiet room.

'Look into the fire Rhianneth,' she said, 'Do you see that tall mountain, and the great grey forest beneath it? Tell me about the things you see . . .'

It was a game they played, following the shifting shapes within the red fire's heart, a game they kept secret. Rhianneth's father disapproved of much concerned with her grandmother, but Rhianneth was already more her child than he knew. Sometimes Rhianneth saw trees and hills, flowers and lakes, and funny things like cow ears or the grey-muzzled face of their old wolfhound. The warmth of the fire and the slow crooning of her grandmother would weave a caul around her that shut out the sounds of the house, so that all her world contracted into that room, and sometimes even further, into the kingdom of the fire itself.

Then she would see other things. Things that came to her from the depths of the fire, quite unlike the shapes that she herself conjured by imagination from the wood, ash and smoke. These were real, or as a dream may be. For that was how they seemed, like brief and vivid dreams wherein she saw scenes strange to her and people she did not know.

But this day was different. Now the wind sang a wild cold song outside the windows and a sense of unease so filled her that she could find no room in her mind for pictures from the fire. At last Grandmother placed a hand lightly upon her bent head.

'The old wolf is watching you, *cariad*,' she said, knowing as always when Rhianneth was troubled, yet knowing too that the grey wolf of fear had not yet taken her by the throat but still slipped like a shadow through the far corners of her mind.

'You must shut him out. Close your mind to him. You must be the stronger, for it is when he prowls that you will need your fire-dreams most.'

There was silence between them then, while the apple-wood shifted and sparked and the wind moaned round the house. Then she said softly, 'Come, look at this. This is for you, when you are grown and have your woman's strength. It is an old thing of power, and when it is truly yours you will need the fire no longer.'

On a thin chain of gold she held a green stone shaped like a small egg. Dark it was, even in the firelight. Then as it moved beneath her hand Rhianneth saw a sudden blaze of cold fire that vanished as she watched, and came again with its turning. She longed to reach out and touch the stone, to steady the elusive fire that moved far below its sombre surface, but because her grandmother held it she did not dare.

Rhianneth held her grandmother in awe, for she knew that the world encompassed immense unseen realms and was aware of great forces in conflict beyond normal vision,, the tremor of which ran through the lives of men, using and changing them for good or ill. Grandmother knew if the crops would grow or fail, if the horses and cattle would thrive or sicken, for she was an old woman and had the sight, and Earth Mother spoke to her in the firelight.

'You see the flame, Rhianneth?' she whispered, 'That is the power source, and many many see it, but it reaches out only to some. Once it was held by the Nadredd, the Old Ones who knew power from the earth, the force that moves through the forests. Now it is mine, and it will come to you. For as I am, so are you, – daughter of my daughter.'

Her words frightened Rhianneth, although she spoke so softly. For those she called the Old Ones were the Druids, priests of a religion so appalling to the Romans that they had destroyed it long ago, annihilating the priests and their holy women in a final battle for the vipers nest, the sacred island of Mona far to the west.

Grandmother leaned down and put the stone into her hand. As Rhianneth's fingers closed, she felt a stirring begin within the stone, as if secret and hidden beneath the surface stillness it spun and sang.

'What is it, grandmother?' she whispered, at last.

'It is power that you feel, *cariad* . Power that will give you knowledge and strength. But not yet. You are still a child, and Glainnader's power is for a woman to use. You have felt it now, you will hold it again, and the third time it will know you and be yours.'

She took the stone away, roughly covering her granddaughter's hand with her own, never noticing the chap-sores which gave Rhianneth such pain every winter. 'Until then, firelight dreams are safer. They are enough for the very young and the very old – for you and for me – who do not stir in the world away from the fires of our own kind.'

'Will Glainnader keep the raiders away, Grandmother?'

'The glass is a wild thing. It cares nothing for us, for the passing of Gods or of empires. It lives. It is. Time it knows, and truth, the only real powers in existence.'

Rhianneth did not understand. She thought of the Nadredd who had held it once, and had been crushed beneath the might of Rome. Of what use is a magic stone if it will not cast a spell against an enemy?

Almost borne away by the wind, a sound came from outside and the old wolfhound Giff raised his great head abruptly. Springing silently up, he slipped away into the dimly-lit passageway. But his tail slapped against Rhianneth's legs as he went, and she knew he had heard the voice of her father. She scrambled to her feet and ran out into the yard, heedless of the thin layer of freezing snow which crunched beneath her boots.

'Hey, what's this?' her father gently ruffled her hair as she pressed her face against the damp thickness of his cloak, 'You run out into the cold and you'll be gathering Rhiannon's flowers before you know it!'

But as she raised her head she saw that his eyes already looked beyond her, to the men who had followed her out and were waiting near the steps of the wooden verandah. He eased her away and moved towards them, his face sharp with cold and his eyes bleak. Lovan was already leading the horses towards a warm stable and winter hay. He gave Rhianneth a wink, but his smile was brief. Then she saw the third horse, and the third man. They had a visitor. She recognised a neighbour, whose land edged, as did theirs, the pastures of the abandoned farm.

In the warm steamy kitchen Olwen began pouring hot drinks, and the men stood near the hot stove, stamping their numbed feet on the red-tiled floor as they talked. Rhianneth crept unnoticed into a corner and sat on the small three-legged stool that Olwen's husband Griffyn had made specially for her.

'A hunting party, we think – too small for a war band,' her father was saying, 'Probably lost their way and wandered too far west . . .'

'Or hunger may have forced them further afield.' Their neighbour's hands were cupped stiffly round his drink, but his face was beginning to lose its pinched look. He took another sip of the hot spiced wine, precious stuff from the south and only brought out occasionally. 'It will have been a bitter winter in Mercia, too.'

'You've no doubt they were Saxon?' Griffyn's bright dark eyes never left her father's face, 'Not bacaudae – or an odd gang out from the towns?'

Her father shook his head. Lovan came in, shaking the loose snow from his feet at the door, smiling his thanks to Olwen as she hurried up with a steaming cup.

'And the fire? Accident, do you think?' Griffyn persisted, 'A

9

hunting party so far from home would hardly want to draw attention, would it?'

The men moved aside to let Lovan come near the warmth of the stove. Olwen hurried away to set the table for a meal and, no doubt, to reassure Grandmother that the fire had been caused by a lost and careless hunting party, now long gone. As she went, the glow from the kitchen fires turned her brown hair to copper like the thick bracelet on her arm. Rhianneth knew that she should go with her, to help with women's work. But small and hidden in her corner she stayed, her heart beating fast as she watched the faces of the men and entered, for a while, their exciting, dangerous and enigmatic world. Her father drained his cup and put it carefully down on the table. His face looked sharper, older.

'The fire?' he said at last, 'Probably an accident. Or it could have been an offering to their Gods for safe passage home. They'd killed something, maybe a boar. There was blood everywhere. We think the original fire was a small one, made for warmth and cooking . . . you remember that fine picture-floor old Gallicus was so proud of, with the mosaics worked by the firm from Corinium? They built their fire in the centre of it . . . '

'The Mercians are savages,' their neighbour burst out, slamming his fist down so that the table shook and the cups trembled. 'A hundred years has changed nothing. Another hundred won't even touch them! By then they'll be squatting all over the island and using the stones of our cities to build their pig-styes . . . '

He stopped abruptly, for Olwen reappeared and hurried to the stove to give a quick stirring to the big black pot which simmered there. Guiltily Rhianneth jumped up to help her and her father swung around sharply.

'Christos!' he exclaimed, 'I thought you were with your grandmother!'

Somehow, she could not reply. But at that moment Olwen called to her, and giving her a flustered and knowing look she piled plates into her arms and sent her off to put them ready on the table.

The living room was a double one, divided into two by sliding wooden doors, which were never used. The smaller area was shaped in a half-circle, and was raised above the bigger by one step. It had once been an elegant dining room, but now a square wooden table almost filled it, destroying the curved beauty of its lines with brutal practicality. Here they sat before steaming dishes of hot meats and winter vegetables, and large plates of new-baked bread, all on the best family pewter instead of the cheerful red earthenware of everyday use. The talk around the table now was of hunting dogs, cattle and horses, and the poor state of the roads. Treacherous roads here in the west of Britain, whether they were the old trackways or the highways built for the marching Roman legions, for the ancient ways turned to mud in wet weather and the military roads were cracked and sagging, with green weeds spreading across the stones.

After a while Grandmother left the table to doze once more amongst her cushions, and Rhianneth curled up at her feet, resting her head against the edge of her chair. Olwen settled quietly nearby, picking up a tiny garment to mend its seams for her coming child. The men stayed on at the table, their deep voices a comforting background to the high moaning of the wind. Her father, with his scholar's face and work-hardened hands, looked thin and tired in the lamplight. Beside him, Lovan the bailiff seemed strong as an oak. His weatherbeaten face, powerful hands and slow speech were part of the security of Rhianneth's life, of their home. His strength, she was certain, could hold back any menace.

She must have slept for a while, for now Geriant and Mostyn and Olwen's husband Griffyn had gone. The talk at the big table was in everyday speech no longer, but in the liquid phrases of what her father called 'nostra lingua' – their tongue, the tongue of the Romans. This, her mother's people had never mastered, but her father had taught her to speak it well, and to read it too, so that she might know what lay within the ornate copper bindings of his precious books, stored in a large two-doored cupboard of oakwood. Something of importance was being discussed, then. Father used Latin to speak of serious matters. Perhaps he felt it added weight to his words. More probably he was using the caution inbred in those who once ruled this outpost of the Empire.

'You'd not heard, Marcus?' asked their neighbour, and Rhianneth shivered, not liking what she saw on his bluff face. An uneasy glance flashed between her father and Lovan. It was Lovan who answered.

'We heard that Elidyr was calling all Mithrasia to arms. That he intends to claim the kingdom of Gwynedd from dead Maelgwyn's son, Rhun.'

'Elidyr was killed, his force scattered. That she-wolf, his wife Myffan, wanted her brother's kingdom and she's ruined Mithrasia trying to get it. Can Rhun stay still, after such an attack? With Elidyr dead and his only son still a child?'

Her father paled. He looked towards where she sat in the shadows. But it was as if he looked beyond her, into the deeper shadows of things, people and times long gone.

'Elidyr dead?' Lovan spoke into the silence. 'Is it really true? Confirmed?'

'Believe it,' said their guest abruptly, 'Rhun has his head.' Lovan nodded, his eyes on her father, who sat so silent and still.

'There are rumours now,' their neighbour leant forward across the table, his stolid red-veined face made almost sallow by the lamplight, 'that Riderch of the Clyde and his northern allies are making a great noise about sailing to Gwynedd to avenge Elidyr – but they have other motives. You knew that Rhun's brother Bridei now styles himself king of the Picts? A war-bond between Pictland and Gwynedd would threaten the whole north. This is what Riderch hopes to smash before it becomes dangerous. That witch has stirred up fires she won't control, and Mithrasia lies directly in the path of the flames. And what of us – with Mithrasia only two days north and Deva less than a day's ride west?'

'Oh, my God!' her father spoke at last, his words dragging raggedly on the air, 'We are roosters fighting in a barnyard – while the wolf-packs circle outside! We did it once – we united under Ambrosius. And then – Arturius. Christos – the victory he gave us at Badon! A generation of peace! If we had Arturius and his cavalry still . . .'

Their guest's fist thudded down upon the table and Rhianneth jumped, her heartbeats fluttering. 'Gone, Marcus – all dead and gone! And the Saxons know it, – Camlann, the whole bloody mess. Maybe they've held back so long because they could not believe it? Loyalty to their chosen leader is the first rule of their life, and it's their strength.' His mouth turned down. 'Wish to God it was ours!'

There was a pause. Then her father said quietly, 'You won't really leave, surely?'

'Marcus, it's been impossible for years. Can't get enough fodder, can't get enough grain, the markets are falling, the roads are like Hell – well, you know it well enough! Elidyr's son Llywarch is a child, only a couple of years younger than your Rhianneth here. The way things are going he'll soon be dead as his father. And after last night? Come with us, old friend. My people in Isca will set you up – get you going with something again!'

For a moment her father did not answer. His face, still pale, had a look almost of pain. Then he turned his head, and it was gone. 'I can't. I'm sworn to the Caer Melot Fellowship; my brother died for it. Besides,' now his tone was light, and he was smiling faintly, 'my family have farmed from this villa for around two hundred years! Incredible, isn't it? An officer of the 20th Legion out of Deva bought the land and built a small house – there, look, is his discharge in the name of the Emperor,' he gestured towards a small bronze tablet gleaming on the wall, 'Now there was a man Arturius would have been proud to know! He'd been here just about five years when the Painted People broke through the Wall and joined with the Scot and the Saxon to smash through the fortresses at Eburacum and Deva, to spread through the countryside and the towns, burning and killing . . .'

'Times were different then,' their guest interrupted impatiently, 'Pax Romana! Rome ruled – the Legions were here. Order and government could be restored. But now – '

The house went up in smoke thirty years later, when Niall of Ireland came plundering with his war-bands and raided

Deva, Viroconium – all the cities of the west,' Marcus went on as if his friend had not spoken, 'Times were spartan hard then. But they built it again – and improved it! That's when this floor was put in, and the old bathhouse.'

'Which we can't afford to use . . .' murmured Lovan, with a wry smile.

'But it was their land, you see? They had to believe times would get better. It's the only way to hold life together. That's why they stayed on even after the Legions left, when refugees were streaming in from Gaul and every city north of the Alps was burning.'

He spread his hands palm upwards in a gesture that was peculiarly his own, but very Roman. 'And they were right. Times did get better, – not for them, perhaps. But for us who followed them. We've lived under Arturius's peace all our lives! How could I leave at the first sign of trouble? My dead are here on the side of the hill, from that first soldier – to my wife.'

'You're still the same dreamer, Marcus,' broke in their guest bluntly, 'Arturius is gone. Caer Melot has gone, in all but name. The Saxons are moving west again. Rhun must be gathering an army in Gwynedd to strike against the north. In God's name, go to Deva! Or to Mithrasia – you've relatives there, your brother's wife and nephew, isn't it? Out here in the countryside . . .' he drew a deep breath, 'Get behind a stout town wall and run your land from there, for the sake of the living – for your daughter!'

'Towns?' her father gave a rueful smile, 'What is it the Saxons call them – "stone tombs"? Should I take Rhianneth there? To the rubbish and the rats in the streets, the ruined buildings, the robbers and murderers – and the yellow plague? That's what killed great Maelgywn of Gwynedd, you maybe heard?'

He picked up his goblet as if to drain the last of the golden barley-beer, then changed his mind and placed it carefully back on the table.

'We are well away from the roads to Deva or to Mithrasia. Whatever comes of the struggle between Rhun and the northern kings, their armies may well not trouble us.'

Almost in anger their guest rose abruptly to his feet. His eyes looked winter-bleak. 'Oh, they'll come, Marcus. And believe me, after them – the Saxons. Like ravens to the battlefield. But this time there will be no Badon Hill in their path . . .'

Her father and Lovan rode with him to the edge of his land through the darkening afternoon, and with their departure the room grew quiet, with only her grandmother's faint snores and an occasional word between Olwen and Griffyn. Rhianneth's thoughts were with the often-told terror of that long ago northern night when Rome's steel-thin defences had snapped and the barbarians had come swarming over the Wall. Long, long ago. But something of that fear had come into their house, since last night. She had seen it, and something else too, on her father's face.

When he came home at last, she ran into his arms. If he felt her trembling he said nothing, but held her close.

'Is the king really dead?'

His hands tightened. She could hear his heartbeat beneath her cheek. 'Even kings die, Rhianneth.' He said at last, and his voice had a bitter edge.

Rhianneth raised her head. He was not looking at her, but at her grandmother. Her old eyes betrayed nothing, but the hands that gripped the sides of her chair were knuckle-white. There was a strangeness in the air, a haunted, elusive quality which slipped away from Rhianneth like the valley mists.

'Is the queen really a witch, a she-wolf, father?'

His eyes left her grandmother and snapped back to Rhianneth. For a terrifying moment she saw both anger and fear clear within them. Then he swung her down to the floor. 'They are just words, *cariad*. Nothing. Off to bed. We'll be up early tomorrow, there'll be lots of dead wood to collect, after this wind. No, Rhianneth,' he added softly, as she began to protest. There was a sliver of steel in his tone she had never heard before, 'Don't. You wouldn't understand.'

But something she did understand, knew within the deepest fibre of her being. This day held within it strands of the unformed weave which would shape her life. They were

15

here, unseen, twining for the loom, and she felt fear and excitement as must a warrior before the battle. Hidden from her then was that other knowledge, cold as salt-waves and hard as the winter north, which would have filled the night with terror.

From that time Rhianneth was no longer allowed to wander alone to the edge of the woods which bordered their pasture-lands. Her freedom was bounded by the small stream which sparkled through the meadow just beyond the gates. She was a willing captive, for she was haunted by a great fear of what might come out the dark woods, where the black crows circled above, breaking the stillness with their harsh cries.

Spring came late and the fires of Beltain were followed by a cool, wet summer. They had a flurry of joy and excitement when Olwen's son was born at harvest time, just before news came that Riderch and his northern allies had sailed to Gwynedd, burned Arvon, and withdrawn before Rhun could gather his forces. That Autumn the men found Deva's market humming with rumour.

'There are few who think Elidyr's young son Llywarch will hold his father's kingdom,' her father told them, 'now that he's caught between Rhun's fury and the deadly friendship of Riderch of the Clyde.'

Lovan nodded. 'There's a lot of talk,' he said, 'of Rhun's possible invasion of the north from the western sea, – helped by a southward sweep of his brother Bridei's Picts . . .'

Rhianneth's imagination ran riot. The Picts . . . the Painted People of the far north. She knew of those ancient enemies of the Roman Empire. She could picture them gathering to strike from their wild cold land, they who had lain quiet for almost a hundred years, ever since the High King Vortigern had in desperation bribed the land-hungry sea pirates of the Saxon leader Hengist to crush them. A gamble which had laid Britain open to the most dangerous enemy of all.

While the rulers of Britain maneouvered for power, and the sons of Hengist inched westwards across the country, life for Rhianneth continued as it always had, and there were no more alarms to threaten by night. Yet the black shadows of these far

16

off events were already reaching out to draw her into the darkness.

Their neighbour left for Isca and a new life in the deep south-west, far from the Saxon territories. Of his leaving, little was said. But the knowledge of his empty farmhouse and lonely meadowlands shadowed their own isolation.

Rhianneth seemed to live in two worlds, with neither of them completely her own. The shabby farmhouse, the thatched bothies of her relatives on the rise above, the soft mists of rain that made the pastures grow green – these were her real world. Yet in her mind she knew another place of sunlit palaces and pillared temples, of flower gardens and well-kept roads, where art and reason were guarded by heroes of dark shining beauty and impossible gallantry. For her father Marcus could never forget that once his family had been members of the togati, and that his great-grandfather had worn in Deva the wine-edged robe and ruby-set ring of a magistrate. It gave him much pride to see Rhianneth eagerly absorb the thoughts and ideals of great men, both of former times when Greece was powerful in the world, and of their own Empire. Rhianneth tinged and altered in her mind the stories he told her of his young days in Mithrasia before he took over the family farm, until they became part of a golden world which was at once past and yet always with her. She would not acknowledge that at the bitter core of his memories was the longing for a way of life which, except perhaps in the hearts of those who lived at the lonely outposts of Empire, had been dead for over a hundred years, or that the world beyond their small hidden valley was no longer that portrayed by the Roman writers of the past.

Close by the house was an old apple tree which she would often climb and lie along a thick gnarled branch to listen to the wind and the rustling of the sweet-scented and sun-dappled leaves. Here she dreamed her dreams, hidden amidst the swaying foliage and the whispering of the ripening fruit against the leaves. She believed with all the strength she could summon, that somewhere in the world that other life existed still. For the words of her Roman writers never changed.

They were solid things she could hold between her hands. They did not fade into the air like the rumours which filtered out from the cities.

Her father was troubled, she knew. He was a gentle, courteous man, but with some inner retreat which no one ever seemed to penetrate. Perhaps her mother had, once. Rhianneth watched him checking their stores of food and animal fodder, running his hand over the hunting weapons which gleamed so brightly now in the winter light, talking with Lovan, with Griffyn, and with Geraint and Mostyn who no longer went home after the day's work but slept in the farmhouse, as their forefathers had done long ago in prosperous times, but now for very different reasons. Marcus had always made time to teach Rhianneth her lessons. Now he made more, sitting beside her while she read aloud from one of his books, or wrote her thin spiky letters on a wax tablet.

They rode together through the pastures, Rhianneth on her little rough-haired pony that Lovan had taught her to ride as soon as she was able to sit safely. When the horses slowed, bent their heads towards the wet winter grass, Marcus talked to her of times past. Of emperors, wars, and worlds that were lost. Sometimes, as the weather improved, they watched the first stars come out as they headed for home, and he told her of Greece and of Egypt, and of the knowledge that had come out of their ancient cities.

He told her stories of Jesus, of miracles under the hot sun of a far-away province of the Empire over five and a half centuries ago. But if he spoke of God, the Father, Rhianneth grew uneasy. For the Christian god was jealous, and would share the world with no other. Marcus never minded the May blossoms brought in to hang around doorways at Beltain to bring luck and life and fertility. On MidSummer Eve they all went up to the beacon-top to light the fire, and he smiled and drank barley-beer and sang till the first magic streaks of dawn lit the sky. But he did not smile when the Old Ones were spoken of, or Earth Mother, or her horned son, Cernunnos. The Old Gods were powerful indeed, part of the land and the people, and their magic was deep and strong and would not be thrust

18

aside. Rhianneth thought of the offerings she left for their own small Gods of the oakwoods, or for the spirit of the shining stream which crossed the meadow, and wondered if her father knew of them. She did not think he would be pleased, but she had no idea how angry he could become.

When April came Grandmother taught her a rhyme, a young girl's spell from out of the shadowed past, to make the fruit grow thick and full on the apple tree near the door. Round and round the gnarled old trunk Rhianneth went, chanting the ancient, magic words, weaving the sorcery through and around each winter-bare branch. The tree bowed and waved to her; she felt light as a bird, breathing life into every twig, gazing up into its empty arms until the sky began to whirl and she turned dizzy.

Suddenly Marcus was beside her. His face cold and stiff with anger, he dragged her back into the house. Grandmother was spinning the long threads from soft-washed creamy wool, and her hands stilled as her heavy wrinkled lids lifted and her dark old eyes turned towards them.

'This is your doing, old woman!' he said, 'I'll not have Rhianneth chanting prayers to the trees like a pagan slave! She is a Christian, and a citizen of Rome, and she will learn to behave like one!'

'And how is that, Marcus? We are far from Rome here – my granddaughter would need to visit Mithrasia in order to learn the ways of the Romans.'

Her father went white. She felt the sudden surge of pain that rose within him, felt it break from some deep pool of anger and bitterness to slash through time-healed wounds once more. His taut face was unreadable. That secret place inside was sealed forever and not anger, nor love, would unlock it.

'I shall take Rhianneth to be baptised into the church of Christ at the green chapel.' His voice shook. 'She will make no more offerings. No more spells. God asks for nothing.'

'Only her mind, Marcus. And her soul.' Her grandmother's eyes were dark, hooded. 'The small gods she serves as a child are not so greedy. A flower, a fish, is enough. Is my granddaughter able to give so much?'

Marcus swung away, dragging Rhianneth with him. The old woman watched them go, not moving, the long spun thread tangled between her gnarled old fingers.

Next day they rode away through early morning mist, the April frost nipping at their fingers, and an uneasy Lovan riding behind. They travelled along the old straight way which led by flash pool and beacon hill right into the far mountains of Gwynedd. But their journey was a much shorter one, for the green chapel stood hidden in deep forest between two roads to the south of Deva. They safely crossed over the first of these, the lonely military road from Viriconium, soon after clattering across an ancient wooden bridge that shook and creaked over a cold-running river. The forest thickened, and the path narrowed, seeming little more than an animal trail. But ever westward it led, until Rhiannenth felt sure they must soon come upon the second road that the legions had made, the one that ran into Deva from all the old fortresses of the western lands.

Then they came into a clearing. It was ringed about with great oaks, and behind them the forest loomed, dark and crowded. The wooden chapel was small, and so covered with green mosses and lichen and trailing plants that it seemed to have grown out of the forest itself. Here the holy man lived and kept his altar. He welcomed them, and accepted with great dignity the sack of flour, the salted meat and the bottle of finest honey-wine, which they had brought as gifts. The horses were tethered. He led the way into a tiny room, where he knelt before the altar.

There was no painted picture of the holy Mother and Child such as they had at home. This altar was covered with a creamy, finely-woven cloth, and on it stood a single lighted lamp. The rest of the room was bare. Where the timbers joined near the roof, a robin watched with black shining eyes. Rhianneth felt the power of the place rise like an ancient shield around them. The aches of the long ride melted, and a sweet calmness came to her. She stared about, breathing in the smells of the damp wooden walls and the green plants that covered them; through the open door drifted the scent of the ancient oaks that stood so close, mingling strangely with the tang of burning oil from the altar lamp. Her father glanced down at her and she hurriedly lowered her head and said her prayer of safe-coming.

They went through a curtained opening at the back of the chapel, where a fire smouldered on a rough stone hearth. The keeper of the altar lit a small Roman lamp and set it down on a table. Thin as a hazel stick, his bare feet were boney and ingrained with dirt within the loosely-tied sandals of thick leather. His face was high-cheeked and narrow, and his nose was long. But his eyes were kind, and his expression held a strange mixture of gravity and humour for an old scar had twisted his lip into a perpetual smile.

'It's been a killing winter,' Marcus said, rubbing his hands together, 'Did you go back to Deva?'

The keeper swung the sack of flour to a high shelf as easily as if it had been filled with hen-feathers. 'And leave the chapel?' he asked, dusting flour from his long strong hands, 'Gifts of food they bring me, from the Holy House there. I manage well enough. It's God's work here, keeping this place safe for Him.'

He turned back to face them, with his odd twisted smile. 'If the altar light did not shine, if it were deserted, they would come back. All the small gods of the forest, who ruled here once. Before them, the Druid priests were here, beneath and between their sacred oak trees, older than Rome. Here they worked their awful magic, made bloody sacrifices.' He shook his head. 'If I should die, another will come from Deva to keep the chapel holy and clean. Besides,' his voice lightened, 'I've the birds to feed, – and one or two other old friends!'

His blue eyes twinkled at Rhianneth, and she suddenly realised that he was much younger than she had first thought. She felt he was teasing, waiting for her to speak. She said the first thing that came into her head. 'Like the old dog fox, with the grey muzzle?'

The room stilled. He looked over her head at her father, then his eyes came back. 'Why did you say that?'

Rhianneth knew that she had made a mistake. But he put

his hand gently enough on her head and tilted her face towards him. 'How did you know?'

She sensed her father's unease. The keeper went on looking into her eyes; she felt no fear of him, only a kind of discomfort, as if she had done a wrong for which she should be sorry, but could not help.

'I have brought my daughter for baptism,' she heard Marcus say quickly, 'We are isolated, and she is too much in the company of her grandmother. I should have seen to it before now, but – ' he hesitated 'the roads are not safe. The journey is rough for a child. Now, I want her safe within the fold. Will you take her for Christ, keeper – here in this chapel?'

His eyes were so clear Rhianneth felt she could see right through to the life-force within him. Like a deep, clean pool of spring water that drew its being from the heart of the living rock, blue-cold and beautiful. Then he looked away, and the spell was gone.

'I will, Sir,' he said, looking at last towards Marcus, 'There is within your daughter a – power, which must be committed to God. But not tonight. Now we will eat, and you shall tell me any news you have of this poor world!'

They ate a simple but filling meal, and afterwards Rhianneth curled up snugly in a blanket and, half-asleep, listened to their talk. The keeper seemed hungry for news, and eagerly devoured every snippet that her father or Lovan told him, although of the great, slow events of the outer world he knew far more than they. Travellers came to him from many parts, breaking a journey to seek his advice, for he was skilled in the art of healing.

The power of Rome was sinking and the Empire had split into two, he told them. Everywhere barbarian tribes were moving in along once secure frontiers, since the great legions had been broken in civil wars.

'The Empire is bleeding to death, it seems,' he said sadly, poking at the fire with a thick, blackened stick, 'and men everywhere are in despair. Only in the east, in Byzantium, does the old life flourish still – long may it do so. Perhaps from there, all may be won back . . .'

'But we in Britain,' Marcus broke in, ' – our eastern lands are already swallowed up by the Saxons, and still we fight amongst ourselves while we drift towards the edge of darkness!'

'Every summer they inch westwards,' Lovan said gruffly. 'You heard of the battle in the southern plain where the great stones stand? With that, yet another city was lost.'

The keeper nodded. 'I heard that it was bloody, and disastrous for us. Christ help us if they ever reach the western sea, then our future will be black indeed, for our island will be cut in half. Split, like the Empire, with the enemy between . . .'

They fell silent, and only the crackle of the stirred-up fire and the fainter sounds of the night forest filled the room. After a while they spoke in low voices of Rhun, and the kings of the west, and of the witch-queen Myffan who now ruled in Mithrasia through her small son Llywarch, the heir of Elidyr.

But already Rhianneth's eyes were closing. She was suddenly tired of the world's disasters and weary of the men who clawed for power as they slid towards chaos. The long journey had taken its toll, and she slept, undisturbed by the rustling of the great oaks, or the calls of night creatures along their hunting trails, or the soft footsteps of the small gods that wandered through the moonlit forest.

In the sunlight of early morning she was baptised with ice-cold water from a tiny stream that sprang out of the earth near the chapel. The April sun was warm on her face, and she could see blue periwinkle flowers scattered like stars at the woodland edge. Her nose quivered at the scents that came from the damp greenness beyond, and she suddenly remembered that it was almost May Day. Soon she would run with Olwen out into the wet grass of the meadow to fetch in may-blossom and fasten it around their doors, ready for the feast of Beltain.

'God keep you, little sister.' Her thoughts jerked back to the present. The keeper's words, with an almost indiscernible emphasis on the first and the last, made her look up into his face. He placed his hand on her head in blessing and she smiled at him, sensing his goodness, his gentleness, as did the birds that came to him in trust during the time of killing cold.

'God's Creation is infinite, and His hand touches all things.'

Voices chuckled and whispered in the stream beside them, and as their eyes met Rhianneth knew that he had heard them too. 'Take care,' he said softly, 'for men fear what they do not understand. But God will be with you always, and there is none greater than He.'

She felt a great sadness as they rode away, for now she knew why he had left his holy brothers in Deva, to keep this lonely chapel in the wild. Yet, after a while, the peace of the place crept back into her mind, and she thought that he had, after all, lost nothing and gained much.

'Strange life,' remarked Lovan gruffly as they joined together once more after leaving the narrow trackway.

'Oh, I don't know,' her father seemed happier than he had been for some time. He leaned forward to pat the sleek brown neck of his horse. 'We are in a triangle of forest here, between two main roads into Deva. It's not so lonely, except in winter. As you heard, many travellers break their journey to visit him, – and I daresay he walks into town sometimes. Look,' he pointed ahead, where the road forked, 'our road to the bridge lies to the right, but we'll climb the hill to the left, just for a moment.'

At the top they paused, the horses snorting in the still air. Deva lay hidden in haze before them, but to the right they could se the road running straight as an arrow, with the river nearby. Further on Rhianneth could see a settlement spanning the river, a sprawl of buildings, some with smoke rising from their roofs, and a large bridge snaking out from their midst to cross the thin gleam of water. Their own small bridge was hidden amongst the trees behind them, for it led only to the old trackway which Rhianneth knew her father thought safer than the main highways.

'Sometimes when you look over there,' Marcus pointed to the left, 'you can see the sea. It's too misty today, but look – see, there's the road from the far western forts, meeting the one from the south that runs to Deva and the north . . .'

Directly below them was a paved road, and joining it was another. This bent sharply after a while and was lost to view amongst the trees, but Rhianneth knew it wound its way through the western hills as far as the sacred island of Mona, to the land of Rhun, great Maelgwyn's kingdom of Gwynedd. So close they were, she could have scrambled down to stand upon them.

They dismounted, and let their horses wander a little way in search of new green grass while they stared into the distances around and sniffed the tang of the sea upon the air. Then Marcus quietly touched her arm, and held out to her his baptism gift. A gold ring shimmering in the sunlight, and around its edge were the words 'Spes in Deo' – Hope in God. There was also a strange symbol which Rhianneth had never seen before.

'Those are the first two letters of Christ's name in Greek,' her father said, 'so that you may think of Him always, though in this life you never see his face.'

She slipped the ring on to her finger, remembering the green chapel deep in the forest behind them and its gentle keeper with the twisted smile. She hardly needed the symbol from Greece, for she already knew exactly how the face of Christ would look. The ring was much too large, but Marcus smiled at her dismay. 'It is meant to be with you all your life,' he said, putting an arm round her shoulders, 'keep it safe. You will grow into it.'

They began to walk back towards the horses. Suddenly, unbelievably, out of the trees where the western road bent away came two horsemen, riding fast. Straight towards them they came, swerving to the north where the roads joined. The wind of their passing shook the green-speckled branches of the rowan tree below, and spattered mud over the yellow heads of coltsfoot standing stiffly to attention at the edge of the road. Then they were gone, their crested cloaks flying, beating their way to Deva.

Before they could move they heard another sound. Deeper, stronger. Hidden until now by the closer thud and ring of the riders, it shook the earth like a roll of thunder that died at their feet.

'Holy Mother of God,' breathed her father, his hand heavy on her shoulders, 'Is everything west of Deva on the move?'

They crouched down into the wet grass, their eyes never leaving the road to the west. Then they saw them. They seemed to pour out of the trees where the road disappeared, and the thudding of their feet mingled with the pounding of the blood in Rhianneth's ears. Down to the hard legionary road they came, passing below only as far from their hiding place as was their old apple tree from the kitchen door. Their accents were strange, and their voices loud and uncaring, as if they were in safe country with nothing to fear. The sun glinted on the fearsome weapons they carried, and they looked rough and wild in their dirty chequered trousers and short tunics of greasy leather. Some wore cloaks of wool flung back in the warmth of the morning, and there were several with thick black bearskins tied over their shoulders. They tramped past, not in step like a Roman legion on the march, but still with an air of purpose which could not be mistaken. This was not simply a movement of people. This was an army.

Wagons and carts rumbled by, and a great many pack-horses loaded with supplies. Then more warriors, looking surly and dangerous, some with dogs running alongside. Several horsemen came riding past the men, shouting orders. One galloped his huge black stallion swiftly along the line, men leaping aside as he swept up behind them, heading for the front of the host. He thudded beneath them, and Rhianneth saw the muscles stand out on his bare brown forearms as he pulled on the reins, saw the long moustaches and flying hair beneath his war helmet, and the long sheathed sword at his side.

'That is surely Rhun himself . . .!' breathed Marcus into her ear. 'See the red dragon crest?'

There on his shield and, careless of any enemy, on the cloak flying back from the shoulders, was the blood-red dragon, taken as their own by so many royal houses of Britain. Rhianneth's blood chilled. here, she knew, was an enemy that her father feared almost as much as the heathen Saxons to the east.

'They're moving north, Marcus,' put in Lovan's calm voice close by, 'they will be nowhere near the farm. We've nothing to fear as yet.'

Marcus made no reply. Rhun's great army moved past them, grim-faced, tired, sweating, dangerous. After a while Rhianneth's legs began to cramp, but she did not dare to stand. Instead she wriggled herself flat on the ground, heedless of the wet grass. Still they came out of the west, wagons, horses, barking dogs, shouting men, silent men, until the sun had climbed high above. Never in her life had Rhianneth seen so many people, nor been so close to them. She was cold now, and stiff with keeping so still, but she could feel panic rising inside to break out in beads of sweat on her forehead.

Her father's hand stayed on her shoulders, holding her still, for a long time after the last of Rhun's armed host had passed by. Then he got to his feet and stood in silence, gazing at the empty road leading north.

'God help Mithrasia,' he said, at last, and she knew he was thinking of his brother's wife and her son, 'and God help us, if that army scatters either in victory or defeat . . .'

CHAPTER 2

Llywarch, the young king, allowed Rhun's great host free passage to the north rather than risk the wasting of his lands by such a powerful enemy. Queen Myffan bowed to a fragile peace with her half-brother. What happened further north no one knew.

But Mithrasia was a frightened city surrounded by enemies and now, through its timidity, without friends. With Lovan, Marcus rode there once to visit his dead brother's wife, Julia, and her son Caius, neither of whom Rhianneth had ever seen. But he would not take his daughter, saying that the roads were still unsafe and that sickness spread where many people gathered.

'Perhaps later, when things are better . . .' he said, softening his words with a smile. But he never said when this might be.

The seasons slid by, and as childhood crept away Rhiannenth's days filled. Now that Olwen had a child, there were more household tasks for her to do as well as the usual work around the farm. The winter feeding of their breeding stock was a constant concern, so besides helping to bale the hay Rhianneth collected acorns from the oak trees which stood near the house, ground tree bark into powder, and tied into sheaves the leaves of ash, elm and oak which Olwen's husband cut from the trees with a large and dangerous lopping knife. She tended her grandmother's herb garden, and brought in whatever was needed for cooking or for curing their ills. As proudly as any Roman general home with spoils from the wars she bore crab-apples, mushrooms, blackberries and sweet wild strawberries into the kitchen from the fields. She ground corn in the quern, and helped Olwen make bread. Now too, she had her own high loom, the warp threads held fast by clay weights, while she sent the shuttles with their coloured weft threads flying from one side to the other, weaving into cloth the wool spun by Grandmother which came from the sheep wandering the slopes of the hillside above the crop line.

Best of all, now that she had grown too big for the shaggy

28

little pony, her father gave her a bay, one of the best horses they had ever bred.

'He's sweet-tempered as his mother,' Lovan told her, unable to hide his pride as he led the horse into the yard, 'but he's got spirit too, and strength . . .'

'He's truly mine?' Rhianneth breathed, cupping her hand as he nuzzled softly into her fingers, 'Oh, but he's beautiful . . .'

The red-brown coat of the horse gleamed, his darker mane and tail grew thick and glossy; there was intelligence in his soft brown eyes, and no wildness there.

'You must give him his name,' Lovan said, glancing with a smile at her father, 'now that he's yours. I've been calling him Taffy, but – '

'Taffy!' Gently she stroked his smooth flank, 'Oh, no . . . that's not a name for him. I shall call him Romulus.'

Marcus laughed. 'Ah, Rhianneth! No mere prince for you – it must be the founder of all Rome, must it?'

She pressed her cheek against the strong neck of the horse. One day, she vowed silently, you and I, Romulus, will ride together over the rim of the world! We'll see the palaces and the flowering gardens by the sea. I shall wear jewels like a queen, and you shall have reins of red leather and a saddle of silk . . .

Now she rode with her father through the pasturelands with more joy than ever, exulting in the power beneath her as they raced along the safe flat-land in the valley, or circled the meadows with the young dogs, when the notes of the hunting horn Marcus used in training them made the air quiver with excitement.

Still she found time to read, to dream, and to gaze into the bronze hand-mirror that had been her mother's. Her hair fell to below her waist and was, as the old saying runs, 'Tiber-dark', despite the russet lights that caught the sun or the fire. But her face lacked the chaste symmetry she so admired, for it bore more traces of Celtic ancestry than Roman. Her chin was pointed but her eyes had no touch of the Mediterranean but were the clear honey-brown of heather wine, flecked with green and tilted like the wide eyes of a fox cub. There was something else, which was not easily defined. The elusive shadow of another strain gave a wistful, elfin look to the already too delicately boned face. It was a look which made her remember the fairy folk, the little dark people who fled to the forests and the hills when the Celts first came to the island of Britain long, long ago.

'It was called "Honey Island" then,' her grandmother said, 'and before that, only "Sea-girt Green Space". Before the Romans came, the land was divided into three: Cambria, Lloegria and Alban. That was when the Old Ones ruled. Under oak, mistletoe, sickle and fire.'

'Wandering priests!' her father mocked gently, when she ventured to ask him, 'who ruled barbarian tribes by magic and fear, and made bloody sacrifices of any who crossed them. We destroyed them – and the power they had over the people, and brought reason and light and progress in their place. Don't look back into the savage darkness of the past, Rhianneth. There are shadows enough gathering around us now.'

She was thirteen by the end of that summer, and Deva was in the grip of a sweating sickness. The roads from the city were choked with funerals. Infected rubbish was piled in the streets, and rats foraged openly. Unclaimed corpses lay where they fell under the warm sun. Frightened families fled the pestilence for the cleaner air of Viroconium or even war-threatened Mithrasia. It was said they left a city breaking apart, with all authority gone. So Marcus set out with Lovan and Mostyn for the market, not at Deva but at Mithrasia, a much longer journey. Rhianneth was full of misgivings, but they had to sell their surplus produce and the summer-fattened beasts, in order to feed themselves and the breeding stock throughout the coming winter.

When a few weeks later Lovan and Mostyn came home, her father was not with them.

'Market went better than ever, *cariad*! The place is packed with refugees from Deva, all eager to buy!' Lovan assured her as she ran towards him across the yard. He swung down and stood for a moment, easing the muscles in his back. 'But Marcus has other business which will keep him there a while longer.'

He walked stiffly back to the house beside her. What business? What business would keep her father away from them in times like these? She wanted to cry. Instead she waited, saying nothing. In her slow, growing years she had become well aware of the advantages of a listening silence, and knew that Lovan would tell her only what Marcus wanted her to know.

'There have been great battles in the north,' he said, as they reached the steps of the verandah, 'but you knew that? The queen has a treaty of peace with her brother Rhun. But Rhun's army is beginning to crack, to scatter. The safety of the city, of the kingdom, overshadows everything.' He paused, glancing down at her. 'The family have always stood with Imperial Mithrasia, and Marcus is helping the cause of the Caer Melot Fellowship now, to try to keep the city strong. The queen hates Rome, and the Empire, and she fears our influence over the young king, Llywarch.'

The witch-queen and Marcus – enemies? Rhianneth thought of him in that far-away place, a city threatened from beyond her walls and dangerous even to those within. She did not know what power the queen possessed, but she knew enough of Rome's history to be afraid for her father. It had always been perilous to challenge Caesar.

As if he read her fearful thoughts on her face, Lovan put his great gentle hand on her head and smiled faintly.

'Don't worry, *cariad*. Marcus sends his love. He'll be home before Samhain.'

But the feast of Samhain, after the Night of the Dead, came and went. Autumn hardened into Winter, and still they heard nothing from Mithrasia. At Midwinter they lit fires on the hill-top to help Llwy, Lord of Light, in his battle against the forces of darkness.

Rhianneth placed a candle on her father's small altar. Its faint light flickered over the painted faces of the Christos and the Holy Lady as they gazed through her into the shadows of the room. She stood for a while, thinking of the lamp-lit altar of the green chapel and wondering how the Keeper fared this Winter night. He was a good man, and she wished him well.

There would be no Midwinter fires of Llwy to cheer him, nor would there be at the house of Aunt Julia. Still the Winter would be made bright with Christian joy, remembering the birth of Jesus, as it would be for those who celebrated the birth of Mithras, on the same day.

The candle flame dipped in the wind that came through the open door behind her. Voices sounded from outside, and further away and faint on the night air came the sounds from the hilltop where the fires were lit. She shivered. All those lonely young Gods, battling out beyond the cold winter stars against the fall of everlasting night . . .

The sweet-tasting hawthorn leaves were out and the wind from the south carried the smell of Summer on its back when a horseman came riding into the yard. Rhianneth set down a water-bucket so violently that half of its contents spilled, and the carved word *'have'* – welcome – set like a stone doormat long ago when the legions had kept the roads safe for visitors to come calling for pleasure, now blazed out a wet sparkling signal in the sunlight. Nothing could have been more welcome than the homecoming of her father. But despite the early sun which dazzled her eyes she knew at once that the rider who came so fast was a stranger. He drew rein before the wooden steps of the narrow verandah and swung to the ground in a blur of dark gold, scarlet and grey. A drift of perfume, strange and spicy, reached out to her.

'I wish to speak to the daughter of the house,' he said, his voice cultured, polite, and distantly haughty.

Rhianneth was speechless. What did one say to a Greek God? Then beyond the stranger she saw Lovan hurrying, and Apollo turned away to greet him swiftly and with obvious relief. She was too confused to hear their brief and muttered conversation, but saw Lovan turn his face away and stand quite still for a few moments. A faint shadow chilled the edge of her mind. Then he straightened, and, taking the stranger's arm, brought him towards her.

'This is Rhianneth,' he said abruptly, his voice strange and harsh. 'I will leave you . . .'

He turned swiftly and walked away. The young man looked at her with shocked surprise on his handsome face, and for the first time Rhianneth was aware of her old dress made from cloth which had dyed in uneven patches, and of the frayed plaid shawl tied out of the way around her shoulders.

'Forgive me , lady. I am Caius Caprilius.' There was a brief pause. 'Your cousin. May I come in?'

Never in her life had anyone called her lady. Although she was now full thirteen years old Marcus still allowed her all the liberties of childhood, and the rest of the household followed him. Now, suddenly, she was desperately ashamed of her bare feet and loose hair blowing in the wild warm wind, and bitterly sorry to be seen so by her cousin from Mithrasia.

She drew back abruptly, indicating with an awkward gesture the open door. He was young; but he wore an air of sophistication with his elegant clothes, and his boots were polished. He was clean-shaven in the Roman manner, and, as his scarlet cloak brushed her arm, she smelled once again a faint, exotic scent.

Griffyn and Olwen were already in the doorway, words of welcome on their lips, their eyes wary. They went into the living room, where the sunlight was streaming through an open window and where her grandmother stood silently waiting. But already a cold awareness was growing within Rhianneth. Her father was dead. She knew it, even before the words left her cousin's lips. Dead of the sickness in Mithrasia. She could not cry. It all seemed too unreal. Even when Lovan returned looking grey-faced, red-eyed and grim, and her cousin pictured for them a city lashed by the tail of the dying plague-monster, which had crawled through its gates with the refugees from Deva.

'The sickness died with the winter, we think,' he said finally, 'most of its venom was spent upon Deva. The city is now considered safe . . .'

Olwen fussed over her, hurrying to and fro from the kitchen with the practical solace of warming drinks for them all. Grandmother took her hand when Rhianneth knelt beside her as she used to in childhood, but she did so in silence, offering no comforting words.

In the shadow of her grief her cousin's presence overwhelmed Rhianneth. Her life had been enclosed, isolated from people such as Marcus had known in his early youth. Now here, suddenly, was part of the world he had known, an heir to the lost legions that had defended them for so long. Caius's father and hers had been brothers and both, she thought bitterly, had died keeping the land and a way of life; one at the side of Arturius at the battle of Camlann, and one in the plague-stricken city of Mithrasia. The swift sword and the creeping sickness, twin enemies that struck at the Empire like assassins at twilight.

Caius stayed with them for several days. He spoke much with Lovan, sometimes with her grandmother, never alone with Rhianneth – save once. It was a morning soft with rain, and the men were all out about their work. In the quiet of the kitchen she stood, lost in blank misery rather than in thought, watching through the open window two swallows dart and dive between the workshops near the gate. Suddenly she had to be away. Away from the overwhelming desolation that filled each room of the house and those within. She ran across the empty yard and leaned against the rough stones of the arched gateway, her breath shuddering with unshed tears as she looked across the meadow. It was covered with golden cowslips. Beyond it, bluebells were spreading like a mist across the forest floor. But Marcus would ride no more with her across the pasturelands, talking of the years long past or of the great world that bustled beyond their small valley, and the damp-earth smell of new growing life was to her like the breath of enigmatic, old and cruel Gods.

After a while she walked slowly out towards the stream which crossed the meadow. She knelt, and quickly gathered an offering of cowslips for the spirit of the little river, laid it gently on the shining waters where it bobbed like a golden ball. Then she turned, sensing a movement nearby. Her cousin Caius stood there.

'I thought you were a Christian,' he said, eyebrows raised.
'Oh I am. I am!' Rhianneth assured him, scrambling to her

feet and dusting the yellow pollen which clung to her dampened skirt. 'I pray at our altar, and I light a candle when I can. But . . .' She grew still, feeling the colour sting her cheeks. 'This is our stream. She waters our meadows, she grows our cresses.'

The blossom-ball spun and turned on the face of the water, racing away from them.

'I sometimes think she is laughing, all the way to the sea . . .'

Caius inclined his head, and his smile sent a jolt of pain through her for it had something of Marcus in it, some elusive family resemblance not noticed before. Suddenly Rhianneth was full of remorse, remembering how Marcus had disliked her small offerings. Her cousin must think her either a fool or wicked indeed, that even while grieving for her father she slighted his God.

She looked at Caius. His hair was Roman-cut, and so clean it slid glossy as a raven's wing when he moved. Marcus and Lovan used to visit the barber in Deva at market times, so that twice a year they came home looking close-cropped and neat as legionnary standard-bearers. Rhianneth swallowed, but the tears stayed hard in her throat. Caius bent and gathered more cowslips, holding them out for her to twist into shape.

'My mother is a Christian,' he said, 'but I serve an older God, as did my father. Mithras, the Unconquered.'

In silence she held the finished blossom-ball out to him, but instead of taking it he murmured, 'She is your stream. Will you help me launch an offering?'

They knelt together in the wet grass, and Caius put his hands around hers to lay the flowers in the water.

'Your grandmother keeps you close, little cousin. And busy.' he said, as they watched the yellow ball go tossing away. 'I have not yet told you how sorry I am to have brought you such news. My mother sends her love, in sorrow, Rhianneth. She grieves that she has never known you, and Marcus's death was a great shock. Perhaps, soon, you might come to our house in Mithrasia? For a visit?'

A trickle of excitement ran through her. Mithrasia! She thought of the paved streets, the shops, the great buildings she had never seen. The sickness had gone. What harm could come in the house of her Aunt Julia? She glanced across the stream and beyond the far meadow to the edge of the trees. Watery sunlight played on the pale green of new leaves, but deep inside was darkness and stillness. For an instant the old childhood nightmare flittered through her mind. Here, in our lonely valley, she thought, is danger enough.

Her cousin's hands were still cupped around her own, his arm and shoulder pressed close. Their eyes met as she slanted a glance up at him. His hands tightened.

'Here's the kin-kiss I should have given you when we first met . . .' His dark head bent towards her, his warm breath feathered her hair, and she felt his lips against his cheek. 'It would truly be a kindness to my mother,' he said, 'if you came to stay.'

Colour flooded her cheeks once more and her heartbeat quickened. She was silent, held in an agony of shyness. Everything about him exuded luxury and polish, the high culture to which he was an heir surrounded him like an aura. What could he know of their ways, out here beyond the cities? Her grandmother would never let her go. Her dislike of the towns was based, not on a logical avoidance of sickness and danger as Marcus's had been, but on a dark and deep-rooted tribal fear.

Caius loosed her hands and put a finger, cold and dripping from the river water, under her chin.

'Rhianneth?'

His voice was soft, lower than the singing of the stream. But she would not turn her head. She could not look into her cousin's eyes again, not yet. She blushed when he spoke to her, and trembled when he was near. How could she bear to see in his eyes only duty between blood-kin, and a casual kindness for an orphaned cousin on an outlying farm, too young and too rough to otherwise notice?

'Why did my father stay in Mithrasia?' she ventured at last, and her voice was so light, so small, that she sounded like a child.

Caius hesitated. Then in one swift movement he pulled her to her feet. 'Family business.'

'To do with the house – the farm?'

'Something like that.'

They began to walk slowly, back towards the gateway. She watched the wet grass leaving shining droplets on his boots of fine leather, and from beneath their feet rose the honey-sweet smell of crushed cowslip flowers. The pale glimpses of sunshine had vanished now, and rain was beginning to fall in a fine mist.

'What had my father to do with the Fellowship of Caer Melot?' she asked, as they passed under the stone archway.

Caius halted. 'Marcus was part of it. As I am.' His glance searched her face. 'What has Lovan told you?'

'Only that you are trying to win over the young king, to keep the city safe. But what has Arturius's stronghold of Caer Melot to do with us, now?'

'When all Arturius had won seemed about to go down into the dark, the Fellowship was formed to stand against barbarism. Either the Saxon kind, or that of our own people.' He paused momentarily, then shrugged and went on. 'Today Constantine of Dumnonia holds Arturius's fortress in the far west – loyal beyond doubt to the Empire. But the spirit of the place flies with the Fellowship, with those few who are left from the old days, and with we who are young and must carry on. As our danger grows, so must our strength.'

'I heard my father, many times, wish we had Arturius with us still . . .'

'Gods, yes!' His face seemed to light up, as if some inner fire had flamed with her words. 'After the legions left, we were all but drowned under waves of terror and blood, did you know that? In exchange for their help against the wild Irish and the Painted People from the Pictish kingdoms beyond the Wall, the Saxon mercenaries demanded more, and more. They knew their strength, you see – and Britain's weakness.'

'I know that they finally burst from their settlements and ravaged the island . . .'

'They took everything they wanted, by fire and sword,' Caius told her grimly, 'because we'd grown timid from years of civilised living under the protection of Mother Rome! And out of that time of darkness, of chaos, one man came with such a hold over the minds of men that the land mourns him still. Arturius! With his stupendous victory at Badon he did what no other man could do. He took the sword from the Saxon, and saved us all! His war-host proclaimed him *'amherawdyr'* – emperor – in the name of their people deserted by Rome. Did Marcus tell you?'

She shook her head, her eyes on his dark face. 'Could I –' she hesitated, – 'be part of the Fellowship? If I came to Mithrasia?'

His slow, sweet smile turned her legs to water.

'When you've grown a little,' he said, taking her hand, 'You will find, little cousin, many more interesting things to fill your head . . .'

Rhianneth watched her cousin shyly as he talked with the men at her father's big table, when the lamplight touched his dark hair with fire and he drank their home-brewed barley beer as elegantly as if it had been wine from the south. She followed him with her eyes as he walked through the cattle enclosures and out into the pasturelands with his scarlet cloak billowing in the wet wind, and it seemed as if that golden world she kept so secretly in her mind had let forth one of its own to come amongst them. But he never spoke to her of Mithrasia again, nor did they walk together in the meadow.

She imagined that it was the family business of the farm that her cousin talked of so often with Lovan and her grandmother, and of this she knew little. But she was not so lost in grief that the half-finished conversations and the sudden silences that so often greeted her appearance did not both hurt and isolate her. Her father had been overworked and unobservant, a dreamer; but they had been close, and he had never questioned her ability to think and to understand. Yet it was only when her cousin at last rode away to Mithrasia that the loss of Marcus came suddenly upon her, and she cried for the first time.

Warm weeks of summer melted by, and stories began to

reach them of a growing lawlessness everywhere, of the destruction of property and the murder of innocent people by wandering gangs of armed criminals, or by remnants of Rhun's great army looking for food and plunder. Empty villas were looted and those still occupied were attacked and ransacked. Fires were lit on once cherished mosaic floors to cook the meat of cattle slaughtered by the raiders, and precious family heirlooms of gold, silver and crystal glass were flung into sacks to be bartered to the highest bidder or shipped to Gaul. Country dwellers were fleeing to the squalid safety of the ruined towns or to the tribal hill-forts of their ancestors, and burying their wealth now, not only in fear of the pagan Saxon, but to keep it from the rapacious and bloody hands of their own people. The old days were coming again, and the farmhouse could no longer be considered safe. At her grandmother's urging, preparations began to be made for them to move to the relative security of the nearby hill settlement. Everything of value or use that could be moved was carried to her grandmother's old round house or packed into the adjoining store sheds, snug within the walls and fencing that surrounded the small dwellings of their kin-folk.

In silent anguish Rhianneth collected her personal treasures and placed them carefully into a small painted box which Marcus once told her had come from Rome itself. Certainly it was very old. Its painted pictures were now mere streaks of colour, and the heavy hinged lid grated with rust as she closed it upon her mother's necklace and earrings of gold, the decorated combs she had worn in her hair, the bracelets of bright copper and enamel. With them Rhianneth put the mirror of bronze, a silver cup and plate, and her father's baptism gift – the gold ring which was still a little loose, and which she feared to lose from her finger as she worked around the farm and the house. Carefully she wrapped around with cloth a small glass bottle, half full of perfume. This, too, had been her mother's. Rhianneth treasured it, sometimes lifting the stopper to breathe in its fragrance; sometimes drawing a faint trace of it across her wrist. All that she longed for seemed locked within its esssence, every precious droplet held dreams of luxury and romance, and a world far away.

'Don't bother with them,' Olwen said sharply, when she began to take books out of the heavy oak cupboard, 'I need help in the kitchen . . .'

She bustled past, a pile of linen in her arms. Rhianneth followed her into the wild disorder of the kitchen, stacked with household goods to be carried up the hill, and heaped with rubbish to be thrown out.

'I need something to carry the books in,' she began, but Olwen rounded on her at once, worry and temper creasing her brow and putting bright flags of colour in her cheeks.

'You can't take them – that's obvious, isn't it?' she cried. 'I don't know where we shall keep half the things we need, and books are no use at all!'

'They are to me! I won't just leave them here!'

Rhianneth's voice rose, despite herself. For she well knew how badly Olwen felt about leaving the farmhouse; she had lived there since before Rhianneth was born, had married there, had her child. Her light warm kitchen with its cupboards, cooking stove and lead-lined sink, and the house itself with its painted rooms and curtained windows, were the stuff of her life. To go back to a small thatched round house like the one in which she had been born and spent her childhood was a dark pain indeed. A pain which must needs be hidden for fear of offending those who offered them sanctuary, and which turned her usually quick temper into bright anger.

'Then put them under the old bath-house, with the other ornaments we can't keep. Go on – before Griffyn seals it up!'

Olwen turned her back and began sorting through the linen pile. Rhianneth thought of the bath-house, never used and falling into ruin, and of its hypercaust beneath where she had loved to hide as a child. Long ago, Marcus had told her, the bath-house had steamed with hot water, and the heat from the hypercaust had warmed the floor of the living room, and one of the bedrooms, too. She suddenly saw her father's face, thin and a little weary, yet alight with the splendour that once had been theirs. Bury his books? It would be like blotting out his memory, smothering all that had been, all that she hoped for

40

in the future! Rage boiled up in her uncontrollably and burst out in a torrent of words.

'I will not leave my books – or anything else that is mine!' she shouted. 'You can do as you like with this –' and she swept an arm around the crowded room – 'but I'll carry the books one by one up the hill, if I have to! And I'll start now!'

She turned to run from the room, straight into the arms of Olwen's husband, Griffyn. 'Careful, *cariad*!' he exclaimed, smiling. 'What is it you are starting now, then?'

'She's being awkward about those old books!' Olwen cried, before Rhianneth got her breath, 'As if we're not in enough trouble with all this! You tell her there's no room – she won't listen to me!'

'I will not put them under the bath-house.' Rhianneth wiped angrily at the tears which ran down her hot face. 'They're mine. I want them with me!'

'Well now –' Griffyn rubbed at his beard, his eyes moving to Olwen – 'they might get a bit damp, at that. We'd best take them up the hill. I'll put them in the old iron tool-box with some other bits and pieces . . .'

Olwen's protests exploded, but Rhianneth threw her arms around him and kissed the rough cheek that smelled so comfortingly of woodsmoke, leather and summer sweat. As she fled to her room she heard him say, 'Ah, Olwen . . . she's lost her whole world this year. Leave her something to hold on to . . .'

For a long while she lay on her bed, until all the hot rage was gone and the tears ran cold and silent over her face, drenching the pillow. Then, shivering, she got up, with the weeping still an ache in her throat. The morning light turned to amber as it filtered through the window. No one made glass any more it seemed, and where a pane had broken the day shafted in like a white sword across the bed. Already the room looked empty, dead.

Somewhere in the house she heard Olwen calling, and slipped silently from the room and out into the warm sunlight. She ran under the yellow-stoned arched gateway and into the meadow, where the clear narrow stream glinted and gurgled in the sunlight on its way to join the Sabrina Sea far to the south. Their old wolf-hound nuzzled her gently as she flung herself face down on the summer-warm grass and plunged her arms into the tingling cold water of the small pool where the cresses grew. She laid her cresses upon the grass and put her wet arms around the dog's rough and greying coat.

'Giff, Giff,' she whispered, smelling the warm dog scent of him against her tear-swollen face. 'Where did it all go?'

The dog whimpered. He was thinner than he used to be, his ribs hard and definite beneath her hands. He was pining for her father, being too old to busy himself with life and forget. Stroking him, she let the tears run unchecked in the quiet sunlight, soft offspring of the violent storm within her.

At what moment in time had the good life ended? For her it had ended on that instant when she read the message upon the face of her cousin Caius. But for Britain? Arturius had held back the rolling tide of Saxon horror for a generation to grow up in peace, and beget children of their own behind a shield of swords and glittering mail that was Arturius's cavalry. The brotherhood of Caer Melot, the hope of the west. The Saxon armies retreated to their territories in the east, and moved no more against the lands of the British. While Arturius lived, the Empire lived still.

But heroism was not proof against the malice, envy and ambition of lesser men, and Arturius had died at Camlann in bloody civil war. Marcus used to say that for the Saxons to be sure of his death in the dark days following the battle would have been a peril most deadly. Into her mind crept a fragment of song she had heard on Lovan's lips when she was a child.

> 'A grave there is for March,
> A grave for Gwythyr,
> A grave for Gwgawn of the ruddy sword.
> Dangerous the thought — a grave for Artur . . .'

Now the Saxon war-hosts were again beginning to move westwards, and the Empire of Arturius was so far shattered that it was said no king of Britain dared turn to face them, for

42

fear of the swords of his treacherous fellow-countrymen at his back.

Giff stirred beneath her hand and silently moved away through the soft grass, crouching low. She watched him until he circled out of sight. He must have scented some small animal and the instinct to kill, to survive, had for a brief time overcome his sad listlessness.

What they needed too was the strength to pierce their fatal weakness with the true will to survive, before barbarian darkness covered all contenders alike. She thought then of the Fellowship, that frail heir to Caer Melot, and the dark face of her cousin came into her mind, bringing with it as always a strange tremor of excitement.

Quickly she bent towards the cresses. Her tears were finished. In a little while she would take home the delicious apology gift to Olwen.

From the direction of the house came a short yelp. Rhianneth froze. Giff, hunting, never made a sound.

Nothing moved across the meadow. Reason urged her to call out to him, but raw instinct clamped tight her lips. After a moment she began to creep silently through the grass, keeping low. Stumbling a little over the tufted grass, she edged her way towards the gateway.

There was a smashing, splintering crash; the noise of an axe against thin wood. Rhianneth's heart leapt as a woman's cry shrilled into the summer air. Olwen!

Lurching against the rough stone of the gateway she stopped, heart hammering with sudden terror. She saw the bright flash of weapons. Men circled in a cloud of dust, shouting in wordless yelps of animal violence. A man – Olwen's husband, Griffyn – broke the circle and ran towards the narrow verandah. But they were upon him immediately. Five men surrounded him, grinning, rough and nauseatingly filthy, with ragged shoulder-length hair and thick unkempt beards.

Rhianneth snatched up a short thick piece of wood used to wedge open the gates in windy weather, and then scrabbled along the wall until she found a small ledge set hand-high, and the hunting horn which lay there, the horn her father had used to train his dogs.

Pure and clear, the note pierced the air. She sucked in a ragged breath and blew again. The men in the yard whirled around. Once more she blew. Then they saw her. Back she ran into the meadow, sounding the horn twice more. They crowded at the gateway, shouting obscenities as she flew along the edge of the grass, close to the fence dividing the pasture-lands. Where she ran to, she had no thought. She only knew that at the end of the valley, the men had been foraging since early morning with the young dogs. Would they hear the horn? If they did – would they know it for what it was?

One of the men was coming after her. She heard the shouts of the others urging him on. His fast breathing sounded close behind. She turned, lashed out with the gate-wedge, and caught him across the side of the head. He stumbled, almost fell. As in a nightmare she tried to force her legs to move faster. She had not stopped him. Suddenly, terrifyingly, he was upon her.

His curses and threats stabbed her ears as his great hard hands pulled her down. Blood streamed down his face where the rough nailed wood had raked it, and his eyes were small and black and vicious. Rhianneth kicked at his legs with her sturdy work-boots and felt them crunch against his shins. But he flung himself forward, sending them both reeling against the fence. She sank her teeth into his hand as it flashed up to grasp her. He yelled in pain and fury, and struck her across the mouth so hard her head jerked back and bumped against the hard interwoven timbers, while the sky tilted as if the earth had moved. His foul breath rasped through big yellow teeth bared in a wolf-snarl. He ripped open her thin summer dress in a series of savage wrenches. His hands on her shoulders and breasts were bruising, violent. Rhianneth screamed as a ring on one of his fingers tore into her bare flesh. Desperately she scratched at his eyes with her fingernails, but he jerked his face aside. As her hands raked the filthy red tunic he wore he grasped her wrists and pulled them apart; her legs were crushed painfully beneath his knees. She was helpless, and the smell of him was a reek that made her wild with animal

44

terror. She screamed frenziedly again and again, until her ears were filled with shrillness.

Suddenly he sprawled half across her, his yelp of shock changing to a snarl of fear as Giff went for his throat. Quick as a rat he rolled away and crouched, his black eyes on the bared teeth of the dog. His hand crept to the knife at his belt, but before it was out Giff's jaws closed around his arm. As the dog's fangs sank deep he gave a harsh scream and swung violently to one side, carrying the dog with him. But Giff's great strength was gone, and with horror Rhianneth saw his fur matted with blood on one side. For an instant he loosed his hold and at once the man shook free and stumbled away towards the house. The dog flew after him, his teeth fastening into the man's leg so that he screamed again, falling heavily to the ground.

Rhianneth pushed against the fencing and staggered towards them. She saw the man's scrabbling fingers close around the nailed wood of the heavy gate-wedge she had dropped in the grass. Appalled, she watched him grasp the weapon, raise it high and bring it down viciously against the dog's head. Giff fell back, his great jaws slack. The man brought the club down again, and again. Blood thudded in Rhianneth's ears, her legs felt heavy as iron; but her mind flamed with the sole intent to destroy the thing that was killing Giff. The world slowed as she reached the man. He was bent over Giff, his back towards her. But the knife at his belt caught the sun as he moved. She grasped it, pulled it free, and as he swung round towards her she thrust it with all her strength deep into his chest. His breath came out on a strangled cry.. He clutched at the knife hilt, doubling up in agony. She backed away and stood panting, her eyes fixed on his bent head. Then terror rose like a silent shriek, as she watched the man get slowly to his feet and start towards her. A dark stain was spreading around the knife in his chest. Through the drying blood on his face his black eyes were fixed, stoat-like, upon her.

A sudden thundering shook the ground. Lovan's great stallion rushed past, so close that the air moved and pieces of loose earth and stone flew up round her face. The man vanished beneath its hooves, and there were voices shouting, feet thudding, a barking of dogs. As in a black nightmare Rhianneth crawled to where Giff lay. One side of his head was shattered into a mess of blood and bone, and although his paws still trembled with a semblance of life, he was quite dead. She knelt on the grass whispering to him, gently stroking his warm rough coat, feeling again the aching thinness of his old body beneath her fingers. The men and the hunting dogs shouted and yelped around her and the trees and the grass seemed to mass and grow darker. Then Lovan lifted her in his arms and rode back to the house, away from Giff and the trampled dead body of the man who had killed him.

When Rhianneth stood in the room where her family had lived for so long in safety and peace, she felt sick. Olwen wept over the big table where her husband lay bleeding from many wounds, while her small son clung to her knees gasping and hiccoughing in between shrill screams that shattered the ears. Grandmother cut away the blood-soaked clothing, applying pads to staunch the flow, her old face intent, oblivious to the noise around her.

Lovan and the other men talked in low and angry voices away from the table, and two of Olwen's sisters moved around the room picking up and straightening pieces of furniture. The doors of the tall cupboard swung loosely from torn hinges, but the precious books were already packed in the locked iron chest which the raiders had neither been able to break open or carry away in their haste. In their cheated fury they had smashed the front of the cupboard with axe blows, broken the windows, and thrown down the brazier which stood against the wall. The small altar in the corner of the room was built of stone and had resisted attack, but the picture of the Holy Mother and her son which had rested against the wall was painted upon wood, and it lay on the floor cracked and splintered as if by a booted heel.

They buried Giff near the old bent apple-tree which had been his watch-post for the house, and where of late he had so often laid, head on paws in the warming sunlight and eyes on the empty gateway, waiting with the patience of his kind for the return of his master.

The dead raider was hidden in a shallow grave just inside the forest into which the others had vanished. Although their dialect had been thick, it had been the Celtic tongue they had spoken. But whether they were stragglers from Rhun's army, or a gang roaming the countryside from nearer home, no one could tell.

Olwen's husband did not die. But after many weeks of fevers and pain he was left with a useless right arm and a leg which stiffened and dragged. He would never wield the great lopping knife for the winter leaves again, nor run with the dogs through the oakwoods for game. Yet he was alive, and they all rejoiced.

It had been the first touch of a cold and rising tide, and behind this lay a dark sea of violence which could engulf them at any time, suddenly and completely, within its mindless depths.

They moved into the protection of the stone-walled, timber-fenced settlement on the hill, and the house was shuttered and left, now to be used only for occasional storage and shelter for the farm animals. The surplus horses were sold. But their finest stallion Lovan kept, and this was a secret joy to Rhianneth for it could only mean that sometime, far ahead, he meant again to build up their stock.

At night, when the bothie grew nest-warm, she would lie wrapped in blankets on a straw-stuffed mattress, listening to the snores of her grandmother and the dream-whispers of their two house-hounds. Sometimes then, the air that was so heavy with the smells of human sweat, stored vegetables, drying herbs and warm sleeping dogs, would seem pierced through in her mind with another scent, spiced and exotic, which she ever associated with her cousin. Caius Caprilius haunted her thoughts with his dark, fine-boned face and Roman elegance. She, who had so seldom wept, now cried herself to sleep in grief for her father, and perhaps for something else: That bright world which she had glimpsed with her cousin's coming, and which now seemed lost to her.

Marcus had baptised her into his faith and tried to teach

her its creed. She had prayed with him to the Holy Mother but in her heart she confused her with Earth Mother, as she confused the Christos with Llwy, lord of light. She remembered her father's distrust of her grandmother, and for his sake tried silently to pray each night to the saviour in heaven who had died to save mankind from the power of evil. But the old gods were crowded close around her and other more ancient words crept into her mind, words they still used at the winter sowing of corn and which had long ago marked the sacrifice of the corn king, who died that his people might live and prosper.

Sometimes a memory would come to her out of the night. *As I am so are you – daughter of my daughter.* The words her grandmother had spoken on that long-ago winter night hissed like a serpent between Rhianneth and her sad dreams of Mithrasia and of Caius Caprilius. Now the old game of reading the pictures in the flames was a game no longer, for she was learning her grandmother's trade. Rhianneth knew that she had the gift, the sight, as her grandmother had, and must eventually take her place, here with her mother's people.

On the beaten earth of the bothie floor her books lay neglected in the ancient iron chest. Useless, save to serve as a stool for her, at her grandmother's feet, for she felt a reluctance to lift them out within the confined, dim and grubby interior of the house. The battered nymphs and satyrs which decorated the lid seemed as incongruous within her grandmother's house as the comfortable wicker chair she had brought with her, or the little Roman lamps which stood like mute and glimmering reminders of that world beyond reach.

Most of the houses within the small settlement belonged to kinfolk. Their cattle grazed with those from the villa, and they planted their grain close by. There were vegetable plots and beehives, and flowers grown for the bees were everywhere in that late summer and autumn. The wind outside the bothies was filled with sweetness, and masked the stench of the cesspit on the edge of the settlement where Rhianneth emptied their refuse.

It was her task to tend her grandmother's transplanted herb

garden, and to bring whatever she might need from it. The subtle scents that rose in the warm sunlight were like balm to her troubled heart, and she lingered often in that quiet corner to breathe in the elusive traces of fennel, coriander and thyme, marjoram, mallow and poppy. Now for the first time she was allowed to help concoct medicines, to grind, mix, distil and store herself the herbs she gathered. Sometimes the men would bring other plants, wild things found in the woods or near the swampy ground where the cattle did not go, and the uses of these too she learned as the year declined and the winds became colder.

Whenever she could escape her grandmother's eye, she left the settlement where children screamed and played on the trodden earth and dogs lay watchfully in the thin sunlight. She would sit on the wind-swept hillside looking towards the warm red roof-tiles of the farmhouse, and the ache inside for the old life was very great.

There had never been a companion of her own age to draw her up the hillside away from the house, and she was not at ease with her kinfolk, nor were they with her. Only with Lovan, who had no blood bond, could she feel truly herself. Often she followed him when he worked, just to talk. He had been her father's friend as well as bailiff and as she watched him, his boots squelching in cold mud and his breath steaming in the frosty air, she thought how like he was to the apple tree which had stood for so long beside the old house. He had been always in her childhood and before it, he was here with her now, and he was her only link with the life of which she dreamed.

His great skill had been in the breeding of their horses. But on the farm he could turn his hand to almost anything. Rhianneth watched him at work in the woodshed, or in the forge at the side of the yard, where things for the house or farm were made or mended. Here, in the glow of the fire, where the thick smoke curled up spark-lit and the air smelled of rust, soot and cold iron, Lovan seemed part of the land itself. She could half-believe he had lived beside each of the seven generations that had farmed here since that first soldier bought the land.

She could imagine him nowhere else. Yet in his youth he had travelled deep into Gaul, and he spoke the Roman tongue with ease. She knew, too, that he had been married once long ago, but that his wife had died very young, and childless. Apart from these few things, Lovan's early life was not known to her, and until this, her own lonely winter, it had not occurred to her to wonder about it.

Sometimes, waiting until he was busily engaged upon a task, she would ask shy questions about her cousin Caius. She learned that because Aunt Julia had been ill for many years after the birth of her son and the death of her husband, Caius had been cared for in the home of Julia's brother Wencam, he who had survived to bring the news of Camlann. The child had been given the name of Arturius's lieutenant, that Caius who had died with his shield held over the fallen body of his great captain. His boyhood had been so steeped in the glories and tragedies of those who once had ridden with Arturius from the stronghold Caer Melot to do battle with the war-hosts of the Saxon, that he now felt himself to be a living, shining sword-arm of that brave company of shadows. Rhianneth blushed when she remembered asking him: 'What has Caer Melot to do with us, now?'

She thought of Caius as she had first seen him, riding towards her with the sun at his back like a figure out of the legends of the past. Now she began to see him as something far more real. Born during those desperate hours when the strength and hope of Britain has gone down into the darkness of betrayal and defeat, Caius was like a bloodied flower sprung from the battlefield, which in the midst of bitter civil wars brought sombre remembrances of the lost brotherhood of Caer Melot. He must be hated then by those who had hated Rome and whose love of personal power made impossible those alliances which alone might hold back the coming of barbarism.

He was close to the young king, Llywarch of Mithrasia. Yet that could be a dangerous friendship in a kingdom much troubled by rival thrusts for power and surrounded by wolf-hungry enemies, and many secret prayers for his safety she sent out to any kind and listening Gods. Her cousin Caius might come no more to see them, but all through that long winter Rhianneth kept close within her the image of a lonely rider, scarlet-cloaked. The last messenger from Caer Melot.

With her hands kept busy and her mind full of dreams, she yet began to notice how quiet her grandmother had become. The winter had been cold but not savage, yet Rhianneth wondered if she might be ill. She was old. Rhianneth's mother had been late-born. But her eyes had not the look of sickness, and there was something in them that was strangely mirrored in the steady blue of Lovan's. With the turning of the year he no longer stayed his work hand to talk with Rhianneth, and sensing his reluctance she fell silent and avoided his company. Yet he spoke more with her grandmother than ever she had known, and often with her appearance their conversation would falter, cease. Fragments she sometimes caught, words on the wind as she neared the bothie, blown to her by some small God of the air maybe, so that she was aware that they spoke of her.

A small fear grew. Already she was fourteen and her cousin had ridden away almost a year ago with no promise to return. Why should he? He had seen her scarcely emerged from childhood, while his manhood was already strong.

The strangeness continued. She did not dare put into words her fears, for then they would take solid shape. Instead she grew silent and elusive, wandering down the hill to the old house to sit amongst the bare branches of the bent apple tree until her limbs were stiff with cold and her mind ached with thinking of times past and the years still to come.

With her father she had heard the wild sea-song of the Odyssey made into their own Latin tongue, had followed Rome's wars with Carthage, and had firm within her the taut and beautiful truths that Roman poets had written in the reign of the great Emperor Augustus. Her mind was feathered and ready for flight.

One day when the pale winter sun gleamed through clouds dark with rain Rhianneth went, warmly wrapped in her thick-woven plaid shawl, to sit on the hillside. She sat for a long

51

time, feeling the silence of the countryside reach away into the dark sea of green forest unbroken to the skyline. There was a woody earthiness on the wet wind, and the young grasses moved with its passing. When Lovan joined her, she felt herself tremble like the green blades before them as she waited for him to speak.

'I have something that is yours. Something I've been keeping ever since last spring, Rhianneth.'

He lifted his hand, and she saw he held a soft leather bag drawn up with thongs. 'Take it,' he urged, 'It holds gifts from your father, kept for you over the years.'

A warm smell of leather came rising up as she opened the bag. Gold and silver gleamed amidst the sheen of copper and enamel and the glitter of stones in necklaces, bracelets, rings and cloak-brooches wrought by masters of metalwork. The exquisite pieces shone and dazzled in the daylight as she lifted them from the soft darkness, dumb with astonishment.

They were not rich. The former grace of the beloved old house had long before her birth been reduced by necessity. This was her inheritance then, and her father must have neglected much that he loved in order to give it to her. Slowly Rhianneth's first shock turned to a puzzled grief, and the colours in her hand blurred as the tears came.

'He should have sold them for the farm. We've needed so much, over the years.'

'Marcus gave them into my keeping when I left him in Mithrasia' Lovan's voice was rough-edged. 'They are yours.'

'But we all had to work so hard, just to keep the farm alive – my father most of all –'

'Marcus,' Lovan broke in abruptly, and then hesitated looking at her with tormented eyes, 'Marcus was not your father, Rhianneth.'

A bird flew low across the hill, the light gleaming on its dark plumage like a flash of purple fire. Somewhere a dog barked, sharp and full-throated. The wind moved, lifting her hair with cold thin fingers, and she sat quiet as the hill itself, as he forced out words. Stumblingly at first. Then steadily, as if this was a long-ago tale like those he told when she was a child sitting on the enclosure gate to watch him gentle his horses.

'Beautiful, your mother was, and wild. We – Marcus loved her always, and when she was of age they were betrothed. We three rode into Mithrasia together that autumn, with the leaves all around us the colour of her hair, and the wedding to come with the new spring green. We stayed with Julia for the time of the market. But when it was over, Julia was ill again. She asked your mother to stay for the winter to keep her company. Later they visited the court, for Julia was kinswoman to Elidyr. Elidyr saw your mother, and . . . she stayed. She loved it all – the clothes, the jewels, the heated baths, the perfumes from the east, the wine from the south. I think she even loved Elidyr, a little. And he – he gave her everything it was possible to give, except marriage. He already had a wife. Maelgwyn's daughter, Myffan.'

He paused, and Rhianneth watched the light in his eyes darken into pain. In silence and in cold she waited.

'After it was known that your mother was carrying Elidyr's child,' he went on, at last, 'the rumours of poison began. Myffan had already lost two children by miscarriage and she was – is – an ambitious and jealous woman. A bastard son for Elidyr while she, as yet, had none, was too dangerous to be borne. So at last, in great fear, your mother fled the city and came home here, to the farm. She and Marcus were married; he was angry and hurt, but he loved her still. The birth was difficult, and Elidyr's child was, after all, a daughter. Your mother died the same day. Marcus brought you up and loved you, Rhianneth, as his own.'

He hesitated, brushing the leather bag with his fingertips, glancing quickly at her and away again.

'Elidyr sent these for you, over the years. He thought you safer here than within sight of the queen. Had he lived, he would by now have acknowledged you openly. As it is, his son, Llywarch, will do that.'

Rhianneth gazed at the shimmering, winking jumble in her hands, but she no longer saw beauty in their depths, only ugliness and danger. She could not speak. It was as if her throat had closed upon a jagged piece of bone that scratched and tore with every effort to dislodge it.

'That last Autumn,' Lovan broke the silence, 'Marcus stayed on beyond his duty to the Fellowship, because he had to make sure of your acceptance by your half-brother. How else could he secure the marriage he wanted for you? He had nothing, and there would be no buyers for the farm, not in these times. You must have known he did not mean you to spend your life here?'

She shook her head. He watched her for a few moments, then got heavily to his feet, pulling her up beside him. For a while his heavy, gentle hand rested on the back of her head. He had shattered her world, and he knew it. Suddenly she turned her face into the felted woollen thickness of his winter cloak, that *birrus Britannicus* which had become so prized by the legions serving in cold outposts of the Empire. She felt light and cold as a blown flake of snow, and there was a singing in her head like the sweet birds of Rhiannon, Queen of the Otherworld, in whose honour Rhianneth had been hastily named when she had stood so close to them in that chamber of death and of birth.

Now she knew why Marcus had kept her so sheltered at the farm. Why her grandmother had so inexplicably appeared to regard Caius more with the respect due to an undeclared enemy than to a kinsman by marriage.

'We kept you close and safe, Marcus and I,' Lovan said. 'Now the old life has gone and you are a child no longer, but the grown daughter of a king.'

Pain slashed through her like sharp slivers of ice. Was she to think it greater honour then, to be the bastard daughter of Elidyr the king, than the true-born child of Marcus Caprilius? Her unspoken words lay like salt tears on the air, and Lovan's hand lifted as he drew back and looked into her face.

'Your father's line goes back to Maximus, Rhianneth. He who built Mithrasia itself as a strong fortress to stand against the barbarians from the north! His blood is not to be despised.'

She dragged her eyes from his, to look down upon the red Roman tiles of the house in the valley below, her mind searching amongst the spoken legends of the past. Magnus Maximus, the soldier, called Prince Macsen by her grandmother; he, who had lived before Arturius or Ambrosius or Vortigern. His name was as a magic word amongst the peoples of the west. Made, like Arturius, Imperator by his troops, he had led them across the Narrow Sea and mastered Gaul, Spain and Africa, until at last he had taken Rome itself. Then, as is their way, the Gods became jealous and turned their faces to smile instead upon his enemy, at Aquileia. There Maximus died, and the flower of Britain's youth who had followed him scattered into his broken empire. But . . . he had reached out and touched the Imperial purple, and his great lost adventure out of their misty and remote island had sent the name of Britannia winging across the Roman world. Within the cold that held her, a faint stirring began, like the silent shooting of the green grasses under the hard earth beneath their feet. Then a thought, storm dark, came.

'She wants me to marry. Now. Here,' she said almost to herself, suddenly sure of what she had previously only suspected. Lovan put a hand beneath her chin and turned her face once more towards him.

'Your grandmother is afraid for you, *cariad*. She's always known that when you were told the truth, the time would have come for you to go away. That she'd lose you. As she lost your mother.'

He gestured towards the jewel-bag still gripped in her hands. 'With Marcus dead, she wanted the protection of marriage here for you first, and these – with what I've just told you – afterwards. But that, Caius and I have crushed. You are Elidyr's daughter, and your half-brother Llywarch will send for you now you're grown. Cai will see to that. He's close to the king, and would be even closer.'

Caius. His name echoed on the wind and sent a shiver through her mind. She heard no irony in Lovan's words, only her own remembered hope of happiness.

'Marcus gave you all his love, and his knowledge. You could not spend your life here, Rhianneth.'

'No,' she whispered uncertainly. 'No. I never wanted that.'

But what it was she did want Rhianneth could not bring herself to say. The wind moved, stirring the grasses into a green pattern of light and dark, and sharp spots of rain began to fall. They left the hillside and walked back through the fence-gate into the settlement. Her eyes were full of wind-tears, and she still shivered beneath her warm wrappings. But she no longer heard Rhiannon's birds, only the sound of her cousin's name in the cry of the wild birds flying low over the hill before the coming rainstorm.

Grandmother was waiting at the door of their house, her brown shawl drawn over her head and half across her face against the cold and wet. She stood very still, only the hem of her long thick skirts moving slightly in the wind. Ageless and full of mystery, belonging to all time, as one with the stoic women of Greece and of old Rome, of whom she had scarcely heard. Earth Mother moved in all of them to give a quality of endurance, an inner strength which steeled them through hardship and danger better than any coat of mail. They knew, deep within, that while man strode through the world wearing his bright fighting colours, always in the shadows sat women, spinning the thread.

'You are wet,' was all she said as the bothie door closed behind them and the familiar warmth and scents enfolded Rhianneth. 'Hang up your shawl and fill your bowl with hot broth before you take cold . . .'

With the spring flooding of the waters and the softening of the iron-hard earth, Lovan rode away to Mithrasia and the house of Aunt Julia – and aunt she still was to Rhianneth, through her kinship with Elidyr. There was no question of Rhianneth going with him, and her tentative questions were silenced almost before they were asked. She did not care. She knew now that she would eventually leave the settlement. The Gods had laid her path long since, on the morning of that golden ride through the fallen leaves to the city of Mithrasia, and she was young and restless to follow where it led.

Olwen was distressed to discover that Rhianneth knew about her father, and angry that Lovan should have told her before he went away. The leather bag of Jewels, she admired. But when Rhianneth mentioned Caius, Olwen guessed what was in her mind, and her voice sank incredulously.

'You want to leave us here, *cariad*, and go to Mithrasia? Even though you know about your mother? It's not safe there, the towns breed wicked people! I was only a small girl, Rhianneth, but I remember it all. People shouting, and your grandmother's tears, and Marcus sitting like a grey ghost with his head in his hands. Terrible it was, and Lovan should have kept it hidden from you – '

'Until I was safely married?' Rhianneth finished for her. 'But I can't marry. The king will send for me!'

'The king is dead!' Olwen retorted angrily, as if the news of five years ago had happened yesterday. 'And his son is only a child! Why should he bother with one of his father's by-blows?'

Her blunt words ripped through the veil of romance Rhianneth had already woven for herself to cover the bare facts revealed on the hillside. A king's love became again only a casual lust, and a tragic tale merely a very ordinary story of flattery and weakness and betrothal vows betrayed, out of which only Marcus emerged with honour.

'Lovan has gone to see Caius . . .' she began again tentatively, but Olwen interrupted with a gesture of scorn.

'Caius! He'd marry you, I don't doubt, to keep those trinkets you hold in the family! But you'd do better to think of Hueill, or Geraint, and stay here safe with us!'

Rhianneth flushed painfully, tears stinging her eyes to hear her deepest and most secret dream-thoughts suddenly spoken aloud with such casual derision. The door of the bothie opened, and her grandmother came in, coughing a little from her small walk in the damp air.

'Tell her she need not go,' Olwen appealed at once. 'Tell her she should marry, and stay at home with us!'

Grandmother stood still, breathing with some difficulty.

After a moment or two she said in a low voice: 'Rhianneth will do what she must, Olwen. And there will be no wedding before the leaves fall.'

Olwen said no more. The bleak note in the old woman's voice held the finality of truth, and no one ever questioned her words. She had become withdrawn, more remote than ever, speaking only when necessary. All her granddaughter's questions regarding her bastard birth she turned away, and after a while Rhianneth no longer asked. Now, in silence, her grandmother picked up the bag of jewels and gazed at the richness that shimmered up through the dark. Then she pulled the bag closed and laid it down.

'My daughter's bride-price,' she said slowly, bitterly. 'Use it well, Rhianneth. Get a strong husband and a sure earth for your cubs.'

She turned away, but not before Rhianneth had seen the fear in her old eyes. She hesitated, feeling a stab of strong affection for her grandmother. The small room seemed to close around them, protective, safe, full of familiar things brought from the old house: her book-chest, Grandmother's chair, the high loom resting against one wall. Rhianneth thought of stocky, cheerful Geraint and of Heuill, so quick about his work and his thoughts tumbling over his tongue in a stammer. Could she really go to an unknown city, to an aunt she'd never seen, a royal half-brother who probably despised her? She almost opened her mouth to tell her grandmother she would not leave the settlement. Then came singing through the dimness of the bothie and into her mind a memory. A drift of spicy perfume from Rome's eastern empire reached out. She seemed to look again into the dark eyes of Caius Caprilius, and remained silent.

In the weeks that followed, her grandmother shook off the darkness that had clouded her mind. Now she kept Rhianneth constantly at her side. She scarcely had time to think too long or too often of the silent choice she'd made, or of how swiftly the Spring had passed into Summer while Lovan remained in Mithrasia. She tried to learn what she could of her grandmother's arts, until the day came when again the old woman held out Glainnader and Rhianneth felt once more the faint throbbing of power within the stone as it lay upon her open hand.

Through the half-open door a shaft of sunlight pierced down and touched the cold fire into golden life, and as it moved beneath the surface the sounds outside the bothie gradually faded.

Pictures flashed within the darkness of the stone, a myriad colours and shapes, layer upon layer, a knowledge of all time compressed and contained. The dense power of the stone could destroy, but Rhianneth had learned with her more gentle fire-pictures to put up a guard and control her mind into its search for what she wanted to know. She thought of the future, and of Caius Caprilius. And at last, out of the shielded darkness came pictures, twisted as in spirals of glass.

A flame, leaping like a burning torch borne aloft in the black wind of a winter night; a great sea-bird that swooped and rose with outstretched wings; a pathway, and a silver sea cold in the light of the moon . . . But Rhianneth could hold back the power no longer, and the darkness cracked open into pain—splintered light before she released the stone and put it from her.

'That you must learn,' her grandmother said, as Rhianneth sat at her feet, head in hands. 'To know the moment when you must let go. Glainnader is not to be used without great care. Come, tell me what you saw. I will read the symbols.'

Rhianneth told her. Her grandmother turned away, as she imagined, in thought. When at last she spoke she did not look at her granddaughter, and her voice was hesitant and old.

'Mark me, Rhianneth. Words fade into nothing, but mine you must lock within you. The flame-bearer, he will be close to you, closer than kin. The bird, and the road, . . . a dream, to unite from sea to sea, to make his people safe. Then will come hope. And hope is . . . an island?'

She broke off suddenly and turned around. Rhianneth saw with dismay that her lined face was streaked with tears.

'Ah, *cariad* – don't go. Choose another path. Don't bargain with the Gods. The price they ask is always too high!'

Rhianneth's blood chilled at her words, and at what she may have left unsaid. She looked at the hooded old eyes, but they were dark and unfathomable. She remembered a winter night long ago, and began to tremble. But she thought of Marcus, and his brother, both dying to keep alive a dream, an ideal. What sacrifice would the Gods demand of Caius to keep that precious light burning as darkness closed in? And she herself – could not she pay the price asked by the Gods as well as he? She had no need to speak, for her grandmother saw the thoughts on her face, and knew her answer.

'Learn well, then,' she said with dignity, and the tears still wet upon her cheeks, 'that which will make your path easier . . .'

She closed the door and shut out the sunlight, and in that close dimness she began to speak of the secrets of the Old Ones, the lore that was never written. Many a dark thing she told that had come to her from long ago, so that Rhianneth might understand the nature of life and laws of sacrifice which are the threads that bind it to the vast deeps of the cold cosmic market place where anything can be bought, at a price. She spoke of the indestructible soul moving in time, incarnating anew as a serpent casts its skin. She crooned snatches of an ancient song Rhianneth had heard Olwen sing, and which she had thought only a memory-teaser beloved of wandering singers, but which now took on a deeper significance within the strange vision of the Nadredd.

'I was born in the region of the Summer Stars . . .
I have been on the Galaxy at the throne of the
Distributor . . .
I have borne a banner before Alexander . . .
I was in the court of Don before the birth of Gwydion . . .
I am a wonder whose origin is not known . . .

While she sang so softly, she drew in the floor-dust that which could be seen everywhere in the art of their people, the Druids' coil of time, so that her granddaughter might see how it rippled out from the first mystic thought to the last great struggle between the forces of evil and good, a true spiral whose end became a beginning.

Rhianneth shivered, as her grandmother whispered of the terror which waited in the dark of the years unborn; of a battle between Gods and Giants on a vast plain when the Gods should fall and fire cover the earth.

'Take care, *cariad*,' she said, 'in the dying of the year, when the winds shake the last leaves from the trees. Then the powers of light and darkness are locked in combat, and the world grows dangerous and cries out for blood.'

Three things she gave her, each full of the power of life rising from the earth. One was Glainnader, the Druid's Glass, that she may see what was hidden within the circles of time; another was a many-coiled golden arm-ring with a serpent's head and ruby eyes to keep away dark evil; a third was a wooden box filled with the distilled and powdered medicines Rhianneth had helped concoct from last season's culling.

But one tiny phial of dark liquid she put into Rhianneth's hand and closed her fingers round it, telling her to keep it always with her for it was the most precious of all the gifts, hardily won by patience and by magic from the life essence of poppy and mandrake and things not to be named. Nine drops of this liquid would open the gates of the Otherworld so softly, so gently, that death would seem only the fading of one dream into another. Rhianneth looked at it with terror, but the gnarled hand tightened around hers so that the small bottle felt hard and strong within it.

'Don't fear it, Rhianneth,' she said softly. 'Use it when you must. You will know when that moment comes. So fine a drink is not for an enemy, but for a friend.'

Her words were beyond understanding, but no more would she say. Rhianneth watched her closed face as she rocked gently in the half-light of the bothie, and all questions died within her.

They had many days of strong winds and heavy unremitting rain. But then the sky cleared, and on that day Lovan at last came riding back, and Caius was with him.

Grandmother was sitting in the sunlight beside the bothie door. Unsmiling, she turned her face away as they approached. Rhianneth stood silent, her heart thudding.

Even with his cloak spattered and his boots thick-coated with mud, her cousin seemed more handsome, more civilised than ever against the background of the settlement.

He took her grimed and stained hands into his and kissed her cheek as the custom is between kinfolk. She blushed as he drew back and looked at her, remembering his kiss as they knelt beside the stream.

'You've grown, cousin, since last year,' he said, in a voice that reminded her with sweet pain of Marcus's cultured tones. 'You're a child no longer . . .'

His dark eyes turned towards Grandmother, and he greeted her formally with a brief bow that sent his cloak swirling. She inclined her head in acknowledgement, and with a gesture she banished Rhianneth to the inside of the bothie.

Caius toured the farm and looked at the sad and shuttered old house, and he slept that night in Lovan's bothie. Next day he came again to her grandmother. Within the space of another day Rhianneth knew she was to leave the settlement with Caius and Lovan, who was entering the service of her cousin.

'Time for us both to go, *cariad*,' he told her with wry cheerfulness, 'I'm no longer needed here with Marcus gone, and the house – and the horses . . .'

'What about Jupiter?' Rhianneth asked, thinking of the loving care Lovan had lavished on the finest of their young stallions, the only one left apart from those for their personal use. 'We can't leave him. We'll have to sell him, after all.'

'I've not bred him up for sale.' Lovan's eyes held a teasing glint. 'It's long been in my mind that you would need a fine gift to present to your half-brother in Mithrasia, and Jupiter is surely fit for a king.'

He laughed at her astonishment and waved away her stammered thanks. When she declared he was the best friend she could ever have in the world, she saw that he was pleased. But all he did was nod and say, 'Off you go then, and find something to take to your Aunt Julia!'

When she went to her mother's grave for the last time, she found Lovan there, but all his smiles were gone.

'She was a beautiful lady, your mother,' he said quietly and without turning, as if he knew she would come. 'Tall as a queen, and with hair red and glossy as a fine fox pelt.'

'I'm not like her, then,' Rhianneth replied, bending to leave a circlet of red-berried rowan intertwined with Roman roses from the bush still blooming near the old house. He turned then, and looked straight at her.

'No, you're not,' he said. 'You have a beauty of your own, Rhianneth, that comes from somewhere far, far back.'

She looked away quickly, filled with the familiar twist of guilt which always came when she thought of her mother, who, in giving her life, had died.

'My – Marcus loved her so . . .'

'Yes, I know,' Lovan answered softly, 'Or I would have married her myself.'

He spoke lightly. But Rhianneth sensed a deadly sharp pain somewhere deep within him, and kept in darkness because he loved them both. She watched him walk away, and was filled with a great sadness for an old sorrow long past redemption.

On the morning they left, Olwen wept and fussed over their belongings, packed into a small two-wheeled cart which Lovan's horse would pull, insisting that Rhianneth must come back next summer to tell them of life in Mithrasia. But Grandmother said nothing. She knew, as Rhianneth knew, that she would not return to see them again.

As they moved along the ridge away from the settlement, Rhianneth kept looking back into the valley at the old villa. Her mother's people would continue on the hill as they had always done, and after a while no doubt the Roman farm-house would be forgotten, like the families it had sheltered through the long years at the edge of Empire. Already it seemed to be settling back into the rich earth, as one with the land.

They rode towards the west in the bright morning, the sun throwing long shadows before them. She turned for one last time, and silently raised her hand in a Roman salute to the dying little villa which had for so long kept alive a dream of order, grace and beauty in a darkening world.

CHAPTER 3

The countryside lay hazy and still as they travelled along the old straight trackway leading west towards the sea, a way so worn that no longer needed were its flash-pools and beacon-heights. But the rains had turned the way into a muddy swamp which dragged the hooves of the horses down deep in some places and had them slipping and terrified in others. Caius had the gift-stallion Jupiter on a lead rein, and it often took all his strength and skill to get the horse, with his own, through to temporary firmer ground. Lovan had even greater difficulty with the wheels of the small baggage cart sinking into the mud, and many wearisome times Caius and Rhianneth had to push behind while Lovan strained beside his horse, urging him to greater efforts with encouraging words.

Flood waters covered the flats and hollows of the countryside. Grass that seemed firm was everywhere a squelching quagmire, so that it was seldom possible to skirt the muddy trackway.

'God's Light!' Caius shouted furiously, as they slipped and staggered through the long hours. 'Will we never get off this stinking trackway?'

Lovan's reply was steadying and calm. But Rhianneth saw his swift glance into the almost imperceptibly darkening sky, and realised it was possible they might not reach Deva before sunset. When at last they came to the hard military road from Viroconium and swung northwards, his relief was plain.

Flocks of birds called across the empty sky, heading for the far southlands. They flew swift and low, for rain was again near and winter cold was coming soon, despite the summer-warm sky.

Her cousin rode close, filling Rhianneth's thoughts. At his side hung his father's sword, dragged from the trampled battle-mud on the day Caius was born. She glanced quickly at his dark, intent young face, and felt the Old Gods whispering amongst the trees as they passed.

But her companions kept their eyes on the road ahead and on the nearby trees, and Lovan's hand rested never too far from the hunting knife at his side. The greenwoods rustled gently at the sides of the road, but they could hide danger, the

more so as they came closer to a city that no longer even pre-
tended to have any remnant of Roman-style civil administra-
tion, but which was already in truth what their Saxon enemies
called a stone tomb, inhabited by frightened people with no
other shelter to which they could flee despite the menace of
sickness, hunger and sudden violence by the *bacaudae*, the
lawless ones who lived on plunder.

Rhianneth thought of the ruin of Caer Melot and the trust
that had come down to them, and fears about her life ahead
battled with a deepening excitement as the sun slid down and
they drew nearer to Deva, the old City of the Legions.

More massive and thick than she could have imagined were the
stone walls of the city that followed the old earthwork ditch and
bank of the tribal stronghold which had been there before the
Romans came. In the dying light of the setting sun the red
sandstone ramparts reared above them like the last bastion of the
gods. Along the walls she caught the glint of helmet and spear, and
saw that shadows moved, watching the darkening countryside.

They clattered across a bridge and under an arched gateway.
Caius spoke to the black-bearded guard who wore a leather
tunic studded with nails and mud-stained plaid trousers of black
and red, cross-gartered above heavy winter boots. He nodded
briefly and let them through, his eyes already on the road
behind, anxious to close the gates before the fall of night.

So they came into the city, where already a few night
torches flared. But the smoky dusk-light revealed no great
white marbled public buildings or colourful shops. Only a
place of narrow streets and crumbling buildings, with broken
window shutters flapping in the wind.

Rhianneth's excitement seeped gradually away, until she
felt only a sick disappointment. A smell of decay came with
the night wind. She caught her breath with a cough, covering
her nose and mouth with the back of a hand.

'Delightful, isn't it?' said Caius. 'The whole place is filled
with rotting rubbish . . .'

'The whole place is dead,' Lovan put in tersely, 'killed
by the plague. Great God, life has drained away and
we're looking at the dregs!'

Empty houses stood with broken and sagging doors, beside some where the flicker of a candle showed shadows within. Where a building had collapsed, a roughly thatched wooden hut stood on top of the rubble, and several small children in the dark doorway sucked grubby thumbs as they watched them ride by.

They passed a house blackened and twisted by fire. The door had gone, with half the front wall. The family living room lay open, forlorn. In a corner lay a broken stone altar, the words carefully carved upon it, to Fortuna, the Home-bringer. A few spots of rain dashed into their faces, and a whirl of cold wind snatched at their cloaks and hissed of more to come.

Before them the road led up towards the dark and silent mass of the fortress. But Rhianneth, who had dreamed for so long, could no longer imagine the proud horses, the red-crested helmets or the triumphant Eagle of the Legion held aloft as they passed through the crowds to the fortress gates. Now gutters were filled with rubbish, and grass grew between stones which once had rung to the clatter of a thronged and thriving military town. She began to wonder what kind of inn there could possibly be in this empty city which had thrust aside her illusions with such a desolate and dirty sword.

The place they came to at last was clean, with whitewashed walls and a swept stone floor, the main room lit by one candle in an iron holder meant for three. It was quiet, with none of the bustle she had imagined in an inn. But it was the sign of the crucified lamb upon the wall which made the back of her neck prickle with uneasy awe, and confirmed her growing realisation that this was a Holy House.

'It's a double house,' Lovan explained, taking her to the window through which she could just make out the domain of the holy men stretching out at right angles to merge with other buildings huddled in the darkness beneath the wind and the rain. 'That's where Cai and I will sleep. You will stay here, with the holy women.'

Rhianneth felt tired, cold and lost. She did not want to be left alone. Seeing the look on her face, Lovan put out a finger and lifted her chin.

'It's the only safe house in town, *cariad*. We had to come through Deva this time. You couldn't have spent the night rolled in a horse blanket, as we've often done. Cheer up, it will be morning before you know it. All right?'

She nodded, pressing her lips tight together. He smiled, raising his hand with thumb upturned in the old Roman gesture for life, for good luck. Tears pricked unshed behind her eyes as she looked into his familiar, weatherlined face. In a changing world he stood firm and deep-rooted, bending with the wind and not breaking as it passed.

The Abbess herself took Rhianneth to a bed in a tiny narrow room, the privacy of which Caius had paid for with a gift for the House. The holy woman accepted his payment without a word. But when the candlelight fell upon the faint mark of Mithras on his forehead, she stepped back quickly from him, her eyes instantly cold.

'By the Light,' Rhianneth heard Caius say behind them as she followed the Abbess from the main room, 'these Christians hate the soldier's God more than they hate the Devil!'

Rhianneth stood very still while the Abbess fumbled with the catch of the window, wishing herself away from this holy place and out beneath the open sky. When she remembered the Christian sign on the wall of the candlelit room, she felt a great unease that Caius should speak in such a way before a most sacred symbol of the God, and her fingers itched to make the ancient sign against evil.

After the Abbess left, Rhianneth lay on the hard bed, covered with a rough, warm blanket, and listened to the rustlings and mutterings, movements and whispers beyond the thin, dividing walls. To the left was a large open dormitory, and to her right was the room in which they had dined on thick stew, barley bread and cold water.

Though her limbs ached from the long ride, her mind refused to slow into sleep. For a long while she lay and watched the raindrops splatter like silver stars against the thick dark glass of the window.

She thought of Mithras, Caius's god of the morning, once beloved of the Roman army. The city of Mithrasia had even been named for him. But the legions had been broken, and now, in the worship of this older god who was born in a cave, was called the good shepherd, the saviour, and whose sacramental meal of bread and water before battle was too much like the last supper of the Christos, she knew that Marcus's Christian church saw a mockery of its own faith. Many Mithraic temples had been desecrated, by the followers of Christ.

The brand on her cousin's brow marked him as a soldier in the army of Mithras sworn to fight the forces of darkness, as his father had been before him and as his uncle Wencam was still.

Rhianneth remembered Grandmother, crooning her charms to make the grain grow or to keep away evil; Marcus, invoking the protection of Christ against the workings of Satan. Perhaps in the end, it was all one. Llwy, lord of light. Mithras, god of light. Christ, light of the world. Different lanterns to hold off the Dark . . .

The strange cold smell, the alienness of the place, made her shiver. She crept out of bed and opened the window. A swirl of wind and a rush of rain came into the room, but she stood for long minutes breathing in the cleanness of the night.

Through the dark air a bell sounded a message for the holy men. Pale candlelight flickered in the dark windows across the courtyard, and, muffled by the thick walls, came the sound of men's voices, chanting in prayer. A lantern swayed in the wind, its yellow light flashing and fading in the rain-swept puddles.

She seemed unable to move. Gradually she grew colder, and the night thickened, reality melted. The chanting began to fill her ears, until it was chanting no longer but a thundering of warrior boots, a spear-rushing and a sword-striking. Here in this Holy House she felt the power of old gods, vast and strange, coming like ice from the dark north, and she was falling, dropping as if through time itself towards an inexorable and unbearable terror. In her ears was the hollow sound of a great bell that changed into the ringing of axe and sword, the stirring of rain-damp wind that was a hissing of spears, and a low singing that turned into screams heard only inside her head.

Gasping for breath, Rhianneth dragged herself down to the

floor, eyes squeezed shut and hands clutching the Druid's Glass which hung around her neck. Glainnader's locked-in power throbbed, faint and steady, while the moments passed and the terror faded. Until she heard again only the night-dark rain blowing cold upon the window.

Still, she stayed. Still as a wild thing when the hunter is close, until her mind was her own and the time-wind whistled away towards the outer depths, searching for other prey. She felt the stirring of the stone warm beneath her hands. For her, if she dared or wanted it, the Serpent's Egg would show what lay beyond the sounds she had heard. But instantly her mind swerved away. She was not ready. She could not yet bear the reality she might see within the stone.

She crawled to her bed and lay shivering, pulling the blanket close. Her thoughts wavered, and for a while she drifted in a deep pool of weakness. But this was a weakness she knew. *As I am, so are you, daughter of my daughter.* She remembered how her grandmother's hands would fall limp, and the curious blankness in her old eyes when she had gazed too long into the fire; for the sight was not really a gift at all, but an often dangerous trading with powerful forces where unsteady time-shifts were glimpsed at the cost of a loss of life force not easily regained.

Tomorrow they would be gone from this place and on the road for Mithrasia. The ride would be long, and her limbs ached and her head burned as if with fever, yet she longed to see the grey new day lift the darkness away.

In the twilight country between sleeping and waking, Caius haunted her thoughts. Since he and Marcus had fought so hard for her acceptance as half-sister to Llywarch, it surely followed that marriage to a bastard daughter of the king was more to be desired than that to the heir of Marcus Caprilius. Elidyr's gifts were riches enough, but the power that came with the blood-royal was treasure indeed. Her cousin was close to the young king, and would be closer, Lovan had said. With a slow trickle of excitement she told herself she did not care what secret ambitions Caius had, so long as he looked on her with favour.

Somewhere a soft bell rang, and through the thin wall to the left there was a shuffling, and a mumbling of prayers.

Rhianneth rolled away on to her side and covered up her ears. But before her eyes closed she whispered twice over the small prayer Marcus had taught her as a child. A prayer to the Christos and the Holy Lady His Mother, for protection from the terrors that come by night. For the house was His, and they slept within its power.

The daylight was thin and cold as they left Deva. Rain drifted in the air and the streets were empty and silent. Only a small black cat arched its back defensively as they passed by, its eyes gleaming tree-green in the pale light. One of the guards muttered something as they rode through the massive gates, and Lovan's reply brought a guffaw of laughter ringing after them, laughter that thinned into the misty air until it died into nothing, and became as one with the hot cookhouse songs and barrack-room laughter of the lost twentieth legion which had made this city its own.

Gone was Cai's brave scarlet. He was cloaked in grey like the morning, and his face was closed and sombre. Lovan gave her a smile as she sat stiffly on Romulus's broad back. But if he noted her pale cheeks and shadowed eyes he made no comment.

Rhianneth had slept heavily after the lonely terror of the night, but sleep had not refreshed her. She felt sick and her head ached. She had already swallowed one of Grandmother's healing powders, and now waited passively for it to work its soothing magic.

They were on the old legionary road to Mithrasia, and when they entered the forest to the north of Deva the trees closed overhead and it grew dim, as if morning had not yet reached into the crowded woodlands and night still prevailed. After a while the misty dampness of the air seemed to creep into Rhianneth's bones and she shivered. Over the sleek dark mane of Romulus raindrops were scattered like glass beads, glittering in the cold light. The forest tangled thickly green to the road's edge, and in the silence around them she felt the fear that had long pervaded this land stir strongly within herself. She knew she was in the dark grip of last night's seeing, but could not shake off the impenetrable horrors.

This road from Deva to the north had once felt the marching feet of the legions, the rolling wheels of pleasure and trade. Now it stretched silently before them, its broken stones offering many a breach through which the rapacious greenwoods were already creeping. Rhianneth thought much of Marcus who had travelled along it before her, and then of the shining lances of Caer Melot, riding beneath the dragon-banner which once had been carried by the auxilliary cohorts of Rome. A lone fox barked once, far off in the woodlands, and she remembered Giff, dying in defence of his old home.

Their world was cracking apart, and life was sliding into an abyss. Soon barbarism would smother their hard-won knowledge, music, poetry, as the briars of the forest were reaching and covering their strong stone roads. She thought of the wretched waifs of Deva, those grey shadows from whom she had been kept apart; many were sick and hungry, some were dying. Where could they go, what could they do, save cling to the shell of a city itself sick unto death? And hope, always hope, that better times would come.

When they paused briefly for a sip of wine and one of Olwen's sweet flat-cakes, Lovan asked if she wanted to rest for a while, his face plainly showing he sensed her unease. She shook her head and raised her chin as she saw Caius glance round, his eyes resting sharply on her pale face.

'I couldn't sleep,' she explained, 'and my head aches. I keep thinking of Deva. I wish I'd never seen it.'

'Ah – Deva!' Lovan said, searching her face. 'I dare say it will survive, somehow. People will crawl back after a while . . .'

'But we, little cousin, are heading for Mithrasia,' put in Caius, stretching as he moved towards his horse, 'and things are different there. We are still very much alive – and mean to remain so!'

As they rode away the men talked between themselves, their conversation at first making only a background for Rhianneth's darkling thoughts, until gradually their words thrust themselves upon her.

'Treachery? It's been bred into us, both from Britain and the Empire.' Lovan eased the muscles in his back. 'You speak

71

much of Camlann. But I've heard it said that even the Great Raid – yes, that far back – was only made possible because of vast corruption in our espionage service, in the Arcani. Even there were men eager to sell anything for gold, for power.'

'And men as willing to give themselves to save what they'd built!' Caius answered swiftly, and Lovan fell silent for a while.

'Will the alliance hold?' he asked then. 'Ida needs our cattle, our corn . . .'

'Not as much as we need his spears at the back of our enemies, and he knows it,' Caius answered dryly. 'The Bernicians are fighting people – Ida claims descent from their war god Woden. They live well enough. What they need, they take. Their fortress of Din Guaryrdi is nothing more than a pirates' stronghold.'

'But to them you would entrust our northern defences?' Lovan thrust in, and Caius took his eyes off the road ahead to look sharply at him.

'To them, I've entrusted my wife,' he said wryly, 'Morvydd is in Bernicia now, awaiting my triumphant return with the sealed war-bond.'

Lovan expelled his breath in a sudden oath. His horse's head shot up with a snort of surprise at his involuntary jerk on the reins.

'Your wife,' he said after a moment, hard anger underlying the held steadiness of his voice. 'She's a hostage?'

They rode on in silence. Shock held Rhianneth still and straight on Romulus, her mind momentarily blank. The fox barked again, farther away now and lonely-sounding.

'Not a hostage. She's with child and could not travel home with me. She's safe enough. They may be barbarians. They are not savages.'

Pain pierced Rhianneth like a cold sword blade. O, Caius, Caius! she cried silently, what have you done? You were my Alexander, my Caesar, my Arturius! Together we were to have diced with the Gods and won back Britain for the Empire. For that, I rode with you though my grandmother's warnings rang in my ears – no, not for that. For you. For you!

The dark Roman face of her cousin had been in her mind and heart since the day he'd come riding into their courtyard. In her dreams they had travelled together into Mithrasia, and then before the first of the winter snows fell . . . She leaned forward, digging her fingers deep into Romulus's thick mane, forcing the tears back into the secret place where her love had grown darkly and in quietness. For now the truth lay before her, winter-bare.

The voices of her companions floated across, far-off, thin, ghost-like. It grew colder, and the sky darkened. Slowly, as if in a dream, she swayed sideways. Even when Lovan had her safely in his arms he seemed insubstantial, not real at all.

Kneeling on the hard stones, Lovan cradled her head on his arm, compassion in his eyes. 'I would have told you, *cariad*. But not now, like this . . .' His voice was a low mumble in her head.

Then Caius crouched beside them, holding to her lips a small bottle cased in leather.

'There's my brave filly!' Lovan murmured as she swallowed, and of Caius he asked abruptly. 'What in Hell is that, Cai? Wine from Gaul?'

'Aquavitae, from Pictland.' Caius was so close his breath stirred her hair. 'You can sometimes get it, up past the Wall.'

The liquid was like fire in her throat and she almost choked. The water of life. Precious, costly liquid made in the secret places of the far north. It was said it could sometimes revive a corpse, and with the life-fire of it burning she could believe it. But ironic, it seemed, that Caius should waste its life-giving force when he had so suddenly and unwittingly killed all that was in life for her.

They travelled on at a slow pace, for Lovan decided that for her sake the journey was best taken in two days. That night they stayed at a roadside inn, rolled in blankets on the warm wooden floor of the upstairs room, with the smell of barley beer and roasted meats coming up with the smoky air through the cracks in the boards.

Across the room the only other guests, a couple with a child not yet able to walk, snapped and snarled their way through a quarrel which only just stopped short of blows as they settled the child and arranged their blankets beside it. Caius gave Rhianneth a wink, and she managed a faint smile; but she was glad to be sleeping next to the wall, with her cousin and Lovan between her and that barely-contained violence.

At last the room grew quiet. But although she ached with exhaustion and with real pain from the long hours of riding and walking, she lay awake and desolate beside Caius, empty of everything except an all-pervading misery.

Light from the room below made grey shadows move in the corners. She could hear the landlord's son playing on the little wooden pipe with which he had entertained them earlier. But then it had been a rollicking merry tune, the words of which Lovan knew but could not be persuaded to sing. Now other notes floated upwards, thin and sweet and sad.

Caius lay turned away from her, on his side. Beside him was his sword, his hand upon it even in sleep. Silently in the darkness Rhianneth let flow bitter salt tears she had scorned to release in daylight. Caius was not for her. He had filled her dreams and her thoughts had been only of him, but he had not waited. He already moved amongst great events and saw her only as a kinswoman, for whom he felt a responsibility. While she had dreamed, cocooned in learning and love, he had taken a wife and fathered a child, and was lost to her.

Caius would bear the torch lit by Caer Melot into the dark of the years ahead, but she would not be the battle-maid at his side. His wife lay waiting for him in the camp of the Saxons, his child beneath her heart.

And yet, she thought, I've looked into the Druid's Glass. My grandmother read for me the signs I saw, and he was there, my torchbearer. Closer than kin to me, she said.

She felt for Glainnader, her Serpent's Egg with its forked pictures that twisted truth and guarded the knowledge of which the Gods were so jealous. That knowledge was hard-gained and dangerous to hold, and the caverns of truth infinite. But she would take it and use it, for there was no safe haven or promise of joy in the life ahead and it was her only weapon, her only shield.

For a while she lay quiet, listening to the pipe's sweet lament, until at last it faltered and stopped. Drying tears stung her face and were warm—washed by others. Then, in the darkness and silence, sleep came.

They were on the road soon after daylight, thankful to be away from the primitive accommodation. For this last part of their journey they rode across heathland where small clumps of stunted trees clung together as though the dark forest which rimmed the horizon had tried to take hold and failed. The quiet air was disturbed only by the soft noise of their passing, and with Deva far behind and Mithrasia within reach well before nightfall, the dangers of their journey gradually faded like yesterday's mists.

The day moved on, until the sun was high above and the warmed air came spiked with the subtle scents of damp woodlands, wild strawberries, marsh flowers and heather. Lovan swore he had fleas, so they sat in the shade of a clump of hawthorn bushes while he stripped and bathed in a little stream.

'Homesick, cousin?' Caius teased her. 'Too late to turn back now!'

'Tired and stiff,' she told him shortly. 'Hungry, too.'

He laughed. 'Little girls are always hungry! Let's eat then. What have we got?'

Suddenly she hated him. So that's how he thought of her. A little girl! Rhianneth could not bring herself to remind him that she was of marriageable age. Not when the desolation of yesterday was still so close.

She turned and rummaged in the travel bags, hiding the twin flags of temper and pain that coloured her cheeks. Their rough overnight inn had provisioned them with meat, bread, sweet honey cakes, apples and barley beer, and when Lovan returned they made a feast of it, with the late summer bees droning between yellow gorse and scattered heathland flowers.

Conversation turned to the great war-horses of Gaul which once Britain had possessed in numbers, but which were fast reverting back into their own smaller sturdy breed. These could not be bettered, declared Lovan, for they were strong and willing and intelligent, and suited the countryside and climate.

Caius shook his head, his hair blowing in the sunlight, half-covering the small scar on his forehead. 'For a cavalry charge,' he insisted, 'you need height and weight – '

'And control,' Rhianneth put in eagerly. 'Roman discipline, like Artur with his cataphracts that could wheel and swerve and charge at his command!'

Caius swung round, his dark eyes shining. 'That's it! That's what broke the Saxons at Badon, those huge horses with their chain-mailed riders acting as one – as if the great dragon itself had left our banner and come glittering down upon them out of the sun!'

Excitement flashed between them. But Lovan was already murmuring wryly. 'For that kind of control you need a commander. A High King, to lead all the rulers of Britain and take for his own war-host the finest of their warriors. A matter of pride then, it was, to be one of the "men of Artur." But now,' he shrugged, 'the kingdoms have closed their gates. Even the united power of the north cracked apart before Rhun's army.'

Caius flung himself back on the rough grass, his arms behind his head, eyes narrowed against the sun.

'The queen's peace with Rhun was sealed with marriage with one of Elidyr's nieces. Mithrasia's greatest danger is not now from the far west, but from the north . . .'

Rhianneth thought, Elidyr's niece? She would be, she supposed, a cousin to herself. One of so many unknown blood-kin she'd yet to meet. Then she realised they would probably never meet. The girl had been handed over to seal a hurried peace, like a load of grain or a few horses. Rhianneth had never imagined how cruel life was. Nor, until she'd seen Deva, how very dark and cold it could be.

'Our problem is how to keep his spears turned to the Saxon east,' Caius was saying, 'and his eyes from the soft south of his fellow-countrymen!'

Lovan tossed away an apple core and got to his feet. 'He

does speak of friendship. That's something, from Urien.'

Urien of Rheged. Though Rhun's name still rumbled like thunder from the west, now in the north stood a young king whose battle-fame was making Mithrasia even more uneasy. Another tall cousin of Llywarch, growing in power.

'If Urien speaks of friendship,' Caius said fiercely, 'the more does Mithrasia need her battle-horses. The kind Constantine breeds still, in Dumnonia!'

'Mithrasia rides only one horse, Cai. It's called Diplomacy, out of Necessity, by Cunning. Now we must make treaties and alliances. Not war.'

Rhianneth watched the light die in her cousin's eyes. Abruptly he sat up, and gazed in silence out across the heath-land towards the dark forest at its edge.

'Yes, I know.' he said, at last. 'We live by balancing one terror against another. That's how it must be.'

Springing to his feet, he threw back his head to more easily fasten the shoulder brooch of his cloak. Then he swung round, holding out a hand to pull Rhianneth to her feet.

'You've learnt more than the poetry of old Rome, Rhianneth,' he said softly. 'Like the red fox, you study strategems. Are you also wild and fierce then, cousin fox-cub, beneath your soft woman-weaves?'

'Marcus was her tutor.' There was a hint of anger in Lovan's voice. 'She might, I think, best you in her knowledge of things past.'

Caius loosed her hand, but his eyes held hers. 'And things to come? Did your grandmother show you the destruction of Britain?'

'If she had,' Rhianneth replied quietly, 'would I not now be riding the other way? Down into the Summer Country and beyond – even across the Narrow Sea?'

He laughed. But a stab of memory – that rain-swept night in the Holy House at Deva – came to her. She turned and ran across to where Romulus cropped the sweet grass at the edge of the road.

'My lady vixen,' Caius called after her, 'you must tell me more of your thoughts on war. If our policies fail, we may need them!'

The teasing note was back in her cousin's voice. She stroked the horse's thick mane, not answering. She amused and interested him, he saw her as a bright young kinswoman with knowledge different from most girls he knew. That was all. What could he know of the Druid's Glass that had shown them as much more than cousin-close?

Her hand froze into sudden stillness. It had not been just the memory of her night-terror at Deva that caused her to break away from Caius. It had been something she'd felt between them as she looked into his eyes. Something she had instantly shut off. Too late. She knew, with the deadly cold certainty of her kind, that what lay between them was indeed the closeness of love, or death.

The sun was low in the sky when they came over the brow of a hill and the city of Mithrasia lay shimmering before them in its golden light. Surrounded by the great walls raised by Maximus, it lay on the southern bank of the River Seteia, where the waters were still narrow enough for a bridge crossing and long before they opened into the great estuary to the west.

'Behold!' Caius declared mockingly, in the Roman tongue, 'Mithrasia Brigantum – the soldiers' city. Flower of all Britain's coloniae!'

He pointed out the fortress of the king, rising from the centre of the city with the red dragon banner fluttering from its square tower.

'The town was originally planned as a pleasant market community,' he said, 'where soldiers honourably discharged from service might bring up their families in peace – yet provide Rome with a sure base of trained men in times of sudden alarm.'

Caius's horse tossed its head, smelling home, and he stilled it with a firm hand. 'Maximus turned it into a garrison town. Part of his chain of defence against raiders from the north. The Auxilliary Legions once had their headquarters here, where three military roads meet.'

Now, Rhianneth thought, it is the fortress of my thirteen-year-old half-brother Llywarch and his all-powerful mother,

78

Queen Myffan. The warm sun glowed over her and she trembled, suddenly cold. Because her mind had been full of dreams, she had come to this perilous place from which her mother had fled in fear of her life. Now grey reality settled like dust. Her father Elidyr had been dead for half a decade. Maelgwyn's daughter reigned in all but name, for Llywarch was still a child. Caius may have persuaded him to send for her, but the witch-queen would not welcome the open presence of her husband's bastard within the walls of her fortress.

Caius meant to use the blood-tie between them to raise the Caprilius family higher, as well as to add strength to the military urgings of the Caer Melot Fellowship which he and his father's brother Wencam kept always near the young king. So she could not expect to stay for long safe beneath her aunt's roof but would, like her mother, venture into the dangerous political cross currents that swirled through the old fortress of Maximus.

Rhianneth knew the path upon which her feet were set. But it led away into darkness beyond which she could not see. When she thought of her grandmother's words as she turned with tears on her old face in the dimness of her house, fear rose within Rhianneth, strong as death.

Then Caius's hand was warm on her arm. She turned and looked into his eager young face, and love-pain overwhelmed her.

She had come for love, for life, for adventure. If love was lost to her, then she would grasp what remained. She was a king's daughter. She had the blood of Magnus Maximus. She had knowledge and power. And she had Glainnader.

One dream was left. To join the Fellowship of Caer Melot and use what arts she possessed to save what remained of the Empire in Britain. She would light her pathway with that tale of lonely heroism in a world grown dark, and Arturius the soldier should have her for his battle-maid.

The elegant town house with its small enclosed paved garden shone with loving care. Everything gleamed, the silver candlesticks, the bronze lamps, the tiled floors. Nothing was shabby, not the curtains or cushions, nor the covers on the beds.

Aunt Julia welcomed Rhianneth with a kiss, exclaiming with pleasure at the roll of fine red cloth, jars of apple-blossom honey, the small bronze figure of Mercury which had been in Marcus's bedroom, though Rhianneth felt the gifts were poor indeed when seen against the quiet luxury which surrounded her aunt.

She was as dark as Caius, small and nervous. She darted about the house touching this, moving that. When she sewed during her afternoon rest-times, her needle flew in and out of the material in an agitated way while she talked of the family, of how worried she was about Cai's wife Morvydd and her coming child; of the latest news, the price of food, the weather, everything that encircled her world.

When first she saw Rhianneth's unpacked belongings, Julia hastily set her woman slave Torfrida to making new garments for her niece. She was horrified by Rhianneth's strong-nailed working boots, pulling her quickly into a bedroom and bringing out sandals and soft slippers for her to try.

'Marcus would never forgive me,' she cried, when Rhianneth protested she would never need so much footwear, 'if I presented you to Mithrasia looking anything less than the sister of the king!'

She threw back a heavy curtain to reveal her own beautiful clothes. Rhianneth ran her fingers over them in pleasure, wondering at their smooth texture and many colours. Some were soft and winter-warm, others of a weave so fine she could see the shape of her hand beneath.

Urged by her aunt, she tried on a dress of bright cornflower blue, loving the feel of its smooth folds against her legs. A twisted belt of silver threads drew the gown closely in, and with a rush of vanity Rhianneth saw how tiny her waist looked, how glossily dark her hair shone against so delicate a colour.

Like a butterfly in her yellow dress her aunt fluttered about the room, hovering at last over a table littered with hair pins, combs, ribbons, tweezers, and small oblong mixing palettes of stone with their neat flat-bladed implements of bronze. Scattered amongst these were little wooden boxes, glass bottles, small alabaster jars, and finely wrought hand-mirrors.

'Come, try this!' Julia insisted, 'Smell this!'

Box lids were removed, jars and bottles unstopped, and the perfumes and lotions within almost stole away Rhianneth's senses with their sweetness. Eagerly she painted her eyelids with malachite-green powder mixed on one of the small palettes, warmed her lips with a touch of red-ochre.

Then she laughed. I look over-coloured, unreal! she thought. But after a while the cosmetics seemed to reveal a strange beauty she'd not known she possessed.

She remembered gazing in her mother's mirror in vain for the classical lines of Rome, finding instead a promise of something else. Now that promise was made true, in the slant of an eyebrow, the high curve of a cheek. All the witchery of Grandmother's ancient honey-island looked back at her from green-shadowed eyes in the mirror, and she felt a power within. A power that owed nothing at all to the lore of any wise-woman.

Torfrida piled materials on the floor for her to choose and their rainbow colours spilled in a fantastic waterfall. Surely, she thought, not even in the land of Rhiannon could there be more beauty than this!

'You must have this,' her aunt shook out a length of green gossamer-fine wool, 'and this one, and this . . . and please, Rhianneth, do not call me "aunt"! Julia will do very well.' She glanced up with a flurried smile. 'I once had an Aunt Julia of my own, with a voice like a drill-master; to hear the names together still terrifies me!'

Rhianneth laughed. She found her aunt delightful, and was grateful for the gaiety Julia brought to the task of smoothing away her rough country edges. Here, where the scent of roses drifted heavily in from the garden to mingle with the exotic perfumes in the room, her childhood dream seemed within a hand's reach. She really could become, as Marcus had intended, an Imperial lady.

Yet, in the dark regions of her mind a small pain stirred. For she knew she would wear the new dresses, redden her lips and perfume her hair only in the hope that Caius would think her beautiful.

Mithrasia was a living city, not dark and haunted like Deva. When Rhianneth went out of her aunt's house into the early morning sunshine with Caius two days later, wearing a new dress green as meadowgrass, her feet in light thonged sandals of softest leather, she was stunned by its size and wealth.

They walked past houses set in walled gardens, where trees grown tall over the years raised heavy green branches towards the sun. The roads were paved with close-fitting stones, and there were even raised pavements to keep their feet dry, as they walked free from the danger of passing horses and carts.

Narrow, open-fronted shops lined the main streets leading to the forum. They passed a cobbler already hammering at his last, with finished shoes and sandals strung around the walls awaiting customers. A wine merchant, more discreet, kept most of his precious wares hidden in cool darkness behind and below his shop.

A draper called to them, gesturing to his stock of colourful cloths, some rough-looking and cheap, some finely-woven and very costly. But Caius tugged at her hand and they walked on, passing a butcher's shop where a small red-haired boy sat at one end of the counter and occasionally moved a long slender-leaved branch up and down to keep flies away from the hanging meat. Next door was a pottery, with piles of ready-made pots stacked perilously one upon the other. Rhianneth saw some shiny red earthenware in a corner like the pots they used at home for everyday, but Caius told her that such ware was expensive now, and scarce.

'It has to be brought from Gaul, no one makes it here any-more', he said, 'which means a long journey up through Dumnonia on the safe western route. Look, here's something that's always cheap, made here at home, and always in demand . . .'

The bone-worker's high counter was full of combs, pins, ornaments, needles, whistles – everything of use or beauty that could be worked. He evidently did not lack for trade, for he went on whistling around his shop and made no attempt to urge them to buy.

Nearer the forum the streets began to stir with life as more people appeared, some walking briskly to begin work, some plodding with baskets on arms towards the market square. Children shouted to each other, racing on errands for early morning bargains of damaged fruit, scorched loaves, broken eggs or cakes.

In the now bustling forum square, the last of many temporary wooden stalls were being hastily hammered into place. Across the square stood the old basilica with its storerooms and offices, and behind it reared the grey stone of the fortress, its bright flag flapping.

Rhianneth thought that Rome itself could surely not be bigger or more splendid, but Caius laughed at her exclamations. Then he pointed out the huge stone over the forum entrance, dedicated in carved and red-painted letters to Magnus Maximus, Imperator.

Rhianneth stared up at the grey stone, red-slashed with straight Roman letters, pride winging through her. 'Am I,' she whispered, 'truly of his line?'

Caius spun her round to face him. 'You are Elidyr's daughter, in direct descent,' he said, his laughter gone, 'never forget that! Marcus spent the last weeks of his life making sure that no one else forgot.'

'Oh, I know!' She was immediately cast down by his frown. 'I only meant – ' She glanced up again at the stone. 'It all seems so . . . magnificent.'

His face changed, softened. 'Come on, little cousin,' he sighed. 'Let's see what the shops have to offer today!'

The roughly erected booths in the centre of the forum were piled with the harvest of the countryside around Mithrasia, with baskets full of cherries, apples, onions, cabbages. One stall was heaped with panniers, plaited baskets, mats and chairs; another sold drinks made of barley and honey and was already doing a brisk trade.

At the side of the square was an arched colonnade, and in its shade was an eating house, shops selling meat pies, and several others displaying brightly-coloured sweets, small toys, lucky charms made in the shapes of birds and animals. From one of these Caius brought a small bronze brooch.

'For you, my lady vixen,' he mocked gently, putting it into her hand, 'a gift of welcome, from Mithrasia. May it bring you luck and happiness in your new life.'

Rhianneth's fingers closed in a rush of pleasure around the cleverly wrought little fox-brooch with its pointed face and thick curved brush. Already she knew that when it was not fastening her cloak it would lie amongst the glittering jewel-gifts sent by Elidyr, and mean more to her than any of them.

'I think I'm lucky already, to have you and Julia.' She looked up at him. 'With such a fine talisman, how can I help but find happiness too?'

Their eyes met, and instantly she looked away, terrified he might read what was in her mind and heart. She forced a smile.

'You are fortunate to have Morvydd and a child on the way. Julia worries, but she is very pleased.'

'Yes, I know,' he answered shortly. 'Morvydd's family were kind to my mother, years ago, before I was born. Their home is in the south, in the Summer Country where my parents lived when they first married. Morvydd was born there, in her grandfather's house.'

She ran fingertips over the brooch lying in the palm of her hand. Her heartbeat quickened. 'Was your marriage then an arrangement between families, not m-made simply for love . . .?'

There was a pause. From out of the bright sunlight the calls of traders came into their pillared shade, the scents of the market drifted in with them.

'All marriages are made for love, Rhianneth,' Caius said, strangely bitter. 'For love of something.'

His hand came over hers, stilling her fingers over the little brooch. She looked up. There was something behind his eyes she could not read, and she shivered. An old woman, muttering under her breath as her laden basket scraped and tilted dangerously, shuffled between them and a stone pillar. Caius

84

drew Rhianneth out into the warmth of the sunlit square, and the odd moment passed. But she could not stop probing.

'I don't understand how you could have left Morvydd to live with strangers. Is she all alone amongst the Saxons?'

Without answering he stopped at a stall selling apples and bought some, handing one to her and biting into another.

'I did not willingly leave Morvydd at Din Guaryrdi. When we married, I meant her to stay with Julia. She would not. When we reached Eboracum, I wanted her to stay there. She insisted on coming into Bernicia, although she knew my business for the king meant I must travel often and fast. She is inclined to hysterics.' He glanced at Rhianneth, his face shuttered. 'I am used to such outbursts of emotion from my mother. But Morvydd was already pregnant. I feared for the child. I gave in. When it was time for me to return to Mithrasia she was ill. She could not travel.'

Rhianneth stared unseeing across the busy square. She could find nothing to say. After a moment, his voice lighter, Caius went on: 'My mother believes Morvydd is in Eboracum. I've let her go on thinking so. But in truth, Rhianneth, she is safe enough. She has her two women with her – one of them an old witch who has seen more births than new moons. By the time I return, the baby will have been born.' He hesitated. 'A new sprig for the Caprilius tree.'

Caius's child. A living chain to bind him close. Here was reality, the dream-shatterer, and jealousy threatened to choke her, despite the casual unconcern of his words.

They walked on, under the stone of Maximus and into the city streets, heading towards the other gate, where the road led north. Now Rhianneth realised where they were going, the real purpose of their morning walk.

As they stood beside the grave, next to the memorial stone erected in honour of Caius's father, silence fell between them.

Julia had wept, as she spoke of Marcus. But Rhianneth could not connect the Marcus Caprilius of the newly-cut stone with the man she had known as her father, and who dwelt for her still in their own house and wandered with the old dogs through the lonely cattle pastures. Her slow tears, when they came at last, were for all that had vanished with her lost childhood, for the hopes and dreams that were even now sliding away.

'What did Marcus want for me, Cai?' she asked. 'Beyond acceptance by Llywarch?'

'Marriage, what else? Through my mother's friendship with Morvydd's family in the south-west, feelers have been put out regarding one of the sons of Constantine . . .'

She gasped, swinging round to face him. 'No one told me! Not you, not Julia – not even Lovan!'

Caius caught her hands, holding her still. 'Marcus wanted you safe, deep in Artur's country. Far from the Saxons and the threats from the north.'

Dark hair blew across the faint scar on his forehead as the sun slanted across his face, highlighting the fine bone structure beneath his summer-tanned skin. He smiled, that sweet smile which turned her legs to water.

'I've watched you playing the lady for my mother, Rhianneth. Delighted as a child with your pretty dresses and soft shoes. But I've seen something else, that not even this can hide.' His finger feathered across the newly-painted shadow on her eyelids. 'Something Artur would have recognised.'

He took her face between his hands. 'There are stormlights behind those beautiful eyes,' he said softly. 'You want far more from the world, my lady vixen, than crops and kitchen and cradle. Am I not right?'

So short a while ago she had wanted nothing from the world but Caius. Even now her heart turned over as their eyes met. She saw again the meadow and the shining stream, the soft crushed cowslips. Felt the kin-kiss on her cheek that had stirred her dreams into pain-filled life.

'You asked me once,' Caius went on, 'if you could be part of the Fellowship. Or have you forgotten that?'

With an effort she pulled free of him. 'I remember,' she answered dully, 'You told me I would soon be more interested in other things.'

'Like this?' Caius lifted a fold of her dress, let it drop. 'It is what interests most girls. But you are different, Rhianneth.'

Different. Because she had a little of her grandmother's ancient lore and uncertain gift of sight? Or because she was Elidyr's love-child with the blood of Maximus in her veins? Already she knew enough about her cousin to realise the strength of the twin forces that drove him, his ambition for the family and his obsession with the defence of the Empire in Britain.

She lifted her chin, turning to look at the road leading away into the northlands, the lands of Urien and Riderch, and swallowed the bitterness in her throat as she remembered the silent vow she'd made, standing before Mithrasia in the sunlit afternoon. Marcus, she thought forlornly, why did you fill me with your dreams, open my mind with your knowledge, if not for this? The sons of Constantine are not for me, nor the safety of the Summer Land.

In the quiet air, only Caius's voice answered. 'Will you join us now, cousin fox-cub? Will you use your cunning and your beauty to help keep Mithrasia safe for the Empire?'

For a moment Rhianneth stood very still, the smooth stone of Marcus's grave hard and cold beneath her hand.

Then she turned, with a smile, towards her cousin.

Rhianneth met her half-brother Llywarch for the first time on a dark windy evening just after sunset.

Stone columns soared upwards into darkness as their footsteps echoed across the basilican hall. Lanterns flared against peeling, painted walls of blue, green and yellow, emphasising the vastness of this place where once officials of the city had gone about their work and merchants from all parts of the Empire had conducted their business.

In the fortress proper, a guard flung open a door. Inside, a big man of middle years played a battle-game with coloured pieces on a wooden board, opposite a serious-faced boy.

The man rose at once, coming swiftly to kiss Rhianneth's cheek. His breath smelt of wine and his long moustaches tickled. When he drew back to look at her she saw that his right arm was stiff and held close-angled to his chest. Like Caius, he bore the sign of Mithras on his brow. This then, was Wencam, Julia's brother, who had survived Camlann and brought Caius up to manhood.

'Well,' he said, staring boldly, 'you have a look of Elidyr, that's for sure! Llywarch, this is your half-sister, my niece Rhianneth.'

The boy looked up, his delicate hand hovering over the pieces on the board. 'Yes,' he said casually, 'I know.'

There was a long silence. Llywarch carefully swept the playing pieces to one side of the board, glancing quickly at Rhianneth and away again. Wencam put his head on one side with a wry smile. Caius said nothing, but his tension was palpable.

'You are a beautiful lady,' Llywarch said unexpectedly, 'and you're young! I'm glad. Nearly everybody is so old. Can you play this game?'

She nodded. 'But I'm only just a lady. I'm about two years older than you, Llywarch. Girls grow up more quickly, that's all.'

Her half-brother gave a faint smile, and motioned her to take the seat opposite him vacated by Wencam. Caius slowly let out his breath, glanced towards the still smiling Wencam. They settled upon a covered bench, watching as the little king set out the pieces once more.

Rhianneth had played the game with Marcus, but had never really beaten him although he'd sometimes encouraged her by losing deliberately. Luck always deserted as soon as she took her place at a games board, and she had no more success now. Soon, as always, she was losing. She chased fallen pieces around the floor, became hot and scarlet-cheeked, and in danger of losing her temper. Llywarch was greatly amused, triumphantly scooping her lost pieces into his hands and laughing aloud at Rhianneth's indignant challenges, her cries of annoyance.

Llywarch was eagerly setting up the board for another game when he suddenly stopped, the laughter dying out of his thin young face. Rhianneth followed his eyes to the door, and her blood chilled as a dark figure came slowly forward.

Wencam got to his feet. 'This is Lucius, the king's tutor.' He made no attempt to hide the sardonic note in his voice. 'A very holy man.'

The priest stared at her with a strange expression of restrained anger and sorrow, but said nothing. She looked into the man's gaunt, shrewd face and black eyes, and suddenly realised what she was expected to do.

'Give me your blessing, Father,' she said, holding out her two hands towards him, 'for I was baptised into the love of the Christos.'

Just for a moment he hesitated. Then he took her hands in one of his and placed the other upon her head as he intoned a blessing in the Roman tongue. She felt Glainnader hard against her heart, and in the priest's piercing eyes thought she saw an awareness of its throbbing presence, a knowledge of the closeness of an old enemy.

'Are you able to read, daughter?'

She nodded, glad to break away from the touch of the holy man, ignoring the sneer in his voice. He beckoned Llywarch. The young king came forward without a word to take Rhianneth's hand and lead her across the room to a cupboard filled with books most beautifully bound in leather.

'This is a sacred book – ' Llywarch held one up, all his smiles gone, and cast a quick backward glance at the silent priest – 'made for me by the monks of Deva. Do you know their holy house?'

Like the single toll of a great bell a shiver ran through her mind. But without waiting for an answer he began to turn the thick vellum pages with their bright jewel colours, peering closely to read small sentences here and there, until he came to the centre. Here were set down the ten commandments of the Christian God, and Llywarch laid his thin fingers reverently upon the words.

'By these words all men should live,' he said earnestly. 'Lucius says my father and your mother broke them. I do not hold it against you, Rhianneth, that you were born in sin. That is not the loving spirit of Christ. We can redeem their souls with our own lives, by keeping not only the statutes of men, but the great laws of God.'

He turned from the book to look at her with pathetically young eagerness, his myopic brown eyes bright with intelligence. She felt a sudden rush of pity for this, her blood brother, living his young life between the coils of his ambitious mother and the strange and austere priest who stood so close behind him. Gently she touched the painted pictures which edged the creamy page.

'For what are our vain laws worth,' she quoted softly, 'without morality?'

Llywarch's anxious face lit suddenly, wonderfully. 'You've read Horacius? Oh, I wish I could write as he did, so long ago! Songs come to me, sometimes, but they are poor things, with no truth in them . . .'

'Llywarch.'

The priest's hand was on the boy's shoulder, though Rhianneth noticed that his eyes were on the book, and they held a hungry look. 'My son, you have other duties which await you. You will meet your half-sister again, when you may resume your conversation.'

A waft of air made the lamp-light waver and dark shadows leap from the painted walls as the book was closed. Llywarch gave her a faint smile.

'I have not yet thanked you, Rhianneth, for the stallion. It is a very fine gift.'

She looked from the dark face of the priest to that of her young half-brother. 'Perhaps we may ride together? Would you show me your city, and the land around it?'

His smiled deepened. 'Perhaps . . . tomorrow? Come with Cai.'

She smiled back. But the black eyes of Lucius the priest as he passed her were cold.

The door closed behind them. There was an explosion of pent-in breath from Caius, and a single word ground out by Wencam that she had heard only once before, from the mouth of the robber who had almost raped her on the day Giff died. Only then, it had not had so much venom behind it.

Gradually, as the first flush of entrancement with the city

faded, Rhianneth saw how a twisted, vicious hatred of Roman Mithrasia snaked out from some who lived within its protective walls and drank its clean water. She read the smears of its poison on defaced monuments, obscene scrawls upon buildings once set up with pride and love; saw it in the filth and decay of homes now used by uncaring strangers. While the forum and the streets close by were kept fairly clear, elsewhere rubbish littered the streets, blew in the wind. By night those streets were deserted, save for nameless dangerous shadows that slid silently between dilapidated buildings, or the occasional gang of drunken roisterers banging and crashing their way home.

Yet Mithrasia was still very much the king's city. Llywarch had no ancestral stonghold to which to retreat for he was, after all, no tribal chieftain of the Brigante people. It was a measure of their regard for the memory of 'Prince Macsen' that his blood-descendant Llywarch now counted as much a king as was Deva's Cynan who ruled from his ancient hilltop and had left his city to rot in disease and decay.

During the days that followed their first meeting, Rhianneth saw much of Llywarch, who seemed to wish for her company and delighted in their long conversations whenever he could be free of the priest Lucius who stood like a shadow between the young king and his court.

But she was not offered a room in the fortress, and Queen Myffan she never saw.

'With the queen's enmity we can do nothing,' Julia cried becoming agitated by what she saw as a deliberate insult. 'Nothing! Llywarch is only a child. We rely on you, Cai, and on Wencam, to manage as best you can. When you go back to Bernicia I really don't know how I can arrange things for Rhianneth! Marriages must be most delicately negotiated, and I lead so restricted a life that without the queen's goodwill I very much fear my niece will be left like a ripe plum unplucked!'

Caius laughed aloud, but Rhianneth hastened to comfort Julia's genuine distress with fierce declarations of independence.

'I have Llywarch's friendship,' she assured her aunt, 'and he's acknowledged me as his blood-kin. I've a fortune in precious metals from my father – why should I rush to find a husband? I mean to employ all my skills to gain a firm place at court, and draw the king away from the spell of his mother and that black-raven priest!'

Julia cried out, made the sign of the cross before her eyes. But no feeling of unease ran through Rhianneth, until she saw the smile on Cai's face die, and watched him turn and leave the room.

She rode frequently with Llywarch, and always Caius and two palace guards accompanied them. Once, while outside the city, Llywarch and Rhianneth urged their horses into a gallop, childishly conspiring to race away from the others for a few heady moments. Her hair shook loose from the braided ribbon confining it, flying out in the wind, and bright colour stung her cheeks, when they drew up, panting, by the grey walls of the amphitheatre which had once been used as a drill-square by the soldiers of Maximus. Rhianneth jumped down to go inside, when Llywarch stopped her.

'It's deserted.' he said, looking at her in surprise that she should not know. 'It's only used as a rubbish tip. There are rats . . .'

Caius and the guards rode up, and angrily kept close to Rhianneth and Llywarch as they all made their way back.

'Things are not what they were, but we'll survive,' Caius said defensively. 'We are packed with refugees from Deva. But the population of Mithrasia has never yet fallen into anarchy like that of some other cities!'

'We have a different population now, Cai,' put in Llywarch with a shrug. 'Honest folk came to us from Deva, yes. But there came others . . . '

Rhianneth said nothing. Though saddened by the decay creeping through the city, she never talked of it with Caius. She could not bear to injure the pride, the hope he bore for this tiny legacy of Rome.

*

Her aunt was frail and disorganised. After a short while Rhianneth realised it was the Saxon slave-woman, Torfrida, who controlled the household, supervised the shopping and the cooking of meals, besides comforting Julia's endless small fears and worries.

With her calm face and hair still the colour of barley in the sun, she was Julia's capable and devoted friend rather than servant and was always treated as such. Her love for Julia and for the Christian God they both worshipped was deep. Her home settlement had been over-run and burned, her husband killed in battle and her little son died of cold and fever. Julia had taken away her slave bracelet and made her a member of her own mourning household, for this was then but a scant year after Camlann. Now, after so many years, the tragedies that had first linked them remained close. But in their evening prayers the dead were now remembered as if they had fallen together, victims of the powers of darkness.

Once, on one of Julia's rare ventures out of the house, Rhianneth watched from the shadows of a Christian church as she and Torfrida bowed their heads before the white-clothed altar and placed an offering in a silver bowl. Though all other traces of her had been swept away, the temple had once been dedicated to a corn goddess, for her sign was still carved above the entrance. Here Christos had triumphed over the Old Gods and people had forgotten that they had ever been. But despite the entreaties of her aunt, Rhianneth could not pray. She could feel no presence of the God here, and the Otherworld had seemed nearer beside Marcus's quiet grave where the wild flowers grew beyond the defensive walls.

Sometimes in the evening while Julia rested on her couch, Rhianneth asked Torfrida to speak in her own tongue. The words sounded alien and harsh at first, like the snarls of a wild-cat from the back of its throat. But after a while Rhianneth began to hear a strange beauty in them which echoed the turning of the year, and held all the keening of the early winds, the warm still days, the wind-rush of flighting birds and the crack-lash of ice-storms. They had a rough wildness, a savage poetry, that belonged not to the elegance of Julia's room but to the elements of storm and battle, of salt-seas and rain-misted forests.

As the light faded one afternoon, Lovan brought a message from Caius that she was to come at once to the fortress. Torfrida made no comment as Rhianneth slipped on outdoor shoes and warm cloak. She went on rubbing red wine over a bronze candle-holder before rinsing and drying it ready for the evening table, but she looked uneasy.

'Cai is with Llywarch,' was all Lovan could tell her as they hurried along flanked by two palace guards. 'There's some trouble over the Saxon alliance. He thinks you may keep the king with us, despite the queen and that bastard of a priest . . . '

Of the antipathy between the queen and her priest, and the Caer Melot faction, Rhianneth had soon become very much aware, and aware too of other things usually hidden beneath masks of civility. But even so she was shocked to hear voices raised in anger well before she reached the king's rooms, and Lovan left her.

The room looked out into the old via praetoria of the fortress, its amber-glassed window not yet covered by heavy night curtains. The people within were fierce in argument and aware only of themselves so that for a while she stood near the door, unseen. Nearest to her, his face dark with anger, stood Caius, and her name was on his lips.

'Rhianneth is Elidyr's daughter, and your son's half-sister. We need her help!'

The only woman in the room turned swiftly. She was as hard and beautiful as a polished stone, and her face was as feline as the eyes beneath their azurite-painted lids. The witch-queen. Maelgwyn's daughter. Her words were plain, shocking in their savagery.

'That stray cat's whelp is no kin to me. I'll not have her called so!'

'She's called so by your son the king, who well knows that only she can lift from us the threats from your brother Rhun, from old Cuneglassus – and Urien!' Wencam stood beside the young king, and spoke in a voice harsh with impatience.

'We're surrounded by enemies, lady! Life has been honey-sweet here – but it's rotted our teeth and we'll fall prey to our carnivorous neighbours unless we make shift to hire guard dogs.'

'Pagan dogs?'

A tall shadow in the corner dimness moved and spoke. It was Lucius the priest, his black eyes glittering with passion.

'Better to tear down Mithrasia stone by stone than defend it with such an unholy alliance. In the name of God, trust in the peace we have with Rhun! Make alliance with Urien of Rheged – and with Cuneglassus, he is aging and would welcome it!'

"Lick the boots of any who raise a sword against us? Kiss the cheeks of those who betrayed us once and will again?" Caius ground out the words, his hand on his sword-hilt. 'The "tawny butcher" Cuneglassus is as deadly in sick old age as he was twenty years ago! By the Light! Is this how you Christians repay your debt to Caer Melot for saving your Church from the Saxon torches?'

'That war host of Arturius,' spat out the priest contemptuously, 'with its glittering mailcoats and great armoured horses had its war-chest stuffed with treasures stolen from the Church of Christ! Our grain taken to feed horses and men. Our gold, silver, silks, our very altar cloths torn down by men no better than the pagans they fought – '

Caius moved with such force that he sent a stool near his foot slithering across the room to crunch against the wall. The priest gasped in sudden fear and pain as a hand closed around his black-sleeved arm.

'Those men gave their blood, holy man, to stand between you and the barbarians. I think you'll find an altar cloth frail defence with Hengist's sons at the gates!'

'Did our neighbours offer help to Constantine, heir to Caer Melot?' Wencam's harsh voice broke in. 'They stood by in silence while Medraut's sons plotted against his life . . . '

'With a holy man. Like you, master priest,' put in Caius bitterly, and Lucius's face went white with rage.

'You see how they drip their poison into the mind of your

son?' he hissed at the queen. Then his eyes snapped towards Llywarch, whose thin figure was half-hidden behind Wencam. 'They were nobly-born and innocent youths. Constantine cut them down with his sword before the holy altar! And I . . . I barely escaped with my life . . . '

'Constantine is a friend, Llywarch, who will never move against you,' roared Wencam, 'Could you ever be so sure of Rhun – or Urien?'

But at that moment the queen's eyes fell upon Rhianneth in the gathering darkness at the edge of the room. She drew in a sharp breath and her eyes dilated as if in fear, or anger.

'How dare you do this,' she said to Caius, her hand trembling towards her throat and her face suddenly white as death, 'when I've sworn I'd rather kill myself than look but once upon her face!'

Caius spun round, releasing the priest abruptly. Before he reached Rhianneth, Llywarch darted forward and came to stand close beside her, facing the queen.

'Mother – ' he took Rhianneth's hand in his, ' – this is my half-sister, who has come to be with us for a while.'

The queen stared at them for a long moment. Her hands trembled against the soft folds of her crimson gown. But when she spoke her voice was steady.

'Rhianneth, is it not? "Little queen." A name both inaccurate and presumptuous.'

Rhianneth watched her in silence. She was indeed beautiful, but her beauty held a wild quality of danger; around her neck shone a magnificent jewelled cross, but the eyes that glistened above it were pagan.

'You are not like your mother,' the queen went on at last. 'It would seem that you know the value of silence, whereas she sang and laughed and chattered like a fool.'

'I'm told I resemble my father,' Rhianneth replied calmly, 'which is what rumour also says of you, lady.'

The room stilled, as if all within it held their breath. Even to Marcus's remote farm had come tales of great Maelgwyn, the dragon of the isle, and his dynastic murders. For he had killed his uncle Ewein to seize power, and later murdered both his own wife and his nephew in order to marry the nephew's wife Myffan's mother.

'There are many who have seen my mother in me too, Rhianneth,' Queen Myffan's eyes narrowed. 'Perhaps you also may come to do so?'

Witch-queen daughter to a witch-mother, for Maelgwyn's second wife had been much more than an accomplice in the murder of her husband and the king's wife. Her meaning was plain, and to Rhianneth her words struck even closer as she remembered the poison threat to her own mother by this woman.

'I see a great many things,' she replied, feeling power within her like a sword in her hand. 'I see the flower in the seed, the sting hidden in the honey comb. I have the look of my father, lady, but the wisdom of my grandmother.'

Myffan drew back uncertainly, and was silent. But her eyes were deep pools of malice which never left Rhianneth's face. The priest came closer, putting a hand on the queen's arm.

'To trust in the pagan Ida is to bring down God's fury upon us,' he muttered. 'Remember Vortigern! His marriage to Hengist's daughter Rowen led to fire and slaughter in our island . . . '

'That was over eighty years ago, priest,' Caius's voice was harsh. 'Between then and now stands Badon – and that is a thing the enemy have not forgotten. Now, while they still remember, is the time for a treaty with the Bernicians to secure our northern borders. Now, before they grasp the true significance of Camlann!'

His glance went towards Llywarch. 'And that, sir, is that we can no longer trust our fellow-countrymen nor depend upon their help against the enemy. While we watch for attack from Rhun in the west or Urien in the north – to the south the Saxon kingdoms of Mercia and Wessex grow in strength. If we can form an alliance with Ida, the Bernicians will keep Urien busy and we may survive a little longer!'

The priest grasped the wooden cross which hung on a long cord around his neck, and held it up. 'Listen to me! It is the heathen Saxon prowling like a wolf along our frontiers that howls at our gates! If we desert our Christian brothers and make unholy alliance with the barbarians, they will over-run us. What then will survive from our burning city, our fallen Church?'

There was a long silence. Then Caius spoke again.

'I hope for only one thing from a treaty with Ida, and that's time. Time for us to build what strength we can. Give our minds that edge for war which was lost at Camlann! Perhaps then we may live secure within our borders – save a little more of civilisation from sliding into the the dark! The Bernician envoys are on their way from the north. If you can't bear to look at them, holy man, take the queen to her brother Rhun in Gwynned and leave Llywarch to barter with them.'

'My son is a child—' the queen began. But Caius cut across her words.

'And they are warriors, lady, who would set at nought an alliance negotiated by a woman and a priest! Llywarch is thirteen and not far from a man. He is also a king. And the barbarians have a feel for kingship. For the blood royal.' He looked at Llywarch. 'Your son knows that we follow an old established Roman strategy. But we'll not make Vortigern's mistake. We give them no land. Merely a little grain and cattle in return for their keeping Urien's army facing east, not south.'

Llywarch's grip on Rhianneth's hand tightened as he faced his mother, avoiding the priest's penetrating eyes. 'Mother, I know you fear for your peace with your brother Rhun. But we've no treaty with Rheged, and Urien grows stronger every year. Our alliance with Bernicia will surely give him pause? He dare not bring his war host south, and leave Rheged defenceless . . . '

Myffan gave an impatient gesture, the rings on her white hand glittering. 'Don't mouth to me the arguments fed to you by the Fellowship! Caer Melot is dead, long dead – are you fool enough to be governed by a corpse?'

Llywarch flushed. 'Lady,' he said quietly, 'I will not long be governed by anyone, save God. As for the Fellowship, those within it have served this city well. I'll not have them slighted.'

For a second the queen's face seemed to slip, as if she saw for the first time the hardening steel of manhood within her gentle young son, realised how fast-flowing were the moments which simultaneously sucked away her strength, her grasp of power, and built up that of the king. Then her gaze fell on Rhianneth, and she smiled. But there was something savage behind her eyes when at last she spoke.

'Then you'd best keep out of sight this lady who claims so much and who could be, for all we know, the bastard sprig of any one of our meanest stable lads!'

Caius's eyes turned black with anger and his hand clenched around his sword hilt. But Rhianneth's pride could stand no more of this brutal confrontation. In the tumult that followed the queen's words she turned and left the room, slipping along the passageway and out into the night where the wind blew clean, sending chill fingers through her hair and lifting her cloak as she ran. She was still in the deserted via praetoria when Caius appeared beside her, his hand on her arm.

'Let me go, Cai. I won't listen to her insults against my mother. You should not have asked me to come! She hates us all, and me more than any!'

Caius's hands were on her shoulders, turning her abruptly so that she looked into his face, sombrely lit by the fire of a street flare on the wall nearby. Even in Rhianneth's distress her heart turned over as his dark eyes met her own.

'Yes, she does hate you. And that's nothing – a woman's jealousy. But that she hates us all, that is something. For she works always to turn Llywarch's mind against the Fellowship. If you are so weak that you run from her tongue, then she will indeed have won a victory. But for Mithrasia – believe it – that victory would be deadly!'

Angrily Rhianneth tried to twist away, but he jerked her back. Then, more gently, he took her face between his hands.

'Wencam spoke the truth in there! We are surrounded by enemies! Those who killed Arturius at Camlann and destroyed Caer Melot – they are the enemies of Rome, who would drag us back into a barbarism darker than the days before Caesar. Between them and the heathen Saxon, the

Empire in Britain may be lost forever. Ah, Rhianneth – here in Mithrasia there lingers still something of that life our fathers' knew! We still have books, and lamps to read and dream by. If we can survive a little longer, then everything may not go; something may be saved to carry with us into the Empire when it recovers. What's a queen's jealousy, against the survival of a world, Rhianneth?'

She began to tremble, both from the enormity of his words and from his closeness. He led her unresisting back into the king's house, into a small candle-lit room, where he called for wine.

Rhianneth sipped the sharp-tanged liquid until she stopped trembling. Caius said no more, but already his words had entered her soul and she felt small and unworthy. She had turned her face from the enemy and betrayed the fine vow made before the walls of Mithrasia.

Caius sat with his dark head bent, his eyes on the red wine as he moved the cup between his hands. At first he made no response when Rhianneth hesitantly renewed her vow to serve the cause for which Caius's father had died, and which was so honoured by Marcus. Then slowly, he drained his wine-cup and placed it carefully on the small table beside them. For the first time since they had entered the room, he looked fully at her.

'Will you listen, Rhianneth, while I tell you how best you can serve your brother's kingdom, and the Fellowship of Caer Melot? Beyond the Wall on the eastern sea-coast lies Bernicia. It's a young Saxon kingdom, carved out by Ida, who came by sea with his war-band from Saxon Deira to the south and made the old shore-stronghold of Din Guarydi his own. Like us, they are surrounded by enemies. They can't trust their cousins of Deira, from whom they broke away; there are Picts on their borders, and the Scots of Dal Riada; there are our British kingdoms of Eburacum and Elmet. Above all, there is Outigern, who once ruled from Din Guarydi and with whom Ida is constantly at war. Now Ida sees, as we do, the growing power of Rheged, under Urien.'

'But Ida is Saxon! Our most bitter enemy,' Rhianneth broke

in. 'It is as if we would tame a wolf to guard us!'

'I know,' he said flatly. His face was expressionless, but his eyes were bleak with cynicism. 'Yet I've found the honour of the Saxon to be a less fragile thing than the love of our fellow-countrymen.'

She felt the black despair within him, so strong that it reached out and caught at her throat. Rising abruptly, he turned away to the window. He grasped the edge of the sill with one hand. She watched the other curl into a fist at his side.

'If Mithrasia and Bernicia stand together, we may both survive. If not, both will surely fall to the same enemies. But we need more than a war-bond.'

'More than – ' Suddenly she knew the thing in his mind, that had grown out of darkness. She trembled from head to foot. 'What sort of bond, Caius?'

'An alliance of peace. A bond of friendship.'

'And – how would you seal this bond?'

He did not look at her. 'For this, Rhianneth – for peace and security – Mithrasia would give Elidyr's daughter in marriage to Ida.'

This then, was the price of the Gods, and it was high indeed.

At last she had her burning torch to carry into the darkness of the unborn years, her lonely battle to fight for the ghosts of Caer Melot. That it was Caius who handed her the torch was unbearable.

He was not for her, that she had already accepted during the long night at the roadside inn. She would never know what it was to be loved by him; but to her he remained all that was gallant in the world, and she could not drive the desire for him out of her mind.

Only one abiding love had Caius – for Rome and for Mithrasia, her daughter. In the service of that love he would gamble with many lives, including his own. Morvydd his wife he'd left with the Saxons while he rode south to fight for this alliance. Why should he hesitate to lay his cousin upon its altar?

His face was sharply etched against the faint glow from a street flare through the golden-glassed window, and in his dark tunic he looked very slender and suddenly vulnerable, like a young soldier keeping his vigil through the long night.

Rhianneth moved, stood, and he turned his head swiftly as he felt her beside him, a hand-touch away.

Hope flared in his face, 'You agree? You'll do it?'

She bent her head, unable to speak. Words faltered and died unborn in her throat.

He drew her to him, kissed her gently on the mouth. 'Brave wonderful Rhianneth. You are your father's daughter, and Marcus's too . . .'

His eyes searched hers for a long moment, and she saw something within them that she knew she would never have seen had it not been for this moment between them. Then he looked quickly away.

'You'll not go alone,' he said awkwardly. 'I – and Lovan – will travel with you to Bernicia. And Morvydd my wife is there. You may take anyone you like to serve you. I – you will find Ida most personable, Rhianneth. He is a warrior, fit and strong. He has many sons, and a fine war-band to protect you . . .'

But already Rhianneth felt the long years stretching before her in that rough land beside a cold sea. How safe would any of her sons be, if Ida should die before they grew old and strong enough to rule?

Her hand stole upwards in a movement that was becoming a habit, to lie against Glainnader and feel its hard sureness beneath her palm. Queen Myffan who, by guile and cunning had kept Mithrasia for Llywarch since the death of Elidyr, hated her for coming into the world. But even she feared the gift that was born in Rhianneth, which had grown in strength with her womanhood. Surely, with the help of the Serpent's Egg, she would be able to protect and bring to manhood the sons of her blood?

Caius began to speak of the land of Bernicia, and of Din Guarydi, Ida's captured fortress by the sea. He told her of winter feasts when the wind howled sea-cold from the north, of the great fire that blazed and crackled and lit the king's Hall with its hot glow while story-tellers sought to enchant with the surging music of their poetry, of the tales which told of stirring deeds past, or of the anguish of love or banishment.

She watched him silently, her dark soldier of the morning god with his dreams of Imperial glory, and love cried out voicelessly within her.

When at last he called for an escort, drew his own sword and led her into the dark of the via praetoria, through the gates of the basilica and along the empty streets towards Julia's house, he was still talking, filling the silence between them.

Rhianneth listened to his words, but she remembered too vividly the priest's hatred of the barbarians that prowled like wolves along their borders. If she were safely to walk this loneliest of paths the gods had thrown before her, and keep but one small lamp alight for Caer Melot and for Rome, then she must become what Caius had in jest called her. Cousin fox-cub. A student of strategem and patience, for Ida did not seem a man to be ruled by his wife.

They safely reached the arched entrance to her aunt's house. Caius dismissed the guards and slid his sword silently into its sheath. Then he took Rhianneth's hands in his and kissed her forehead, his lips cool as the night wind.

'Mithras light your way, cousin. May your sons fight with us against the dark.'

Voices came from the house then, and lantern-light spilled from windows and opened doors into the paved garden beyond the archway, so that the shadows drew back and shrank against the high walls.

But somewhere in the shadows of Rhianneth's mind, a deeper shadow moved. For if she mated with the Saxon, then her sons would surely run with the wolves.

CHAPTER 4

When Caius told his mother that the alliance with Bernicia would be bonded by marriage she turned so white Rhianneth thought her about to faint.

'This is the queen's doing!' Julia's hand fluttered to her throat.

'It is the hope of the Fellowship – and me.'

'You! In God's name, why?'

He shrugged. 'To buy a strong ally against Urien.'

'Buy? With Rhianneth?' For a heart's beat, she closed her eyes. 'Caer Melot obsesses you, Cai. It killed your father. Will you let it destroy Rhianneth, dead though it is?'

'Dead? Caer Melot lives within the Fellowship! With loyalty. With honour!' Caius flushed with sudden anger. 'It was men – men without either – who killed my father!'

Trembling, Julia sank lower in her chair. 'Can't you see? That child's mother died because of me. I took her to Elidyr's court all those long years ago. I dressed her up, painted her face, was amused when she flirted with the king!'

Her voice became a whisper as tears welled up and ran down her cheeks unheeded. 'I was lonely, Cai. I'd been ill. I was bored – and I broke Marcus's heart! I can only mend what I did by getting for Rhianneth a good marriage. A noble marriage!'

She looked up at him her mouth working piteously. 'You told me once that you wanted that too!'

Cai's hand clenched as if around the hilt of a sword, but he did not reply.

'Is this what you meant?' Julia cried, 'For your cousin to live with a heathen murderer?'

Caius looked across his mother, at Rhianneth. Something flickered behind his eyes for an instant, then it was gone. 'Mother, the bargain's made. It needs only to be sealed, and will be. Despite the queen and her black priest. Or your conscience.'

Appalled by his callousness, Rhianneth ran to Julia and threw her arms around the thin shoulders. 'No one has forced me! I do this because I, too, am pledged to the Fellowship . . .'

But Julia sat quite still, clenched fists pressed against her face. 'I went there, with Reburrus my husband. To Caer Melot. I saw them, those who filled his days and his dreams. Arturius, the Bear. And gallant Caius, whose name we gave our son. Bedwyr, Gawain . . . all gleaming like stars in the summer twilight, with the shine of swords and lances, the shimmer of the wine-cups. To Reburrus, Arturius was a god worth dying for, and Caer Melot the last bastion of civilised freedom to the north of Rome. But I was a young bride, Rhianneth! Sharp with jealousy of these rivals for my love, and uneasy in an atmosphere I did not understand. I saw the anger that lay behind Arturius's eyes, and the fatal indifference in those of his wife Gwenhwyvaer. She moved amongst those with malice on their lips and ambition and greed in their souls. If Caer Melot had splendour, God knows like Rome it had squalor too!'

Her eyes wandered away, bleak with the coldness of an old memory. Her voice grew taut with anguish.

'I begged Reburrus to leave. But he was bound too tightly in love and honour to Arturius. At last, heavy with child, I went alone to the villa of friends in the Summer Country. He did not follow. His bride of a year, his coming child – neither meant more to him than his oath to Artur's Brotherhood.'

Drying tears made streaks of light across the carefully applied paint on her cheeks and the red-ochre colouring on her lips had smudged where her fingers had pressed. Rhianneth thought with pity how much older she seemed suddenly, how ill.

'At Caer Melot, you see, they lived always as an armed camp,' she went on, 'and on the fringes were weak and brutal men, bitter in their lack of power and dangerous in their hatred of the Empire. They wanted Britain swept free of Saxons, yes. But free of Rome too, so they might themselves carve out kingdoms to rule as petty tyrants. They attacked Arturius at Camlann. With that battle Caer Melot broke apart, and all my life with it . . .'

105

Rhianneth knelt down and took Julia's hands in her own. 'Those men, and men like them, are threatening Mithrasia now. They would tear all Brigantia between them and make this city into a marrowless bone to be fought over, with every vestige of Roman life gone.' Carefully she steadied her voice. 'That is why Cai is fighting for this alliance with the Saxons. To buy time for us to survive, in peace.'

'You sound like Marcus, Rhianneth!' Her aunt's eyes swung, startled, into focus. 'you must not let them trap you into their politics. You're too young to know the price of men's dreams. The price that women pay.'

Her hands struggled free and she clutched at Rhianneth's arm. 'I lay, with Cai not one month old in my arms, and watched Wencam press the hilt of my dead husband's sword between his baby hands. I was too ill. Too stunned with grief to care. But from that day I had lost him, as I had lost my husband. We always lose, Rhianneth!.

There flashed into Rhianneth's mind a picture of Caius on the road to Mithrasia, his father's sword at his side and the wind lifting away the dark hair to show the scar-sign of his god. A god who himself had been born already armed with a sword and a torch. She raised her chin and looked first at her cousin and then back at Julia, feeling the raw energy of youth flowing through her, tide-strong.

'I won't lose, Julia! I'll enter the camp of an enemy, without weapons, and turn that enemy into a strong friend.'

'By marriage with a barbarian?' Julia choked, 'Imagine what your life may be! How could you survive in some mud-caked hut in an unholy pagan camp.'

'I think,' Rhianneth began gently, 'that amongst the Saxon people Ida is considered as much a king as Llywarch . . . '

'They do not read, they do not write! They guzzle in their mead-halls all night, and they raid and burn and murder by day . . . '

Torfrida knelt beside her distraught lady, the usually calm face creased with worry. 'Lady, some Saxon princes are very fine,' she said in her slow, dignified way. 'Their women do not lack beautiful jewellery and soft clothes.'

106

But nothing would comfort Julia. She pleaded with Rhianneth. She stormed at Caius. She slapped Torfrida. When her sobs began to rise into hysteria, Rhianneth became really afraid. She had never seen anyone so possessed. It was as if the bitterness of her life, and the twisting guilt that followed the fatal autumn visit which destroyed both Marcus's hope of love and the life of Rhianneth's mother, had gathered during the long years between to rise now in one gigantic wave of raw emotion.

Torfrida talked constantly to her mistress in a low voice, stroking the back of her head with strong, gentle hands. Caius's voice grew louder, harsher, as he tried to reach his mother with cold reason.

Their impotence exasperated Rhianneth. At last she could bear no more. She had the power to stop this. Dare she use that power? She took a deep breath, and left them. When she came back she carried a small cup of wine, well laced with a strong dose of her grandmother's sleeping potion, culled from the blood-red poppy.

'Drink this, Julia,' she said flatly, pushing past Caius.

Her aunt's eyes were salt-sore with tears, her breath came in rasping gasps. She seemed about to knock the cup from Rhianneth's hand, but something she saw in her face stopped her. Obediently she drank the potion.

Soon, even that great storm which had its origins in the lost years and dark places of her mind gave way to the power of the poppy, and she slept.

The Saxon envoys from Bernicia rode into the city to the fortress of Maximus. Their horses' hooves rang through the rubbish-blown streets, and Llywarch's own red-dragon banner snapped before them in the wind. Silent, in their battle-garb, they were both splendid and terrible. The light gleamed on chainmail and shield-bosses, glinted yellow on the brazen boar-crests that reared fiercely over their helmets.

'Hell's teeth!' muttered Lovan, as he hurried Rhianneth back to her aunt's house. 'They rode under the stone of Maximus as if the whole city was bought and paid for!'

Rhianneth laughed, unwilling to let him see that her unease matched his own. She had persuaded him to take her to see the Saxons come into the city, had coaxed him as far as the Forum entrance, and now almost wished she had not.

Easy it had been, to boast to her aunt of walking into an enemy camp and making them allies. Now she had seen her first Saxon warriors riding insolently along the streets where she'd walked with Caius, and her courage faded before them.

When they reached the archway of her aunt's gate Lovan stopped, his hand on the rough stones.

'We can leave, *cariad*,' he said quietly, not looking at her. 'We can go home. Marcus wanted a marriage for you with Constantine's son, down in the south-west. He knew nothing of this. Neither did I, till we came to Mithrasia with Cai.'

Rhianneth looked at his strong, weatherbeaten face; at the large hands that had gentled their farm horses for so long, had protected her since the day she was born in so much sadness. She had only to speak, and Lovan would risk Cai's anger, and Llywarch's, and the fury of the insulted Saxon's, to take her away from here and from the marriage with Ida.

'I've given my word to Cai, to the Fellowship,' she said, swallowing. 'I can't leave. Marcus would understand. He lived by honour.'

Lovan did not answer for a while. He straightened up, turned and looked at her. 'Yes, he did,' he said, his eyes tired. 'We all did, in the Fellowship. But time is running out for us. God knows whether this bond with the Saxons is right or wise. I have a feeling that in the end it won't matter. We shall be swallowed up, either by a sworn enemy or a strong friend. In the meantime, Rhianneth, you – '

'In the meantime,' she said quickly, before he could go on, 'I shall be married to a king! Marcus would love that!'

'King? A bloody pirate, from what I've heard!' he retorted, and then as if he saw what lay beneath her pert smile, recognised the fear and the resolution, he let out his breath on a sigh and ruffled her hair as if she was still a child.

'You've got you mother's spirit. But what is more, you have the discipline, the determination, that she never had. Marcus taught you that; may it serve you well.' His hand suddenly stilled, hard against the back of her head. 'God go with you, *cariad*! And with us all . . .'

Torfrida washed and combed Rhianneth's hair till it streamed dark and shining down her back from under a small gold-netted cap. kept in place with polished bronze pins.

She put on a dress of deep green, and soft thin slippers of pale leather with padded soles to keep out the cold. From Elidyr's gifts she selected a many-stranded necklace of gold, and filigree earrings with emerald beads. But on her arm she slid her grandmother's talisman against evil, the bangle with a serpent's head and ruby eyes.

At last, beaming and satisfied with her efforts, Torfrida left her. But tumultuous emotions, both in her aunt's house and in herself, had left their mark. Rhianneth felt drained of energy and a dull grey pain encircled her head with a grip of iron. Listlessly she opened a big wooden chest, thinking to find one of her grandmother's potions, but with the sound of masculine footsteps outside her door she slammed it shut and swung round.

When Caius came into the room, she saw astonished admiration leap into his eyes. Her heartbeat quickened. She felt the colour flame into her cheeks and turned to look into the tilted mirror, large as a shield, which swung loose between its stand-fastenings. Through it, she watched him lean back against the wall, darkly handsome in red, a thin band of gold around his brow catching the lamplight, and a smile teasing the corner of his mouth.

'Well?' After a moment she turned, holding out her arms like a dancer. 'Does your little cousin look like an Imperial lady, a daughter of Elidyr the king?'

Caius's dark eyes met the challenge in hers. He pushed upright and took both her hands in his. 'She does, indeed,' he said softly, and there was no mockery in his voice. Gently he turned her in his arms so that she could see herself in the mirror, her eyes wide, catching the gleaming green of the gown.

'There will be no lady more beautiful than you in the king's rooms tonight, Rhianneth.'

They stood like lovers. Phantom lovers reflected in a mirror. Caius's hands were warm around her waist, his breath soft, quickening against her hair. If only she could stop time – hold this moment forever. Then the moment passed, and Caius was flinging a cloak around her shoulders.

'We must hurry,' he urged her towards the door. 'We must be there, to stand beside Llywarch when the Saxons come.'

They entered the king's apartments through dark-polished carved double-doors. Rhianneth's breath caught in her throat. Here, in this room, the son of Maximus had entertained his family, his officers, and the important citizens of his city. It was enormous, with the illusion of even more space given by a beautiful and life-like painting of a green garden with apple trees and flying birds which covered the whole of one wall.

Although cool autumn winds curled around the high stones of the fortress and made the dragon-banner crack like a falling axe, the air in this room was soft as summer, and the floor beneath her feet felt warm. Half a hundred fat wax candles burned steadily and slowly and did not waver, so that the room was as bright as day and the people moving within it glowed like coloured butterflies. There was no sign of the queen.

Llywarch stood alone, slender and still in cream and gold, a heavy twisted torque gleaming about his neck. Gone was the eager boy she knew. Kingship was now a shining mist around him.

Silence fell as Rhianneth walked up to him. With so many eyes upon her, her face burned. But Llywarch welcomed her warmly, kissing her cheek.

Then he turned and said in a clear voice: 'My friends, God has smiled upon me – upon us all. He has sent my sister Rhianneth to us. Be pleased to welcome her to our father's city.'

A low murmur rippled through the room. Rhianneth looked swiftly towards Cai, saw his smile, the glint of triumph in his eyes. Then people came forward to greet her, curious but friendly.

Wencam, Julia's brother, gave her a kiss, and brought forward his wife, Sibilla. Her plain face was creased with the small worries of many years, but kindness and goodwill shone through like a candle. Before her splendidly dressed little person she clasped together plump hands ringed with the trophies of her husband's many battles.

Rhianneth smiled at this lady who had been foster mother to Caius during those early years of his life when Julia's world had collapsed. How often she must have tempered Wencam's well-meaning roughness for the small boy!

'Welcome, Rhianneth,' she said now, 'It makes our hearts glad to see you.'

'I'm happy to be here,' Rhianneth responded at once. But she thought, how easily we lie to those we like, and for the best of reasons . . .

With Llywarch by her side she slowly made her way through the room, and nodded and smiled until she felt her face would never lose its creases, trying all the while to judge by the warmth or coolness of a greeting who were of the queen's party and who were of the Fellowship. There was as yet no sign of the Saxons.

Time slipped by. Her skin felt damp with sweat. The band of pain around her head tightened. Sometimes clearly, mostly muffled by the voices of the guests, musicians began to play. Still the Saxons had not come.

A burst of laughter erupted nearby, and in turning her head she caught a glimpse of Caius pushing his way towards them through the moving crowd, his eyes giving a signal to Llywarch.

Silence fell upon the room, as if a blade had cut through the talk, the laughter and the music. Rhianneth stood up straighter, holding her aching head high as Llywarch turned to greet the Bernician envoys.

She had to remind herself that this was Llywarch's fortress, his city. These tall Saxons, so overwhelming with their bright hair and wolf-snarl voices, were but a few warriors on a mission of peace, far from home.

They wore richly-bordered tunics above their breeches,

111

and wide rings of gold on their arms, and their mailed coats and terrifying helmets were gone. But swords still swung at their thighs, and about them was an alien savagery that no fine clothes could hide. Seeing them, Rhiannetho's mind trembled.

It was not too late. All she needed was to tell Caius she could not do it. Then she could go home to her grandmother. Put out the torch the gods had lighted for her. Forget Caer Melot, and let someone else move within the great arena of the coming years.

But even as the thought flickered through her mind she knew with chilling certainty that it was already too late. It had always been too late. For the gods had planted in her a dream as strong as that which held Caius fast. She could never, now, use what power she had – as her grandmother did – simply to make the crops grow and keep the storm winds from their hill-top. A dark wind was blowing over the whole of Britain, and against that wind she must weave a shelter, stronger than the lost shield-wall of Artur.

Her eyes fixed on the man who strode ahead of the others to greet the king. A wolf in a flower garden, she thought, as he towered over Llywarch. Beside him her half-brother looked remote, imperial, very young – and very vulnerable. She felt his thin hand tremble slightly as he drew her forward.

'Here is my sister, Rhianneth.'

The Saxon's hair and short beard were the colour of their grain-field at home, sombred by rain. His handsome blunt-featured face was darkened by sun and wind.

'I am Aethelric, sent by Ida to bring you his greetings, lady,' he said in their British tongue, though his words had a strange cadence.

Gold flashed at his wrist and on his shoulders as he gestured to one of his followers. The man came forward, knelt, and held up a heavily carved applewood box.

Rhianneth hesitated, unsure whether she should just thank him, or open it now. But the room rumbled with excitement, and all eyes were on her expectantly. She lifted the lid. On a lining of scarlet lay a purse of softest leather. Its ivory lid was

ornamented with strange birds and animals in gold and gar-
net, and edged with interlaced patterns so intricate they could
have been wrought only by a master artist.

Carefully, she lifted out the purse. It was filled to
bursting point with silver coins. Some were Roman, for she
recognised the head of an emperor. Others were of a strange
design unknown to her. She gasped, both at the beauty and
richness of the gift, looking swiftly up into the Saxon's
face.

'A gift from Bernicia.' A smile twitched the corner of his
mouth. 'Half craftsmanship. Half plunder.'

His eyes were cool and grey as northern seas whose depths
are never moved by storms nor ever warmed by the brief summer sun. As they met hers Rhianneth felt a tremor run
through her, an awareness, as if something secret and hidden
had passed between them.

'Thank you,' she managed. Then words failed her. But her
awkwardness was smoothed over by the bringing in of hot
spiced wine, which the Saxons viewed with suspicion. The
small pies, cakes and other delicate offerings suitable to the
reception of honoured guests into Llywarch's city, however,
they ate with speed and relish.

Music began softly once more. People drifted around the
room drinking and talking, casting covert glances at the
enemy in their midst. The Saxons stayed together and talked
amongst themselves in their own language, staring about the
room with their fierce light eyes.

Rhianneth stood between Llywarch and Caius and sipped
her wine, listening in silence as they talked with Aethelric and
his two brothers. Wencam joined them. The talk turned to
war, and to his years of campaigning as a young man against
the Picts and their northern allies.

'God, it was hard!' Wencam said, already in his mind once
more with his troops, armed and waiting for any signal of
trouble, 'Years, I had of it. Bloody years . . .'

'You rode with Artur,' Aethelric said. It was a statement, not
a question. Wencam glanced swiftly at Caius, and back at the
Saxon. He drew himself up, eyes wary.

'Oh, yes,' he replied pleasantly enough, but the word Badon was written plainly on his honest face. 'There are still some of us left.'

Aethelric nodded, his smile showing he could read Wencam's expression as well as anyone. 'A great war-leader. Our warriors speak of him still.'

Llywarch broke in to ask eagerly if he might look at Aethelric's sword, the boy in him overriding his careful dignity. At once the Saxon drew the deadly weapon from its fleecy-lined black wolf-skin sheath. It had a grip of wood, bound with leather, and the blade flashed as he handed it to the young king.

'What is this pattern – is it writing?' Llywarch's eyes shone in the candlelight as he peered at the blade of the sword. Rhianneth, too, leaned forward to look at the strange inscription cut into the blade with thin, stick-like markings.

'Those are rune signs. They make a charm, a magic for protection in battle.'

'What does it say?'

'If I told you, the magic would drain away.'

'Come, Sir, you'd best hand it back,' Caius put in, smiling faintly. 'Already you have been greatly favoured. A Saxon's sword is his friend. He lets few others feel its weight, in peace. Does it have a name, Elric?'

'It's called Dreamweaver. It gives me sweet dreams by putting my enemies to sleep.'

Rhianneth was startled by his subtlety. She had thought them all barbarians, not far removed from the mead-swilling monsters depicted by her aunt. But he, at least, was something more.

His sword slid back into its sheath, and the talk swirled away to hunting dogs and their stamina in the chase for the wild boar.

More food was brought in. Rhianneth ate nothing. Her stomach churned at the very smell of the savoury pies. But she clung to her wine-cup as if to a talisman, taking tiny sips from time to time. Over its rim, she watched Aethelric. Compared with Caius she thought him rough, lacking in breeding and

114

civilised polish. Yet she sensed the force of his energy lying like a coiled wire waiting to spring, and felt uneasy and vulnerable in his presence.

The conversation paused, and in that instant he looked directly at her. She swallowed, saying the first thing that came into her head.

'You speak our tongue very well, for a foreigner.'

Her innocent choice of words sounded dangerously near an insult. But the momentary tension which fell upon those within earshot was broken, as the Saxon laughed.

'Why I thank you, lady,' he said, as the colour ran up under skin. 'We usually claim to master peoples, not their language. But I had a British nurse.'

Rhianneth's discomforture changed to anger at the cutting edge of his voice, at the scarcely hidden arrogance in his words. He looked at her in a cool, almost insolent way which belied any deference he made, and she suspected that behind his façade of politeness he was laughing at her.

The last of her wine swirled darkly at the bottom of the cup and she quickly drank it, drowning her thoughts. Deliberately, she turned away to gaze at the scene around; at the rich fabrics and the candle-lit jewels which flashed with the turn of a head or the wave of a hand.

Strange and beautiful perfumes drifted on the warm air, and sent her mind winging back to the expression on her cousin's face when he first saw her in her frayed plaid shawl on the broken wooden steps of their old colonnade at home. Suddenly she felt sick, needing desperately to feel the cool night wind which moved in the garden beyond the room.

Murmuring something, she wandered over to the open door and stared up at the thin streaky clouds drifting across the face of the moon. Her stomach cramped painfully, and the ache in her head was like a grey weight.

Caius came to her side, his smile a flash of triumph. 'It's going well, little cousin. The alliance is as good as sealed. We can all give thanks that the queen stayed away!'

'I want to go home, Cai,' she said abruptly, 'I don't feel well.'

He stared at her, astonished. 'We can't leave yet! Aethelric – '

'I don't like him.'

'You don't have to like him, Rhianneth. Just be polite. He is Ida's son. The best of the old wolf's cubs.'

Dismay swept through her. Ida's son. Bernicia's king was not young, then. The half-formed picture in her mind of the warrior bridegroom awaiting her began to shred. Ida's son . . . that great arrogant man, with his cold grey eyes? What then, could she expect Ida to be like?

Before she could speak, Caius muttered something about getting more wine, and left. Rhianneth took a few deep breaths and walked out through the door.

The garden was small and mostly paved, the area nearest the house lit by torches which flickered dangerously in the wind, constantly under threat of extinction. Sinking down upon a long low bench of stone beside a small ornamental pool from which the water had long since gone, she put her head in her hands and tried to slow the thoughts that whirled as aimlessly as the dead leaves skittering around the empty pool basin.

Now that the Saxons were here, the full meaning of her part in the alliance was breaking over her. She realised the truth of what she was undertaking, the enormity of it. She was to travel with them into their northern fastness, to marry their chieftain Ida – she would not call him a king, not tonight – who actually claimed descent from their pagan war-god Woden.

A dark demoniac picture of Bernicia was forming in her mind. So far north. Past the great fortress town of Eburacum, and on beyond the Wall to the cold edge of the North Sea. A storm-tossed land, cruel and violent as their Gods, incapable of rearing gentle men amongst its craggy hills. Yet what vows she had made to Caius, to Julia – to herself! Arturius's battle-maid! Her stomach churned again, and she let out a small moan.

'Lady Rhianneth?'

She snatched her hands from her face and looked up into grey eyes staring straight into hers. Her hand shook as she took the cup he offered, spilling some of the wine.

'Thank you, Aeth – Aethelric.'

To her humiliation her tongue twisted, stuttering around the unfamiliar consonants. Easily, he leaned back against the slender trunk of a rowan tree.

'Will you call me Elric? It is how I am known to those closest to me.' He raised his own wine-cup a little as if in a toast, looking amused. 'And you will find it easier to say.'

Dislike of him rushed upwards. 'I am nimble-tongued enough in both Latin and my own language,' she snapped. 'Until now, I had not thought to speak with barbarian tribes.'

'Ah,' he said softly. Nothing more. Against the background of laughter and music coming from within the room, silence deepened between them. Rhianneth averted her head and let her gaze wander around the dim shapes of bushes and small trees beyond the torchlight's rim, over the smooth limbs and foldeld dress of a slim stone statue near the doorway. Someone came through the open door. Seeing them, he raised a hand in a gesture, half salute, half apology, and disappeared.

Where was Caius? she thought resentfully. How did he dare leave her here, alone with the son of Ida? Swift as a sword-thrust came the answer. Caius would dare anything for Mithrasia, for the Empire. Had he not left his wife and unborn child in the Saxon fortress of Din Guarydi? Soon she, too, would be alone there, another piece of Cai's desperate war-game set in place.

But the battle she had vowed to win was beginning for her here and now, if Ida's Saxon wolf-pack was to guard Roman Mithrasia from the ambitions of the British kings of the far north. And that meant being polite to this cool, odious man beside her.

Rhianneth turned and looked into the face of the enemy.

'My cousin's wife,' she said, 'was she well, when you left?'

His sea-grey eyes openly studied her face, until she raised her chin higher, angrily fighting down the colour beginning to rise under her skin.

'The lady Morvydd naturally looks forward to her husband's return,' he answered at last, 'but she is well enough, I think.'

'We will all be in Bernicia before winter,' Rhianneth hurried on without pausing, without thinking very much. 'Do you get a lot of snow?'

'Yes,' he replied bluntly, 'and great banks of mist that roll in from the sea. And rainstorms, when you can watch lightning leap from hill to hill and hear the thunder roll like the voice of the great god Thunor.'

She stared at him, her face blank. Not for anything would she let him see the dismay that filled her, the dark depression his words created.

'Bernicia is not lush and fruitful, like lady Mithrasia. More like that enchantress of which our legends speak – she who rides the wind as a wild sea-bird and sometimes takes shape as a woman to steal away men's senses.' He drained his cup of wine in one swallow. Then he smiled, showing strong white teeth, as if he had seen through her careful mask to the emotions moiling beneath. 'But our long winter nights are times of feasting, and magic. Singers we have, and players of the harp. And there are those who hold in their minds all the past years and the deeds that were done then. They are the memory of our people, the keepers of the word-hoard, who can count back through the generations and name the dead who were before us. It is they who speak our present hopes, who hold for us our dreams of the future.'

After a moment Rhianneth broke free of the strange thrall of his words. 'That must be quite a feat. I understand that Ida traces his origins back to the god Woden?'

He shrugged, his mouth twitching at the corner. 'I believe that you and your brother Llywarch claim descent from Prince Macsen and a maiden called Elen of the Hosts?'

'But they were real, not Gods!'

Now he actually laughed at her. 'Yet you write his name in letters of blood on stone outside your market place. To your people I think he has great magic. He has become a god!'

Rhianneth gasped. She could not think straight. How could she explain a legend that grew from a fact to this barbarian? Savages, the men at home had called those other Saxons from Mercia, savages that not even one hundred years

118

would change. She could see their warm kitchen now, as the men came stamping in from the snow, and sudden tears pricked behind her aching eyes. Saxons from Mercia, or from Bernicia, they were all one. They were destroying the world she knew.

Elric's head turned sharply, and following his gaze she thankfully recognised Caius coming towards them. But as she sprang to her feet to run to him, the ground slid away, the torchlight blurred. She felt Elric's arm shoot out to steady her. She tried to speak, and instead was violently, shockingly, sick.

Sweat broke out cold on her face when she raised her head. Stained and wet, Elric's arm still held her upright, though her legs trembled, weak as straws. Above the wild drumming of her heartbeats a woman's voice shrilled from the open doorway.

'It's the sickness – it will kill us all!'

Terror exploded inside Rhianneth. She heard Caius's voice close by, rough with alarm. Her eyes closed as her head whirled.

Then the Saxon swept her up into his arms and strode towards the door, people falling back before him. There was a babble of voices and a blur of colour, and Rhianneth's head fell back against his arm as a rush of warm air met them.

Caius was looking down at her, his face pale in the lamplight. Somewhere outside the small room Rhianneth could hear subdued voices, a frightened whispering. There was fear on Caius's face too, and her heart stirred with sweet pain. He knelt and took her icy hands between his own.

'Don't die, Rhianneth,' he murmured. 'Please . . . '

The warmth from his hands seemed to fill her whole body, his low words were like balm. 'There's only you, cousin foxcub! No one else could . . . '

His voice died away, and as she looked into his eyes she saw the truth. His fear was not of the killer that lurked so close, nor did his concern stem from fondness. Her cousin plainly thought she was about to die, as Marcus had died, and so bring about the ruin of everything for which he had worked and schemed. He got to his feet.

'Lie still,' he said, his voice unsteady. 'We've sent for the surgeon from the barracks . . . '

With arms folded, the Saxon Elric stood in the shadows, his face inscrutable. Rhianneth turned her head to the wall and shut her eyes.

She felt too ill to think of anything but getting through each succeeding minute. Her head pounded, and there was an increasing pain in her back which got no easier however she twisted and turned.

The surgeon was a thick-set man, with strong muscular arms covered with fine dark hair. But his hands were gentle as he made a swift examination, and his voice was steady and reassuring.

'Can't tell yet. I'll know for sure in a couple of days. Keep her warm. Plenty to drink. I'll be back in the morning. In the meantime, get everyone out of here. And, except for the slaves, I do mean everyone!'

Rhianneth thought the room grew darker, but strangely no more lamps were lit. She tried to ask why, but no one seemed to understand what she said. Gradually day and night merged until time was completely lost. She no longer knew light from dark, or how many days had fled since she had stood in the torchlit garden trembling in the grasp of sickness. She lay, shaking and burning, while panic rushed through the fortress. No one came near save the surgeon and one old woman who seemed constantly at her side.

Her high fever passed, and there came a time when pain ebbed away and Rhianneth felt herself drifting warmly down towards sleep.

A commotion startled her awake, and she struggled to see, but the pain behind her eyes shot back and made the room blur. She sank back, covering her face.

Then Caius was beside her, gripping her limp hand so tightly it hurt. Each time she began to slide away into sleep he dragged her back to the hot bright awful world of sickness. She knew there was something she had promised to do, that she must not sleep until she found out what it was Caius

120

wanted. Gradually the region of darkness retreated.

When at last it was certain that Rhianneth was not going to die, that this illness, dangerous though it had been, was not the monster plague which had destroyed Deva, the surgeon allowed her to be carried in a covered litter to her aunt's house. There, in the care of Torfrida and the safe comfort of her own room, she made a rapid recovery.

Urgent preparations for the wedding journey began, and the quiet house was filled with an untidy bustle as Torfrida cut and sewed new winter-warm garments to be placed in the great wooden chest bound with iron bands.

Rhianneth kept busy because she did not want to think of the future, and to remember the past made her sad. The days of her illness were a confusion of pain and fear, a wild high tide of nightmare which had all but drowned her. But bright and clear in her mind was a picture of that torchlit garden, and the humiliation of her vomiting over the son of Ida. Remembering his cool grey eyes, she grew hot with shame. How could she ever look into his face again?

Aunt Julia was pale, subdued, her brittle gaiety broken. She would not speak of the alliance, but trailed around the house in silence or sat pensively in the late sunshine that warmed her pretty paved garden. One day she swept all her cosmetics and perfumes into a wooden box and gave them to Rhianneth, saying that she was an old woman and had no more need of them.

'Julia,' Rhianneth pleaded, 'please, don't do this! You will certainly need them again, just as soon as you feel better . . . '

'I can't be bothered with them.' She was wandering restlessly around her room opening doors, pulling out drawers and closing them again, as if searching for something.

Dismayed by her frail appearance, her strangeness, Rhianneth said more sharply, 'Julia?'

Torfrida shook her head, pushed her out of the room and softly closed the door. 'It's no use. Take them. Put them in the big chest, out of her sight. It is as if she has to be rid of everything that reminds her of the old days. Of your mother . . . '

She looked anxious, almost distraught. Rhianneth swung round and caught her hands. 'She'll be better when I've gone. When the house is back to normal.' She forced a smile to bolster her words, but Torfrida made no response except a quick nod, her eyes darting away as if seeking escape.

Rhianneth sensed there was something else behind her agitation besides her anxiety for Julia. But Torfrida eased her hands away and walked on, down the stairs. Rhianneth followed her, puzzled and uneasy. At the bottom of the stairs she placed the cosmetic box in the almost full chest, just as Caius came in from the garden.

'This is Alda. She's a gift,' he said carelessly. 'From Llywarch, to you. He thinks she might be useful, being Saxon-born.'

He pulled forward a girl of about her own age. Rhianneth straightened, staring at her, too taken aback even to smile a welcome. She wore a slave-ring on her arm. Her curly brown hair was streaked with gold, and her face had the kind of strong and gentle beauty Rhianneth had seen come to their wolfhound bitches with their pups.

'Saxon?' Torfrida tensed. 'Where do you come from?'

'From the edge of the great plain, in the south,' the girl answered without a trace of accent. 'I was taken at the age of eight by a raiding party. It was after a battle. But I don't remember much about that. I've served in two households before I was brought to Mithrasia last year, and I can mend and sew.'

Caius seemed unmoved by the girl's tale. But Rhianneth felt both pity that she should have known so much violence and bondage, and amazement that despite it her eyes should be so merry and her smile so ready.

Torfrida did not answer for a while. Then, unexpectedly, she shook her head, letting out a shuddering breath that was almost a sob.

'I have been here so long,' she said huskily, 'that I had almost forgotten my own people, the scent of my own kind.'

Memory, and some old grief, filled her eyes with unshed tears. 'But there is something in the blood. A need for kinfolk, for the remembered places, the familiar tongue. For the old stories that bind one generation to the next and weave a girdle to make a nation . . . '

When she spoke next it was in Saxon, and she held out her arms to the girl, Alda. The slave-girl's own eyes filled with tears as she went into them, and impulsively Rhianneth put a hand on each of their shoulders, smiling a welcome into the girl's face.

She and Caius left them together, and went to sit amongst the last of the summer roses. She thought Caius looked tired, his face withdrawn. He lay back in one of the wicker chairs near the door, and closed his eyes.

'I don't know what I shall do with her, Cai,' she ventured after a while. 'I've never had a maid before . . . '

'You don't have to do anything,' Caius replied dismissively. 'She will do it. She's your slave – you own her.'

Rhianneth studied his face. His eyes remained closed, but a tell-tale muscle in his jaw betrayed his taut nerves. Something was troubling him. Was it the alliance? Hardly, or Llywarch would not have sent a Saxon slave for her. The queen then, or Lucius the priest. Or perhaps he was simply worried about his mother. Or his wife. Of course, that was it. What an unthinking fool she was! His child must already be born, for Rhianneth's illness had delayed the journey to Bernicia by several weeks.

'We'll soon be on our way,' she said. His eyes remained closed.

'The sooner the better,' he answered tersely.

'I'm sorry.' She moved in her chair, helplessly casting round for words of comfort and finding none. At last she asked, hoping to steer his thoughts from Morvydd, 'Are the Saxons becoming restless?'

'Of course. They are not at ease in our towns. Deep down they suspect magic or treachery.' His eyes flashed open. 'And this time, they are right.'

'What?' She stared at him.

'Oh, Rhianneth!' Suddenly he sat up, running a hand through his dark hair in a gesture of futile anger. 'Your illness put a weapon in the hands of the queen and with it she has made a wound which she hopes will fester!'

'I don't know what you are talking about.' But her heart was thumping, remembering the malice in the eyes of the queen.

'I'm talking,' he said bleakly, 'about the fact that I refused the surgeon's advice – and more to the point, Llywarch's command. I did not keep away from the sickness. I came back, to be with you. After we left, the queen's party fell upon that old woman who nursed you. She was overcome by their flattery. She made much of little things, she winked and nodded until the fortress fairly rocked with excitement. By now there can be no one in the city of Mithrasia – including the Saxons – who has not heard that Caius Caprilius is so mad with love for his pretty cousin that he intended to die beside her!'

Rhianneth sat in stunned silence. Caius's anger was so intense it was almost tangible. She thought of the queen, and shivered. Beneath the surface show of injured bitterness she displayed towards her husband's bastard, was the deadly coldness of true implacable hatred. Yet even she could not have realised that the weapon with which she slashed at the alliance was cutting so deeply into Rhianneth's heart. For it was not love that had kept Caius at her side. He was aware of nothing but his mission to save Mithrasia, and he saw her only as a counter in his dangerous game of chance.

She watched the sunlight falling dappled on his hair through the moving leaves of her aunt's young ash tree, lighting the planes of his face, so sun-darkened by their days of riding with Llywarch. Her whole body ached to touch him, to feel his lips on hers once more. If only it were true that Cai loved her, she thought bitterly, she would open the gates of Rome herself to the barbarians, for one night in his arms.

'Have you spoken to Elric?' she asked, hesitantly.

'The alliance is sealed. Safe. But I would not have Ida look on you with suspicion when this slander reaches Din Guaryrdi!'

'And – Morvydd?'

His head shot round, his eyes blazing. Then he seemed to see her face for the first time. His mouth twisted, and he slowly let out his breath. 'We may not marry for love, Rhianneth. Yet within a marriage there must be pride, and honour.'

In a whisper, she asked: 'Then where will you find love, Caius Caprilius?'

For what seemed an eternity they sat still, Caius's eyes locked with hers. Then he said softly, 'Never, I hope, where I might bring dishonour and danger to the lady in question.'

She had underestimated him, had thought him blind, but he understood more that she knew. She closed her eyes, feeling hot tears of weakness start and knowing they must never fall. If anything had passed between them, it was much too dangerous ever to acknowledge. A dream to be kept well away from the clear light of day.

After a while they walked back to the house, the scent of roses rising around them as they moved.

'It's all so stupid,' Rhianneth said, 'they can prove nothing . . . '

Caius·stopped, swinging her round to face him. 'They don't have to, do they? Ida's mere suspicion will be enough to ruin me, and any good I can do for the Fellowship in the north.'

She stared at him, fear washing over her like a wave. 'You mean you might have to leave Bernicia?'

'I mean just that, little cousin.'

Llywarch gave a farewell feast to honour the Saxon envoys on the eve of departure for Bernicia which Caius insisted they attend despite Rhianneth's pleas that she was still unwell.

'Stay away, and their slanders will be given credence,' he told her roughly. 'We'll face the queen's party tonight and toss their lies down their throats! What are you wearing?'

She told him. He crossed swiftly to the clothes chest and began sorting through the contents, throwing aside beautiful dresses of bright or subtle colours, until he held up a dress of soft cream wool, patterned with a border of gold.

'Wear this,' he ordered, 'Tonight I want you looking pale, young, and virginal. Gods, how I hate them! I swear I could strangle that witch and her black-crow priest with my own hands!'

Llywarch greeted her as before with a kiss and a smile. But as they took their places Rhianneth was sickeningly aware of the sudden hush, and her imagination supplied vividly the covert nudges and smiles of the guests.

Down the length of the room tables were placed together, covered with fine white cloths which reached to the shining mosaic floor, and on them stood delicate dishes of glass piled high with fruit, and large glossy-red bowls filled with salads, the green of the cresses and the lettuce spiked with scarlet radishes opened like flowers.

To Rhianneth's horror she found that not only was Lucius the priest at the feast, but the queen herself. She sat at the table in a drift of perfume, jewels shining like stars, her painted eye-lids reflecting the purple of her gown. Rhianneth heard her laughter, and saw from time to time her eyes slide maliciously sideways in her direction.

Beside the queen, and directly opposite Rhianneth, was Elric. A thick jewelled chain around his broad shoulders flashed as it caught the light reflected from the gleaming dishes before them. His hair shone gold in the soft candlelight, and to Rhianneth's distress when he looked at her she blushed all over, as if still hot with fever.

'I am glad to see you well, Rhianneth.'

His deep, alien voice cut through a sudden silence at the table, and her uneasy speculations on what he really thought of the rumours concerning his father's bride vanished as a vivid picture of their last meeting rushed into her mind. She nodded, giving a polite smile. But she could not meet his eyes.

'Such a long ride to your fortress by the sea!' the queen drawled, her delicate fingers twisting one pendant earring so that its silver gleam reflected against the creamy column of her neck. 'But then, Rhianneth will have her cousin Caius for company. He will keep her amused, as he did on her last journey.'

The conversation of those nearest faltered, fell into a momentary bowl of silence. Rhianneth was unused to insults, and the queen's words were veiled by her soft sympathetic tones. It was a second or two before their poison bit. By then people were talking again, louder, faster than before. Small dishes of savoury eggs were being brought in, to whet appetites for the meal to come. The queen waved hers aside with a faint smile. But her eyes, glittering coldly, were fixed upon Rhianneth, waiting.

Against this woman Caius had struggled for the mind of Llywarch, for the survival of Roman Mithrasia; riding her insults, slashing through the slanders she sowed like bindweed. Feeling came flooding back through the numbness of Rhianneth's brain, a burning anger fired in love that brought hot words bubbling to her lips.

'Try this wine,' Wencam said clearly, deliberately, as his hand closed firmly over her arm. 'It's light, not too sweet.'

Somehow Rhianneth broke free of the mocking challenge in the queen's eyes, her glance sliding from the wine-cup before her across the table to Caius. His dark face was watchful, tense. Very slightly, he shook his head. Her hand trembling, Rhianneth picked up the wine-cup and drank. Of course, Caius was right. To the Saxons within their gates they had to seem a strongly united kingdom threatened only by outside enemies. No civil strife must appear likely to upset the flow of grain and cattle agreed by treaty, and the queen's slanders against the bride chosen for Ida must be made to seem merely the poisonous outpourings of a jealous woman frustrated in her bids for power.

They had cooked fish in muria sauce, and with it came mulsum, a wine well sweetened with honey which the Saxons found much to their taste. Rhianneth had never seen such appetites, not even when the men at home had come in hungry from a day-long hunt. They wolfed down the food, and the small hot bread-rolls which were meant to be nibbled between courses disappeared like magic.

There was red warm-wine ladled from large bowls into cups of shining pewter, and ham spiked with honey and baked in pastry. Roast goose, pigeons, hares, and dishes of vegetables piled high and steaming, lay between bowls of plums, apples, nuts and dishes of sweet cakes and pastries.

But Rhianneth had no appetite. She toyed with her half-empty cup of wine, avoiding the queen's eyes, talking to Wencam on her right and to Llywarch when he remembered enough to pause in his conversation with Elric. It seemed that during her illness her half-brother had formed a great attachmnent to the Saxon leader, for he laughed and talked so easily with him it was obvious they had spent much time together.

She noticed the black eyes of Lucius the priest turned resentfully in the direction of Llywarch, and felt a sharp pleasure in seeing the priest's power over her half-brother temporarily broken. His long fingers played constantly with the pepper bowl, raising the tiny spoon and letting the precious stuff – so expensive a luxury Rhianneth had never before seen it – trickle back like golden sand. His dislike of her and his held-in hatred of the Saxons was dark and powerful. She remembered the keeper of the green chapel, in all his gentleness and strength, and wondered that two such different men should serve the same God. His baleful stare shifted suddenly to her and she shivered, feeling for the comforting coils of the golden serpent bangle on her arm as she turned quickly back to hear Llywarch eagerly asking Elric to describe his city.

'There is no city,' the Saxon said, his eyes on Rhianneth. 'Din Guaryrdi stands alone, high above the sea on a great rock. It is very old. The Romans took it for a signal fort and built the stone buildings which stand today. When Ida drove out Outigern, he repaired the broken walls and made it strong enough to withstand a siege army. It would need treachery – or all the armies of the northern kings – to threaten Din Guaryrdi, and they hate each other more than they fear us. They would need to be desperate indeed to make such an alliance.'

'A dangerous thought though,' murmured Wencam, rubbing his moustache, 'but unlikely. Urien is on his way to making Rheged the most powerful kingdom in the north. He needs no allies.'

'Not yet.' The Saxon's teeth glinted in a smile which took the edge from his words. But from the corner of Rhianneth's eye she saw a dark movement as the priest leaned forward.

'I've been told that you Saxons have a dream that one day the most powerful of your kings will rule over the whole island of Britain,' he called, his eyes glittering. 'Bretwalda – Wielder of Britain. Is this not what you call this fantasy-king?'

Elric turned towards the priest, his smile fading. 'You call us all one name – Saxon? Yet we in the north and east of this island are Engles.' He shrugged, candlelight flickering on the jewelled chain about his shoulders. 'Bretwalda? Our cousins in the Saxon south may hope for such a title. We are content to call all our little northern kingdoms merely Engleland.'

To avoid his eyes, Rhianneth looked away down the length of the table. Semi-barbaric, magnificent in their bright colours, glittering arm-rings and chains of gold, the Saxons were rough and had no fine manners. But their cold eyes held all the slow patience of the northland, and in their strong faces was written a grim steadfastness which seemed suddenly to hold a terrible and silent threat.

She thought of Wencam with his bitter memories and withered arm. Of Caius with his tense young face. Of Llywarch so excited and trusting, and she trembled for Mithrasia. Was the Fellowship right – or were they inviting a pack of wolves into the city?

She remembered Rhun, riding to the front of his army as they marched towards Deva, and the fear she had felt then. Now there was Urien in the kingdom of Rheged to the north, whom Caius thought as dangerous as Rhun. And Saxon Mercia growing in power to the south and east. Mithrasia was trapped between them. A jewel, surrounded by thieves. What could they do but adopt the old Roman strategy of bribing one enemy to fight another for them?

As the evening lengthened the room grew hotter, talk and laughter louder, and the music of the harp rippled through the air, sighing and falling like the sound of the wind through the trees.

A glass dish filled with a mixture of chopped fruit and thick cream appeared before Rhianneth. Her head swam. The legacy of tiredness which her illness had left swept over her.

She wondered how long this meal could go on. And afterwards – how long would they sit around talking and drinking?

Caius was listening to Llywarch, his dark head bent. Rhianneth tried, and failed, to will him to look her way. Next to her, Wencam was turned away, his hand half covering his wine-cup as he recounted yet another of his youthful battles, this time with the tribes of the Scotti, north of Dal Riada.

Suddenly Rhianneth stood up. Perhaps the wine had gone to her head. She had no clear idea what she was about to do, or say. She only knew she could sit there no longer and must make her excuses and leave, with or without Caius. The chatter and clatter died away as all eyes turned, startled, towards her. Then, before she could speak, the queen's voice broke the silence with a laugh.

'Your cousin is looking pale, Caius. I think she wants you to take her home to bed.'

There was a muffled gasp, a hiss of indrawn breath along the table, and an oath from Wencam as his hand jerked against his cup, sending the red wine streaming away. Rhianneth knew that in some way the queen had insulted her again and worse, had insulted Caius. She heard mockery in the sly tone, and venom behind it. But the wine, combined with her tiredness, enabled Rhianneth only to understand the words the queen spoke; not the meaning behind them.

'All I need is fresh, clean air,' she told her carefully. 'I do not think that is found much in your presence, lady.'

The queen flushed angrily, and when the hot colour drained away, her face was icy beneath its mask of paint.

'Ah, forgive me, Rhianneth!' she ground out. 'Seeing you in your new finery I had forgotten you were born on a farm!' She made a mocking sweep of the table. 'We Mithrasians must seem very stuffy, when you are used to living amongst the beasts of the field!'

Dimly Rhianneth was aware of Llywarch's voice raised in protests of a crashing sound as Wencam sprang to his feet and of Caius in a blur of movement across the table. Her mind, her vision, was centred on the face of the queen. It swam before her, eyes shining with hate, mouth smiling in triumph.

Rhianneth was filled with a murderous rage against this woman who had tried to poison her mother, who hated her and hated Caius, and would do anything to wreck the dream of the Caer Melot Fellowship. Yet, strangely, it was the mockery of her childhood home which goaded her most, their gallant little outpost in a dangerous and darkening land. The Saxons, Llywarch, Caius, this splendid Roman feast, all slid away and were forgotten. Only this woman remained and all Rhianneth desired in that moment was to blot her forever from her sight.

She snatched up the bowl beneath her hand and hurled it unerring and straight, into the face of her enemy. In triumphant horror she watched it empty over the queen's elaborately-dressed head and purple gown, pieces of fruit lodging amongst the combs in her black hair while cream slid down her face and dropped like pearls from the ends of her silver earrings.

Pandemonium broke out as the queen's shrieks rose into the air. A fierce joy swooped up in Rhianneth at the sound of those penetrating cries of rage, mingled as they were with the lower exclamations of the Mithrasians and, unexpectedly, the deep hearty belly-laughter of the Saxon envoys. Then Wencam's one strong arm lifted her from the table and half-dragged, half-carried her out of the room to push her, none too gently, on to a bench in the cool lamp-lit ante room.

'Oh, she is vile!' Rhianneth was trembling from head to foot. 'I could kill her!'

'What the Blinding Light did you think you were doing?' Caius was beside them, his face a mask of fury. 'Have you lost your mind? Gods help us, Ida won't take a mad woman to wife!'

As she stared at him, stricken, she heard Wencam bellow towards the outer door. 'Street escort!'

A soldier appeared, his sword already in place, throwing on a thick night-cloak over his tunic. Wencam's heavy hand fell on Caius's shoulder.

'Get her home, Cai. I'll sort this lot out.'

'Sort it out?' Caius's reply was an explosion of anger. 'We've lost Llywarch – you realise that? He'll never forget such a humiliation! As for the queen – she'll already have decided an assassin is a better bet that slander. We'll be lucky if we even reach the forum.'

In one swift movement Wencam turned, pulled Rhianneth to her feet and pushed her urgently against Caius. 'You can do nothing here, that's certain!' He glanced swiftly towards the shadows at the lamplight's edge. 'So go! Now!'

For an instant longer Caius hesitated, his eyes brilliant with fury. Then he nodded briefly and swung away, dragging Rhianneth with him. Their escort silently turned as they passed him and followed behind. With the night guards near the entrance to the king's apartments Lovan also waited to escort them home through the dark streets. He sat at a table shaking dice with three men, a little apart from others who sprawled around the room talking and chaffing, long legs out-stretched. Torchlight flared across his face as he looked up and saw them, lighting the surprise that jerked his features at their leaving so early.

'By all the Gods, don't ask!' Caius ground out as he hurried Rhianneth towards him. With raised eyebrows Lovan got up, picked up his dice with a muttered apology to his fellow-players and followed them from the room. They walked so fast through the empty forum and the dim narrow streets, the men with their swords naked and ready in their hands, that all Rhianneth's triumphant elation vanished with her breath into the cool night air. Once safely inside Julia's garden, Lovan slid his sword back into its sheath and stood for a moment irreso-lute, looking from one to the other. Then at an almost imper-ceptable movement of Caius's head, he turned and left them.

Rhianneth sagged, panting, against the house wall as weariness surged over her. Nothing seemed real any more. Far from home, she was moving into a nightmare filled with people wearing masks that hid their true intent, who could smile in the teeth of an enemy and wade through lies and abuse in order to reach their own secret victory.

She was not yet the clever fox-cub Caius had so teasingly

named her. She had been born amongst those who showed their anger or pleasure plainly. How long would it take to learn the art of hiding her hot emotions, forging them into weapons? Within her was a growing sense of isolation and fear, bursting through the thin armour of proud resolution she had worn since her first brave vow to the Fellowship. To Caius she was obviously not a flaming sword against the enemies of Rome, but a dangerous fire-risk within the murky alleyways of Mithrasian power politics.

Suddenly he moved, and she saw the anger still glinting like ice in his dark eyes.

'Remember this, little cousin,' he whispered savagely, 'I have endured much to ensure this alliance, and risked more. I'll not let you or anyone else wreck it now!'

He did not touch her. Yet the force of his fury washed over her like a wave, leaving her cold and trembling, nerves taut as harp strings.

'I will not apologise to that woman,' Rhianneth said, gritting her teeth, 'I will not see her again.'

As he swung away from her, she caught at his sleeve. 'I won't!'

'Go to bed, Rhianneth. And give thanks to whichever god saw us safely home tonight!'

'Cai, wait! Would your Saxons have thought more of me if I'd swallowed her insults? Are you deserting me because I stopped her slander instead of suffering it?'

Now he turned back. 'Deserting you? I'll be your second shadow until you are safely in Ida's bed!'

She stared at him, stunned into silence by the brutality of his words. The Empire, Caer Melot, the Saxon alliance – all dream-words that were a part of her dream of Caius. Never had she allowed the reality of what she had undertaken to touch that dream. Perhaps, in truth, she had not recognised it.

Sudden tears welled up and spilled over. His concern was all for the safety of Mithrasia, for the alliance. She had always known that. He cared nothing for her. But for all her bravado she was desolate, and could not bear that there should be bitterness between them. Something of her despair must have shown in her face, or perhaps he saw the shimmer of tears through the darkness, for he let out his breath on a long sigh, slightly touching her wet cheek with his hand.

'Gods, you're so young, Rhianneth,' he groaned, 'I don't know why I'm treating you like this – saying such things. But this is not a game we are playing. We're on the brink of destruction, and every unguarded moment brings us nearer to the edge . . .'

She pressed the back of her hand against her face to dry away the tears, and he covered it with his own. They stood silent in the shadows, while the rose-scented wind lifted her hair and she struggled to stem the flood of her tears.

'Tomorrow,' he said, at last, the anger finally drained from his voice, 'we will be away from here. Away from the queen and all her ill-wishing.'

Away to the north, to the land of the mountain passes. To Ida and his stone-ringed fortress beside a cold sea. To the lands of the pagan invaders. To Cai's wife – and his newborn child. As if he read the thoughts on her face, he drew closer, until she could feel his heart thudding beneath his cloak.

'My brave lady vixen, you can do it,' he whispered. 'For Mithrasia. For Rome. For me?'

His hand slipped under her chin, raising her tearful face to his. 'If the Saxons saw us now,' he said unsteadily, 'the alliance would break into fragments!'

But she could not smile. Her love for him was an ache which twisted into pain at the nearness of his dark face, the sweetness of his warm breath across her cheek. She tried to speak, but her voice faltered and her mouth opened beneath his as Caius kissed her.

'You can be sure of me, little cousin,' he whispered, his lips feathering across her cheeks, her closed eyes. 'Hold fast to that, when you are afraid.'

Warm joy ran swiftly through her. She reached up and locked her fingers in his hair, feeling his hard young body suddenly tense and still. Then his mouth came back to hers once more, and she felt his growing desire in the rough tightening of his arms as she sank against him, letting all her long hidden love pour out into the honey-cup of his kiss.

'I love you, Cai,' she breathed against his mouth when at last their kissing broke. 'I love you so!'

He stopped, his arms rigid. Slowly, he drew back, his breathing slowing. She clung to him, her fingers twisted in the folds of his cloak.

'You do love me, just a little? Cai?'

For a moment he looked down into her pleading face. Then he said quietly, 'Love – Llywarch's sister? Ida's bride?'

His words fell like ice between them. Gently he loosed her fingers and held both her hands in his. He smiled faintly, but it was a smile of bitter, savage regret.

'You are what my love for Mithrasia made you, Rhianneth. Untouchable. I should have left you with your grandmother, little cousin.'

She could not speak. One word would have choked her. He pulled her close for an instant, for a heart's beat. Then he flung an arm about her shoulders so that she was drawn into the shelter of his great cloak, and walked through the doorway of the house.

Rhianneth turned on the stairs, looking down at him. He was watching her, his face sombre in the dim lamplight, and her heart turned over with love.

'Cai . . . ' It was no more than a breath. But he heard.

'Don't,' he whispered, not moving.

The bleak word, spoken with difficulty, drained all hope away and left a cold void within her. Had she really thought that Caius, to whom honour meant so much, would abandon it for a fragile emotion sprung probably, on his part, from the bond that held them both?

She turned and ran up the stairs. Arturius's battlemaid . . . The years stretched before her like the cold miles between Mithrasia and Din Guarydri, like the dark gulf between Rome and the sea-wolves of Bernicia, and she shivered as if the bitterness of the northern winter was already upon her.

CHAPTER 5

The forum was crammed with scurrying people, lined with loiterers enjoying the mid-morning excitement. The autumn sun blazed on the helmets of the mounted escort and fired with colour the flags which fluttered like bright leaves.

Rhianneth waited with Cai near the basilica wall. After a sleepless night her nerves were raw, her stomach queasy. Beneath a thin mask of green cosmetic, her eyelids were swollen with weeping. Cai scarcely looked her way. Beyond briefly urging her to hurry, he had not spoken to her since last night.

She glanced now at his profile as he watched the crowd. The ache inside her jagged with renewed pain. She had to thrust away the sharp desire to grasp his arm, force him to notice her.

Nearby, slaves were loading a four-wheeled supply waggon, thumping and bolting its tail board into place. The two mules harnessed to it dozed, indifferent to the rolling clatter that saturated the square with sound. But Rhianneth's horse Romulus shuddered with nervous impatience, the muscles shivering in his smooth flank as he nuzzled reassurance from the stable-lad holding his bridle.

Rhianneth patted his neck. You're like me, Romulus, she thought, longing to be away into cool empty country, away from people who stare with veiled curiousity, or insolent admiration.

Wencam pushed towards them. He was followed by Idwal, Llywarch's kinsman and captain of the palace guard, who was to ride to Bernicia to see the marriage sealed. Black-haired and powerful in leather tunic and big riding cloak, he bowed toward Rhianneth and turned aside to talk to Cai. Wencam, as closer kin, planted a rough kiss on her cheek. The wine he drank as a pain-killer was sour on his breath. He fumbled in his tunic pocket.

'Where is the blinding thing . . . ?' he muttered, twisting round to reach into yet another pocket directly beneath his useless arm. Awkwardly, he drew out a gold chain with a pendant disc swirled like the rays of the sun.

'Live with Light, Rhianneth.' He slipped it over her head and then, suddenly serious, laid his hand against her brow in a strange ritualistic gesture. 'All our hopes go with you.'

Rhianneth's gaze slid across his watherlined face and met his eyes, puffed, weary, bloodshot. And she saw the years fall away to reveal, not the Wencam she knew now, but the Wencam he once was. Strong, fired with dreams. She felt what it was to be young in the days before Camlann, knew the brief fierce glory of battle, the future hopes bought with the sword's edge. Felt his agony as the great brotherhood broke, and the image of youth faded before her eyes. His face grew old again, and harder. How heavily the Caer Melot dead lay on Wencam's heart! No tears from the living through all the weary after years could wash away the blood debt he carried. Not Julia's, she thought, not mine. Until the debt is paid in full by those who betrayed Arturius, Wencam will spare nothing and no one. And he had made Cai into an image of himself.

'The king!'

Cai's tense voice broke her thoughts. She caught a warning glint in his eyes as Llywarch approached. So he still had a lingering fear that she might prove as insolent to Llywarch as she had been to the queen?

Cai's voice sank lower. 'Show respect, for the Gods' sake!'

She noticed the pallor beneath his sunburn which, wrapped in her own misery, she had not seen till now. She shivered, as if touched by a cold finger of mist. But it had nothing to do with Llywarch.

The humiliation of the feast was not mentioned. But the old ease had gone. Llywarch was stiff, formal. As if they had never played wargames together, nor rode outside the city walls under the hot sun, nor talked in the dusk-light until the lanterns grew brighter than the stars.

Any hope Rhianneth had that her half-brother the king would offer his regrets for the base slanders of the queen was shattered. If, on his part, he expected to carry her apology back to his mother, he would be disappointed. She kept her head high and her replies brief.

Yet, unwillingly, her resentment softened. Llywarch looked

so young, his eyes screwed up against the bright sunlight. When he turned to answer a question from Wencam, she noticed that for all his careful dignity that wayward lock of short hair stood straight up from the crown of his head, still defiant. His position was difficult, dangerous even; a heavy burden on his thin boy's shoulders. Yet as king, she thought, he stands here beside us, before the gathered citizens of Mithrasis. His very presence proclaims that his heart's hope is with the Alliance, and diminishes the sinister shadow of the queen's intent.

She felt shame, that she should have added to his troubles. Her heart melted. Gently she touched his arm.

'Take care, Llywarch. Be steady, and brave. I'll think of you, often.'

Cai and Wencam fell silent. For a moment Llywarch did not reply. When he turned to face her she saw to her distress that his eyes were full of tears.

'I shall . . . miss you.' His voice cracked, half boy's, half man's. 'It was good to have a sister for a while. Someone young to talk to and – ' he managed a faint smile – 'argue with.'

He blinked, swallowing hard. Then he raised a hand, beckoned. A man hurried forward and, with a slight bow, handed Rhianneth a square, flat box.

'Open it!' Llywarch urged. She lifted the lid. It was the 'ludus' game at which he had so soundly beaten her at their first meeting. Despite the tear-shine that still caught the sun he smiled again at her expression.

'I thought you might practise during the winter,' he said sadly, 'perhaps to beat me when we meet again?'

Elric rode up then, swinging down from his horse to present Llywarch with a finely-wrought Saxon sword. The tension was broken. Men were laughing, admiring with Llywarch the beauty of the deadly thing, with its ringed blade and decorated pommel. But Rhianneth turned away hiding her dislike while pretending to soothe Romulus before handing her gift-box to Alda to store in the baggage. She had nothing to say to Ida's son. His very presence disturbed her.

The dragon-banner was raised. The cavalcade rumbled out under the stone of Maximus. Young people ran through the narrow streets, heedless of danger from the great iron-rimmed wheels of the supply waggons or the hooves of the nervous, dancing horses. When the procession was through Mithrasia's open gates and riding along the soldiers' road, the city tumult faded. Rhianneth let out a sigh of relief.

No more hornblasts, no more bangs or shouting; only Lovan's deep reassuring tones, and Alda's voice, breathless with excitement as she sat timidly on the broad back of the placid sweet-tempered mare Rhianneth had demanded for the maid from Cai before she would leave her aunt's house.

'If Alda is my slave,' Rhianneth had insisted, 'I want her near me at all times – not perched on the sleeping waggon at the back of the line!'

She had scarcely cared what she said, feeling drowned in tears, both her own shed during the night and Julia's which flooded in with the morning. Cai had listened, looked into her determined face, and agreed. Now he rode beside her, as silent as Rhianneth herself.

Romulus tossed his head and flared his nostrils at the strange wild scents blowing in the wind. She ran her hand down his loose mane, feeling the great neck quiver in response. As she had promised him long ago, they were to ride together to the rim of the world. Of their world.

Best forgotten were last night's memories of hurrying from the palace through the dark streets, fearing the vengeance of the queen; of those moments alone with Cai in the sweet shadows of Julia's garden.

But her eyes were still salt-sore from the night's weeping, and in her heart was a growing bitterness that fate should twist all her dreams into such dark reality. Cai's love was not for her. It was not even given to his wife and his unseen child. It was pledged to the Empire and the ghosts of Caer Melot. It ran so deep that any lesser loves must drown in its depths.

Desire and love were not the same, she knew that. But that Cai had kissed her, had fleetingly wanted her, she locked in her memory like a bright picture to warm her in the winter of her life.

At a crossroads, the cavalcade halted to rest and eat. Rhianneth sank down on the grass, close to the stone which marked the road east. It had toppled backwards and was time-eaten, covered in moss. But the long dead stonemason had cut deep. She could still trace the words: *'Ad Legionem Sextam'*

'It doesn't mention Eburacum on the waystone,' she turned to Lovan, as he looped the reins of his horse over a branch and dropped down beside her. 'Isn't that odd? Just "To the Sixth Legion".'

'The Sixth Legion was at Eburacum for three hundred years,' he pointed out, easing his back muscles. 'It became inseparable from the city itself. It was enough to know you were heading for their base, the most magnificent fortress in Europe. but we shan't see it this time, *cariad*. We're taking the hard high trackway over the hills to the Wall.'

She shot upright in dismay. 'Not to Eburacum? Then how will we reach the big road north?'

Lovan's expression softened as he took in the pinched look round her still childish mouth.

Christos! he thought. What in Hell am I doing? I should be taking her south, deep into the west country where Marcus wanted her to be, if I had to kidnap her to do it! But her eyes moved past him, looking for Cai. He sighed.

'We can't take that road, Rhianneth. Eburacum rules the whole Vale and although it is a British kingdom, it's close to Saxon Deira. Too close. There's some kind of war-bond between them – and the Deiran king Aelle is no friend of Ida's. If this party rode in through Eburacum's gates, do you think we'd ever ride out again? With his bride and sons as hostages, Ida would find a sharp sword at his throat.'

Lovan rummaged in his saddlebag and brought out apples, offering one to Rhianneth.

'And if we'd taken the western route to the Wall we'd have found ourselves in Rheged.' He bit into his apple. 'I don't want to find out at first hand what Urien thinks of our alliance with Bernicia.'

The maid Alda brought food and barley beer from the supply wagon. She walked stiffly. As she knelt beside them her eyes filled with sudden tears, and she gave a cut-off gasp of pain.

'You'd better ride in the waggon from now on,' Rhianneth said sharply. Remorse that she should have insisted on a horse for Alda made her angry. 'I'll ride with you, for a while.'

Lovan winked at Alda, with a sympathetic smile. Brief resentment surged up through Rhianneth's already shaken emotions. Although no older than Rhianneth herself, the Saxon girl was woman-rounded, her breasts thrusting against the fall of her tunic and with no sharp angles in the smooth curve of shoulders or swell of hips. Even in pain, her movements were graceful, deft.

She handed Rhianneth a cloth napkin containing cold roast meat and bread, and poured drink into a cup. A glass-beaded bracelet slid down her wrist towards smooth plump hands. Suddenly Rhianneth felt awkward, clumsy, unformed. Her misery and sourness of temper grew. She took a few bites of her apple, then hurled it into the bushes.

'In a way, it's a pity.' Lovan stared into his cup. 'I'd like to have seen the city. It's twenty years, more, since I was last in Eburacum.' He raised his cup as if in a toast, giving a wry smile. 'To the Great Army!'

'What great army?' Rhianneth pulled her cloak closer against the breeze that ran from the western sea over the peat bogs before it swept the upland crags to the east.

'There's no great army!' Cai grinned, dropping down beside her, a large chop-bone of pork held in greasy fingers. 'Not any more.'

'Did I say there was?' demanded Lovan with mock belligerance. 'But once, once it meant something, after the Roman Command left and we still had order here, men appointed with overall authority. The northern headquarters was at Eburacum, and the commander there was Coel – Coelius. Most of the northern kings claim blood descent from Coel; Llywarch, Urien – even the kings of Manau Gododdin in the far north – they are all the heirs of that Roman army. Of Coel's officers, perhaps. Men flocked to Eburacum to swell the

141

spears there, to keep the "legion" alive.' He shrugged, looking briefly at Cai. 'But bad times came, as everywhere. Defeats. Plague. Till only the memory of the Great Army remained. Now Peredur and his cousin Gurci govern Eburacum as magistrates. They do not, as yet, call themselves kings.' He drained his cup and smiled. 'I'm told they are more Roman than the Romans ever were!'

'So why isn't our alliance with them?' Rhianneth asked resentfully, thinking of the long weary journey ahead over the hills on the old military patrol roads.

'They play a deep game,' Cai put in, his smile gone. 'They have links with Rheged and Manau Gododdin, let alone their agreement with the Saxon Aelle. They did nothing to help us when Rhun came marching through Mithrasia. I'll not forget that. To be plain, they don't need us. And we can't trust them.'

He sprang up, seeing Elric and his youngest brother Theodric approaching. Even now, Rhianneth thought as they drew near, there is a swagger to their walk, as if they owned the world!

Theodric was of slighter build than his tall fair-haired brothers; fifteen years old, with curling dark hair and a lazy smile that hid a sharp mind. The comments he made during the conversation that followed were brief, shrewd, often funny. But the talk gradually became a conversation between men, full of hunting and battle tactics. Rhianneth found little to say. She tried to keep her eyes from resting on Cai, and avoided looking at Elric. Theodric's gaze was on Alda, and Rhianneth guessed that his wit was being deliberately sharpened to impress the attractive maid.

Feeling out of things and a trifle jealous, Rhianneth took Alda's hand and walked across to the small stream that rushed past the bushes nearby. She scooped up some water in cupped hands and drank. It was ice-cold, so cold it made her teeth ache.

Her temper worsened. She felt sick with the pull of her ravelled-up emotions, frightened of whatever fate lay ahead. How she envied the people of Eburacum, with their strong fortress and wily magistrates! Perhaps they even had warm baths.

*

There was a magic about the days when they rode through the forest country, with the leaves breaking and drifting down as they passed, rustling in wind-blown heaps underfoot.

Rhianneth's spirits rose. She was young, Cai was by her side in a heroic venture worthy of a minstrel's song. Even Idwal, captain of the Mithrasian escort, lost the wary reserve that had been in his eye and in his speech ever since leaving the city; she heard him laughing as he rode beside Elric's other brother, Adda.

Near the ruined fort of Mancurian a few children ran alongside the wagons and horses. Their elders stood in the doorways of their turf-tiled huts to watch with puzzled eyes as the cavalcade turned away from the Eburacum road on to the small track that led northwards towards the hills that are the backbone of Britain. Washing blew like gay flags between the trees close by. But the place stank of pigs.

When they rode through the empty fort at Olicana, they saw grass growing on its thick broken walls. A raven paused to blink a fierce black eye at them, as it tore at its kill. Now they kept their cloaks on even at midday. The dragon-banner was furled against the wind that gusted across the open moorland.

Once, Rhianneth watched a red kite eagle sail across the empty sky, its white tail feathers catching the light as it rested lazily on the air. Then it was gone, rising effortlessly above the hills in the distance.

The high places were craggy with grey rocks, haunted by bird calls and the thin keening of the wind. Now fires were lit at night. Not only for warmth, but to keep away the grey wolf which might catch the scent of horses and mules. Sometimes as the company, tired from the long day's journey, sat around the leaping flames to eat and talk, Rhianneth would fall silent, withdrawing into herself to wander uneasily amongst her own thoughts.

Soon it would be Samhain. The year would end, another begin. What would it bring? A glimpse she might have caught, in the fire's glow or in Glainnader's elusive flame; but for that she needed solitude, and more courage than she had been able to scrape together since the seeing in the Holy House at Deva.

Already the things that sang through her mind in these desolate places brought a coldness to her back. It was not the eerie, deserted forts that disturbed her. Their ghosts were only the ghosts of men.

The road skirted a great mound. A burial place of people dead long before the coming of the Romans. Strange stone-shapes stood on the lonely moors, with carvings dug into the hard rock face. Gods older than any she knew had walked these wild places once. Always she was aware that beyond the little circle of flickering fire-lights lay the cold, ancient hills. And that within their silence, something waited and watched.

The weather changed as they neared the Wall. Rain sagged the strong hide covers on the supply wagons into pools of wind-whipped water. It soaked through their cloaks until they ceased to talk but rode in silent, sodden misery.

Rhianneth was glad to climb into the waggon which had been brought for her use, and rode with Alda under its shelter, in privacy and with her personal baggage, including the heavy box containing Marcus's precious books.

A main legionnary road led from Rheged's western shore to the old fortress settlement at Catraeth. When they crossed, it was empty and rainswept, and from the deserted fort at Lavatrae only wild birds sounded their alarms as the cavalcade passed by and vanished into the rain-mist beyond.

Rhianneth was tired of the smell of human sweat, wet leather, dripping matted cloaks. Her temper grew short as she brooded on the lost comfort of Eburacum's fortress; on the steaming water and soft linen that doubtless graced the magistrates' apartments in the old headquarters of the legionary commander. When she thought of Ida's stronghold, her mind panicked and veered away. Julia had prophesied that she would live in a mud-caked hut in an unholy pagan camp. The further north they travelled through such unrelenting rain, the more she came to believe it.

Woodsmoke drifted on the wet air when at last they slipped past the dark outline of Corstopitum at dusk, and there was a smell of cooking meat that made Rhianneth's mouth water.

But even these shabby comforts were not to be theirs, for they rode unseen along a narrow road built in the old days so that traffic to the Wall could avoid the centre of this once bustling Roman military station.

'There she is!'

Lovan rode up beside the waggon, pointing ahead. Beneath the hood of his birrus his face was wet in the spitting darkness, and droplets of moisture shone amongst his beard. 'We've reached the Wall!' he shouted to her, spurring away to the front of the line.

'If it only has a roof,' Rhianneth said to Alda, 'I won't care if we've reached the Halls of the Dead!'

The road led over a deep ditch and through the massive earth-mound that marked the approaches to the old frontier. Then they were rumbling under an arched gateway and into a small military post which once commanded the passage of goods and people where Agricola's eastern road crossed the Wall.

It offered shelter from the rain and wind, though the sound of them moaned around its thick walls like lost spirits. Lovan said they were very near a big cavalry fort which lay to the east. But Rhianneth was glad they did not attempt to reach its empty barracks and stables, its echoing streets and eerie broken-windowed houses and offices. She felt safer in this small place built on either side of the big road.

'God, I'm stiff!'

Lovan stretched his back, rubbing his beard with the palm of his hand. A weary gesture that sent a pang through her, for it was one she had seen him make many times in the warm kitchen of the old house after a day in the fields or stables.

Why, it's apple-time, she thought. Time to be gathering and storing. Grandmother is mixing her potions and ointments ready for the winter ills. Olwen is cleaning the apple barrels, and preparing to salt down the meat killed at Samhain. What are we doing, Lovan and I here at the edge of the world? We ought to be at home.

'Pity about the big fort,' Lovan's mouth twitched with sudden humour. 'We might have got the old bathhouse working . . .'

They were up before it was light. But an early start was frustrated by a broken harness. For a while Rhianneth watched the men working within the circle of swaying lanterns, her cloak pulled close against the dawn bite in the air. Then she grew restless. Leaving the grunts and muttered curses behind, she went through the archway and up the worn stone steps into the darkness beyond, looking for Cai.

Out here the air struck colder. She smelled the sharp tang of wet grass. But the rain had stopped, and the night stars rode glittering across the sky. Somewhere nearby, a tawny owl let cry.

Dimly lit by the lanternlight faltering up from below the steps, Cai leant against the breast-high wall, his back to her. He stared out to where the great fort lay deserted, but his head shot round as she came up beside him.

'Rhianneth? Have they fixed it yet?'

His breath cooled into mist between them. She shook her head, letting her hood fall back.

He swore softly. 'We should have been away from the Wall before daylight! We're too close to Aelle. And within range of Urien's scouts. The wagons slow us to crawling pace!'

'It's nowhere near dawn.' She looked up as clouds scudded across the sky and it grew darker as the stars winked out. A breath of wind lifted her skirt, swirled round her ankles. And yet – there, where the fort lay in silence, was there not a faint greyness in the sky, or was it a last glimmer of starshine?

'You're cold. You'd better go back.'

'Oh, not yet! I want to be with you, just for a while. It may be the last time we can talk alone.' She shivered, hugging her arms across her chest under the thick travelling cloak. 'There are so many last times. Sometimes we don't know it is the last time.'

'Ah, Time,' Cai said lightly. 'First Lord and Master of the Elements, of Heaven and Earth. Creator and Destroyer of everything.'

It sounded like a litany. Perhaps it was. If so, Rhianneth preferred her grandmother's ancient lore wherein nothing

146

created was every destroyed, and the ring of life spun eternally through the spiral of time.

'Listen!' Cai's hand was on her shoulder. From out of the darkness came a sweet, brief, tentative shrilling. 'A song-thrush?'

They waited. The tawny owl cried again. One bright star glimmered for an instant, and disappeared. Then the birdsong came, stronger this time.

She stole a glance sideways at her cousin. He looked at her and smiled. Her heart turned over. How can I live, she wondered, through the long years that will feed my love-hunger as they eat away my future?

She did not know that longing had softened her lips and set witch-lights shimmering in her eyes; she only saw that, as he looked at her, Cai's smile slowly faded.

'Gods, Rhianneth!' he whispered. 'Look at me like that and the Alliance will blow apart!'

Love was a shooting pain inside her. Time was slipping away; their frail love could have no flowering, it was like an autumn bud that withers in the cooling air. She knew it, and turned her head away before the pain of his nearness became too much to bear.

The greyness in the sky was more definite. Ground mist rose up from the dark wet earth beyond the Wall.

'I'll go,' she said, shivering. 'They will be ready soon.'

But as she turned, suddenly she was in his arms, crushed against his chest.

'God's Light!' he muttered, and then his lips came down upon hers. Not tenderly as she had so often dreamed they might, but as if anger surged behind his kiss, and she tasted blood where her lip pressed against her teeth. Fierce hunger swept through her, and a savage longing.

Cai swung her round as their kiss broke, pushing her hard against the wall. His mouth found hers once more. Weakness, and wild joy, filled her world.

His head lifted. 'Gods help us,' he groaned, his warm breath against her face. 'What am I doing?'

147

Rhianneth pulled him closer. Fear tightened the clasp of her hands as she pressed against him in the agony of longing. 'Kiss me again . . . tell me you love me, Cai! Say it . . .'

But he jerked back, holding her at arms' length. His hair tumbled over his forehead, and in the dim light passion fought with anger on his face.

'What sorcery did your grandmother teach you, Rhianneth? What ancient love-spell that keeps you in my mind?' His grip hardened hurtfully. 'All these days of hill roads and foul weather – and still my thoughts are only of you in the darkness. Of that last night at home!'

The trilling of the thrush came again, gallant, heart-catching in its lonely welcome to the slow-coming new day.

'And that?' He stared over her head into the thickening mist, his eyes still bright with anger. 'Is it real? Or have you called one of Rhiannon's singing birds to make me forget why we're both here on this bloody Wall, in this gods-forsaken place?'

A nervous muscle twitched in his jaw. 'Small lusts I have had before.' His voice shook. 'But this – wildcat – tears into my stomach whenever I look at you. It could tear apart the Alliance, destroy us both, unless it is smothered. Now.'

Slow, sick anger washed over her. 'Let go of me, Cai.' She twisted out of his grasp, stumbling sideways against the wall, spreading her hands behind her on the damp stones. 'Don't say any more. I know well enough why we are here. But I have loved you, since the day I watched you ride up to our house in your brave scarlet cloak. You were everything I had ever dreamed of; you were . . . gallantry, and hope. And to know, now, that I had your love, would warm the unborn years without you . . .'

Her voice trailed away into his silence. They stared at each other.

'Wrong, cousin fox-cub,' he said at last. 'It would rot your soul, and mine. You little fool!' There was sudden violence in his voice. 'I'm trying to protect you, safeguard us both! And not only from Ida – though it would freeze your blood if I told you what he might do. Love turned back on itself is a deadly thing, Rhianneth. You've seen Julia, broken apart. Not because her husband died in battle – but because he held his pledge to Artur above their lives together! And Marcus. You must have realised that somewhere inside he was scarred, pain-twisted? Need I go on?'

'You . . .' Her throat was choked with unshed tears, and the sound of Marcus's name was like a sword-edge. 'You don't know what love is! You can't even give an honest name to lust. It has to be magic that turns you away from duty – even for such a small thing as a kiss!'

She was trembling now, shaken with a sharp desire to hurt him. 'I'm tired of all your talk of the Roman Empire, and honour! I'm the one who is sealing this bargain with the Saxons. It is I who must marry Ida!'

She saw him flinch. He looked beyond her. His fingers curled into fists.

'Honour and duty are all I have known.' His voice was bleak. 'I grew up with them. Even my marriage was made to redeem an old debt which was not mine. If it's love-words you want, Rhianneth, I won't say them. I will not spell-make us into destruction.'

She pushed herself away from the wall. Pride stiffened her back. 'I should not have come up here,' she told him bitterly. 'Don't worry, Cai. I will not fall into your arms again.'

'If the Gods love us – that's right, you won't . . .'

'You! You talk of sorcery!' she said, stung into a renewed burst of fury, 'Caer Melot possesses your soul – that is real enchantment! Twice I've begged for a little of your love. I'll not ask a third time. You have none to give. It is all in thrall to a lost dream!'

'Not lost, Rhianneth. Not yet. But this is our last throw. And whatever it is between us, my lady vixen, it is not worth the loss of everything we worked for – that so many died for.'

Cai watched her, forcing himself into stillness. When, after a moment, her head came up and she pushed the heavy fall of hair away from her face, a tremor ran through him. He recognised something of Marcus's stubborn pride in the set of her jaw, the straightening of her back. Gods, but he'd taught her well! The desire to gather her into his arms and show his love with kisses blazed, sudden and fierce, within him. He moved, almost took a step towards her.

Instead, in silence, he left.

White mist touched cold fingers to Rhianneth's face. Her teeth chattered. But she could not go down into the lantern-bustle below. Not yet. She was more alone than she had ever been. Even when Marcus died, she had been comforted by kinsfolk, nestled in the house of her birth. Now she must live amongst strangers beside the cold North Sea. Without love, Cai's love. Hardest to bear was the knowledge that he was right. Hers was a dangerous dream; one which could prove, not a solace, but a seeping sore in the long years ahead.

Yet Glainnader, the druid's stone, had shown him close to her. Shown his torch aflame against the powers of darkness, revealed his dream of holding safe a part of the Empire in Britain for the future. She clutched at the stone, felt it hard and unyielding beneath the soft stuff of her tunic.

'Serpent's Egg . . .' she whispered, in cold anger, 'with your twisted pictures! But I'll read you plain yet, however tightly you ravel up the truth . . .'

A sound, standing out from the muffled movements of the company below, and not part of the stirrings of wild life beyond the Wall, made her turn.

The Saxon, Elric, stood within the stone archway that led out to the ramparts of the Wall. He moved forward, his face unreadable in the faint light.

'I waited as long as I could,' he said, as insolently self-assured as always, 'but the cold forces me to disturb you, Lady Rhianneth.'

His expressionless eyes studied her face. She felt hot blood stinging her cheeks. Was the turmoil of her mind apparent to him? How long had he stood within earshot in the shadows of the archway? How much had he heard?

'You do not disturb me,' she kept her voice level. 'There was no need to wait.'

'I think there was.' He moved closer. 'There is a time to speak, a time to be silent. I am not quite the barbarian you

150

seem to think me, lady. You may find Ida, my father, more so.'

An icy trickle of fear chilled her. There was an implied threat within his words. Her voice sharpened. 'You talk in riddles.'

'That is not usually one of my failings.'

His hand reached out and closed slowly round her flowing hair, twisting it gently through his fingers. 'What it must be,' he said mockingly, 'to be possessed by such a love. A love for which you would risk a crown, throw away an Empire . . .'

Rhianneth froze with terror. He knew! Rumours were but empty whispers on the air. But if Elric had witnessed the scene between Cai and herself – perhaps for the entire time between the fading of the stars and the coming of dawn-light! Her mind went blank to everything but fear, the feel of his hand on her hair, his look of angry derision.

'My cousin has a wife, and a child,' she managed at last, gathering her wits. 'Caius is an honourable man. He is not in love with me. Ida need have no – '

'That I know. But Ida isn't marrying Cai. He is taking to wife a girl sick with love for another man.'

Rhianneth jerked her hair free. As always, pride and anger came riding to her aid. 'It's my body he is buying with his war-spears. Not my soul!'

'He believes they come together. Intact. Are you still a virgin?'

A shred of sanity held back her hand from striking his face; from clawing at the grey eyes, glinting and narrowed, so close to her. One flash of temper now, one hot lie, and Cai's hopes would come to nothing. His dreams would fall, with hers, amidst the ashes of her vow to Caer Melot. She moved away from him, lowering her lashes to hide the anger behind her eyes.

'No man has touched me, Elric.'

She forced softness into her voice. He said nothing. After a while she slanted a glance towards him. He still watched her.

'What would you like me to say?' Suppressed fury sparked behind her words, 'I have a fondness for my cousin which he does not return. If that makes me an unsuitable bride for your father, then tell me now!'

151

'It could make you a vulnerable bride. Ida will have no rivals. Not for his land, nor his women.'

She drew her cloak tighter, staring straight into his face as she tried desperately to hide her immense dislike of him and at the same time think of a dignified reply. Unexpectedly, as their eyes clashed, his mouth twisted in a grin.

'It's no use. Your little cat-claws are showing, lady. Ah!' His hand shot out and grasped her shoulder as she spun on her heel to leave him. 'I helped your cousin forge this alliance between our peoples, Rhianneth. I'll not break it because you fancy yourself in love with him.'

A sudden murmur of voices came from the room below, and he released her. 'But grow up enough between here and Din Guaryrdi to hide that hungry look in your eyes.'

Footsteps rang on the stone steps and Cai appeared.

'We are moving off.' He paused as he saw Elric and shot a glance towards Rhianneth.

She brushed past him without a word. As she ran down the steps Elric spoke, and she heard relief within Cai's quick answering laugh. But her own emotions of love and anguish, fright and anger, following so quickly one upon the other, had extinguished every feeling in her.

Except an intense dislike of Elric, son of Ida.

As they neared the sea the air grew salt-cold. Rain stung like needles of ice. Mud made the road treacherous, the wagons were slowed almost to a halt. Idwal, captain of the escort, rode up and down, bellowing orders. But nothing could make the sweating terrified horses increase their speed. Rhianneth rode in the wagon with Alda, jolted and bruised with every lurch of the wheels. If she pulled aside the wet leather awning she was blinded by rain; wind snatched at her breath.

Her first sight of Ida's fortress was awe-inspiring. Huge, gaunt, impregnable, it crouched upon a great black crag high above the sea. A few small dwellings clung to the base of its foundation rock, their thatched roofs dark-wet and dripping. But Elric had spoken the truth. There was no city. Din Guaryrdi stood alone.

Led by Elric, the Saxons rode up the narrow trackway towards the arched gateway of the stronghold. Massive wooden doors began to swing open. People spilled out through the widening gap, shouting greetings. Dogs leapt forward with deep-throated barks of excitement and ran towards the waiting wagons and horsemen at the bottom of the hill. They hesitated, snarling. But they came no further. The intruders were not yet on their territory.

'Ride with me, Rhianneth.' Cai rode up close, holding out a hand. 'They'll have trouble getting the wagons up that slope.'

She scrambled from the wagon and slid across to ride before him on his great stallion, painfully aware of his arms around her. His eyes were narrowed against the rain, and rivulets of water ran down his face. From within the warm dampness of his cloak rose the familiar spicy scent he wore, brought at great cost from the Empire in the east.

His horse began backing and dancing, worried by the extra load and unfamiliar noises.

A bellow, carrying above the shouts of greeting, parted the crowd like a wind through corn. Striding through the gateway, a warrior on either side of him, came a figure that could only be Ida himself.

Rhianneth's blood ran cold.

Ida's sons she had met within the civilised confines of Llywarch's palace. Here, on this windlashed outcrop, his grey fortress rising behind him, Ida was a figure out of the nightmares of her childhood.

Giant-tall, broad-shouldered, tawny hair blowing loose to his shoulders beneath a narrow gold headband. He was bearded, with a long moustache. A golden torque gleamed round his thick muscular neck. Rings of gold flashed on his forearms. He was every Saxon pirate that ever burnt a farmhouse or plundered a town.

He greeted his sons with great shoulder-blows of affection, shouting a stream of Saxon into the wind that blew between them, whipping their cloaks into wings. Another tall, fair-haired man came through the gateway and joined the family group.

'That's Hussa, the second of Ida's four sons,' Cai murmured against her ear, adding, 'Into battle, cousin fox-cub . . .'

But her eyes were upon Ida, who came towards them, arms stretched wide, as Cai urged the horse up the slope, loose stones slipping and grinding beneath its hooves.

'Caius Caprilius! You are welcome!' He shouted in the British tongue. His accent was barbarous.

Cai swung down from his horse and grasped the great hand Ida held out.

'Ida! *We sindon gecumene!*'

They both laughed, as if they had achieved something clever. Then Ida turned to Rhianneth, still and erect on Cai's horse, frozen with cold, wet and fright. Cai's smile died.

'Lady Rhianneth,' he said, making a hand movement in her direction.

When she looked in Ida's face her courage almost failed. A hard face. The face of a man who had lived long with treachery and danger; who dealt with both ruthlessly, fear-lessly.

Without ceremony he lifted her down, sweeping her to his side as if she had been a doll. He threw back his head and spoke to his sons in a speech full of drum-rolls of the tongue and soft sea-sounds at the back of his throat. Then, fit-ting his strong-hands around her waist, he roared with laugh-ter. Laughter that was taken up by those Saxons gathered around.

'Ida bids you welcome, Lady Rhianneth.' Elric was at her side. 'He – er – he hopes he may have many more sons . . .'

Rhianneth flushed. Ida had certainly said more. Looking round at the laughing faces she guessed it had been coarse; probably to her detriment. She blinked back tears, as bright anger and pride drove down fear.

'Tell Ida – ' her voice was level – 'tell him that Llywarch's sister is not a tame brood-mare!'

Elric interpreted her message. Ida listened, his hands still around her waist. Incredulity and sharp interest grew in his blue eyes, fixed so firmly on her face.

'Ha!' He swung her around in a shower of flung raindrops and let out another flow of Saxon that made the company burst into fresh laughter. The wind whipped at his yellow hair flowing loose below the gold band around his brow; beneath his moustache his teeth gleamed in a wolfish grin. Rhianneth's stomach muscles tightened.

Then he released her, setting her down as gently as Lovan would a new-born foal. He bowed his head in mock humility and held out a huge hand for her to take. Ida's sons pulled the weary horses aside to give their father and his bride passage through the gateway.

Inside the old ramparts, made even higher with timber fencing, were many buildings of wood and thatch. The blackened, broken tower of a Roman beacon reared defiantly skywards. Dominating even this was Ida's thick-timbered mead-hall, its doorway guarded by the murderously jagged antlers of a giant stag, dripping in the salt-wet sea wind.

Rhianneth glanced back over her shoulder, fear still spearing strongly within her. Elric was so close behind that he obscured her view of the crowded gateway.

'Where is Cai?' she cried, the shrillness of fear in her voice.

Elric wiped the back of his hand along his jaw line, sweeping away rivulets of rain that poured on to his soaked shoulders.

'I would guess already with his wife and child?'

The grey eyes met hers with a flicker of contempt. I hate him, she thought. On the Wall he had made her love for Caius seem like the green longings of a half-grown girl; now he looked at her as if she were a jealous harlot.

She turned abruptly, flung back her hood, straightened her aching back. With her head held high and her mind low-laden with fear and anger, she walked beside Ida into the heart of Din Guaryrdi's fastness.

That night Ida gave a feast. Sprawled laughing in his huge carved chair in the centre of the north side of the long hall, he shouted across to Cai and Idwal seated in the place of honour

155

against the south wall. Between host and guests the hearth-pit blazed with crackling logs and dogs prowled and snapped after tossed scraps.

Torches flared. At the end of the hall, a giant baulk of timber lay in its iron cradle barring the doors, a gesture symbolising that the king was at meat and not to be disturbed. Heavy wooden candle-rings swung from the high rafters, glinting on gold and silver jewellery and the precious metal of cups and dishes, flickering over shields and weapons hung amongst bright woven tapestries on the wooden walls. As Rhianneth's eyes wandered over them, it was borne in upon her that here survival was too urgent a matter for diplomacy and depended upon war-gear always being close at hand.

The fire's glow reddened the face of Ida's young warriors as they sat, Idwal's Mithrasian soldiers amongst them, at the long trestle tables. But in the strange custom of the Saxon people, Rhianneth sat not beside Ida, but with the women on cross benches in front of a wooden screen which cut off the end of the Hall; a screen so intricately carved with monstrous serpents and strange bird-like creatures that she could not tell where one ended and another began. A weird, alien thing of superb and delicate craftsmanship. The rough splendour of the hall in which it stood was a fit setting for its virile magnificence.

Beside Rhianneth sat Gwen, British wife of Ida's only married son, Hussa. On her other side was Cai's wife, Morvydd.

Morvydd's blue eyes had pale silky lashes; her light russet hair had been twisted with rags so that it fell in tiny waves. She was not beautiful. But she had a thin patrician nose, a skin creamy fine and faintly flushed with colour. On her long delicate fingers she wore many rings. Even here, in the Saxon camp and still recovering from childbirth, her Roman elegance matched Cai's. Rhianneth's heart sank when she looked at her.

Beside her, Rhianneth felt herself the unpolished farm girl Queen Myffan had once called her. She hid her suntanned

156

hands and half-grown fingernails in her lap, and tried to keep her unsteady emotions from showing. That Morvydd so casually accepted all that was beyond her own reach brought an ache of envy to Rhianneth's throat. Jealousy tied her tongue, settled like a cold stone in her stomach.

After a while the Lady Gwen rose, and carried a large silver cup down the Hall to Ida. He got to his feet and raised the cup into the air, his sudden shout of *'Waes haeil!'* startling Rhianneth. Benches tumbled, mead spilt, as the whole male company sprang up and raised brimming cups to toast the alliance and each other in a mighty roar of acclamation.

The cup was carried across to Cai. He drank, then raised a hand in salute to Ida, and the cup began a long journey round the Hall, from one warrior to another. Ida began to speak.

His deep guttural tones blended with the storm rattling the closed shutters of the window behind Cai; his great height, wide shoulders covered by a flung-back cloak of thick black fur, the fire-flames flickering across his wolfish face, made him seem a living, brutal part of the dark barbarism that threatened the land.

Rhianneth quivered. The thought of marriage to Ida rose like a thorn-wall before her. What had possessed her, that she had agreed to this?

The answer was already in her mind. The spell which bound Cai had reached out and touched her, through him, Marcus had opened her mind to a world and way of life fast slipping away. In Cai she found its most stalwart defender. Her vow had been as much to him as to the Fellowship of Caer Melot.

She threw a glance towards her cousin. Cai was watching Ida, his face unreadable. Was he remembering how they had stood together in the shadows of Julia's garden? Or how the dangerous thoughts which had swirled between them had iced into bitter kisses on the Wall at dawn? No, he had put her from his mind; she felt the emptiness which lay between them. Perhaps, as he watched Ida, he was remembering the story of Vortigern, who had paid the Saxon leader Hengist with land and gold to drive the Picts back into their hills. That

157

alliance too, had been sealed by a marriage. To Hengist's daughter Rowen. Yet in the end the Saxons took everything, by right of fire and sword.

What had the priest Lucius cried in that dark room of Llywarch's palace? ' . . . *what will remain then of our fallen church, our burning city . . .?*'

Cai knew this marriage was a gamble. Our last throw, he had said. But to him, Vortigern and Hengist were people of the past, almost a hundred years dead. Between them and now stood Artur and the great victory of Badon. Closer still was the black nightmare of Camlann, its bitter treachery. Greater than any fear of attack from British enemies, was the overwhelming desire for vengeance. Vengeance, which was to him a pledge for the future, given to the shadows of the past. That was what drove Cai.

Gwen returned to her seat and leaned forward, concentrating on Ida's words. 'He bids you welcome,' she whispered. 'A noble lady, he says. A pledge of peace between our peoples . . .'

As the softly spoken translation of Ida's gruff words went on, Rhianneth looked past him to Elric. Hands cupped round a drinking horn, a thumb traced the silver pattern around its edge. What were his thoughts? As conflicting as her own perhaps, in a different way. He plainly despised her for so obviously loving a man who did not – could not – love her. Yet he too, wanted the alliance. For the moment that desire was overlord to the contempt in which he held her.

After a while a minstrel sat cross-legged by the fire and lifted his small harp from its carrying bag. The hall hushed at the soft sweet sound. Then the minstrel raised his head and sang in such a warm full-throated voice that his sad-sounding songs caught at Rhianneth's already vulnerable heart.

Song after song he sang. Servants scurried up and down the hall carrying huge platters of roasted meat shoulder high, their faces gleaming with sweat in the firelight, while slim boys darted between them to keep the mead cups full.

At last the minstrel put away his harp. A story-teller sprang up and began a long tale, egged on by shouts and applause.

The Saxon words meant nothing to Rhianneth, yet within the story she could clearly hear the clang of combat; see, by an outflung arm, the size of an army, the rough waves through which surged the Saxon war-boats!

The Bernician warriors, already flushed with wine and the heat of the hall, grew more excited, louder in their acclaim for the story-teller. They banged their fists and stamped their feet, and when Ida rose again to speak, he was greeted with a roar of cheering.

'Ida says that, since he brought his people here, riding the salt-grey waves,' Gwen whispered, 'they have stood alone. No hand of friendship was ever given. Only their heroes and their gods have kept them from destruction . . .' She smiled, glancing at Rhianneth, 'Now there comes to Din Guaryrdi the Lady Rhianneth . . .a peerless princess, a peaceweaver . . .'

When Gwen touched her hand later, murmuring, 'Time for us to leave, Lady Rhianneth,' she was glad to go. The atmosphere had gradually changed, roughened. The very air was becoming charged with a strange and violent force, like the gathering of a storm. So it must be in war, Rhianneth thought, when brothers-in-arms link together in mind and body to face an enemy. Or when a wolf pack howls in the night as the scent of prey drifts towards the hunting runs.

She had been given a guest house, a separate building close behind the Hall, and with Alda tucked into a pallet bed close by she was glad to creep into the wide bed, made soft and warm with furskins.

Through the wooden walls, above the sound of the wind and the spitting rain, came singing and laughter from the hall. But the footstampings and shouted brags, the frequent crashings and shatterings, sounded more like the frenzy of battle than merriment.

Trembling with nervous excitement and cold she slid down beneath the furs, pulling them up over her ears. With hammering heart she remembered Llywarch's elegant dinner party where she had seen her first Saxon warriors. Now she could hear them roistering in their own fortress, feasting and drinking to the success of a war-bond between friends.

How barbarously they would celebrate as conquerors in the hall of a defeated enemy she could imagine only too well!

The marriage ceremony was delayed so that she might recover from the long journey. But even after several days Rhianneth still found the Saxon capacity for enjoyment astonishing. They ate, drank, shouted and laughed aloud with a gusto unmatched by anything she had known. Their songs and poems were heroic. Gods, heroes, battles, adventures with weird creatures of the Otherworld – all spoke of a high code of loyalty, honour and selfless bravery. Yet in the hall of their king the noise often became cataphonic. Drunken fights broke out. It was so at odds with the measured coolness she saw in their eyes that she found them ever more enigmatic.

One morning, when she knew that Cai and Lovan were talking together in the horse enclosure, Rhianneth made her way to the house where Cai's wife stayed. Morvydd had not seemed particularly friendly. Cai had kept, perhaps deliberately, out of the way. Yet Rhianneth felt she should make some gesture of goodwill, of fellow-feeling, since they were both in a stranger's camp. Besides, she wanted to see Cai's son.

Like all the fortress dwellings, the house had walls and a floor of strong oakwood, rafters of ash, and a thatched roof supported on hazel hurdling. She was beginning to understand the Saxon dislike of stone-built towns and villas, for the sweet scent of the sawn wood was held like a soul within these small houses, as it was in Ida's mead-hall. Its elusive fragrance met her as she entered to find Morvydd sitting beside the cradle, carelessly rocking it with a crimson-slippered foot.

A cooking fire smoked near the doorway. A little bent old woman hung garments in the warmth above it. She cast one malevolent glance towards Rhianneth and then carried on with her task, muttering under her breath.

Rhianneth's smile of greeting to Morvydd did not reach her eyes, and faded as she bent over the carved Saxon cradle. The baby slept, dark as Cai, one tiny fist curled beside his face. Her stomach tensed with the desire to lift him into her arms, to put her mouth against the petal softness of his cheek.

'He is beautiful,' she whispered, afraid of waking him.

Morvydd shrugged. 'He cries a lot. I'll be glad to get back to Mithrasia and let Torfrida look after him. My young maid-servant is an idiot, she doesn't know a thing. The surprise nearly killed her when he was born.'

She glanced towards the door, but the old woman had gone outside. 'Megan is good, but so old. She tires quickly. She was my nurse. And my mother's before that.'

She leaned forward to brush a speck of wood-dust from the baby's face. He stirred, but did not wake.

'He's her first boy-child. She's proud as Caesar's lap dog and twice as jealous! She won't let my maidservant touch him. Perhaps just as well.'

'What will you call him, Morvydd?'

'Reburrus, after Cai's father, of course.' She sighed. 'I wish it had been a girl. Boys are so boring after babyhood. A girl might have been fun for me. But I suppose he'll trail around after Cai, with the men . . .'

'I suppose so.' Rhianneth could detect no humour in what Morvydd said, no loving pride hidden beneath the flippant words at which they could then have smiled together. Morvydd meant every word.

Watching her, Rhianneth sensed uneasily that something within Morvydd was unsteady. Not thrown off balance as was the bedrock of Julia's being, by the blows of life, but flawed by nature. She seemed to have no inkling of the motives, the thoughts of others. Her own needs filled her mind, like those of an infant.

Into Rhianneth's mind came the memory of Cai's eyes, bleak in the dim dawn light on the Wall. Even if he had loved Morvydd, the years of marriage would have eaten that love away; as it was, his marriage was barren from the start, its soil unsuited to hold roots even of comradeship, and scattered with irritation's sharp stones. Even so, it had given him a son.

Forcing a smile, she said goodbye to Morvydd. Alda waited outside, and together they began a stroll around the fortress. The servants who hurried to and from the kitchens, which were separated from the hall itself, chattered and joked, always in the British tongue. The were Votadinian people, like Hussa's wife Gwen, brought in from the surrounding conquered land. Little wonder, Rhianneth thought, that the younger Saxons speak our language so easily, when they have British servants and slaves from birth.

Ida's young warriors practised with sword and spear, others kept a look-out from the high ramparts. A few sheep, brought in from the thinly-grassed slopes at the base of Din Guarydi's rock, wandered aimlessly, nibbling at the scant grass. Around the houses, hens scratched at the earth, and the stench of a pig-pen against the western wall occasionally blew back against the wind.

They passed a granary, the grain for which would now largely come from Mithrasian fields as part of the treaty. Other small buildings were used as workshops. Some, Rhianneth noticed were stone-built, as if they had once been part of the Roman beacon-fort.

The familiar smell of an iron forge stung her nostrils, reminding her sharply of the hours she had spent watching Lovan and Griffyn, their faces sweat-beaded and ruddy in the fire's glow. She watched for a while from the doorway the giant blacksmith and his apprentice, her mind saddened with memories of home.

Peeping through another doorway she saw women working at looms, chattering as they wove the brightly-dyed wool. Their talk stopped when they noticed her, resuming more quietly as she moved away.

Everywhere was bustling, busy with life. But she felt alien. The eyes of some she met shifted uneasily, as if they were afraid to look into hers. Suddenly Rhianneth wanted Olwen and her grandmother, and home. To be with her own people, safe and loved.

Grandmother's snores in the slow afternoon, she thought; Marcus coming in from the fields. I want Olwen to scold from the kitchen . . . I want old Giff to get under my feet, the way he used to . . . Her eyes filled with tears of homesickness.

'Let's look at the sea.' She grasped Alda's hand, 'Up there . . .'

They climbed the rough log steps and stood on the narrow path that ran along the inside of the ramparts. Wind slapped into their faces, sent Rhianneth's hair streaming back like a banner as she raised her head over the timber-top.

She caught her breath. Silver-bright before her stretched the sea. Murmuring, moving, until it met and merged with the clouded sky far, far away. Near the shore it broke into cream-white waves that hissed and rumbled amongst the sand and stones. Rhianneth was filled with wonder. Never could she have imagined the immensity of that moving, living water, or the salt-edged cleanness of the wind that swept its surface!

'Look, lady!' Alda gasped, holding her flying hair with both hands. 'Islands in the sea!'

Small, dark, desolate, the islands rose dramatically from the waters, some to the east of Din Guaryrdi, some to the south. The sea churned at their base, the blown spray making the wet rocks gleam in the grey northern light. No life moved there, only the sweep of sea-birds above.

Northwards was another, larger island. It was further away, and the distance gave it a veiled magic, lent it more mystery than had the bare rocks before her.

'That island is called Metcaud,' said a voice in her ear, and she swung round, joy leaping within her.

'Cai!'

Alda had slipped away. He was so close beside her that his arm brushed against hers.

'It's a strange place.' His eyes caught the light off the sea. 'Half island, half not. At low tide you can walk across from the mainland if you are careful, but the sea rushes across and cuts it off completely for most of the time. I've been there with Elric and Hussa –' he pointed to the shore below – 'in one of those. Not something I'd like to repeat.'

Rhianneth scarcely glanced at the boats pulled up on the beach. 'Cai, I've hardly seen you since we arrived . . . and where is Lovan?'

'With the horses. I have something to say, Rhianneth. I may as well say it here.'

His closed, unsmiling expression, the tremor of cold in her

stomach, rang a warning. But nothing prepared her for his next words.

'I'm taking Morvydd and my son home, to Mithrasia. We leave tomorrow, with most of the escort.'

Numb with shock, she stared at his half-averted face. 'Tomorrow!'

'I'll be back late next summer. Before Samhain.'

'But the marriage? The wedding is only a few weeks away. You can't . . .'

'A few weeks can mean a lot at this time of the year. I want Morvydd home before the worst of the weather sets in.'

Cai taking his wife and child home! Now? Leaving her here amongst barbarian strangers? Could he not even wait to see her married to Ida and the alliance finally sealed?

'Lovan will stay with you,' he said quickly, reading her thoughts, 'Not as bodyguard, but as your "kinsman". We don't want to offend Ida. You have Alda. The Lady Gwen will be a good friend. Idwal and his escort soldiers will stay until after the wedding. No one will harm you. You are quite safe, Rhianneth.'

His soothing tones lit a flame of anger inside her. 'Don't!' Her voice shook. 'Don't tell me you think I'll be safe amongst these tow-headed savages! You – you don't care if I live or die. You made that plain on the Wall. You have the Alliance. That's all you ever wanted. Now you can't wait to get home before winter!'

His eyes darkened with leashed anger. 'That's not true, Rhianneth. You know why I must leave. We both know!' He held his voice low, taut. 'I can't guess what Ida has heard. Nothing, it would seem. But if I stay to watch you wed, he would have to be blind not to realise! Just a look, a touch . . .' He stopped abruptly, swallowed. 'You – don't know Ida. In anger he shows just how near the surface barbarism lies . . .'

The sea swept rhythmically in upon the deserted shore. Behind them the life of the fortress went on. Dogs barked, women called, children shouted and wailed. Rhianneth trembled with anger and a vast despair.

After a long silence he said, 'I will come after next summer.

With a year between, the rumours will have died. Whatever it is we feel for each other may have cooled.'

So, she thought, he will still not consider it love that we feel! But then, he never has. Remembering again the dawn scene in the fortlet on the Wall, she clenched her fists, feeling the sharp edge of a jaggedly growing nail stab into the soft flesh of her palm.

'Yes, come next autumn,' she said. 'By then I'll probably be too busy producing an heir for the Alliance, a little Saxon warrior, to remember ever having once flirted with my cousin . . .'

He looked as if she had struck him. But not even the knowledge that her words could wound him was enough to lift even a part of the bitterness she felt.

They made their way back, in silence, past stone altars to the Saxon Gods, standing in the shadow of the high walls. Here, a tall wiry man with thin yellow hair turning grey was brushing away ash with a peculiar circular movement of his hand. As they approached, he limped off.

'That is Wermund, priest to their gods, keeper of the altars,' Cai murmured. 'He hates and distrusts me; always has. He believes, I'm told, that my true name is not Cai, but Loki. That I'm building a ship made of dead men's nails, in which I shall come against them at Ragnarok with a crew of giants! By the Light,' he laughed grimly. 'I swear I'm bedevilled by mad priests, here and at home.'

He stopped, seeing the light catch the pendant round Rhianneth's neck. He lifted it between a finger and thumb.

'This gift from Wencam – it's a symbol of Mithras. You realise that?'

'I do.'

'But of course you do. I still remember the little offerings to the spirit of the stream. You will always hedge your bets, Rhianneth. It's part of your strength. Not for you the darkness of a fanatic faith like that which blinds Lucius – or Wermund.' He slanted a glance towards the retreating Saxon priest. 'But beware the Saxon Gods, cousin fox-cub. They are wild and strange – and cold. Do not dice with them.'

He turned to face her, one hand resting against the

rounded timber of a door post. 'Forgive me, Rhianneth,' he said softly, 'when you can. I put things badly. But you will understand, sometime, that I have no choice. Take care, till I come back.'

That day Rhianneth went out no more. When darkness came she pleaded tiredness due to her recent illness and did not go to supper in the mead-hall.

Next day, when Cai and Morvydd prepared to leave with their military escort, she was calm and in control. Only once, when Lovan moved close beside her, did her outer shield of resolve falter. She clung to his arm as so often she had done when a child, feeling comfort in his strength.

'He'll be back,' he promised her, the wind whipping his curling grey hair about his forehead, 'and we're snug enough here for the dark months. You've still got old Lovan, *cariad*, and always will have while I live and breathe!'

While the little wizened old nurse rocked the baby in her arms, Morvydd and Cai came forward to kiss Rhianneth's cheek. Still her shield-wall held. She was the daughter of both Elidyr and Marcus, and must stand proud and erect while her world toppled, or lose all respect amongst these Saxon barbarians. A little to one side she saw Ida's son Elric watching her, without expression.

Forgive me, I have no choice, Cai had said. Because of Morvydd and the child? Because rumours from Mithrasia had reached Din Guaryrdi and Ida no longer trusted or welcomed him? No! Rhianneth thought. His leaving was the price of Elric's silence, and she hated the Saxon with all the force that was in her.

The cavalcade wound its way down the steep trackway and across the flat land on the narrow Roman spur of roadway that once had led from the main road to the beacon fort. Before it was swallowed up into the forest Rhianneth walked back into her house, fastened the door, and lay on her bed.

When the tears came, it seemed they would never stop. All the tension, excitement and pain of the last days welled out of her in a great tearing flood. She covered her face with her hands and scalding tears ran between her fingers.

Alda brought food and drink, which she could not touch. Lovan sat beside her for a long time, while she lay limp, weak, drenched in tears. He spoke slowly and gently of loved and remembered times past, or of his small day-to-day adventures amongst Ida's large stable of horses. Once she heard Ida's great voice roaring outside, and Alda's high, frightened response. But he went away, and she fell asleep.

When next she woke, the Lady Gwen was beside her. A small cooking fire glimmered near the door, and Rhianneth could see Alda stirring a pot hanging above it. In the soft glow of the fire and the paler gleam of a candle beside the bed, Gwen's face was calm, kind. She leaned forward, a cup in her hand.

'Drink this, Lady Rhianneth. It is soothing warm-wine.'

She waited, a small still girl only a few years older than Rhianneth, with bright eyes like a bird.

Dark, spicy, sweet as honey, the liquid coursed down Rhianneth's throat, warming and reviving. She emptied the cup, and felt strength and hope begin to creep back.

'And now, eat.' Gwen turned to take a bowl and spoon from Alda, who was watching with frightened, worried eyes. 'This is frumenty. Delicious and nourishing wheat cooked in milk, with honey and spice. Try it.'

It was a kind of porridge, such as Olwen made. But this had a subtle, different flavour. While she ate, Gwen sat on the edge of the bed, stroking the soft fur covers.

'I know was it is to leave home and family, to marry a stranger,' Gwen said quietly. 'You know I'm not Saxon? I am of the Votadinian people. We lived a little way along the coast, near the island of Metcaud. Hussa saw me, wanted me, and brought me here to Din Guaryrdi as his woman. I was lucky. He's a good man. He made me his true wife, paid my bride-price. That first year I was homesick from Beltain to Samhain, resentful to have been forced from my kinfolk into the camp of the Saxons. But now?' She smiled, flushing faintly. 'We have a little son, and I am content. Now, nothing could make me leave Hussa!'

She took the empty bowl. Rhianneth lay back exhausted, but calmer, the wild grief and bitterness seeping away.

'You feel a stranger,' Gwen went. 'You do not yet speak their tongue. I, at least, could do that. But then, the young ones mix so often with our people that most of them have some British. You will be sick for home, for a while. But when children come – ah, suddenly, this *is* home! You will see . . .'

Rhianneth drifted towards sleep. The murmurings of conversation by the cooking fire gradually faded. On the edge of her dreams, lance in hand, rode the lonely hero, Artur. And in the midst of her misery, a strange thought came. If she could instil, drop by drop, into the mind of the Saxon people the golden essence of that world he had fought to defend – what a dark victory that would be over the enemies of Camlann! Within the pages of Marcus's books she would find her weapons; weapons to preserve the best of all Rome and Caer Melot stood for. Everything those enemies had tried to destroy.

And the victory would be won here, in the camp of their most deadly foes.

Rhianneth gradually regained her strength and her spirit. She wandered freely around the fortress, and even found her way to the shore, crunching over the wet sand between the drawn-up boats. She would stand at the very edge of the sea, staring out at the restless, flint-grey waters that stretched away to touch the sky, laughing while Lovan told her wild tales of sea-serpents and sirens, embroidering without shame the old stories of Homer the Greek.

Alda and Gwen started to teach her some words of the Saxon tongue, which here in Bernicia they called Englisch, so that occasionally during the fire-lit suppers in Ida's Hall she was able to understand some small part of a song or story. But Ida's loud voice and rough manners she could not grow used to. His great hunting dog Bron followed him everywhere, even leaping unchecked on to the supper table to reach the sweet honey-wine for which he'd developed a taste. When Rhianneth watched the animal lapping from Ida's own cup amidst roars of laughter from those nearest the king, she remembered Llywarch's elegant dinner parties, or their own quiet table at home, and her chin jerked upwards in disgust.

One day Ida shouted for Elric to saddle up. Quickly a small hunting band gathered. Rhianneth watched, her desire to ride out with them so plain that even Ida noticed.

'Follow the hunt if you're set on it! Although by Woden's Eye I'd rather pull an oar than sit on a nag's back!' he roared, and Alda's swift translation into her ear made Rhianneth laugh aloud for the first time since she had left Mithrasia, as she ran to the stables for Romulus.

They rode across moorland and into the forests, along windswept headlands and down wolf-slopes where cold mountain streams plunged through rocky fissures, always following the hoarse, deep roaring of the stags.

The sharp air lifted Rhianneth's desolation, put a sparkle in her eyes and bonny red flags in her cheeks. She began to forget that she was a stranger, and unhappy; remembering more that she was young, Artur's battle-maid, riding Romulus on a fine autumn day.

Not even Ida's rough kiss on her mouth as he swung her down from her horse, nor Elric's cool eyes on her flushed face, dampened her spirits.

That night, when the fire was lit in Ida's mead-hall and the cresset torches flamed by the heavy barred doors, the minstrel plucked his harp and sang a new song. A song to the beauty of Ida's bride.

Colour flooded Rhianneth's face as Gwen whispered the words of his song into her ear. She lowered her eyes. But not before she had seen the look on Ida's face. It was the look she had seen when he closed for the killing of the stag.

Her stomach cramped, her heart hammered. The marriage would be delayed no longer.

A pile of wood grew tall in the practice yard, ready for the marriage-fire that would burn through the night until sunrise. Excitement rippled through Din Guaryrdi. The hunt now rode out daily for the feast-meat, small boats set out to cast nets for the fish that swam in the grey deeps of the sea.

The trees of the forest to the west were bright as flame in their autumn yellows and russet-reds, with here and there branches already bared by the winds to the coming savage knife-cut of winter.

Rhianneth watched, fascinated, as men carried in armloads of green forest trimming. She smiled as, chaffing and laughing with the servant-girls, they hammered up branches of evergreens and red-berried holly over every doorway, with sprigs of rowan slipped amongst the greenery to guard against evil.

She had lost trace of time, since Cai left. She knew the year must be almost at an end. Now she realised with a shock that turned her cold that the wedding would be sealed on Samhain eve.

Samhain, the end of summer. The turn of the year. The dark time when winter's grip tightens on the bare land above the newly-buried grain. When Balor triumphs over Llwy and the sun sinks into the power of darkness. She remembered the Samhain fires at home, burning bravely on the hilltop and outside the meadow gateway. The voice of her grandmother came whispering down the years.

'The fires are lit to guide the spirits of our dead, Rhianneth. They search for warmth and comfort before winter comes. On Samhain eve, the doors of the Otherworld inch open . . .'

Not only kinfolk came through that open doorway. There were others, seeking vengeance. There were evil ones. There were dreadful non-human creatures who roamed abroad in search of prey . . . Suddenly the teachings of Marcus were as nothing. She was all her grandmother's child. The hunt was back, and she hurried to the stables to find Lovan.

He was nowhere to be seen, but Ida stood half-turned away from her, draining a drinking horn. Thick mud caked his boots and trousers, and was spattered across his tunic and flung-open cloak as if he had been thrown from his horse.

Beside him, Elric was running his hand over the shivering withers of Ida's great black stallion. He muttered something. Ida tossed the horn towards a waiting stableboy, wiped his mouth with the back of his hand. His snarling reply angered Elric, for he let out a blistering stream of Saxon that made the stableboy cower and brought a red flood of rage to Ida's face. Like wolves about to fight father and son stared at each other.

Then Rhianneth's foot set a broken harness buckle ringing against the stone. They turned and saw her. Elric's eyes glinted dangerously. There was no smile for her from Ida, who stared through her, consumed by his inner rage, as if she were an unwelcome slave. She raised her head higher, unwilling to admit even to herself that she should leave. Retreat would have been an admission of fear. Fear of the anger that whipped between the two men.

'I have to speak to Ida,' she said steadily. 'It can't wait.'

Elric let out his breath slowly. 'Yes?'

She swallowed, disliking the necessity of speaking to her bridegroom through him. 'The wedding. It is a bad day. Samhain eve.'

'So?'

'I will not marry on Samhain eve. Tell Ida.'

By now Ida's anger was towards her. It burned the air between them. Elric started to speak. But Ida cut across his words with a stream of Saxon, finishing with a sweeping gesture of his two hands that was clear even to Rhianneth. He swung round, yelling for his slave Rolf. Then, as if she were of no more account than a troublesome servant, he left her standing there and limped away, leaning heavily upon Rolf's shoulder.

Rhianneth was so full of cold fury she was speechless. Elric handed the black horse to a stableboy with a brief word. Then with the remnants of his anger still hardening his face he surveyed her, his flint-grey eyes moving slowly over her loose hair, down the length of her dark green tunic to her feet in the soft leather shoes Aunt Julia had given her when first she arrived in Mithrasia.

'Ida's had a fall. He's a sailor, not a horseman. That's why he is angry. I lost my temper because he nearly killed a good horse.' He paused, then went on: 'Wermund the priest has cast the runes. The day of the wedding has good omens for us. Ida will not change it.'

171

'Runes? What are runes to me? I will not marry on Samhain eve! Tell your father!'

'No need. Ida has a little British, he understood you. It's useless. Wermund sees a new beginning for our people in the flames of the wedding fire. The birth of a great kingdom. The runes are the gift of Woden, they never lie. They mean everything to Ida.' He smiled, eyes mocking. 'Samhain means nothing.'

She stared at him, clenching her fists to keep from striking him. 'I will not marry on Samhain's eve. Tell Ida that, if you dare!'

She turned to walk away, but his next words stopped her dead.

'You should know, lady, that the accident to Ida involved Lovan, and your horse Romulus.'

She spun round. Her eyes went instinctively to Romulus's stable where Lovan spent so much time. Perhaps deliberately Elric misinterpreted her reaction.

'Don't worry, your horse is fine,' he said dryly. 'Your man Lovan is over there, near the gate.'

She ran past him, stumbled blinking into the dim light of the shed. Relief flooded over her. Lovan lay propped up against a bale of hay. His weatherbeaten face was pale; blood caked his hands. But he was alive, and smiled a weak welcome.

'Ah, it's nothing, *cariad*! Looks worse than it is. These –' he raised bloodied hands – 'I got falling into a bramble bush, that's all . . .'

She dropped to her knees beside him. Until this moment she had not realised the love that was in her for Lovan, her strong old apple tree. She had grieved for Marcus. But to lose Lovan would cut through the roots of her life.

A shadow moved. She looked up to see the lean figure of Wermund the priest. He carried water in a bowl, and his tunic was smeared with blood. Lovan tried to pull himself higher against the hay, but the priest pressed him gently back with long strong finger. Beads of sweat broke out on Lovan's face.

'My leg,' he said, breathing fast. 'He's cleaned it up. It just needs . . . to stop the bleeding . . .'

His eyes closed, his head fell back. Rhianneth turned her head sharply, and saw his right leg for the first time. A deep jagged gash from mid-thigh to mid-calf steadily oozed blood, seeping through the already drenched straw beneath him.

She sprang to her feet. The wound must be closed, the bleeding stopped, and quickly. So much blood lost already! Frantically she tried to think. To remember how her grandmother dealt wih injuries such as this. But she had never seen a cut so deep, so terrible, not even amongst the many wounds Griffyn had sustained in his fight with the robbers.

The priest moved her aside. He had narrow swathes of linen, and a small dish filled with a mixture she could recognise neither by its green-grey colour nor sharp, bitter smell. Alarmed, she tried to stop him. He looked up at her from his kneeling position, his eyes cold with dislike tinged with fear, and spoke in Saxon before returning to his task.

'Let him be, Rhianneth,' Lovan murmured weakly. 'He tends their battle-wounded. This was only a bloody stag horn . . .'

His face twisted in sudden pain. 'Just bring me one of Grandmother's potions . . . her pain-slayer . . . and I'll be all right . . .'

In a mesh of indecision Rhianneth looked from Lovan's white face to the tense figure of the priest, intent on his work, the long fingers pressing, holding, winding. Then she ran to her house and scrabbled in the great chest for her wooden box of precious medicines.

When she returned, the priest had finished. He rose, and put out a hand for the cup. She hesitated. His long sallow face was set, his thoughts unreadable, as he stared back at her.

For the first time she recognised marks of pain in the deep lines of his forehead and around his mouth. Bitterness was there too, far below his present dislike of her. She wondered briefly as she gave him the brimming cup if that old hard core of hatred might not so press against his surface resentment that he would throw the potion to the ground.

But he held it to his face and drew in a deep breath. His eyes met her over the rim, and something within their dark grey depths reminded her of the black eyes of Lucius. It was as if he looked at an adversary, measured an enemy. Then the moment passed, he was calling for help to move Lovan to the comfort of Cai's empty house, and the stable filled with rough Saxon voices and brawny arms.

There would be full days ahead, Rhianneth thought, but with Alda's help she would nurse Lovan back to health. The thought that he might yet die she pushed to the back of her mind, where she had already hidden the fear that Cai would not come back with the autumn.

At supper that night Gwen handed to Rhianneth the great engraved silver cup.

'It is for you to take into the hall now,' she said smiling, in no way resenting the loss of her position as first lady. 'You are Ida's chosen one, soon to be folk-queen of the Bernician people.'

The harp stilled as she walked down the hall. Silence fell. She felt as if a thousand eyes burned her skin. The great cup, full of mead, was heavy. Her progress was slow. Blood pounded in her ears, enough to make her dizzy. I must not fall, she thought. I mustn't drop it . . .

Then she was looking straight into the face of Ida. The old warrior heaved himself stiffly to his feet and began to speak gruffly, softly, just to her.

'Ida asks you to forgive his – roughness,' Elric translated. 'He had been thrown from his horse. And worse, had missed his stag.'

Smiles lit the faces of those around her. She lowered her eyes to the heavy cup between her hands. 'Did you give him my message?'

'I did.'

Now she shot a glance at Elric from beneath lowered lids, and away again.

'The answer is no,' he said softly. 'He will not change the day.'

Ida waited. The silence unnerved Rhianneth. When she looked up at last to meet his fierce blue eyes they were filled with a kind of angry pain that blotted out any words of protest she might have made. He's so old, she thought suddenly, and shivered. He could be my grandfather! Old and ill. That fall . . . She passed the cup to him, and he drank.

Drops of mead trembled on his moustache and beard as he raised the cup between his great hands, high into the air.

'*Waes Haeil!*'

As always, his cry was taken up to roll like thunder between the wooden walls. Ida's mouth widened into a smile. It was more than a wish for good health. It was a cry for reassurance of faith. Of loyalty between kin, between battle-brothers.

Rhianneth turned away, but had hardly taken more than a few steps when she became aware that the noise in the hall had changed in character. Horror filled the faces of the women. Gwen rose slowly from the bench, her hand over her mouth. Men at the trestle tables started to their feet, craning to see down the length of the hall.

Rhianneth spun round. She froze with shock. Face down across the table, clenched fists stretched out before him, Ida lay as if for sacrifice amongst the scattered dishes of meat and bread. Spilled wine from the *Waes Haeil* cup trickled to the floor.

Uproar broke out. Benches were knocked backwards, dishes flung aside. Men sprang over the table to reach Ida's side. The dogs leapt with them, sensing violence and fear. Meat, drink, all were swept to the floor as Ida was lifted bodily on to the table. She saw Wermund the priest bend close with an ear against Ida's chest. Then men crowded between, and the scene vanished behind shouting, jostling warriors.

Rhianneth stood still, heart thudding as if it would burst through bone and flesh.

Silence fell, more dreadful than all the noise and tumult. The voice of Wermund fell like a stone. His words hissed through the crowd and out of the hall to the whole of Din Guaryrdi.

'The king is dead.'

Men's voices echoed through the lofty Hall. Women sobbed. Shrill voices rose outside in the darkness. Shocked into

175

immobility, Rhianneth waited. At last a shadow fell across her feet, and she looked up to see Elric standing between her and the fire.

'Go to your bed, lady,' he said, his voice unexpectedly gentle. 'Ida is dead. You can do nothing.'

Something she saw in his face made her turn and walk trembling away without a word. As she reached the open, crowded doorway, people moved aside, averting their eyes so swiftly it seemed more in fear than respect. Alda ran to meet her, and together they stayed inside their small house through the following dark hours, listening to the sounds of weeping and confusion.

Rhianneth had never seen such grief as that which overtook the Saxons upon the death of Ida. A black shadow covered the fortress, made tangible by the smoke of altar fires and the stench of blood from sacrifices.

Ida's four sons rode off to a high place amongst the hills to the north, sacred to Woden, dragging behind them the pathetic bleating sacrificial victims.

The branches of forest green were cut from the doorways, and the great woodpile dragged from the practice yard out on to the wild headland beyond the fortress gate to the north.

Riders were sent to summon Ida's thanes, those chieftains who formed the king's council, to the funeral and to the naming of the new king which must follow. Within a day these great lords began to arrive at the fortress, together with Ida's ceorls who once had manned his war-boats and now farmed the land he had won for them.

In his own candle-lit, silent house, Ida lay alone, splendid in his cold chain-mail and the rich colours of a fine woven pall.

Rhianneth kept herself busy helping Alda and Rolf, Ida's former slave, to take care of Lovan. She did not want to be alone, to think. To acknowledge, even to herself, that she was very frightened.

But at night as she lay awake, she found it impossible to repel the thoughts that stormed and harried her mind, and she wept scalding tears both for Cai's lost venture and her own bleak and miserable future. She had feared marriage with Ida and life with the Saxon people. Yet her Caer Melot vow had given her a design for the future which if achieved would have planted strong seeds from the shaking Empire in the hard soil of this alien world.

What could she do now? To return to Aunt Julia meant living with Morvydd and the baby – and Cai. She would be desolated by conflicting ties of love and honour, and vulnerable to the taunts of Queen Myffan should she venture to keep up her position as Llywarch's half-sister, Elidyr's love child.

She could go home to her grandmother. Learn her trade. Marry Hueill or Geraint, grow old, and eventually take her grandmother's place. But the old deserted house rose up, ghost-like, to haunt her. Here, Marcus had filled her mind, rallied her dreams. She could not live on the hill and watch them crumble with the villa.

Thoughts of her mother tormented her. She too, had been young and full of dreams. Laughing in the sunshine, her hair as bright as the autumn leaves, she fluttered through Rhianneth's mind along the edge of sleep.

'Take care!' Rhianneth tried to cry. 'Oh, take care!'

Then with a start she would come back from the dream borders, cold with sweat, knowing that the warning voice in her ears was not her own, but that of her grandmother; the words were echoes of those once constantly on her lips as she had watched Rhianneth's inexpert fingers break open a plant to reach its precious essence.

CHAPTER 6

The last rays of the setting sun slanted across the land and tipped the wave crests a giant's stride away, as if an army of
spears waited just within the edge of night.

The tide had turned. Already the holding ropes of Ida's
high-stemmed, shallow-draughted boat were taut. The dead
king lay amidships, a sword in his hand, spears at his side; his
shield lay on his breast and around him his great war-cloak
fell in folds. In death his face had lost any touch of the mead-
hall. He looked what he had always been. A lean and hungry
sea-wolf, bound for Woden's Waelhaell and the arms of dead
comrades, to feast and fight until the ending of the world. At
his feet lay the body of his favourite hound, Bron; valiant in
life, faithful in death.

Upon the sea-soaked salted timbers of the boat glinted
copper and bronze and bright enamels, the gleam of pale
polished horn. Coloured tunics and warm-woven cloaks lay
against the empty oar-benches; leather mead bottles stood
beside cups and plates of silver and arm-rings of twisted gold.
Gifts from Ida's living followers, each giving the best he had
for his dead lord.

'God keep you, Ida.'

The words she had often heard Marcus say at her mother's
grave came to Rhianneth's lips as she laid a heavy gold chain,
that had once been Elidyr's, upon Ida's dark cloak. At the
edge of his shield she tucked a sprig of rowan to ensure the
protection of Rhiannon against the force of evil.

One of the half-naked warriors waiting in the surf to launch
the boat lifted Rhianneth down to the beach, as Ida's sons
came riding across the sands. They wore full battle-gear.
Fearsome helmets of engraved iron and chain-mail covered
their faces, and they carried naked swords.

In silence the four men drew rein and waited, their horses
tossing their heads and stamping their hooves on the wet rippled sand. In the crowd a child cried, and was quickly hushed
by its mother.

Wermund raised his arms and called upon the high god

Woden, Lord of the Spear. The dying sun blazed back from the gift-shields and helmets and bright coats of mail that hung upon the boat. The square sail caught the wind and swelled towards the east.

Flaming spears whistled through the air towards the boat. Thin black smoke wavered upwards. Then sudden flames roared into life dimming the sky with their brightness as the sail caught fire, banners of wind-blown smoke billowed out across the sea into darkness like sombre messengers of the king's coming.

They slashed the ropes, and the muscles of the men in the water swelled as they strained to heave the great boat outwards through the surf, until with a rush the tide took her. She slid into deeper water where the current and the wind swiftly took her out into the lonely sea. Gulls, disturbed by the roar and crackle of the burning boat, shrieked overhead as they circled the drifting smoke.

To Rhianneth, the barbaric scene had raw magnificence. A true heroic ending for Ida, she thought. Floating to the halls of his gods like a blazing star in the night-dark sea.

She remembered small sad funerals at home; her grand-mother mumbling, scattering her charmed flowers; Marcus's prayers. Marcus, so pleased and proud as he slipped the baptism ring on her finger, that she might never forget the Christos. Something within her stirred uneasily, and she snapped off the memories before they could take hold.

The wind blew stronger. She pulled her cloak tight. Wermund turned to walk back towards the fortress. Some of the crowd followed him.

Then a woman began a high keening that chilled Rhianneth's blood. An eldritch wail that rose and fell, riding on the back of the gusting wind. Others joined their voices to hers, until the skies were filled with weird echoing lamentations.

Ida's sons moved, raised their swords in salute to Ida, who had taken by storm the citadel and the lands around it for his people. Up and down the edge of the sea they rode, calling out towards the swift-coming darkness in harsh Saxon. To Rhianneth they looked like phantom warriors, with the sombre light glinting on the chain-mail that swung from their helmets, masking their faces.

'What are they doing?'

She turned to the group of council chieftains who stood nearby, with the ceorls who acknowledged no lord but their king.

'They call the Waelcyrian, lady,' a tall, bleak-eyed man with a deeply lined face and greying beard answered her, 'calling them for Ida. Asking Woden to open the doors of Waelhaell for our great warrior king.'

Wild, cold and strange, Cai had said of the Saxon gods. A world apart from those sprung from Britain's ancient earth, or those that had come from the warm lands across the southern seas. But as she looked around at the gathered people, and the women's wailing joined like a wild harp's song the hoarse shouting of the riders at the edge of the sea, Rhianneth felt the true force of their power, and was afraid.

Reason started to slip away. Her child-time promises to Marcus faded. Now, above anything, she feared to see the terrible daughters of Woden come riding down out of the night sky.

'And – will they come?'

'They will come.' He must have seen her fear, for he added gently, 'For Ida. Only the dead, or dying, see the Waelcyrian.'

But tonight, she thought, tonight is Samhain Eve. The Night of the Dead. The gates of the Otherworld stand wide open and anything may ride the sky or wander the earth. Whispered terrors echoed from the nightmares of childhood. She looked from Ida's burning death-ship to the cloaked mourners huddled on the windswept shore. They too, seemed full of menace.

She ran across the sands and snatched Alda's hand, dragged her, panting, up the path towards the northern gate of the fortress.

People had gathered in the space behind Ida's Hall. As she and Alda approached they fell silent. The faces that turned towards them were strangely sullen, closed. A pang of new fear shot through Rhianneth. They would have to go through the group to reach safety and privacy.

Now Wermund raised his voice. One word hissed through the night air. *Wealas.* Without knowing its meaning Rhianneth felt its menace. Heads turned. The word was taken up, spat from many throats.

Wermund saw her.

Raising his head high, he pointed a long bony finger and began to speak in slow, measured tones, thick with venom. Alda clutched Rhianneth's arm, jerking her backwards in her fright.

'Come away, lady! Come away!'

The flare of torches showed more people moving near the main gates. Dark shadows stirred between the houses. There was no way they could reach the safety of house or meadhall. Behind them was the northern gate to the beach, soon to be slammed against the night. Beyond that, blackness. Sea and wild country to the borders of Pictland, and the dark terrors from which she had just fled.

'They are saying we are wealas – foreigners! That you are a sorceress, evil . . . a child of the black priest of the west. That you put poison in Ida's cup . . .'

Alda gasped out the words, her eyes fixed on the priest. Horror-struck, Rhianneth stared from the grim and sullen faces before her to the face of Wermund, sharp-angled and deep-shadowed in the harsh torchlight. The body smell of the crowded people stung her nostrils as she took in a ragged breath of smoky air. The priest pushed away those before him and strode forward.

'White blood of the mistletoe fruit,' he said haltingly in the British tongue, 'In Ida's poison-cup. Only that could kill Baldur, son of Woden, beloved of the gods! Only that could kill Ida! The golden bough, sacred amongst the black druid priests – '

'Druids?' Rhianneth gasped. 'There are no druids!'

He came near, till he was not a sword's length away. In his narrow, bone-hard face pain and sorrow were written deep, and there was hot hatred in his eyes.

'Who knows what dwells in the far west? You are named for their goddess. Was it not through her enchantments that the

181

great stag was hidden from Ida's sight until it charged out to kill? When that failed, you took another way. Poison!'

His hand shot out, gripped her shoulder. He called aloud something in Saxon which ended in the name of Woden, and the war-god's name was shouted again and again by the crowd, like a chant to charm away evil, or call up a demon.

Alda's scream lanced through the noise and confusion, and Rhianneth jerked free of the priest's grip, spinning around and running with Alda straight towards the northern gateway; towards the dark shoreline and, she remembered suddenly with leaping joy, Idwal and his six remaining soldiers!

In the light of the wind-blown torches, sword in hand, stood Elric. Behind him the gate was a black hole, leading to nothingness.

Rhianneth stopped, the breath rasping in her throat. A wild glance over her shoulder showed the black moving shape of the crowd coming fast. She never doubted that she and Alda were in mortal danger. She felt Alda's hand shake, heard the girl's breath shudder as she searched the darkness for somewhere to go.

Then Elric moved. In two strides he reached them, thrust them behind him.

The Saxons were still shouting Woden's name, as if to open the very doors of Waelhaell by the force of their chanting. Those at the front hesitated, stopped when they saw Elric's naked sword. They shouted back over their shoulders as others bumped against them, knocking them forward.

Elric's voice rose above the noise, calling the names of his brothers. The crowd shrank back into itself as Ida's sons appeared from the blackness to stand beside him, swords gleaming in the red torchlight. Like Elric they were still fully armed, save for their helmets.

But Wermund pushed slowly forward, his eyes glittering in his craggy face. He spoke in Saxon, pointing towards Rhianneth. Elric's answer was brief. Then the priest let out a stream of words. Harsh spitting growls that halted and dried to nothing, when Elric's sword was raised slowly until it pointed straight and unwavering at Wermund's throat.

In the silence that followed Rhianneth could hear Alda's trembling breath even above the thudding of her own heart. The priest's eyes fell away. He took a step backwards. After a moment, he turned and walked into the darkness.

Elric grasped Rhianneth's wrist and jerked her forward to stand beside him, never for an instant taking his eyes off the hushed crowd.

He began to speak. Short snarling wolf-barks of words that made the Saxons look from his face to Rhianneth's, and then to slant glances towards each other.

An old man with a twisting scar down one side of his face said something, shooting a worried look at Ida's other sons as he did so. It was young Theodric who answered, and what he said brought a tentative rumble of laughter from somewhere in the crowd. The old man shrugged and turned away, making a gesture of compliance.

Suddenly the unbearable tension eased, the violence that had tinged the air diminished. Elric strode forward, dragging Rhianneth with him, swinging his sword to clear the way. The crowd parted before them, falling back like shadows.

Inside the frail safety of the house, Alda began to cry, her eyes still round with shock.

Elric silently slid his sword into its fleece-lined sheath of black wolfskin. He reached for a jug of mead and splashed the golden liquid into wooden cups. Briefly his eyes met Rhianneth's, before he tossed down his own honey-wine in one swallow.

His face was pale and his eyes had the burnt-out look of one who had not slept. Marks left by his iron helmet were darkly imprinted on his forehead. Rhianneth remembered that he and his brothers had kept armed vigil last night beside the body of Ida in the king's house.

He had loved Ida. She was a stranger, whom he disliked. Yet he had defended her against Woden's priest and his monstrous charge of poison. Rhianneth told herself that she was overwhelmingly grateful for his presence, and his power.

Alda crouched behind the fire, still crying, her tears dropping like rain into the cup she clasped. Rhianneth was about to go to her when Idwal thundered to the door, eyes blazing with rage.

'Sweet Jesus, lady, is it true? While the funeral boat still burns?'

'It's all right,' she answered swiftly, a new worry assailing her on seeing his familiar face. 'Please, will you go to Lovan, tell him that nothing has happened. That Alda and I are safe. Elric spoke to the priest, to the people – that's all. It was a . . . mistake. Elric put it right.'

'Did he? If I'd been quicker up from the beach it would have been more than a sweet tongue I'd have licked around that bitter pagan priest!'

He started to say more, but seeing her face he stopped, holding up a hand. 'Right. I'll go to Lovan. But we stand guard outside here overnight. And tomorrow, we'll sort it out. I'll have food sent over to you. And you, lady, don't leave this house tonight.'

Still breathing hard, his face set in lines of anger, he left.

Rhianneth turned back into the room as Elric was refilling his cup. His great height and broad shoulders towered close in the light of the low-burning fire. Sharpened now by the acrid smell of greased chainmail, came the familiar masculine tang of fresh sweat and warm leather, reminding her of Lovan and the men, home after hunting with the dogs.

She was shaking, grasping her cup so tightly the liquid slopped around the inside. Quickly she gulped down half the contents, feeling the sweet fire warm her stomach and steady her nerves.

'There is great sorrowing here, Rhianneth,' Elric said, watching her. 'Ida was our strength. Our power that comes from one folk, one king. He was not an old man, nor sick. So, when people ask why he should die, Wermund gives an answer.'

She glanced quickly at him, at his thick straight hair and level gaze. Grateful as she was, she wished he would go. She was still trembling. She wanted to be alone with Alda, and he seemed to fill the room with his presence.

'But perhaps,' he persisted, 'Ida was not meant to die. Just to fall ill. To avoid a wedding on your Night of the Dead? Your grandmother, I'm told, is wise in such things.'

There was a long silence. 'If you think that,' she whispered at last, 'why did you stand against Wermund?'

'He wants to hang you, lady. On the sacrificial ash tree. Send your treacherous little soul to Woden. Will Llywarch keep the alliance, do you think, while the crows make a feast of you, and Cai comes hunting for my blood?'

The raw brutality of his words crumbled her thoughts into nothing. Somewhere outside she heard men's voices raised in anger. A clammy sweat broke out on her cold hands.

'Ah, yes,' he said, reading the blank horror on her face as she stared at him aghast, 'when we scent treason, Rhianneth, we do become the barbarians you think us, and worse.'

'I want you to know –' somehow she kept her voice level, her eyes steady on his face – 'that it is not true. I did nothing. Ida just – died.'

From the darkness beyond the door the night shattered with shouting, and the bump and scrape of a sudden brawl. Further away a woman's voice shrilled out in anger. A child started to cry. Rhianneth's heart thudded and her brain seemed to burn as panic crept nearer. Yet not for all the gold of Rome would she have him know the depths of her fear.

'If you harm me,' she went on, swallowing, 'Cai will come. And with Mithrasia's army at his heels!'

'Why should I harm you, when we row to the same purpose? I understood the alliance was greatly desired by Cai's Caer Melot Fellowship. Are you not one of them?'

She raised her head higher. 'Yes.'

'Then we think as one, Rhianneth. The marriage that seals the alliance will go on, despite the death of Ida.'

Her mind stumbled through his words, until the meaning of what he was saying burst upon her. She felt a shock as sudden, as great, as if he had struck her across the face.

Was this what Idwal had meant? 'While the funeral boat is still burning . . .' he had said, and she had thought he was talking about Wermund's attack!

'Is that what you told them – out there?' she gasped, remembering the faces in the crowd staring, glancing at one another. 'I know how little you think of me, Elric, but this, this is beyond belief! With your father just dead, already you insult me.'

'Insult?' he asked dangerously. 'Ida's gone. I claimed you as mine, my woman. Under my protection.'

She looked at him. At the powerful shoulders beneath the linked-ring tunic, at the untidy light hair, blown by the sea wind. Never had he looked more Saxon, more foreign. What he said was alien too, made more frightening because he spoke as if he had acted in all honour. If he had, it was the honour of a sea-pirate, she thought, and rage rose in her and, swelled by fear, broke.

'Yours? By what right? I'm not a gift, to be tossed down a line of barbarians! Yes, Ida is dead! My part is finished. And I want . . . I want to go home!'

She turned away blindly, knuckling at the hot tears before they ran down her face as she used to do after a childhood argument with Olwen. But he was suddenly behind her, grasping her shoulders, spinning her round to face him so that her head swam and the salt tears in her throat almost choked her.

'Why else are you here but to seal the alliance?' he demanded, his voice rough. 'I've still to win over Wermund. I hardly thought I'd need to persuade you!'

There was an urgency in his face, in the hardness of his hands, that shook her. Then his eyes ran over her flushed cheeks and storm-filled eyes, and his grip slackened. Her chin trembled and she caught her lip between her teeth,.

'Hel's Gate,' he muttered through his teeth, 'you're really only a little girl, aren't you?'

His hand came up to touch her wind-tangled hair. His voice softened. 'Too young for girdle-keys, let alone fight your way through this mess. Don't cry, Rhianneth. You're quite safe, I promise you. Whatever killed Ida was not in the Waeshaell cup you handed him. Hussa is your champion in that – he saw the dogs lapping up the spilt mead. And I . . . I

186

don't believe your powers of ill-wishing are strong enough to kill – if they exist at all . . .'

Suddenly she was in his arms. She could not speak, hardly think. She only knew that for this moment the one safe place in all the world was here, held close against the hard young strength of his body, his hand at the back of her head blotting out thought, stilling her mind.

She felt his breath stirring her hair. He was speaking, softly, but the words were in Saxon. Rhianneth closed her eyes.

Then, infinitely slowly, thoughts began to creep back into the drained stillness of her mind. This was Elric. Elric, claiming her as his bride before the ashes of his dead father had blown across the cold sea waters.

The dregs of her anger seeped through and joined the desolation that had been in her since Cai left, until she could no longer push her thoughts away. She became aware then that she was crushed against the meshed rings of his mail-shirt, that the scramasax, the short blade that hung from his studded leather belt was pressed painfully into her side. Violently she pushed away from him, broke free of his arms.

'I won't marry you, Elric! Unless word comes to me from Mithrasia – from Llywarch . . . and from Cai!'

There was something in his face that she saw and did not understand, and which vanished instantly. When he spoke it was with that faint mockery which had spurred her hatred of him on the Wall.

'Is this Cai's heroic shield-maiden? I'm not asking you for marriage, lady. Not yet. A betrothal will be enough to win over the council and secure the kingship – and the alliance.'

She shook her head, backing away. She wanted time. Time to think. She felt cornered, nowhere to go. Lovan was sick. Idwal had but six soldiers. The civilised safety of Mithrasia lay far across the high hills. At this moment she was in Elric's power, with only her own wits to guide her.

Elric needed this betrothal to secure his inheritance. Why should that be, unless he feared a scramble for power amongst his brothers? Yet they had gathered to him at the gate to face Wermund's hostile followers; they seemed close,

close in friendship and in arms. The alliance had been made with Ida, the strong old wolf. The council would now, perhaps, support for kingship the strongest of his sons, the one who held the Mithrasian marriage bond in his hand.

'Your brothers –'

'My brothers are not entered in this contest, save that they stand beside me. It is Guthlac who will seek to take Ida's place. If he succeeds there will be no alliance, with or without the marriage bond. He is sour with hatred for all your people.'

'Guthlac?'

'Ida's brother, who holds the stronghold at Gefrin. He is away with his war-band to the west. But messengers have gone after him. He will appear soon enough. We shall hold Ida's funeral feast, and he will lay claim to Din Guaryrdi. I need your betrothal pledge now – and Wermund's acceptance of it, to convince the council. Before his banners come into sight.'

'Wermund accept it? He thinks I murdered your father! If I'm betrothed to you he will surely support Guthlac!'

'I don't think so.' Elric's smile was grim. 'It was in Guthlac's boat he smashed his leg. Guthlac left him to die. No, our priest will find himself between ship and shore. Nothing will make him support Guthlac as king. Which leaves him with me, and you – and the alliance.'

Rhianneth stared at him in silence. Like the priest, she seemed to have no choice. Unless made with Elric, there would be no alliance, and the prayers of the Fellowship for this bulwark in the north would be blown into fragments.

She remembered Wencam's face on that bright last morning in Mithrasia's old forum. All that young summer glory under the weight of winter years. 'All our hopes go with you,' he had said.

'I'm sorry to have offended you, to have spoken in the way I did,' Elric was saying carefully, his eyes on her face. 'I have not the art of wrapping my words to deceive an enemy – or please a lady. Time is short. My messenger must soon be on his way to Mithrasia. The message, I fear, will be worded bluntly. But I do not doubt he will return with Llywarch's agreement. Have I yours?'

Marry Elric? His physical presence filled her with a sensation of intense unease so powerful she could feel reason crumbling with every thud of her heart.

Ida was dead. How could she, alone, seal with marriage a new alliance with one of his sons? Yet this seemed the way she must take. Quickly, before Guthlac came.

Unwillingly she looked at him. 'You have my word, Elric. I appear to have no choice but to join with you. But a betrothal only. No marriage till I hear from my brother.'

Unsmiling, he held out a hand. After a small hesitation she put hers into it.

'A betrothal is good enough.' He drew her closer, tilted her face up to his. As their eyes met warily he lowered his head and kissed her on the mouth.

'And may the Gods, both yours and mine,' he said sombrely, 'be with us.'

Two days later the council met to choose Ida's successor, closely watched by the people of Din Guaryrdi. Rhianneth had imagined they would be old men, wise elders of the folk. But they were tough, fighting men, some contemporaries of Ida, some younger, who deferred to no one and owed their allegiance only to their chosen king.

The priest Wermund raised his thick staff which had the eye of Woden carved upon its head. Serpentine shapes, ending in dragon-heads, intertwined about its length. He called for silence, and asked the Gods to guide the minds of the council chiefs. Then the lord of a shore-line fortress to the south spoke. After him, others.

At last Wermund struck the ground three times with his staff, calling again for silence. And, although he spoke between his teeth, the name on his lips was Elric's. When the voting came, there was no doubt by the roar of acclamation that Elric was indeed the new king of Bernicia.

Lovan rubbed his bearded chin thoughtfully when Rhianneth ran to tell him that it was over, that the alliance was safe.

'Maybe . . . but they won't hold the funeral feast until Guthlac comes, let alone the oath-taking ceremony. They

hold him in that much respect. He is lord of their big stronghold at Gefrin, Ida's only surviving brother.'

'But not heir to his kingdom, nor even to Din Guaryrdi!'
She stirred the pot of stew that simmered over the fire. 'He
can't lay claim to anything of Ida's, not when Ida leaves four
sons, all grown to manhood!'

Lovan pulled himself painfully to a higher sitting position,
the knuckles of his gnarled brown hands white with effort. A
few beads of sweat started on his forehead.

'Their ways are different, *cariad*. Ida was not all-powerful.
Not a god-king, though he claimed descent from Woden. But
they hold kingship in awe. They believe a power, a force, runs
through the blood of the whole royal race, bringing good fortune to king and people. They call it *mana*. It's their royal
blood that raises them above the rest, so kinship with the king
gives a man the right to be amongst those from whom the next
king is chosen. But no right to the crown, without the will of the
leaders of the people. Usually, a king's son will succeed him; but
if it's felt that his *mana* has drained away, that he is in any way
weak or unfit to lead, another is chosen from the royal stable.'

Rhianneth handed him a bowl of stew and he began to eat,
blowing on each steaming spoonful. She sat carefully on the
edge of the bed, thinking that in spite of his weakness he
already looked much better. Ida's young slave Rolf had
attached himself to Lovan, dressing his wound, sleeping in his
house. Wermund did not come near. His work was done, and
reluctantly Rhianneth admitted his skill as a surgeon. He had
done, that day in the stable, what she could not. There had
been no time or opportunity for her grandmother to teach her
the dressing and healing of wounds. Yet it had been her mix-
tures, her potions, that had dulled Lovan's pain, sent him
blessed sleep. Wermund and I would make a good team, harnessed together, she thought wryly, were it not that he plainly
wishes me dead.

'They would not choose a child then?' she asked. 'As
Llywarch was when he came to Mithrasia's throne?'

'They are a fighting people. They need a war-leader. A
strong battle-captain.'

190

'Then Elric it must be, despite Guthlac.'

Lovan looked at her, his spoon half-lifted from the bowl. 'There may be trouble, *cariad*, before the oath-taking.'

'But I did the right thing, didn't I Lovan? To agree to a betrothal?'

He thought for a moment. 'If Elric is determined to keep the marriage pact, he won't let you go. But as you said, it's only a betrothal, until we hear from Llywarch. Meanwhile, we'll see what Guthlac does. If he wins, he'll send us packing. This stew is good, Rhianneth! Tastes better than Olwen used to make!'

He winked, and her heart swelled with pride, for she had made every bit of the meal herself, just for him, as he well knew.

'I wonder what Cai will say?' She kept her head bent, her eyes on the thick wool of the sheepskin rug she teased between her fingers. 'He trusts Elric. Do you?'

'I don't know him, *cariad*. I only have what Cai told me, and scraps picked up from the British servants around the kitchens and stables. He seems straight. Strong, without temperament or nervous shying. And he's young. More to your fancy, I should think, than an old war-horse like Ida?'

Her cheeks flamed. 'He is overbearing and arrogant.'

Lovan finished the stew, as if he had not heard. Then he handed back the bowl and lay back with a sigh.

'I know how Griffyn must have felt, all those weeks he was laid up. Helpless you are, without the means to walk. On the night of the funeral I heard the shouting and brawling, and somehow I crawled to the door. But I was weaker than I knew and fainted clean away. Young Rolf found me, got me back to bed. Idwal told me you were safe. So I'm thankful as you are to Elric and his brothers, for their protection of you that night . . .'

Her eyes flew to his face. But there was nothing there to reflect the reproach she fancied she heard in his words. Swiftly she rose, and put his bowl to be washed.

'Elric wants the alliance as much as Cai,' she said flatly. 'They need our grain and cattle since Urien's raids are coming further into Bernicia, burning their harvest crops. Both he and Cai see me as the means to an end.'

'The alliance does not stand or fall upon a marriage,' Lovan said to her back. 'Sure, it's a strong thing to bind us in blood. Nothing better, with children as living links. But a military agreement only would still serve. Elric may decide to stick to that, and not saddle himself with a foreign wife who resents and dislikes him. We may yet go home, *cariad*.'

Home! A longing ached through her for Marcus, for long winter days winding wool for her grandmother before the glowing brazier; for bright days of summer running with Giff through a meadow thick with cowslips, the air heavy with their scent. Gone, all gone. She remembered walking through the same flowering grass with Cai, his scarlet cloak edged with damp, and all her young being aflame with pride and love, yearning to serve the Fellowship as he did. As Marcus had done.

'Three times I've given my word,' she tried to keep the bitterness from her voice, 'to Cai, to the Fellowship, and now to Elric. And –' she took a deep breath – 'after Cai left, I made a promise to myself. For the future, here in Bernicia. If I can, I'd like to keep it.'

Lovan raised his eyebrows. 'And what would that be? To tame an arrogant young wolf-cub into slinking at your heels like dear old Giff, maybe?'

'What?' Angry words rushed to her lips. But at the sight of the old teasing smile on his face, so drawn by fever into unfamiliar fragility, they died unspoken. Instead she sank upon the bed and caught his hand. 'Oh, Lovan! What would I do without you?'

His mouth twitched again with humour. 'As you please, I imagine, as you always do!'

At the betrothal supper that night Rhianneth sat beside Elric and put her hand under his around the silver loving cup, while they pledged faith before the whole company. Then he placed into her hands his betrothal gift, a narrow belt set with semi-precious stones, to girdle her gowns.

She sipped morat, a sweet, dark and precious drink made from mulberries. Elric turned the cup to drink from the place where her lips had touched. Then he caught her chin, and bending his head, kissed on the mouth.

'I realise now why Cai broke away from you so violently, that morning on the Wall,' he whispered against her ear. 'Your kisses have a quality of danger, best confined to the marriage bed.'

She blushed scarlet with anger. That he should at this moment have Cai's name upon his lips showed his complete insensitivity. But to make a jest of something almost unbearable to her in its anguish proved him to be as coarse, as brutal, as his pirate ancestors. When she told him so, he laughed at her.

Next day she rode out into the damp, blustery air with a small hunting party, glad to be free for a few hours of Din Guaryrdi's high walls and the people within them. Wermund avoided her. But she was aware that many others, too, turned aside when she approached, their light eyes sliding away as if they feared to meet hers. So it was with a great lifting of spirits that she left Alda sitting with Lovan and, with Romulus warm beneath her and the smell of leather like perfume between her hands, she trotted beside Elric down the long trackway and away towards the woods.

They passed by the huge old ash tree on the edge of the forest, and its bare branches swaying in the light wind. She shivered, and turned quickly to look at Elric instead. She knew his reason for saving her, even though he half-believed she had spell-wished Ida to die. But the morning sun briefly broke through the low-flying clouds and lit the dark gold of his hair, deepened the russet hue of his thrown-back cloak, and suddenly her joy in life bubbled uncontrollably upwards, bringing with it a rush of belated gratitude so warm that she smiled impulsively as she caught his quick glance.

Surprise flashed across his face, and something else which she could not read. Then they were entering the woods and Romulus started to skitter at the crackling leaves beneath his hooves, needing all her concentration to calm him.

When the cry came that the quarry had been sighted, Elric leaned across and held her reins with one hand while the riders galloped past. She watched with surprised apprehension as the last of them plunged out of sight behind the trees.

'We shall lose them,'' she said. 'Why don't you follow?'

'I'm not in the mood for the bustle of the chase; we will take a different path.' He smiled, and loosed her reins. 'Let me show you a little of Bernicia.'

They rode for the most part silently, occasionally brushing the forest. The trackway grew rougher, and after a while she dismounted, leading Romulus, and becoming hot despite the breath of winter in the air.

They came to a lake, and she let Romulus loose so that she could walk to where the clear water lapped up to the shingle edge. Huge and silent, the hills curved darkly round it, their frozen heights merging into heavy clouds.

'I used to come here with Hussa,' Elric murmured softly, coming up beside her. 'It seemed a place to sit and think, to dream. Many times we've ridden from Din Guaryrdi on such a day as this, just to see it, to smell the wet windy air.'

She turned to look at him, suddenly conscious that they were entirely alone. It was very still. The hunting party had vanished into the forest and she could not even hear the faint sounding of their horns. Now the unease which she had always felt in Elric's presence held her; she floundered around in her mind, unable to think clearly. At last she ventured hesitantly:

'Could Guthlac really claim Din Guaryrdi?'

'My uncle will try for more than that,' Elric answered dryly. 'He will claim captaincy of all Bernicia, despite the council. Whoever holds Din Guaryrdi rules Bernicia. If it comes to a fight and he wins, they will sway towards him. They won't risk civil war. Not with the Picts on our borders and Urien panting for our blood.'

'You don't like him, do you?'

'Should I?'

'He is Ida's brother. Your uncle.'

'He is Ida, made smaller and more vicious.' He picked up a stone and hurled it skimming across the lake. 'If I lose, Lady Rhianneth, be out of the gate before he takes my head – for he'll smash the alliance, and you with it.' He smiled grimly.

Quickly she looked away to where the lake rippled with the force of his flung stone, spear-tipped with silver as the wind passed over.

A battle! she thought. Surely it would not come to that? Guthlac may dispute Elric's claim to kingship but the council cannot be ignored! They did not choose Guthlac. Elric has three brothers. Does he expect me to believe that Guthlac could overtide the council, be allowed to murder all four of Ida's sons?

She tilted a sideways glance. He watched her, the reflected light of the water and the dripping trees turning his grey eyes green. 'That's the trick of an enchantress,' he said softly. 'Is that how you spell-bound Cai?'

He gathered a thick handful of her hair, weighing it in his palm. 'You need no spells, Rhianneth. With your sweet face and this, like dark fox-fire, I am already at your feet . . .'

In one angry movement she pulled away, tossed her hair back over her shoulder. She knew mockery when she heard it.

'At my feet you are useless,' she hissed. 'I need you upright and armed, facing the enemies of Mithrasia!'

He burst into a shout of laughter as she swung away and caught up Romulus's reins ready to go. His talk of fighting with his uncle, she thought furiously, is calculated to frighten me, to draw me further into the net of his protection while his messenger returns with Llywarch's agreement to the new marriage bond.

Slowly, they rode back towards the sea. Elric talked to her of the coming of Ida and his followers to Bernicia, after a long bitter quarrel with the Deiran king. Her resentment gradually faded. She pictured the grey waste of the northern seas and the curved boats clinging as close as they dared to the broken coast, treacherous with strange currents and jagged rocks. He made her see the huddled women and children in the narrow bows, drenched with sea water; the straining muscles of the warriors at the oars, their bright shields slung along the bulwarks like a defensive wall, their hands calloused from rowing.

She could almost feel the stiffness of cramped muscles, the soreness of a wind-chapped face, sea salt grating in hair and clothing. Unwillingly at first, her admiration grew for Ida's grim, determined warriors, and for the women who came with them, who shielded their children from ice-needled weather and bloodied foe alike.

'Ida's landings were many, and bitterly contested,' Elric told her. 'Until he fought his way into Din Guaryrdi we children scarcely set foot on dry land, and we were always ready for instant sailing if the battle went against us. All my early memories are of the boats. They were our home. Our refuge. The safe place, on the sea. I still dream, sometimes, of the great square sail swelling and cracking above my head as we found a following wind, or of the roar and thud of the sea as we swept shuddering in through the waves to make a landing.'

'I pity your mother,' Rhianneth said, with feeling. 'How did she care for four little children in such savage conditions?'

He fell silent. The sea wind was blowing stronger now, bringing flurries of rain that made Romulus snort and toss his head, dancing sideways against the pull of the reins.

'Ida knew many women,' Elric replied at last, 'and had two wives. One was my mother – and the mother of Hussa and Adda. She died at Adda's birth, before I had seen five winters. His second wife, Theodric's mother, died while Theo was still a baby.' He stopped, shooting a quick glance at Rhianneth. When she made no comment, he went on: 'Old Nesta, our British slave-nurse, brought us through the boat time. For a woman, it was a hard life. A hard country.'

Again he paused, and when Rhianneth still said nothing he commented dryly, 'But you need not fear, lady. We have it tamed. Now our boats are used for catching fish.'

In silence, Rhianneth reflected on the strangeness of the Saxon people. These Engles of Bernicia celebrated in song and saga battles fought to the death for a hopeless cause, and made jests around past tragedies and bitter hardships. They lived by a harsh battle-code of honour and loyalty. Even in their religion there was no comfort, no reward. For the Gods were themselves ultimately doomed to destruction in one last great battle against the forces of darkness and terror.

They tied the horses to some wind-bent, stunted bushes, and made their way down towards the shore through a ravine which cleft the low cliffs. The salt wind blowing off the sea stung Rhianneth's cheeks. But the waters below were dark and mysterious, crested with white foam, and she could see Din Guaryrdi high upon its rock a little way down the coast, as if it were carved from the earth itself. On the beach below it were the curved ships, and the small fishing boats, drawn up above the tide, waiting.

She thought of Ida's wave-tossed funeral pyre, flowing out with the tide and swift currents into the lonely darkness of the sea. And at last she understood. Saw beyond the alien barbarism that had shaken her into flight, that night of the funeral. They had sent him, their old warrior, into the arms of Woden and the Hall of Waelhaell. Dressed as a king and decked in gold, with the ship he loved better than any woman. A ship that had sheltered his sons and his people, and brought him to a kingdom for the winning. His storm-racer. His foam-crested wave skimmer . . .

She caught at her thoughts as, in her head, Alda's voice murmered the words of a mead-hall tale. Easily, it seemed, she was beginning to learn their tongue; as easily as once she had learned *nostra lingua*, the language of Marcus's Rome.

When they were halfway down the rough pathway, Elric took her hand and led her along a narrow ledge that led to a cave.

She gazed around, listening to the hollow echo of the sea and trying to see what might lie in the darkness beyond the rocky entrance. They were close to Din Guaryrdi, but she had heard wolf howls at night that sounded too close to have come from the far slopes beyond the forest.

'I have spent nights here,' Elric said, running his hand over the rough wall of the cave with an affectionate gesture, 'wrapped in a blanket, watching the sea pound and roar below. Sometimes the sound of it echoes round the cave like thun-

197

der, and the waters spume up like dragon's breath!'

'Were you not afraid,' she glanced at the dark recesses of the cave, 'to be all alone?'

He grinned, his hand falling to the sword at his belt. 'I have Dreamweaver. Besides, no enemies come here, so near to Din Guaryrdi, but hidden.'

'There are other things, unseen . . .'

She touched the warm coils of her serpent bracelet as she spoke. Elric took hold of her wrist to look more closely at it, running a finger over the ruby fire of its eyes.

'My sword defends me and nothing else. Charms, spells, most of them useless. Even above the Gods, Fate is strongest. Only that is real.'

'Have you forgotten your sea-bird enchantress?' she whispered, remembering the night in the garden of Llywarch's palace.

'A tale of long ago. A dream. Are there enchantresses except in the minds of men?'

He studied her face. A sea-gull hovered outside the cave before rising on the air with a harsh cry.

'Wermund claims you have strange powers, Rhianneth. Unpredictable. Dangerous. That sometimes you seem to be listening, waiting. What is it you hear on the wind that escapes me? I hear only the cry of a sea-bird – do you think to hear the echo of the enchantresses singing, and truly hope to learn their wiles?'

He smiled as he spoke, but there was a question behind his eyes as they met hers, and his hold on her wrist tightened. She could not think how to answer him. Then his hands moved upwards to rest upon her shoulders.

'Close your ears, my lady. You will learn nothing from the voices in the wind. Woden is stronger. He rides on the wind, his breath stirs the tree tops; he can hear a blade of grass grow. And he alone gives us victory in battle! Join with me, and I'll pour the treasures of two kingdoms into your lap, place a double crown on the head of your son – build you such a fortress that all the powers of darkness will find it unassailable . . . Ah, Rhianneth!' His voice softened. 'Forget your enchantments. If it's real power you want, I offer you Bernicia now and a double kingdom for your heirs!'

'A double kingdom?'

Her words were whispers, thin echoes of the growing confusion in her mind. Was she not already upon the path set before her by the Fellowship? There was no way back, if Llywarch agreed to the new marriage bond.

His hold tightened. 'We shall take Deira before long. It's always been like a dagger at our back. They wink at our enemies, make pacts with the British of Elmet, of Eboracum. But Woden is with us! Wermund's runes tell us so. There will be one kingdom, for all the folk north of the Humber. And one queen, Rhianneth . . .'

'If your war-god can sweep Urien from our borders and keep Mithrasia safe,' she answered, through stiff lips, 'then I'll acknowledge him master of all sorcery, and you his warrior to be immune to the wiles of enchantresses!'

Elric twined his fingers in her hair, turned her face up to his. 'But not, I fear,' he said, 'to those of a mortal woman . . .'

Her heart began to thud. Even as she realised his intention, his arms went around her and his mouth came down upon hers. The fire that burst upwards within her drew all her strength with it, so that she would have fallen but that his hold tightened. They stood pressed together in a moment of hot honey-sweetness that seemed outside time, for the sea-sound beyond the cave and the high screaming of the gulls died away into silence.

Elric bent her head back across his arm and began to stroke her hair with his free hand whilst his kiss deepened, hardened. She felt a shaking excitement, as if all her being was melting into his and she had no will left except to yield to the pressure of his mouth upon hers. His hand slid over her shoulders and her body and she made no resistance; it was as if nothing mattered in the whole of eternity, save this moment. His body was powerful, hard. As she swayed against him she opened her eyes and saw naked desire in his face, and something deep within her exulted.

At that moment some trick of the wind brought a sound into

the cave. It was a hunting horn far off in the forest, faintly heard and gone in an instant. But it broke the spell that held her.

She twisted loose and sprang back against the cave wall, hands outstretched to hold Elric off. He grasped her wrists and pulled her toward him once more, but she jerked her head aside and pushed against his hands as violently as she could, her panting breath spiralling between them in the cold wet air. Elric easily caught her two wrists in one hand, and with the other grasped her hair to hold her head still. The hardness of his hold made her gasp with sudden pain, tears filling her eyes.

'Why do you fight,' he asked, but he loosened his hold somewhat, 'when we are already pledged?'

Desperately she gathered her wits. 'Let me go, Elric. I will not be tumbled like a captured slave! This alliance must have the blessing of the Gods – and you will treat me with honour!'

Abruptly he released her wrists. But he kept his hold on her hair so that she could not move away while he ran his hand gently over her face where the tears had overspilled. She was trembling with shame and anger that this Saxon barbarian should think her so easy a conquest. That she could have been so easily delighted by a kiss, when her love for Cai should have turned her response to ice.

Elric's eyes were on her mouth, but even as she stiffened in expectation of another struggle, he suddenly laughed and loosed her.

'By Woden's Eye, lady, you do not flatter me! You are the first woman to weep because I wanted her.'

Rhianneth leaned back against the cave wall, hands pressed together, watching him warily. He was so tall, the breadth of his shoulders emphasised by the folded bulk of his tossed back cloak. Beneath the glint of twisted gold bracelets she saw the strength of his wrists and hands, strength that came from hours of practice with spear and sword. He was hard, aggressive – and handsome. Should his head turn in their direction she could well imagine that women came to him only too willingly.

Well, she thought, he'll not find me amongst them. I am in thrall, still, to one who once filled my heart and mind and lingers yet in the haunted shadows of my dreams.

'There were also tears in those beautiful eyes when we met on the Wall, Rhianneth,' he said softly, 'but they were not for me. Used as a weapon, it seems they are more effective in defence than in attack. Or could it possibly be that for Cai, honour shines more brightly than the tears of an enchantress?'

Her anger burst with such force that she sprang away from the rock wall with fists clenched to strike at him. He caught them and knocked them aside. Then he pulled her brutally to him, holding her so tightly that all her fierce struggles were as nothing.

'Ah,' he said, into her ragged breath, 'have I said the magic word that unsheaths those sharp little cat-claws? What was it? Honour – or Cai? Or is it only when they go together that you become dangerous?'

'Let me loose!' she demanded between her teeth, while the blood pounded behind her eyes with impotent rage. One of his hands tangled in her hair and he pulled her head back to look into her face.

'Is it safe?' His eyes mocked her. 'Or will you sink your claws straight into my heart?'

'You –' She struggled to think of a word vile enough to call him but her brain was too hot with fury. 'You – savage! Take your filthy hands off me! I can't bear you to touch me!'

Only the sound of the sea broke the silence for a long awful moment. They stared at each other, while a measure of stillness seeped back into Rhianneth's mind. His face revealed nothing. But in the frail light his eyes echoed the icy depths of the waters below them.

'Well,' he said at last, 'that should prove interesting, after the wedding feast.'

His hands dropped away, and she was free. In silence they made their way back to the horses and rode slowly along the coast track and towards Din Guaryrdi.

By the time the fortress loomed blackly before them against the clouded sky, Rhianneth's temper had cooled so much that icy trickles of remorse started to flow. Had she truly called him a savage, Ida's son? Cai's friend, who had saved her life on the night of the funeral? She cast a quick look towards him, and swallowed.

'Elric, I'm sorry . . .' she stopped, and started again. 'I didn't mean what I said. I was angry. Frightened . . .'

He did not reply. He was staring ahead toward the fortress. The gates were open, and Hussa strode down the trackway to meet them, his usually cheerful face grim.

'Guthlac's on his way.' He steadied the horse's head as Elric swung down from its back. 'He's called at Gefrin to pick up his wife and child, and he's coming straight on with his war-band, still in their battle-gear. They're armed to the teeth, and it means trouble.'

'Not before the funeral feast,' Elric said. 'Not before the first cup's drunk and the first praise-words spoken.' He drew in a long breath. 'Not even Guthlac would quite dare that. How long have we got?'

'Our messenger had a good horse – he very nearly flew. But they can't be far behind now.

'Then let's buckle on our best gear, gather the council round us, and welcome our uncle to Din Guaryrdi with real princely dignity.' Elric threw an arm around his brother's shoulders, grinning. 'That should kindle his temper nicely . . . he always did react like a bull to the goad!'

CHAPTER 7

Guthlac came in force to Din Guaryrdi, the thunder of his war-band through the open gates making Rhianneth quiver with nervous doubts. Why should he bring so many armed men, unless to challenge Elric? The chieftains of the hastily summoned council, though armed, had brought only a handful of followers, leaving the remainder to guard their strongholds. Guthlac would not leave his fortress Gefrin undefended – so his army was considerable.

'He means no good, lady,' Rolf told her gloomily. His young face was intent upon binding Lovan's leg with clean linen, his mind elsewhere. 'He has with him Caldis, his wife, and her little son.'

'Then – he intends peace, surely?'

'They are the sting to bring Aethelric to the fight! And, maybe, weigh down his sword arm, too!' Rolf suddenly flushed, glanced quickly up at Rhianneth and back to his work.

She remembered Elric's grim smile by the still lake as he described Guthlac. Her doubts deepened. A black hatred there, too bitter to have sprung solely from a contest for the kingship. Where did its root lie? From what seed had it grown?

For her meeting with Ida's brother Rhianneth chose a gown of purple, of a rich fabric brought from the banks of the river Bosphorus in the Eastern Empire. Elidyr's jewels gleamed at her ears and throat. A slender gold band encircled her brow.

'Oh, lady!' Alda's eyes widened. 'You look as magnificent as Queen Myffan!'

With that unfortunate compliment ringing in her ears, Rhianneth entered the Hall. Elric stood with his brother Adda, but his eyes were on the doorway. He came swiftly to lead her towards his uncle.

Guthlac lacked Ida's height. Thick-set, his burly shoulders strained beneath a brown tunic edged with gold. His hair and beard were red. Only the bright blue eyes that glared into Rhianneth's held any reminder of Ida. Hostility was plain within them.

He spoke to Elric. Short, growling sentences in Saxon.

'Guthlac says he has been misled.' Elric's voice remained level as he translated his uncle's words. But his grey eyes were dark with anger. His fists curled, a hand's breadth away from the scramasax at his side. 'He expected a British lady. He sees a daughter of Rome.'

Rhianneth knew well enough what that expression meant amongst the Saxons. Her temper smouldered. Head high, she met Guthlac's gaze.

'Your uncle is mistaken. Only the new king's promised bride stands here.'

Guthlac's lady, Caldis, stood beside him. She darted a fearful look at her husband, clasping a hand to her throat. Her eyes turned to Rhianneth then, and they were neither blue nor grey. Golden, like a falcon's Rhianneth thought, and a small chill touched her.

Elric's reply to Guthlac was careful. His uncle's only response was a slow expelling of breath through his nostrils as he turned away, pulling his wife with him.

He pushed his way through to a group of his own men whose guttural laughter was loud enough to drown the crackle to the fire-pit flames. His lady sank down upon a bench close by and turned her face away.

A boor, thought Rhianneth, after a king! With all his roughness Ida had still been royal. In this hall he had raised the Waes Haeil cup, had received the roar of loyalty from those sheltered beneath his roof. Now scavengers flocked here, dangerous scavengers who threw out insults and were not rebuffed.

'You did not give him my answer.' She turned to Elric. 'Will you let him insult me then, and do nothing?'

Elric too, gazed down the Hall. But his eyes were on the forlorn figure of Caldis, sitting alone amongst her husband's warriors.

'Until the funeral feast,' he answered softly.

Rhianneth's heart missed a beat. It was said like a vow and a threat combined, as metal is twisted together to forge a sharp sword.

*

204

A Bernician funeral feast was an affair for men. But, in the area cut off from the main hall by the carved screen of oak-wood, Rhianneth sat with Gwen and several Saxon ladies, to listen as men rose to speak of Ida's bravery, his kingly generosity, his cunning and his wisdom. Some were there only to honour Ida. Some, like pack-wolves, to be at the nerve centre of the imminent struggle for power.

Already the two camps had shown themselves in small incidents, vicious scuffles within the fortress. Now violence brooded over the mead-hall, rippled along the packed benches, scented the over-heated air so that even the dogs padding around the fire looked sideways and snarled.

Time passed. Rhianneth grew more uneasy. Elric had not appeared. Ida's great chair stood empty. Guthlac had not dared to claim it for his own. Not yet.

An old man had quavered out a poem in praise of Ida's wars with Outigern, when Elric came at last. Silence fell. Then Guthlac's voice roared gruffly, his sentences short, stabbing, angry.

'Guthlac says that Aethelric is late,' Gwen whispered. Her frightened eyes darted back and forth across the scene in the Hall. She was measuring the distance between her husband Hussa and the nearest of Guthlac's men.

'He says he wants Aethelric's pledge of loyalty. He wants it now. And that of the council . . .'

Rhianneth looked from Guthlac's anger-filled face to the armed strangers who sat near him. Fear fluttered through her like a night-moth. Guthlac's voice rumbled into silence. Then Elric spoke.

Gwen gazed throught he carved screen-wall, one plump hand trembling as it rested against the twisted serpentine shapes. The other ladies pressed close to see through the screen. Angry at not being able to understand the words thrown like weapons across the Hall, Rhianneth tapped Gwen's hand urgently.

'Not while I live, Elric says,' the girl responded. 'He is challenging Guthlac for the kingship. But why? The council have chosen!'

Have they? Rhianneth wondered. Or will they sway this way and that? Had Elric known that a battle was inevitable – that with Guthlac alive he would have no security?

'Now Guthlac is shouting that he and Ida beached the boats and fought together for this land! Ida has gone and he claims his brother's fortress, his right to rule the kingdom . . .'

Uproar filled the Hall, drowning Gwen's words. Benches were thrust back. Rival factions yelled at each other. Swords and scramasaxes flashed, unsheathed.

Fear grasped Rhianneth in earnest now. But the scene held her in horrid thrall and she could not move. She heard Elric's voice roar above the noise, and Guthlac's answering bellow of fury.

'Aethelric claims kingship by right of blood and the council,' said a low voice close to her ear. 'My husband says he will send him to Hel . . .'

Caldis stood beside her. The pale beautiful face was calm, her yellow hawk-eyes steady. Only the fingers of her right hand moved, turning round and round a narrow ring of silver on her left hand.

Pity tinged Rhianneth's admiration of the lady's control, as she stood alone amongst the wives of Elric's war-band. Even so, caution made her glance towards Caldis's braided belt. But there was no small dagger there, such as was favoured by many Bernician women.

At Gwen's gasp, her eyes flew back to the Hall in time to see Guthlac lunge forward, sword upraised. His followers rose to a man to defend him.

And suddenly in that packed Hall men were leaping, grappling, amidst a roar of oaths, the ringing of blade across blade. Blood stained the floor. Bright tapestries were spattered and rent.

'Hussa, Hussa, Hussa . . .' Gwen whispered, as if the sound of her husband's name hissing against the screen was a charm against hurt.

But Rhianneth's throat was too dry to speak, and Caldis made no move.

206

Slashing, thrusting with the savagery of men who knew their combat was mortal, Elric and Guthlac circled each other.

Guthlac was a man on fire. Fury coloured his face to match his flaming hair, gave him dangerous strength, as with a series of short, powerful onslaughts he slowly drove Elric backwards towards the screen.

Between their grunts of effort, the rasping breath, Rhianneth heard the high death-song of their iron blades. Her blood chilled.

Others came between them, and for a while they were out of sight. Noise filled her ears, a clamour which might have followed Cernunnos, the Lord of the Wild himself.

Her lips moved, soundlessly forming a pattern of words so ancient its origin was forgotten, its meaning obscure. Only its function remained. to create a protective sheath around the corn in the earth, the child in the womb, the warrior in battle.

The knot of men in front of the screen parted suddenly. She saw Guthlac's sword sweep in a great arc upwards, missing Elric so narrowly its sliced through the sleeve of his tunic as he twisted aside. Then his uncle was upon him, upraised weapon glinting down to deal a death blow. Rhianneth's breath stopped.

Swift as a cornered wolf, Elric spun about, thrust his sword straight and true into Guthlac's tensed body.

For an instant they stood still as figures of stone. Then Guthlac slowly sank to the floor, his own sword clattering down before him, blood frothing from his mouth.

Elric stood panting, wiped the running sweat from his face with his sleeve. Then he straddled Guthlac's body and lifted Dreamweaver, red-wet with blood, high into the air.

Rhianneth clenched her fist hard against her mouth to stop the scream that rose in her throat. She knew what he was about to do. With a rush of wind the blade swept downwards. Blood gushed now like a river undammed. Guthlac's body quivered as Elric bent and grasped the severed head by its flaming, bloodied hair.

Now Hussa was beside him. Holding his own gory sword, he roared above the clash of conflict one repeated phrase in Saxon. He heaved himself up on to a heavy table that still stood upright. A thunder of jubilation broke out as Elric tossed up into his brother's hands the still dripping head of Guthlac, drowning another sound that was half-groan, half-snarl, as Guthlac's men clawed back their fading strength and renewed their onslaught.

Suddenly a hand grasped Rhianneth's shoulder. She gave a scream of terror that shrilled out and was lost amidst the noise in the Hall.

'By Christos, Rhianneth, what are you doing here?' Lovan shouted into her face. 'Come away!'

His eyes went to Gwen, to the other women crowded in the small space. 'All of you, come away!'

Leaning heavily on a thick staff, his face grey with effort and his eyes bright with pain, Lovan looked like a messenger of vengeance and death. The women fled, although some, at least, had no idea what he said.

Rhianneth was shaking, her muscles clenched hard as iron. Lovan's arm came round her shoulders, pulled her close.

'You're not hurt, *cariad*?'

'No. Guthlac's dead.' Her voice choked in her throat. 'But his men – they are still fighting. Elric is slaughtering them!'

Lovan's hold tightened. He stared through the screen at the broken and bloody wreckage of Ida's proud mead-hall.

'Holy Mother of God . . . '

At that moment Idwal, captain of the Mithrasian guard, burst through the open doorway at their back, sword in hand. His cloak hung torn, his tunic darkened with blood. He stopped short when he saw them, lowered his sword till its point rested on the floor.

'This is no place for you, Lady Rhianneth.' He was breathing hard. 'I ran to your house searching for you, and to the Queen's Bower – '

'What of your men?' Lovan asked, 'Any dead, wounded?'

'All of us safe. We fought our way to the doors and got out.'

'You did not fight, then, against Guthlac?'

'What?' The word shot from Idwal's mouth, iron-hot with angry resentment. 'They wear no war-crests at a funeral feast! How could we tell friend from foe? To us they are all Saxon. You, sir, should not be out of your bed!'

He swung round and signalled to his men, who crowded the doorway. 'Help him to his house, and quickly. Gareth, stay with him. On your guard. And you, lady, come with me!'

The turmoil of battle still filled the Hall. But the heart of the conflict was now at the other end, where Guthlac's warriors had formed a tight shield-wall. Men leapt across the central fire-pit swinging their swords, others ran with deadly intent along the Hall's length to their comrades, scramasaxes ready in their hands. Rhianneth turned to go, and froze.

Within a small circle of warriors to the side of the Hall, Guthlac's wife Caldis stood before Elric, her hair loosed from its braids and falling freely down her back like an unwed maid's.

Rhianneth watched Elric hold out his hand and slowly pull Caldis into the shelter of his arms, his short shoulder-cloak swinging round her protectively. As her golden hair fanned out against his chest his lips moved in words that were lost in the noise around them.

Idwal was urging her away. When she looked briefly back again there were only warriors filling the Hall, some of them coming fast towards the screen.

'It's almost finished,' she heard Idwal say grimly. 'Not one of Guthlac's men will leave the Hall alive. That's a deadly kind of honour, isn't it?'

But she could not answer him. She stumbled through the doorway. The cool night air stung her face like a slap. Suddenly she felt drained, sick, and cold to the bone.

Victory was bought at a bitter cost. When Elric rode out with his brothers to his uncle's stronghold, he was able to take with him little more than half his war-band. Warriors of the council accompanied him, bearing Guthlac's body wrapped in fine scarlet cloth bordered on gold, as befitted Ida's brother. Under the eyes of these thanes Elric would offer war-gear, gold, and a place at his hearth, to any of Guthlac's men at Gefrin who would now swear allegiance to him.

'With Guthlac already dead,' Idwal had remarked cynically the previous night, 'how can they refuse?'

Lovan, his leg wound open again and seeping, his eyes hot with fever, said nothing. But Rolf shot a glance edged with contempt towards Idwal.

'If they desert their dead lord to serve the one who killed him,' he said thinly, 'will any man trust them again?'

'But Aethelric will offer – '

'That is custom. They cannot accept.'

Idwal gave an incredulous laugh. Civilised men, he protested, would never tolerate that iron battle-code, such brutal laws of honour!

Now, as Rhianneth watched Elric's cavalcade depart in a dawn mist that hung the trees with ragged banners she knew that death rode with them, hard as ice. But it was Idwal's remembered laugh that made her shiver, for within it she seemed to hear the distant crack of the Empire's cities falling before the barbarian onslaught like fat corn before the summer scythe.

Cold, miserable, she walked back to her house. The savagery of the struggle in the mead-hall haunted all her waking hours. That bloodied head swinging by its flaming hair from Elric's clenched fist! And Caldis, freed of her husband by means as bloody as any tale of revenge sung to the minstrel's harp. Had her pale beauty been the seed from which sprang the deep hatred between Elric and his uncle? Doubts, nebulous as the dawn mist shrouding the morning, darkened her spirits as she entered her house.

The fire was ashes and there was no hot water. Nothing simmered in the pot.

Shivering, white with cold, Alda crouched in a corner. When Rhianneth went to her, the girl flinched away.

'Alda?'

Then she saw the bruises, darkening across the girl's arms and face. The torn tunic. The bloody scratches on smooth bare shoulders. Horror ran through Rhianneth like a high cold wave.

'Alda?' she said again, and knelt beside her. 'What happened? Who did this?'

The girl fell weeping into her arms then. Rhianneth held her close, sick with the sense of animal violence that sprang up unfettered with every sharp-jagged word. Her memory swept uncontrolled back through the seasons of her girlhood to the moment when the robber had caught her by the pasture fence, and she herself had felt her world dissolve into an ancient terror.

'I went to the well for water . . .' Alda sobbed, 'although it was still dark. You . . . had been sitting up with Lovan and I wanted to be ready when you came . . .'

'Who was it, Alda?'

The girl shook her head, her face gleaming wet with tears. 'He came from behind, from somewhere . . . He dragged me into the old beacon tower. He hit me, he kept hitting me . . .'

The man had beaten her into silence. She could not describe him, save tht he had long hair and a moustache, and smelt of pig grease. And that, thought Rhianneth, could apply to most of the slaves and servants who had followed the council lords into the fortress since Ida's death.

She helped Alda into the big bed, gave her a drink and covered her with warm furs. Then she ran for help.

The mead-hall was silent, empty of life, the fire-pit grey with wood-ash. Along the side aisles lay the battle dead, cloaked together under tapestries torn down from the walls. Like tombstones, shields rested upright at their heads.

The Queen's Bower was crowded with wounded men. Some sat propped up, others lay groaning. Several looked near death. Although the door was wedged open to let in fresh air, the place stank of blood, sweat and sickness. Rhianneth's stomach churned as she searched quickly, desperately.

Gwen was not amongst the women working there, and those who were paused to watch Rhianneth suspiciously. The air was thick with the sharp smell of healing pastes, possets and potions. She had never offered any of her own precious store, for too close were the poisonous accusations of Wermund the priest; too many were those who still distrusted her. She read it in their eyes, in their superstitious gestures.

Near the doorway two old women crouched on either side of a wounded man, each holding the other's hand and grasping one of his to make an unbroken ring. Cunning women, the Saxons called them. Wise women, skilled in birth-coming and death-slipping.

She watched them sway, each in her own small circle, eyes closed, crooning a healing charm to help injuries mend. No different, Rhianneth told herself, heart pounding, from my grandmother . . .

But the charm-words were simple enough for her to translate, and they brought memories of the mead-hall rising up like nighmares.

'Bone to bone,
Blood to blood . . .'

Across the room, Wermund paused in his work to shoot a venomous look towards her. Retching, she backed away and ran along the narrow pathway leading out between the mead-hall and the Queen's Bower.

Oh, Caius! she cried silently; how could you leave me in this terrible place? I cannot bear it. No, not even for the Fellowship. Not even for you.

She leaned against the wall of a house to get her breath, calm her thoughts. Since the day she left her grandmother's house she had been adrift on an endless rushing stream, barely surviving the swirls and rock-strewn torrents. Like the flower-ball she had made for Cai to offer to the spirit of the stream, she thought wildly.

If Marcus had lived, if she had never known Cai, would she now have been travelling south-west into the Summer Country, towards a gentle courtship and a fine marriage with one of the sons of Constantine?

She closed her eyes, picturing one of the king's villas nestled in the soft green countryside. There would be children, learning, as she had, the universal tongue of the Empire, the civilised wisdom of Greece and Rome. There would be

dogs, like old Giff, sleeping in the sunshine instead of slavering as war-dogs at the heels of warriors. Long summer days
and the soft rain of winter. Safe, safe in the warm Summer
Land.

I must get back to Alda, she thought dazedly. Help her,
myself. Later I can raise the alarm, hunt the man down.

She pushed herself away from the wall and went to the well,
found the bucket lying on its side. As she carried it, full,
towards her own house, she met Idwal.

'Lady Rhianneth!'

He looked at her with as much astonishment as if she had
been carrying a live snake. Swiftly he took the bucket from
her, spilling a quarter of it, still staring at her. I must look as
strange as I feel, she thought.

Aloud she said, 'Alda has been attacked.' He continued to
stare blankly. 'She doesn't know him. He's probably a servant
of one of Ida's thanes . . .'

'Alda?' he repeated. Then, as if the words at last penetrated
his mind, he jerked into action. He dropped the bucket and
seized her arm. 'Rape? Here – in the fortress?'

His dark face turned ugly with anger. 'Christ's blood! What
kind of animals are they? The mead-hall is full of slaughterd
men and they've turned it into a glory-shrine while they go off
to kill some more! Ida's son inherits you as if you were family
property and now – ' he paused, breathing fast – 'now, even
your serving-maid is treated as a whore!'

Rhianneth's face whitened before the sudden force of his
fury. As if he saw for the first time that she was already half-
numbed with shock, realised the further stunning impact of
his words, his voice tightened into control.

'Come, lady, I'll get you home. See that you have help,
everything you need!'

At his demands people came running. The house filled
with softly exclaiming female voices, willing hands, the sweet
smell of herbs. Alda was bathed, her scratches and bruises
tended, her mind soothed by a healing potion.

At last, only Gwen sat on, quietly stitching narow strips of
linen for bandages, while her baby son Hrothgar played at her

213

feet with a string of coloured beads. Beneath the bed-furs, Alda slept.

Rhianneth's mind surged back and forth like a wild high tide. She could not keep still, but fidgeted restlessly round the small room.

Alda's attacker had not yet been found. The fortress slaves and servants had been questioned, to no effect.

Rolf had stormed up to the door in bright-eyed rage, his impotent distress on seeing Alda so great that Rhianneth wondered, not for the first time, if his fondness for her maidservant was deeper than she knew. Despite his Saxon name, Rolf was the son of a British slave-girl. If, as he so passionately wished, his unknown father had been one of Ida's hearthhorde, it showed neither in Rolf's looks or temperament. Small, lithe, dark, with an equal capacity for wild elation and black despair, he seemed all Celt. But his heart's core was Saxon, and that ruled his life. He had been born amongst them, had come as a small child in the boats from Deira. His loyalty was total, his only ambition to join Din Guaryrdi's army of spears.

Rhianneth swung restlessly back towards Gwen. Something about the way she sat so quietly sewing, head bent, was sharply reminiscent of Guthlac's demure wife, she of the hooded yellow eyes.

'The lady Caldis,' the words were out before she knew, 'she's still in Din Guaryrdi?'

Gwen stopped stitching. Her eyes moved sideways under the shielding lids.

'Why, yes,' she replied after a moment. 'Where else would she go? This was her home before she married Guthlac. Her parents are dead. She only has – '

'Elric?'

Gwen's cheeks flamed. She kept her head bent.

'I was about to say "her son". He is heir to Gefrin. She may make her home there again, after a while.'

'But for now she will stay here, in Din Guaryrdi?'

There was a long silence. Then Gwen sighed, swallowed, and put down her needlework.

214

'I know very little, Rhianneth. They – Caldis and Aethelric – were once in love and wanted to marry. He was seventeen and she a couple of years younger. But Guthlac wanted her, and her father gave her to him while Aethelric was on a summer war-trail with Ida into Rheged.'

She glanced up. 'That's all I know. Just a small love story, over and forgotten. The only one really happy was Guthlac. She gave him a son, a bride-night child. He'd been married twice before, to barren wives. You can imagine what that did to his pride – when Ida already had four strapping sons!'

'Yes, indeed,' Rhianneth murmured. But her mind was busy forging links between Gwen's words, iron hard. A child well within the year. Two wives and no children in all the years before. And no child afterwards?

Gwen hastily gathered her needlebox and swung her baby up into her arms, saying she would be back in a little while. Then she caught the look on Rhianneth's face, and stopped.

'What you are thinking,' she said, her voice low, 'no one has ever dared to say. Guthlac would have killed her, and the child. Now that he's dead and Aethelric betrothed in this great alliance, you may be sure Caldis will tolerate no slur that seeks to make her son merely a bastard sprig, no more than several young heroes of Ida's hearth-horde.'

She held her child closer. 'Why should it bother you, Rhianneth? Hussa has bastards all over the countryside. But I'm his true wife. My son is his heir. Nothing can alter that.'

She left, her face troubled. Rhianneth sat on beside the sleeping Alda. She thought of big, laughing Hussa raising his cup and foot-stamping in the Hall; swinging his sword around the stuffed straw-men in the practice yard; throwing up his baby son to make him laugh, or lifting plump little Gwen way off her feet to plant kisses on her down-turned face, Yes, she could imagine Hussa tumbling willing girls in any handy bush or cow-byre.

But Elric . . . it was not the same. He had loved Caldis then, and, from the way he looked at her now, loved her still. It was indeed a tale worthy of the minstrel's harp, its eternal theme of love and parting curving down to complete the ancient shape with an act of revenge. That slow-burning anger she had sensed within Guthlac – was it really fuelled by his claims to the kingship? Or had he known, deep hidden within himself, that he had neither his wife's love nor a true-born son of his own flesh?

As for Elric, with one fatal blow in the mead-hall he had secured his kingdom, and freed his lost love.

Silent and grey, the dawn scene on the Wall swam before Rhianneth's eyes. A girl sick with love for another man, Elric had taunted her. A blade-thin sliver of anger shot through her, remembering his strong ruthless face in the dim dawn-light as he derisively flung to the winds her secret love for Cai.

Was his own youthful pain really still strong enough to sour him, even after five years? She could not believe it. No man with his arrogance would allow a woman, even one with hair of gold and untamed falcon eyes in her madonna-face, so much power to wound him.

Guthlac's men at Gefrin gave no allegiance to Aethelric. They carried the body of their lord into his stronghold and barred the way with a solid shield-wall. Elric's war-band, the warrior lords of the council beside them, fought their way in, killing all the armed defenders. Guthlac's servants fled as, with the fortress stormed at last, the bodies of the slain were piled around Guthlac's and Gefrin burned to the ground. Grim and grey-faced, the war-band returned.

Rhianneth went to make her complaint about the attack on Alda, and found Elric alone. A line of ugly bruises ran from beneath his eye to the point of his jaw where a sword had slashed across the linked-mesh of his helmet mask. Blood-stained linen bound his sword arm.

'Rhianneth – ' he cut abruptly through her words, and there was no welcome in the look he gave her – 'I've just come from Gefrin. Half my men are dead or wounded – '

'My maid-servant was beaten and raped within your own walls, Elric! She is Saxon, like you! Don't you even care – '

'You are not listening to me.' His voice softened dangerously. 'Word has come that Outigern's son Morcant is burning settlements within our borders. He's wreaking havoc in revenge for Guthlac's western raids, and we are so much weakened that I – '

'A girl in my service, under my protection! I demand that you – '

'What in Hel do you expect me to do?' he roared, startling her into mouth-opened silence. 'Ride round Bernicia shouting vengeance because of a tumbled slave-girl?'

He turned away, letting out a string of Saxon oaths from between clenched teeth as he eased his injured arm into a more comfortable position. Rhianneth stood, indecisive. Then without answering she walked to the door. Not for the world would she humble herself before him.

Julia is right, she thought bitterly. These Saxons are as harsh as their remote gods. Without mercy. They had not even been softened by luxury, as the Romans had, into a smooth cat-like cruelty that hid its claws in silken sheaths. They were like the wolves that roamed their forests and hill-slopes, openly howling for blood.

In the corner Elric's helmet and chain-mail shirt hung gleaming and full of menace on a cross-pole. Her courage shrank, as she imagined facing him in the raw, sweating reality of battle. She had been a fool to come asking for his help, to place herself in the position of supplicant. Idwal was doing all that could be done.

'Was she a virgin?'

Rhianneth stopped, her back to him. 'I don't see what . . .' She drew a deep breath, steadying her voice. 'Yes.'

'Not that it matters. It happened under my roof, so I'll pay you wergeld anyway. For damaged goods.'

Slowly she turned, looked straight at him. His tunic was unlaced from throat to waist and she saw the silver flash of an amulet against his chest. The hammer of Thunor, mighty god of battle and storm. Elric was his warrior . . . and a barbarian whose mind she would never understand.

Against the pallor of his face his eyes were storm-dark with pain. But easily she crushed down compassion, for every word he uttered spoke of his own unrelenting savagery, a code of

217

honour untouched by the gentle light of the star of Bethlehem or by any other pathway to pity. He lived by a harsh masculine creed, accepted uncaringly a world made for men.

More powerfully now than she had thought possible, she hated him.

'Wergeld . . . man-money?' she asked, her voice cold. 'Tell me, Elric – what is a slave worth?'

'Whatever you want. Hel's Gate, Rhianneth – can't we settle this later?'

He looked ill, death-weary, as she left. She did not return. But several times she sent Rolf with a cup spiked with drops of her grandmother's potent pain-slayer. From him, she learned that Caldis was now tending Elric.

'You should be there, lady,' Rolf told her, his young brow creased with concern. 'It is your place. You are promised to Aethelric.'

'He doesn't want me there,' she answered carelessly. 'And I'm needed here with Alda and Lovan. Besides, he's not much hurt. The lady Caldis can give him all he needs.'

Din Guaryrdi honoured the warriors who died with Guthlac in Ida's mead-hall, sending them to Waelhaell together with its own dead heroes in one immense funeral pyre, built around the wedding-fire timber out on the headland. But though the fire's fierceness threw a glowing red pathway across the sea and blotted out the stars, no blaze of glory could burn away the hideous memories, the welter of blood that still reeked across Rhianneth's mind enough to sicken her.

When the council lords knelt to swear allegiance to Elric, each one pressing the hilt of his sword to his lips, it was the fearful magic running beneath the rough splendour of the ceremony that made Rhianneth's breath catch in her throat. Some force, that made old men feel young again and young men burn to follow their new king to adventures, conquests and rich booty.

She thought of Llywarch's court beyond the grey hills; the hates, fears, jealousies and crosscurrents of ambition that swirled through that citadel of Maximus. With a boy king, its

218

great lords divided between the queen's party and the Fellow-ship of Caer Melot – Mithrasia was in powerful need for sure of a strong ally to keep Urien's army at bay.

Elric held out his own sword, gleaming flat across his open hands, to make his vow of service to Bernicia. If any trace of wound-weakness lingered, it did not show. In his height and breadth of shoulder, his heavy cloak of deep red lined with dark fur in thick folds about him, he was the epitome of a Saxon warrior king. Ah, yes, Rhianneth told herself, his friendship was the strong bulwark Mithrasia needed against her treacherous northern neighbours!

Yet, watching him, feeling his physical power and the *mana* that he held like life-blood for his people, a cold finger touched her heart, bringing with it a memory, a name, out of the past.

Vortigern.

No, not the same. Reason stifled the thought before it grew enough to make her afraid. So very long ago it was, since Vortigern made his fatal alliance with the Saxon Hengist and married his daughter Rowen. The cold weight of all those years lay between what was happening here and now, and the eruption of fire and slaughter as that old alliance broke and Hengist harried the land from sea to sea.

Bernicia was undeniably a kingdom, not just a marauding wolf's lair. A small kingdom, clinging to the coastline and in as much need of friends as was Mithrasia across the hills. The priest Lucius had cried 'Vortigern' in a last throw against the alliance, because his heart was with the enemies of Caer Melot. Would she, now, be swayed into doubt by so nebulous a thing as a drift of alien magic?

But magic, her grandmother had once said, was the strongest force in the world, for it held in thrall not the bodies but the minds of men . . .

Resolutely Rhianneth crushed the thought away and fixed her eyes upon the scene before her, as the last of Elric's thanes sheathed his sword and stood to one side.

Caldis came forward, bringing her fair-haired little son to kneel before Elric amidst murmurs of approval.

But when Caldis paused before her, with head inclined just

enough for politeness, Rhianneth's hard-won confidence slipped. Caldis was so slender and tall, so palely beautiful in her dress of creamy-soft wool, she once again reminded Rhianneth of the Christ-child's holy Mother.

The Saxon ladies wore fine dresses in the mead-hall and their craft-wrought jewellery glittered with every movement. But perfume was precious to them and they had no cosmetics such as those to be bought in Mithrasia. When Rhianneth shadowed her eyelids with soft green and touched her lips with red, rosy as Eve's apple, she told herself with a touch of defiance that though she lived amongst barbarians she was still a citizen of the Roman Empire, and should be seen as such.

Yet now, with her skin still honey-toned from the summer sun and with Julia's exotic colours tinting her eyes and lips, Rhianneth felt like Cleopatra confronted by the irreproachable wife of one of the Roman Senate.

If only I had my mother's height, she thought, and her glowing mane of fox-red hair! Before that, Caldis would have paled like a candle in the sun. As it was, Rhianneth felt her own dark elfin beauty elusive, her cosmetics tawdry, beside the golden purity of this northern lady.

She raised her chin a little higher. I am Elidyr's daughter, she thought fiercely, in direct descent from Magnus Maximus. Maximus, who had won an Empire and worn the purple! Proud indeed she could stand before this pale widow of a Saxon sea pirate.

Then, for a second, Caldis lifted her careful veil of lashes. There, in the yellow depths of her eyes blazed something that for a crystal-thin sliver of time belied completely the gentle calm of her face. Then it was gone.

As the woman walked away, the child's hand clasped in hers, Rhianneth recognised that she had yet another enemy. Not for what she had done, or thought, or felt. But because of what she was. Queen Myffan's jealous eyes had looked through her and seen the shade of her dead, laughing mother. Lucius the priest had recognised in her the weakening of his power over the young king and the triumph of the Fellowship.

Here in Din Guaryrdi Wermund saw her as a living, poisonous link between his folk and those who were close kin to their most bitter enemies.

And Caldis? It needs little effort to find the root of her hostility, thought Rhianneth wryly, when I stand here at the side of the man she loved once, and loves still.

So many enemies crowding round her, deadly blossoms of that wild autumn sowing so many years past; and with the fruit yet to come, and the gathering time . . .

A voice spoke close beside her. Elric held out his hand, the movement making the jewelled chain about his shoulders flicker with kindling fires. He seemed bigger, more dangerous than ever, and she caught her breath, tried to gather her thoughts.

'My lady?' he repeated. She put her hand in his, feeling the warm strength of bone and sinew, the hard callouses that came from gripping a battle-sword.

'Bernicia is one again,' he said quietly. 'With one king, like a well-wrought blade. When we've licked our wounds and got our breath, Urien shall feel the edge of it!'

There was a shadowed tenseness in his face, a few beads of perspiration on his forehead. So, Rhianneth thought, even of Elric have the last grim weeks taken a toll, though he hides it as fiercely as any soldier of old Rome! Yet neither grief for Ida nor battle-weariness from his struggle with Guthlac has quenched the spring of his energy, nor weakened the arrogance that is a part of him. Already his thoughts leap across time to winter's end and the routing of Urien. Obviously he expects to win!

With reluctance she acknowledged a kind of brutal gallantry of spirit, such as had carried Maximus into Rome and Arturius to victory at Badon.

But even that bright link could not bridge the dark cleft that yawned between the poorest civilised Briton of the Roman Empire, and a Saxon king. Rhianneth had not forgotten the attack on Alda, nor Elric's answer. The coffer of coins he had sent her had a value far in excess of anything she could have anticipated, but it only served to further outrage her sense of justice. For the attacker had not been found, and no searchers had been sent to the strongholds of Elric's thanes. She had been tempted to toss back the coins in a gesture of contempt. But some part of her that was of her mother's people, the earthy thriftiness of her grandmother, prevented her. Instead she handed the box to Alda.

'Lady, I can't take this!' The maid-servant's eyes grew wide. 'What would I do with it?'

'Keep it, Alda. Have it as a marriage dower.'

Alda turned away, her face troubled. 'Slaves don't marry, lady.'

'If ever you asked, I would set you free . . .'

'I've nowhere to go. Nothing of my own. Before long I would be a slave again, with another mistress.'

'Not if you married Rolf.'

A slow flush crept up the girl's face, but she made no answer. Rolf, Ida's slave – to whom did he belong now? Elric, Rhianneth supposed. Would he free him, if she asked? Her stomach revolted at the thought of going ever again as a supplicant, and she pushed the idea to the back of her mind.

'Whatever you want, it can be made possible, Alda,' she said aloud, with more confidence than she now felt. 'I will make it so.'

But Alda shook her head, eyes bright with unshed tears. 'No, don't, lady! I don't want any man. I can't marry Rolf. Something in me freezes when he touches me. I'd be no fit wife for him. I am spoiled.'

Spoiled? Rhianneth's eyes flashed from Alda's pathetically bowed head to the box of shining coins. Elric's wergeld. For damaged goods. O Gods, yes! The world was ruled by men, for men. That was the natural way of things, and as life grew more dangerous the rule tightened.

But she remembered Julia, weeping for the lost years, and set her teeth as bright anger ran through her. No man will break my spirit, she vowed. No, neither through love nor fear! And no one will entirely rule me either – nor any of those dear to me. Not while I have strength and wit enough to claw back at life!

Now, she looked up into Elric's face and smiled, unaware that anger had brought a flush to her cheeks, made her eyes glow like honey-wine in firelight. His hand tightened over hers and he drew a swift breath, but not by the flicker of a muscle did his face change.

They walked together through the gathering, and out into a clear space near the beacon tower. Elric lifted his face to the sky, ragged with wind-blown clouds.

'Winter.' He took a deep breath of the cool air. 'Long nights and dark days.'

Then he looked down at her. 'Perhaps you will keep me amused by speaking for me the words the Romans wrote in the books you have? I would like to hear of Odus, and the great sea voyage that lasted ten years.' His free hand came under her chin, fingers framing her face. 'That is,' he said softly, 'if we can find nothing else to do.'

So, he had seen her smile as a challenge, and had picked it up. She had always known it would take more than a smile to put Elric off his guard. He would not easily forget the insult she had flung at him in the sea cave.

'If you mean Odysseus the Greek,' she replied cuttingly, jerking aside her head to free herself, 'his story is long, his adventures many. I'm sure they will outlast a Bernician winter.'

His eyebrows rose. 'Oh, I hope not. That might try even my patience.'

They were circling each other like fighters in the arena, throwing not weapons but words, every one double-edged. Suddenly weary, she turned her head away to gaze up at the gaunt ruin of the beacon tower.

Elric watched her, silenced. Out here in daylight her youth was very apparent, from the pure curve of her neck under the small pointed chin to the smooth unblemished brow with its narrow band of gold imprisoning her dark hair. He had a sudden desire to wipe away the scarlet colour from her lips, to taste again their soft naked sweetness as he had in the cave with the sea surging and rumbling below.

Then he saw a longing in her face as she stared up at the old

Roman stone-tower; a longing that was not for him, that shut him out as completely as if she had slammed shut a door between them. His hands curled into fists at his sides and the soft oath that escaped him brought her head round.

'How many warning signals must have flamed from here to relay down the coast, and inland too.' She made an angry gesture towards the dark bulk of the tower. 'Maybe to bring troops from the nearest fortress on the Wall, or from Eboracum. All for nothing, in the end. Only this, and ruined forts, and a few dreams, remain.'

Bitterness tinged the sadness in her face. ' "Why do we aim so high" ', she quoted, ' "when time must foil our brave archery?" '

'One of your Roman poets?'

She bit back tears. 'Yes. But he's dead. They all are.'

'His words live. They hold a great truth.'

She shot him a resentful look, half suspecting mockery. Today she was tired of the game, the battle always between them. Marcus was too near. The pastures of her childhood and the warm walls of home flowed into her spirit and filled her soul.

'Give us time to master the art of writing, and our saga-masters will unlock such a word-hoard from Engleland as will outlast Fimbulwinter itself – and put glory into the hearts of the Gods at Ragnarok!'

Elric's soft words scarcely touched her mind. Then his hand closed on her arm. 'That is why we aim so high, Rhianneth. For that brief wisp of glory as our arrow-tip catches golden fire from the sun. It is all we have. A thread of gold in the web of Fate, to light the dark of that last bitter winter when the wolf Fenrir devours the sun and the stars fall; to put strength into our Gods as they ride into the final battle against monsters and frost-giants on the cold plain of Vigrid!'

She stared at him, half astonished, half appalled. Threads of gold tossed up from time's beginning, to await Ragnarok when the great Gods, doomed themselves, must yet destroy the forces of chaos so that their sons might survive, and the world struggle towards a new beginning. A bond between men and Gods in the fight between good and evil, darkness and light; a bond, close as that between lord and liege-man. It gave heroic meaning to the warrior's death, the poet's striving.

But when she thought of those dead warriors riding out of Waelhaell into oblivion with their gods so that the armies of the night should not prevail, and of the kin-given glimmer that lit their way, it was such a bleak ice-edged picture, twilit and terrible, that a chill ran over her.

'Real Gods don't die.' she said, 'They live forever. That's why they are Gods.'

'Nothing lives forever, Rhianneth. Not even the Gods.'

As he spoke, suddenly she was a child again. Held close by Marcus, seeing the inexplicable pain in his face as he stared beyond her towards her grandmother. Even kings die, Rhianneth ...

With an effort she remembered their prayers together before the picture of the Christos and his holy Mother. Forever and ever . . . Marcus had said then. And Grandmother, with her dark hooded eyes, tracing for her the endless spiral of time with a sharp stick on the hard trodden earth of her old round house ...

Yet – had not her grandmother, who knew nothing of the ways of the Saxon people, whispered to her once of a battle on a vast plain, when the Gods should fall?

She shivered. Elric unpinned his cloak and threw it round her shoulders. The dark fur lining was warm from his body. Gratefully she snuggled into its comforting protection.

'We must see that you have some really warm clothes,' he said, 'before winter roars in from the north. Up here, the wind off the sea has a bite like a whetted scramasax . . .'

Despite her darkling thoughts, a small smile of amusement curved her lips. 'You think of everything in terms of weapons and fighting!'

Their eyes met, and his hands stilled in the act of fastening the cloak-pin.

'That is my function in life, to defend Bernicia. If ever I tire of battle, be sure that Urien will throw us back into the sea!'

'And what is my function, Elric – apart from producing sons to take your place when you grow too old, too feeble, to fight?'

For a moment he did not answer but watched her narrowly, trying to read in her face whether her question was asked seriously, or in jest, or in the mock seductive vein of her earlier smile.

'You must guard my interests when I am away. Give me comfort when I'm here. Teach our children to read so that your Roman poet's words may even outlive the Gods.' Unexpectedly he grinned. 'Make sure the war-band's tunics are patched and darned . . .'

That night was given over to celebrating the coming of the new king, and a joyful optimism surged like a wild tide through the fortress.

Wearing the jewelled girdle that was her betrothal gift and glittering with as many of Elidyr's jewels as she could decently pile on, Rhianneth carried the waes-haeil cup to Elric. The laughter in the Hall died as he took it from her. For a heartbeat's length he hesitated, as if Ida's ghost muttered close by. Then he drank and raised the cup high, his words bringing reassuring thunder back from his people.

Back in her seat once more Rhianneth ate little, but sipped mead from a polished silver goblet and gazed beyond the fire's glow into the dancing shadows at the outer edges of the hall. The gift of Rhiannon, her grandmother used to call it, the tawny essence she distilled from each summer's flowering. Just a few drops had brought a calmness to Rhianneth, slowed her racing thoughts and unsteady emotions.

She watched Idwal swirling his drink round his goblet, his dark face closed and brooding. Since the night of Guthlac's death he had changed. His old suspicious unease in the company of the Saxons had returned in full and amidst the laughing company around him he remained remote, watchful.

On the other side of the fire Elric sat in the king's chair. Without antagonism, Rhianneth saw his glance fall and linger on the beautiful regal figure of Caldis, her long braids falling over her breasts like plaited ropes of pure gold. For why should I care, she thought, if he loves her still – if I am just a means to an end? Am I not myself using this marriage merely to secure our northern borders, fulfilling my vow to the shades of Arturius's Caer Melot?

A log moved in a shower of sparks, sending hot light slanting across Elric's hair and his hard, handsome face. Momentarily she closed her eyes and was back in the sea-cave, in his arms. Join with me, he had said, and I will build you such a fortress that all the powers of darkness will find it unassailable!

A double kingdom for my unborn sons, she thought, Bernicia and Deira. And the Mithrasian alliance would reach across the island, straddling Rome's great Wall like a giant. Who of Caer Melot's enemies then would dare stand against the combined power of the Dragon and the Wolf?

But those were dreams. Disturbing, exciting dreams with which, she now realised, Elric had sought to seduce her. He had wanted the betrothal bond tightened before Guthlac came to Din Guaryrdi or the messenger arrived from Llywarch. To make quite sure of the Mithrasian marriage by taking her, there on the sea-cold floor of the cave.

Like any harlot bought with promises. Like her mother, bought by Elidyr with jewels and luxuries.

Elric's motives had been hidden, then. But she had once smelled the animal tang of murderous lust on the robber in her own quiet pasture, had dreamed bitter dreams out of an ache of longing for Cai, and now some instinct for survival – muted in her mother by the high spring tide of womanhood – sang strongly in Rhianneth. Nothing will I give willingly, she vowed silently. Not my body, nor my mind. Not until I stand safe within unassailable shield-walls of honour and trust.

A minstrel began to play, the sweet notes of his harp rising to die somewhere amongst the shadowed rafters. With her grandmother's potion slipping along her veins, Rhianneth fell to dreaming as she used to dream when a child, isolating herself from her surroundings with an old, practised ease that once used to set Olwen's temper flaring.

The densely-carved supporting timbers of the Hall, the

weapon-hung walls – bare now of their torn and bloodied tapestries – dissolved. In her mind stone columns soared, painted walls opened imaginary windows upon sylvan scenes. Dark pools of water cooled the air, and she walked through the imagined gardens of old Rome.

Then slowly, the childhood fantasies changed, became dreams which held some substance of a past reality. She knelt in wet grass, and Cai was filling her arms with sweet yellow meadow flowers.

'She is your stream . . .' he said, and put warm hands round hers to lay a blossom-ball on the water. The delicate offering swirled away with the stream towards the distant sea, far from the quiet meadows of its flowering. Then Cai's lips were touching her cheek, claiming the kinship kiss which had ended her childhood. Her dreaming died on a spear of pain, and the harp's voice trembled into silence.

Gwen smiled beside her, wearing beads of red amber, her eyes fixed on Hussa who was attempting his favourite trick of balancing one stemmed wooden cup within another and pouring mead into the topmost one till it overflowed like a golden fountain. Shouts of encouragement and laughter accompanied his efforts, the weather-tanned faces relaxed and friendly in the warm glow of the firelight.

But Rhianneth's eyes wandered behind the long tables to the dark outer edges of the Hall where shields and masked helmets hung, and a spear-rack was filled with grey-tipped weapons. Near it, the skull and antlers of a stag threw a monstrous shadow across the Hall, like the watching presence of an ancient God.

Rhianneth shivered. Here, in this hall, one might dream for a little while amidst warmth, light, laughter. But always within sight were harsh reminders of the dangerous world outside. How close within herself she must hold those frail dream-seeds she carried! For now was the time of the hunters, of the wolf and the raven, when nothing grew.

CHAPTER 8

Rhianneth crossed the open space where hens scratched at the trodden earth and the odours of sheep and pigs mingled with cooking-pot smells from the houses and the mead-hall kitchen. She climbed up to where the wooden ramparts reared high above the old stone walls, making a platform that ringed the fortress, with an out-jutting thatched shelter below for animals brought in for winter's siege.

Here only the sound and smell of the sea pervaded the air. She flung her new fur cloak around her shoulders and stood watching the white breakers dash into foam against the rock islands, with the coastline of Bernicia fading into mist on either side. The wind was seeded with ice and dark cloud turned the sea a sullen grey, but she found a strange comfort in the height and loneliness, in the endless swirling of the sea and the far soft sound of it.

Only when rain began to spatter in earnest, did she reluctantly turn to go. By the time she reached the bottom of the steps rain was sweeping across the fortress like a grey curtain. She darted under the animal shelter where a few sheep bleated. Catching her breath, she leaned back against the tall wattle-fence dividing the space and pushed away her dripping hair.

Running feet, gasps that turned to panting laughter, indicated that other people had found shelter beneath the ramparts. Rhianneth straightened, hidden behind the frail barrier fence. She still felt ill at ease with many of Ida's people.

They began to speak. She tensed. It was Elric, and with him was the lady Caldis. She heard, too, the high piping of Caldis's little son, Brand. His mother's voice, hushing him. Then Caldis spoke again, this time in the British tongue.

'The child won't understand us. Guthlac would not have a wealas slave or servant in the house for fear of a dagger in his back or poison in his meat.'

'Caldis . . . ' Elric said slowly, as if the word was dragged from him, 'let it be. The marriage is pledged. It is done.'

There was a small silence. 'I can be to you anything you

want, Elric. As I was, once. I was always merry when you were so, do you remember? I never wept when you went off on the war-trails. My blood is your blood. I have no kinship with the wealas enemy!'

Above the thudding of her heart, Rhianneth heard the child begin a thin singing chant in Saxon, his voice fading a little as if he moved away from them.

'She has powers to bind men to her – I know it!' Caldis's voice trembled now. 'Some dark magic. I have heard that she holds her cousin, King Llywarch's envoy, in thrall –'

'Don't, Caldis! Caius Caprilius is a friend I hold in honour.'

'Honour! What do they know of honour? They are all cunning, treacherous. Even the great Artur of whom they now boast in song – they turned on him like wolves and destroyed! Ah, Elric – keep Ida's spear-bond if you must. But marry Llywarch's sister, and you'll take a serpent into your bed!'

Though rain trickled coldly from her wet hair over her face Rhianneth dared not move, could not even cover her ears though she felt sick with fear of what more might be said. It was as if some malicious God had arranged a reversal of her dawn meeting with Cai on the Wall, and she was now the eavesdropper. She knew their story. She had no desire now to witness the crumbling of Caldis's careful dignity, or the raw pain that lay beneath Elric's arrogance. Yet having heard this much, she was terrified of discovery.

'By all the gods, Caldis – you know I loved you!' Elric's words were jagged, his voice sharp-edged. 'For you, once, I would have stormed the walls of Asgard! If you had fled Gefrin and come to me then – '

'You know I could not!' her voice rose. 'I was already pregnant. I would not have my child made bastard!'

'I know,' Elric said more softly, his words muffled as if he pulled Caldis close against him. 'I knew it then, in my saner moments. Guthlac would have had us killed if he could, we would have been outlawed by the council. It was never possible. Your were right to safeguard Brand, to stay quiet. And I – ' he drew a quick breath – 'I was lucky to have Hussa at my side, dragging me away to spread fire and havoc amongst the enemy instead of riding like a madman to Gefrin to try for Guthlac's head!'

'Guthlac is dead. I am free – '

'Ida is dead. I am king.'

His voice remained soft. Yet some strand woven within the words gave them menace. 'You once shut me out, Caldis. Denied me our son. I thought they – your father and Guthlac – had beaten you into submission. Then you told me you had agreed because of the child you had just conceived. Because then he would be heir to Gefrin, not bastard born to one of Ida's sons. A son already out somewhere amongst the enemy, who might have been slain before the summer's end – or any summer's end. Ah, Caldis!' He went on at her low cry of protest. 'I've told you – you were right. But as your responsibility was then to Brand, so mine is now to Bernicia.'

'Are you saying these things to wound me, to punish me?' Her voice was sharp with anguish. 'I was fifteen, Elric! Guthlac had wanted me for months, the marriage settlements were already made although I did not know it. I was beside myself with worry and fear – how could I help but be persuaded by my mother that what I did was best for the family, for the child – for me! That once I was lady of Gefrin and the child born, all the pain would begin to fade. But in all those five years, Elric, I never stopped wanting you, loving you!'

'Five long years. Years of clinging to this great rock with Outigern hammering at our gates; quick skirmishes, bloody battles crashing through the forests. Living off the land, sleeping under the sky with nothing but a bag of dried meat and a couple of flat cakes if we were lucky. You were safer at Gefrin.'

Caldis began to speak again, swiftly, passionately. But he cut across her words. 'My dear, you are wrong. I am no longer the boy who rode with you across the sands, beating the tide at Metcaud. You don't know the man I have become. Now, I'm a king, and must act like one. I've sworn before Woden that I'll make the northern rulers tremble before Bernicia! But power, Caldis, is useless if it crumbles with my death. I want my sons to claim as their birthright not only Bernicia, but Deira and

Mithrasia too! Three kingdoms into one! Who then will dare raise arms against the Englisch north of the Humber?'

'You talk like an eagle. But that girl is just a pretty caged bird – '

'Whose blood-line goes back to Rome. I need this marriage to tie Bernicia's princes into that line. Llywarch is a boy ruled by his mother. More suited to join their priests than father-sons. It is his sister who will bring Mithrasia into our hands.'

Rhianneth froze with shock. She heard Caldis begin to cry softly.

'I cannot bear that you should marry her, Elric! I cannot bear to think of you kissing her, touching her, taking her . . .'

The child cried out then, frightened by his mother's tears. Elric's voice deepened, murmured something in Saxon.

Rhianneth crouched back against the woven fencing. She watched them walk back through the still-spitting rain. But not for a long time could she force her own limbs to move. Then, unthinking, drenched and shivering with cold, she ran straight to Lovan.

He was asleep. Rolf sat beside the bed, quietly whittling a piece of wood to make a bobbin for thread. He nodded reassuringly, smiling faintly. But Rhianneth saw the fever-sweat that beaded Lovan's face and her heart sank, distress for him rushing to join the tumult already in possession of her.

Lovan was still weak, his wound slow to heal. The only real remedy was time, she knew that. But she ached with a helpless longing to see him stand without help, to watch him gentle the stable horses with strong brown hands once more.

'Where is Alda?' She controlled her voice with an effort. She could not add to Lovan's burden of pain.

It was as if a shutter came down, darkening Rolf's face. 'On the beach. The fishing boats are in, with a good catch.'

Once outside, she held herself still for a moment, taking a deep calming breath. She forced her steps to a normal pace, went to her house and changed her cloak, fumbling with stiff fingers at the strong brooch pin. Her mind was a cold confusion into which thoughts dropped like icy rain.

Watching the Saxons ride into Mithrasia she had felt a

flicker of fear, sensed a darkness in them beneath their light hair and bright garments. Even when they roistered in their own rough fortress, laughing and fighting, tossing down barley-beer and honey-wine like water, it was there. A strange coldness buried deep, that gave them the calculating patience of the hunting wolf shadowing its prey.

Ida had grown old, tired, fighting his long wars against Outigern, and glad enough of Mithrasian friendship. Their grain and cattle for his spears against Urien, with marriage to seal the bond. Cai's alliance with Ida had been well made.

But Ida was dead, and Elric was young, strong and – he had seen Mithrasia. Seen the frailty of her luxury, the vulnerability of her faded glory.

Rhianneth's breath caught in her throat. She leant for a steadying moment against the door-post, trying to grasp her thoughts, gather them together.

Already Elric had shown himself ruthless, murderous. Now she knew him to be in thrall to nothing save ambition, ruled by nothing but his own cool reason. He intended to raise a new Empire, through marriage and by conquest, and not even Caldis's golden beauty could divert him from his path, a path which she had learned from his own lips would end in a half-Saxon prince in the fortress of Maximus, ruling Mithrasia. His son, she thought, trembling – and mine.

Cai would not pay that price. Not even to annihilate the enemies of Caer Melot.

Hard on the heels of that thought came others, colder still. Her eyes closed in horror against a vision of opposing armies battling across the countryside, squatting in the towns. The whole north at war. And Cai, his dream shattered and his blackest nightmare reality! For how long could the city stand in the teeth of such a wind? It would either be swallowed up into the maw of kinsmen like Urien, those enemies of Arturius – or taken by Elric's Saxons.

Engles, she corrected herself, not Saxons. And they call their little kingdoms with their ever-shifting boundaries, Engleland. They are truly one folk, she thought fearfully, and

233

one day they will know it, and that day will be black indeed for my own people. For they do not want our cities. Rome means little to them, or our way of life. What they want is our land. They want to roll their Engleland over our ruins till it stretches from sea to sea.

Blindly she pushed aside the door and took deep breaths of the rain-dashed air. Gradually the cold dread that gripped her began to release its hold.

I'm being stupid she told herself. Colouring this with dyes too deep for the cloth. Whatever Elric's ambitions for the future may be – the truth today is that Bernicia is a tiny kingdom clinging precariously to its sea-edged lands and facing formidable enemies. Why, only days ago Urien plundered their territory and burned their western settlements! Elric will find it hard enough to keep his part of the bond without being driven into the sea, to even survive long enough to keep the northern kings occupied!

Calmer now, she thought, I'll go down to the beach and find Alda. We'll talk together and walk a little, and watch the fishers unloading their catch. Alda had been hurt and badly frightened by her attacker, and her abrupt rejection of Rolf's love had wounded him as deeply. He had withdrawn into proud remoteness. Yet under the fiercely protective kindness of the fortress women Alda's natural buoyancy of spirit was returning. Born Saxon, though she had lived as a slave amongst Britons since childhood, the belief of her people in the implacable power of fate was deeply imbedded in her. What could not be fought had to be endured, and with as much grace and gallantry as could be mustered.

And that, Lovan had ruefully told Rhianneth once after cursing the uselessness of his wounded leg, gave them some edge in war, in life itself. To look at fate with a level eye and neither be crushed by despair nor dizzy with elation. Yes, Alda would give her revelations regarding Elric their due weight, and no more.

As she left the house Idwal appeared. He came straight towards her, breathing hard.

'Lady, the messenger is back from Llywarch,' he said. 'Aethelric is waiting for you. Now.'

For a moment she could only stare at him blankly. 'In the mead-hall?'

But she swayed as she spoke and Idwal's eyes sharpened. 'Are you not well?'

Rhianneth bit her lip, seized by dread now the moment had come to know whether this marriage would go ahead blessed by Llywarch and the Fellowship. And Cai.

'Would you tell me something, Idwal?'

'If I can, Lady Rhianneth.'

'What do you really think of all this? What do you hope Llywarch's answer is?'

He hesitated. 'The truth?'

She nodded. For a bare instant in the dark depths of his eyes, something flamed. 'Then I'll tell you what I told Lovan and that boy Rolf, the day they burned Gefrin.'

In his face, suddenly naked of its tight control, was something that unknowingly she had sensed in him since the morning they had left Mithrasia. Something more than dislike, more than unease.

'Lady, I can't wait to get home,' he confirmed slowly, 'and take you with me. And to Hel with Caius Caprilius. I wouldn't leave my stable droppings here to feed their soil, let alone Llywarch's sister to grace their pig-styes.'

'You don't trust them?' she managed after a moment of shock, realising how inadequate the works sounded in the face of such strong emotion. Why, he truly hates them, she thought. All of them, not just Ida or Elric.

'About as much as I'd trust a pack of wolves. When have Saxons ever hesitated to break a treaty with our people if they could gain by doing so? We made this alliance in fear of our kinsman Urien – and the Saxon scents fear like a wolf. Some day, when we least expect it, they'll be at our throats!'

Three kingdoms into one . . . She told him then, everything she would have told Alda, everything she could not pour out to Lovan in his sickness. All her nebulous doubts and fears, culminating in Elric's explicit words overheard beneath the ramparts.

Idwal listened in silence. When she finished he said, deadly

235

quiet, 'Jesus Christ, you can't stay. We are not dealing with the old wolf now. Aethelric boasts of ruling Mithrasia while you are only his promised bride – his ambitions will grow once he has you as wife. And I fear that Llywarch's answer will be "Yes".'

Her heart lurched. 'Then there is nothing I can do. Except, perhaps, once I am his queen, try to influence Elric as best I can for Mithrasia's sake. . . '

'Influence? Aethelric wants you by his side to weight his future bargainings with us, and ultimately to give his cubs the quota of Mithrasian royal blood they must have to claim Llywarch's kingdom!'

The silence that fell between them was total. Idwal had gone too far, and he knew it. Eventually he said stiffly, 'Forgive me, Lady Rhianneth. My concern for Mithrasia makes me rash. But if you will trust me, there is a way out.'

She stared at him. Grimly he met her eyes. 'Llywarch's official scroll was not the only thing the messenger brought. To me, he gave this.'

From his tunic he drew a short, squared wooden stick, with strange notches cut across its four edges.

'A different message.' he said, handing it to her. Rhianneth touched her fingertips to the marks along the length of the stick. 'Are they runes?'

'Runes! This is nothing to do with Wermund's damned magic. It is Latin, of a sort. But not the Roman letters you know, and only understood by those who have learned the art from the travelling monks of the Scotti people, in the far west. The message is short, but clear. "No wedding. Lose the bride."'

'What?'

He gave a short bark of a laugh. 'Lady Rhianneth, you – we – are as good as hostages here. What can Llywarch do, but agree to this new marriage, openly? Not to do so would be to smash the war-bond. But if the bride disappears, absconds of her own volition – why then it is Llywarch who will have the grievance against Aethelric, for his lack of care for her safety. It is Llywarch who can threaten to break the bond, cut off the grain supplies. And when Aethelric has apologised enough the war-bond can be confirmed once more. But no marriage. Simple.'

'But where could I go? Not to Mithrasia – '

'That, apparently, is left to me. And since I am to be your accomplice, or abductor, whichever the Saxons care to think, I would prefer it to be deep inside our own lands, far from the jaws of the wolf.'

Rhianneth shivered. Her mind skittered as if on ice, unable to grasp the full impact of what Idwal was saying. Two messages. One open, for Elric. One secret, for Llywarch's loyal captain of the guard. It seemed incredible, yet here in her hands lay tangible proof.

Her mind clutched at a memory. Somewhere safe, in friendly country? The far south-west . . . The Summer Land? Where Marcus had wanted her to be.

'Dumnonia . . . ' she asked. 'Is that far enough?'

'If I can get you there, we'll both be safe. I can offer my sword in service to Constantine.' His lips twisted into a smile. 'When things have quietened, maybe Llywarch will arrange a Christian marriage for you with one of Constantine's sons. It's a good life still, down there.'

His words echoed uncannily what was in her own mind. Her thoughts flew back to the sea-cave, to those moments of near surrender in Elric's arms. If he had taken her then, she would now be lost. For no son of Constantine would take to wife the leavings of a Saxon pirate.

Idwal watched her curiously. He hesitated, then held out a hand to escort her to the mead-hall. 'I need time to think and plan. We'll talk again. But for both our lives, say nothing of this – not even to your maidservant. One word could ruin us. Aethelric must think of you as a willing sacrifice.'

She took his hand, then hesitated. 'But – Lovan? I could never leave without a word. It would break his heart!'

His face changed. 'Lovan is ill. He can't travel. He must be left behind. I beg you, lady, if you love him, tell him nothing! His devotion to you is plain, so, forgive me, his honest distress will guarantee his safety. We'll get a message to him when we reach Dumnonia.'

Llywarch was indeed officially pleased to give his sister in marriage to Ida's heir. The fortress plunged into preparations for the wedding. The days fell away, and Rhianneth lived through them in a state of confusion that drove out rational thought, her mind sliding between certainty and fear. She had seen what Elric had done already in his thrust for power. If he now mated with the blood of Elidyr's royal house, would it not be as if Mithrasia itself had flung wide the city gates, inviting invasion?

Yet the happy bustle all around her was intoxicating. Like honey-wine, it shook her fears and blurred her reasoning.

Alda was full of excitement, her own troubles thrown aside before the stir that filled the fortress. Her admiration for Elric was as obvious as had been her fearful respect for Ida.

'How lucky you are! After all our troubles, to be married at last!' She sighed. 'And to such a man!'

'You think him a happier match for me than Ida?'

'Oh, lady!' Alda laughed incredulously, and blushed. 'Aethelric?'

Even Lovan smiled through his weakness, misinterpreting the look in Rhianneth's eyes, the flush on her cheeks. Again her mind shifted. The wedding but two days away, and Lovan smiled? He loved her. What did she really know of Idwal?

She longed to fling herself down beside Lovan's bed, grasp Alda's hand tightly, and tell them everything. But Idwal was right. Lovan was sick. She could not leave him here with such dangerous knowledge. And Alda was so full of joyful anticipation, chattering around the fortress like a nesting bird; it would need only a hint, for Alda's open smile and sparkling blue eyes to fade, for suspicions to be aroused.

At last she grew desperate enough to send Alda to sit with Lovan, saying she wished to be left quite alone. Then she closed her door, and took Glainnader into her hand.

Afterwards she wondered why she had not died with the seeing. Died of the terror that came as the power of the stone ran through her hands, pain shot between her temples.

A torch flicked briefly against darkness. *He will be close to you, the Flame-bearer* . . .

But then came fire. Fire, across mountains; flames, that swept roaring up the arch of the sky. In its ashen wake lay the end of a world. Grey country, where a serpent stretched glistening coils up from the sea's edge, breathing out poison.

Distant battle-horns called to invisible armies, and the tumult of a terrible conflict grew, until even that was swallowed up by the slavering snarl of a monstrous terror.

A terror that rose until, wolf-eyes burning, open yellow-fanged jaws dropping blood, it filled the skies.

Slowly, slowly, its head turned, looking for prey.

Rhianneth heard her own silent scream ring down through the darkness of the stone.

Then there was only the sound of the wind blowing off the sea, moaning round Din Guaryrdi's salted stones.

For a long, long time she lay on her bed staring into nothing, willing her limbs to stop shaking, her heartbeat to slow. As strength seeped back into her body, Rhianneth's mind crept painfully and slowly around the edges of the seeing, looking for a pattern.

Once more she had seen Cai's torch – and after it? Symbols, she reminded herself fearfully. Only symbols, and always their meaning forked as a viper's tongue.

But symbols, all of them, of death and disaster. Urging her to act, now, before it was too late.

That night as she left the mead-hall after supper, she was halted by a whisper. Idwal moved forward out of the shadows, his finger to his lips. He took her hand, drawing her further into the darkness.

'Lady, I have a plan. I had to wait until now to tell you.' He shot a quick look behind him. 'Tomorrow is the day of the hunt, the wedding-eve. It's no pleasure hunt, it is to provide meat for the marriage feast. But if Aethelric asks you to ride with them, make some excuse. My men will go with the hunt. They must be above suspicion. I shall not go. Some little while later, come to the stables, seek me out. Tell me you have changed your mind, you want to catch up with the hunters. Together we will ride out of the gates, and away. The hunters will think you in Din Guaryrdi, Din Guaryrdi will think you with the hunters. With luck, we will be out of reach before they even realise you are missing.'

Rhianneth felt the colour drain from her face. She had known it must come, and within the next hours. After seeing the horror within the Serpent's Egg she was ready to act. Yet, now, hearing Idwal's words, all she could think of was the fury that would possess Elric when he realised she had cheated him, had flown, on the eve of their wedding.

'I am pledged to him,' she whispered wildly. 'I – '

'A betrothal is easily broken!' Idwal's face sharpened in the dim light. 'a marriage is not!'

He caught her shoulders, shook her gently. 'And through such a marriage Aethelric will claim your brother's kingdom. Though it takes him twenty years of fire and blood!'

Fire . . . She was trembling now, her mind helplessly sliding down once more into the terror of the stone. There was a roaring in her head that blotted out everything except the horror that waited in the years to come. Her whole body trembled, like a leaf before the fury of winter. Just once Idwal's voice pierced through, calling her name sharply. Then the world dissolved into black silence.

Next day she had, after all, no need of excuses. She looked, and felt, too ill for the energetic uproar of the chase. Alda urged her to stay in bed, blaming everything on the excitement of the wedding preparations. But Rhianneth insisted on first seeing off the hunters from the gates. It was irrational, she knew. But she could not be easy in her mind until she had seen the hunting party actually leave the fortress.

'I'm sorry you are not well, Rhianneth.' Elric held her hands loosely, as if anxious to be gone. His eyes were cool, remote. 'I trust you have everything for your comfort?'

She nodded, wordlessly. Since their walk by the beacon tower after the oath-taking he had not touched her. They had scarcely spoken together. Yet when he took her hands in his, she felt the force of their mutual antagonism leap into such life that the very air trembled between them.

As the company rode through the gates she watched him hold back his horse, waiting until Caldis drew up beside him. When she came close enough he leaned towards her and spoke. Seeing Caldis's unbound hair blowing in the wind and Elric's eyes upon her lovely face, Rhianneth went cold.

Suddenly every lingering doubt vanished. She knew what she must do. Ride with Idwal away from here, away from Elric.

She would warn Llywarch, tell Cai what she had overheard, open the eyes of the Fellowship to the truth of Elric's ambition and the danger of making any marriage bond. Let Elric re-negotiate another, merely military alliance. Pay wergeld for her loss, she thought savagely, if Llywarch felt himself insulted enough by Elric's careless protection of her!

She called to see Lovan. He looked better, his fever gone and a large bowl of Alda's frumenty rapidly disappearing beneath his spoon. She dropped a kiss on the top of his head and nodded a smile towards Rolf.

Lovan would be safe, she assured herself, walking away. Her box of medicines must stay here, and already Alda had acquired knowledge of the potions he needed when the fever came. She and Rolf between them would nurse him back to full health. Negotiations would begin again, for the bond itself was too valuable to loose entirely, and Cai would come. When he returned to Mithrasia, he could take Lovan and Alda back with him. Maybe Rolf too, since he had become so much Lovan's man.

She was not a child, but a woman grown, who could manage her own affairs. Not for anything would she endanger Lovan by seeking a few words of comfort and reassurance.

Outside her house, Alda was washing her hair ready for the great day, the thin sunlight flashing on the water in the big copper bowl. Rhianneth moved past her, into the house.

Swiftly then, she lifted the heavy lid of the great chest. She knew how very little she could take with her without arousing suspicion. All her lovely clothes must stay behind, her pretty soft shoes and sandals and her light cloaks. Her heart sank lower as she surveyed the strong heavy box which held her books. How could she bear to leave them?

Setting her teeth resolutely, she stripped off her finely-woven dress. With shaking fingers she threaded a narrow leather thong through the loops of the bag holding Elidyr's jewels and tied it tightly round her waist before pulling on a dark-dyed dress of thick wool. She pushed her feet into strong winter boots, catching her breath sharply at the hardness of the cold leather. When Alda opened the door she was already fastening her warm travelling cloak with the fox brooch that had been Cai's gift to her.

'What are you doing, lady?' Alda stood stock-still with astonishment. 'You should be in bed!'

'I've changed my mind,' Rhianneth answered carelessly, 'A ride with the hunt will do me good. Idwal knows where they are heading. He will take me.'

Avoiding Alda's eyes she turned, gesturing towards the corner. 'As soon as I've gone, get someone to carry those books to Lovan. Now he's recovering, he may like to look at them. But see that the box is carried with care, Alda. They are very precious to me.'

Alda scarcely glanced at the box. 'I'll do that. But please, I'm sure you should stay here! It's the wedding tomorrow and you're not well.'

'Don't fuss!'

Instantly regretting her sharpness Rhianneth added more softly, 'I'm too restless to sit about, Alda. My mind's flying like a bird. I need to be doing something.'

Alda's face reflected her doubts. 'But the hunt? Lady, surely – '

Rhianneth kissed her cheek, still damp beneath her wet hair. A goodbye kiss, she thought. A sudden wave of sadness swelled up from the cold depths of trepidation she was just managing to contain. Through all the dark time after Ida's death Alda had helped her, and now this moment of parting had come with such suddenness and need of secrecy that no farewells could be made. But it won't be for long, she thought. Not too long till we are together in the south-west.

She forced a smile. 'Don't worry! I shan't try to keep up with them. I'll just ride with Idwal in the rear, and breathe green forest air, and calm down . . . '

Idwal was waiting. In no time Romulus was saddled, and they were out of the gates and down the trackway towards the woods, leaving no trace of suspicion behind.

They passed the Wall and travelled on down the Roman road, through the shabby bustle of Catraeth, into the vale of Eburacum with its lonely marshes and fenland where flocks of wintering wild ducks and geese foraged, and an occasional raven or buzzard flew overhead.

Winter's coming was plainly to be seen in the hardening bark of the trees, the wet cold smell of the earth. Leaves lay dead or hung dying on the thinning branches. Only the rowan tree blazed defiance, its leaves thick around the bright berries. But even that brave showing did little to lighten Rhianneth's spirits. Her muscles ached from their long ride and although tiredness blurred her conscious thoughts, it could not overcome the tenseness of her nerves or allow her eyelids to droop during their short periods of rest.

They avoided the centre of Isurium by taking the north eastern by-road, but then found themselves riding through a sprawling outcrop of old shops and trading huts, most of them boarded up and abandoned, some completely derelict, as if the traffic which once brought prosperity had like a high river-wave washed through, and died away.

It seemed to Rhianneth they had chosen a dangerous route and she urged Romulus to a trot. But Idwal dismounted by a shop that seemed open for business and disappeared inside to buy bread and beer. She drank the beer and looked dubiously at the rough chunk of bread Idwal handed her. But she was so very hungry that, after all, it took little effort to forget its grimy origins.

When at last they clattered under the stone archway of Eburacum's north gate, Rhianneth felt her throat dry and her palms grow damp. Catching her nervousness, Romulus began to throw up his head, dancing sideways so that for a few moments she found it hard to hold him.

The huge grey fortress brooded like an eagle over the city that had sprawled to life in its shadow, and the wide main street led straight to the old legionnary headquarters, the *principia*. Here, once, Constantine the Great sat in state, and here now Eburacum's two magistrates, Peredur and Gurci, wielded king-like power.

Other streets, narrow and mean, twisted away between old stone buildings, new timbered houses and thatched huts. In one of these streets they found an inn. Their horses were stabled and fed, but they themselves had scarcely begun a meal when there was a disturbance at the door.

Three men pushed the landlord aside and came into the room, halting when they saw the two people within.

Her heart thudding, Rhianneth saw the boar crest on their tunics and knew they were palace soldiers. Impossible that they should be seeking her! Only within the last hour had she and Idwal slipped quietly into the anonymous shelter of this small travellers' inn.

One of the soldiers said: 'If you will come with us, sir – and Lady?'

The innkeeper sidled in past the soldiers, his face a mixture of curiousity and anxiety. Idwal got slowly to his feet. 'Take good care of the horses till I come back, Innkeeper,' he said, and threw a small bag of coins into the man's hands.

Rhianneth sprang up, backing away until she was brought up by the wall behind her. Idwal turned and held out his hand.

'Don't be afraid,' he gave a faint smile, but his eyes glinted a warning. 'These are strange times for two people to be travelling alone. The city guard will want to know our business, and any news we have from the north. Is that it?' he asked the soldier who had spoken.

The man looked at him without expression. 'I believe so, sir.'

Idwal moved, grasped her hand and urged her to his side. 'Come. A few questions, and we'll be back. Keep it hot for us, Landlord!'

At the *principia*, Rhianneth was left to wait in a small room

244

while Idwal went with the soldiers.

The sounds of the palace seemed full of menace instead of the normality of everyday life. Impossible! Impossible, she told herself over and over again, that her identity should be known. It was, as Idwal told her, just a routine check on two strangers entering the city. They probably took every tenth traveller.

But there was a dark shadow in her mind that would not be reasoned away. A shadow that grew relentlessly as time passed.

When, at last, the thud of boots sounded against the old thick stone of the passage outside, she stood up white-faced but with a fatalistic calm that did not flinch as the soldier's words confirmed what she had now accepted.

'Will you follow me – Lady Rhianneth?'

The floor of the large room was scattered with ankle-deep rugs of dark fur. Roman lamps sent light shimmering across painted walls so that the figures pictured on them seemed to move and whisper together. Rhianneth had thought the magistrates' room would be filled with people, but only the painted people on the walls stared at her curiously. Except for two guards who stood immobile, their sword-points towards the floor, Eburacum's two rulers were alone.

'You are Llywarch's bastard sister?'

The man who spoke was tall, lean, with sharp intelligent eyes above a hooked-beak nose. There was no insult in his tone. Rhianneth raised her chin, her eyes brilliant in the lamplight.

'I am Elidyr's daughter, Rhianneth.'

'Great God in Heaven, so its true!' The other man left the table littered with maps and came towards her. Shorter, more thickly built, his face was as ruddy as the other's was sallow. He gave a throaty chuckle of laughter and reached forward to take her hands. Rhianneth stepped back as if stung. His bushy eyebrows rose.

'What's this? Eh? I'm your kinsman, girl! Peredur. Peredur

Steel-Arm! You've no call to fear me, nor my cousin here, Gurci!'

'Perhaps the lady has had her fill of warriors, Peredur.' The tall man straightened up, a faint smile on his tired, cynical face. 'My cousin means to welcome you, that is all, my dear.'

'Where is my escort? Where is Idwal? What have you done with him?'

'Done with him?' Peredur growled, 'Why, what would we do? He is making a report for us of the happenings in Bernicia. A report we'll want you to verify later.'

'I don't understand.' She stared at them, wide-eyed, her heartbeat quickening.

'Don't you, Rhianneth?' the mocking voice came from the doorway behind her, and it turned her blood to ice. 'Not even with your great powers?'

Queen Myffan came past her, cat-eyes sliding maliciously sideways, to stand beside Peredur.

Rhianneth felt her throat had frozen, cleaving her tongue to the roof of her mouth.

'Idwal is my man, Rhianneth. I appoint the palace guards. They answer to me.' The queen watched her, as if studying a trapped bird.

'Why, of course!' Peredur put in gruffly, 'Did you think we were torturing the fellow? Relax, little lady. You are amongst friends!'

'The child has been so pitilessly used by the Caer Melot faction,' the queen said, 'that she hardly knows friend from foe!'

Peredur nodded agreement. But when Gurci joined them, he glanced shrewdly from Myffan to Rhianneth's face, which was white with shock. Comprehension came into his eyes.

'You intended to slip through Eburacum. You did not wish your presence known to us?' he asked softly.

Rhianneth could only stand speechless, possessed of a deep foreboding that this wrong path she had chosen was leading to disasters greater than she could imagine. Myffan's unrelenting hatred and the coming anger of Elric seemed to merge into one enveloping aura that held the fate of many within its menace.

She thought with bewildered bitterness of Idwal. He had brought her out of Din Guaryrdi, only to deliver her into the hands of these kings whom the Fellowship did not trust. The queen's man. Owing his position and his loyalty to Myffan.

He must have sent a message to the palace as soon as they entered the city! She could scarcely believe it. Yet, thinking of his dark brooding face, she acknowledged that there had always been something. She had thought him a soldier made hostile to the Saxons by his battle experiences. Never had it occurred to her that he rode into Bernicia carrying secret orders from the queen to wreck the alliance, when chance came.

Now she saw that with Ida's death the way had opened to complete his assignment. That stick with its strange writing had been no subtle device of the Fellowship to stop the marriage without breaking the war-bond. The only message to come from Llywarch and the Fellowship, Elric had held in his hand.

'No wedding. Lose the bride . . . ' Rhianneth whispered aloud the words that hammered with each wild beat of her heart. The face of the queen blurred. 'You sent that message?'

'Not quite that message. One word is wrong.' Myffan's lips parted in a smile that was not a smile. 'But then – truly – Idwal did not expect to find me here in Eboracum. He was as shocked as you, for a moment. But Idwal is never dumb-struck for long. He quickly explained to me the advantages of having Aethelric 's bride here as a bargaining counter, rather than . . . lost.'

Gurci asked quietly, 'Had you other plans for the girl, then? I'd understood your only object was to stop the Saxon alliance?'

'What matters is that he got her out! And brought us the best news for years!' Peredur burst in before the queen could reply. 'Ida's gone. Half Aethelric's troops are out of action after a skirmish with his uncle, that old rat Guthlac! It's a shaking kingdom, ripe for attack. We'll never have a better opportunity to drive them back into the sea for good!'

Gods help us, Rhianneth thought, they cannot mean to attack Elric! The kings of Eburacum have kept out of conflict for years, loosening or tightening their links with the British kingdoms, or with their Saxon neighbour, Aelle of Deira. Even to Rhun's great drive north they had closed their eyes with their city gates, Cai had once told her resentfully.

Her heart almost stopped when she thought of Cai.

By her own stupidity and through Idwal's treachery she had betrayed the Fellowship. Broken the hard-won alliance. When he learned that his promised bride had fled to his enemies in Eburacum and that Bernicia's present weakness was now known to them in detail, Elric would never again speak of friendship with Mithrasia. The alliance could never, ever, be re-negotiated into a plain military pact.

Elric's dreams were but formless shadows in an unborn future. But our northern shield, she thought in despair, will be shattered. Shattered when we most have need of it.

It was a nightmare. A black dream from which she must soon awake, or die.

'I believe our little bargaining counter is about to drop out of the game . . . ' she heard Gurci observe dryly, and the room tilted as physical exhaustion and the shock of Idwal's treachery made her head swim.

But she did not faint. She only curled, ashen-faced, into the corner of an old-fashioned Roman dining couch, piled with cushions and pushed back against a wall. Wine and food were hastily brought for her.

The room began to fill with men. Important men, judging by the richness of their clothes and the freedom of their manners in the presence of Eburacum's two kings.

Rhianneth was the object of all their scrutiny as they entered the room, and of glances filled with curiosity from then onwards. But they swiftly became absorbed in talk and no one spoke to her until one, younger than most, limped across to her.

'I am Gwgaun, Peredur's son,' he announced abruptly, pouring himself wine from the jug beside her, 'You look as doom-blasted as I feel.'

Rhianneth watched him toss down the drink and pour another. 'Don't worry about this.' He caught her look and raised his cup in a mocking salute. 'I can out-drink old Bacchus himself. It's all I can do,' he added bitterly.

Her glance fell from his aggressive short-bearded face to his feet. 'You have hurt your leg?' she managed at last, her voice almost inaudible above the growing noise.

'No,' he retorted carelessly. 'God and his angels – and the bloody midwives – managed that on their own the day I was born. Have more wine, Llywarch's sister. You may need it before this day's work is done.'

He lifted the jug with his left hand, and Rhianneth saw with pity that his other arm hung at his side, as maimed as his leg.

She watched the precious liquid tumble blood-red into her cup. It carried the scent of the south, the memory of some long-ago summer hotter than she would ever know. Suddenly, unbidden, Cai was before her, sunlight glossing his dark hair, blazing in the swing of his cloak. 'I am Caius Caprilius,' He was saying, smiling into her eyes, 'your cousin.'

She swallowed more wine. That was wrong, she thought. He had not smiled at that first meeting. Not really. Only in her thoughts could she make him smile at her, kiss her, love her.

Cai would never smile at her again. She was cold and lost. Everything was in ruins. She wished she was dead. But even her grandmother's deadly sleepmaker – even that was left behind in Din Guaryrdi.

She swallowed more of the sweet, strong wine. It blurred the edges of everything but the hard core of dread that remained untouched within her.

If I survive this, she vowed silently, and if ever that death potion comes back into my hands, I swear by all the listening Gods it shall never again leave me. I will keep in my power the means to send my enemy – or myself – into oblivion.

Gwgaun stared at her curiously. Beneath the unbound dark hair her delicately-boned face was pale, with faint smudges of tiredness beneath her eyes. But by God, he thought, she's a beauty. And with promise there to be even more so in a couple

249

of years. Ida's wolf-pack is no place for her! She needs warm luxury, butterfly trivia. All the softness the Empire can still provide, sometimes, and at a price. Like this wine, shipped in from Gaul to the one ramshackle wharf that remained usable since the yearly floodings destroyed our riverside docks and defences.

He drank, watching her over the rim of his cup. Ah, yes! Given the right setting Llywarch's sister would glow like one of the rare small pearls found along the Deiran coastline, for which they traded with Aelle.

Yet, crouched amongst the piled cushions, both hands clenched round her wine-cup she did not seem the wild and wilful little lady he had expected. Within those wide beautiful eyes, with their almost imperceptible upward slant at the outer edges, lay something that spoke not of defiance but of despair..

He must learn more about Llywarch's bastard sister.

'We heard about Ida,' he ventured. 'We hoped his death would finish the alliance. But we never imagined anything like this. A runaway bride! Aethelric's pride will be in the dust!'

She stirred, casting a look at him from beneath her lashes. 'I have broken no marriage vows. It was only a betrothal.'

'Only?' he commented, and sank down on the couch beside her, easing his maimed leg into a comfortable position. 'But their ways are not ours. We may follow the Romans and slip in and out of betrothals as it suits us. To the people of Deira a betrothal is as binding as marriage. A solemn pledge between families. I cannot imagine their cousins in Bernicia are different.'

She stared at him, her eyes darkening. Then she let out a ragged breath, turning her head away. She drained her cup, then held it out to him for more. He raised his eyebrows. She made no response, and with a shrug he refilled her cup.

The rumblings of conversation in the room grew in strength. An argument was in progress, so great that it seemed the lamplight shook in the blast of heated outbursts, sending a shudder across the painted walls.

'I say Aethelric is as full of wind as his miserable fortress towers!' shouted one. 'Let him sight our army on his borders and he will collapse with never a blow struck!'

'The old wolf is dead and half the pack with him!' Peredur roared in his gruff voice, 'They've already wiped out Guthlac and his stronghold for us. We'll never get a better chance!'

There were shouts at this. But then one deep, strong voice surfaced along the ever-rising tide of sound.

'My lords of Eboracum! Let us not rush headlong on to Aethelric's swords! Why must we act alone? Send for Urien. Let Aelle show his true face at last. With a three pronged attack we can toss the Bernicians back into the sea like Neptune spearing fish!'

Through a rumble of agreement, Gurci spoke. 'Urien is far to the north, still tangled in a bitter struggle against Bridei and his Picts. He'll already be looking over his shoulder for winter quarters. It would be weeks before he could join us. We cannot wait! The weather is breaking. Aethelric will never expect an attack so late in the year. That's why we must march now, within days! Aelle we can reach.' He gave a cynical smile. 'He may even be persuaded to show his hand, if it means a real chance to rid himself of his troublesome kinsmen!'

Peredur thumped the table and roared in a voice that rocked the room: 'What say you now, my lords? Will you rouse yourselves and march north to crush Bernicia while she is licking her wounds? We will never again have such an opportunity! By next harvest the wolf-pack will be strong enough to run at will through our lands with fire and scramasax!'

This time there was an explosion of sound as the gathering responded to Peredur's call.

'Your queen looks like a cat who has found the cream,' commented Gwgaun dryly, 'and it seems it is to be war.' He turned to look at Rhainneth. 'God help us all, if Fflamddwyn proves as cunning and tenacious as the old wolf . . . '

But the rich wine had taken effect. Llywarch's sister had slid lower amongst the cushions, her eyes half-closed, heavy with sleep that was already carrying her away from the scent of war around her and the despair and exhaustion within.

*

Messengers pounded away into Deira to call upon Aelle's help. Amidst the turmoil of preparation in Eburacum, Peredur was jubilant.

'Under heaven,' he roared, 'the very earth of Bernicia will shake under our feet, we will smother them with our banners!'

The boar-crested banners, the coats of mail, vanished northwards. The war-horns died away. The stamping of hooves, the tramping of feet, faded. The great legionnary fortress fell silent.

Gwgaun was left as chief magistrate during the absence of his father, Peredur. He sought Rhianneth's company, seating her beside him at supper, and never failing to present her in the light of a heroine before the city elders who ate with them.

Her room was luxurious, with thick rugs on a coloured mosaic floor, painted walls, a maidservant – and an armed guard outside her door.

Every day Gwgaun sent a tiny gift to amuse her, brought into her room on a silver tray. A pretty glass phial of perfume. A rosy apple wet with dew. A tiny wine jug filled with aquavitae, the fiery liquid from the far north which, at her first sip, made her choke on too-vivid memories of the ride from Deva when she had heard of Cai's wife for the first time.

She recognised an innate kindness beneath Gwgaun's defensive mask of cynicism and the touchy belligerence that sometimes broke through it. His curiosity too, about her. He knew, now, that she had been deceived into flight. That she was not the headstrong princess he had first thought her, dragging her captain of the guard in her wake. But he would never know the depths of desolation, the despair which never left her.

Queen Myffan was at first openly jubilant that her strategy had worked so well. The marriage was finished. Bernicia itself about to be annihilated. The power of the Caer Melot Fellowship was broken, its influence blown away. Once Urien's Saxon enemy in the east was destroyed she knew he would turn southwards. But she cared not at all if her son Llywarch's little kingdom of Mithrasia was swallowed up in Rheged's growing power. Urien would strengthen the links about to be made with Eboracum, would form a vast northern alliance which one day would march west to attack her step-brother, Rhun.

Cut deep into her heart were the words her father Maelgwyn had uttered as he lay in delirium, dying. His two sons by his former wife were useless, as nothing in his eyes, he had cried. He would as soon the kingdom of Gwynned passed to his daughter.

Once, she had tried to claim it, and lost Elidyr, her husband. Now she worked more subtly, through others, for Rhun's destruction. Soon now, when Peredur and Gurci returned in triumph, the negotiations she had begun in secret could continue openly. She would return to Mithrasia with a treaty of friendship, and the offer of Gurci's niece as a bride for Llywarch. That should be enough, she thought, to ensure Eburacum's help when it came to filling Rhun's empty throne.

The days dragged by, but no news came from the north. Only a blustering wind came that rattled the shutters, and every day's dawning found nerves more ragged. If only the clash and clangour of battle had rushed in on the back of the north wind! But a deep quiet lay across the land as far as eye could see or ear could hear, and slowly the queen's triumphant smile faded. Her face grew harsh. Her mouth set in a tight line.

Rhianneth dreaded each silent suppertime, when she felt the hatred of the queen touch her very bones. Even Gwgaun spent most of the time morosely tossing back wine, or staring into space.

Then late one evening a messenger came in from the north.

Rhianneth was summoned to the magistrates' room. She flew along dark corridors, heart thumping. But when she entered the large lighted room and saw the scene within she stood suddenly still, her blood running cold.

Gwgaun was there with several of the elders, and the queen. Myffan shot one glance at Rhianneth, her eyes glittering green in a strangely white face, then gave her attention again to the messenger who stood in the centre of the painted room, covered in mud and dried blood.

'By God,' he was whispering, tears of exhaustion furrowing down his travel-grimed face, 'I have never seen such slaughter . . . We got near to the old fort of Caer Greu, well inside Bernicia. And still we'd not seen any sign of the Saxons. Then, suddenly they were amongst us! They were everywhere, their war-horns echoing to the skies like the wail of demons out of Hell! Banners dragged along the wet grass and shredded. We floundered in the mud as they forced us back. We were covered in blood and dirt . . . our mounted men trampled our own foot soldiers. We fell into more and more confusion.' He rubbed a fist across his wet cheeks. 'I saw Gurci cut down. When the cry went up that Peredur was killed, confusion turned to panic and men fled as best they could, caring nothing for friends left behind. We broke in great disorder and the Saxons pursued us for miles, killing all they could. . . '

His voice died away. Silence seemed to tremble on the air. The queen stood without speaking, head bent, her face hidden by her long black hair.

'And Aelle? Where was he?' asked Gwgaun at last, deadly calm.

The messenger shook his head. 'The Deirans were moving along a wooded ridge to the east of us. I'd seen their camp fires. Just before the attack I saw their weapons glint in the light.' His face twisted and he closed his eyes momentarily. 'They did nothing. They just melted away. . . ' He stopped, throat working as he strove to stem the tide of his emotion.

'Christ's Blood.' Gwgaun's lips were white, stiff. 'They were waiting. Waiting to see which way the battle went. . . '

The queen raised her head, tossed back her hair from her face. 'All cannot be lost!' she broke in passionately, 'I won't believe it! Your army will re-group. They will turn again, and fight!'

The messenger looked towards her. 'Our army is scattered, lady. There is no hope of returning to battle. Peredur and Gurci are dead.' He swung bloodshot eyes back to Gwgaun. 'I beg you, sir make shift to defend the city before the Saxons reach the gates!'

254

Defend the city?' Gwgaun gave the ghost of a mocking smile. 'We can just about hold the fortress gate! Will Urien come to relieve us in mid-winter, when there's no more meat and we are down to the granary sweepings?'

Stunned by the sudden calamity that had befallen the army of Eburacum, Rhianneth looked round the room, freezing as she met the look on Queen Myffan's face. Myffan's eyes were gleaming savagely; she seemed more that ever feline, and a wounded wildcat crouched in the grass could not have emitted such an aura of menace. She would kill me now, if she dared, Rhianneth thought. She has made her last throw in this deadly game, and lost. But I have not.

Suddenly her mind cleared. 'You still have your bargaining counter,' she said to Gwgaun, and all eyes turned towards her. 'If Aethelric will turn back from the city , I will go with him. I don't believe he will choose a winter seige, not with Urien and Morcant at his back.'

She heard the queen gasp, and a rumble of astonishment went through the room. Gwgaun's eyes narrowed.

'I admire your courage,' he said. 'Were I a woman betrothed to Fflamddwyn I would have chosen the seige – or flight.'

At his words something stirred at the back of Rhianneth's mind. Then the half-formed thought was swept away in the clash of talking around her.

'Is Eburacum grown so timorous you would send Elidyr's daughter back into the wolf-pack rather than stand a few months seige?' cried the queen derisively, not in Rhianneth's defence but in angry fear least the Saxon alliance yet be completed. 'By God, were Peredur and Gurci the last real men of the city?'

Gwgaun flinched and grasped the back of the chair he stood by as if he must keep his hands from her throat. Anger choked his voice.

'I will not hazard the lives of Eburacum's citizens on the chance that Urien might come in mid-winter to raise the seige. They have lost husbands and sons, their kings are dead. In this fortress we can last only a few weeks before we starve, and the Saxons meanwhile will be camped in our city streets, or plundering the countryside without mercy! Aethelric will pillage and burn, and slaughter our people; if he takes the fortress by storm – '

'Then your father's gallant venture was in vain!' quavered one very old man, his eyes bright with unshed tears. 'Peredur and Gurci are lost, and our sons died for nothing . . . '

'That disastrous venture was none of my doing!' Gwgaun said bleakly. 'I'll not have it laid at my feet. I cannot bring back your son, Janus. Nor even keep the kingdom's honour. I can only try to save what we have left, and the lives of our people, by whatever means I can find!'

The remnants of Eburacum's proud army straggled back in small limping tattered groups. Behind them came people hurrying before the Saxons to the frail protection of the walled city. As every weary party staggered into Eburacum, fresh tales of terror ran through the city streets.

Elric was indeed moving south, ravishing the countryside, spreading fire and havoc. The Saxons seized everything of value and slaughtered anyone who withstood them. The smell of burning began to pervade the air, brought on the wind from the north. Such was the fear they inspired that settlements and small towns emptied before them, the people hiding in the forests or fleeing south.

Then, for Eburacum, time ran out. Elric's banners came within sight, his spears glinting in the distance like a grey forest tipped with sunlight.

'If this were Mithrasia I would have made it a gigantic funeral pyre rather than barter for it with the Saxon wolves!' the queen spat out with a final flash of fury.

'You'd best leave us, lady – .' Gwgaun threw the words over his shoulder as he limped away – ,'and take your man Idwal with you. Better the winter road south, when Fflamddwyn learns of your part in this catastrophe.'

Myffan's mouth tightened into a vicious line as she turned on Rhianneth. 'So, Gwgaun tells me that Elidyr's sly little by-blow does indeed mean to stay! I wonder what personal advantages you hope to gain by acting the heroine and facing Aethelric's barbarous rage? Or has your passion for Caius Caprilius made you too stupid to care?'

Rhianneth met her eyes with a rush of loathing. Not for her life would she give this woman the satisfaction of knowing her afraid.

'I've nothing to fear from Aethelric,' she replied, holding her voice steady. 'He may have brought Eboracum to its knees, but he still needs the alliance. Still wants a marriage link with Mithrasia.'

'I hope he kills you,' Myffan ground out between her teeth, 'as Ida killed his second wife!' Then she gave a brief, contemptuous laugh, put a cold hand on Rhianneth's arm and squeezed painfully. 'But there is no fear of that – is there? As you more delicately put it, the Saxon pirate needs you for his royal brood mare. . . '

Rhianneth dragged her arm free of the bruising hand and gave Myffan a stinging slap across the face. Then she ran from the room and down the empty corridors to fling herself panting upon her bed, gulping down waves of nausea while she strove to conquer her wild thoughts.

The turmoil of the past days, the queen's vindictiveness, even the very real fear that gripped her when she thought of looking once again upon Elric's face – all these paled before the dark shadow rising in her mind.

Fflamddwyn – the Flamebearer.

That was what they called Elric here in Eburacum. *Flamebearer.*

She covered her face, trying to shut out the memory that would not be shut out. Twice now she had seen it, through her Serpent's Egg. The torch, flaming in darkness.

'It does not burn for Rome. Or for Cai,' she whispered, and black despair filled her. 'It burns for Ida's son. Aethelric Fflamddwyn. The Flamebearer.'

Ida's son. Ida! Rhianneth's eyes flew open behind her shielding fingers. She would not, dared not, lift away the layers of venom that wrapped the queen's words lest she discover a truth, ugly and riddled with fear. A truth that could finally break the tight-wound threads of her courage.

Ida was dead. He could not touch her, nor could anything he had done in the past. It was not Ida she would soon face now, but Elric.

Her door opened suddenly and she sat up, expecting to see her maidservant. But the tall figure of Idwal stood there, dressed for travel.

She had not seen him since their arrival in Eburacum. Even now the memory of his treachery was so bitter it closed her throat. She turned her head away.

'Lady Rhianneth,' he said after a moment, 'I ask your forgiveness. I had a prior commitment to the queen. But I would have you know that within that commitment, I did my best for you. When the queen wrote "lose the bride", she really meant it. You were not intended to survive.'

'You were to kill me?'

He hesitated. 'I – I believed Eburacum to be a compromise. The alliance would be broken. But you, at least, would live. I did not envisage, not in my wildest thoughts, that the queen would be here. Or that Peredur would drag Eburacum hot-foot into Bernicia to attack Aethelric.'

At last she looked at him. 'And now?'

He shrugged, his face bleak. 'I am leaving. Alone. By the south gate. I can never return to Mithrasia, not while the queen lives. I've failed her, twice. She will never forgive that.' He nodded slowly as Rhianneth's eyes flew to the dagger at his belt. 'Yes, lady. She sent me here. One last attempt to be rid of you. But I can't do it.'

Rhianneth caught her lower lip between her teeth to stop it trembling. She could find nothing to say. He turned to go.

'I wish you luck, with the Saxons. As for me, there is always work somewhere for a good sword.' He paused, his hand already at the latch. 'Bolt your door, lady. And before you open it, be very sure you know who is standing on the other side.'

He was gone. She slid from the bed and ran to the door, slamming home the bolt and leaning for a moment with her back against it. Then she crossed the room and picked up a small hand-mirror.

Her thick dark hair was a tangled mass, her eyes wide and brilliant with shock.

She took a deep breath, straightened her shoulders and threw the hair back from her face. The doubts and fears that made her weak must be wiped from her mind. Later, there would be time to think. Now, as befitted Artur's battle-maid on the eve of conflict, she would wrap around her all the imperial dignity inherent in the blood of Maximus.

Her broken vows between them, in proud silence she would face Elric. Never would she ask his forgiveness, not even if in his anger he raised his sword to strike her down.

Her lips curved into the shadow of a smile. No, he would not do that. She knew the mind of Ida's son, knew his secret ambitions for the years yet to come. He *needed* her, for through her blood he hoped to secure his claim to Mithrasia. Though it seemed his reputation equalled Ida's in ruthlessness, he would not harm her. No anger, no passion, not even desire for the beautiful Caldis, ruled Elric entirely. It was his strength that hot emotion never melted cold reason, and that would prove to be both her shield and her sharpest weapon. For she, to whom his ambitions had inadvertently been made plain, was fore-warned, fore-armed. She would prove a traitor in his very bed.

CHAPTER 9

The Bernician army camped outside Eburacum, eager for more spoils, but reluctant to sleep within the city walls for fear of magic.

'I'll make what bargains I can for the city.' Gwgaun limped into Rhianneth's room. 'They'll fill their war-chests with everything they can lay hands on. Then slink back to their wolf-rock for winter and leave us to lick our wounds. Thank God they've not the means nor the will to hold the land they have ravaged. Not yet.'

He poured out two cups of wine. 'Here – ' he pushed one into her hand – 'drink some liquid courage. And take heart, Queen Myffan has gone. So has your gallant escort.' He drank deeply. 'We shall tell Aethelric you were abducted. Taken by force. That should soothe his pride.'

'He'll never believe that.' She raised her eyes from the wine-cup in her hand. 'And I don't have to lie.'

'You do.' Gwgaun gave her a level look. 'My God! Even now you don't realise what you've done. Broke your betrothal vow. Rode off with the captain of your guard! What's more, the information that left with you was all my father needed to trumpet this kingdom into war. Aethelric won. But you exposed him to ridicule. He won't stomach that. Retribution – savage retribution, if I know the Saxon mind – is what he'll want.'

He tossed back the rest of his wine. 'Believe it, Rhianneth. Use your wits. I'll explain how you were carried off on orders from the queen. Describe the state of shock you were in when I first saw you. That, at least, will be no lie. You stay in your room, practice fluttering and weeping and looking fragile.'

His mouth twisted in the ghost of a smile, but there was no laughter in his eyes. Only a tiny flame that flickered once and died. 'You'll manage. You may not know it yet but you have in you witchery enough to twine any man so deep in love he'd forget anything.'

She thought of Cai, and turned aside. 'Not any man.'

'Aethelric is as susceptible as the rest,' he said, misunderstanding the forlorn meaning of her words. 'God! I wish it had all gone right for us and we'd swept the whole bloody wolf-pack into the sea! I'd have stood between you and your brother's anger, Rhianneth. Even the half-man I am, in time, I'd have made you queen of the north.'

She swung round, startled. But already he was limping towards the door. His back to her, he paused to set down his wine-cup on a small table.

'Forget I said that.' He threw a wry grin back over his shoulder and raised his sound hand into the air, palm outwards in a gesture of denial. 'This Gaulish wine is too rich. Even for me.'

Rhianneth spent a sleepless night. She had trusted Idwal. She had made only what she had wanted to make of Glainnader's symbolism.

'The glass is a wild thing,' her grandmother had said. 'It cares nothing for us, for the passing of Gods or of empires. It exists. It *is*. Time it knows, and truth, the only real powers in existence . . .'

I'll never read it, Rhianneth thought, staring wide-eyed into the dark. Grandmother's precious gift is wasted upon me. I have the sight but it is erratic, unfocussed like the eyes of the new-born.

Pictures in the fire are simpler: they became easy for me to read as I absorbed Grandmother's skill.

But the Druid's Stone is different. Powerful. Dangerous to hold. There was no time for me to gain that deeper knowledge my grandmother took a long lifetime to acquire. *Serpent's Egg.* The stone is well named. All that it holds within itself is forked, coiled, intertwined like the fearsome snakes that writhe around the carved timbers of Din Guaryrdi's Hall.

The failure of her wild, foolish flight was bloodily surmounted now by the agony of Eburacum's tragic defeat. Peredur and Gurci were dead, their army shattered.

Again Glainnader's grim pictures rose up in her mind but instantly, her flesh turning cold, she pushed them away. Another coil, and one she could not think of now. For that nightmare had nothing to do with this battle of Caer Greu. Of that she was sure. So dark a terror was still to come.

Withered was her brief dream of reaching Constantine's kingdom, where Rome's influence was still strong. She had deceived herself, and been deceived. For the Fellowship had accepted without question Elric's offer to take up the marriage bond when Ida died. Now Elric was here, and like the booty seized on his drive south, like the spoils demanded from the city itself, he would carry her back. Back to the bitter north.

She was trapped, a vixen gone to earth. Yet within the lie Gwgaun offered, she might be safe, treated even with sympathy and respect. Her vows both to the Fellowship and to Elric would appear whole again, as if they had never been broken. Let the future take care of itself. Now she must use everything she could for her own protection. She could never swerve from that lie, not as long as she lived. At daybreak Elric would ride into the city and enter the fortress to accept Gwgaun's submission and claim back the lost bride. Before then, she must plan her strategem, sharpen her woman's wits.

Before dawn Rhianneth rose and lit the lamps in her room. Carefully she washed in a large bowl of gleaming bronze, and dried herself on a cloth of such fine soft linen it felt like a caress against her skin. Gwgaun's little glass phial of perfume lay close by her hand. She sprinkled it on lavishly, catching her breath as the exotic scent of Rome's eastern Empire rose sensually up from her warm skin.

She had witchery, Gwgaun said. Witchery her grandmother practised, for she was old and so steeped in ancient knowledge that she could sometimes catch a small thread of power, and for an instant twist it to her use. But it was not power such as her grandmother knew that had been in Gwgaun's mind. Only the magic that some women hold for some men.

Rhianneth took up a hand-mirror and stared into it. Her newly washed hair hung thick and dark, with an occasional ripple of fire caught from the slow-burning lamps. She tilted her head until her eyes also stole golden light from the small lamps, gleaming behind their black lashes like green-flecked jewels. Unbidden, Elric's words came into her mind, soft as the surf-whisper that echoed round the cold walls of the sea-cave: 'Are there enchantresses, except in the minds of men?'

Ah, yes, there are, she thought wryly. But had I the powers of Circe herself Elric would still see only a small girl with eyes that made him think of a cub-vixen. The tall golden beauty of Caldis had woven a charmed circle about him long ago, too strong and bright to be broken by dark foreign witchery.

She put down the mirror and pulled from a chest the clothes she had travelled in. Sombre colours and winter thickness would add strength to her story of abduction and virtual imprisonment here in Eboracum. She hoped that after all his gallant kindnesses Gwgaun would forgive her if she played this part of frightened captive to the full.

Finally dressed, she picked up her travelling cloak and sat down to wait, summoning to her aid the childhood lessons in composure instilled by her grandmother as necessary first steps towards learning the elusive secrets of her own magical lore.

So far away were her thoughts, that at first the loud knocking seemed part of her reverie.

'Rhianneth!'

Her mind sprang into wakefulness, eyes widening as she recognised the Saxon roll in the voice that called. Taking a deep breath, she stood up and smoothed her skirts. Then sliding back the heavy bolt, she opened the door. Relief, and a warmth that was almost affection washed over her at the sight of Elric's younger brother, Adda.

Tall, fair-haired Adda was the middle brother; too old for affectionate teasing like Theodric, too young to be Elric's close boyhood companion like Hussa. Yet within that brotherhood he held his own, possessing a cool strength of mind and body in no way overshadowed by Hussa's bold and cheerful energy or Theodric's sharp wit. Rhianneth liked him, though of them all in character he most resembled Elric, to whom he gave complete loyalty. In Adda she sensed a gentleness beneath the strength that she had not yet found in Elric.

He stared at her, his face stiff, anxious. Then he took both her hands in his. 'Are you well, lady?'

Rhianneth caught her lower lip between her teeth, moving into her part. 'I am now, Adda!' She gripped his hands as if she feared to let go. 'Oh, I've been so afraid. I thought you would never come!'

'They have not misused you?'

'No, oh no! Gwgaun protected me from the queen, he has been so kind –' She stopped, looking past him. 'Where is Elric?'

'He sent me to find you. He's with Gwgaun.'

Rhianneth's heart plummeted. Was this the action of a man whose abducted bride was found safe and well? To have sent his brother to her while he calmly stayed to bargain with Gwgaun was surely a deliberate insult both to her, and to Mithrasia. A coldness whispered through her telling her that Elric believed not a word of the abduction story; that he could not bear to look at her – she who had exposed him to mockery by stealing away on the eve of the wedding and riding into the city of his enemies with news of Bernicia's weakness so detailed as to encourage them to attack. Her mind went blank as sick fear filled her.

Then she looked up into Adda's steady blue eyes and concerned face and her heartbeat slowed. Elric must accept Gwgaun's story, if only in public. It salved his pride. It even gave him an edge in his dealings with Mithrasia, since Idwal had been Llywarch's trusted officer. All she had to do was keep her head and lie into his face. If anything went wrong she would slide to his feet in a faint, like a vixen playing dead in order to escape later.

She recognised several of Elric's war-band, and two of his thanes, as she entered the magistrates' room beside Adda. Gwgaun turned his head towards her. He looked white, exhausted. There was a warning in his eyes that made her pause. Then, bracing herself, she walked across the room as the tall figure of Elric came to meet her.

'Rhianneth.' He drew into his arms, bending his head to kiss her. 'You are not hurt?'

Rhianneth felt hot colour run under her skin at his touch. She glanced quickly up, and his eyes were like ice. His back was towards the men in the room. They saw his swift embrace, heard his greeting. Only she saw the cold glitter in his eyes, and stiffened in his arms.

'I'm quite well,' she answered awkwardly, and then floundered in to the part she must play. 'But I've been in great fear for Bernicia. And for you, Elric!'

Fool! she thought instantly. But too late to bite back her last few words. He would know them to be a lie. Had she not once called him a savage, spat out that she could not bear him to touch her? Swiftly she lowered her eyes.

'You were wounded?' She ran her fingertips over a sword slash in his tunic, over old dark bloodstains on his sleeve.

'That's not my blood, lady.'

There was an odd note in his voice that made her glance up. He watched her curiously, and she saw a flicker of doubt cross his face. 'But we've had a rough enough road since we left Din Guaryrdi.'

He reached inside his tunic. 'I bring you this,' he said, and held out the jewel-encrusted girdle that had been his betrothal gift to her.

Rhianneth stared at the beautiful thing, gemstones glistening in every gleaming link of metal, understanding that this was Elric's token. That he took her back, without suspicion, as his bride. Publicly at least. His private suspicions she had already glimpsed, chillingly.

With his other hand he seized her wrist, turned it, and laid the girdle across her open hand.

'Take it. It is yours,' he said quietly. 'It has lain near my heart through the wet marches, the battle at the fort, all those burning miles after the enemy scattered.' The familiar mockery was back in his voice.

Rhianneth drew back clutching the girdle so tightly that the smooth-edged metal bit at her hand like fire. He must not rouse her with his soft-edged taunts. She had given Eburacum no information dangerous to Bernicia, that must be laid at Idwal's feet; and whatever Elric privately chose to think, he knew that to voice his suspicions aloud could cost him the Mithrasian marriage. He would not risk that. So, whether drawn in by fear or by ambition, they were both now captive within the strands of the abduction fabrication woven by Gwgaun.

That thought gave her such confidence that she smiled into his face. 'Thank you, Elric. As you see,' she made a pretty gesture of compliance, 'I'm ready to travel with you whenever you wish to leave.'

That is, she thought sardonically, as they moved further into the room, if there is room for me amongst the other spoils in your newly-loaded war chest . . .

Once into Bernician territory and with the Wall behind them, the war-bands began to break away as each thane headed for his own lands and fortress. The army that had destroyed the invading kings of Eburacum melted until, a bare day's ride from Din Guaryrdi, only Elric's warriors remained. By that time, Rhianneth ached in every limb and dreaded yet another night huddled against the cold on the hard earth.

But when they reached the forest clearing that was to be their night stop, she found there was shelter, of a sort. Several small huts, and a large open-sided timber shack stood green-walled with moss under sagging turf-tiled roofs. Woodcutter's huts, long abandoned.

Rhianneth slid from Romulus's back and ran her hand down the loose mane, leant her cheek against the smooth coat as the horse turned a graceful head to nuzzle her.

'Your gallant captain at least allowed you to ride,' Elric had remarked softly as he helped her mount in Eburacum, 'we feared he might have simply thrown you across his own horse to carry you off . . .'

She remembered looking down at him from Romulus's back with wide innocent eyes. 'Idwal was the queen's agent,' she had replied truthfully enough, 'he betrayed me, and I can't bear to speak of him.'

Elric's look of cynicism had faded as he stared at her, replaced by something else. Something she could not read. Then Adda rode up, and he had turned away in silence.

Now she was too bone-weary to do anything but watch as

Romulus was taken from her and led into the big open-sided shelter, huts were banged open, armfuls of wood carried into the clearing and a fire started.

She gratefully preceded Elric into one of the small huts, in which blankets were spread on a wide bench.

'Can I bring you meat and drink?' Elric rested a hand against the door post, his hair tossing in the rising wind. 'I hope the roof stays sound,' he went on, glancing upwards, 'it's going to be a bad night.'

Even as he spoke faint thunder rumbled, and there was an agitated flurry in the bushes as a bird swooped away, screaming its warning.

The fire glowed comfortingly in the clearing behind Elric's tall figure. The men sprawled around it, tension beginning to relax now they were nearing home. She herself was beyond worrying about anything, be it leaking roofs or an enemy attack. As soon as she stretched her aching limbs out upon the rough warmth of the blankets she fell asleep.

She woke to darkness and to thunder so close, so deafening, it sounded like the end of the world. She sat up, heart thudding. A terrified whinnying had her scrambling to her feet and jerking open the door. Romulus!

Men were running for shelter in the dying light of the fire and dark clouds obscured the moon as the storm rushed towards them.

Rhianneth ran across the clearing towards the horses, the wind snatching every breath she took. Before she reached shelter, the storm broke. She was drenched, half blinded, by the fury of the rain. Lightning ripped across the sky like a sword slash. The answering thunder roll made her crouch close to the earth, in the grip of primitive fear.

She heard a shout. Elric grasped her shoulders, jerked her to her feet. She was pulled stumbling back to the shelter of the hut. He pushed her inside roughly.

'You little fool!' He shook her violently. 'Why did you leave?'

'For Romulus! He needs me! I heard him!'

'Romulus?' Elric flung an arm towards the open door beyond which the trees moaned and tossed in the eerie flickering light and the earth shook with thunder. 'Do you hear that? When Thunor strikes, whole forests burn! Would you cross the spear-flight of a god's anger, for a horse! Hel's Gate! How can a wise-woman's granddaughter be so stupid?'

Rhianneth stared at him, speechless. Stupid was she? To care for Romulus, who was terrified by storms? Scalding words bubbled within her, but she was suddenly too hot to shape them. Instead she struck him with all her strength across the face.

His head jerked back. Then anger such as she had never seen before flooded his face. He caught her shoulders roughly and pulled her against him. She could feel the trembling of his arms as he fought to contain his fury.

'Rhianneth!' he breathed, but anger made him inarticulate. One of his hands tangled in her hair to jerk back her head, while his other arm held her so tightly her breath almost stopped. She caught a glimpse of his eyes, blazing in the blue storm-light, then his mouth was on hers, forcing her lips apart.

Heat flamed through her body, melting her bones. Through her rain-soaked dress she could feel sensual power pulsing from him and before it she lost mind and will until only her senses remained. She began to tremble. Dark waves of excitement crept slowly over her, so that she felt both exhilerated and yet so weak that she relaxed helplessly against him, her hands sliding upwards to link behind his bent head.

He lifted his mouth from hers, muttered something in Saxon before swinging her round in his arms to lay her down on the rumpled sleeping-blankets.

For an instant the hut blazed with light as the sky slashed open. In the following darkness the air shook with the fury of the gods, and Rhianneth cried out in fear. But Elric held her close, his warm strength a shield against the terror of the storm as she hid her face in his chest.

'Wermund is right –' his breath stirred her hair – 'you really do have the blood of an enchantress.'

She felt him unpin her brooch and slide the wet dress from her shoulders. He untied her shift, pushed it aside. She heard his swift ragged intake of breath as he lifted his head to look at her in the flickering storm-light.

'Aelfsciene!' he said unsteadily. 'Beautiful as one of the elf-kind . . .' Are you as dangerous to men as they are, Rhianneth?'

The thick blankets beneath her now seemed to have become soft as her fur-lapped bed in Din Guaryrdi. She touched his mouth with her fingertips and a strange fierce joy ran through her as she felt his body tremble. Then Elric's lips were moving against her neck, but his words were so soft she could not hear them. She only knew they were of tenderness and desire, and her fear of the ferocious forces thundering in the night vanished before a sense of power more heady than rich Gaulish wine, beside which the sudden blaze of her own passion was as nothing.

For Ida's arrogant son was caught in a double trap. His own ambition had driven him into the marriage contract. Now, even while in his heart he distrusted her, he was snared by lust. She had him fast, for a while. And for as long as the witchery lasted, she meant to use its power to her own advantage.

His fingers trailed fire along her bare skin. She felt a dark arrow of desire shoot within her, and she shivered.

'Don't be afraid, Rhianneth,' he whispered, between kisses on her lips and throat. 'For this, we were pledged together before all Din Guaryrdi . . .'

His voice grew husky with passion as his lips travelled downwards to touch her breasts. She arched towards him, her arms stealing around his neck, fingers entwining in the thick hair at the back of his head.

Suddenly he paused, breathing unsteadily. 'What's this?'

Unthinkingly Rhianneth fumbled, unloosed the thong of leather around her waist and let the small heavy bag fall away. 'My jewels.'

She felt him grow still. 'You carried them with you – even when you thought only to ride for a morning's hunt?'

Silence closed around his words and her heart leapt, for into that silence she heard a bright danger sing, rising even above the wild song of the storm.

Fool! To have forgotten the jewels! Now Elric's unspoken suspicions were confirmed. Now, he had proof that there had been no violent abduction, that she must have prepared and planned, and willingly flown with Idwal even while Din Guaryrdi prepared for her marriage to their new king.

Lightning flared. Gods, she thought, his eyes are like the drowning depths of the northern seas which lap Din Guaryrdi's shore. She felt her courage plummet. Then as thunder came, and died, he got up and fastened the door.

'Why Rhianneth?'

His tone was soft. He made no move towards her. Desperately she tried to think, but her thoughts scattered like the blown leaves outside in the storm, leaving only the bleak and naked truth in her mind.

'I know about you and Caldis, your uncle's wife,' she said after an agonised pause, 'and I know you would marry her, if it were not for your ambitions to push westwards. To claim Llywarch's kingdom for your son, through me! I meant to warn the Fellowship, to warn Cai . . .'

'Everyone knows about Caldis. It's an old story, and closed. As for the rest, do you think Cai is a fool? It is a jest between us. Beneath the smiles, we both know that one day there may be a contest, a reckoning. But that day is not yet. May never come. I may have no sons. I may be killed in battle. Cai is willing to chance the future because now, now is the desperate time for Mithrasia, as for us. Oh no, Rhianneth. You would not have blown apart the alliance for that.'

She felt her mind begin to slide. She had told him the truth, and he had tossed it aside as of no account. Worthless, the revelation of Elric's intent that she had thought so vital to carry to the Fellowship.

It had all been for nothing, all these terrible last weeks. A game for the gods. A game that had ended in the ruin of Eboracum and the deaths of Peredur and Gurci in the bloody carnage of Caer Greu.

What was it Elric had told her, on the night of Ida's funeral? 'You're really only a little girl . . . too young . . . to fight your way through this mess . . .'

Not too young, she thought; too naïve. I really am still the simple farm-girl Queen Myffan called me. But I shall learn. One day I will dice with the Gods, and win.

'Or did you never intend the alliance to take place, from the beginning?' Elric broke into her thoughts, and now his voice hardened. 'Ida died . . .'

'Are you daring to accuse me of that again?' she cried, in a sudden blaze of real anger at the implication in his words.

There was a silence. 'So you would have married Ida?' he said. 'Therefore, it really is just me that you hate . . .'

In the flickering darkness he seemed wolfish, dangerous. She felt like a cornered animal seeking escape and finding none. Elric was between her and the door, and beyond that door were his warriors.

'How did you persuade Idwal to take you. With them –' he gestured towards the jewels – 'or with something else?'

Rhianneth sprang to her feet and backed against the wall, clutching her shift across her breasts. She flung back her hair and looked straight at him.

'Get out, Elric,' she said. 'I don't want you to touch me.'

'So you told me, once before.'

In two swift strides he crossed the space between them and grasped her wrists, jerking her hard against him.

'You also cried then, lady, that you wanted the blessing of your Gods upon our alliance. That I should not tumble you like a slave, but treat you with honour!' His hand came up to hold her face. 'That's not a word we use lightly, Rhianneth!'

'If you believe I've dishonoured you, send me back to Mithrasia! Break the alliance!'

For an instant she thought he would strike her, as the jibe reached him. She felt the sudden tension in the muscles of his arm as his grip tightened. Yet like a wildcat drawing blood with her scratches she was overwhelmed with the power of her sharp claws.

'Or would you rather kill me,' she taunted him recklessly, 'as I'm told Ida killed his second wife?'

A dart of fear shot through her, for his hand was on her

271

throat. Then she knew; knew that what she had crushed down into the far shadows of her mind was not some venomous lie of the queen, but a dark truth. A truth that had been kept from her, even by Cai.

She could hear Elric's unsteady breathing, felt it fan warmly across her face. But for a long moment he did not reply, and she was reminded of an animal waiting to spring, betraying only by an occasional flick of its tail the dangerous tumult within.

Then he said softly, and with menace: 'Kill you, Rhianneth? Never. For I do want sons. Sons with the rich blood of Rome and the hard strength of the northlands in their bones . . .'

Thunder growled. The air quivered with violence. But Rhianneth felt something of the storm's wild brave spirit enter into her.

'Let me loose!' she cried passionately. 'I will never marry or breed sons with a man who distrusts and despises me!'

Violently she wrenched herself free and started to push past him. But in an instant he had spun her round and was holding her crushed against the damp wooden wall.

'By Hel, you will!' he said roughly. 'You made your pledge to me, Rhianneth. You will not slip away again. I'll bind you closer than any spoken word of honour, for I'm taking you now!' He laughed, deep in his throat. 'And we'll have a son, lady. Conceived in lust, spawned in hate, his birthright bathed in the blood of two kings – by all the Gods, he'll prove a warrior to make the earth tremble!'

She struck at him with all her strength. Her nails tore down the side of his face and she felt a savage exultation to see the jagged trail of blood they left, black in the strange storm-light. With an oath he swept her off her feet, flinging her down on the blankets as if she was nothing, as light as the elf with which he had compared her.

Elric's mouth closed over hers while he tore aside the shift she had been holding and slid his hand across her naked breast. His hand was hard, his kiss rough; he was forcing her clenched teeth apart and she was smothering beneath his weight.

She hit him with her clenched fist, then fastened her fingers in his hair and pulled viciously. He jerked his head free, and as he looked down at her she saw desire blaze behind his eyes, like a flame caught from the lightning fire of the gods.

Beside herself with anger and now with real fear of his obvious intent Rhianneth struck at him again, clawing and biting until he caught her hands in one of his own. He held her with so little effort that her own impotence raged in one long silent scream. Against his strength she was helpless, and they both knew it.

The night shook, flickering with light as the storm rolled back and forth across the heavens. She had a frightening glimpse of his face. He looked like one of his own storm-gods, ice-cold and intent. She knew then that for Elric this was no love-struggle. It was no longer even lust, but war. A war he meant to win.

Hatred rose like a hot wave, engulfing her. But she would not plead with him, not for her very life. Her mind racing, she lay still as he bent over her, caressing her trembling body now with a touch more gentle. The warmth of his lips roused memories of the sea-cave where once before he had intended to make sure of her, before his uncle Guthlac should contest the kingship. Then, she had thrust honour between them like a cold sword-blade. Now she had nothing.

'Where did you intend to go – straight to Cai?' he demanded thickly. 'He has never been out of your thoughts, has he? Not for a day, or a night. But he wants the alliance more than he wants you, Rhianneth. As for me, I'll never win your heart. But by Woden's Eye, I'll make sure of your body . . .'

Her heart lurched under his hand. Love or esteem between them she could have used as a shield. But there was neither. She had only the tears that were every woman's last frail defence, and because she was completely at his mercy she choked down her fierce resentment and cooled her pride into shining droplets that quivered on her lashes and ran cold down her cheeks.

For an instant as his lips touched her wet face, he stopped, and his head lifted.

273

'Don't bother, Rhianneth.' he said then. 'Oh, you are really very good – these are even more touching than your tears in the cave. But this time, it's not worth the effort.'

Blood pounded loudly in her ears as fear and fury mingled and rose uncontrollably. If she could only drag her nails once more across his dark, hard face; pound and pummel with her clenched fists until she could no longer see the grey eyes staring into hers! She let out a long shrill cry of pure rage that did battle with the roaring of the storm itself, until his mouth stopped her with a deep, savage kiss.

And suddenly it changed, as if the separate streams of their anger merged, became one overwhelming torrent. Within his arms, her lips bruised with passion, and with instincts she had never known slowly aroused to a pitch of intensity that was almost unbearable, Elric's final possession of her was both brutal and an ecstasy beyond description.

* * *

The day was so warm, so still, that the sea rolled to the shore's edge in long langorous waves and a haze of heat hid the islands. Baskets of fish being unloaded from a boat nearby stung the air with a sharp sea smell, and within the shouts and laughter that welcomed the late-comer home Rhianneth heard the roughness of anxiety relieved.

She closed her eyes momentarily against the now familiar scene, remembering that autumn of a year ago, the first days of her arrival in Din Guaryrdi as Ida's bride. Then, the weather had been cold and wet. Now, in this last blaze of the dying year, the sun was burning her face.

Her eyes flew open and at once, protectively, she drew the thin blanket higher around the baby in her arms. Looking down into the tiny face of her sleeping son, she was filled with a sensation too deep, too thickly woven, to be called simply happiness, or joy. For out of fear and anger, out of desire and pain, had come love. Love at last, born to her two weeks ago.

The edges of her memories were becoming blurred concerning the return to Din Guaryrdi with Elric and the warband, the marriage itself. Her abduction by Idwal was exclaimed over and accepted, it seemed, by all. If there were

274

some who wondered, they wisely kept silent. Never by even the flicker of an eyelid did Elric move from the story. But the flash of hostility occasionally glimpsed beneath those lids, though swiftly hidden, was a constant reminder to Rhianneth that between them there was not peace.

On her part, though other memories had softened, his taking of her in the midst of the storm remained vivid, violent. For that brutal humiliation she would never forgive him.

With her early pregnancy she became queasy, sick, and Elric began to sleep in the mead-hall, as the young unwed warriors of his war-band did. Almost before winter ended he left on a war-trail to the west, taking half his war-band and gathering behind him as he rode a pack of young warriors yielded to his service by the thanes who had won with him the battle of Caer Greu.

All summer he was away skirmishing with the enemy, harrying the lands of Urien and Morcant until the grey-hills rang with the terror of his war-horns and people fled before the coming of Fflamddwyn, Flamebearer.

Rhianneth grew languid and, relieved of Elric's disturbing presence she gradually relaxed in the warmth of the summer days, sitting out in the sunshine beside Lovan with Alda fussing around them both.

Passively she listened to the highly coloured accounts of Elric's battles related by the messengers who occasionally pounded in shouting their news to an excited fortress; she cared for nothing but the child growing within her. Only that gave meaning to the cruel and snake-like twists of the life-path upon which the Gods had set her feet.

Then, unexpectedly, even while the late summer still bloomed, the war-band was back, swaggeringly triumphant. They were invincible, and Elric sent by Woden to make them so!

Suppers in the mead-hall became almost feasts as drink flowed until deep into the night and tales were told and retold of the triumphs over the kings of the north. Even Wermund, usually so dour and watchful, smiled into his mead-cup and drank with the rest. Elric poured into Rhianneth's hands booty seized from the enemy. Belts, bangles, brooches, plate and cups, things of silver and bronze and gold. But her time had almost come, and once more he spent his nights with the young warriors in the hall.

The birth was long and difficult. The air was stifling, made smoky by the fire kept blazing to scare away demons who might steal the new-born soul. The quavering of charms by one old cunning-woman and shrill vigorous exhortations from the other, were a reality Rhianneth gratefully clung to in a turmoil of sweat and pain. For always, haunting the hot shadows of the birth-house, was the memory of her young mother's death.

But when at last through one great flame of agony she heard the thin pure cry of new life, all her fears shrank away before a sensation of relief and triumph such as that which swept across the victors of battle.

Elated exhausted, already sliding towards the edges of a sleep swiftly induced by the fierce potency of a drink they held to her lips, Rhianneth thought Elric stood in the doorway, bringing the cool night air with him. In slow dream-time she watched the cunning-woman triumphantly place his son in his arms, saw him shake his head and hand the tiny bundle back to the astonished woman, push past her into the room.

'Do not touch her, Aethelric!' A strong skinny arm shot out to stop him. 'She sleeps this night in Eostre's arms – would you anger the Gods?'

Her shrill laughter cackled out as the scene blurred and dimmed into sleep's oblivion, and afterwards every memory that was not of heat and pain became a strange mosaic of jumbled pieces, none of them quite real.

'Lady – look!'

Alda's laughing cry scattered Rhianneth's thoughts. The girl ran towards her holding a dripping skirt away from her legs, bare brown feet sticky with sand.

'One wave,' she panted, cheeks flushed beneath her curling hair, 'bigger than all the rest! It crept in so quietly it was there before I knew!'

How pretty she is! Rhianneth thought wistfully. But how

long will Rolf wait for her? Sometimes she seemed to warm towards him, but always shrank from a final commitment. Already he had ceased to press for a betrothal, and it seemed to Rhianneth he was growing more remote, avoiding Alda when he could.

Alda peeped at the baby, smiling. 'You must not get tired, lady. Let me carry him back for you. We'll settle him in his cradle, in the shade.'

She stopped, staring over Rhianneth's shoulder, the colour fading from her face. Half expecting to see Rolf, Rhianneth turned, and all the breath left her lungs. Cai stood on the beach near the narrow path leading up to the northern gate of Din Guaryrdi.

In the warm autumn sunlight he appeared in no way altered, his body as lithe, hair as dark, face as handsome, and the sudden sight of him turned Rhianneth to stone, silencing and stilling lips and body.

Then he was coming towards them.

She felt Alda lift the baby from her arms. Now I can move away, she thought, faint – or die. But she only went on standing there, until he took her hands in his.

'Rhianneth.' He bent his head to touch her cheek in a kin-kiss then slowly drew back still holding her hands, his eyes on her face, and said again more softly, 'Rhianneth. Are you well?'

Before she could reply the baby stirred, whimpered. Cai turned, letting her go. 'So this is your son.' His face tightened into a faint smile. 'I can scarcely believe it, little cousin!'

Gently pushing aside the blanket, he let the tiny hand curl around his finger.

Somehow Rhianneth forced words to her lips, her voice like cracked ice. 'Take the baby back, Alda. We will follow later.'

'Yes, lady.' Alda spoke quietly, but she looked worried as she turned and walked away from them.

Cai led Rhianneth to a flat rock in plain view but away from the busy scene around the fishing boats. She sat in silence, unable to form words amongst the frozen wastes of her emotions. Great black-headed gulls flew in out of the mist to hunt along the shore's edge, screaming hungrily as they hovered above the baskets of landed fish. A slight breeze touched her and died away, leaving a smell of sun-dried seaweed on the air.

At last Cai said abruptly, 'We knew nothing at home. Not till news of the battle at Caer Greu came and we heard that Peredur and Gurci were dead and Eburacum wide open. Aelle has moved in there, did you know? It was part of his bargain with Elric, to keep Deira out of the fight. About Idwal, and you,' he went on, as she made no response, 'we only learned when the remaining soldiers of your escort returned to Mithrasia after the wedding.'

'Surely the queen . . .'

'Queen Myffan never came back. She's at the court of Rheged with Urien, doubtless plotting our downfall.' His voice was bitter. 'It was her doing. All of it. Idwal was sworn to her service before ever he entered Llywarch's.'

'Where is he now?'

'Maybe the Gods know. I don't. But the Fellowship are oath-bound to kill him and we will, one day. If Elric doesn't find him first.'

Inwardly she shivered, not so much at his lethal words but at the coldness in his voice. 'How are you, Cai? And how are things at home?'

'We carry on.' His face seemed to close. Abruptly he said, cutting off any more enquiries: 'He has Ida's eyes, your little Saxon warrior. Is Elric pleased?'

She shrugged. He stared at her for a moment in silence. 'What's wrong, cousin fox-cub?' he asked then, softly.

'Wrong?' She kept her gaze on the sea, a tremor running through her as the old, teasing, special name left his lips.

'A first-born son usually turns a Saxon into a flaming braggart. Elric seems – different.' He hesitated. 'Idwal did not touch you, did he, Rhianneth?'

For an instant she was shocked into silence. Then a bubble of laughter that was almost hysteria rose, threatening to choke the words unborn in her throat.

'Elric wants to carve out an Empire for the Englisch north of the Humber river, and he'll use the Mithrasian blood in his sons to give him a right even stronger than conquest.' She turned her face towards him. 'Do you understand me, Cai?'

Cai was watching her, his expression unreadable. How she had schemed, planned, finally risked everything to bring word of Elric's ambitions to Cai! Now those very words sounded simple, trite. It hardly seemed to matter at all.

'But not even for that, I think, would Elric accept another man's bastard as his heir,' she went on, swallowing. 'There is no way he could believe my child to be anything other than his own son. He knows, without a shadow of doubt, that I came to him virgin.'

'I see.' Cai's face tightened, a nervous muscle jerking in his jaw. His thumb worked across his clenched fist. Their eyes met, and suddenly it was as if they stood above a chasm of fire as between them swirled terrible, unspoken words. One slip, and they would be lost.

Painfully, Cai drew back from the edge.

'Julia has entrusted me with gifts for you,' he said tonelessly, 'things she believes you might be missing.' He hesitated. 'She has been ill, from early summer. As for my wife Morvydd, she . . .'

As his voice died away his shuttered expression cracked open for an instant, revealing a glimpse of pain that appalled Rhianneth, jerking her out of the mesh of her own troubles. She realised he was not, after all, unaltered. Now she saw that his face seemed thinner, more tightly drawn. There was a tenseness within him that had not been there before, not even in their blackest moments.

'Sometimes I feel,' he went on quietly, 'that I'm living in the screaming heart of madness. If it were not for Torfrida the house would collapse in on itself, and all of us with it. Morvydd neglects the child, steals my mother's clothes and jewels —'

He stopped abruptly, as if already he had let slip too much. Before Rhianneth could gather the words to speak he changed the subject.

279

'I can't believe that Elric ill-treats you in any way, Rhianneth. He has always seemed concerned for your safety . . .'

'So concerned,' she cut in, 'that he told you to go home and leave me here! To go, even before the wedding with Ida could take place!'

'Yes, he did,' Cai admitted carefully. 'He was anxious, I know, that Ida should not misunderstand the fondness between us. Elric had heard the slander the queen spread through Mithrasia, and he knew Ida. He thought it wiser I should not stay. Because of the alliance and because –'

'Because of Ida's second wife?'

Cai froze. After a long pause he said, 'What do you know about that?'

'Only that she is dead, and that it was Ida who killed her. Why did you not tell me, Cai?'

There was a silence, while only the laughter of the fishermen and the screaming of gulls lay upon the still air.

'I didn't want to make you afraid.' he said at last. 'It was all a long time ago. When Elric was scarcely as old as Llywarch is now. Ida found his wife – Theodric's mother – with one of his war-band. He killed the man on the spot. Later, he took his great sword and killed her too. And he made sure that Elric was there.'

'A young boy!' Rhianneth's blood ran cold.

'But not just any boy, Rhianneth. Ida's first-born. The likely heir to the kingship. Ida would want him to see a king's power in action. To understand how a king may need to use that power to keep the loyalty, the respect of his warriors and his people.'

Gently he took her hand, held it hidden amongst the folds of her dress between them. 'Ida was always a barbarian at heart. But Elric is more than that. I value hs friendship. I like him, as a man. I was –' he hesitated – 'glad for you, cousin fox-cub, when we heard that he had offered marriage. I thought with him you might find a happiness you would not have found as Ida's queen.'

Ida's queen. Rhianneth shivered, remembering the sword that hung now in the house she shared with Elric. Ida's war-sword, that had not gone with him to Waelhaell but had passed to Elric. But Elric had Dreamweaver, and unless that broke in battle it would be Ida's grandson who next grasped its carved hilt.

As if he half-guessed her thoughts Cai said, 'You never liked Elric, I remember that. But Rhianneth, if it is hard to be a king's son it's harder yet to be king. To be alone. Oh, not physically. That, he rarely is. But here –' he touched the side of his head – 'where no comrades ever walk, there you could be always. Whatever it is between you and Elric, can't you put it aside? For the sake of your own little son, who may one day inherit.'

Inherit what? she thoughty wearily. A bloody sword, an enemy-ringed land, backed by the sea? Or a growing Empire, stretching westwards into the heartland of my people?

A small memory struggled into wakefulness. A dream that had briefly flared, once. If the Gods threw an Empire open to her son, then it was she who must be certain that it was ruled by the dying light of Arturius and Caer Melot, not by the savage cruelty of Ida's ancestral halls.

'I'll try,' she said aloud, and Cai's slight smile wounded her like a spear-thrust. He drew her to her feet, releasing her hand as they walked slowly towards the rough pathway up from the shore.

'My Saxon is almost non-existent,' he said, 'but they tell me the child is called Aethelfrith, which I take to mean "prince of peace." Is that a good omen for us, do you believe?'

Rhianneth's heart suddenly surged with love for the tiny scrap of life born to her with the summer's dying, and she quickened her step.

'He has a Saxon name,' she answered, 'but until he's grown old enough to fight, he is mine. And I shall win his heart for us, Cai – or break mine in the losing . . .'

He shot a quick glance at her, and paused. Then he shook his head, letting out his breath on a low laugh.

'That's my true battle-maid!' he said softly. 'Ah, Rhianneth! Cousin fox-cub, if only . . .'

But when he spoke again the longing she thought she heard

in his voice was overlaid, cooled and crisped as if by a fall of snow.

'We've brought cattle and grain from Mithrasia. Come and see the granary, little cousin! It's stuffed full enough to last a whole winter's siege with Urien camped hungry outside your gates!'

CHAPTER 10

The Beltain fires flared and died. Summer was coming and the world was astir. Din Guaryrdi hummed with activity. Doors were flung wide, blankets and furs aired in the wind, lines of washing flapped in the sunshine. The stables were cleaned out with great vigour. Amongst the hiss and smell of hot metal the forge fire glowed with a fearsome heat as household knives and pots were mended and weapons were made or hammered into shape, ready for the coming warm months, the fighting time.

Rhianneth stepped out of the king's house and stood for a while, lifting her head to breathe in the musty smell of may that lay heavily on the air. Oh, the sweet memories of home it brought back! All those childhood springtimes when, careless of scratched arms and tangled hair, she had run to Olwen with her arms full of the creamy hawthorn blossoms to beautify the house fot the feast of Beltain.

Her heartbeat quickened. Need rose in her like the springtime sap. A fierce desire for greenness, for damp new grass and the whisper of trees instead of the relentless sound of the sea. Bluebells were spilling out of the forest into a pool of blue at the foot of the great ash, and from its branches the cuckoo called seductively to his mate, while deep in the hunting woods other birds were busy nesting. Rhianneth wanted to leap astride Romulus and gallop away.

When Lovan walked towards her, his limp almost gone, she ran to meet him like a child, eager to share with him the restless urgings that filled her.

'How's my best filly this brave morning?' he cried, his smile broadening into a grin. But before she could answer, his eyes moved past her, and she heard her baby son laugh, and Alda's greeting as she carried Frith out of the dwelling house close by, so close it was almost a part of the king's house. Here Alda now slept with the baby, his Saxon nurse Freda, and little Gwynne, a Rhegen slave-girl no more than twelve years old, who cleaned, washed and mended.

'Here he is!' Lovan swelled with pride as Alda placed the

child in his open arms, 'And what do you want to do today, eh? Fly like a bird?'

Alda gave a scream of protest as Lovan swung the baby into the air. 'You'll make him sick!'

'Sick? Take more than that to make him sick!' Lovan protested. But she snatched the child back and set him down on his sturdy legs, steadying him under the armpits. He began to cry, holding out his arms to Lovan.

'You see?' Lovan was triumphant, laughing. 'Now, leave him to me. It's all right, I won't swing him up again. We know what we're about, don't we, Master Frith?'

He took two small linked iron rings from his belt pouch and rattled them enticingly. The child toddled unsteadily across to him, tears forgotten.

'Don't let him put them in his mouth,' Alda warned tartly. 'They look like horse-trappings . . .'

'I won't. Just fetch me a stool, and we'll be happy here for a while.'

The stool was brought. Lovan settled with a contented sigh. The baby leaned against his knees chortling a stream of nonsense. Ruffling the soft butter-blond hair Lovan remarked, 'He's nearly as bonny as you were, *cariad*. But bigger, much bigger!'

Rhianneth sank down beside them, smiling. The baby shook the iron rings with a gurgle of laughter and her heart swelled with love for them both. As a small girl she had followed Lovan around the farm, watching him tend a sick horse or hammer home a new fence-post. Marcus had stirred her imagination to dream of times and places far beyond the small world she knew. But always, it had been Lovan who pointed out the swallow's nest in the yard, or the sweet-smelling dog violets that flowered beneath their feet, under the snow.

Suddenly the longings that only moments ago had been so powerful, weakened. She had her little son, and not even to undo the ravelled-up nightmares that had gone before would she wish him unborn.

He was her blood, her bone, her life. For his sake she would endure anything. Aethelfrith. Frith, her little prince of peace. Now over a year and a half old.

284

'Go on down to the beach!' Lovan's voice cut into her thoughts. 'The men are working on the boats. I'll stay here with Frith. If I need help I'll call Freda!'

Alda was hovering, strangely indecisive, before them. She looked at Rhianneth, hesitated, and looked away.

'Oh, go with her, *cariad*!' Lovan caught Rhianneth's eye and winked. 'Go and see the boats.'

Then Rhianneth understood. Rolf was down there. She smiled at Lovan, dropped a kiss on the baby's head and jumped up to take Alda's hand.

As they walked, they watched swifts scream over the beacon tower searching for nesting places. The whole world was moving, restless, driven by the yearly need to re-make, re-create. Surely soon the ice in Alda's heart would melt for Rolf?

They passed through the north gate and down the pathway to the shore, giggling, chanting together softly in Saxon an old song Alda had taught Rhianneth, a song to please the northern goddess Eostre whose festival had been celebrated just before the British fires of Beltain; Eostre, who made the seeds swell into life and protected all helpless newborn things.

> 'Now the green blade rises
> from the buried grain,
> Wheat that in the dark earth
> many days has lain.
> Love lives again
> that with the dead has been,
> Love is come again
> like wheat that springs up green . . . '

Gwen was on the beach, rocking her new baby girl Bebba in her arms. She and Hussa were laughing together as their small son Hrothgar ran in circles around them, holding a long trail of seaweed aloft like a banner.

Something stirred faintly, sadly, in Rhianneth. How lucky they were in their contentment, to have been overlooked by the gods!

All this past winter she had lived in the king's house with

Elric. Carried the waes-haeil cup to him in the mead-hall, slept beside him on the fur-lapped bed. Yet even through the warm stirring of her senses, her mind remained cold and closed against him in pride and anger.

Never again had he used force in their physical relationship. He hardly had need to, for a look in his eyes or the touch of his hand made her tremble with a weakness she despised, the more so because she suspected Elric was well aware of it.

'You are soft and warm in my arms,' he whispered once, 'yet your heart is cold as ice. What would it need to melt it, Rhianneth?'

'That's something you will never know,' she retorted, resentful as always of his arrogance and his power over her; a power that had somehow twisted her dislike and fear of him into a dark desire that made her writhe inwardly with shame. 'You've made sure of my body.' Mockingly she flung his own words back at him. 'And you have your son. What more do you want, Elric?'

'What indeed?' he had replied savagely, and left her.

' "Now the green blade rises . . . " ' Alda sang again quietly to herself, searching amongst the beached boats for a glimpse of Rolf's dark head. ' "Love is come again, like wheat that springs up green . . . " '

Suddenly Rhianneth was filled with longing for Cai. For him the ice in her heart would crack, and her mind would open like a flower.

She heard Gwen call her name and she waved a hand in greeting. As she walked across the hard wet sand, sunlight shafted across the great moving waters of the sea, dazzling Rhianneth's eyes. Only when she drew close, did she see Elric.

'Elric is going to the island of Metcaud alone,' Gwen said quickly, looking from one to the other. 'He has made a wager with Hussa that he can row there and back before the incoming tide reaches that rock over there.'

Hussa laughed. 'I'm making him a gift! The tide is already running north, to Metcaud. And there's a following wind! Even Gwen here could do it!'

'Then I'll do it with cargo. Come, lady –' Elric advanced on

Gwen – 'Will you slow me down by sitting in the stern?'

Gwen shrieked and shrank behind Hussa. Elric looked at Rhianneth, held out his hand. 'Rhianneth?'

Dumbly, she shook her head. He moved towards her. She stepped sideways hurriedly, grasped the curved prow of a large boat.

'Never! Go out on the sea – and in that?' She glanced, appalled, towards the tiny boat that waited, small waves lapping around its bow.

'Trust me. You'll love it.' He was beside her, gently lifting her clutching fingers from the wooden prow.

He meant it. Panic added venom to her words as she hissed into his face, 'Stop it, Elric! Play your rough games with someone else! Try Caldis!'

His expression changed. Without warning he twisted her away from the boat and tossed her over his shoulder like a sack of grain.

'Let me go! Let me go!' she shrieked, hitting him with clenched fists. She glimpsed Alda and Rolf, saw them stop short, dumbfounded. Rolf's mouth dropped open.

'Alda! Help me!' Rhianneth screamed as Elric strode to the small boat and dropped her into it. Hussa roared with laughter. Gwen's face was a mixture of incredulity and sympathy, and a growing amusement which she swiftly hid by lowering her face towards the sleeping baby in her arms.

Through Rhianneth's continued cries, Elric pushed the boat outwards, wading in the surf until it floated freely, then jumped in and seized the oars to pull her over the rising waves.

As they rushed through the foaming breakers Rhianneth's breath stopped, and her cries with it. She was stiff with fright. Even when they reached calmer waters a little way from the beach she still clutched the wet boat-edge on each side of her with rigid hands, her eyes enormous.

She could hear Hussa's laughter behind her, but dared not turn to see how far away the shore was. A quick glance to either side increased her terror as she glimpsed foam-laced grey-green waters heaving and rolling within an arm's reach.

Elric sat easily facing her, his bare feet braced against a

piece of wood across the bottom of the boat, swinging his body with each strong pull on the oars. The muscles of his arms and shoulders were taut, hardened by years of gripping his battle shield and wielding Dreamweaver. He looked up, and something flashed for a moment in his eyes before his usual coolness masked it.

'Don't be afraid, Rhianneth. I won't let you drown.'

She forced herself to relax her fierce grip on the sides of the boat. Not because of what he said, but because of that brief glitter of triumph she saw in his eyes.

Elric swung the boat round. She slid a glance sideways towards the shore. How far away it looked! She recognised Alda's yellow dress, standing out like a spring flower amongst the knot of people watching, but already the familiar scene was fast slipping away behind them. On her right the sea stretched out glistening until it touched the sky and froze into a still, dark line.

Rhianneth shut out the slap of waves against the boat, the shudders that ran through her hull as she dipped and rose. She sent up a silent prayer for mercy to any listening God able to bind the awful waters of the sea, and fixed her eyes on the island of Metcaud towards which they skimmed.

The sun was warm, tempered by a breeze cooled by the sea. As her first terror subsided, there were moments when Rhianneth felt a new and strange pleasure in the calm, clean emptiness surrounding her. Then she remembered how flimsy was their craft, how unimaginable the depth of water below them. Into her mind crept the words of Homer the Greek, of how Laocoön and his sons had been devoured by terrible serpents who rose up from the sea, and she trembled anew.

Yet when after a while Elric stopped rowing and brought out food and drink from under his seat she discovered she was ravenous, and not even her fear prevented her from tearing into the cold meat and taking her share of the barley beer.

Soon Metcaud was no longer the strange mist-laden island Cai had once pointed out to her from the ramparts. Now, green and gold in the sunlight, it floated like a flower on the face of the sea.

Nearer still, and Rhianneth saw thin columns of smoke rising into the blue sky from a few houses huddled together beneath a huge jagged pinnacle of rock at the tide's edge. Elric rowed on, edging round the island until at last they crunched up on a deserted beach. He carried her clear of the water, and she helped him drag the little boat safely beyond the seaweed-strewn edge of high tide.

She wondered how long he meant to rest. Even more than that, she wondered whether she could screw up courage enough ever again to step back into that frail vessel.

Elric held out his hand, fair hair tossing above a tanned face sweat-beaded with effort, his eyes teasing. 'Come, and see Metcaud.'

The cool sea wind lifted the hair from Rhianneth's hot brow, and the scent of crushed grasses and small herbs rose around her as they paused on the downward slope of a flat-topped hill. From the top she had gazed all round, as with the eyes of a drifting sea-gull, seeing the green island bright with buttercups and daisies all the way from the gaunt rock on one side rearing up at the sea's edge, to the pale sands where their boat lay.

After the bustle of the fortress, here was peace indeed. Silence, broken only by the murmur of the sea and the cry of gulls on the wind. The last of Rhianneth's anger vanished.

'I once thought Metcaud an eerie place, covered in sea mists.' A small, reluctant smile curved her lips. 'But it's beautiful!'

'You've forgiven me then, for carrying you off?'

'Never.'

He laughed. 'Never? Is that a word my peace-weaver should use?'

'Peace-weaver?'

'Wife. Have you not heard our poets describe the sexes neatly with such words? Women create order from chaos. Men must fight to protect them.'

Stung by his amusement she snapped, 'Does that include humiliating them with a show of strength?'

As gently as if to a wild creature he reached out and touched her cheek. 'Are we still talking about our little skirmish on the beach?'

'You know we are!'

The wind spilled her hair over his hand in a dark stream and she tossed back her head impatiently. He looked at her with a level gaze, as though assessing an enemy.

'I never know, Rhianneth,' he said flatly. 'So often your lips say one thing, your eyes tell me another.'

Silence fell between them. Yet it seemed to Rhianneth that for an instant she had looked beyond his hard male arrogance and glimpsed another part of him. She thought of the boy he must once have been. A boy who spent nights alone in a cold rock cave, listening to the voice of the sea. She remembered the succession of nurses who must have filled his early years after his mother's death, the rough company of warriors that succeeded them. Had anyone truly looked with understanding into his grey eyes then, soothed his hurts, kissed away his tears?

Perhaps he had loved his father, but it had not been a soft relationship. Ida had mercilessly made sure that his eldest son knew just what kingship meant. A king was guardian of his kin. No personal weakness could be allowed which might undermine his power or place his people in jeopardy. To love was to be full of fears, and therefore to be vulnerable.

After the brief affair with Caldis, Elric had known only the rough affection of his brothers and the comradeship of war, the flaring excitement of conquest. How then, could he know anything of the respect, of the dignity there should be between men and women? Rhianneth tried, and failed, to imagine Griffyd throwing Olwen over his shoulder and carrying her across the yard before everyone. Or Cai, seizing herself in some like manner in front of Aunt Julia.

That thought ceased abruptly as Elric's hand slid round to the back of her neck under her blowing hair, and he drew her towards him.

'Tell me I'm forgiven,' he said against her ear, sending little shivers over her skin.

'Tell me you're sorry.'

His breath fanned warmly over her cheek as he laughed softly. 'You never give in, do you?'

He pulled her into his arms and held her close, his mouth near hers. Slowly he bent his head until their lips met. Her head fell back, her lips parting beneath his kiss as the familiar fierce pleasure speared sweetly through her. The sky tilted and she closed her eyes. Elric pressed her down on the grass, amongst the scent, the feel of growing things bursting with life.

'I am sorry I treated you roughly,' he whispered. 'Am I gentle enough now, lady?'

She touched his face, ran her fingertips over the healed scars where once a sword slash had driven into the iron-meshed face-guard of his war helmet. He grasped her hand, stilled it against his face.

'You have been a lot of trouble to me, Rhianneth. Yet I burn fiercer for you now than when you first stirred my blood.' His slow smile held a hint of mockery. 'You stood so fearful and proud beside your brother in Mithrasia. A Roman lady before the barbarians. How could I not desire you? Only then, *deorling* – ,' now the mockery sounded clear in his voice as he murmured the Saxon endearment – 'you were promised to Ida. In love with Cai. But now . . .'

His free hand stroked her hair gently, sensuously, as if she were a wildcat he would tame. Warm excitement filled her, the blood began to pound in her ears.

By all the Gods, she thought furiously, what kind of creature was she that she could still dream of Cai, still long to be in his arms, yet whenever Elric touched her tremble with what she had once called hate or fear, but now knew by its true name.

Elric was what he was born to be. His ambitions were as plain as his reputation on the field of battle was ruthless. He wore no mask, as the enemies she had so feared in Mithrasia wore masks to hide their intentions. As Idwal had worn a mask.

No, it was not Elric's demands that unnerved her, but her

own response to them. The hidden flame that had flicked into life the first time she had looked upon his face, and which now threatened to consume her. A dangerous flame, that licked around the edges of her silent and guarded love for Cai.

'You are like a hunter that needs his kill!' She threw the words like weapons into his face, as if by so doing she might wrench out the treason inside herself. 'Physical pleasure is all you know!'

'It is all I get,' he answered, the mockery suddenly gone from his voice.

Riding the wind, a gull called to its kind and was answered. Stronger now, the peace of the island flowed over her. No clang of weapons as the war-band exercised. No loud laughter or rolling Saxon voices. No barking of dogs or squealing of pigs. Only the sea wind breathing across the hillside to make the grasses move and the small flowers bow their heads, like silver and gold strewn before a God.

Elric's grey eyes were on her face, waiting. Long ago it seemed, that moment in the woodcutter's hut when she had promised herself she would use the lust he felt for her own advantage. That was before, in his great anger, he had taken her with such savage violence. She thought back over the strange, cold months following Frith's birth, when Elric had seemed an indifferent stranger. By the coming of summer he was still coldy courteous towards her, even in bed. There, no words of affection passed between them, only a mutual slaking of passion.

Gradually, as the months slipped by, the tension had eased. Elric smashed out his energy with the war-band, although the skirmishes with the enemy were light that summer. Rhianneth's attention was concentrated on her baby son. She had no time, and little interest, to spare for what went on in Elric's head. She thought she knew him well enough. She believed that when he looked at her and Frith, the memory of that night on the road back from Eburacum simmered in resentment. He, who planned his battles and fought them with such calm deliberation, was bitterly ashamed that in those flaming moments he had lost his normally cool reason. He hated her for causing him to lose control, almost as much as for her treachery.

His carrying her off from the beach today had not only humiliated her. It had also acted as a warning signal, arousing her. For it must never happen again. She herself must control the situation, fan or smother the dangerous flame that smouldered between them. Keep the promise made to herself and use Elric's lust to further her own ends. Grant favours. Tame the male urge to conquer.

'You are forgiven,' she said softly, 'for bringing me here. Metcaud is an enchanted place.'

He drew a swift breath. 'It could be so for us, Rhianneth.'

His mouth came down to touch hers briefly, and she tasted the clean sea-salt on his lips before he moved on to kiss her fluttering eyelids, her ears, the pulse that throbbed in her throat.

'We can't stay,' she whispered, 'you will lose your wager with Hussa.'

'What wager?'

She opened her mouth to argue, but he smothered her words with his kiss. Though her mind was filled with cold calculation, desire seared her body like a flame and soon she could not remember what she had wanted to say for she was lost in the turbulence of a growing storm of passion. Even her resentment of Elric's easy mastery of her emotions was like the sting of spray which but excited her senses more.

The true wild heartbeat of the island rose from deep beneath its soft earth-breast to mingle with her own. Ancient magic twined them about with a power, a strength, older than Eve. The gift of Earth Mother to her daughters, hard to find, harder to hold. For the brief span of its enchantment they came together as lovers, equal partners in the long duel between them, and in the sweetness of that triumph every cool deliberation in Rhianneth's head was consumed utterly.

Warm, languid, she lay quiet in his arms and through part-closed eyes watched the slow passing of small clouds across the great vault of the skies. Beneath and between the crying of gulls, other birds called. She recognised their low, crooning voices, and remembered a bright coverlet Gwen had given her for Frith's cradle, padded with small soft breast feathers from those birds, painstakingly gathered from the lining of the nests they had deserted as summer deepened. So warm and light a thing, she had never before seen.

Thinking of Frith she stirred and sat up. A long column of gnats danced carelessly in the warm air, but the sun was already upon its slide back towards earth. A cold finger of unease touched her at the thought of floating in darkness across the green sea-miles between Metcaud and Din Guaryrdi.

'Elric, we must go,' she said, leaning over him.

He opened his eyes, instantly awake with an ease born of long years of danger and now as instinctive in him as in a hunting wolf.

'The tide has turned, and you have surely lost your wager with Hussa.'

'Ah, how sad!' His eyes laughed at her, his fist brushed her chin. 'But then, *deorling*, there's no need to hurry, is there?'

He sat up, and suddenly their positions were reversed. He held her beneath him with easy strength, and began to kiss her again. Slowly, gently.

They came back through the twilight time, while the moon rose steadily into a still pale sky. Elric wrapped an old length of sailcloth about her and she huddled into it gratefully, for the air was chill when the sun had gone, although the wind from the south which had aided their outward journey had fortunately died down.

Rhianneth slid several times into sleep beneath her rough blanket. Then, while they were still far away, she saw the lights of Din Guaryrdi flaring out across the sea like a beacon guiding them home, and they came in softly, with the tide.

News came of Urien, who had with spring shed his wintertime of quiet and was riding the countryside gathering followers, urging his allies to raise arms against Bernicia. Even before spring swelled into full summer the war-band left to rouse Elric's thanes, to strike at the enemy before he grew too strong. Amongst those who went with Elric was Lovan, as guardian of the horses, and Rolf, spear in hand and iron helmet on his head, his joy so great that even Alda hid her fears and rejoiced with him.

The days slipped by. Din Guaryrdi settled quietly to sit out the long warm weeks of waiting for news, watching for danger.

Rhianneth kept Frith with her during his waking hours, only handing him over with reluctance into the care of his nurse at bedtime. He was such a true little Saxon, sturdy and blond, that it pleased her enormously when the words he now began to string together were in her own tongue. It could not last, or course. Soon enough he would use British only as a second language, and she would lose a precious link in the invisible chain that held him close to her.

Gwen's baby daughter Bebba thrived, a tiny red-haired scrap with an enchanting toothless smile and fierce tantrums, quite unlike her brother Hrothgar who at three years old was an oddly solemn little replica of his vigorous and cheerful father, Hussa.

'I believe that I'm with child again,' Rhianneth told Gwen shyly, as they sat together watching the children play around their feet.

Gwen's face lit up. 'Ah, I'm so glad!' She laughed. 'This old fortress begins to blossom like a garden without thorns!'

But one thorn in Rhianneth's life went on pricking blood. Guthlac's widow, the lady Caldis, still lived, with her six-year-old son Brand, in her guest house within the fortress.

She had refused an offer of marriage from one of the Council lords, pleading that she still mourned her husband. Elric had shown none of the anger that such a patently untrue and dangerously tactless statement should have aroused. Rhianneth's already growing resentment quickened. Any compassion she had ever felt for Caldis vanished. Quite apart from the disturbing knowledge of the lady's past involvement with Elric, she found she disliked her, at times intensely.

The room at the back of the hall called the Queen's Bower

was where the women gathered, often with their small children, to chatter and sew. For a long while Rhianneth avoided going there. She could not follow their quick Saxon, nor did she like the scarcely veiled distrust in the pale eyes of many older women.

When, at Gwen's persuasion, she at last began occasionally to spend time in the Bower, she found that Guthlac's widow was the centre around which all other conversations flowed, as if she were queen and the room her own domain.

In her dealings with Rhianneth however, Caldis moved carefully, gracefully. Her soft-spoken words seemed honey-sweet until, too late, the sting left buried in them was discovered.

'How I envy you your night-dark hair,' she said one day to Rhianneth, with an exaggerated sigh. 'To keep the sun in mine I must gather rainwater and drench it with endless showers!'

There was laughter, for the Saxons loved playing with words. But Rhianneth saw the glint of sharp malice in Caldis's eyes as they swept her from head to foot, and knew that she was emphasising her own immaculate beauty.

At once Rhianneth felt unkempt, slatternly. Her own hair flowed untamed over her shoulders, for she rarely braided it as the Saxon women did. Now its loose freedom seemed sluttish, unbecoming in one no longer a maid unwed. Looking down, she noticed for the first time on her skirt an ugly dark splatter of the endless courtyard mud that never seemed to stain the pale dresses that so complemented Caldis's golden grace.

Rhianneth flushed with anger. With all her heart she wished Caldis gone from Din Guaryrdi.

Summer chilled into autumn, the leaves of the great ash tree were loosened by frost and shaken by the first winds of winter before news came that Elric's banners were within a day's march of home.

He came into Din Guaryrdi like the north wind itself, and the fortress was at once thrown into feverish life, a bustle of preparation. The tedium which had prevailed vanished as if blown away. The air echoed with the loud rolling boasts of the returned warriors.

Lovan and Rolf swaggered in, eager to relate their adventures. Lovan was burned as brown as a nut and seemed ten years younger despite the harrowing events in which he claimed to have taken part. His descriptions of skirmishes with the enemy were vivid, but suspiciously all encompassing, such as might have been the view of a watcher keeping the horses at a distance. Rhianneth kissed him in the middle of a story, her heart suddenly overflowing with love.

The days which followed were bright and filled with laughter. Elric was pleased and triumphant when she told him of her pregnancy. Whatever had gnawed within him at Frith's birth had vanished. Rhianneth knew that his grey eyes grew softer when they rested on her amidst the heat and chatter of the mead-hall suppers, and nothing could hide the newly tender passion which possessed him when they were alone in their house and he took her into his arms. He swept aside her attempt to fasten her hair into matronly coils, scattering pins everywhere.

'Leave it,' he said, burying his fingers in its thick darkness, 'I like it loose . . .'

But Rhianneth held down the heady sense of power that again rose within her. She wanted more. If he would once say 'I love you' then she would truly have won. She would have him fast. Love was a word seldom used by Elric, and that word had not passed between them, however much it appeared to tremble upon his very breath. Perhaps he kept it, clean and shining, for Caldis.

With that thought came a surge of emotion that was raw, savage, so unlike the sad jealousy she had once felt of Cai's wife Morvydd that momentarily she was almost ill.

So Rhianneth pushed it out of her mind. She concentrated on being docile, responsive, and she bided her time.

Wermund had returned with the war-band. As ever, he made no attempt to approach her in friendship, and their encounters were of the briefest. Caldis's son Brand followed him around the fortress, and often Gwen's solemn little

Hrothgar would run out to join them. Then Wermund would show them small tricks with stone and fire and water, often within sight of the king's house so that Frith too would toddle out to watch the magic.

Rhianneth knew it to be a harmless game of wonder for children. Yet she was uneasy. It was Wermund who was master of the game, and she felt in her bones that hidden behind the innocent magic was a true cold sorcery. All her senses screamed danger, but her reason could as yet give it no form.

Once too, she watched Caldis in conversation with Elric and Wermund, and felt a pang of real fear as she noticed for the first time how Caldis's beauty had heightened since Guthlac's death, like that of a captive freed into sunshine. As Caldis turned towards Wermund the expression that had been in her eyes as she spoke to Elric had not yet faded. Rhianneth remembered that glimpse of ruthlessness she had once caught behind Caldis's pale serenity, and shivered. She wondered how far Caldis would go in order to win what she so obviously still desired.

Always in her presence Rhianneth felt a sense of disquiet, as if Caldis brought with her a shadow of . . . something.

Gradually this, and the more open unease she felt about Wermund, merged together in her mind into one enveloping aura which held her within its menace.

Gefrin was being re-fortified because of its strategic importance in war, and its custody was in the hands of an old shrewd soldier called Cuthwulf. Now, surely, was the time for Caldis to take another husband? To take one more step away from Guthlac's treachery and so increase her son's hope of being officially restored as lord of Gefrin.

Yet she refused yet another marriage offer, still declaring she mourned Guthlac and needed time to continue her supplications to Woden, to lighten the doom-weight of his crime. But the supplications Rhianneth saw were the ones in Caldis's eyes whenever she looked at Elric, and the only grief was for time lost and fate's malice.

At last, Rhianneth drew Alda aside and told her to gather secretly any information regarding Caldis, from whatever source. She was aware that Alda would use the slave-child Gwynne to collect kitchen gossip, or listen unnoticed to chatter from the shadows of the mead-hall. She knew she should feel ashamed to stoop to such action. She felt nothing.

As the scraps of intelligence, mostly gossip, came into her hands, Rhianneth made secret notes in the careful Latin script of her childhood lessons. These notes of names, events, dates, she stored in her locked medicine box. Occasionally she checked, to make sure they had not faded or blurred, just as she remembered Marcus looking over the hunting weapons after their neighbour's farmhouse had burned.

'Aye, prepare for the evil day,' her grandmother had nodded then, 'and the Gods may change the rules of the game in your favour.'

What the game might be, Rhianneth did not yet know. She could only gather what weapons came to hand, and hope that one might prove sharp enough to turn the odds.

Winter roared in, and Rhianneth heard in its storms an outer echo of the powerful forces of destruction she felt building up close around her. She became restless, nervous. Gwen told her it was pregnancy that made her so and Alda gave her soothing drinks made with herbs to calm her mind.

She felt the very depths of winter creeping into her bones and chilling her blood. The dark and icy nights were pierced by the hungry howling of wolves prowling the forest, and the sound of the sea came muffled by the wind, like a far-off multitude crowding unseen in the black night.

Snows came, piling up around the fortress. The air grew so cold that the seas threw up great lumps of ice against the shore.

Rhianneth wrapped herself in her warmest clothes and always kept a thick cloak nearby. But her hands cracked with cold, and chilblains made her feet so sore even the softest shoes pained her.

At night she curled within the warm curve of Elric's body, listening to the wind as it howled around the ramparts until it grew in her mind into a living thing trying, like the snows and the forest wolves, to find a way inside Din Guaryrdi.

Then one evening, terror really came.

The little slave-girl Gwynne fell staggering through the door in a blizzard of snow, crying out that Frith was missing.

He had played with Hrothgar and Brand earlier and at first it was thought he had crept out to be with them again, while his nurse Freda dozed and the little maid had been laughing with friends in the big hot kitchen near the mead-hall. But both the older boys were safe at home, and Frith was not with them.

Rhianneth flew into a rage of fear, boxed Gwynne's ears and threatened worse to the nurse who had neglected her son by sleeping. The whole fortress was roused, and when through tears of hysteria the nurse admitted the child could have been missing for more that an hour, a search began in earnest.

The cold was intense. Snow filled every crevice and piled up against the sides of the houses in deepening drifts. The wind was strong and from the east, tearing away the shouting voices, blowing out torches.

Rhianneth, grown clumsy in pregnancy, paced the floor of the king's house, too full of fear even to weep. Gwen and Alda did their best to reassure her, but she would not be comforted.

All her darkest fears now clung about her, most of them too hideous to speak of. Frith had played with Brand. And behind Brand, stood Caldis. Beside them both, Wermund. She covered her eyes and saw Frith's sturdy little body in the icy sea, or fallen from ramparts, or down the well.

Every house was searched. Men inched along the rampart platform, unable to stand upright for the force of the wind.

After kicking away the snow and forcing open the door, they found him at last, huddled in the beacon tower.

The door must have slammed shut, they said. The latch was too high for him to reach, and the howling of the wind had silenced his cries.

He was alive, but cold as ice and blue around the mouth. He wore only his indoor tunic, and his feet were bare.

They wanted to lay him in his own cot, but Rhianneth would not let him out of her arms. She lay down naked beneath the furs of the big bed and held him close against her own warm body.

Whispering to him, rocking him gently, she gradually felt the terrible coldness of him relax.

'There, *cariad*,' she murmured, 'now you're safe. Safe . . . '

The child's eyelids fluttered. 'Brand,' he said almost inaudibly. 'Come get Frith . . . ?'

Rhianneth's eyes met Elric's. Without a word he left, to fight his way to Caldis's guest house and haul her son from his bed.

Brand admitted he had told Frith he was going to the beacon tower after dark to test his courage. Frith was only a baby, he protested, he had never asked him to go too. And although very frightened by Elric's grim face and furious questions he repeated again and again that he had not gone after all because of the snow. He had not shut Frith inside the tower.

'What are you trying to do, Elric?' Caldis cried at last. 'Please stop – he's only a child! He's told you all he knows. You can't believe that Brand shut your son in the beacon tower! Why should he?'

And Elric, looking at the boy's thin pale face, eyes shimmering with unshed tears, let out his breath on a long sigh.

'Why, indeed?' he said heavily, ruffling Brand's soft fair hair.

Rhianneth listened in silence when he returned, her eyes above the dark bed-furs cold with disbelief. The door had been slammed, she knew it. And not by the wind which blew from the east and should have held it open. But she watched Elric's face and saw beneath his tenderness as he looked down at Frith, some other emotion to which he would never admit. A suspicion that gnawed at him like a rat, and for the first time, and strange amidst her anger, she felt a stirring of pity.

She reached out and took his hand. 'Come to bed, Elric,' she said. 'It was an accident, that's all. It's over.'

Now her nights were either sleepless or else filled with nameless terrors and sudden starts into wakefulness. Often she dreamed vividly of Cai, called to him as he walked towards her across the meadows at home. But he never reached her side before the dream changed, or died with waking.

Sometimes her old childhood nightmare came back. She would be there with a burning farmhouse, the black birds screaming overhead circling the smoke, while in the dark forest were huge savage men, waiting.

One night Wermund invaded her dreams, muttering a stream of alien curses and rattling the bag of rune-stones at his belt. Caldis stood at one side, holding her son Brand close against her skirts. Then slowly, as if invoking a God, she opened her arms wide in a ritualistic gesture. Freed, the child ran to the priest, snatched away the rune-stones and flung them at Rhianneth. They flew over her head like birds, calling aloud with voices of ice, and death was in their flight.

She awoke cold with terror, the sound of her sobbing filling the room. Elric bent over her, shaking her awake. She clung to him, weak with relief to find herself safe. For a while he cradled her in his arms, murmuring reassurances until she stopped trembling.

'What frightened you, *deorling*?' He stroked the damp hair back from her forehead. 'There is nothing to harm you here. You have protection wherever you go.'

'In the kingdom of dreams we all walk alone,' she whispered, pressing her face against his warm neck. But when he asked what dream had made her so afraid she told him she had forgotten. Some deeply primitive part of her mind clawed upwards, crushing reason, hissing that to speak her fears aloud would make them more real, give them substance where now was mere shadow.

After a while he rose and lit a candle, then poured out two cups of honey-wine. In the faint shifting light his face was shadowed, inscrutable. Yet there was something there she found disturbing.

He moved back to the bed and handed a brimming cup to her. Suddenly she wondered just what she had called out in her sleep, or to whom, on this and many another night. She took a deep swallow of the mead, feeling in its warmth a comfort as much to her mind as to her body.

302

'I thought,' he said lightly, sitting on the edge of the bed, 'that, as we've given Urien such a bloody nose he'll be skulking at home all next summer, we could make a visit to Mithrasia.'

He watched, without expression, the slow penetration of his words upon her senses and the sudden upward swoop of joy which painted a picture clear as crystal on her face.

'Ah, yes!' she exclaimed. 'Oh, Elric, yes! And we'll take Frith, and the new baby. Aunt Julia will be so – .'

'Frith stays here,' he broke in, 'safe in the fortress. And you'll have to find a wet-nurse for the baby, when we leave. He won't be weaned yet.'

There was a long silence. Rhianneth sank back against the cushions. When at last she spoke there was a note of resentful petulance in her voice. 'You know I can't leave Frith, nor the new baby either.'

'No, I don't know, lady. I know you are nervous, restless. I'm willing to escort you to see your kinsfolk – and Cai. I thought that would make you happy.'

'Are you mad?' she cried. 'After Frith nearly died in the beacon tower? I'll never leave him alone here – not while Caldis is in the fortress. She watches me. She watches Frith. Send her away, Elric! Get her out of Din Guaryrdi. Unless – ' her chin came up, challenging him, – 'your obsession with her has made you weak!'

'My obsession,' he echoed blankly, 'with Caldis?'

They stared at each other, and for an instant it was as if time stilled, waiting. Then Elric's face changed and when he spoke there was a thin edge of ice to his words.

'No dreams lay seige to my sleep, Rhianneth.' He got up abruptly, poured more wine. 'And I can't send her away. There is nowhere she can go. I killed her husband, you may remember? Burned Gefrin. Her nearest kin are in Deira.'

Rhianneth gazed at the back of his head, stinging with helpless exasperation. Send her to Deira then, she wanted to scream at him, marry her off! But she knew he would not do that. And not because he owed her protection. Because he loved her. Had always loved her.

With a flash of suspicion Rhianneth wondered if he had actually taken Caldis again as his mistress while she, his wife, had been too occupied with pregnancy, or too sure of her own physical power over him to see. She tried to picture them together in secret, stolen hours, but instantly her imagination failed. She would know. In Din Guaryrdi's small enclosed community such a thing could not be hidden. And Elric would be different. Worst of all, she would see the scarcely disguised triumph in Caldis's amber eyes. No, it was not possible.

Yet her tongue burned with unformed, unspoken questions and her cheeks grew hot as she sipped her wine, watching him. She was tired, weary beyond sleep. The fragile chain which passion had forged between them was becoming thin, brittle as winter-frozen leaves.

She felt helpless, big with child and no longer desirable. Her hair was lank. She hadn't the energy to paint her face. Her hands were swollen with winter sores and her skin blotched-red every night in the heat of the mead-hall.

She almost laughed when she remembered her fierce vow to tame Elric through his lust for her. Instead, a tear rolled down her hot cheek and fell into her cup. Here lies Artur's battle-maid, she thought, all her weapons broken, crying into her wine.

The baby kicked vigorously within her and she drew a sharp breath. Elric swung round. 'What is it?'

'Nothing. Just your son, getting ready for the birth-battle.'

Swiftly he was beside her. He let his hand rest lightly, fingers spread, over her stomach. '*Our* son,' he corrected. Then he glanced at her face. 'Ah Rhianneth, don't cry! Do you feel ill? Shall I call Alda to you?'

Wordlessly she shook her head, and he gathered her into his arms, rocking her gently against his chest.

'You'll be better when the baby's here. You'll see. Shall we have a feast, to welcome him? And a new dress for you, of finest weave, dyed crimson which will never fade?'

Sniffing, she gave a muffled laugh. He caught her chin and turned her face up to his, dropping a kiss on her nose.

' "A splendid folk-queen you will be!" ' he quoted, in excellent mimicry of a tedius storyteller who occasionally held the mead-hall in boredom, ' "With two brave princes at your knee!" '

Rhianneth's daughter was born while snow lay thick over the countryside; a hungry time of year, with the celebrations of Yule passed and the wind whipping like a knife-blade from the sea.

It was an easy birth, and with it her dark thoughts and imaginings lifted. Winter's broken, despite the snow, she thought, as her spirits returned. Why, even now the foxes will be mating, and at home the first blackbirds will be singing at sunset from the branches of the apple tree.

'Are you disappointed?' she asked, with studied indifference, as Elric held the tiny bundle in his arms.

'Why should you think that?'

'You wanted a son.'

'I already have a son.' He bent his head towards the baby, his expression hidden. 'She's beautiful, *Aelfsciene!* What shall we call her? Wulfruna, after my mother?'

'What?' Rhianneth exclaimed in dismay. 'Not another Saxon name, all thunder and storm!' Her voice softened. 'I know it's winter now, and bleak enough. But she first came to me in springtime, when the island of Metcaud was covered in flowers. Don't you remember how peaceful it was? I want the essence of that tranquility captured in her name. I thought – Serena?' The colour ran warmly beneath her skin, remembering. She added swiftly, a note of challenge in her voice, 'Anyway I'd like a name that remembers Rome, for my daughter.'

'After three years you still call us Saxons, my *deorling*,' Elric remarked mildly; 'And you'd burden our Englisch daughter with so Latin-sounding a name?'

He glanced up and their eyes clashed. Rhianneth stiffened, ready for battle. But he merely said carelessly: 'Yes, why not? Even the great Saxon Hengist's grandson bore the British name Cerdic.'

From his father, Vortigern. A cold shiver ran through her. But she said nothing.

Gwen brought her a gift, a soft woollen shawl.

'She came more easily than Frith,' she remarked, admiring the baby. 'Just as well, for Elric . . . '

'For Elric?' Rhianneth was astonished. 'Why, I had the child, didn't I?'

'Of course!' For a moment Gwen seemed flustered. 'I only meant . . . Well, you can't imagine what Elric was like, the night Frith was born. He was so desperately afraid. I truly believe he would have strangled the cunning-women if anything had happened to you.'

To me? Rhianneth thought disparagingly. Or to the son he begot with such angry violence?

Aloud, she said: 'And bring the curses of the Gods down upon his head? I hardly think so. With Elric, cold reason would surely have prevailed!'

She smiled, to take the sting from her words. But the uncomfortable expression on Gwen's face showed she was undeceived. At last she rose to leave.

'She is a lovely baby, Rhianneth.' She hesitated, and Rhianneth's heart sank. She did not want a discussion. Not even to Gwen would she entrust those secrets most painful to her. For Gwen was Hussa's wife, and Hussa was Elric's loyal brother and battle-friend, a comrade cleaved closer that a mailed shirt.

But all Gwen said was: 'I don't believe you know Elric at all. Or any of us, really.'

She opened the door and the wind swirled through, lifting the hem of her skirt and bringing with it sounds of the fortress.

'But your baby and my little Bebba are so near in age, they must surely grow up sister-close.'

CHAPTER 11

Time slipped by. Spring days, when offerings were made to Eostre and to Woden as the people of Bernicia planted their seeds and put their lives and their battle hopes into the hands of their Gods.

Then came summer, when fishing was good and the forest alive with game but when danger from Rheged was high, and the war-band often away.

After Samain was the Saxon Blodmonath. Blood month, when animals which could not be maintained through winter were sacrificed to Woden for victory in battle. Although this month held the greatest feast of the year, Rhianneth found it always a time of dark, chilling foreboding, made more so by the weird and lonely cries of seal packs who came to the off-shore islands for the cubs to be born.

With winter's wild days the wind howled in from the sea cutting hands and faces till they bled. But at night fires blazed high, and through the old minstrel's magic, sweet music filled the air. Storytellers conjured great heroes into life once more. Weland the Smith and Sigmund Dragon-Slayer strode through the mead-hall, burnishing for these Englisch adventurers the dim folk-memory of their ancestral homeland across the sea.

Two years had passed since Serena's birth. Rhianneth began to be reconciled to life in Bernicia and more at ease with those around her. She had an ability with strange tongues, a skill once used to learn Latin, and her Englisch improved rapidly.

Since Elric had freed him to become part of the war-band much of Rolf's bitterness fell away, though it was plain that his feelings for Alda were unaltered. Then one day he approached Rhianneth and asked if she would release Alda.

'She has agreed to become my hand-fast wife, lady,' he said, reddening with embarrassed excitement, 'and I would buy her with this.'

He held out a gold arm-ring on the palm of his hand. 'I

have a house close by where we may live. If this is not enough, I can get more,' he added anxiously, as Rhianneth made no move to take his war booty from him.

She shook her head, eyes shining. 'Rolf, I give her into your care with all the goodwill in my heart. I want no payment. Give the arm-ring to Alda, in place of her slave bangle. You are both free now, and my dearest friends. May all the Gods go with you, and bring you every joy!'

Her own life with Elric was on the terms of an armed truce, outwardly easy but with neither lowering the shield that guarded their innermost thoughts and feelings. Rhianneth's great joy lay in her children.

Frith was afraid of nothing. He yelled with delight when Elric swung him shoulder high, threatening to toss him into the sea. He fought in the snow with bigger, stronger boys and trailed reluctantly after Rhianneth, to protest loudly as she dried his curling damp hair and wet rosy cheeks.

The boldness that was such a source of pride to Elric made Rhianneth apprehensive. She had never forgotten the episode of the beacon tower, and she loved Frith with such passionate intensity that when Lovan found the child in the stables amongst the dangerous war-stallions, or Rolf pulled him down from the high ramparts, her fear for him burst out in a storm of scolding.

She was thankful that his closest friend was Gwen's son, his cousin Hrothgar. They were always together, and, although Hrothgar was the elder by two years, Frith grew so sturdy and tall that they seemed of an age. Hrothgar's cautious nature curbed Frith's impetuosity, for he often saw danger where Frith saw none.

But Gwen's often expressed hope that her little girl Bebba would also be fast-friends with Serena, was proving futile. Bebba was a small-boned little thing, at three years old as delicate and chirpy as a sparrow. Hrothgar's red-gold hair was, in his small sister, deepened to autumn russet, and his solemn tongue-tied silences were incomprehensible to her. She chattered away, often to herself, and Serena's baby games held no interest for her. Her overwhelming desire, always, was to be with Hrothgar and Frith. To do what they did. Her repeated cry was, 'Wait! Wait for Bebba!'

Caldis and her son Brand remained in Din Guaryrdi. Another offer of marriage had come from a cousin, Siward, in Deira, but Caldis as yet showed no willingness to accept.

Brand had grown tall, and was as pale of skin and hair as his mother. There seemed nothing of Elric about him and little that resembled his younger cousins. Although Rhianneth smouldered with resentment if ever Elric appeared to favour him, she had to admit that in truth the boy seemed afraid of him, preferring instead the company of Wermund.

One night after supper Rhianneth lingered in the Bower talking amiably with Gwen and a middle-aged lady with a sharp nose and even sharper wit. She was the wife of the steward of the fortress, who herself oversaw the business of the kitchen and kept the serving maids in order. Their talk circled gently around the children, the breathless heat of the fine weather that showed no sign of breaking, the need for the grain that would be coming soon from Mithrasia.

At the other side of the room Caldis and her several friends sat near the young minstrel. Later that night he would be summoned into the mead-hall by his master, the old musician, to play soothing music when the men grew tired of bawdy riddles and far-fetched stories and were heavy with drink and meat.

Caldis's long slender fingers plucked at the minstrel's small harp, encouraged by the cries and banter of the small group.

As always in Caldis's presence, like a wild thing sensing a nearby predator, Rhianneth felt a prickling of her spine. Her disquiet was made more intense by Caldis's occasional low amused laugh, the slanted glances that were sent in her direction.

Gradually the chattering group dispersed, and when her own two friends also rose to leave, yawning, for their beds, Rhianneth unwillingly got up with them. She told herself that it was a warm night, bright with a huge moon, and that she was not tired. But at the back of her mind was a ridiculous sour reluctance to leave Caldis here, in the Queen's Bower, like an empress in an empty court.

Caldis stood up suddenly, smiling, and held out the carved instrument to Rhianneth. 'I'm hopeless! Why don't you try, Lady Rhianneth?'

Rhianneth stiffened, suspecting an opening to thinly veiled mockery. She opened her mouth to refuse, but Caldis was already at the doorway. 'My puny efforts can't compete with the noise from the hall anyway! I'll say goodnight, lady – ' she threw a backwards smile towards the minstrel, – 'and Aesc.'

She was gone, and the little harp was in Rhianneth's hands, the carved wood warm and smooth from long handling. Gwen hesitated in the doorway, questioning eyebrows raised. But with Caldis's going, the sense of oppression had vanished. Rhianneth felt wide awake, a little triumphant, and her fingers itched to release the harp's silver notes into the air.

'I believe I will stay a while,' she said. 'It's too hot to sleep.'

Aesc the minstrel was about seventeen, slender, with light brown curly hair and gentle eyes. His face flamed as Rhianneth smiled at him. Her perfume drifted around him, blurring his senses. For a long time he had loved Elric's lady in silence, and with an adolescent intensity only matched by the awe he felt for the king himself. Only sometimes, with a sad song of love that had hardened old warriors, made maudlin by drink, weeping into their cups, could he pour out the longing within him.

Now his sensitive, strong fingers trembled as he placed her hands in position. Her loose hair was so close that had he turned his face he could have pressed his mouth into its darkness.

He watched her catch her lip between small white teeth as she plucked at the strings, and her delighted laugh as the first thin, pure notes sang out was to him more lovely than the voice of the harp.

In the hall beyond someone was telling a story. An old tale, many times told, that demanded at intervals set close together a chanting, footstamping response from the listeners. A response that needed to grow louder, longer, as the story headed for its climax.

The music of the little harp was lost as the shouts and

310

laughter grew. At length Rhianneth swept to the door, beckoning as Aesc hesitated behind her. 'I can't hear right notes from wrong! Come to the king's house it will be quiet there.'

The king's house was empty. A thick candle burned slowly, mingling its pale light with the red glow of the banked fire. Aesc entered with reluctance, uneasy in Elric's private domain. Outside in the shadows, a darker shadow moved.

But Rhianneth was already sitting on the edge of the fur-covered bed. She pulled up a stool for him, but her whole attention was on the harp.

'It's all right,' she said with a touch of impatience, seeing his glances towards the door, 'you'll hear them if they call you. Some of them have voices louder than war-horns!'

He smiled uneasily. 'It's not that – ' he began, but she missed her note and twanged the strings so badly she burst into laughter.

'Show me again,' she pleaded. 'I've already forgotten what you told me!'

Gradually, very slightly, he relaxed. And although her nearness remained disturbing, the light was soft enough to hide his flushed response.

At last, sighing, she handed back the harp and begged him to play for her. His soul basked in the admiration on her face as the sweet notes rose into the warm air.

In the mead-hall a thin figure behind the king's chair bent forward to whisper.

When the music stopped Aesc laid the harp aside carefully. She was not watching him now. Her eyes blank, as if her thoughts were far away in another place and time, she stared into the shadowed edges of the room. Tears glistened on her cheeks.

He caught his breath, his heart aflame at the elfin beauty of her small pointed face. At once Rhianneth became aware of him, that the harp was still.

'That was enchanting, Aesc.'

She unclasped her hands and held them before her, smiling ruefully. 'I don't think my fingers were made for harp-plucking.'

311

'They are beautiful, lady!' Gently he took her hands in his. 'as you are . . . '

Rhianneth felt the tremor of his arms through her fingers, and a sliver of unease pierced her. For the first time she noticed how flushed his young face had become. She tried to withdraw her hands. His grip tightened. She stood up and he rose with her, so close she could see the pulse beating wildly in his throat. His breath was ragged as he pressed against her.

'Ah, lady.' he whispered hoarsely, 'how often I've thought of this! My songs were all for you – '

Suddenly his lips were on hers. Gasping, she tried to push him away. He loosed her hands and threw his arms around her to hold her even closer. His breathing came more quickly as his kiss roughened with a rising passion.

His back was to the door, but he must have felt the rush of cooling night air. Or perhaps his musician's ear caught a sound. He swung round, pushing Rhianneth to one side. In the open doorway, his face dark with fury, was Elric.

For one nightmare instant there was total silence. Then Aesc fumbled for the small dagger at his belt, for words were useless.

Before it was half out of its sheath Elric moved, and his fist cracked sickeningly against Aesc's jaw. The boy staggered back against the bed, blood running from his mouth.

The look on Elric's face filled Rhianneth with terror, for never had she seen murder written so plainly. With a scream of protest rising in her throat she sprang forward and caught at the minstrel's sleeve, sure that Elric was about to kill him. Before the cry ever left her lips Elric gave her a blow with the back of his hand that knocked her to the floor.

'You stay still, lady, and keep your mouth shut.' he said unsteadily, as if he fought to control himself and feared to lose the battle.

The doorway suddenly filled with armed men. Elric slowly drew back, as if against all nature he forced his muscles. His eyes stayed on Aesc and never once glanced towards Rhianneth.

'Get him out of my sight!' he said thickly, pointing at the boy, and his hand shook.

There was the ring of metal, the thud of feet, the sound of many voices. Then the door closed, the noise fell away. The room was as before, but the air quivered with violence.

'Get up,' Elric said quietly. Rhianneth could not move. She seemed held in shock, hands covering her mouth, her breath coming in short, sobbing gasps. Elric bent, grasped a fistful of hair, and dragged her to her feet.

'By all the Gods – ' his voice was hoarse, – 'have I mistaken you, lady? Are you true to your Roman breed after all – with the heart of a whore?'

Abruptly he released her. She caught at the doorpost for support.

'What?' she gasped, more shaken by his words than by his violence. 'Why, you – .'

She caught back the words, watching his hands slowly clench. Unbelievable as it seemed, she suddenly realised that the life of the young minstrel depended upon what she said, now. How she reacted. If all else was confusion, she was certain of that.

'That was unforgivable,' she said at last, her voice held low. 'And yet – yes, I am to blame. The Bower was full of the noise of your men. I wanted to hear the harp's notes. I brought him here. What harm was there in that, in my own house? But I should have seen his fondness. His calf-love, for he is only a boy. You won't harm him, Elric?'

With dismay she heard a rising note of panic beneath that hard won control in her voice, and wondered if he heard it too.

'You seem unconcerned for your own safety, lady,' he replied softly, and with menace.

At once her eyes flashed fire. 'Are you now threatening me?' she demanded, raising her chin. 'Llywarch's sister?'

Elric's hand dropped suddenly and crushingly on her shoulder. 'Aelthelric's wife!' he said roughly. 'Who moons with the mead-hall minstrel behind closed doors! You dared to come here, in my house! How often did you contrive your meetings?'

She felt the tension in the muscles of his arm as he kept his hand rigid on her shoulder, and the anger behind it. She had never seen him drunk. Not even after the longest feasts, when most of the war-band lay sprawled across the tables or under them. Despite the hot sweet mead on his breath, he was not drunk now. When his eyes met hers she saw they burned with a cold flame like the light that flickered sometimes in the icy sky of the northlands. Yet his very sobriety frightened her. He did not believe her.

'Don't be ridiculous!' She forced her voice into calmness. 'That boy has never been here before. I've not even been aware of him. He stole a kiss, that's all! What of that? When my slave-girl was raped you thought it of such little importance you did nothing! Yet now, you come blustering in, accusing me –'

She stopped. Caldis. Suddenly, she was sure. Caldis had watched, waited. She had made certain Elric came. Anger burst up even through her fear, scattering caution.

'You fool!' she exclaimed. 'To be duped by that woman! She whispered in your ear, didn't she? And you leapt up like a dog hearing cat, just as she knew you would!'

'If you mean Caldis, she has not been near the hall.'

'Her messenger, then!'

For an instant something wavered behind his eyes, then it was gone. He said deliberately, controlled anger behind every word: 'No matter how I came. And it is your good fortune that only I saw the pretty scene in here.'

'You struck me!'

'I stopped you screaming your defence of that boy into the ears of my men!'

Silence. The significance of his words crept into her mind, coldness spread within her. She saw the glimmer of metal behind his head, where Ida's great battle-sword hung on the wall. Memory caught at her throat. A king must keep the loyalty, the respect of his warriors and his people . . .

The cold entered her very bones as she thought again of Caldis. For that woman had sought no mere domestic upheaval. She had meant to endanger her life, and with it that of the boy, Aesc. As once she had planned for Frith's death, alone in the cold of the beacon tower.

Rhianneth drew in a ragged breath. 'If Aesc truly needs my

defence, Elric, then you are as much a barbarian as Ida ever was! And more of a fool,' she added bitterly, beneath her breath.

His eyes narrowed and his held anger was suddenly unleashed, violently, as if it broke crashing through a hard held fastness of many years. She thought he would strike her again. Instead he shook her till her head rocked on her shoulders.

'You stupid bitch!' he ground out. 'I should break your damned neck!'

The room spun, the candlelight blurred. He flung her, half-stunned, on the bed. Gasping, she looked towards him. His face was white, and although his breath came hard his voice was now controlled again, and deadly.

'I've shielded you,' he said, 'from the moment I saw you weeping for Cai in the darkness, with Queen Myffan's slanders slithering at your feet. You cared nothing then for our customs. You care nothing now. You flaunt your Roman freedom in my face. I've swallowed your contempt. Your insults. Even your treachery. For the sake of our son, I'll swallow this.'

His hand shot out and pulled her to her feet. She sank against him, the strength seeming to drain out of her body at his touch. 'But if you so much as look sideways at any man again, I'll have your head, lady.'

Now she should have twined her arms around his neck, kissed away his anger, softened his humiliation with her tears. His desire for her was as great as ever, the witchery still held. The passion she aroused in him when they lay together beneath the furs was more powerful now than it had ever been. But she could not do it. It may have been the stabbing thought of Caldis, or the naked arrogance of his words, but she was overwhelmed with a dangerous desire to wound him.

'I've never looked sideways at anyone,' she said thinly, 'nor ever will. There is only one man I've ever wanted. I thought you knew that.'

His hand dropped and he turned away, and stood facing the

315

door. She watched the muscles of his shoulders tense beneath his tunic as he gripped the doorpost, and her mouth dried. She had surely gone too far.

He swung back towards her then, his grey eyes storm-lit and spiked with pain. 'By the Gods, Rhianneth,' he whispered unsteadily, 'were you sent to destroy me?'

Before she could deny his words by even a gesture he had flung open the door and was striding away towards the mead-hall.

She sprang forwards, grasping the doorpost. 'What of Aesc?' she screamed after him. 'You won't harm him?'

He halted for an instant, but did not turn.

'He's already dead.' he said, and walked on.

Rhianneth stood rooted in horror, feeling every drop of blood drain from her face.

The roll of the sea and the rumble of voices from the mead-hall faded before a growing thunder in her head. Her hands rigid on the doorpost, she took gulping gasps of air, fighting faintness.

She backed slowly into the room and sat on the bed for a long time. Out of the hot chaos of her mind, only one thought was clear. She must get away. Out of here. Out where the trees sang with the night wind and the land lay cool, cleaned by moonlight.

The stableboy ran to do her bidding, staring open-mouthed as she mounted Romulus and rode for the gate. At her command the guard leapt into action, protest dying on his lips as he saw the look on her face. In a moment she was through the part-opened gate and away, the horse's hooves pounding against the rough trackway that led to the forest, stones ringing and scattering as they flew behind them. Rhianneth's loose hair blew tangled about her shoulders. tears ran freely down her cheeks.

They entered the forest, rushing through pools of moon-light and black shadows that shuddered with the wind of their passing. The track was a thin band of light, the trees crowded black and eerie on either side. Romulus's breath puffed out like silver mist. It was a dreamlike wild gallop from some hideous truth, through a landscape perilous with shifting enchantments.

Rhianneth's chilled wet cheeks stung as she swayed on the brink of reality. Out of the forest and on to the bleak sloped, territory of the hunting wolves.

Romulus was tiring now, slowing to walking pace.

Her head spinning, Rhianneth fell forward with eyes closed, rested her head against the silky mane. Romulus plodded on.

Somewhere a voice called. She roused, looked back and saw a horseman coming up swiftly behind her. She tried to urge Romulus into a canter but instead he stood still. The shout came again, nearer now. Romulus turned back, as if to greet a friend.

Then a hand was catching at her reins, and without surprise she recognised Lovan.

'*Cariad, cariad* – what are you doing?' Breathing hard with the effort of his chase, Lovan lifted her down from Romulus. 'Come on now, you're safe with old Lovan. You're safe now.'

The warm sweaty smell of his old leather jerkin rose familiarly, comfortingly, around her. She clung to him, hiding her face against his chest as if she were a child again. His big hand felt strong, warm against the back of her head, crushing the wild-blown mass of her hair. His steady words of reassurance gradually slowed the whirling of her thoughts.

'There, my lovely . . .' he murmured soothingly, drawing back a little after a while. 'Now, this is no safe place to be. Let's get back to the fort.'

Behind them, Romulus threw up his head and whinnied softly, scenting some wild thing on the wind. Slowly Rhianneth turned her head and looked about her. Only then did she become conscious of where she was, how far she had come from the fortress gates. Beyond the forest. Out on the hunting trails in the dangerous moonlight of a summer's night.

'Oh, Gods!' she whispered, her voice cracking. 'Oh, Lovan, what shall I do?'

'Come home, now. Home to Din Guaryrdi. To your husband and your babes.'

317

He watched her eyes widen in horror and distress, and eased her once more against his solid bulk, held her steady, stopping her as she broke into jagged, incoherent protest.

'No, don't bother to tell me. I got the gist of it from the mead-hall uproar. Before the stable lad dragged me out shouting that you'd gone off on Romulus! And I don't want to know what went on between you and Elric.'

She pushed away from him then, shaking her head. 'I can't go back. I won't! He hit me. He called me vile names. I hate him! And he said he would kill me!'

Lovan was used to gentling wild and frightened fillies. He stood quite still, made no attempt to touch her.

'Elric?' he said, gently. 'He'll never harm you, *cariad*. He loves you. Any fool can see that.'

'You don't know him. He loves the alliance, the spears and the grain that come every autumn.' She wiped her wet cheeks with the back of her hand. 'And that woman.'

Lovan made no reply. In the moonlight his face was without colour and carved into smooth high planes and dark crevices. The same, yet unfamiliar. As though the night forest had thrown a strange enchantment around him.

'Aesc is dead!' she flung into his silence. 'Should I go back and lie beside his murderer? Gods help me, I must get away from here. I must!' Her voice suddenly broke. 'Lovan, I want to go home . . .'

'Someday, maybe.' Lovan threw a glance over his shoulder. 'But not just yet, *cariad*.'

A group of horsemen had come out of the forest, and were heading towards them. Lovan threw up a hand, and Rhianneth heard their leader's far-away shout of recognition, saw them begin to slow their pace. Lovan grasped her shoulders and gave her a little shake.

'Listen to me, Rhianneth,' he said urgently. 'When a husband finds a man with his wife at night behind closed doors what in Hel should he think? Gods, by now you should know these people! At the very least you've smashed aside a custom designed to protect their womenfolk. Don't make it worse, now! Let it stay a feather in the wind, not a snowstorm.'

Rhianneth stared at him. The drumming of hooves against the dry summer earth grew louder as the horsemen approached. 'Aesc is still dead . . .'

'And you are still Aethelric's queen, remember that!' Lovan's voice was harsh, each word bitten off. 'Leave this to me, Rhianneth. You just keep your mouth shut.'

His words echoed those of Elric as she had lain half stunned by his blow, and she flinched. As the horses came snorting up in a cloud of hot breath, she turned aside, her hands to her face to still the trembling of her lips.

A murmer of conversation, then Lovan was helping her mount Romulus. A few beads of sweat gleamed coldly on his forehead. He gave her one tight smile before he swung up onto his own horse.

She straightened, grasping the reins. Their escort was made up of Elric's younger men, probably the quickest on their feet when the gate-guard reported to the mead-hall. Their leader, a lusty red-haired giant who could hurl a spear or swing a sword with equal ferocity, met her gaze with sympathy, even admiration. Fleetingly, she wondered what Lovan had said to him. Then she found she was too weary to care.

The ride back seemed long. In the cool air her face ached and stabbed, and it felt swollen. The rumble of conversation was subdued, spasmodic. No one spoke to her. But she heard Lovan's deep voice several times as they passed through the woods, along a path no longer moonwitched but dim and dangerous with dust-filled pot holes.

They clattered into the fortress. Lovan held out his arms and she slid from Romulus's back into their steadying grip.

'You made this ride because you were beside yourself, hardly knew what you were doing. Don't ever forget it.' He spoke against her ear, under his breath. 'And by the way, Aesc is alive.'

Relief flooded through Rhianneth, her hands tightened on his arms. But Lovan drew back, straightening, his eyes like stone. 'Elric had him branded with a hot iron, Rhianneth. He's gone. Din Guaryrdi's gates are closed to him forever, and no thane would dare risk Elric's anger by taking him into his service. He is a wanderer without a lord, an outcast of the Bernician people. A marked man and as good as dead, they tell me.'

Rhianneth shook her head, hearing that remorseless echo of Elric's final words to her. She tried to speak, but no sound came out. As always, Lovan softened in the face of her obvious distress.

'Ah, *cariad,* a bad business. But he'll survive. He'll reach Deira.' His voice lowered. 'They say the lady Caldis, overwhelmed with pity, ran to the gate and put his harp into his hands. Elric did not prevent her, even though she probably gave him something else – a ring, maybe, as passport to her kinsman Aelle. And the Deirans would love to spit in Elric's eye.' He smiled faintly. 'But it was a kind act, from a beautiful and gracious lady. God send her good fortune for it.'

With the grain from Mithrasia, came news from Cai. Julia was ill. His wife Morvydd had gone south to her father's house in the Summer Country. Political affairs kept him busy in the city.

That was all. But immediately Rhianneth suspected that behind the tersely written communication lay a call for help.

'I think my aunt is dying,' she told Elric, abruptly breaking into one of the many silences that now lay between them.

'Why should you assume that? Cai says merely that she is ill.' The grey eyes rested coldly on her. 'And that his wife has left.'

Rhianneth flushed. 'To visit her father, yes. I'm not concerned with Morvydd. I want to see Julia again. You offered once to take me back, Elric. Now I want to go.'

Elric turned away, shrugging out of the old sleeveless leather jerkin that had protected him through many a battle and which now served merely to keep out the wind.

'I can't take you. Not this year. Urien and Outigern are stirring again. They're planning a joint attack next spring and I must be ready for them.'

'Then let me go with the grain escort, now,' Rhianneth urged. 'I can't wait until next autumn!'

He grew still. 'You're willing to stay away, for a year?'

'A year? I'll be back before Midsummer!'

'You will not.' He turned then, to face her. 'By Eostre's festival the whole countryside north of the Wall will be dangerous. I won't present Urien or that bloody butcher Outigern with my woman as hostage – or worse. If you go, you'll stay there until the next shipment of grain comes up under guard. Will a year be long enough – with your aunt?'

Resentment quivered in Rhianneth at the implication behind his words. But she controlled it. Elric could so easily refuse to let her go. She wondered why he did not, and the thought of Caldis slithered up to her and would not leave.

'Julia was kind to me, when I was lost and very frightened.' She looked away from him. 'Gods, but I've dreamed of her warm bathhouse, with all the perfumes of the Empire rising in the steam! Besides I want her to know Frith, and Serena.'

Elric did not answer. A chill finger of unease touched Rhianneth. 'Elric?' Her head shot round. 'You will let me go?'

'Why not?' He was regarding her with a brooding savagery. 'But Frith stays. And Serena too.'

Instantly Rhianneth's caution vanished. 'I won't go without them! Serena can ride with me, and Frith is old enough to –'

'Frith is an aetheling. The probable heir to the kingship. I won't let him leave Bernicia. Not for you – nor for perfumed baths!'

His last words enraged her, as the derision behind them stung. 'You think he's safe? While the lady Caldis is here? Don't you realise she wants him dead – and nearly succeeded once, through her own son Brand!'

'You are being ridiculous! That was a child's game, an accident! You never stop, do you? I've told you any link between Caldis and myself is broken. Dead! Are you still trying to strike at her, through the children?' He grasped her shoulders, jerking her against him so that her head was forced back. 'Until she accepts a husband the lady will remain here, under my protection. Do you understand me?'

'One of her kinsmen from Deira is in the fortress now, offering marriage to her and the protection of his house to

Brand!' she spat back at him, 'Why has she refused him? What is she waiting for?'

His face was suddenly hard. 'You know that Brand cannot, ever, come near the kingship. Everyone knows it. Including Caldis!'

'Guthlac died for it.'

'Gods grant that Brand is not like Guthlac!'

'He's not likely to be, is he?'

There was an ominous silence. Rhianneth stared into his face, willing him to deny the relationship, knowing he could not. Suddenly his eyes reminded her of deep sea water, hiding many things. A tremor of fear shot through her.

'I gave a pledge of silence, once.' His voice was quiet. The coolness she had heard in it turned now to ice and all the mockery had gone. 'Then, it was a question of life – or death. Now, it is a matter of honour. You'd best guard your tongue, lady. Or by Woden's Eye, I'll seal it for you!'

He turned on his heel and left her.

Rhianneth stood for several moments shaking with suppressed rage. Then she darted to the chest that held her books, lifted the heavy lid and moved aside the precious volumes to reach the locked medicine box which lay beneath. Her fingers sorted rapidly through the many bottles and jars sent over the years by an anxious Aunt Julia from the best apothecary in Mithrasia. Deeper, past her grandmother's dwindling supply of potions and ointments, until she grasped the tiny bottle of poison. Her grandmother's last gift.

Held safely now in a specially fashioned casket on a cord of twisted silver, it was ready to lie hidden between her breasts if ever she should leave safe Bernician territory again. Rhianneth stared at it, so small and deadly in the palm of her hand. Nine drops.

Then she put it carefully aside. So fine a drink is not for an enemy but for a friend, her grandmother had said.

She thought with loathing of her enemy's calm pale face, behind which coiled such ruthless, murderous designs. Aesc was gone. His name was never spoken. Did he shelter now in Deira, or lie dead somewhere in dishonour? How could she leave her children here, where such a viper nested so snug?

She picked up another bottle, like its dark twin unopened. A quick poison, cleverly culled from the foxglove. Slide this into Caldis's cup, and all her fears would vanish.

Then suddenly, she thought of her own mother, with the king's bastard in her womb. And Queen Myffan, with poison in her heart and mind. Her blood ran cold. It was like gazing into a mirror.

Her hand was shaking. She clutched it hard against her chest and the tiny bottle clinked against the Mithraic pendant she wore.

Live with Light, Wencam said, that bright morning she left Mithrasia. All our hopes go with you. She remembered his pain-blurred eyes blazing for a brief moment with all the doomed glory, the shining dreams of Caer Melot. And she had vowed in her heart, to serve them all. All those warriors of Arturius who had so gallantly ridden into the darkness under their banners of Light.

Gods, what am I doing, she asked herself wildly, am I about to stain my vow with black evil, evil by stealth?

She thrust the lethal thing to the bottom of the box. Her hand brushed against her old wooden writing tablet and small iron-pointed pen. She opened it and stared at the notes scratched so carefully on the waxed inside. Names and dates and scraps of gossip, all collected secretly for her by Alda and Gwynne, and all about Caldis.

Slowly her mind cleared. She pushed the tablet to the bottom of the medicine box, and locked it. Then she replaced her books and shut the lid of the big chest. She knew now, what she could do.

There are other ways than murder, she told herself, for I know my enemy.

Caldis wanted everything that had been Guthlac's and much more, for her son Brand. For herself, she wanted Elric. Events had ensured that Brand never could aspire to the kingship. If he was Elric's son then it was too late, for Caldis was too proud and too wise to admit it. She had filled Brand's head with tales of Guthlac's cunning and strength against the enemy, of his lost stronghold Gefrin where he had once ruled in as much splendour as his brother Ida. Elric would have made promises regarding Brand which she meant to see fulfilled.

Meanwhile Caldis remained Elric's first love. Forlorn, beautiful. And deadly, thought Rhianneth. For she's trapped on shifting earth and can only reach solid ground by pushing me aside. If she marries again, she will lose her hold on Elric. So she waits. She is but one step from his side, after all. Should I die in childbirth – or in some contrived accident – or if Elric could be persuaded to put me aside . . . With a flash of rage Rhianneth recalled the dark winter evening when Caldis sent a slave to whisper in Elric's ear; saw again blood trickling down the minstrel's chin, the fear in his eyes, Elric's murderous anger.

She seized her cloak and ran out of the house and up to the ramparts.

The waters below were sullen, iron-grey. A great flock of birds wheeled against the clouded sky, changing from black to silver as they all turned together and their white breasts caught the light. They were flying south to spend the winter.

Flying south. And by all the gods, so shall I! Rhianneth vowed. I must strike now. Now, before another day has passed.

She stared out at the cold waters, and gradually a plan formed in her mind. The pieces fell into place, locking like the iron rings of a battle-shirt, until the pattern was complete.

The wind rose and she shivered. From inside her dress she drew Glainnader up on its slender chain and held it against her breast, close in the hollow of her hand. It sang, throbbed in her fingers like a living thing, but she did not look down. She kept her eyes on the grey waters. This was not a time for seeing, but for something else. Something her grandmother had known, but which she could not be certain had passed to her.

She grew cold. Beads of sweat chilled on her forehead. Her muscles ached with tension. Still she stood motionless. Behind her eyes was a fire that burned until the pain of it forced tears down her cheeks that felt like crystal on her icy skin.

She grew colder.

Then, it was done. She turned, her hand still hiding the Druid's Stone, to face Wermund the priest.

Often he had looked at her with dislike, even hatred, although since the birth of Frith he had mellowed somewhat. Now what she saw plainly on his thin face was fear.

'You – called me, lady.' It was a statement, not a question.

'No.' She lied easily and at once. She had never forgotten the warning given her long ago by the keeper of the forest chapel. Take care, he had said, for men destroy what they do not understand. Wermund understood only too well, and he was a dangerous enemy.

He stood quite still, watching her, reading the marks of effort on her face, in the tremor of her limbs.

Rhianneth took a deep breath. 'But, since you are here, I would speak with you privately.'

He waited, and watched. 'How may I help you?' he asked at last, uneasily. He had feared this foreign woman when first she had come here from across the grey hills. He believed then, he believed now, that she had killed Ida. If not by poison, then by some sorcery unknown to him.

Aethelric had not listened to him. He had laughed when Wermund warned him that she was in magic league with her dark kinsman. He had threatened him with his sword when Wermund wanted to sacrifice her to Woden for her murderous treachery. But then she had bewitched Aethelric with her elfin face, even before his father died.

Now, the years had slipped by. She had given Aethelric a fine son in Aethelfrith, and a daughter too. Great Ida's grandchildren. Wermund had begun to soften.

Until now. Now, when she called and he had come to her.

'I believe we may be able to help each other,' Rhianneth said. 'I speak of the lady Caldis.'

Wermund eyed her narrowly, but said nothing. Rhianneth swallowed.

'You may know that I wish her gone from the fortress, for reasons that must be plain enough.'

He nodded slowly. 'And how does this affect me?'

'The boy, Brand. I've seen him following you, watched you talking together. He is not happy away from you. And you want him, do you not? As your pupil, your successor?'

Wermund grew still, his eyes sliding away from hers. 'That cannot be. He is high born. Such do not become Keeper of the Altars.'

'Caldis thinks Gefrin will be his one day, with all Guthlac's authority passed on to him. It will not. Elric has three brothers who will not be pushed aside. Not for a traitor's son. Or Elric's bastard.'

Wermund's gaze shot back to her face, momentarily shaken by the brutal plainness of her words. She shrugged. 'He'll never rise past the royal princes. They will see to that. If he had the makings of a hero, another Ida, things might be different. But he'll never make a warrior, though Elric tries to make him one.'

There was silence, broken only by the sullen movement of the sea. Wermund avoided her eyes.

'What you say may be true,' he answered at length, careful of every word, 'but the lady Caldis is rightly ambitious for her son. As for herself. She also has a certain influence with Aethelric which she will use quite ruthlessly to further her purposes.' His faint smile was without humour. 'She is not as resigned to her position as would appear on the surface.'

'I want her married to her Dieran kinsman,' Rhianneth stated bluntly, 'and you want her son. We have common cause. Will you join with me?'

'And do what?'

'It is whispered to me that you have knowledge of – certain events. Knowledge that could cut forever any obligation Elric now feels towards Caldis.'

The priest's eyes narrowed. After a moment he said cautiously, 'And her son?'

'He will be part of our price, for silence. You shall have him, I do not doubt.' She smiled derisively. 'Forget the Altars, Wermund. Persuade Caldis that to be Keeper of Runes is power indeed.'

There was another long pause. 'Aethelric is not always dis-

326

posed to believe what I tell him,' Wermund said sourly. 'The lady will realise that. Besides, all this was years ago. What can it matter now?'

'It will matter to Caldis that it be kept from Elric. That is the heart of the thing. And I mean to use it. With your help.'

Slowly he shook his head. ' I find this too subtle, lady. Too fragile a weapon to be of use . . .'

Rhianneth threw back her hair impatiently. 'Leave it, then, to me! I will see Caldis. Only give me your word that you will stand by the knowledge you possess, and I will guarantee you shall have your apprentice before nightfall.'

A hungry look crossed his face. Seeing it Rhianneth smiled faintly. The priest stepped back, his expression changing as their eyes met, to one almost again of fear.

'By Woden's Blood,' his voice ran quiet beneath the rumble of the sea, the crying of gulls, 'these last years I'd begun to forget what I first saw in you. Poison-keeper. Oath-breaker. Child of the Serpent.'

She made no reply, but watched him with eyes that revealed nothing. Alien eyes, reminding him of honey-mead. Sweet to taste, potent enough to steal away a man's senses.

'This –' his long fingers spiralled the air – 'is but a small thing. You fight now, for yourself. But some day there will be greater matters. And then, like the she-wolf you will destroy anything that offers danger to your kin.' His voice sank even lower. 'You will spare not a crumb of pity . . . for anyone.'

'Don't shake your rune-magic at me, Wermund.' Rhianneth's words fell between them like slivers of ice. 'I don't need your foretellings. Just your word in this one small thing. Are we in league?'

The glow from the fire set just inside the doorway cast a warm light around the house, on the sheen of furs, the glint of silver. The lady Caldis sat on a cushioned stool, her skirts in elegant folds around her, a piece of embroidery in her hands. her beautiful face was carefully calm as ever, but her amber eyes gleamed with mockery.

'Lady Rhianneth, I do not understand you. You tell me that

if I am to keep the regard of Elric I must accept my cousin Siward and leave with him for Deira? Are you suggesting that Elric is weary of my presence in Din Guaryrdi?' Her head tilted provocatively sideways. 'I do assure you, he is not.'

She returned to her sewing, the needle piercing the cloth smoothly, evenly. 'I have had one disastrous marriage, lady. I've no intention of rushing into another.'

Rhianneth felt her skin flush with angry colour. You smug bitch, she thought fiercely. How I loathe you, and that sly son of yours!

'I'm sorry your marriage to Guthlac was not a happy one, ' she said aloud, raising her chin in determination, 'but it was a marriage made of your own choosing, was it not?'

Caldis gave a short laugh. 'Hardly. My late father forced me into Guthlac's bed when I was scarce fifteen –'

'Scarce fifteen, and with an eye on Gefrin! And Guthlac's claim to the kingship? A much better bet, you evidently believed, than mere wife to one of Ida's sons, and trailing a bastard.'

Caldis's head shot up, her face blank with astonishment. After a few seconds she regained possession of herself sufficiently to exclaim, 'How dare you, lady! Brand is Guthlac's son, and heir to Gefrin!'

Silence. She lowered her voice to a whisper, her eyes glinting dangerously. 'You have the audacity to challenge my honour? My son's birthright? You foreign slut, bastard-born yourself, who must needs seduce even our song-maker when your black-haired lover is away!'

Such savage dark anger ran through Rhianneth then that as she sprang to her feet she saw Caldis flinch.

'I'm telling you to be gone with Siward for a marriage in Deira before the Mithrasian grain escort leaves this fortress! Or Elric shall have the truth about your famous forced marriage. I have the messenger who was sent to Gefrin to persuade Guthlac to make an offer for you. A boy then, a man now, and ambitious for a place amongst the war-band. He still remembers the message, word for word. Every last ring of dower gold! Every inducement of goods, servants and land!'

'My father arranged the marriage. He forced me! He bribed Guthlac –'

'Forced you? I'm told you demanded Guthlac for a husband! When your father protested you were too young you laughed in his face!'

Caldis went white. 'That is a black lie! Who told you that?'

'A servant who once worked for your family.'

Caldis relaxed, her voice contemptuous. 'A servant! No doubt with a grudge. Is that your threat? Elric would not stoop to listen to him.'

'To her,' Rhianneth corrected coldly. 'She was your mother's handmaid. She says your mother was already ill with the sickness that killed her. She had brought Wermund the priest to the house to see if his magic might draw out the elfshot, for the cunning-women had failed.'

'Wermund?' Caldis's voice held a faint tremor.

'They were halted at the door by the argument within. They overheard everything. Your mother's tears. Your father's protests. And your demands for an immediate marriage with the king's brother before, and I think Wermund's words were, 'you dropped your bastard brat in the mead-hall for any one of half a dozen young warriors to claim.' Did he quote you correctly?'

Caldis sprang to her feet trembling, her eyes flashed gold. 'Lies! Elric was my only lover, ever! I said that only to force my father's mind!' She shook her head confusedly. 'No, I don't mean that! It's all lies. Elric would never believe any of it. He would never listen to you!'

'Would he listen to Wermund the priest?'

She stared at Rhianneth, hatred blazing like a hot sun from her yellow eyes. 'Why? Why should Wermund do this to me?'

'He wants your son Brand. As a pupil.'

The silence that came then filled the room more thickly than the loudest scream. Rhianneth felt sweat trickle coldly down her body. Her muscles ached with the effort of keeping still, when every instinct urged her to fly.

She moistened her dry lips. 'This way, lady, you can return to your kinsfolk in Deira with an honourable marriage. With Elric's regard for you untouched.'

'Gefrin is Brand's!' Caldis replied vehemently, ignoring Rhianneth's last statement. 'And Elric must restore it to him.'

Never, thought Rhianneth. Aloud she said, 'You must know that Elric will guard Brand's interests.'

'With you – and Wermund – whispering in his ear?'

Rhianneth smiled wryly to hear herself linked with the priest. 'Elric acknowledges Brand to be Guthlac's heir,' she said. ' I do not want that changed.'

'Of course not!' Caldis's tone was bitter. 'Any wife prefers her husband's legitimate cousin to his bastard son! But no aetheling becomes a priest of Woden, a Keeper of the Altars! Elric will never agree.'

'You will persuade him.'

Rhianneth started to go, suddenly sick of it. But Caldis grasped her arm, the slender fingers strong as talons.

'Yes, I chose Guthlac because I wanted wealth and position. To be lady of Gefrin! Not just one of Ida's daughters-in-law, like Gwen. And I believed that if Ida was killed in battle, Guthlac would take his place. Then I would be queen.' Colour flooded her face, and faded. 'He was vicious, cruel. I loathed him. He knew Brand was not his child, though he would have died rather than admit it. For Ida had four sons. Guthlac needed Brand. But he saw to it that I paid for my deception in so many vile and secret ways.'

She paused, her eyes gleaming with a still-living hate. Her hold on Rhianneth grew tighter. 'Do you imagine Elric's love for me so frail that he would be rid of me because I was once overwhelmed not by force but by youthful ambition?' Her lip curled. 'His own ambitions are being achieved by means more bloody. No, my lady serpent, I'll call your bluff and let you spill your poison. He'll never send me out of Din Guaryrdi!'

Rhianneth's hands grew clammy. She fought to keep her head clear. 'Perhaps not. He may weigh your unhappy hours of marriage against your betrayal of his love. He may keep you here. But he will no longer hold you in his heart.'

Caldis laughed, an ugly sound. 'Do it! Let Wermund tell Elric the truth! What will you gain? He'll not fill his heart-gap with you! And I will still be here.'

Rhianneth clenched her fists till the nails bit into her wet palms. 'Having lost the only thing for which you stay? When Elric remembers those dark years after you denied him, and his child . . . why, if I died tomorrow he would not make you his queen!' She bent forward. 'And Brand?' Will he love you for making him just a royal bastard and no longer heir to Gefrin? Over the years, Caldis, you've spun a fine dream for Brand! Of his heritage, of his heroic father Guthlac. But all your hopes would crumble like wood-ash if he, himself, came to believe his rightful place was with Elric's hearth-horde, along with some of Ida's bastards!'

'You lying witch!' Caldis's pale face flamed with hot hatred. 'If Elric himself repeated that to my son, Brand would believe it to be a slander designed only to dispossess him of his rightful lordship!'

'Your son would believe Wermund. He makes the priest his hero and his friend.'

Silence, broken only by the ragged sound as Caldis drew in breath, and in that silence Rhianneth felt victory begin to slide warmly towards her.

'Go with your kinsman to Deira, Caldis, and leave your image still bright in Elric's heart,' she said quickly. 'Give Brand to Wermund, until Gefrin is restored. The boy has no zest for battle-training.'

Caldis flared again into anger. 'He is my only son . . .'

'In Deira you may have other sons.'

Caldis watched her in silence for a moment, breathing hard. 'The game is not yet over,' she hissed, her beautiful madonna face white with fury. 'I will destroy you, or that which you hold dear. I've made attempts at subtlety, but I have not your foreign cunning. Your son survived the cold night of the beacon tower. When I sent Elric to your house to find you behind closed doors with the minstrel I prayed, in vain, that his fury would be such he would kill you. Now I will be straight, and certain. Though it flies over half a lifetime, be sure that, with my curse within the runes on its shaft, my spear will reach you!'

Staring into those hate-filled eyes, a thin streak of horror

331

darted through Rhianneth. The past years rolled away. All the familiar domestic trivia that had filled them, had given her a sense of belonging, of safety, fled. She was back with an alien people, whose gods rode the storm winds and sent the lightning. A people who fearlessly called down the terrifying daughters of Woden to carry their battle dead across the skies. Who used the strange magic of the runes to protect or to curse. An exotic magic that Rhianneth truly and secretly feared.

Some deep part of that knowledge inborn in her through her grandmother, shrieked danger. Danger both terrible and sure, hidden like an assassin's knife in the folds of the years to come.

A sense of dread covered her, as if Thought and Memory, Woden's ravens that wandered the world in their master's service, hovered close in the confines of the house.

Her hand shaking, she opened the door wider and let in a rush of cool air. Stepping through, she paused, gathering her courage.

'Play what games you will.' She turned her head for last a look into the room. 'Just go, Caldis.'

CHAPTER 12

Rhianneth held her cup with both hands, grateful for the warmth as she sipped the hot spiced wine. The morning air was chill, and she shivered as she stood in the kitchen doorway, staring out into Julia's small vegetable garden. Yet she was unwilling to turn back into the warmth of the kitchen, heavy with the odour of roasting meats and the pungent smell of raw onion and chopped herbs.

Surprisingly, she longed for the sweet comfort of a plain dish of frumenty. But the kitchen girl had never heard of it, and Rhianneth hesitated to trouble Torfrida. Her aunt's faithful Saxon maid was full of care in this house nowadays.

Somewhere out of sight she could hear Cai's six-year-old son Reburrus shouting as he rhythmically banged a stone against one of the wooden rainwater barrels that stood beneath the house guttering, while his pet dog barked in excitement.

In the garden before her, Morvydd's old witch of a nurse, now more shrivelled and bent that ever, placidly lifted a weed from the onion row, deaf to the noise. A short while before, the child had pulled violently out of Torfrida's grasp and darted out barefoot into the damp cold morning, clad only in a thin house tunic.

'You'll not hold him!' the old nurse, cackled, throwing a thick shawl over her shoulders as she followed the child out. 'He's a real boy, is that one!'

'The old fool!' Torfrida glared after her. 'She'd deny him nothing, not even the sweating sickness!'

'Don't worry,' Rhianneth comforted her. 'I doubt he'll come to real harm. My own little Frith runs around in all weathers and scarce ever takes a cold.'

'If your boy is like his sweet baby sister upstairs then at least he'll take to reasoning. But Reburrus! He's growing like a wild colt and with as much sense!'

Rhianneth smiled. 'Frith is nothing like Serena. He's big, bold, too cock-sure for his own good!'

But not wild, like Cai's son, she thought. Not wilful, uncaring. As if driven by a raw resentment gnawing inside.

'She makes my life unbearable.' Torfrida looked worn, her once-bright hair dulled with a scatter of iron-grey. 'And she indulges Reburrus in everything. Encourages him to defy me. He's growing so quickly, and he's bright. I know he's bound to be a handful. But he's becoming indisciplined and insolent through that old hag's doting. I do my best with the boy. But I need to spend my day caring for my poor lady; I've no time to cope with a spoilt child and a cantankerous old woman!'

'Can't Cai keep him in order?'

Torfrida's expression softened. 'Ah, he tries. But he's so seldom at home. Always at the palace with the king, or with his uncle Wencam. Or riding down to Deva on some other business. I haven't the heart to worry him with such small domestic trifles. He suffered enough of that when his wife was here, God help him.'

'Morvydd? They left Bernicia soon after I arrived. I scarcely knew her.'

Torfrida's plain face flushed angrily. 'Lucky for you.' She glanced over her shoulder, lowering her voice. 'Holy Mother, but we've had our share of scenes here! She really is a prize bitch!'

Her lips compressed. As if she realised she'd said too much, she hurriedly shook and folded clean linen into a basket ready to carry upstairs to lay in large scented chests.

The noise outside suddenly stopped. Rhianneth heard Lovan's deep voice, and then Reburrus was chattering, excitement trembling through his childish treble. The desperate defiance that had sounded like a cry of pain with every blow, every shout, was forgotten. Pushed back into the darkness where childhood's fears fester or fade through the growing years.

Thank the gods for Lovan, she thought. Soon after their arrival Reburrus had started to follow him around like a puppy, pathetically eager to help as Lovan began his self-imposed tasks of repairing and decorating Julia's house, rebuilding the crumbling garden wall.

'If you've finished your drink, we'll go up to Julia.' Torfrida shook out the last of the linen. 'Little Serena has been with her long enough. Though she loves her company, my lady's too frail to cope with anything for long.' She paused, watching Rhianneth place her cup on the heavy wooden table. 'You're looking a mite pale yourself.'

'I – I find I don't sleep well. Not yet. After all this time, the city noises are strange.'

Torfrida regarded her shrewdly. 'You're missing your home, maybe? You have your baby with you, at least. She'll keep the worst at bay.'

She picked up a warmed drink for Julia and went towards the stairs.

Rhianneth stared after her, astonished. Homesick . . . for Din Guaryrdi? After only two months away, including the journey? Why, she had been frantic to get away! So much so that with Caldis safely vanished into Deira with her newly-betrothed Siward, she was happy to leave both Frith and Serena in the care of their nurses and under the sharp eyes of Alda and Rolf. Then, seeing her mother getting ready to leave, her placid little daughter had fallen into such uncharacteristic storms of tears that even Elric had surrendered. Young Gwynne, in the years since Frith's brush with death in the beacon tower, had grown into a capable, responsible nurse-maid. Rhianneth felt thankful that at least Serena was not another burden added to the upsets in Julia's once quiet house.

True, her private visits to Llywarch were not as she had imagined they would be. A man now of nineteen, her brother was kind, gentle. But the ease between them of six years ago had gone. There was a guarded remoteness in his manner towards her that made her careful when she spoke. His mother the queen he never mentioned. Nor Idwal. Sometimes she felt strongly that he had wiped the past deliberately from his mind, and that her coming was a disagreeable reminder of it.

And then . . . Cai was not here. He had gone into Dumnonia after his wife Morvydd.

She hid her bitter disappointment well. But when she woke

at night, all defences had vanished. She would listen for the sound of the sea, turn for the warmth of Elric beside her and be filled with a brief panic at their loss. Then, to fight the desolation creeping over her, she would think of Cai. His dark, closed face, the sudden sweetness of his smile. Pray that when he came at last, he would not have Morvydd at his side.

Yet she had been officially welcomed with warmth, and respect. As Llywarch's sister, queen of his northern ally Aethelric, she had dined in fine dignity in the painted room, and had an armed soldier who guarded the house and escorted her wherever she went.

Homesick? Why, the idea was ridiculous!

She became aware that Torfrida was waiting at the foot of the stairs, and hurried out of the kitchen towards her.

Suddenly she stopped, feeling sick and giddy. She put a hand against the wall to steady herself, closed her eyes and swallowed hard. The feeling passed.

'What is it?' Torfrida watched her steadily, 'Are you ill?'

Rhianneth managed a laugh. 'I swallowed the wine too quickly. Your recipe is so delicious it makes me greedy!'

Julia lay propped up with cushions on a long Roman couch, watching Serena sort through a box of coloured beads to make small shining treasure mounds on the floor. Already her face was too flushed, eyes over-bright with excitement, and she made no protest as Gwynne was called to carry Serena off, though her expression was fond as she watched the little girl wave from the doorway.

'Is everything all right?' she asked Rhianneth anxiously, when they had gone. 'I heard noises from the garden . . .'

'It was only a game Reburrus was playing. He's helping Lovan now.'

Julia sank a little lower against her cushions, her smile wistful. 'Reburrus was such a beautiful baby, so like Cai. It's strange, but there seems little of his mother in him, Rhianneth.'

'Thank God,' said Torfrida in a low voice against Rhianneth's ear, as she bent to place Julia's drink on a small table.

Rhianneth wandered round her aunt's room, touching the

full, costly curtains of Imperial purple, lifting the stopper of a glass bottle to sniff the perfume captured within.

'You stayed in Eburacum on the way down.' Julia followed her with her eyes. 'Is Gygaun there still?'

Rhianneth turned, feeling the familiar pang of regret twist within her when she remembered Gygaun.

'They tell me he's fled to his cousins in the kingdom of Elmet. There's nothing left for him in Eburacum, Julia. Aelle of Deira rules there now, through his regent Wulnoth. He received us courteously enough – for Elric's men escorted us into the city.'

It was with faint disgust that Rhianneth remembered Wulnoth, a flaxen-haired giant with an ale-swollen belly and cold green eyes, whom she did not trust. When she thought of the Deiran treachery at Caer Greu she hoped Elric placed no great reliance in the present link with his slippery Deiran kinsfolk.

For her, Eburacum's fortress would forever be haunted by its two slain kings Gurci and Peredur. And by Peredur's son Gygaun, crippled by the Gods. Such gallantry of spirit she doubted ever to see again.

'Ah, Eburacum!' Julia sighed weakly. 'I have never seen it. Nor ever will, now.'

Rhianneth looked at her aunt, at the thin hands plucking restlessly at the folds of her dress. So gentle, so delicate a lady. She felt a stir of pity that Julia had been born too late; she should have lived at the height of the Empire, when the world lay secure.

'You would not like it,' she answered bluntly. 'Any remnants of Roman elegance have vanished. It cannot now be compared with Mithrasia.'

And that's no lie, she thought. Not with Saxon thatched huts in every open space and Wulnoth's soldiers sleeping, spitting, swearing in the painted rooms of the *principia*.

Seeing the faint tremble of her aunt's lips, she forced a smile and hurried to hand her the soothing drink left by Torfrida.

'Have this now, Julia, while its warm. And I'll sit with you,

337

and tell you about a marvellous dye the Saxon ladies have, made fromn oyster shells. It produced a most beautiful crimson for their gowns, which never fades . . .'

One afternoon Rhianneth took Serena to see Wencam and his wife Sibilla. The child's grey eyes widened with awe as they entered the large town house with its attractive black and white tiled floor. In the enormous living room decorated in gold, cream and green she hung back, asking to be picked up. Her little hands tightened around her mother's neck as she gazed open-mouthed at the long rich curtains with their patterned borders, the bright coloured pictures painted on the walls. When their hosts hurried forward to greet them, Serena clung harder, and would not be put down.

'Rhianneth!' Wencam's wife kissed her, led her to a couch and sat beside her as Rhianneth settled the little girl on her lap. 'And – Serena?' Sibilla smiled as the child pressed closer to her mother, peeping from the corners of her eyes. 'A Roman name?'

'How did you manage that?' Amusement gleamed in the tired eyes Wencam turned on Rhianneth.

'With the Saxons it is the *sperehand* that matters,' she explained wryly. 'The spear-hand. The right hand. The male line of descent. The female line, the shield-hand, is not quite of such moment. So, I was able to save her from some hideous battle-screech of a name.' She smiled, flicking a glance from Serena's small solemn face to that of Wencam. 'My poor little Aethelfrith I could do nothing about. But at least he's become just Frith, to us!'

She looked from one to the other. 'But you? How have these past years treated you? You seem just the same as when I left . . .'

This was not quite true. Sibilla remained much as Rhianneth remembered her. But Wencam was altered. He looked so much older, and the lines of pain were scored even deeper on his face.

'Oh, we survive, what else?' he answered carelessly. But Rhianneth did not miss the slight fading of Sibilla's smile as she glanced up at her husband.

'I thought by now to be find my brother married,' she remarked lightly, deciding to veer away into less personal matters. 'But he seems not even to be casting his net. Are the available fish not suitable?'

'Something like that,' Wencam muttered, after an almost imperceptable pause.

With a tinkle of bracelets, Sibilla got to her feet. 'You will take some wine with us, and cakes? I'll just make sure all is prepared . . .'

As the door closed behind her small plump figure, Rhianneth looked at Wencam. 'Sorry. Have I blundered into some secret negotiation?'

Wencam shrugged. 'It's no secret. Cai's in Dumnonia treating with Constantine. We want his youngest daughter for Llywarch.' He blinked tired eyes, gave her a faint smile. 'Your husband's kept his part of the Bernician alliance well. Keeps Urien busy in the north. What we need now is a friend in the south to watch our backs. Constantine. But Llywarch at the moment will only play the game so far, and no further.'

'I see.'

He gave a short laugh. 'I doubt it. Maybe I shouldn't be talking like this to you. You're Llywarch's sister. But I dare say Cai will tell you everything fast enough. In any case I'm too tired, too old, to care what constitutes treason these days.'

'What?'

'Llywarch has no mind to marriage. None at all.'

Rhianneth's mouth softened. Poor Llywarch. She could well imagine it was true. He lived for his poems, his books. The cares of kingship sat heavily. What was it Elric had said of him years ago? More suited to join their priests than father sons . . .

Wencam sat beside her, wearily letting out his breath. 'Even if Cai's successful, I've a feeling Llywarch may baulk at actually marrying the girl. Then we'll have lost Constantine's friendship. Probably gained his enmity. I remember him as a touchy youth, stiff with pride. I doubt he'll have altered much over the years.' He shook his head. 'But that's another matter.

339

The truth is, Llywarch's heart is not in the kingship. Maybe it never was. And, by God's Fire, we need a strong ruler! Someone shrewd enough to twist events to our advantage, turn one enemy against another. I'm getting old. Without me, will Cai have strength enough to push aside men already seeking power through the weakness of a king who's a dreamer, a poet?'

Rhianneth stared at him, shocked. 'Oh, but he will. He must!'

'Rhianneth, I've lived almost thirty years at court. For much of that time all my hopes were centred on Elidyr's son, Llywarch. I should have remembered, now and again, a fact as old as Rome. A kingdom with a weak king will be torn apart by ambitious men. Maybe I didn't care to recall that in the years we spent battling for Llywarch's mind against the queen's party.'

He raised a hand, a dismissive gesture, like brushing away a fly. 'Ah, to hell with it! You'll have to forgive an old man's ramblings. I left my youth at Badon. My strength at Camlann. I object to having what's left of me ground so fine in a fruitless struggle to keep Llywarch's eyes off Heaven and on the enemy!'

Rhianneth stared at him in silence. He looked straight back into her eyes, reading the distress there.

'Oh, yes,' he said, 'there are plenty to take Llywarch's place. Cai for one. Or his son Reburrus, should your brother take so long to exchange his palace for a Holy House.'

He got painfully to his feet and eased his shoulders with an almost inaudible curse. He walked slowly to the window and stood with his back to her.

'Your brother has more than a touch of the Roman sickness,' he said softly, brutally. 'Do you understand? He doesn't like women. And what he does like he will never, for love of his God and all His Angels, take. You know the strength of his belief! He'll never betray it by acting what he calls the Sodomite, as others do. I don't think he was born so. Maybe that bloody witch, his mother, eventually smothered all that was natural in him. He's full of pain. Only truly happy

340

amongst books. Or with the temple priest.'

Rhianneth blanched. 'Lucius? Still here?'

'Hell, no!' Wencam turned back to her. 'That black crow flapped away after his mistress, to brood amongst our enemies in Rheged.' Now his voice was full of bitter satisfaction. 'Llywarch's new priest came up from Deva's Holy House. And he's no palace priest, scheming and plotting. He keeps to the Christian temple in town, where he's gathered a few other holy men around him. They do good work there, I give them that. Healing the sick. Copying precious books like otherwise to be lost. God's Light, I sometimes wish Llywarch would join them and be done!'

Sibilla returned then, followed by servants bringing refreshments. Wencam said no more about the king, and the conversation turned to lighter matters. But for Rhianneth the sunny afternoon had become tinged with sadness, and it was with something like relief that she entered her aunt's house once more, to hear the familiar uproar of a domestic battle between Torfrida and Reburrus, with the cackling of the old nurse in the background.

A month past the festival of Samain, which was never celebrated in Julia's Christian household although fires lit the dark countryside beyond Mithrasia's gates, the weather continued unseasonably warm.

Rhianneth sank down on to a seat by a stone pillar, the shouts of stall-holders filling her ears as they urged every loiterer to buy: 'Fine fish, lady, fresh caught today. . . !' 'Here's apples, rosy as a maid's first blush . . . !'

But beneath this colonnade that flanked the forum the shopkeepers were less insistant, for these were not the roughly erected temporary stalls of the market folk in the square, but real shops with all the dignity of permanence.

She watched Torfrida lean over the counter of a jeweller's shop, pointing out the broken clasp of a necklace. This was the place where Cai had bought the fox-brooch for her. But the old shopkeeper had gone now, his premises taken over by a fat woman with a Cornovian accent.

Serena nudged against Rhianneth's knees, face expectant, small hand reaching out towards the sticky sweets skewered on a stick in her mother's hands.

Beside her, Julia's kitchen boy Gareth moved restlessly, shifting the bag of purchases he carried from one shoulder to the other and muttering some rueful jest to the palace guard who accompanied them. The elder man shrugged, blowing out his cheeks with an air of resignation as he stared about the forum square with world-weary eyes.

Rhianneth popped a sweet into Serena's mouth and glanced towards them with sympathy. 'Here – ' she proffered the stick of sweets – 'Take one, I'm sure Torfrida's almost finished now . . . '

The guard said nothing, accepting a sweet glumly.

But Gareth grinned as he stretched out grubby fingers. 'I'm used to shopping days, lady. We're never finished till we're back inside the house. There's quite a few street pedlars between here and home, and maybe one of them will have a pretty thing for my lady Julia, or some new thing come up from foreign lands that can't be done without . . . '

Rhianneth laughed. Watching her mother, Serena gave a gurgle of laughter too.

'That's a right nice little maid,' the boy said. 'Wouldn't mind ten of her, she's no trouble to anybody!'

Sensing an admirer, Serena turned her wide grey eyes upon him and toddled to his side. He crouched down beside her, swinging his load to the ground.

'Can you remember what I've got in here, eh? All the things we've bought?'

Rhianneth watched them, the young boy and her tiny daughter, and faint sadness touched her. Long though a year seemed, in a lifetime it was nothing. There was no future here for Serena. She would not grow up in that world Rhianneth had once longed for so passionately. A world of richness and culture, gowned and perfumed with all the sophistication at the heart of a vigorous thrusting Empire; a world of which this city of Mithrasia, civilised as it seemed, was but a far-thrown echo, as the thin voice of old age is the echo of strident youth.

She suddenly thought of the resentful bitterness that had

soured Olwen's temper when they left the villa for the bothies on the hill. Now she understood. Olwen had wanted for her children the comparative comfort and civilised amenities of the old Roman farmhouse, as now Rhianneth herself desired the rich environment of Roman culture for her daughter.

Her mouth curved into a wry smile. Though Serena's silky curls were more subtle in their fairness than Frith's thick blond hair, the child's grey eyes were Elric's and all Saxon. Elric's daughter would make a Saxon marriage. One that was politically expedient.

But Rhianneth comforted herself with the thought that that was years away. In the time between she must begin to fulfil her vow to the Fellowship. To confound the betrayers of Caer Melot by the utmost irony of passing the flame of Rome's culture to those Arturius had called his 'honest enemies'. And she must start by awakening the minds of her own children.

Gods, how she ached for Frith! The year that had seemed nothing in the ice of her battles with Elric now stretched like a wasteland. She remembered the feel of his sturdy little body pressed against her as she explained that his great-aunt Julia was sad and ill, and very far away. He'd demanded to come too, until she told him his father needed him at his side. Then he'd accepted without question that her journey with Serena was but women's work and his place was with Elric.

Elric. Without warning her stomach muscles contracted as he came suddenly into her mind, his powerful young body gleaming in the candlelight, the sea-grey eyes mocking in his sun-darkened face.

They had parted neither friends nor open enemies, but with a cool reserve that reflected faithfully the atmosphere of the previous days. And the nights between, when Elric had stayed long in the hall. Only once had they twined together, and then in a strange fierce silence that fitted Rhianneth's mood of defiance and uncertainty like a mailed shirt.

She thought of the long Bernician winter ahead, of the deep thunder of waves at Din Guaryrdi's foot and winds howling in from the far north, spitting ice. Would Elric miss her, lying alone in the night? Or would he warm his bed with a willing maid from amongst the slaves and servants?

Torfrida approached, and Rhianneth got to her feet abruptly, thrusting her thoughts aside. They started to walk back towards the forum archway, then Torfrida paused outside an eating house to rummage in her coin purse.

The smell of the hot greasy food brought a rush of nausea to Rhianneth. She swallowed desperately to keep back the salty saliva that gathered beneath her tongue and felt herself go cold, felt sweat break out on her face.

'Dear God, what is it? You're white as spilt milk!'

Rhianneth saw the dismay of Torfrida's face, but could only shake her head, fighting sickness. She walked quickly away from the eating house, back into sweeter air. They hurried beside her, their anxious voices merging in her head. When she stopped, shivering, Torfrida took her arm, urging her on, until at last she found herself sitting on a wooden bench inside the Christian temple with the old goddess still carved over the entrance.

Someone held out a cup of wine, and she took it with a shaking hand. Gratefully she looked up, and froze.

Her mind jolted backwards. She heard again the small rushing stream chuckling beside her, felt the sun that had warmed her face that morning so many years ago. She stared up once more into those same periwinkle blue eyes that saw so much, that same twisted smile that was formed not by laughter but by an old injury.

'But you . . . ' Her voice faded, gathered strength, 'You're the Keeper! The chapel in the forest . . . ?'

He put his head on one side, looking back at her in silence.

'And you,' he said at last, 'are the little maid, too much in her grandmother's company?'

They stared at one another, while Torfrida hovered, uncertain in the face of this unforeseen development.

'This is the lady Rhianneth,' she broke in, bewildered but anxious there should be no unintended slur upon Rhianneth's dignity or status, 'kinswoman to my lady Julia Caprilius, and half-sister to the king.'

The Keeper nodded, but his eyes never left Rhianneth's

face. 'Wed to the Saxon lord in the north, who keeps Urien from our gates,' he said, adding softly, 'you are very welcome, lady.'

'Mama!' The small silence shattered as Serena pulled free of Gareth's restraining hand and came to clutch at Rhianneth's skirts, her face crumpling into frightened tears.

'My daughter, Serena.' Rhianneth pulled the child close, smiling reassurance. 'Mama's fine, *deorling*. This kind man is an old friend.'

She drained the cup and held it out. 'Thank you. I'm very grateful.' Then she hesitated, shook her head. 'Forgive me, but I still can't believe you are here, in the city. When last we met you seemed a part of the forest, as if you would never change.'

'Everything changes.' he said quietly, 'God sent someone else to tend his altar, keep the chapel pure. I admit it was hard for me. Hard to leave a life I loved, the little wild creatures who became my friends. But I was needed elsewhere, as I found when I reached Deva. I set my face northwards and made my way here, following the crying in my head. And God's power had not misled me. Llywarch was in great distress.'

'Lucius had fled to Rheged. To the queen,' Rhianneth said flatly.

'He had. Taking with him, incidentally, several of the little king's most precious books. Llywarch felt lost. Betrayed by a man he had trusted. A man of God. I realised then the task God had set before me. To rebuild Llywarch's trust in man, strengthen his faith in God. I came here – ' he gestured around the temple – 'because I felt it best to have a place apart from the court. In the heart of the city itself, where any citizen might come to worship, or be healed. Where Llywarch could come, safe from whispering corridors, listening rooms. Together we began a great undertaking here. A work held higher than most, in Llywarch's esteem. And over the years, in God's good care, we have achieved much.'

'You heal the sick?'

'That, yes. But to soothe Llywarch's spirit I had to reach

345

into his mind, find the thing he loved. When you are rested, would you care to see a little of what we do here?'

Rhianneth left Serena sitting on Torfrida's lap sucking a sticky blob from the sweet-stick as, tears forgotten, she watched Gareth open his bag upon the floor and begin to sort out their purchases once more.

A door to the side of the altar led into a small living room containing chair, bed and table. A heavy brown cloak lay tossed on the floor. The Keeper bent to retrieve it.

'Is your father well?' he asked unexpectedly, hunching the cloak over a hook on the wall.

'Marcus died of the sickness here in Mithrasia, some years ago.'

'Ah.' His bright eyes fixed on her face. 'I'm sorry for it. He was a good man. But not, I now realise, your father, since you are half-sister to Llywarch.'

Rhianneth threw up her head to meet his gaze. 'I am Elidyr's acknowledged bastard. Marcus married my mother, brought me up as his own child when she died.'

He nodded. 'A good man,' he repeated. 'And now you are queen of a Saxon kingdom. A pagan people. Is this our chance, do you think, to safely send one of our priests to bring them to God?'

Rhianneth blanched. She pictured Elric and his brothers riding along the edge of the sea, black figures against pagan flames that roared into the heavens. Ida's sons, calling down Woden's daughters to fetch a dead king.

'I . . . Not yet.' She cast round for something to soften the bluntness of her words. Then she saw the gleam of humour in his eyes.

'You, yourself, little sister, are still not truly one of us. I fear you wander at the edge of the flock, a prey to the grey wolf.'

She looked down at her hands. 'I have this ring, my baptism gift. But sometimes – yes, I wear the sign of Mithras, and often a serpent bracelet of the old Gods, for protection. And I must warn you that the Gods of my husband's people are most powerful and dangerous. They will not be easily pushed aside, to let in the Christos.

'That, I know.' The Keeper's voice was quiet, his tone flat. He turned, pushed open a door and beckoned her to enter. 'In God's own good time, perhaps?'

Before her lay a long narrow room, well lit by glazed windows set high in the walls. Three men in the rough brown tunics of holy men sat at sloping tables, copying manuscripts. Close by each one was a sturdy bench holding small jars of inks, brushes and sharpened pens of quill and reed.

'Our writing room.'

The Keeper pointed ahead where another door stood slightly ajar. 'Beyond is where the brothers of this small community sleep. Where we cook and eat. And beyond that still is our surgery, where we treat any who seek what skill we have in medicine. All this was added on to the temple by Llywarch, so we might truly make a centre of Christian work and worship. And, as the extensions covered the original temple garden, your brother even made over to us the land adjoining, so we might grow food to eat, plants for healing.'

Rhianneth wrinkled her brow. 'I can't remember what lay behind the temple.'

'Pigs,' he replied, 'and a pork butcher's slaughterhouse. He was happy enough to sell the land at a profit and move his animals elsewhere. Unfortunately he kept the slaughterhouse.'

'Oh dear.' Rhianneth had unhappy memories of the Saxon slaughter of pigs during Blodmonath, a time that yearly brought both the excitement of Woden's great festival and the bloody business of killing animals and salting meat for the coming winter.

The Keeper smiled at her expression. 'Oh, it's not too bad. Serves to remind us of our own mortality. Come, see what we are doing here . . . '

He led her along the aisle between the desks, pausing to watch the scribes as they carefully copied from older manuscripts on to new-made vellum.

'Most of these are city records, some of the originals near falling apart. They must be copied and carefully stored if we are not to lose them forever, and with them all trace of the city's history. We make copies of other things, too. A book by

347

the Roman Cicero that belongs to the king . . . We've even made copies of several of Llywarch's own poems, so he might present them to friends. And then, there are the Gospels, of course.'

Rhianneth stopped by the middle desk, fascinated by the sure-handed skill of the young man. Under his fingers the faded writing of a tattered manuscript was born again in bold black script upon a smooth clean page.

He glanced up at her, flushing slightly with the readiness that came with red hair and pink-toned skin. But his sandy-lashed light blue eyes were friendly, and Rhianneth smiled at him. His mouth fell open and his flush deepened. He was very young, probably no more that sixteen.

The Keeper leaned across, lightly touched the page's edge. 'Here we are making copies of the annals kept by successive priests of this temple. On these sheets are recorded events of note, both here in the city and elsewhere in Britain. We can't be sure they are even half complete, for these holy men could only put in what news came to them, as can we ourselves. News often comes late, and there is sometimes a confusion of dates, and items are scribbled where they can be squeezed in. For these new copies we do attempt to tidy up the mess – and trust that some kind souls will do the same service for us, in years to come.'

Rhianneth bent closer to study the immaculate Latin script of the new copy, her lips moving silently. '517. In this year Brother Julius came to us from Deva. Fire destroyed six houses and a bone-worker's shop. There is plague in Gaul. 518 . . . '

She stopped, heart lurching, as a memory stirred. Her eyes shot to the next year entry.

'519. In this year did Christ Jesus ride with us against wicked heathen men. At Mons Badonicus the savage armies of the enemy were scattered, their might destroyed. Arturius the soldier took the sword from the stone and is therefore now hailed as true ruler of Britain. Brother Giraldus died. The new altar given by Vassilis the Greek was consecrated to God . . . '

'*Badon*' Rhianneth whispered aloud, the hair prickling along her arms and up the nape of her neck. All her life, Badon had been more that just a word, a name. It had become a dream, a brilliant starburst of light in the dark of the years after the legions left. A symbol of hope. To see it written in plain Latin was almost shocking.

She stared at the clear new lettering, once again silently mouthing the sentences. Then she hesitated, read it again. There was something wrong, something nonsensical, in the last lines. Stone? Arturius took a sword . . . from a piece of rock?

She looked from the newly written copy, across to the old manuscript. There it was, the line she wanted. The writing was crabbed, as if the entry had been made by an old man. A man who found using a pen difficult. The ink had faded, and the last sentence was crammed in above the following entries, as if added with hindsight. Afterwards.

Arturius . . . took the sword from the – Saxon. That was it. *Saxon*.

She straightened, her gaze running once more over the new copy. She could not guess exactly how much Latin this boy knew. Probably just enough to get by. But Marcus had taught her well. No matter that the Latin of the original was bad, the lettering faded and cramped, never would she have written the Roman word *Saxum* – stone – when she thought she was writing *Saxon*.

As she took a breath, about to point out the error, she caught the eager look on the boy's fresh young face. Saw the pride in his eyes as he glanced up at the Keeper, then back to the new page lying before him, so carefully penned on its bed of pale expensive vellum.

And she could not do it. Not even to preserve Mithrasia's temple annals from the mockery of some future reader better versed in the tongue of the Romans. What would it matter, after all, the raised eyebrows, the distant disdain of some future holy man for the error that marred this one year?

For it was a year like no other year. And it was Badon itself that people would remember in times to come. Artur's shattering victory. That star of hope to all who struggled against great odds. Beside that immutable fact, the amusing fantasy evoked by one mistaken word would be quickly forgotten.

They were waiting for her comment. She took another deep breath, casting around for words to convey what she felt.

'As a child,' she ventured, 'I was made to practise my letters by copying wise sayings from Rome. I think I've forgotten most of them. Except one. "People who forget their past. . ." '

' ". . . forfeit their future," the Keeper finished, his expression wry. 'I know it well. My old tutor, God rest his soul, used to call it the epitaph of fallen empires!'

Rhianneth smiled. Her glance fell again to the half-finished manuscript page. 'Here, at least, you keep our memories bright. You must be proud to have such skilled craftsmen in your community.'

'Pride is a sin, lady, one that brought down Lucifer,' he reminded her, though his blue eyes twinkled. 'We try only to be thankful for the talents God has given us.'

She raised her chin. 'Well, I would be proud indeed to show even this one page to my children! It marks a great year in the history of our people. And sometimes, when all seems lost –' her eyes grew remote – 'pride is the only horse which will carry you on her back.'

The Keeper said nothing, only held out his hand. Rhianneth took it, and after nodding farewell to the young man, they left the room.

'I'm sorry,' she said, as the door closed behind them. 'I should not have said that. It was not polite. As you so rightly observed, I do wander at the very edge of your flock. And so I hear other voices. Other calls, from the wild country beyond your meadows.'

'I know. I kept the chapel in the forest for too many years not to realise that the old Gods do not die because we no longer call upon them. They wait.' His twisted face shadowed as if with sorrow. 'God knows what sacrifices His shepherds may yet be called upon to make, to keep safe His lambs.'

Rhianneth felt foreboding feather across her flesh like the touch of a black raven's wing. She shuddered, as something clawed at the back of her mind, and slipped away.

But she looked up into his eyes, saw the bright goodness in their depths. Hard, fierce and splendid, invincible as the deathless realms of light.

A cloak of stillness fell around her. Fleetingly, she felt once more like the trusting child she had once been, when she had ridden with Lovan and Marcus through the greenwoods in the early spring.

Then the Keeper shattered her calm by asking, as if he read her thoughts: 'Would you take one small step nearer to Marcus's God? Would you bring your little daughter to me here, for baptism?'

'How can I?' Rhianneth cried yet again, her patience near snapping. 'Elric would kill me!'

Julia's thin face was flushed, her eyes overbright. 'Then why tell him? Serena is too young to do so. He need never know. And your darling will be safe, in God's care. Surely you want that? Rhianneth?'

Rhianneth pressed her lips together. 'I don't know,' she managed after a while. 'She is Elric's daughter . . .'

'And yours! Oh, Rhianneth, if you only knew what this would mean to me! I already love her so. After you've gone, this is all I'll have – this knowledge that she has come to us, is under God's wing.'

Rhianneth was silent. Elric never bothered to ask about her beliefs. He merely assumed that she accepted his gods as well as her own. But just how furious would he be should he find out that she had placed his child into the hands of a priest of the Romans? She had once heard Ida growl that he would rather open his gates to a plague-carrying beggar than to a Christian priest. He'd believed they worshipped a dead god, that they drank blood and ate human flesh in disgusting ceremonies of resurrection. And Elric? Strange, that after six years she could not be sure of his thoughts.

'Llywarch would be overjoyed, I know,' Julia said innocently.

'Llywarch? Why should he care?' Rhianneth flared at once.

'He pretends to be so devoted to his faith. Yet he sent me, his sister, to Ida without a qualm. I wonder he does not consider my children heathen bastards, my marriage empty!'

Julia gasped. 'Rhianneth! Your brother was only a boy then. What could he do? The Fellowship demanded the Alliance, even though Ida was pagan. But I know Llywarch commanded that for seven days the temple priest should pray for you, should bless the marriage. You must believe that!'

Rhianneth stared at her. 'Must I?' Then she shrugged, ashamed to have upset Julia by bursting out with a niggling resentment she had thought long forgotten. 'Oh, what does it matter, anyway?'

What harm could it do? It would greatly please Julia. Almost without knowing it, Rhianneth began with her usual pragmatism to view the protection of the Christos and his Lady Mother for her little daughter as something desirable, another shield against the dangers of the world.

Then Julia used her sharpest weapon. 'How pleased Marcus would have been,' she sighed, lying back with closed eyes, exhausted.

Julia was not strong enough to leave the house. Her baptism gift for Serena, which she pressed against her lips before placing it in Rhianneth's hands, was a pretty silver fish gleaming on a thin neck-chain. Rhianneth hid it away amongst her own jewels. She did not want anything that might remind the child of the temple. Not yet. Time enough when Serena was older to explain her aunt's gift.

With only Torfrida beside her, and with faint but persistent feelings of unease, Rhianneth took her daughter once more into the temple.

When Lovan found out about Serena's baptism he was deeply angered.

'I didn't tell you because I knew you would raise some objection!' Rhianneth cried, her eyes defiant. 'Although why should you? You're Christian yourself. You should be glad!'

'I'm a lot of things, Rhianneth. But one thing I'm not is a fool!' His eyes were bleak. 'Yes, I'd have stopped you. If you'd asked my opinion, as you used to, once upon a time.'

'I did it for Julia!'

He made no reply to that. Rhianneth threw back her head, fixed her eyes on a corner of the ceiling, unable to cope with the emotions aroused within her by his words. By the hurt in his eyes. Mixed feelings of guilt, resentment, and a small quiver of fear.

'I did it for Julia,' she repeated, when she had recovered enough to look back into his face, 'and to protect Serena too. If you're worried about Elric, don't be. He won't care.'

'If you believe that,' Lovan said quietly, 'you really don't know him, at all.'

'And you do?'

'Enough to offer you a late piece of advice. If you want it.'

'And that is?'

'Forget this. Don't go to the temple again. If Elric does find out, plead there was sickness in the city and you were desperate to enlist the aid of any God who might offer the child protection. Otherwise, keep quiet.'

Quiet. Keep quiet. Gods, she thought, with a fresh spurt of anger, had she become such a chattering fool over the years? As a child, as a young girl, she had learned to listen, had been much praised for her silences. Now, it seemed that at every crisis in her life some man told her to shut up.

But this was Lovan. She knew she had wounded him. Perhaps in her heart she had known what he would say, had not wanted to hear it.

'I really do want the protection of the Christos for Serena,' she ventured miserably, 'and that of the Holy Lady, too. Is that so wrong?'

Lovan looked at her downcast head, and into his mind came a picture of the terrified child she once had been, her dark hair loose and tumbled as she clung to Marcus that night the Saxons burned old Gallicus's farmhouse beyond the wood. He remembered her too, crouched dazedly by the meadow-fence, hands sticky with her dead attacker's blood. As for the years since then . . .

He swore softly under his breath. Was it any wonder she gathered Gods around her like a cloak, wore their symbols as talismen?

353

'Oh, *cariad*!' He reached out, gently lifted her chin, already in his mind sorting and discarding words. Words he knew must already have been used, in vain. For Marcus had been far more committed to the Christian faith than he was, or had ever been.

But before the appeal in her eyes, his thoughts crumbled. What use was it now to remind her again that Marcus's God brooked no rivals? Not the small Gods of her childhood, nor those of her grandmother. Nor, more dangerous still, those Gods of the north to whom she fearfully made obeisance.

Lovan expelled his breath on a long sigh. 'May Christ be always with you, and with all those we love,' he said simply, and added, 'but I meant what I said, Rhianneth. Keep this business from Elric – if you can.'

Some days later, Llywarch sent for Rhianneth. She found him sitting in the small room where they had first met, six years before.

'Rhianneth.' He smiled at her, rising to his feet. She thought he looked tired. He was so tall now, and had grown very thin. Once again, she felt a faint regret for the boy that had gone. Even the rebellious lock of hair that used to stand upright from the crown of his head was now tamed into submission and lay flat with the rest.

What fierce games they had played at this table, and he had beaten her every time! With a pang she remembered how angry she had become. His childish glee. Gone the few happy hours spent with her half-brother. Lost amongst all the spent years streaming away into eternity. Now they were both adult, polite strangers.

'I asked you to come,' Llywarch said, offering her a chair, 'because I have something for Serena. A small gift to mark her baptism.'

He smiled, waving aside her gratitude, as Rhianneth exclaimed over the beauty of the jewel-encrusted silver cup. He picked up a linen-wrapped parcel from the table and handed it across to her. 'And this, Rhianneth, is for you. With my love. I – I believe it is something you will be proud to own.'

His mouth twitched, as if he held back a smile. Puzzled,

Rhianneth laid aside the linen wraps and with a gasp of pleasure brought out a slender leather-bound book with clasps of gold.

'It covers about thirty years, I believe.'

Llywarch watched as she gently opened the book, saw her tense, saw her eyes go carefully down each page. She stopped, looked up uncertainly to meet his gaze.

'Yes, it's still there.' He was grinning now, like the boy he had once been. 'Lovely, isn't it? When I mentioned to our temple priest that I'd like to make a gift to you, he told me you were greatly taken with a page they had just finished working on, that it might be made into a small keepsake book. Then, when I received it and read it through . . . at first I was furious. I was about to storm off to the temple, when suddenly I . . . ' He paused, looking sheepish. 'Well, I remembered the sort of things we'd laughed about, that autumn before you left for Bernicia. And then I knew. I was sure you'd seen it too. That you wanted that manuscript, not only because it was Badon, but because it was so funny. Was I right?'

Her smile answered him. Then they were shaking with laughter held only in check by reluctance to hold the temple craftsmen in even affectionate ridicule.

'It's so poetic, too!' Llywarch spluttered. 'Like Alexander cutting the Gordian knot! It really is priceless!'

'Llywarch, I do thank you,' Rhianneth managed, after a moment. 'I shall treasure this always. It's such beautiful work, and so . . . '

'So imaginatively copied?' Llywarch finished for her, as their shared laughter bubbled out once more. 'And you know, I have the barest suspicion that my wise, wily priest is fully aware of every error that goes through his workshop . . . '

The days passed, and Julia grew no stronger. Rhianneth spent hours beside her as she dozed, stitching at something taken from the cupboard piled with unmended linen, while Serena played at her feet.

She was grateful for the time spent in Julia's room, time in which to gather her thoughts. She had counted the days, knew the signs well enough. She could no longer hide the truth from herself, and she was gripped by resentful anger. For there was no doubt that she was pregnant.

It was almost as if Elric had made sure of her. Made certain that if she spent a year away from him she would spend it carrying his child. Swollen, ungainly, undesirable to other men. It would be born next summer, here in Mithrasia. Elric's child . . . born in Julia's house. Cai's house.

Openly now she acknowledged to herself that her urgent desire to return to Mithrasia had little to do with Julia's illness. Her quarrel with Elric, the realisation that Morvydd had gone away, that she would have Cai to herself – that had been the sharpest spur.

Now her dreams of time alone with Cai, riding in the autumn sunshine or talking through the darkening afternoons while winter rain slashed against the window glass, seemed but a bitter jest.

CHAPTER 13

Sounds of battle often rang out from beyond the peace of Julia's room; Torfrida's angrily raised voice, protesting cries from the old nurse, howls of temper from Reburrus.

The sound of feet pounding upstairs would herald the arrival of Serena's nursemaid Gwynne, out of breath and her face red with indignation.

'That old woman's a witch, I swear it! And she'll turn the boy into a fair demon before she's done! He needs a strong hand, that one – and the sooner the better!'

Rhianneth agreed with that, although watching the boy with Lovan she felt also that what he most needed was reassurance. If what Julia and Torfrida said was true, then his life until now had been lived under the shadow of flaring quarrels dangerously near the edge of violence. A precarious world, made more so when his father left on the king's business; periods of absence incomprehensible to the child. Yet though she felt pity for Cai's rebellious son, Rhianneth took care never to leave Serena alone with him. So far he had virtually ignored the little girl. But Rhianneth did not intend her baby daughter to be within reach during one of his outbursts of temper.

One afternoon, when it had grown dark enough for Rhianneth to put aside her sewing, there was yet another commotion downstairs. She sighed, getting to her feet to light the lamps. Whatever it was this time, she would soon hear the details.

As the first lamp glimmered into life, Julia opened her eyes, a frown creasing her forehead. 'More trouble?'

Her voice sounded hoarse, and Rhianneth poured a drink of honied water to ease her dry throat. 'Sounds like it.' She kept her tone light. 'Don't worry. They'll sort it out. There –' she smiled, for the noise below stilled – 'You see? All over.'

Julia sipped the drink gratefully. 'I must try not to nod off so much. It must be so boring for you.'

Rhianneth shook her head, as footsteps thudded on the wooden stairs. 'Here we go – ' she forced another smile – 'news from the battle already –'

The words froze in her throat as the door was flung open and Cai strode into the room.

He had not troubled to remove his heavy boots, and around his shoulders his travelling cloak glistened with damp from the fog which had thickened as the day wore on. In the thin glimmer of the single lighted lamp he appeared pale. He stopped short, staring at Rhianneth.

'So it's true!' His voice shook as he swore softly, and the breath rasped in his throat.

At once Julia turned her head, struggled upright. 'Cai! My love, you're safe home! Ah, come here, where I can see you!'

He went down on one knee beside the couch, taking Julia's thin hand in his own and kissing her cheek. 'Mother. You're looking better than when I left. How do you feel?'

'Oh, I grow stronger every day!' Julia assured him. 'I'll soon be well. But Cai, look at the surprise we have for you!' Her eyes flew past him to the foot of the couch where Rhianneth stood as if turned to stone. 'Here's Rhianneth with us again! With both of you here, how can I help but get better?'

Cai rose to his feet and looked towards Rhianneth. There was a moment's silence. Then he said: 'When I first saw Lovan here, I thought you were dead. That he'd come as messenger. Then he explained that . . . '

He stopped. Shock was still evident in the pallor of his face, the set of his mouth. It showed in his voice as he burst out in anger: 'Just what in Hel are you doing here?'

He ignored Julia's sharp cry of protest, holding Rhianneth's eyes with his own until at last she found voice enough to reply.

'I came to visit your mother. To bring my daughter to see her.'

'Elric let you come?' Disbelief was plain in his tone.

'I didn't know I was his prisoner!' she snapped back, recovering control of herself as the numbness that had possessed her upon Cai's appearance eased. Then she added more gently: 'Don't worry, Cai. I assure you I have his blessing. I came with the grain escort.'

He shook his head, incredulously. 'How will you get back? It's winter. And with a child?'

'With the next supply of grain.'

'Next year?'

She watched as disbelief and a growing puzzlement flickered across his face. But she was spared any further explanation by Julia.

'Is this any way to greet your cousin, Cai? My love, how can you say such things? Rhianneth is our guest, our very welcome guest!'

Cai took a deep breath, glanced down at his mother's worn, anxious face, then back towards Rhianneth. 'Of course. I – I thought some disaster had come to Bernicia. Forgive me, Rhianneth.'

He came quickly to her side, kissed her cheek. Leaving his hands on her shoulders, he stepped back.

'Well, cousin fox-cub. After five years, how goes your world?'

His smile was forced, his eyes remained unfathomable. It was as if he walked on cracking ice. Several days' growth of beard darkened his chin, and his normally Roman-clipped hair now touched his cloak. But the sight of him, so close, after so long apart, was enough to rob Rhianneth of the power of speech. She struggled to find words, while the emotions sweeping through her at his nearness, at the familiar exotic scent that stung her nostrils, made her heart pound.

'And you have a daughter now?' Briefly his eyes flicked over her before returning to her face. 'Motherhood suits you, Rhianneth. You've rounded out, where once you were all angles. Fox-cub no longer, eh? My lady vixen now takes her place.'

'Little Serena is an angel!' Julia broke in. 'Do see her, just for a moment, Cai. Will you fetch her, Rhianneth?'

Cai released her, swung round to face Julia. 'Mother, I'm filthy. I'm tired. I'm still in travelling gear, putting mud all over your floor . . .'

Julia bit her lip, her hand at her throat. 'I said just for a moment, dear. By the time you've washed and shaved and changed and had something to eat, the child may well be asleep. But still, if you'd rather not . . .'

Cai turned back with a sigh, lifted his eyebrows and spread his hands in a gesture of resignation. Rhianneth gave him a tight little smile and hurried to fetch the child from Gwynne's care, thankful of the opportunity to take a firm grip both of her thoughts and her leaping emotions.

Negotiations regarding Llywarch's marriage with the Dumnonian king's daughter had gone well. Like his father Cato, Constantine had fought beside Arturius, and he welcomed Cai with all the grave respect due to the son of a dead comrade-in-arms.

Cai had left Caer Melot triumphant, heady with the growing assurance that yet another good alliance was certain. Soon neither Urien nor Rhun would dare move against them – not with the spears of Mithrasia's allies now pointed at their backs.

He'd turned in the saddle to look back at the great fortress dominating the surrounding land from its high limestone plateau. The early morning sun slanted across ramparts of stone and timber, caught a flash of metal from one of the lookout towers. Over five hundred feet above the ground mists that swirled below, the place looked remote, impregnable. Almost, he could imagine Arturius still there. That Camlann had never been.

God's, he'd thought, how often down this trackway must his father have come? He could almost hear the red-dragon banners flapping in the dawn wind. The jingle of harness, the creak of leather, would have mingled then, as now, with the alarm calls of birds fluttering up from the bushes.

Here in Artur's country, Constantine was keeping faith. Keeping Caer Melot alive. From this bastion in the west Cai could feel the spirit of Empire still streaming outwards, and with Constantine's reassuring messages tucked inside his tunic, he felt a great surge of confidence roll through him that all would yet be well, both for Mother Rome and her lost child Britannia.

His exultation dropped when he visited his wife. In the luxurious family villa he was treated with cold courtesy. His

360

attempts to reason with Morvydd met with blank hostility. Nothing had changed. She disliked Mithrasia. She despised his home and held his mother in contempt. She hated him.

With resignation he heard the familiar shrill note of hysteria start up in her voice and, suddenly murderously weary of the whole affair, he turned abruptly and left her. When he mentioned divorce, her father went white with anger.

'You'd cut us off from our grandson?' he demanded. 'Whom we've seen but once, since his birth in a Saxon hovel!'

'I would remind you, sir, that your daughter insisted on travelling with me into Bernicia. Just as she chose to leave Reburrus and come to you when Mithrasia became too distasteful to her.'

'So?' Contempt flashed in his father-in-law's eyes as he looked down his autocratic Roman nose. 'Is divorce your answer to Morvydd's spirit?'

A cold anger settled like thin ice, stiffening Cai's muscles. 'Spirit? Morvydd is vain, wilful. Selfish to the bone. She considers no one but herself. Not even her own child.' He hesitated, still unwilling to wound this proud old man, choosing his words with care. 'You may continue to indulge her, as no doubt you have always done. After seven years I'm no longer willing to do so. Nor, sir, will I ever again allow my son to be exposed to her . . . her whims.'

Bitterness followed him on the long road northwards to Mithrasia. Accusations and recriminations echoed through his head, and regrets turned in his stomach like sour wine.

Now, he'd had a week of meetings about the Dumnonian alliance. A week of arrangements and settlements. Of arguing round the edges of the agreement terms. Of seeing Llywarch nod, and watching his eyes slide away. The shining enthusiasm with which he had departed Caer Melot had grown wafer-thin.

Suddenly the atmosphere closed around him like a cloak, muffling action, stifling thought. He could not spend another night in the palace. He walked home, careless of the late hour, of the dangerous shadows that haunted the crumbling boarded-up civic buildings, the deserted streets.

The house was quiet, everyone in their beds. Thank the Gods for that, he thought, as he pushed into the dim-lit dining room. He needed wine tonight. Gaulish wine, the richer the better.

Rhianneth sat alone at the table, crumbling the last of a small bread roll between her fingers, a half empty wine-cup before her. Cai halted barely an instant, then walked on across the smooth tiled floor towards the wine table set ready against the far wall.

'You should be in bed,' he said quietly, pulling out a chair to join her. He saw her hand tremble slightly as she lifted her cup and drank.

'I don't sleep well.'

She was pale, he thought. He crushed down the warm ache of longing that seemed to melt his very bones whenever he looked at her. His tone remained admirably light as he said carelessly: 'I still find it hard to believe you are really here.' His glance rested for a moment on her slender body in her loose green gown before returning to her face. 'That Elric would let you stay away so long.'

Rhianneth turned her head away, a soft fall of hair partially hiding her face. What could she say to him? she asked herself. During daytime she might have tossed out some light remark, knowing that other things were going on, other people around to make a distraction. But Cai had not been home for as much as half a day since his return. And now that the house was quiet, and they were alone, she found neither the strength to lie to him, nor to tell him all the truth.

'Is everything all right between you and Elric?' Cai asked, when she made no reply. 'Rhianneth?'

'Hasn't Lovan told you?' She raised her head, striving for indifference, trying to draw it around her like a cloak.

'Told me what?'

Rhianneth hesitated, her heart thudding. To say that she and Elric had quarrelled seemed inadequate. She still felt sick whenever she thought of Aesc. Of the murderous tension that had quivered in the air that night as the young minstrel staggered back from the force of Elric's blow. The only bleak

362

satisfaction she had was in remembering the look on Elric's face when she told him there was only one man she'd ever wanted. And that was something she could never repeat. Not to Cai.

She threw a glance towards him, at the winged eyebrows and the dark hair, now trimmed once more into his neck. Her heart jerked. Wasn't this how she had dreamed it might be? Just the two of them in a dimly lit room, with the night and the winter world shut out? Yet now, it was different. Suddenly she could not bring herself to describe her relationship with Elric. It had been too much like standing on a bridge of ice above a smouldering fire. Cold, and ultimately dangerous. No, Elric held too powerful a grip on her emotions. She wanted him out of her mind. The bitterness between them had no place in this quiet, elegant room.

'Elric and I have crossed swords too many times lately,' she managed at last. 'Then, when I knew Julia was ill, I wanted to come home for a while. Finally he agreed. By the time I get back, the air will have cleared.'

Cai looked at her sharply. The colour came into her cheeks, and faded. When she offered nothing further he said: 'I'm sorry. I imagined by now . . .' He broke off, gulped down some wine and closed his eyes briefly. 'God's Light, I'm tired!'

She twisted the cup between her hands, watching him covertly from under her lashes. He was no longer the twenty-year-old who had captured her heart with his Roman elegance and shining ideals. Now he was a man with faint marks of disillusion on his face, a shadow of cynicism in his eyes. Yet if anything, he was even more disturbingly attractive. She yearned to smooth away the tenseness around his mouth, the fatigue from his muscles.

Ah, Cai, she cried in silence, why could you not have looked beyond the child I was when first we met, and asked my grandmother for me? Before there was Morvydd. Before Elric. Love is surely only one step away from desire . . . and I could have made you love me.

Aloud, she asked: 'Are things not going well?'

'For me? Or for the new alliance?'

She gave a slight smile. 'Isn't it the same thing?'

His jaw tightened. 'Yes, by Hel,' he said after a moment. 'It always has been, hasn't it? Rome and the Fellowship. Maximus, the Empire . . . they've been in me since the day I was born. In so deep, they're there till the day I die. How else do you imagine I have strength enough to keep from kicking our dainty young king into the monastery he yearns for?'

Rhianneth flinched at his contemptuous mention of Llywarch. He and Wencam see my brother only in terms of what they want for Mithrasia, she thought resentfully. They don't care any more that he is clever, or kind, or gentle.

'I've had to convince the Fellowship that we need Llywarch as king, if only because of Constantine's obsession with blood-line', Cai went on. 'He sees an alliance with Elidyr's son as good because Mithrasia has an unbroken royal line stretching back to the son of Maximus. Without Llywarch, to Constantine we'd be just another unstable kingdom. He wouldn't touch us.' His face tightened. 'It took all my persuasive power to convince him that our alliance with Bernicia was a well-tried Roman strategy in an already perilous situation. He kept mentioning bloody Vortigern, just as I knew he would.'

'But you did persuade him?'

'Just about. Oh, Constantine has no love for Urien, nor any of the royal breed of Rheged! He understands our danger well enough. Luckily for us, maybe, the Dumnonians have experienced treachery at really close quarters. He's learned to recognise its smell. Years ago, their neighbours, rulers of the Belgae people, turned on Ambrosius and killed his ally, Constantine's grandfather, Gerontius. When they also joined up with the Saxons at Badon, Constantine's father Cato made damned sure they were annihilated. Now Dumnonian rule extends right over the lands of the Belgae, stopping only at the frontier made by the Great Dyke. And then, of course, Artur named Constantine his heir. We couldn't find a more loyal ally.'

'He's Christian, isn't he, like Llywarch?' A memory from childhood stirred at the back of Rhianneth's mind. Something she had overheard Marcus say. 'Didn't he once put on the robes of a holy man and go into a monastic retreat?'

Cai drained his cup. 'That's right, he did. After Camlann. By all the Gods, that battle shattered more than limbs! It broke everything apart. A world that Artur had clawed together for us out of chaos. After that, there was no more trust, no loyalty. Can you imagine what it did to Constantine, leaving the mounds of the dead and riding back into Caer Melot – to a heritage of nothing?'

He reached for the wine jug, offered it to her, then refilled his cup. For a while he stared broodingly into the red wine before him. Then he drew a hissing breath.

'And even in a Christian Holy House, still Camlann reached out to touch him; did you know that? Encouraged by their mother, two lads barely in their teens forced their way past the altar and tried to kill him. Perhaps to avenge their father's death. More likely to snatch at what they claimed should have been theirs. They were the sons of Medraut.'

'Medraut?'

'Artur's bastard. And enemy.'

'They wanted Caer Melot?'

'They wanted everything. I imagine they thought Constantine easy meat in his holy man's tunic and sandals.' He smiled faintly. 'Unfortunately for them, the habits of a fighting man are hard to break. Constantine was armed beneath his tunic. He killed them both. After that he left the monastery, and came back to piece together what was left of Artur's Caer Melot.'

'What's it like, Cai?' Rhianneth asked eagerly. 'Bigger than Din Guaryrdi?'

He really smiled then, relaxing suddenly, his eyes teasing her. 'Oh, it's big,' he assured her, 'and intact. I didn't mean it was in ruins. Far from it. What I meant was – '

'I know what you meant,' she said softly. 'You're talking about something that lasted for only – two decades? The time between Badon and Camlann. But something so bright, so gallant, that its light warms us now and will shine like a beacon across the years to come . . . '

He touched her cheek with a finger, his smile broadening into a grin. 'You see it still, don't you? As clear as on the day you rode with me along the high ridgeway away from your home. I get thwarted so often. Baffled. Angry. Often too damned tired to remember what the Fellowship is all about. I'd forgotten what an inspiration you are, cousin fox-cub!'

'Fox-cub no longer, remember? Now I have cubs of my own!' Her heart began to beat irregularly at his touch, his closeness. Swiftly she said, 'Cai, about Reburrus. . . '

His hand fell away abruptly, his smile vanished. 'Yes, I know. I'm away too often and too long. I'd have liked him to go to Wencam, as I did. But that's not possible. Wencam is sick, and getting old. So, I've arranged for him to go into the house of Falco. A good friend, one of the Fellowship. He'll grow up with Falco's three boys, share a tutor with them. He'll be happier there. Besides, he needs discipline.'

Rhianneth was aware that it was common custom amongst those who clung to even a shred of old Roman nobility to send their young sons into other households, especially if they themselves were often away at war. Implicit in these arrangements was the understanding that if orphaned, the child's future would be secure. Even the great Artur had been brought up in the family of one of his companions, that most loyal of friends after whom Cai himself had been named. Yet when she thought of Reburrus, with his defiant pain-filled eyes that were so like Cai's, she felt a qualm.

'He needs to be sure you love him, Cai,' she ventured. 'That, more than anything. Perhaps if Morvydd . . . ' Her voice trailed, inviting information.

'I'm going to divorce Morvydd. He won't see her again.'

Shock held her speechless. Cai smiled sardonically.

'He won't miss her, Rhianneth. Any stray street-cat would make a better mother. Reburrus is my son. But I'm not prepared to keep a strumpet in my bed, or raise any bastard brats as my own.'

Rhianneth gasped. 'I can't believe you're talking about

Morvydd – '

'No?'

'I know she's – difficult. You told me once that she had fits of rage, that she stole your mother's jewels, but – '

'Did I? But that must have been over five years ago. Since then, my high-born wife has had any number of hot little affairs during my absences. Lovers she collected and discarded like so many new gowns.'

He raised his cup and tossed back the wine in one swallow. Rhianneth stared at him, horrified. She thought of Morvydd, sitting beside her in Ida's mead-hall. How she'd envied her then, possessing Cai! How jealously she'd gazed on Morvydd's cool classic features, her air of impeccably bred sophistication, had wretchedly imagined her such a good match for Cai's Roman elegance. It can't be true, she thought now. No one looked less like a wanton than Morvydd.

'Are you sure – ' she began, but he interrupted her.

'Oh, I'm sure.' His tone was bitter. 'I've had it from diverse and undeniable sources, one of them being the lady herself. The palace has been whispering for years. But after one of her cast-off lovers threatened to kill her, and killed himself instead, Morvydd decided to leave. Not for all the gold in the Empire would I take her back. It's finished.'

He stood up abruptly, filled his cup to the brim and picked it up. 'Can I see you to your room, Rhianneth, and wish you goodnight? Perhaps you would care to ride, or walk, with me soon? I may be in better spirits by then.'

'A walk would be pleasant.' She rose quickly, feeling as if she spoke with a stranger. 'Could we, perhaps, visit Marcus's grave?'

Their eyes met briefly. 'I'm sorry you should have come home to this,' he said quietly, 'My marriage to Morvydd was already dying when I last came to Bernicia. You've arrived in time for a final memorial ceremony.'

A few days after the celebration of Christ's Mass, Rhianneth found Cai waiting for her at the bottom of the stairs. He held out a hand and smiled that sudden sweet smile which held such power to twist her heart. Together they walked out into the winter streets.

Standing once more beside Marcus's quiet tomb she shivered and pulled her thick cloak tighter. The weather was breaking for clouds were banking towards the north, but she did not want to go back yet. This was a rare and precious time alone with Cai. Even the guard who usually accompanied her was absent, for she was under the protection of her cousin's sword.

The rain reached them with frightening speed, its fury such that they were drenched within moments. They hurried through the city gate and into the nearest shelter, an inn which once had offered respectable accommodation for travellers into the city, but now looked run-down, sleazy.

When Rhianneth would have shaken back the hood of her cloak, Cai stopped her. His eyes went past her into the room, poorly lit against the darkening day by ill-smelling mutton fat candles. Men sprawled around tables stained by the grease and ale of years. He spoke in a low voice to the red-faced leather aproned landlord, and there was the chink of coins.

The man led them down a passage and into another much smaller room at the back of the inn. He lit a candle on the table. After a moment a blowsy, sloe-eyed girl brought in a jug of wine and two cups.

'Anything else?' she demanded, pushing long greasy hair behind her ears. Cai shook his head, tossing a coin into her hand, and she flounced out with a smirk, thudding the heavy door behind her.

'You should take off your wet cloak,' Cai said into the sudden silence. 'Sorry about this. It's the only spare room they've got. I couldn't take you into the other place.'

'No.'

She hung her cloak on a peg. Cai flung his own over a stool, then poured wine for them both. Restlessly he pushed open the small window that let on to a sour-smelling back alley littered with kitchen rubbish. Rain was still beating down, and the candle flame swayed perilously in the sudden draught. He closed the window quickly, came back to the table and picked up his wine cup.

'The sooner we can leave, the better.'

Rhianneth glanced round the grimy room, bare of furniture save for the table and a few stools, and silently agreed.

'Have you been here before?' she asked, after an awkward silence.

'Once, only. About five years ago. On my way back from Din Guaryrdi. I felt . . . I felt the need of drink, of company. But there are much better places.'

'I can imagine.'

This time he glanced at her with faint exasperation. 'No, you can't. How could you possibly know how it feels, when a whore-house holds more comfort than your own home?'

'Is that what this is?'

'That's right. Of a sort. The rooms are upstairs.'

She sat down on a stool, silenced. What had that woman been like, she who had given Cai a brief solace he never found with Morvydd? 'There are better places' he'd said. So there had been others, too, over the years, faceless creatures he'd held in his arms for a few brief hours. She was not jealous. Jealousy was the aching envy she'd once felt of Morvydd. Or the tearing animal hatred she'd known for Caldis . . . Abruptly, she cut off her thoughts.

Cai remained standing, watching her. 'It's all right, Rhianneth,' he said, misunderstanding the expressions crossing her face. 'No one will disturb us. As soon as the rain eases, we'll leave by the back door. Or would you rather we left now?'

'No.' She shook her head. 'No, of course not. We had to find somewhere. It's not that. It's just . . .' She sighed, caught her bottom lip between small white teeth. 'Nothing works out as we think it should, does it? There's always a twist in the path.'

'Of course. How else can the Gods keep one step ahead?'

He hooked out another stool and sat down, his smile only faintly bitter. The candlelight caught a glint of the slender chain Rhianneth wore round her neck. On it swung a casket smaller than a little finger, delicately carved in silver.

'You always wear this,' he said, touching it lightly. 'This –

369

and that green crystal Serpent's Egg. Yet you must have many other pretty things. Things of more value?'

Rhianneth caught up the tiny cage and held it hidden within her hand for an instant before dropping it inside her dress to lie where it usually lay, safe between her breasts.

'It's precious to me. My grandmother's last gift. It would take much – ' A sudden chill ran over her and she shivered, looking away from his curious eyes – 'Almost too much, for me to part with it.'

At once he pushed her wine cup nearer. 'Swallow some wine. It will warm you. Sorry, does it upset you to be reminded of home? Perhaps,' he hesitated, 'perhaps it might be possible, if Llywarch agrees, to get an escort after Beltain when the roads are better, and –'

'No!' Sharply she cut across his words, and then at his look of surprise added more gently, 'No, I wouldn't want that. It's been too long. I couldn't bear to see the house again. Or to know which of my relatives live and which are lost. It's a part of my life that has closed. I don't want it . . . reopened.'

And by Beltain, she thought sourly, I'll be in no fit state to travel anywhere. Once more, hot resentment against Elric erupted, flooding her face with colour, her eyes glittering with swiftly suppressed tears.

Immediately Cai changed a subject he imagined distressing to her. 'I'll be going down into Dumnonia around harvest time.'

She raised her cup and sipped the rough red wine, trying to regain her composure while he made conversation.

'If all goes well, I'll bring back a bride for Llywarch.' He paused momentarily. 'And a string of the fine big horses Constantine has promised as a bride dower. Stallions we can use as the basis of a cavalry unit for Mithrasia. Mares we can breed from, too!'

'Cai, that's wonderful!' She saw, for the first time since she'd been here, a gleam of excitement that briefly erased the cynicism in his eyes. 'It's what you've always wanted!'

'It's what we need. Thank the gods we still have a few old

cavalrymen, like Wencam, left. They'll have to teach us how to fight from horseback. Train up a new breed of warrior to equal Artur's cataphracts. Let's hope it works.'

He tossed back his wine and, getting to his feet, opened the window. The rainstorm had passed, although its force could be still heard in the water pouring down pipes and rushing along the street gutters.

'Well, cousin fox-cub?' He turned back, lifted her sodden cloak from the peg. 'Shall we go?'

'That's twice you've called me that.' She smiled wanly. 'Yet for a lady with two children it's no longer appropriate. Or so you told me.

She stood up, too close.

'Whatever I said, my lady vixen,' he answered slowly, his eyes on her mouth, 'to me you will always be as you were the day we walked together across your meadow to the stream.'

'Even when I have grandchildren around my feet?' Her eyes danced, teasing him.

'Even then.'

For an instant they were so still she heard the quick breath he drew. His lips touched hers in a light caress that lasted less than a moment. Her lips parted on a gasp. He swore softly, and turned aside. Then without warning his mouth was back on hers again, this time in kiss so intimate that a sweet spear of remembered desire stabbed through her. She slid her hands behind his head, into the thick dark hair, and his arms tightened around her. When he dropped the cloak he was holding and his hand cupped the swell of her breast she quivered, but did not pull away. Her whole mind was on fire with the realisation that after all these years, after all her dreams, she was here at last, alone with Cai.

And he wanted her. She could feel desire running through him has he drew her closer against the hardness of his body. His lips travelled from her mouth to the hollow of her throat and her head fell back as she trembled against him.

His breath quickened. 'You are more beautiful than ever, Rhianneth,' he whispered, 'and I've never stopped wanting you, loving you . . .'

371

His mouth covered hers in a deep kiss of naked longing. Rhianneth felt herself lost, swept away on the tide of his sudden passion. Her breasts tautened beneath his hands and her heart began to beat with slow powerful thuds as the blood raced through her body. His head lifted and he looked down into her face. His eyes were dark pools, swirling her into oblivion. His hands moved, caressing her back, sliding down to grip her waist.

'One brief moment for us Rhianneth. What is that against eternity, against the shrine-cold annals of honour . . .'

But with his words, she thought of Marcus, and the grey rain darkening the stone of his tomb as it swept down from the northlands. And then a shaft of real fear shot through her, deadly enough to pierce the dream she was in. Elric! If he ever knew . . .

When Cai's hand moved to her shoulder, closed over the fastening-brooch of her dress, she jerked away so violently the pin ripped his flesh. She half fell the few steps away from him to stand shaking, her hand gripping the thick wooden windowframe.

There was silence behind her.

When finally, she turned to face him, he had not moved. Even in profile she saw his face was white. The air in the shabby room seemed to press down, thunder-weighted.

'Forgive me, Rhianneth.' he said, his voice not quite steady, 'I had no right to do that. To ask anything of you. I was . . . briefly carried away by your charms. It must be this damned place.'

He straightened, turned his head to look at her. For an instant all the austere discipline, the pride and the arrogance that had once made Rome great was stamped there on his dark and lean features. Then she saw blood running down his fingers, and the spell was gone.

He shook his head as she sprang towards him with a cry of distress. 'It's nothing.' Awkwardly he lifted the soft linen scarf from his neck. She snatched it from him and dipped it in the wine before wrapping the small wound.

'Did you learn that from your grandmother, or from our

army surgeon?' His voice was taut with the effort at lightness.

'Neither.' She tucked the scarf end into his wrist. 'Wermund the Saxon priest is a wise old man in many ways. Although he still hates me.'

Cai half smiled. Silence fell between them, awkward, thick.

'Do you remember when last I held you in my arms, that morning before dawn, on the Wall?' he asked then, his voice low. 'When I accused you of conjuring up one of Rhiannon's singing birds to make me forget? I half believed it, you know. I wanted you so much. But then, I was ablaze with the dreams of the Fellowship . . . it wasn't really hard for me to find strength enough to act rationally. Today, I believe I would have dishonoured you and betrayed Elric, had you not stopped it when you did. I have no excuse, save an abysmal heaviness of spirit. A disenchantment with the demands of my world. But –' he took a deep breath – 'if my strength seems to have crumbled, it appears that yours has grown iron-hard in these last years.'

She looked away, unable to meet his eyes. It was not strength that stopped me, she thought, with a flicker of hot anger. It was Elric. Even here, amongst my own people on the far side of Britain, he invades my thoughts. Governs my actions. Holds me in submission.

' "What's needed, usually grows",' she managed at last, bleakly quoting her grandmother's herbal lore, 'And there have been times, believe me, when I have needed much strength.' She turned away, picked her fallen cloak. 'I daresay there will be plenty more. Shall we go?'

When they reached the house she started up the stairs to her room without a word, but Cai caught her arm, pulling her to him.

'Why did you really come here, Rhianneth? It wasn't just for Julia, was it?'

She shook her head, misery washing over her. 'I wanted to get away from Elric. To see you again. Find the dreams I once had.'

'Oh, Gods!' he said softly, and then she was in his arms once more, but gently this time, without passion, her head cradled against his chest as he stroked her hair.

'I'll make it up to you. We'll go riding in the spring, all round the city walls just as we did when you first came, do you remember? And I'll get back from Dumnonia in time to travel up with you and grain escort in the autumn . . . You'd like that?'

She relaxed against him. 'Yes! Oh, yes . . .' she began, then her voice trailed away as she remembered. And she knew, now, that she had to tell him. 'But no spring rides, Cai. I . . . I'm with child. Pregnant.'

She felt him stiffen. 'What?' He eased her away and stared down at her, holding her face between his hands. His throat contracted as he swallowed. 'Are you sure?'

'Quite sure. It will be born around midsummer.'

Very slowly he let out his breath. 'I see.'

He released her and stepped back, a bright glitter of anger and pain deep in his eyes. When he spoke again, his voice controlled, cool. 'You'd better get out of those wet clothes. I hope your shoes are not ruined.'

A shadow moved in the doorway nearby. The thin bent figure of Morvydd's old nurse stood there, her eyes malevolent. But even as Cai looked round sharply, an oath on his lips, she melted away into the dimness of the unlit passageway.

'We should send word immediately to Bernicia,' Lovan insisted. 'Elric must be told, and now!'

Cai listened in silence. Then, brushing aside Lovan's offer to go himself to Bernicia, he left to secure Llywarch's permission to send an official messenger.

It was the worst time of year for travel, but Lovan was right. Cai cursed the brooding introspection that had filled his mind for the past days, the self-absorbed rakings amongst a mass of frustration, jealousy and resentment he had no right to feel. There should have been no need for Lovan to jerk him back to reality. He ought to have known what had to be done, and acted immediately. In Lovan's carefully blunt words, birth was a chancy business. An infant could arrive weeks earlier, or later, than might be expected. There must never be any doubt in Elric's mind as to when this child was conceived.

Already that old witch would have sent the news to Morvydd. He knew she had her ways, had often watched her make her way to one of the back-street scribes. This time her message would drip with spite. Every look, every word of his conversation with Rhianneth at the foot of the stairs would be embellished, coated with innuendo. If she were here when Elric came . . .

Cursing, he planned action. Despite his father-in-law's undoubted interpretation of his decision as one of malice arising from the old woman's revelations, arrangements must be made for her immediate return to Dumnonia. With any luck, and the winter roads the way they were, the old witch would not survive the journey.

Spring came, flooding the countryside. The water gradually soaked into the hard earth, swelled rivers into roaring torrents spilling into the sea. But the messenger sent to Bernicia did not return.

'It's been a bad enough winter here, around Mithrasia. Further north . . . They say the drifts were roof high. I don't think he made it.'

Cai looked at Lovan. 'Llywarch's accepted that. We're sending another.'

They both turned, instantly silent, as Rhianneth entered the warm kitchen, Serena's hand in hers. She had deliberately closed her eyes against Cai's growing tenseness. As the winter days passed she had spent more and more time with Julia, and not even Lovan's gradually deepening unease would she allow to touch her.

Now, she looked from one to the other. 'Why bother?' She kept her voice cool, ignoring Lovan's steady gaze, the darkening of his expression. 'Elric will only be interested when the child is actually born. And only then, if it's another boy.'

The second messenger returned a few weeks later. Bernicia's winter had indeed been the worst in living memory, and snow still lay thick on the high hills. His predecessor had never reached Din Guaryrdi. He himself had arrived to find

375

Elric gone, already fighting the fire and sword attacks with which Urien and his allies had promised to devastate the lands north of the Wall. Bernician messengers would reach Elric's war-band if, and when, they could.

Rhianneth's son was born late. The birth was as easy and quick as Serena's had been. But the baby was small, and so weak that for some time he seemed not likely to live.

She held the tiny scrap close in her arms, willing strength into the fragile thread that held him to life, nurturing with silent tears the first faint bloom on cheeks that looked so pale in contrast to the child's soft tufts of hair as dark as her own.

When at last Gwynne lifted him away and gently tucked him into the cradle that had once held Reburrus, and Cai before him, Rhianneth sank back against her pillows, limp with exhaustion.

As the days passed, the baby took a firmer grip on life. But Rhianneth did not recover her strength. A wet-nurse was hurriedly found, and gradually the child began to thrive. Rhianneth grew weaker.

Most of the time she slept. Whenever she awoke, the room shivered, blurred. People drifted through, transient as summer shadows. Familiar faces came near, and faded before she could think or find strength enough to speak. Doors opened and closed. She heard whispered voices.

One day she heard a woman's muffled sobbing, and briefly her mind cleared. The baby was dead. A single tear rolled hot down her cheek, before her eyes closed once more.

When she opened them again, Cai was sitting on the edge of her bed, watching her. This time she managed a croaking whisper. 'The baby . . .'

'He's doing well.' He stroked back the damp hair from her forehead with gentle fingers. 'And you, my love – please, please try . . .'

He bent his head, but not before she'd seen tears in his eyes. With enormous effort she reached out to touch his tightly clenched fist, and at once he seized her hand and held it pressed against his cheek.

From then on, she grew stronger. Soon she was able to sit up in bed, to accept the nourishing soups, even swallow the awful bitter medicines so lovingly prepared by Torfrida.

Each morning as she awoke she looked across at the cradle, at her baby son rosy with life, and sent a silent thanksgiving winging into the summer skies to whichever Goddess was looking kindly upon her.

Lovan edged into the room, standing stiff and awkward beside her bed, his honest face creased and shining with relief. When full of pride, he bent over the cradle, she felt she'd never loved him more.

Soon she was able to sit propped with pillows on a couch, while Serena played close by. Then, on a cushioned wicker chair in the tree-shaded garden. Julia kept her company for a while each morning, but she soon tired.

Then, Cai would come. They would sit through the long warm afternoons, sometimes in lazy quietness, sometimes making slow conversation. Whenever he talked to her, it was only of happy things. He would relate the latest gossip from the palace, or boast of how Reburrus was leaping ahead with his studies, resolved to beat the Falco boys and looking set to do so.

But the thing that lay uppermost in both their minds – the fact that Elric had neither come nor sent word that he had received Cai's message – they discussed not at all. Whatever lay at the root of the Bernician silence, whether it was merely Elric's indifference – or a disastrous scattering of his warband by Urien – would prove bitter enough in the tasting.

One day Cai tossed a small box into her lap, watching her face light up as she opened it to find a pair of long pendant earrings, delicately wrought in gold.

'Out of the east, from Byzantium.' he told her carelessly, as she admired their strange exotic beauty. 'I thought they would look well against your dark hair . . .'

But later, when she looked into Julia's tilting mirror and saw the earrings beside the whiteness of her face, her pale lips, the lankness of her hair, she burst into tears.

'Ah, there!' exclaimed Torfrida, hurrying into the room.

'What can you expect when you've been so ill? But you're young and pretty! Some good food and a few weeks of summer air, and we'll have your hair glossy and your cheeks glowing again!'

Then suddenly, there was no more time for her to grow pretty enough to wear Cai's earrings. All at once he was leaving for Dumnonia. Her heart dropped like a stone when she realised they had been a parting gift, and her whole being seemed to wither.

'Will you be back before I leave for Bernicia?'

The summer breeze gentled her hair with soft fingers, and the dusty smell of the streets mingled with the sweet scent of the last of Julia's roses. Rhianneth felt as if a part of her was dying with them.

'I don't think so.' Cai smiled, but there was shadowed anguish in his eyes. 'It's . . . better, if I'm not.'

His smile faded as he stared down into her pale haunted face. God's Light, he thought savagely, where in Hel is Elric? It's well over three months since our messenger returned. Wherever the bloody war-band is, word must have reached him by now.

She reached up and kissed him briefly on the lips, ruthlessly crushing back the tears that smarted behind her eyes. He stiffened, then pulled her into his arms, his mouth coming down on hers in unfumbled contact. She felt thin in his arms, light as a wild bird and as fragile. Immediately he drew back, holding her gently away from him.

'One goodbye kiss is all I'll steal from Elric,' he said huskily, softening his words with a faint smile. 'This time! Take care of yourself, Rhianneth. And of our new little Saxon warrior.'

When she made no reply, he lightly touched her pale cheek with his fingertips. 'I'll try to come up next year, with the grain escort.'

His horse waited outside the gate, tossing its head with impatience. He watched Rhianneth swallow, force a smile. Then his hand dropped to his side and his boot ground into the broken stones of the narrow pathway as he swung away and strode through the arched gateway into the street.

She stood until the sound of hooves faded on the warm air and were lost under the general noise of the town.

Lovan's voice made her jump, jerking her back from her reverie. She turned to see him striding towards her with Serena in his arms.

'She's tumbled over. Scraped her knee. Gwynne's cleaned and put ointment on it, but she won't be comforted. She wants her mother.'

Rhianneth looked at her woebegone little daughter's red tear-swollen face and running nose and swept her into her arms, finding release from her own aching sense of loss in the feel of her baby's warm sturdy little body.

'*Deorling, deorling,* don't cry! Come close to Mama. There . . . who's my brave girl?'

She stroked the mouse-soft hair, murmuring reassurances, unaware that it was Saxon she spoke until she noticed Lovan's wry expression.

'I think,' he remarked slowly, 'it must be almost time for us to go home?'

Rain pattered hard against the windows. The air of the room was cool and still. Rhianneth lay back against pillows, grateful for a few more hours in this small timeless world within the old fortress of Eburacum.

The journey from Mithrasia had been taken easily, with frequent stops. But by the time they'd entered the city Rhianneth had been so deathly white with exhaustion the captain of their escort had been forced to agree to Lovan's demand for a few days rest, despite his very real concern for the safety of his precious grain wagons in this Deiran-held city.

They should have left at dawn, but the weather had delayed them for these few extra hours. Rhianneth knew they must leave by noon if they were to reach their next stopping place before nightfall, and she felt time slipping by in the sound of the rain. Invisible, inexorable.

The door opened. She turned her head, thinking it was Gwynne.

Elric stood, cloaked against the rain, his broad shoulders

almost filling the doorway. Her heart gave a great leap. Her spirit sprang to life. Relief flooded through her and her whole body relaxed before the power of his presence, the sureness of his strength.

'Elric?' she croaked, from a throat suddenly dry.

Swiftly he crossed the room and bent to kiss her. Then he knelt beside the couch, took her thin hand in his.

'How are you Rhianneth?' His voice was low, rough. 'They tell me you've been so ill they thought . . .' He broke off, then went on more evenly, 'But you're better? Really recovered?'

She nodded, wordlessly. She had forgotten how potent was his virility, the masculine aura of horse and leather that was as much a part of him as the elusive scent of salt-sea spray. He was deeply tanned, his forehead scarred where his iron war helmet had pressed all summer long. His hair had grown shaggy, the ends bleached fair as Frith's thick blond mop. For a moment she was aware only of the hard strength of the warm hands holding hers. Then she realized that his dark cloak was sodden and his eyes looked as tired as if he had ridden through the night.

'Elric, take these wet things off!' she exclaimed in dismay, touching his shoulder. 'Are they sending up food for you? How long have you been on the road?'

He grinned with relief to hear the faint echo of the old spirit in her voice and stood up, wincing as his leg muscles cramped.

'I'm not sure.' He flung his cloak over a stool near the corner brazier, and stretched stiffly. 'Hussa's with me, and Theo. We sent the war-band on its way home. I knew the grain escort must have left Mithrasia, that if I used the road I couldn't miss you. I came as soon as I could.'

'Did you?'

She remembered the long waiting time after the second messenger returned. The glances between Cai and Lovan. Her own careless attitude and inner rage.

He turned, looked at her sharply. 'I've been paying for that grain in blood and sweat, Rhianneth! Keeping Urien occupied, in case he should fancy Cai's Roman city for his southern power base. The message about you took a long time to find us. When it did come, it was at the worst possible time.'

His expression softened as he took in the disturbing slightness of her body, the tautness of the skin over the bones of her pale face. He came back to her side, trailed his fingers gently down her long dark hair.

'We had them, you see? Trapped in one of their own hill valleys! We were about to attack. Above anything we meant to have retribution for their burning of what spring crops the floods hadn't ruined. For the slaughter of our people. And by Woden's Eye, we did! Old Outigern is dead at last. And Urien's so mauled it will take him ten years to recover!'

Rhianneth tried to summon up interest, and failed. It all seemed as strange, as far away as Rome's old wars with Hannibal. With a soft knock at the door, a servant silently brought in food and drink.

As the door closed behind him, leaving them alone once more, Rhianneth said quietly: 'I've been fighting a battle of my own, Elric. Here is your son . . .'

She moved slightly, drew back the coverlet that had hidden the baby lying snugly between the back of the couch and her own warm body. He slept, sated with milk from the wet-nurse they had persuaded to travel with them.

Elric was silent. Her gaze slid back to him, trying to read his reaction in the grey eyes. He was staring at the baby, at the soft rose-petal cheeks, the dark fluff of hair, with a brooding intensity.

'Lovan tells me he looks very like I did, at a couple of month's old,' she said wanly. 'But he almost died . . .'

Elric eyes moved to her face. after a strange awkward moment, he said: 'Yes. Well, maybe he's inherited your strength of will, too.'

He hesitated, then picked up her limp hand and turned it within his own, appearing to study it though obviously his thoughts were elsewhere. 'It was a long cold winter,' he said oddly, at last. 'but I take it your aunt still lives?'

The hurt she felt at his disinterest in the baby, and the

unease beneath the hurt, smothered the last scrap of pleasure that had leapt up so wantonly at first sight of him. After a year apart, and despite his obviously hard ride to meet up with the grain escort, he was not really different. He had deliberately made her pregnant before she left. There had been no spontaneous burst of desire in that last cold coupling, she had long since realised that. Now the resentment she had long held suppressed rose up sour again at the way he used words that meant far more than they said. At his double-edged questions that cut so deep.

With an effort she slid her hand from his. She felt his eyes on her, almost as if he held his breath, waiting. And even drooping as she was, almost too weary to barb her shots, somehow she gathered strength to answer him in his own coin.

'Yes. Nothing has changed. I found everything – everyone – much as I left them six years ago.'

'Seven,' he said.

She threw a sharp look up into his face and was appalled by a glimpse of flame-hot anger deep within his eyes. Then it had gone, and he smiled with faint bitter-laced mockery. 'It's been seven years, my *deorling.*' He gestured towards the table. 'May I get you some food? Wine?'

Now that the storm had passed, the shadows of clouds slipped across the sea's face like wraiths against the moving fabric of time. The shore was full of sound, echoes of the sea wind and the gull's cry and the rumbling of waves as they surged over the sand and rocks.

But they were quiet sounds, with nothing left in them of the fury of the storm when the wind broke out of its northern lair and howled across the sea to fling wild witch-green waters as high as the fortress ramparts. Now the wind was only a faint whispering that touched her cheek like a caress, cooling the tears that ran unchecked as Rhianneth stared out over the low murmuring sea.

Romulus was dead. Over the years his fear of storms had grown worse. This time, heading home beneath a darkening sky from a morning's exercise, his panic had been uncontrollable. At the first lightning flash he had reared, thrown his rider and bolted.

Whether by instinct or by chance he made for home. Sweating, wild-eyed, tail and mane streaming, he raced through the rising wind as the storm roared in from the sea towards him. At the bottom of the steep trackway to the fortress gate he'd swerved from restraining hands to gallop away across the leg-breaking tummocks of rough grass, the dangerous rock-strewn terrain of the broken shoreline.

Rhianneth was glad it had been Lovan. Others, younger, quicker, had found him. But it had been Lovan, whom he trusted, who had set him free from pain and fear with one swift thrust of his hunting knife. Rhianneth pressed her clenched fist against her mouth as her mind swept back through the years to remember with bright clarity the moment she had realised Romulus was to be hers. How warm and sweet his breath had felt on her face! How smooth his coat beneath her hand while she whispered promises, secrets for him alone. Ah, Romulus, she thought, we rode together over the rim of the world, and never found the white palaces or the flower gardens by the sea . . . With his death another piece of her childhood world had slipped away beyond reach.

Marcus's words came whispering with the wind into her mind, to make the tears flow faster. *'Even kings die, Rhianneth . . .'* Queens, too. With a fresh pang of sadness she remembered that Llywarch's bride, Constantine's daughter, had died within a year of marriage; and that Llywarch himself had become withdrawn, retreating steadily from the world and his duties as king.

After a while she drew a deep breath and wiped her eyes. No use to lose herself for long amongst sad memories and childhood dreams. She had to look clear-eyed towards the rising years, recognise the shadow-shapes of coming events. Aim her arrows true and hold her shield high.

Baldur ran to meet her as she approached the king's house, and immediately her heart lightened. Her youngest son, now almost ten years old, was a joy to her. Of her three children he was outwardly the one most like herself, being dark and slightly built. But he was slow and gentle and full of dreams, and his tongue had none of the sharpness that hers had acquired over the years.

She had wanted to call him Marcus. But Elric would have none of it. She often wondered resentfully whether his choice of the tongue-twisting Saxon name Theodbaldur was deliberate. Fortunately, because of the need to distinguish between the child and his uncle Theo, Elric's youngest brother Theodric, he quickly became known as Baldur.

'Mama!' He stopped short, seeing her red eyes and puffed face. 'Mama? Are you all right?'

She smiled, ruffling his hair as she preceded him into the house. 'I've been thinking of Romulus, and all the rides we used to take together. But . . .' she hung her cloak on a peg, took a breath – 'there's nothing to be done. And we must get on with our work.'

Three pairs of eyes watched her solemnly. Baldur, Serena, and Gwen's young daughter Bebba.

'Perhaps Woden will take Romulus into his great stables, for the heroes of Waelheall to ride to battle.' Baldur sat down cross-legged beside the girls, his face troubled. 'He might even ride him himself.'

384

'He's g-got his own horse, Sleipnir,' Bebba said, 'eight-legged, and swift as an arrow.' Then seeing Baldur's face fall she added quickly. 'B-but he's sure to keep Romulus safe.'

'If the gods have been very kind,' Rhianneth said softly, 'I know just where Romulus will be.'

'At your villa!' put in Serena, with sudden insight. 'In your meadowland, by the stream?'

'I'm sure of it!' Rhianneth smiled at her daughter, brought up, like all her children, on tales of the old farmhouse they had never seen. And maybe he'll find you there, Marcus, she added silently, for where else were you ever truly happy?

She watched as Bebba painstakingly copied a Latin sentence on to her waxed tablet, her mop of red hair half obscuring her face, her tongue peeping out at the corner of her mouth. Bebba's many deep sighs, her covert glances towards the open door, were signals that the girl was even more bored than usual. Only because her mother Gwen insisted did she even try to read and write the strange, difficult language of the Romans. Bebba's interest only awakened when Rhianneth brought out one of the precious heavily-bound books, and told stories from within its pages; wonderful accounts of gods and magic, of giant one-eyed monsters, and witch-maidens whose singing lured men to madness and death.

But then, for such tales even Elric – and Bebba's own father Hussa – would pause to listen. For though the islands of Greece might seem unimaginable, glittering with fierce sunlight and strange enchantments, the stories told of sea-rocks and storm winds, dangers only too familiar. They felt at home in the company of those long-ago sailors on their heroic voyages of adventure.

How Frith hated lessons! He'd resented having to sit still when he was restless to be following the hunt on his pony over wild country, armed like the men with spear and bow. He thought writing and reading a waste of time when he only wanted to be with Hussa's son Hrothgar; to swim, or wrestle on the shore, or slash with his sword at the straw-men as the warriors did in the practice yard.

Rhianneth had tried hard to instil a little love of learning into her firstborn, but it was no use. She had gradually realised that, much as she loved him, it would not be through her eldest son she would fulfil her vow to the Fellowship, for only when she spoke of Rome's wars with Carthage, or the taking of Troy, did his interest quicken.

What was it Elric had so grimly prophesied of his unborn son, that night he was conceived in such a storm of anger and passion beneath the wildfire and thunder of the skies . . . 'a warrior to make the gods tremble?'

No, never! She thought. True, Frith was tall and strong, quick to grasp the arts of war. Certainly he would be a leader to equal Elric one day. But he was also open and trusting as a near-grown puppy, generous, brave . . . and kind, too. Even to Bebba, Hrothgar's little tomboy of a sister, who ever since babyhood had trailed after the two boys whenever she could escape her mother Gwen's eye.

Bebba was so like Frith, Rhianneth thought, watching with resignation Bebba's bright head come up yet again as laughing voices sounded outside. Small, spirited, agile, she could leap across tide pools, climb rocks, ride breakneck across the hunting trails like a boy.

But now her brother Hrothgar was a man at Hussa's side, for their father's territory shielding Din Guaryrdi's northern flank was land once held by Ida's old enemy Outigern and was therefore always under threat of attack by his son Morcant. Frith was now intent only upon proving himself a man grown before Elric. The childhood circle was broken, and not often nowadays was heard along the shore or round the fortress her cry, 'Wait – wait, for B-Bebba . . .'

Another heavy sigh rose up. Then, like magic, Lovan appeared in the doorway. Immediately, amidst cries of greeting, work stopped. Rhianneth threw up her hands in despair.

'Oh, give me your tablets. We may as well leave it for today . . .'

'Sorry!' Lovan looked at Rhianneth. 'Have I interrupted their lesson? You've usually finished by this time.'

Bebba grinned gratefully up at him as she darted out, the

others following more slowly. Rhianneth placed their waxed tablets on a small bench.

'I started late. They were already restless.'

'Even Baldur?'

She smiled, touching her son's tablet with its uneven but accurate letters. 'He is clever, isn't he Lovan? Already he knows far more Latin than Frith ever did. He'll soon be able to read anything . . . every book I possess.'

'And Serena?'

'Serena's quite good.' She glanced at Serena's neat script. 'But Bebba!'

Lovan looked across at Bebba's effort, at the untidy smudged line and a half that was all she had managed to complete. He smiled.

Two out of three is not bad, *cariad*.'

'Two out of four,' she reminded him, 'I had no success with Frith. Not a scrap.'

'Frith's all right,' Lovan responded at once, his tone defensive, and Rhianneth laughed at him. She knew his affection covered all three of her children; but Frith was the one who held his heart and always had, from the day he was born.

'I know,' she sighed gently, after a moment, 'I know. But I have this hope, you see? That I can somehow light a Roman lamp in Bernicia. For Cai. For Marcus . . . and Arturius. So that all they knew once won't be forgotten.'

In silence Lovan picked up Baldur's waxed tablet. 'You know, Rhianneth,' he said carefully, 'I loved Marcus. But there was another reality to the Rome he dreamed of. Great cruelty and depravity at the heart of the Empire to which Marcus closed his eyes and which Cai will not acknowledge. Rome sent the best of her sons out into her provinces. They lived and died in her service, and their children and grandchildren grew up knowing only the power of Mother Rome, the light she brought to a dark and savage world.' He stared down at the tablet in his hand with unseeing eyes. 'In my travels as a young man I learned quite a bit. Most of it gossip, and probably true. I gradually realised just how squalid the old struggles for power really were. And it grew worse, you know. More murderous, as authority weakened.'

Rhianneth stared at him, a chill of dismay washing over her. Lovan's hair was now completely grey, his weather-beaten face scored deep with lines. He was as strong, as tough as ever save for the leg once torn by a stag's antlers, which still gave him pain at times. Yet suddenly he looked all of his three score years and more, and she could not bear it. That Lovan, her strong apple tree, should grow old, frightened her more than any of the words he spoke.

Unthinkingly, he was passing a thumb across the soft wax of Baldur's tablet, obliterating the script. His eyes followed the action but saw other things, in other places, other times.

'Loyalty, chastity, duty . . . old values became a joke, in Rome. The army that held the Empire together had to recruit more and more auxiliaries, many of them half-wild barbarians. All over the Empire, old enemies were bribed with land, gold, Roman citizenship, while the legions broke and the Empire cracked.

Rhianneth opened her mouth to protest, but he held up a work-calloused brown hand. 'Hear me out. I want you to understand, *cariad,* that even knowing all this, I believe with the Fellowship that what we still have is worth keeping. Only don't close your eyes to everything that doesn't fit Cai's picture. And when you light your Roman lamp look, occasionally, into the faces of Elric's people. Those virtues the Empire forgot, they still possess. There's strength there, strength we're going to need if we're to save anything of Rome's Britannia. They'll defend this land more fiercely than Rome ever did, because that's something they understand; something they can touch and hold. What you're trying to show them is more . . . elusive. An alien way of life with different customs, strange Gods.'

Lovan paused. His eyes focussed on the blurred letters of the wax tablet in his hand, and he gave a half-smile of apology as he placed it back on the bench.

'They're not all like Baldur, with a scholar's mind, curious to learn,' he said. 'Some, like Frith, will need more than just a lamp and book. They'll need some . . . bright scrap of magic, to stir their blood and open a door into their hearts.'

Rhianneth sighed. 'They listen well enough to the stories from Marcus's books.'

'And why not? They're gripping adventures. What is more, no matter how many enchantments are woven into their fabrics, it is some real . . . essence, of old Greece or Rome that holds them together. Just as some spirit of their ancestral homeland shines through those fantastic tales they tell in the mead-hall. That's what we need. A link between Rome and the glamour of their sagas. Something to bind them closer to Britain than to that homeland none of them ever knew.' He shrugged, spreading his hands. 'But then I suppose for that, *cariad*, you need the sort of spellmaking their saga masters do so well . . .'

'You really are happy here.' It was a statement, not a question. Even so, her tone held a faint surprise.

'I find, after all these years, they are my kind of people,' he answered simply. 'I'm beginning to understand them, at last. I've always admired their cool courage. Even their final grim acceptance of what they call *wyrd* – fate, what will be. Now I've come to appreciate their many kindnesses, even their peculiar sense of humour! I've never been lonely here . . .'

A faint sadness underlined his last words, as if an old sorrow stirred and died. Rhianneth wondered if it was the thought of his lost young wife that shadowed his face, or the memory of her own mother. Of the three of them riding together under the eyes of the Gods, her mother's fox-fire hair blowing like a bright-bannered challenge between Marcus and himself.

He had loved her in silence, because he also loved Marcus. Had her loss been the more bitter then, because of that unspoken hunger? The love of his young bride was his, forever. But that other, which he had never held . . . did it haunt him down all the empty years?

Rhianneth tried to speak, but words refused to come. Instead, she touched his arm, smiling her understanding. He nodded, returning her smile, and age left him and her heart lightened.

*

'Bebba's old enough to be wed, yet she can scarcely sew a straight seam!' Gwen wailed, as she stood with Rhianneth on the shore watching Bebba's bright mane of red hair fly in wild curls around her flushed face as she raced bare foot along the sands after Frith. 'What am I to do with her? Why can't she be more like your Serena, a little lady!'

Rhianneth laughed. 'She'll settle soon enough,' she assured her sister-in-law, but her attention had already passed to where her own daughter stood some way off, talking to someone. A year younger than Bebba, Serena was tall, graceful. Her silky hair blended subtle shades of gold and her dark-lashed eyes were Elric's, cool and enigmatic. Already softly rounded into womanhood, she held the promise of great beauty.

Rhianneth felt a faint prickle of unease as she realised it was Brand, son of Caldis, with whom Serena spoke. Caldis had never returned to Din Guaryrdi, though Brand made frequent trips to Deira to visit his mother. A man now, he had proved a skilful pupil for Wermund the priest. But he reminded Rhianneth always of his mother, with his pale face, pale hair, and his cold, watching eyes. She was never at ease in his company.

A moment later Serena was walking towards her alone, and Rhianneth's brief disquiet vanished.

When Gwen left them, Rhianneth took her daughter's hand to stroll slowly along the water's edge towards the mass of jagged rocks gleaming spray-wet in the warm sunshine.

Ahead of them Bebba and Frith chased each other, shouting and laughing as they splashed through rock-pools and kicked at the creaming waves of the incoming tide.

Serena made a soft click with her tongue and cast her eyes skywards. 'She'll never grow up,' she informed her mother, with a grin. 'Did you know she goes swimming with them, in her shift?'

'No, I didn't!' Rhianneth gasped, 'You mean with Hrothgar – and Frith?'

Serena shrugged. 'Hrothgar wanted me to go too. But I would not.'

She tilted a glance sideways at her mother, inviting her to become a partner to their secrets, smile at their fun. But Rhianneth was suddenly vividly aware only that the tantalizing aloofness within her daughter's cool grey eyes held more allure than any blatant invitation, and her heart sank.

Gwen's right, she thought. They are cubs no longer. For their own safety Serena must now be guarded, and Bebba tamed.

Frith had left the beach and was climbing the rock-cliff. He looked back over his shoulder towards Bebba and shouted something, but all Rhianneth heard clearly was Bebba's answering cry of 'Frith! W-wait for me . . .'

Elric was on the beach; crouched low, feeling for damage along the timbers of a boat pulled up above high tide reach.

Gods, she thought with a flicker of anger, to come unexpectedly upon him even now sends a quiver along my spine.

She saw him straighten suddenly and move, cutting across the sand towards the tumbled rocks at speed. The tide was racing shorewards now, covering the sands swiftly below the rough cliff slope. Water spurted up glittering from under his feet and fell back into a foam wake. Then he reached up and pulled Bebba backwards into his arms, just as she was about to scramble up the treacherous rocks, slippery with sea-wrack and black lichen, after Frith.

Over her head, he roared out an oath-laden order that brought Frith leaping back on to the sands, red-faced.

'I w-was all right!' Bebba protested. 'I c-can take c-care of myself!'

'No, you can't!' Frith panted, unexpectedly. 'You're a girl. But I can look after her!' he added, staring at Elric belligerently, his blue eyes hot.

'Not unless you have eyes in the back of your head, you can't!' Elric retorted harshly. 'Now get her off this beach before Hussa bloody well tears your ears off!'

Stiff with anger, Frith muttered something almost inaudible as he strode past his father. But Elric heard him.

'If you think you're a man,' he threw after him, 'you'd better start treating her as a woman.'

Frith halted, swung round, his face taut with fury. For a few seconds anger battled with discretion as words fought their way to his mouth, but no further. Elric waited, raised an eyebrow. But Frith was as yet no match for his father's strength, and had no wish to demonstrate the fact.

From then on, Frith would have none of Bebba. Each day he was off with the war-band, hunting, wrestling, swimming, slicing the air with his practice sword until his shoulders groaned. He ignored her appeals to go with him, until gradually, like a mewed bird, she grew silent.

Only occasionally, during the cheerful noise of the supper table in the hall, his eyes slid towards the women's table where she sat in one of her pretty new dresses, her wild autumn hair smoothed with unaccustomed sleekness down her back and her vivacious little face wan.

In autumn Cai came, bringing word of Wencam's death, another link of the Fellowship, broken.

But more ominous was the news he carried of affairs south of Mithrasia.

While the north had been quiet for almost the whole ten years since Baldur's birth, save for occasional skirmishes with Urien or with dead Outigern's son Morcant, in the south the Saxons had been steadily pushing westwards. That summer, under their leader Ceawlin, they smashed their way through the combined forces of three western rulers, captured their fortified Roman cities of Corinium, Glevum and Aquae Sulis, and pushed on till they reached the Sabrina estuary.

'Three cities gone. Three rulers, dead on the battlefield,' Cai said in a low voice, as they stood in the mead-hall. 'All friendly to us and to Constantine.'

'Coinmail, Condidan and Farinmail,' Rhianneth murmured, and their names fell like a casting spell from her lips. Cai shot a look towards her, his face sombre.

'The southern Saxons have sliced us in two,' he said. 'Dumnonia's cut off. Which means that Constantine – and Caer Melot – are now isolated from the rest of Britain.

Into the silence that fell Lovan said slowly: 'By God, they've got their revenge for Badon at last!' And Rhianneth shivered, as though the sun had gone down.

But when Elric joined them, Cai played down the disaster, and instead brought out some astonishing news of his own. Some weeks after news of the battle reached Mithrasia, a panting messenger had summoned him to the southern gate. There, the unbelievable sight of a herd of fine horses met his eyes. Originally the gift of Constantine to his neighbour Farinmail, they were all trained cavalry steeds. But Farinmail had never used them as such, merely following the ancient custom of riding to battle, then sending the horses to the back and fighting on foot. When the battle had swept past them, leaving them isolated on the wooden hillside, Farinmail's horsemaster seeing all lost, with a Saxon army between him and Dumnonia, made haste to slip away northwards, bringing to Llywarch a gift worth more than gold.

'An honest man,' Elric commented dryly. 'He could have sold them for a fortune. What reward did Llywarch make him?'

'None,' returned Cai bluntly. 'He brought the horses to the gate . . . and rode-off. He left a message with one of his stable-boys.' His mouth twisted into a strange smile. 'Oh . . . and his name. Idwal.'

Silence. Then Cai went on: 'His message suggested a troubled mind. And a worried man, after witnessing such a battle. He greatly fears the Saxons following up from the south, maybe to join with the Mercians. He also fears Rheged – because his former mistress Queen Myffan shelters there. And she would dearly love his head on a shield! I gather he sees Mithrasia as a bastion against them both.'

'So . . . where is he now?' Rhianneth asked, surprised that after all these years her stomach could still churn at mention of Idwal's name, or that of the queen.

Cai shrugged. 'No idea. Maybe he's gone into Gwynned. It's of no account. For the gift he's made us, the Fellowship are prepared to forgive his past deeds. What matters is . . . ' he drew a sharp breath, 'Do you realise how many years it takes to build up a stable of cavalry horses? And we've got the lot! With those that came to Mithrasia as dowry with Constantine's daughter, we've enough to train a cavalry wing here in Bernicia as well as at home!'

Cai talked on, like a man inspired. He made Rhianneth see the confusion, the noise of the battlefield as fortune rolled one way and then the other. Made her realise the impact upon both sides as the warhorses suddenly swept down out of cover upon the enemy.

There was silence as he finished. Rhianneth looked from Cai towards Lovan's suddenly intent face. But it was Elric who spoke, and his expression was remote.

'Fighting from horseback is not our way.'

'Artur's cavalry won Badon!' Cai retorted swiftly. 'The day might have been saved at this summer's battle, if Farinmail had had the sense to use Constantine's horses as was intended, instead of leaving them tied uselessly behind the lines.'

Elric's voice grew colder. 'We use our horses as we use our boats, to get us to the battleground. A Bernician warrior using his horse as an extra weapon I'd find hard to imagine!'

'So would Urien,' Cai answered quietly, pointedly.

Rhianneth felt the air move, the atmosphere change. No more was said, for the moment. There was no need.

Then Baldur ran into the hall, his face alight with eagerness to greet his Mithrasian uncle, and Cai strode laughing to meet him, throwing an arm around the boy's thin shoulders.

But Elric walked away, his anger evident in the dark moodiness of his face.

'A delicate situation.' Lovan commented softly, 'Cai's right about the cavalry, if we're ever to stop the menace of the northern kings. But I'm not sure it helps to remind Elric of Badon. Still less to assume he's as shattered as we are by the Saxon victory in the south. Why should he care? What are our southwestern kingdoms to him? His interest would only arouse if Ceawlin's Saxons came further north, threatened his Mithrasian grain and cattle supply.'

Rhianneth nodded absently, her eyes on Cai and Baldur.

Her mind had drawn back from the conflicts of the world outside, to fret at something much closer.

'I wish Elric . . . ' she hesitated. 'I wish he would take more interest in Baldur. He doesn't bellow at him like he does at Frith. He's never beaten him. Yet Baldur is afraid of his father, I know it. And Elric . . . well, because Baldur's not tall and strong and full of energy, because he – '

'Because he reminds Elric of Cai'?'

For a second her mind went blank with shock. Then fury rose, its eruption strangely the more violent because it was Lovan who provoked it.

'What in Hel do you mean?' she hissed, her eyes wide and glittering in a face suddenly filled with angry colour, 'Are you telling me that Elric thinks Baldur might not be his? That I –'

'No, I'm not!' Lovan said swiftly, appalled by his own thoughtless words and even more so by her reaction to them. The news from the south must have hit me harder than I knew, he thought savagely, I'm not usually so bloody senseless. He glanced around. Cai and Baldur had gone out of the doors at the far end. There was no one else in the hall. He grasped her shoulder and felt her trembling. His next words came more slowly, each one emphasised: 'Of course Elric doesn't believe that. Not for one single moment!'

She waited for him to go on, her breath uneven, her hands clenched into small fists. It was too late now to draw back. He took a deep breath.

'Rhianneth, Baldur was not born here. Elric did not even know you were pregnant when you left for Mithrasia. I never really understood why he let you go.'

'You know why I went, Lovan. For Julia's sake. And, because of the minstrel, Aesc. Because I could no longer . . . I could no longer bear to live with Elric. Not without a barrier of time to heal the violence between us!'

Lovan looked at her. 'Yes, I know why you went. What I said was, I didn't understand why he let you go. Maybe he just got tired of trying to hold wild fire in his hands?'

Impatiently she shook back the hair from her flushed face. 'I don't know what you're talking about!'

His mouth twisted in a sad half-smile. 'No, you really don't, do you? Even now. You'll never get Elric to come to heel, *cariad*, as you once hoped. He's too proud to play that game. But he loves you. You must know that.'

'Whatever Elric feels for me,' she answered at once, 'it's not love. You said something like this to me once before, Lovan. It was after that mad moonlit gallop out on to the hunting trails, do you remember? After Elric had called me a whore? Threatened to kill me?' Her lip curled and her short laugh held a sour amusement. 'No, Elric's heart is bound to that certain lady he takes Brand to visit, in Deira. He still believes her to be a wounded dove!'

'And you think that is love?'

She stared at Lovan's gently derisive expression, and thought of Cai. But not even to Lovan could she speak of that. Instead she said quickly, 'I know that love is sweet, and gallant. And dignified. Once having known it, it's easy to recognise in others . . . '

'That it is,' Lovan murmured.

Remorse shot through her as she heard the irony in his voice, for had not Lovan himself drunk deep of love's bitter-sweet waters? More sharply than she intended, she reminded him: 'You were about to speak, not of Elric's feelings for me, but for our son . . . ?'

Lovan hesitated. 'You must be aware – ' he paused feeling his way through the words – 'that Elric found it difficult to come to terms with the birth of a son, so far away? And then, Baldur is so unlike Frith and Serena . . . '

'He takes after me.'

Lovan shook his head. 'He's like Elidyr, Rhianneth. Same dark eyes, dark hair. A dreamer. Indecisive. Easily persuaded by stronger wills. Elric contrasts him unfavourably with Frith. Even his skill in Latin is like an affront. When he looks at him, Elric sees only Rome in those dark eyes. Just as he does with Cai. And the mind is a strange, complicated thing, *cariad*. He must remember the greentime fondness you once felt for Cai. It could seem to him that the child's appearance and character were some God's malicious jest, mocking his manhood.'

Rhianneth stared at him, all the hot colour draining from her face. She went slowly cold as she thought of the years since Baldur's birth. She remembered the silences, the bleak look she had often caught on Elric's face as he watched her play with the child. The irony of the situation hit her with the force of a blow. For, had it not been for the caprice of the Gods, the son that Elric found so disturbing could have been truly Cai's. She thought of the Mithrasian inn, and the sound of the rain, and the dark passion in Cai's face . . . 'One brief moment . . . against the shrine-cold annals of honour . . . '

'Can you try to understand?' Lovan was saying quietly. 'I put it badly, I know.'

His words penetrated the chilly flow of her thought. After a moment's silence, she straightened her shoulders.

'Thank you, Lovan, for always being honest with me. I'll remember what you said about Baldur. But you really don't have to worry about Elric and me. We know where we stand. We don't need to fight any more.'

As darkness closed in on Samhain Eve, Llywarch's gift to Elric arrived, as promised by Cai when he left for home some weeks previously.

Though the idea of riding into battle, vulnerable to spear and sword thrusts from the surrounding enemy on foot seemed madness to Elric, yet Badon was a Saxon disaster still strong in memory, and Artur's mailed battle-riders too potent a legend to be easily dismissed. Cai's Roman war tactics might be made to work, and Elric was willing to test the practical possibilities.

Big, heavy horses clattered through the gates, drawing exclamations from the watching warriors and screams of excited fear from the scrambling children. Women clutched their crying babies close as the strings of horses were led past them towards the new stables block hastily erected during the past days.

After a couple of night's rest, the horsemen would ride back to Mithrasia, unencumbered by their precious charges. But three had come to stay throughout the winter, to train Bernicia's warriors in the Roman art of cavalry warfare. Two were tough, weatherbeaten soldiers of Llywarch's own cavalry wing. The other was Cai's seventeen-year-old son, Reburrus.

They stood before Elric in the spitting, blustering twilight, their heavy travel cloaks thrown back over their shoulders to reveal Llywarch's red dragon emblem on their chests.

'Welcome to Din Guaryrdi.' Elric spoke in the Celtic tongue. But as the light from a nearby torch moulded his features in bronze and the thick bracelets of gold that encased his wrists gleamed with a barbaric richness, he had never seemed more Saxon. He gestured towards the wagons following. 'I see our gift horses will not go hungry. Cai thinks of everything.'

'I hope so, sir.'

Rhianneth could scarcely take her eyes off Reburrus. He was unmistakeably Cai's son. Dark, slender, upright, with the same fine-boned face and olive skin.

'Unbelievable, isn't it?' Lovan spoke close to her ear. 'Can this truly be that little tyrant who almost drove Torfrida out of her mind?'

Rhianneth laughed. 'He's had many years of schooling with the sons of Cai's friend, Falco. Besides, he was never really bad. Just unhappy and afraid. Cai told me he's a natural battle-rider, and a good leader, too.'

'Maybe being so close in age he'll be able to influence Frith in favour of cavalry,' Lovan said, but he looked dubious.

As the weeks passed, Din Guaryrdi swelled almost to bursting as young men flocked in from all over the Bernician territories to join the king's new battle-riders. Only the best, the most promising, were chosen. Excitement filled every corner of the fortress. The short daylight hours echoed to shouted orders, the thud of hooves, the panting of breath as horses swerved, galloped, stopped short, reared, crashed down with deadly iron-shod hooves.

Elric watched, narrow-eyed. Although under his ultimate command, he was content for the moment that the untried cavalry wing should be led by Reburrus, whom he readily acknowledged an able leader and skilled horseman.

Baldur talked incessantly of the big horses, sliced his thin arms through the empty air in imitation of the cavalryman's slash, and developed a bad case of hero worship for Reburrus. Fortunately, Cai's son took an immediate liking to the young boy and talked with him as if he were an equal in years. Baldur flourished under this unexpected attention, for Frith had never bothered much with his young brother. He had treated him with a rough kindness — whenever he noticed him.

Now, with the coming of Reburrus, Frith's attitude changed. His careless, teasing good humour vanished and he became belligerently protective of Baldur and touchily resentful towards Reburrus. Often, only Hrothgar's steadying presence prevented hot words dissolving into open combat.

The last of autumn passed by, dragging its flaming colours behind. The annual cries of the seal packs with their new-born young warned that winter was coming and soon the world would begin to shake with the first of the ice-winds from the north.

The air was already astir with tensions, undercurrents. Elric dismissed them as no more than rivalries between growing pups. But Rhianneth could not be so easy. It was the merest tremor, a feather brush along her nerves. Yet it served to make her shiveringly aware of something moving, edging nearer from out of the dark.

If Frith's temper was disturbed by the arrival of his dark Mithrasian cousin, Serena's self-contained calmness was shattered. Rhianneth's wry amusement was spiked with sadness as she watched the girl blush and tremble, stumbling over her Celtic whenever he spoke to her. That was one match, Rhianneth thought bleakly, Elric would surely never countenence.

Reburrus was confident, sometimes almost recklessly so. He looked forward with enthusiasm to future combat with Mithrasia's enemies. But it was the enthusiasm of a young man who had theoretically mastered his art and had yet to practise it. He lacked his father's burning obsessions. Caer Melot had not stolen his soul. Yet his charm was potent, and when Frith saw even Bebba's shining eyes and blushing reaction to Reburrus's stories from the kingdoms beyond the grey hills, his attitude became even more hostile.

At Yule time, on the night of the midwinter celebration, Din Guaryrdi feasted on the spoils of the previous day's hunt, upon stag-meat and wild pig and mountains of sweet honey-cakes, and the mead-hall rang with merriment.

A storyteller had come from Deira, and with him some brightly-dressed tumblers who turned somersaults, cartwheeled on their hands and performed fantastic feats of contortion, never stopping for a second. They contrived a number of clever tricks with two large ferocious birds.

Rhianneth shivered as she watched the cruelly curved beaks hover, then pounce upon a morsel of food held between the teeth of one of the performers. The birds were wild and angry, straining restlessly against their imprisonment and stretching their great wings as if in readiness for the moment of escape, longing for cold air and freedom and finding no way out of the glittering trap into which they had been lured. Rhianneth felt pity for them, but she could not help but be relieved when the birds were returned to their cages and the tumblers announced they were about to enact the drama of the coming of the seasons.

The huge fire leapt and glowed and lent the hall an aura of barbaric mystery as the green forest trimmings shivered in the hot rising air and the carved serpents appeared to writhe along the huge supporting pillars of ancient forest oak.

The warriors kept up a continual stamping and laughter as an exaggeratedly pregnant Autumn trailed around the hall bewailing fate, and the actor played up to them in his woman's skirts. Frightened by Winter, he produced an enormous offspring of nuts, apples, loaves, and a few mice which provoked startled shrieks as the bundle was tossed towards the women's table.

Winter, a dry old man with a false red nose, then reigned supreme, shuffling around the hall coughing and blowing his nose with a sound like a rutting stag, threatening those nearest with an icicle which sparkled marvellously, and a bunch of prickly holly, until he was chased away by Spring, played by the only woman in the group.

She was clad in a tunic of green, with a string of bright cloth flowers on her head. Her slow dignified progress down the length of the hall was made with so many enticing gestures and with such outrageously lascivious smiles that the coarse, bawdy jests of the warriors rose in volume and quantity until the hall rocked with red-faced ribaldry.

Spring was pursued by Summer, a portly, jolly-faced man in red, holding aloft a giant horn spilling with honey wine. They performed their love dance of pursuit, catch and escape, leaping the edges of the fire, until at last they bowed, panting, before Elric, with shouts and applause ringing through the hall. The girl tore the flowers from her hair and held them out to Elric, who caught her hands, pulled her close and kissed her, to the jeers and chanted encouragement of the war-band.

But Rhianneth watched the smile Elric gave the girl and was hard put to keep her own smile in place through a sudden surge of emotion that was raw, savage.

What is the matter with me? She thought. It must be Yule, that midwinter fire deliberately stoked to bring our autumn crop of babes. It captures us all with its hot passions, why should I be immune on such a night, to the sting of jealousy?

Not for the first time, she wondered whether Elric might want more children. She had not conceived again since the birth of Baldur. Not even on the Night of the Mothers, when the fertility goddesses Hreda, Eostre, Erce and Fricg were especially close. Of course, she had never eaten of the awful mixture prepared each year by the cunning-women for those desiring a child, a vile-smelling concoction of oats and blood, bitter herbs and other potent ingredients wisely kept secret. Nor had she slept with a rune-stick beneath her. Elric had never suggested she should. She suspected he had as little faith in such endeavours as she had. Certainly no such magic worked for Alda and Rolf. After all these years, they remained childless.

But surely better so, she thought sadly, than be like poor Gwen, who had endured so many miscarriages in the last ten years, and was even now pregnant again.

She glanced sideways at her sister-in-law, here to celebrate Midwinter with them. Gwen's face was pale and beaded with sweat. She looked exhausted, almost ill.

'Do you want to leave, Gwen?' Rhianneth felt a swift thrust of pity as she touched the small plump hand lying so listlessly on the edge of the littered table. 'I'll come with you, if you do.'

At once Gwen stirred, her brown eyes going to where Hussa sat beside Elric. 'No, of course not! Why, I'd miss the storyteller . . . '

And Hussa would miss you, Rhianneth thought shrewdly. Gwen loved him so, would endure any discomfort rather than worry him by her absence. How close they were, despite Hussa's blatant and constant betrayals with women who meant nothing to him!

She glanced towards Elric, and at that moment he turned his head and looked straight at her. He raised his cup in a half-mocking salute and she smiled, inclining her head. A quiver of excitement ran down her spine.

She thought once more how heavy with sensual pleasure was the atmosphere of Yule. Offerings soberly made to the gods during daylight were for good fortune in the coming year. But during these Midwinter nights, when the smell of roast meats and honey-wine, the pungent fragrance of evergreen boughs intensified in the heat of the hall, something stirred that was older than Woden, older than Thunor. The Gods of storm and battle stood aside, for the world was cold and dark, and there was a great need to renew life.

The storyteller was a tall man with a grim, bearded face and eyes like blue ice. His voice was deep, resonant, and from the moment he began to speak, silence fell. He used words as if casting a spell. As Rhianneth looked at the intent faces around her, she remembered what Lovan had said; of their need for more enchantment than plain truth could offer.

To honour the Battle-Riders, the saga master told a new tale of great courage. He spoke of Beowulf, a warrior of the old country across the sea. A hero whose strength and bravery surpassed all others, who came with his war-band to the hall of a neighbouring king and found it menaced by Grendel, a monstrous being who murdered by night.

When the storyteller described Beowulf's comrades in their bright mail-coats and masked helmets, his rapt audience smiled. But then he spoke of the night, and of the grim monster slinking across the lonely moors towards the kings hall. Smiles faded, and a few uneasy glances were cast towards the great doors. Now that the hall was quiet, the wind's thin whine and the lonely beating of the sea could be heard when the storyteller paused. Rhianneth had heard tales of dragons and monsters before, but this one chilled her blood.

Suddenly the deep voice rose to a shout, as the monster burst open the doors of the hall where Beowulf's war-band lay, snatched up and devoured a sleeping warrior . . .

Rhianneth knew she would remember that moment forever, and shiver. The storyteller had made it too real; too close to her own childhood nightmares, and the terror that had lurked in her mind beyond the edge of the trees, where the burned farmhouse lay hidden.

Beowulf slew the monster, and its even more hideous mother. In old age he even slew a dragon that was slaughtering his people, though he died doing it. It was a tale of heroism, marvellously told and rapturously received. Yet the first sombre pictures of a place menaced by evil would not leave Rhianneth's thoughts nor would her dread of the monster fade.

Outside, the Midwinter fire lay waiting to be lit, symbol of the coming again of summer, the triumph of warmth and light over cold and darkness. She stood beside Elric as he thrust the first flaming torch into the bottom of the towering pile of wood. Then other torches were thrown. The wood caught, blazed towards the black sky. The wind took the flames and smoke upwards, blotting out the faint cold light of the stars.

People moved around the fire, some tossing into it flat oblongs of wood inscribed with runes that as they burned would waft the desire of the last one to touch them to the ears of the Gods. She saw Bebba run up, then turn and wait for Serena. The two girls clasped hands and threw their pieces of wood into the heart of the flames. Rhianneth did not have to ask herself what their secret wishes were.

'Have you no desires to be granted, lady?' Elric's arm slid around her waist, pulling her back against him.

'Do I need the power of the runes?' she smiled, and felt him draw a swift breath. His lips trailed along her cheek, then he turned her round to face him.

'You'll never need them.' His hands moved upwards, holding her face, his mouth coming down on hers with a demanding intensity. The fire burned fiercer, hot against her back. Voices around them ebbed and flowed on a tide of laughter. Somewhere a dog barked. He swung her up into his arms and carried her away into the night. She wound her arms around Elric's neck, the grim memory of Beowulf's story fading before the comfort of his strength.

We are safe, she thought. The fortress standing on its great basalt rock was impregnable against any evil thing that crept over land or slithered up from the sea. Surely, here in Din Guaryrdi, they were safe.

A few weeks later, at Solmonath time, a sickness struck their winter fastness with a dreadful swiftness against which the potions and charms of the cunning-women were useless. Even Wermund's aelfthone, his powerful remedy made from enchanter's nightshade against an attack by the whole dark race of elves, proved impotent.

Like the monster Grendel it struck fear into all as it reached out and devoured its chosen victims. Most of those who died were very young, or enfeebled by age.

All except one. After a day and a night of burning fever, Gwen miscarried. By next midday she was dead, and a pall of sorrow lay over the entire fortress.

Hussa was like a man walking in his sleep, all his gay bombast gone. He and Hrothgar drew closer, seeking strength from each other. Hrothgar had always been steady, even solemn. Now he showed a rock-hard control beyond his years. But Bebba simply abandoned herself to misery, eating nothing for days and crying, until Rhianneth was frightened

404

the girl would make herself ill.

It was as if this calamity was the final crushing blow after the past miserable months of enforced decorum and restricted freedom. Rhianneth could only do her best to comfort her, and Bebba clung to her like a small lost sparrow.

At Eostre's time, Elric took down Ida's great sword and put it into Frith's hands.

'But I . . . ' Frith turned scarlet, his voice shook with suppressed excitement. 'Surely . . . it's yours?'

Elric shook his head. 'Dreamweaver and I suit each other. Your grandfather's sword has been kept for you, until you were man enough to hold it.'

Their eyes met, cool grey and bright blue. Frith looked away first, smiling as he held up the heavy sword. 'Does it have a name?'

'Battle-light.'

Frith brought the sword round with a rush of air, his smile becoming a grin. 'Battle-light! By Woden's Eye, I'll make it a name to remember!'

Rhianneth came in at that moment and stopped dead, seeing the weapon in her son's hand. 'What's this?'

When Frith told her, she turned pale. Since the night of Ida's death, his sword had hung on the wall of the king's house. She had never touched it. Not since the day Cai told her about Ida's second wife. Now seeing it grasped so eagerly by Frith, she felt sick. All her old fears came rushing back. The thing was tainted. She could not bear to see Frith with it, even though Ida's blood ran in his veins.

Elric watched her, the warning in his eyes quite plain. This was men's business. If she hampered Frith's sword-arm with a woman's nebulous fears he would never forgive her. She swallowed. 'He is surely too young, yet?'

'I was with Ida on the war-trail long before I was Frith's age.' Elric's voice was hard, brooking no protest. 'He'll ride with me this summer, bearing his grandfather's sword.'

Frith looked from one to the other, sensing more between them than a mother's natural fears. He judged it a good time to throw down a diversionary request.

'Since I'm now acknowledged a man grown,' he said quickly, 'before I leave with the war-band, may I claim Bebba as my wife?'

Elric and Hussa agreed to a betrothal, with the wedding to follow after Frith's first summer campaign.

The past weeks had been miserable as Bebba moped and pined while Frith strutted with ruffled feathers, aggressive, moody, uncertain and angry in an emotional limbo. Now the young pair flew together like matched falcons, and the whole fortress smiled.

At the betrothal supper Bebba sat with shining eyes beside Frith, her small hand covered by his large one as they shared the loving cup. Rhianneth's throat ached at the sight of her big, rough, reckless son turned so touchingly gentle by love.

As was the custom, Elric made his gift-offer to the betrothed couple. Anything within his power to give, he declared, was theirs.

Frith avoided his father's eyes as he rose to answer. He affirmed his undying allegience to Elric. He muttered something about gathering, in time, his own war-band to serve Elric. The hall grew so quiet the crackle of the fire was the only sound apart from his voice. Elric's eyes narrowed ominously. He sensed trouble.

'If it pleases you to grant it,' Frith went on, his voice rising through the stillness, 'I would like Gefrin, the land and the new fortress. Your seneschal is old and sick and unlikely, I hear, to recover. I would keep Gefrin as it should be kept, a stronghold to guard our western approaches.'

The silence became deathly. Elric was trapped. He had made the gift-offer, spoken the age-old form of words. He could not now, with honour, withdraw.

Openly dismayed, Hussa shifted uncomfortably in his seat, wondering whether Elric suspected him of secretly urging his future son-in-law's request.

His brother Adda looked furious. Now that he had a small family, he'd had plans of his own for Gefrin.

Theo, Elric's youngest brother, merely allowed himself a faint smile as he observed the silent consternation around him. That young cub's a force to be reckoned with, he thought, turning his gaze on Frith. Better away at Gefrin, maybe. Here, snapping at Elric's heels, he's liable to be savaged.

Elric raised his head at last and looked into his son's face. Grey eyes cold with anger locked with blue, quelling Frith's assurance into shamefaced defiance.

'Cuthwulf as yet still holds that fortress for me.' Elric's voice was expressionless. 'But I have given my word before this company. Should he surrender his charge through incapacity or death, Gefrin is yours.'

Frith flushed deeply, seemed about to say something. Instead he inclined his head in thanks and sat down amidst a sudden outburst of noise that faded as Brand leapt to his feet and came swiftly up the centre aisle to stand before Elric.

'I challenge your right to give away my father's property!' His voice shook, he held his hands tightly clenched at his side. 'Gefrin should come to me!'

Elric's face was white. A muscle jerked along his jaw. 'Everything Guthlac owned was forfeit when he raised his sword against his king. That is the law.'

'And I'm a traitor's son who must be nothing, have nothing? Is that your law?'

Slowly Elric got to his feet and leaned towards him, his hands flat on the table. 'Have you wanted for anything since you came under my protection?'

Brand made no response. He was breathing hard, as if he had been running.

'I promised the lady Caldis your mother that Guthlac's treachery would not taint you, and I meant it. You are treated with all honour, Brand. But Gefrin I never intended to be yours. There are other places. Now let it be!'

Later, in the privacy of their house, Rhianneth turned a dismayed face towards Elric. She had never seen Brand possessed by such rage. It frightened her. Though she had always known he would never be allowed to claim back Guthlac's powers, she had imagined Gefrin would one day quietly come under the command of Hussa, or Adda, even Theo, and that Elric would soothe Brand with something else.

But for Frith to have claimed the place for his betrothal gift before the entire mead-hall! It was like throwing a lighted taper on straw. Why had he done it? As far as she was aware, he had no personal animosity towards Brand. Of his love and loyalty to Elric, she had no doubt. Yet he'd reached manhood, and frequently there were clashes between two strong wills, Perhaps now, with Bebba, he just needed a place apart?

'I can't believe Frith meant to cause such trouble,' she pleaded, 'I think he asked for the first thing that came into his head . . .'

'Like Hel he did! He and Hrothgar have been riding out towards Gefrin often enough lately. He planned this as soon as he realised old Cuthwulf's sickness was mortal!' Elric slammed one fist into the other. 'Yes, by Gods, he meant to force my hand tonight! He did just what I would have done if it was the only way to get it.'

His anger was so intense that only when he saw Rhianneth's expression did the incongruity of his words penetrate. He let out a Saxon obscenity that might once have made her wince, but which now brought a faint smile of amusement to her lips.

'God's spawn,' he said, his face twisting into a reluctant grin, 'But he's Ida's grandson! A true wolf's cub, full of guts and cunning. You know the British servants already have a pet name for him? They call him the Twister. Some say because he can wrap the women round his little finger. Others, that his battle-practice makes the men think of a whirlwind, smashing everything in its path. I think they've merely recognised he can be devious. Which I've failed to notice until now, Gods help me!'

Frith, devious? she thought at once, incredulously. But then she wondered whether Frith had pondered the covert speculation that still occasionally rippled regarding Brand's birth, and had intended to establish on firm ground his own position as Elric's true-born son and heir.

'What . . .' she ventured, hesitantly, 'what will you do about Brand?'

At once his face sobered. 'Only the gods know. Frith's made an enemy there, the young fool. And I . . . ' He paused – 'I'll do – something, to save the situation. I'll not have Brand dishonoured.'

Elric was as good as his word. He made Brand lord of broad acres of fine grazing land south of the Wall, and set a seneschal to oversee them until he should wish to build his own hall. This was land close to the Deiran border and to Caldis his mother, and would be safe under the protection of Adda, whose territory stretched below Catraeth.

Brand's simmering anger cooled, and he seemed gradually to accept both the present situation and his future comfortable prospects. Yet Rhianneth saw the swiftly hidden hatred in his pale eyes whenever they fell upon Frith or Hrothgar, and remained uneasy. She felt once more the warning prickle that bespoke of something, some danger unknown, inching nearer.

It was a cold wet spring. Before the birds were in full song or the blossom was out on the hawthorn, news came from Gefrin of Cuthwulf's death. Elric rode off at once with a large company of men to honour the old warrior at his funeral. Frith went with him, unable to suppress completely his excitement beneath a sombre air.

Rhianneth watched them go, feeling depression creeping over her. The disastrous winter of sickness and loss had left her weary and far from well. She hated the thought of the summer months to come with Elric away, with no Gwen at her side as the days dragged by. She wanted to ride on Romulus far into the blessed silence of the grey hills, leaving her fretting thoughts behind. But Romulus was dead. And she was Elric's queen, his peaceweaver who must try to smooth the turbulent currents that were sweeping the fortress.

CHAPTER 15

At summer's end, Frith and Bebba married. Frith behaved with an awkward gallantry, endearingly at odds with his normal, good-humoured carelessness; he seemed scarcely to take his eyes away from his enchanting, elf-like bride.

Watching Bebba, her autumn-hair curling loose, a flush of love-desire tinging her cheeks, Rhianneth thought of Gwen. How she had stood with Bebba in her arms, laughing beside Hussa on the shining sands. And now . . . she shivered. Fate cut through a life-thread so quickly, between one heartbeat and the next. She touched Glainnader's hardness through the soft stuff of her dress. So many years had passed, more than Frith's young lifetime, since she had last looked into the Druid's glass. Now, she feared to do so. Feared what it might reveal, and her own inadequate reading of its twisted truths.

Her hand moved upwards to rest upon the many-stranded gold necklace that looked so magnificent. But her fingers felt beneath it for the hidden silver chain that held Serena's baptism gift from Julia. One day, she would give it to her daughter. But today, though they would never know it, she wore the talisman of the gentle God and silently asked His blessing for Frith and Bebba.

Her thoughts went back once more to that May morning, when Elric had carried her off to the island of Metcaud . . . a special love-time, when she and Elric had together found such honied oblivion of passion amongst the brief flowers of spring, and Serena had come to them.

Now their daughter was a maid grown, with dreams of her own. Serena was so in love it was painful to watch her tongue-tied silences, her efforts to manoeuvre a few moments alone with Reburrus.

Yet, Rhianneth reminded herself, Serena was still very young. By next spring Reburrus could be replaced in her mind by any one of his own dashing young battle-riders. Girls changed. Their thistledown emotions and green first loves were easily blown away.

Though not mine, she thought swiftly. Cai was all I ever

dreamed of, from the day he rode like a dark Greek god through our gates.

She looked across to where Cai, up with the grain supplies in time for Frith's wedding, now stood deep in conversation with Lovan and Rolf. His body had hardened to a whiplash leanness over the years of riding as royal envoy, training with Llywarch's cavalry. But those same years had drawn lines of cynicism on his face and left a bitterness in his dark eyes that nothing now would entirely erase.

Sometimes, when everyone was laughing and applauding at supper, their eyes would meet. But she never surprised any betrayal of emotion in his expression. Reason told her that here in Din Guaryrdi danger stood behind every smile. Yet, perversely, she was wounded by his careful self-command.

That day in the Mithrasian inn Cai had wanted her. There, as the rain slashed down cutting off the world outside, she would willingly have given herself to him. Until . . . Elric had lanced into her mind, like a thrown spear. The moment had been lost and would not come again. Yet still woman-like, Rhianneth needed to see held-back desire smoulder on his face, the shadow of dangerous dreams darken his eyes.

She moved across to join him. 'What are your plans for Reburrus?' she asked with a smile, careless of Lovan's eyebrows raised in warning.

'Plans?'

She gestured towards Frith and Bebba

Cai shook his head. 'Reburrus will make his own mistakes. From experience I've found they are not quite as unpalatable as those made for me by others.'

Morvydd. Rhianneth's smile faded. After an awkward pause she said quietly: 'You should have taken a second wife, Cai. One of your own choosing.'

Lovan's face grew darker. Rolf looked uneasily from one to the other, feeling tension in the air.

'Maybe I should,' Cai said, meeting her eyes at last. His mouth twisted sardonically. 'But harlots are a damned sight cheaper. And easier to get rid of. Out of your bed, out of your mind.'

Faint colour stained her cheeks. He watched her broodingly, moiling over in his mind the tangled mess of his divorce from Morvydd. A mess created by his own stupidity. As he'd once fervently wished, the old nurse had indeed died soon after her return to Dumnonia. Too late he'd realised how much weight her sudden journey home added to the rambling reports she had previously sent by messenger, and death certainly raised her credibility.

Because Morvydd's father was an honourable man, once the divorce was complete the matter was closed. But the price of his silence – the burning of that last slanderous message, the quiet divorce itself – had been raised to a ruinous level.

Now, Cai wondered whether Rhianneth had any notion at all why he had paid over such an enormous part of the family wealth in order to be rid of a wife, when he had no intention of re-marrying. No, of course she had not, he thought cynically. Hadn't that been the whole idea? To protect her, and her new-born child? And the Alliance, of course.

Under his sombre, disturbing scrutiny, Rhianneth's colour deepened. Some emotion she could not read burned darkly within his eyes, made her uneasy. Was it pride? Pride that made him reluctant to speak to Elric of Reburrus, and unwillingness to risk his son's rejection?

Rhianneth resolved to approach Elric herself, in private, as soon as the wedding celebrations were over.

When she did, she was totally unprepared for the violence of his reaction. Elric slammed the door shut and swung round to face her, eyes blazing in the flickering firelight of their quiet house.

'It won't work, Rhianneth! You can't bring your daydreams to life through Cai's son, by spinning your illusions into Serena's head!'

She gasped. 'I don't know what you're talking about!'

'I'm talking about your encouraging our daughter to be moon-eyed over Cai's hot-blooded young whelp! I've other plans for Serena. Do you want me to tell Reburrus now, to save him the trouble of asking?'

Rhianneth's eyes flashed. 'Don't you dare insult him by

such a thing! He'll think you hold the Caprilius blood in contempt!'

'I don't give a hornet's gizzard what Reburrus thinks.'

'Nor how Serena feels! Nor how I feel - you never have! Besides, Cai would . . . '

'Ah yes, Cai!' He cut across her words. 'I thought we'd get to him before long. He's never been out of your heart and mind, has he? Not in all these years. And I've never had time, nor been love-sick enough, to jostle for space amongst your fantasies.' His mouth twisted in an ugly smile. 'There's never been quite enough room for the three of us inside that beautiful head, has there? Not then, when the Alliance was made. Not now.'

Once she might have turned away. Long ago she would have flared up into angry words. Now she did neither. Her hand swung across his face in a slap so hard his head was turned by the force of the blow.

There was an instant of silence. Then he pulled her into his arms and jerked her face up to his. Her knees began to buckle beneath the savage intensity of his kiss. His head lifted a finger's breadth and the look in his eyes made her heart leap wildly between fear and the desire his touch always aroused in her.

'You're a fool, Rhianneth!' he said brutally. 'But this at least, has always been mine! As for your dreams of Cai . . . ' he drew breath – 'you hardly know him! Over the years, you've created a man who doesn't exist. The young cub you were so green-sick for has changed. We all have!'

'Love doesn't change . . . ' Her lips were stiff, her throat seemed to have closed.

'Love? We're not talking about love!' His expression was suddenly savage, his hands iron-hard, and in his eyes a strange hunger that made her tremble.

Then inexplicably, he released her so abruptly that she staggered. The thin silver chain around her neck snapped. By the time she recovered her balance, Serena's baptism gift dangled gleaming from Elric's fist.

The silence between them grew ominous. Rhianneth felt

413

her palms prickle. She said quickly: 'It's Serena's. A gift from Julia, years ago. It – carries the blessing of her God.'

'I know well enough,' Elric said slowly, 'what the sign of the fish means to Christian priests. Are you telling me that you took my daughter into their temple? That they touched her with their filthy hands?'

'Never!' Rhianneth lied at once. She recognised danger in the chilling of his voice, the levelling of his gaze, and cast any future exposure into the hands of the gods while she dealt with the immediate situation., 'Julia thought only to please her. Serena was just a baby!'

'Then she won't miss it.'

Before she could move, Elric tossed the necklet into the fire-basket. 'Those bloody priests won't cast their nets in Bernicia. Not while I live!'

Rhianneth stood aghast. Only the certainty that Elric could easily prevent her stopped her from darting to snatch it from the glowing logs. Christ's symbol melted before her eyes. Her ears rang as if a thousand shrieks streamed across the bowl of heaven, and a terrible fear gripped her.

'The sacred talisman of the Christos!' she whispered. 'His God will surely strike us down!'

Elric gave an exclamation of derision, standing arms akimbo in the glow of the fire. 'God? Which God? There's nothing greater than Woden save Fate itself. And this – ' he jerked a thumb inwards towards the Hammer of Thunor that gleamed on his chest – 'this is the only talisman a warrior needs to turn spears, blunt the swords of the enemy!'

She hardly heard him. 'The protection is burned through! It's no longer whole! How could you dare to do it . . . ?'

'As easily as I'd burn the first black priest who tried to use such a talisman as a pass into Din Guaryrdi!'

Then slowly, his expression changed, as he saw the very real fear on her face. 'Hel's Gate!' he said softly, 'I want the truth! How did Serena get the necklet?'

Something in his quieter words reached her. She pulled herself together, took a deep breath, and looked straight into his eyes. 'It was truly a gift from my aunt, Elric. Just before

414

Baldur was born. When I asked for the protection of the Church for Serena, as Marcus once asked it for me.'

Silence. Silence so deep she heard her own heart beating.

'By Woden's Eye,' he said, at last, 'how is it I've never actually killed you, Rhianneth?'

Winter came. A wild wind buffeted the fortress, churning the sea into a roaring white foam. Two great stones from the top of the beacon tower crashed to the ground, and a black jagged crack half a man's length appeared ominously below the place where once they had lodged.

This outer turbulence Rhianneth shut out. But the tremors of human emotion within her small circle she could not avoid. It was true that Frith's antagonism towards Reburrus had gradually faded and he and Hrothgar were moving tentatively towards friendship with Cai's son; even Frith's former furious resentment of Serena's infatuation with Reburrus changed into brotherly teasing. As for Reburrus, his fascination for Serena was plain to see in the way his dark eyes sought her out. He went out of his way to speak to her, to hear her soft, prettily accented British. But Serena was so in love that Rhianneth worried, knowing her daughter must be hurt. For she could see no chance of Elric contemplating a match between Serena and Cai's son.

The silver talisman also preyed on Rhianneth's mind. Elric had listened in stony silence when she spoke of Christ's doctrine of forgiving love, and had brushed contemptuously aside her protests that His priests were not eaters of the dead. Elric considered that his destruction of the Christian symbol cleansed Serena of any contact with the hated church, and for him the episode was finished. But Rhianneth still trembled when she recalled the sacred silver fish sliding amongst the burning logs as if it was alive. Surely, not even a loving God would let pass such an insult without retribution?

After Yuletide, the rough weather was replaced by clinging sea-frets that blanketed the coast, and gradually the soft grey days and windless nights had a strangely soothing effect. When they lay together beneath the furs Elric did not now

415

speak of plans for attack or defence, decisions and policies, but of far-off days in the old land across the sea where the legends of Bernicia were born. He drew Rhianneth into a world where mighty heroes strode and enchantresses rode the wind with their black tipped wings.

Fascinated by the magic of his words, it sometimes seemed it was Marcus's voice she heard, spinning tales of the ancient south as they rode home through sweet-smelling damp grass under the evening stars. It was as if two worlds touched within the circle of her own faint firelight, and the continuity of all things seemed assured. Yet often, Lovan's words fretted at her thoughts. Something was needed to weld Elric's people to Britain, he had said; Rhianneth would fall asleep while her mind still sought for a third singing ring of magic that might interlock, strong and true, like the links of their shining battle shirts.

By Solmonath it was clear Bebba was pregnant, and that the child would be born around harvest time. This happy news augered well for the new year, and Rhianneth determined to shake off her worries and settle snugly down to prepare for the coming event.

When Elric, his face taut, told her he'd just seen Brand, she stared at him blankly. 'Brand? About what?'

'He asked for Serena.'

For a moment she could not answer. The colour faded from her face. Then she drew a hissing breath. 'What did you tell him?'

'The truth, at last.' Elric's voice was devoid of expression. 'Serena is his sister. What else could I say? I'd given Gefrin to Frith. Brand won't forget that, ever. Whatever other reason I might have given for refusing him Serena would have made him more bitter.' He let out a long breath. 'What a bloody mess I made of it, all those years ago.!'

Rhianneth moistened her lips, suddenly dry-mouthed. 'You are quite sure that Brand is your son?'

Immediately she would have drawn back the words, if she could. She began quickly to speak again, but his look stopped her, his face naked and vulnerable to hurt as she had never before seen it. 'As sure as any man can be, who puts his trust in a woman.'

'I see.' She looked away, thinking of what she knew about Caldis. What Wermund the priest knew. Dangerous knowledge which could never be proved, and which could cause only more pain. Knowledge best buried with the past. 'Where is Brand now? Would it help if I went to see him?'

'No. What in Hel is there to say? He may forgive his mother, they were always close. He'll never forgive me, even if I build him the finest hall in Bernicia and load him with gold rings from wrist to armpit!'

'What did he say?'

'Very little. If he'd had a scramasax at his belt I fancy he'd have said even less.'

His grim humour failed to hide the pain behind his eyes. Rhianneth took both his hands in hers, feeling the taut hardness of his muscles against her fingers.

'You – and Caldis – did what was necessary at the time. Guthlac was a dangerous man. And afterwards, it was too late. Kinder to say nothing. When Brand has time to think, he'll come to understand. The past is dead, and bitterness better buried with it.'

Fractionally, he relaxed. 'You're right,' he said, 'It's all done with and best forgotten.'

But the past is never really gone away, Rhianneth thought, even while she murmured more comforting words. And bitterness is a plant that throws up poisonous shoots.

The weeks passed, and the time of Eostre's feast drew near. One night when supper was finished, they sat at the still littered tables listening to a slow melody plucked out on the minstrel's harp. The fire settled, sending a shower of sparks into the air that made the dogs leap away and the shadows shudder as they danced upon the walls.

Suddenly above the harp's voice came the sound of a commotion outside, men shouting and a thud of hooves. The music died away as all heads turned to the doors and the great bar, signifying that the mead-hall was at meat, was hastily raised.

Immediately there came a clang of metal against stone, and then a thud as the door was flung wide.

Several men strode into the hall, and the entire war-band sprang to their feet as they did so. Rhianneth's heart lurched in alarm. Then she saw Elric's wolf-head emblem on the tunic of the foremost, and breathed again.

The man pushed his way towards Elric, his face white beneath the sweat and grime. Elric was already on his feet shouting something, but for a few seconds the man seemed unable to answer.

'Urien . . . !' he panted at last, leaning across the table for support. 'He's moving! Moving fast! Already he's got command of the great road north out of Eburacum where it splits westward into Rheged, east towards us!'

'Catraeth?' Elric's voice was harsh, incredulous. The man nodded. Elric ground out an obscenity, smashing a clenched fist down with such force the solid table shook. 'What in bloody Hel is Aelle doing? Cowering behind his miserable walls hoping they don't come south?'

'It's us, Urien's after!' Frith was flushed with anger and excitement. 'He's cutting off our supply routes from Mithrasia! Then he'll close in, try to push us into the sea!'

The messenger nodded, breathing hard. 'Looks like it. And this time he's not alone. There's some sort of alliance. Morcant's with him. And Dunaut. Old Riderch and his sons. Gaullauc . . . '

Elric's teeth glinted in a snarl. 'So he's got a pack behind him, has he? We'd best be moving then – before the mongrels are at our throats!'

The fortress was in turmoil as the men prepared for war. Bright battle shields were stacked around the hall, and the long ashen spears with their deadly iron tips. Men crouched in the courtyard, polishing weapons with sand, sharpening the edges on whetstones till they would slice a hair.

Messengers rode breakneck to summon the thanes to arms. Hussa and Hrothgar arrived with their war-band within a day. Adda and Theo soon afterwards.

A vast army it seemed, that eventually started southwards towards the Wall, and Catraeth. But Rhianneth remembered how once Peredur and Gurci had marched as bravely out of Eburacum with banners flying, and fear clawed in her stomach.

'Take care!' she had said when Elric bent to kiss her farewell, and for once had allowed her fear to show as she clung to him, heedless of the meshed rings of his battleshirt hurting her breasts.

'I'll be back.' He caught her chin, his mouth coming down swiftly on hers and lingering with growing intensity. Then he lifted his head and grinned. 'And I'll bring you Urien's head for a loom-weight!'

'And Frith . . . ' She could not smile. Not with her stomach churning and her heart fluttering like a bird. He stroked the hair that lay in a silken stream down her back.

'Frith was born for this, my *deorling*. He's a true son of Thunor. With Ida's sword in his hand he'll slice through the enemy as though they were no more that straw-men in the practice yard!'

As she caught his hand and held it against her cheek another sharper pang of fear slanted through her, for she realised that even in the haste of preparation Elric had remembered to cut short his fingernails in case he should die in the coming battle. The ship of monsters let loose at Ragnarok would be built from the nails of dead men, and no warrior would willingly give the smallest paring towards its completion.

She wondered then what Wermund the priest thought of Cai's Battle-Riders. For had he not once, long ago, believed Cai to be the sinister Loki who would steer the ship of nails?

'Will Wermund be with you?'

'Not this time. He's too old for real campaigning. He'll stay here in the fortress, with some of my war-band. Theo's in command, with a few of his closest hearth companions. There'll be enough drunken fight-wounds to keep Wermund happy.' Momentarily he hesitated. 'We'll have Brand to patch us up, if we need it.'

She nodded, thrusting down her unease. Brand had appeared to accept the situation. But he was so silent, so watchful, that her sympathy was over-ridden by the more

419

primitive instincts of survival. She felt, deep inside, that Brand was dangerous. But to whom, and how, she did not know.

Days slid into weeks. Rhianneth kept busy with household tasks, anything to stop her thinking. She made sure there was a good supply of medicines and clean linen for men who might return hurt, and kept up the spirits of the fortress by ensuring that supper each night in the mead-hall was hot and savoury.

When news came, it was good. The army had recaptured Catraeth, the nerve-centre of the north. Urien's ally Dunaut in whose charge it had been, had barely escaped with half his men. Now Elric had taken his army into Rheged, scouring the countryside as he went.

Theo was overjoyed. 'Hel's Gate,' he cried, his eyes shining, 'I wish I was with them!'

'Would you leave us here unprotected?' Rhianneth demanded, laughing, her spirits rising for the first time in weeks.

Theo glanced towards his wife Elfwyn and their twin girls, whom he'd brought into the shelter of the fortress. He smiled back at Rhianneth. 'Thank the Gods for Din Guaryrdi,' he said sincerely. 'This rock is virtually impregnable.' He winked. 'You don't really need me!'

The year moved into summer, and the air grew heavy with scent. But as time passed without news, it began to seem as if Rheged had swallowed up the army.

The hot days made Bebba exhausted. Her anxiety over Frith caused fretful nights, and her appetite dwindled alarmingly. Rhianneth kept her occupied as well as she could, soothing the girl's fears with a calm and cheerful aspect. But beneath the façade her own apprehension grew.

'Could there have been a disaster with the Battle-Riders?' she asked Lovan anxiously. 'They are in unknown territory. Urien's country.'

Lovan studied her face, his expression brooding. 'If they go too far into Rheged, with the Dal Riada Scots ready to sweep down across their backs, its not just the cavalry we'll be losing, but Elric's whole army. There's something wrong. I smell treachery. But I can't quite sniff it out . . . '

'Treachery?' cried Rolf, stopping abruptly as he sharpened a spear-point. 'You mean a lure-on? A trap?'

He had not fought since an arrow had smashed the bone of his left thigh three years back, but he still thought and talked as one of the war-band.

'Keep your voice down when Bebba's within earshot!' Alda hissed at him reprovingly. 'The babe's due by harvest and she needs Frith home safe before then!'

Summer drifted on. There was no news from Rheged.

Baldur spent his days with Theo's men, listening to their stories of long-dead battles, or singing with them the ribald songs that mirrored the cheerful optimism of Theo's small war-band. His interest in learning diminished, and Rhianneth could no longer summon the energy to persuade him. It was the uncertainty of the present situation, she told herself. When the army comes back, and Theo left them, everything would return to normal.

Then, the horseman came. Riding as if pursued by the hounds of Hel, out of the woods and along the trackway, the horse panting as it galloped up the fortress slope and through the gates. Men sprang forward to catch the rider as he slid from its lathered back. Theo came running like the wind.

It was Cynric, Wulf's son, and the youngest of Elric's war-band. Sudden dread iced Rhianneth's blood. She caught Baldur to her, held him iron-fast when he would have run to the gate to hear the boy's first stumbling words.

There had been a big battle, when the Bernician war-bands had come upon the British encampments somewhere north-east of Urien's city of Caer Luel. It was near an old Roman fort, in thickly wooded country where cavalry was useless. But the boy was in pain from a badly-torn shoulder muscle, and very confused.

'The enemy kept changing,' he repeated, as Wermund tended his wound, 'melting away into the forest till we hardly knew who we were fighting . . . '

One thing he was sure of. The army had been deceived,

was even now chasing shadows deeper into Rheged, while Urien's main force had turned eastwards and joined with his allies Morcant, Gaullauc and old Riderch of the Clyde to strike straight into Bernicia's heartland, at Din Guaryrdi itself. Only by chance, as he edged homewards with despatches, had Cynric come upon the great host of the British as they rallied beneath their bright-coloured banners. Then, realising the extent of the danger, he had ridden break-neck home to warn the fortress.

'You should have let Brand tend this wound before you left,' Wermund said. 'It would have spared you much pain.'

The boy shook his head. 'I couldn't find him.'

Wermund's deft fingers stilled momentarily. A faint chill touched Rhianneth's skin. Wermund finished his work, straightened, and looked straight into her eyes.

'At least the captains of our armies are safe, as yet,' he said. 'We are not leaderless in that nest of serpents.'

Rhianneth's lips thinned. 'What of your rune-craft now, priest?' Her voice was brittle with scorn. 'Where is the ruin of Rheged your gods promised?'

'The runes cannot lie. They said victory. A road, sword-hewn across this island from sea to sea . . . '

A memory slid into her mind. Her grandmother's face wet with tears as she read the symbols in the Druid's stone. From sea to sea . . .

Wermund watched her, saw her eyes darken as she caught her breath. 'Victory,' he repeated, nodding in silent recognition, 'and soon.'

He spoke quietly, with implacable faith. But lines of weari-ness scored his face beneath the thin straggling yellow hair, and she glimpsed uncertainty in his eyes. Wermund was grow-ing old. He was but a man after all, as anxious as she. Nor could she honestly think of him as her enemy. For many years now there had been a truce between them, never broken even in times of greatest stress. Sympathy suddenly welled up in Rhianneth, breaking through her hard-held control.

'Yes,' she assured him, 'victory.' But when, she thought, and at what price? And her heart grew heavy with foreboding.

Two riders were hastily despatched to evade the enemy host, cross Rheged, and summon Elric to Din Guaryrdi's aid. One more rode southwards to Deira, to appeal for Aelle's help.

Din Guaryrdi closed the gates and crouched back upon its rock to await the coming seige army.

Rhianneth was walking with Bebba and Alda towards the Queen's Bower when suddenly Bebba stopped, raising her head. 'L—Listen!'

From far away they heard a rumbling, like thunder in the earth. Rhianneth turned cold. She had heard that sound before. Long ago, when she had lain in the damp grass with Lovan and Marcus and watched Rhun's great army come out of the west, heading for Deva.

'Urien!' she whispered. 'By all the Gods – how many are marching with him?'

The beseiging army was numbered in thousands. As darkness came, the lights of their camp fires flickered between Din Guaryrdi and the forest like summer stars; noise swelled towards them, thick with menace.

That night Rhianneth did not sleep. At dawn Urien laid seige in earnest, and the day passed in a confusion of noise and choking grey smoke as the defenders fought to smother the fires that sprang to life both within the fortress itself and along its timber ramparts, wherever the deadly flaming arrows lodged. As one person tired, another took up the task of hauling water from the well, and the line of buckets never failed.

In the enemy camp the giant trunk of an axed tree was openly being prepared as a battering ram, mounted on wheels and fitted with a sharp iron snout.

'Nothing but show!' Theo declared with derision. 'Our trackways are too steep and they know it.' He glanced at Rhianneth's smoke-smudged face and heavy eyes. 'Why not rest, lady? I've got men posted all round the ramparts. There is no way they can take us by surprise. But it's going to be a long wait before our army gets here . . .'

But not until daylight faded did she fall at last, fully-clothed, upon her bed and close her eyes in exhaustion. Her sleep was shallow, strange; time and again she started up from dreams full of alarm and confusion.

It was fully dark when Lovan shook her awake. She thought for one bewildered instant he was part of the sequence of nightmares. But his grip on her shoulder was real, and urgent.

'Move *cariad*!' His voice was rough from the smoke-filled air. 'We're getting out. Into the boats.'

She sprang to her feet, heart thudding, 'What's happened?'

'Treachery!' Brand's with the enemy!'

Already he was dragging her towards the door. She jerked free, darted to her box and flung up the lid. She snatched up the leather bag of jewels, a small box of medicines.

'Wait!' she screamed, as Lovan seized her arm once more. Fumbling in her haste she slammed down the lid on her precious books, turned the key and dropped it into the jewel bag.

'Christos!' Lovan bellowed, 'One blow with a battle-axe and that lock's gone! Leave it! Theo's holding the north gate clear – but we've got seconds, that's all, before he's over-run!'

'Where's Serena . . . Baldur?' she panted as they ran out into the night, 'And Bebba? Oh, gods – where's Bebba?'

'Gone ahead – keep close, *cariad*!'

The night was filled with noise and terror, a confusion of faces red-lit as demons in the light of a blazing house. They ran down the narrow treacherous pathway to the shore, stumbling, breathless. Then between two rough lines of jostling warriors, beyond whom Rhianneth glimpsed the enemy streaming across the beach towards them.

The huge bulk of a boat loomed blackly before her, already afloat. She was lifted, thrown into it.

The warriors put their shoulders against the old salted timbers and heaved. Smoothly the shallow-draughted boat slid through the surf. Willing hands hauled the men aboard.

Arrows sang through the air. Spears whistled, thudded against the timbers. Rhianneth crouched low, heart hammering. But already the boat was in deeper water, moving fast beneath the desperate strength of her oarsmen. The enemy's deadly hail soon parted only the surf behind her stern.

Rhianneth felt sick with fright and shock as she looked at the people around her, and at the dark shapes of the other boats floating nearby. Din Guaryrdi to fall within a day of seige! It was unbelievable.

'Believe it.' Lovan's voice was low and grim besides her. 'Brand deserted our army and went straight to Urien, with an offer to open the way into Din Guaryrdi. There's an old Roman tunnel running into the fortress not far from the Beacon. Guarded, of course. But Brand told the guard he'd slipped past the enemy in the darkness to bring urgent news from Elric. Why should the man doubt Brand? He lifted the bar, and Brand killed him. The guard's lad got away, raised the alarm . . . but the enemy were already streaming in. The rest you know.'

This was the reality within the shifting sense of danger she'd felt for so long. This betrayal was Brand's vengeance. His answer to Elric's denying him Gefrin. And Serena. How it must have bitten into his soul to realise he was bastard-born, and not Guthlac's son . . .

Ever since Frith was locked in the beacon tower that bitter winter night, Rhianneth's instinct for danger had always over-ridden any compassion for Brand. Perhaps if it had not, she might have healed his deep-burning resentment before it came to this.

Now, her heart ached for Elric. And for Wermund, who had opened up to Brand the secrets of his precious magical lore. She raised her head and looked across to where the priest huddled within his cloak. He sat immobile, a hooded shadow, lonely in the darkness, and pity stirred within her.

The long sea-oars dipped under the hardened muscles of Theo's warriors as the heavy tillers swung the big boats out towards the safety of the open sea, to ride at anchor while anxious eyes scanned the shore, and the dark wastes around them. They had done what had been done so often in Ida's day. They had launched the boats, and put their lives into the hands of their Gods.

The wry, often ribald comments of the men kept spirits raised. But after a while it began to rain, and the air grew cold.

The sea stretched in long glistening swells under a black sky. The stark bulk of Din Guaryrdi vanished behind thick dark mist.

Baldur pressed against Rhianneth. His face had a sweat-beaded pallow, and when she touched his hand it was ice-cold. She flung her cloak around his thin shoulders and held him close. The colour of his face frightened her, despite Lovan's assurances that it was only sea-sickness. He tried to get Baldur to take a drink from the small leather bottle he carried, but the boy shook his head and turned away.

Rhianneth looked worriedly across at Bebba. The girl lay warm-cradled between Serena and Alda, and managed a faint smile.

The long, cold night crept by. When dawn came the wind grew gusty, and the waves rose higher around them as the boat dipped.

Baldur was violently sick, as were many others. Anxiety clawed sharply, as Rhianneth watched Bebba's face whiten and her bright head bend over a bailing bowl while Alda's arms encircled her shaking shoulders.

The wailing of children rose above the thud of waves against the boat's timbers. The wind grew stronger, and the boat began to pitch dangerously amidst the white-crested waters.

The stench of vomit filled Rhianneth's nostrils and rain ran coldly down her neck. Her limbs were cramped and stiff. She had never felt more miserably helpless in her life.

Then Serena touched her arm, fear in her eyes. 'Mama, it's Bebba. Alda thinks the baby is coming.'

The boats crunched up the beach on the seaward side of the island of Metcaud, and at once the cunning-women took charge. A shelter was made for Bebba from upright spears driven into the ground and the shields that had been slung like a defensive wall along the bulwarks of the boat.

The sombre day inched towards night, every hour interminable. Rhianneth paced restlessly, never moving far from Bebba's shelter. There was something wrong. She read it in the grey faces of the cunning-women. The child was taking

426

too long to come, and Bebba was narrow-hipped, frail-boned as a small bird.

Darkness fell. Torches were lit. The thin drizzle ceased for a while and the moon gleamed fitfully behind wind-driven clouds.

Rhianneth's head shot up at the baby's first cry, her heart thudding. When at last one of the women placed the warm-wrapped child in her arms, she almost laughed aloud with relief. It was a boy. She gazed down into the small, crumpled face, and love spread through her like a warm tide. Frith's son she thought, safely born at last!

Then she saw the expression on the woman's face, the fear in her eyes. All her joy vanished.

'It's the bleeding that won't stop, lady. I've seen it often before . . . '

But already Rhianneth had thrust the child back into the woman's arms and was running towards the shelter.

She and Alda tore up shirts, shifts, tunics, fighting to staunch the deadly flow of blood. Bebba grew weaker.

'Is the b—baby all right?' she asked after a while, as rain beat down once more and the wind gusted against the shields.

Rhianneth stroked back the damp red curls from Bebba's forehead. She had to lean close to hear her whispered words.

'He's perfect,' she said. 'He looks like Frith.'

Bebba's hand moved gently in acknowledgement.

Rhianneth's own hands were shaking. She felt light-headed with exhaustion.

A little time crawled by. Then Bebba said, each word coming slow and faint, 'Tell Frith I l . . . love him.'

Cold tears ran silent and unheeded down Rhianneth's face. Desperately she summoned every scrap of strength she had left to keep her voice steady. 'He'll come soon, Bebba. Then you shall tell him yourself.'

'No . . . ' The word floated feather-light along her breath. Then a smile briefly touched her lips. 'Strange . . . for just this one time, it is I . . . who c—can't w—wait for him . . . ' she said, and died.

In the silence that followed Rhianneth heard neither wind nor rain, nor the subdued voices nearby. She went on kneeling beside Bebba, stroking the bright tangled hair, her mind locked in ice.

'Oh, my God . . . '

Slowly then, she turned her head to look up into Lovan's grey face.

'Come, *cariad*,' he said. 'Come away with me. Let the cunning-women in.'

Gently he lifted her from her knees, led her from the shelter.

They carried Bebba across the tiny island, and the people of the turf-roofed houses helped build a cairn for her beside their own dead. A fitting thing to do, for they were kinfolk of her mother Gwen, who had been born just across the causeway.

The sand bar between Metcaud and the mainland lay bare at low tide. But it was narrow, treacherous, completely covered by the sea for many hours each day. Theo confidently declared that it could be defended by his fighting men. Everyone else he ordered back to the far side of the island, close to the safety of the waiting boats.

Here, grateful for the rough shelters and fires of dry land, they made camp as best they could while they awaited the inevitable coming of Urien's armies.

Rhianneth remembered how she had lain with Elric amongst the soft new grass of Metcaud, that sweet May morning; how in contrast to the everyday clatter of the fortress the peace of the little island had seemed almost a holy thing. Now fear was all around her, and the far hillside belonged only to Bebba's elfin shade.

She gazed along the beach at familiar faces rough grimed with sea-salt, taut with strain. And she realised that it was to her they looked, Elric's woman and their folk-queen, for courage and guidance.

She set her teeth, and resolutely closed her mind against the withering grief of Bebba's death. She comforted the old ones and soothed the children. Tirelessly and for the first time in all the years since she had come to Bernicia, she worked alongside Wermund and the cunning-women, tending those wounded in the flight from Din Guaryrdi.

Her strength did not falter, not even when at last they felt the monstrous rumble of the enemy approach shake the earth. Not even when the deep-throated roar as the gathering host chanted out its challenge sent terror winging through the air.

Every so often the same challenge would thunder out, swelling as it gathered force. At other times the warriors stamped in unison, and beat their weapons against their shields in a slow relentless rhythm that chilled the blood.

Rhianneth knew they faced ultimate disaster. Huddled on this far beach, their only hope Theo's warriors who stood ready to defend at low tide, their only comfort the sturdy bulk of the boats, the escape route of the open sea. Their food could not last. Even if one of their messengers reached Elric, his army would be in no state after a forced march, to face the might of Urien's host.

'I wish they'd go away!'

Baldur's hands clenched as the menacing sounds of the enemy rolled towards them yet again. He bit his lip to hide its trembling.

'It's just noise,' Rhianneth soothed him, 'To make us afraid. Like a dragon roaring and puffing out smoke . . . '

And what is the surest way to kill a dragon? she thought suddenly. Why, to cut off its head!

'I'll do it!' Rolf burst out, 'I can still row a boat. And aim true for Urien's black heart!'

'With that thick Saxon accent? You'd never get near him.' Lovan replied quietly. He glanced down at his own filthy tunic and torn cloak. 'I'm British, and shabby enough to pass unnoticed. But I'm no sailor. If you could just get me across, after nightfall? It would mean a long pull northwards for a safe landing.' His smile was grim. 'Those so-called allies are enemies under the skin. Give them the scent of Urien's blood

429

and they'll turn by instinct, rend each other apart!'

All the old hatred of the Caer Melot Fellowship for Urien and his kin shone coldly in his eyes. He bowed slightly to Rhianneth.

'A right true vengeance, *cariad*. One they above all, should appreciate. Kill the Pendragon and the kingdoms fall apart!'

One of the islander's small boats lay ready to push out into the dark sea. Rhianneth shivered at the sea's edge, sick with anxiety as Lovan crunched over the sand towards her carrying on his shoulder the leather stable-bag of medicines he'd possessed ever since she could remember; a horse-doctor was welcome everywhere, even in a seige camp. He carried no weapon except the sharp hunting knife thrust into his belt.

'Take this too, Lovan,' a tiny phial lay in the palm of her hand. 'It's swift, and deadly. It may prove safer for you than a knife.'

'Grandmother's best?' he joked, tucking the phial beneath his cloak.

Rhianneth shook her head, unable to return his smile. Ah no, she thought, not for Urien, the gentle oblivion of her grandmother's last gift which lay, still unopened, between her breasts in its sinister casket.

Then she drew a quick breath, for something feathered across her mind. The next instant, unrecognised, it had gone.

Lovan was watching her. Bebba's death had affected him deeply, and in the clouded moonlight he looked drawn, old; yet a pale fire burned behind his eyes.

'Don't worry,' he said gently. 'I'll stop him. One way or another.'

Rhianneth reached up to kiss his tough, weatherd cheek, her throat aching with unshed tears. Then Rolf came, with Theo and several of his men; and Alda, Bebba's baby son in her arms.

Theo grasped Lovan's shoulder. 'Good luck,' he said, as the older man turned towards him. 'May the gods, both yours and ours, stay with you both!'

Long after the boat had vanished, Alda went on rocking the

child against her shoulder, staring into the dark mist that rose from the sea's face. Rhianneth put an arm around her waist, sensing a fearful apprehension that surpassed even her own.

'Rolf will be all right! He's only to wait, hidden, with the boat.'

'He'll never leave Lovan.' Alda turned, her face ravaged, the salt and dirt streaked by dried runnels of tears. 'I thought you'd realised that.'

When day broke on the fourth day of seige, the Bernicians were in despair. Their food was fast running out. Blankets were sodden, and what clothes they managed to dry around camp fires were swiftly drenched once more by almost continuous rain.

Several of their men had been killed fighting off attacks at low tide along the sand bar, and many more wounded. Mutterings began about taking to the boats and throwing themselves on the mercy of their wily kinsman Aelle of Deira. But Theo would have none of that.

'I'd as soon go north amongst the Picts than trust that Hel-Snake!' he cried, eyes burning with exhaustion in his grimy face. 'If I live through this I swear I'll roast Aelle and his whole skulking pack of bloody cowards over his own hearth fire!'

The deep roar of the enemy chants started again. Taunting, threatening.

Rhianneth's nerves tightened to breaking point. Lovan's failed, she thought. It was a stupid hopeless throw of the dice. Now he's dead, and I've killed him.

'Mama?' Serena knelt beside her on the damp sand. 'Baldur says there's one Mithrasian banner amongst the enemy flags.'

'He's mistaken. He must have seen Gwynedd's banner, which bears Maelgwyn's old device – the Dragon of the Isles.'

Serena shook her head, fumbling for her mother's hand 'Baldur said it bore Mithrasian colours, and flew next to Urien's.'

The Queen, Rhianneth thought, come for the kill. Her mouth dried. There would be no mercy for her or her kin if that woman found them alive . . .

'The noise,' Serena whispered, raising her head to listen, 'It's not the same. They're not shouting together any more!'

'Oh, gods! They've broken through!'

Serena shook her head. 'The sea is still covering the sands . . .'

But her face lost colour, and her eyes were suddenly bright with fear. Rhianneth threw her arms around her daughter and held her crushed against her body in a fierce, animal urge to protect. She would die before she let Urien's warriors touch Serena – yes, and take as many as she could with her! She must get a weapon. A knife, to hide beneath her cloak . . .

'Something's happened!' Baldur ran stumbling towards them, his thin face hot with excitement. 'Theo says the British are fighting amongst themselves, right there at the edge of the water! They're all milling about!'

Urien was dead, and it was Lovan who had killed him. That much was sure.

But rumour ran wild through the countryside as the great seige collapsed. Some said that Morcant's jealous anger was behind the murder, for Urien had rashly offered Din Guaryrdi as a bribe to his Irish ally Fiachna, even though he was well aware that the fortress lay in territory seized by Ida from Morcant's father, Outigern.

Seeing their father slain, Urien's son Owain and his brothers ran amok with their swords amongst the erstwhile allies, thus ensuring their lasting enmity. Old hatreds flared into violent life. The alliance dissolved into carnage. The British host disintegrated as thousands of warriors streamed homewards to defend their own kingdoms against their neighbours' wrath.

When the waters fell away from the sand bar, Theo with some of his warriors crossed cautiously over to the mainland, silent now save for the harsh cries of birds.

Until once more the sea flowed over the sands to make Metcaud an island, they searched the littered remains of the great encampment. But if amongst the scattered British dead under its gory cloak of battle-crows they ever found Lovan or Rolf, they kept silent.

As the big boats floated out with the next tide, heading for home, Din Guaryrdi's minstrel was already making a song, twining words into a poetry that would ensure the everlasting fame of their two heroes.

Rhianneth sat cold and dry-eyed as the island slipped away behind them. The soft murmurings of the minstrel blew towards her on the wind, and she remembered the excitement, the boastings and the laughter as the pair of them returned from their first campaign with the war-band. Perhaps after all, she thought bleakly, Lovan and Rolf would rather be remembered in legend, than have the brief glory-blaze of a Saxon warrior funeral.

CHAPTER 16

Bernicia's army limped back, weary and badly mauled in running battles with the splintered British force heading west.

Elric's anger was intense. He had been tricked by his enemy, betrayed by his son. Such was his bitterness he would not speak of Brand, not even to Rhianneth. But she saw the expression in his eyes when he looked on the wreckage within Din Guaryrdi and it was not one of grief. It was iron-hard, murderous. The war-bands were weakened, they had lost men and horses and much precious war-gear, but Elric's sword would not stay long in its sheath. He was already planning his next campaiagn.

Though its woven hangings were sword-ripped, its furniture smashed, the mead-hall was standing. It served as their refuge, for many houses had been destroyed by fire, including the king's house.

In her sturdy box, dented and smoke-blackened though it was, Rhianneth's books lay untouched. Yet inexplicably, amidst her brief joy as she lifted them out, realisation finally came to her that she would never see Lovan again. Her anguish was slow, and deep, a pain too great to cope with except in solitude, where none could see her grief. Tears she shared with Alda, in plenty. But nothing touched this, the hard secret rock of her sorrow.

Never again would any of them feel entirely safe within the fortress walls, or beyond them. Serena's self-composure had gone. She was moody, nervous, jumping at the sound of a hunting horn. Baldur had such bad dreams he woke screaming in the night for a sword to hold off the enemy, and had half the fortress scrambling to arms.

It was a time of desolation for them all. But Frith . . . Rhianneth's heart sank whenever she thought of Frith.

He had heard how Bebba died, in unmoving silence, staring down at his tiny son with dead eyes.

'Hussa thought to call him Eanfrith,' Rhianneth ventured gently, at last. 'And of course we'll care for him here in Din Guaryrdi, until Gefrin . . . '

'Call him whatever you like,' Frith answered thinly. 'But never call this fortress by that British name again. Not if you love me. Not if you ever loved Bebba!'

He spent hours alone on the ramparts or scuffing along the beach, staring out to sea. In the mead-hall he sat silent, brooding. Rhianneth watched him toss down cup after cup of potent mead, and her unease grew.

Winter came. Frith remained solitary and taciturn.

Soon none of the slaves or servants dared give Din Guaryrdi its name within Frith's earshot, and gradually everyone began to call it Bebbanburgh. Bebba's fortress.

Long before Eostre's feast Frith was pressing to be off in pursuit of Urien's son, Owain. He laid Bebba's death at the door of the northern kings, and meant to destroy them all, one by one.

'He needs vengeance,' Elric said, 'to slash at the enemy now, before it burns his heart out!'

Rhianneth's cheeks paled. For her, memories of last summer were too painful, too close. And there was something about Frith's implacable determination that chilled the blood.

On the morning the warriors set out to hunt for Owain, Frith tossed out taut jokes amongst the men. But Rhianneth saw behind his grin, to where a terrible and savage grief made his eyes colder than death. She shivered as he rode off beside Elric. Sensing his impatience his horse danced restlessly. The swinging masked helmet hung menacingly from the saddle reminded her, irresistibly, of a severed head.

Whatever had awakened in Frith when Bebba died had changed him. Altered his inner self, the very core of his being, into a dark, demoniacal force of destruction.

Summer passed, and the warriors returned after harrying the enemy from below the Wall to the borderlands of the Picts.

'Rheged's on her knees!' cried Frith fiercely, 'scoured like a black pot for us! And by Urien's own bloody neighbours! So much for the great alliance!'

But Elric now had other concerns, arising from their own dreadful battle losses of the previous summer and their urgent need for more weapons, horses and armour.

'We need fresh supplies, and quickly,' he muttered to Rhianneth afterwards, his voice still raw from shouting orders, 'We'll not find them in Rheged's ruins . . . '

Through Cai, Elric speedily began negotiations with Llywarch. So that Bernicia might continue the harassment of the northern kings, Mithrasia agreed to send all the supplies Elric demanded from his ally.

The bargain was sealed by marriage, between Elric's daughter Serena and Reburrus, son of Llywarch's most trusted kinsman, Caius Caprilius.

Elric shrugged off Rhianneth's astonishment. 'With Urien dead, Llywarch might have felt a lack of urgency towards our needs,' he stated baldly. 'I made sure Cai would press hard. That's all.'

She stared at him. 'But – you had other plans for Serena, you said.'

'Aelle's son, Edwin?' he laughed briefly, dismissively, 'I'd never stomach a Deiran alliance now, not while Aelle lives.'

'You insisted you wanted a Saxon marriage for Serena! Yet now you're quite willing to bargain her away in exchange for war gear from Llywarch – '

Eyebrows raised, he surveyed her. 'I thought you'd be happy? It's what Serena obviously wants.'

'That is not the point! What kind of father can use his daughter as a – a lever, to get what he wants? What kind of man are you, Elric?'

'I am a king, Rhianneth.' He gave her a level look. 'A war-leader who must never leave the kingdom at risk because of a . . . personal conflict. Who cannot allow emotion to rule him, ever.'

Staring at him, she seemed to catch a glimpse of Ida. Ida, raising for the good of his people the great war-sword that now was Frith's.

'Ah, Elric!' she shivered, held out her hands to him. 'Say you arranged it, just a little, for the happiness of Serena and Reburrus . . . ?'

His face relaxed into a smile as he pulled her into his arms.

436

'If it pleases you' *deorling*,' he whispered against her hair, 'I'll say anything . . . '

The months turned into a year, into two years.

Frith moved to Gefrin, taking his own small cohort of close war-brothers to join the warriors already there. Once, he'd hoped to make Gefrin a home for Bebba and their child. Now it was simply a war base, his whole purpose concentrated on annihilating the enemy.

Baldur was fast growing towards manhood. Already he was a head taller than Rhianneth, although it was obvious he would never reach the height of Elric or Frith. His nightmares were forgotten. But the more Rhianneth watched him practise his cavalry skills with Reburrus, the more terrified she became of the day when Elric should judge him ready to ride with the war-band.

Then she would look at Frith's little son, Eanfrith, and feel her courage lift. For Bebba's child had survived, for all that his life had so often seemed vulnerable as a candle flame. As Bernicia itself had survived, when all hope seemed lost. And through the child, Alda had conquered her grief for Rolf, cherishing the frail infant with the same tenderness she'd shown when Bebba was a tiny scrap wandering into her house searching for Hrothgar and Frith. In the midst of despair it seemed, some God always left a grain of promise.

Soon after Solmonath Cai arrived, bringing the last of Llywarch's promised war supplies. Cavalry horses, trained and ready, to refill their depleted stables.

He also brought disturbing news.

Rhun's heir Gorthyn, with one hundred mounted warriors, had been in Manau Gododdin to the north of Bernicia for the past six months, an honoured guest in Mynyddog's stronghold of Din Eidyn. Acceptable, for he had old blood ties with the Gododdin kings, and his uncle Bridei still ruled the Picts.

But sometime around last Samhain, the Dal Riada princes had joined them, with a war-band.

Now Owain's youngest brother Elphin, flame-haired and

437

hot-tempered to match, had left Rheged to ride north-east with a band of followers.

Elric looked broodingly at Cai. 'Hel's Gate, what do you do – train crows?'

Cai's tensed muscles relaxed. 'No. Just human spies.' A brief smile lifted the corners of his mouth. 'Over the past few years we've needed to keep a closer watch on the neighbours.'

But it looked ominously like a conference of war. Elric moved swiftly, and with purpose. Fast riders alerted the thanes to danger. Tall beacons stood ready to blaze into life. The fortress burst into a storm of action as they prepared for an attack.

Cai stayed with them, determined to ride with Reburrus's cavalry.

Baldur . . . Rhianneth's heart sank. Her youngest son was not made for war, as was Frith. His body was slight, his mind full of dreams. But since the seige his determination to be one of the Battle-Riders had become so obsessive it was as if dark elvish forces drove him on. He looked so resolute, swerving and rearing his horse at the practice ground. And so vulnerable, that Rhianneth drew her shawl closer across her face and turned away before he saw her.

Her hopes rose as weeks slid by and the year passed into harvest time.

Then, at last, a fire flared its warning into the waiting sky, and the signal came from the south.

A force from Manau Gododdin was indeed coming. But it had moved in a vast sweep down through the west, and only when it had crossed the Wall did it turn eastwards.

This was Adda's territory. His war-bands harried the enemy, edged them slowly further south, delaying their progress until Elric's armies arrived. He then withdrew his tired warriors well to the south, and stood by to cut off any possible escape route.

Near Catraeth, Elric split his force around the enemy like the claws of a crab and closed in for the kill, his war horns rending the air.

The Bernicians were numbered in thousands, vastly outnumbering the Gododdin army. Yet from his southern viewpoint Adda watched anxiously, knowing that in battle the odds were never certain. His ears were filled with the cries of men, the screams of horses, the ring and clash of weapons. He rubbed a grimy hand across red rimmed eyes, trying to make sense of the blurred confusion before him.

There was a sudden hissing through the air as a rain of arrows fell amongst his men. A warning shout went up from behind him: Treachery! Adda's men whirled round, as a mass of Deirans came at them from the undefended rear.

Adda's war-bands went down before them, taken off guard and overwhelmed. The exultant Deirans smashed their way north, until they reached the edge of the main battle-ground.

They stopped. Their war-howls strangled in their throats. Out of the tumult before them only one thing was clear. Elric's victory over the British was total. The entire Gododdin force was annihilated.

Aelle's warriors fled in panic when they saw the size of the triumphant Bernician army bearing down on them out of the carnage, covered in filth and blood. Hot with victory, enraged by the Deiran treachery, they howled like wolves catching the smell of blood. Their gaudy banners hung torn, their shields splintered, some sword-hacked away till nothing remained but the central iron boss, now used as a mailed fist to maul and ravage their way through Eburacum and pour on into the heartland of their perfidious cousins.

Aelle had badly miscalculated. For once, he had allowed his survival-cunning to be clouded by the casting of the runes. By the potent magic of one who burned with a strange inner fire. A fire Aelle perceived as coming from the gods to inspire this part-priest, part-prince, part sorcerer. To this compelling son of Ida's murdered brother Guthlac, Aelle had almost promised his daughter Acha.

Three times the runes were cast. Three times they prophesied his royal house would rule the northlands. But the ambitious, too-vigorous sons of his old rival Ida had made him more uneasy that he'd been for years; Aelle was fatally persuaded to honour his tentative alliance with Manau

Gododdin and attack from the unsuspected south.

And the gods deserted him. His darkest fears became reality. Now his fine timbered Hall blazed around him and he lay dying of a single thrust from the sword of Ida's son, Aethelric.

The breath hissed in his throat as he crawled inch by inch towards his carved stone judgement chair. His hand thrust out, spread-fingered, towards the cold unmoving stone, and slid in blood. A body sprawled in his way, on its flung arm the brand-scar of a lordless man. It was Aesc, his minstrel, loyal to the last.

Aelle's words came bubbling, hoarse and inaudible through the noise, the crack of burning timbers. With a shattering roar the roof collapsed, burying his curse in fire.

Ale and mead flowed amidst laughter and oaths and much loud boasting. Dogs barked a welcome to the returned warriors. Maids made bold shining eyes at the men and shrieked protests at their careless smacking kisses.

Outside a raw wind cut like a knife. Hailstones rattled against the doors. But her men were for the moment safe, and Rhianneth wished the fortress encased in ice nine feet thick to keep them so.

So many dead in the battle at Catraeth and the running fights through Deira, including Hussa's son Hrothgar. Three quarters of Adda's war-band lost in Aelle's attack. And so many wounded . . . including Baldur.

They'd thought him dead, she'd been told, when the Deiran spear had grazed his temple and knocked him senseless. There'd been so much blood.

A shadow stirred from the past. Malice, in Caldis's voice, so long ago, '*Though it flies over half a lifetime, be sure my spear will reach you. . .*'

Ridiculous, Rhianneth told herself sharply. A jealous woman's empty threats. Stupid to think of them now, for Baldur was recovering with only occasional head pains and blurring of the sight which Wermund assured her would fade in time. She stiffened her back, pushed the memories away. Yet depression crept over her.

Serena ran into the hall through the Queen's Bower door, her husband Reburrus following close behind with Frith's little son Eanfrith on his shoulders. They paused by the carved screen to shake melting sleet from their hair. The child laughed and tossed his head like a puppy.

How fast he was growing! Already four summers had passed since the seige. Summers that once had been loud with alarms and noisy preparations for battle, and were now vanished into silence.

Rhianneth's depression deepened and her mouth drooped, as the words of a long-dead Roman poet reached into her mind. 'Ah, how they glide by . . . the years, the swift years . . . '

'Sad, cousin fox-cub? When we're home in triumph?'

Cai pushed a brimming cup into her hand. She looked up quickly, her heart warming at sight of him.

'I was . . . wishing Frith was here. His son hardly sees him.'

'Frith's better at Gefrin for a while,' Cai answered. Then surprise flickered briefly in his eyes. 'You don't know?'

She was instantly alarmed. 'He's hurt?' Her hand jerked and mead spilled, spattering her dress.

'No, not at all!' he assured her, but now he was guarded, wary. He swallowed some of his own drink, casually placing himself between her and those nearby. 'You heard Aelle's son Edwin escaped? Aelle's daughter Acha we picked up only because one of our soldiers recognised the man with her. It was Brand.'

'Brand!' Rhianneth stiffened. So he'd been active at the Deiran court? And Elric . . . Elric would have killed him, she never doubted that. Yet he'd kept it from her. Why? She tried, desperately, to remember if there had been some subtle pain in his eyes when the war-band returned, anything that might have warned her. But then, she had been so bound up with Baldur's injury . . .

Cai watched her. A sharp stab of familiar longing went through him, to comfort her. To pull her into his arms, touch her lips. As if words choked in her throat, she waited in silence for him to go on. His fingers tightened around his cup as his unease grew, but it was too late to stop now.

'Brand cursed us all, by every God in Asgard.' He kept his

441

voice low. 'He boasted to Elric's face how he alone convinced Aelle to attack us. He claimed to be betrothed to the king's daughter Acha, and went half-mad with rage when Frith touched her. All eyes were on Elric, waiting to see what he'd do.' He drew a quick breath, his lips tightening. 'But I saw Frith look at the girl, then back at Brand. I watched him smile. Then his scramasax went into Brand like a hunting knife into a boar's belly.'

Silence. Rhianneth swallowed, moistened her lips. So, it had been Frith. Frith, who had carried the death of Bebba in his heart like a dagger waiting a chance to strike. In the sombre aftermath of the seige he'd sworn many oaths of vengeance, including one against Brand who had let the enemy into the fortress. Now Deiran treachery had killed his closest friend, Bebba's brother Hrothgar. With the agent of that double betrayal before him, he would not hesitate.

She drank, felt the honied liquid run like fire down her throat. Steadied, she looked again at Cai. 'Then Frith has done Elric a great service. Are you telling me he's not now welcome here? Is that his reward?'

'No, by the Light, I'm not!' Cai's face darkened. 'Elric tossed Aelle's daughter into his hands – and the royal jewels she had with her. That was his reward! But Elric was shrewd enough to tell him to keep her at Gefrin. Some of his most loyal lords still have old kin-links with Deira.' His mouth twisted derisively. 'They gladly ripped the place apart for him. But they would not like to see a lady of the old blood-royal treated as a harlot!'

Rhianneth's face went blank with shock. Aelle's daughter? Numbly she grasped at scraps of half-buried knowledge. Hadn't the girl's mother been born further south, amongst the east coast Engles who called themselves the People of the Wolf?

Elric would want no blood feud with them! Not until his hold on Deiran territory had been strengthened by the rough rule of his loyal Bernician overlords.

Cai must be mistaken. The girl had been taken as a hostage against any Deiran rebellions.

'Hostages? We took only booty!' Cai muttered, a haunted

442

look passing like a shadow across his face. Momentarily he fell silent, back amongst men hot with fury over the Deiran betrayal, violence reeking on the air, black as the rolling smoke from Aelle's blazing Hall.

Then he shook his head abruptly, took a swallow of mead and veered abruptly to the safer edges of a dangerous subject. He spoke of Catraeth, though the battle itself was a blurred confusion in his mind.

'The only part I remember clearly, was the beginning. The Gododdin warriors themselves, with their high-raised banners . . . their mailshirts glinting blue in the sunlight. And they were singing! I suddenly thought of . . . Arturius.'

'Artur!' Rhianneth's eyes focussed on him now, with a glint of anger. 'Those men were in league with Aelle! They would have destroyed us if they could!'

'Instead, we slaughtered them. Every last one.'

'Would you have spared them, for their bonny songs?' Elric was suddenly beside them. His voice held a light mockery, but his eyes were like ice. We've heard the tunes before, here in Bebbanburgh!'

For a moment there was silence, between and around them. Cai looked at Rhianneth. Elric was so close she stood almost within the curve of his arm. A small coldness unfolded within Cai like a flower.

'A momentary weakness,' he admitted wryly. 'It must be the mead. I haven't the stomach for it.'

'When you know more of battle – ' Elric slanted back a grin, though his eyes were still hostile – 'You'll find it sweeter than wine.'

In their own house, Rhianneth turned to Elric. 'Is it true that Frith has Aelle's daughter at Gefrin?'

'That's right.'

'Elric, you can't allow it!'

His eyes rested on her troubled face. He seemed genuinely surprised. 'Why in Hel not? Let Frith keep her if that's what he wants.'

'All Frith wants is vengeance!' Somehow Rhianneth muffled the dead names that beat remorselessly through her mind. In this, her only concern must be with the future. 'Acha is a royal lady!'

'So? If she'd been Aelle's son she'd be dead.'

'But Edwin is alive, and wherever he goes he'll stir up trouble for us!' Rhianneth's resolve stiffened.

'At least draw the teeth of his uncle in the south. Get an honourable treaty with him, instead of his enmity – which you'll certainly incur if you treat Edwin's sister, his niece, as if she were a captured slave!'

'Raedwald? He's no threat. He's too busy watching his Saxon neighbours to bother over much about the north.' Elric's gaze sharpened. 'Is this by any chance Cai's idea? Is he worried I might use Mithrasian war gear against the Wolf People – instead of chasing the northern kings?'

Colour flooded her cheeks as she flared into impatient anger. 'Cai said nothing but that Frith had the girl at Gefrin! But I am telling you, Elric – if you don't care that half your Council will think shame, or that Raedwald will bear a dangerous grudge, then consider this! Any bastard son Frith gets from that girl could well turn out as another Brand.'

His face whitened. If she had set out to wound him she could not have succeeded more. He drew in a ragged breath, but before he could speak Rhianneth pressed herself close to him, her fingers curling into the material of his tunic.

'Elric, listen! You have a chance now, to create one great kingdom north of the Humber. If you dishonour their royal blood, you'll never rule the Deiran people in peace. Don't embitter future years to feed Frith's vengeance! Ride to Gefrin tomorrow – tell him he must marry Aelle's daughter!'

That night Elric's loving was fierce and splendid.

'I need you, Rhianneth!' he muttered harshly, 'not only your body and your sweet face, but your strength . . . '

Afterwards Rhianneth lay in his arms, curved against him in the warm firelight, his face buried in her long hair. A faint echo of unease rippled across her mind as she recalled the small incident in the mead-hall. Cai's reluctant admiration

444

for the Gododdin warriors, his remembrance of Artur's cavalry. Then she reminded herself that Cai's life had been spent in the shadow of dead battles, old treacheries. Warfare had been only a rumble from the past, or a future threat. Nothing, not even Rhun's great army surging through Mithrasia so long ago, could have prepared him for the raw brutality of Catraeth.

'I need your strength . . . ' Elric had said. Strength? Strength was to face the enemy time and again as Elric did. To be aware that the lives of his people depended upon him, and yet to keep his mind cool and hard as a sword-blade.

For her, the swift danger of combat was as distant as it had once been for Cai. She was a woman, who knew only the slow endurance of the turning of the years, the inexorable reality of birth and death.

For the moment, thank the Gods, her world had righted itself. The summer's danger had rolled away, a new year stretched ahead. And never before had Elric admitted that she had become a necessary part of his life . . .

She smiled, as her thoughts drifted slowly down towards sleep.

When Cai returned to Mithrasia he was able to take Aunt Julia good news. Baldur's head pains and sight-blurring were now so infrequent that after a winter's rest the boy would doubtless be back to normal. And Serena, Aunt Julia's special god-child, was carrying Reburrus's child . . .

Of Frith's carelessly shrugged assent to an immediate marriage with Acha, Cai said little. He knew that with the first touch of spring Frith would be off with his war-band into the north-west, as he so grimly put it, headhunting. Cai had no wish to arouse in Julia any sense of the unease that inexplicably prickled the back of his neck whenever he thought of Frith.

Within days of the birth of Serena's daughter Rowen, Frith's wife Acha was delivered of a son. Frith's indifference was such that the fact that he had recently slain yet another of the siege kings, Morcant, gave him far sharper cause to rejoice.

'Have you chosen a name?' Rhianneth bent over the cradle, stifling a sigh. She felt sorry for Acha. Heavy-featured, with protruding pale blue eyes and a sulky mouth, how could she compete in Frith's mind with Bebba's elusive, elfin ghost?

'Oswald,' the girl answered, reluctantly. 'For my grandfather.'

Well, thought Rhianneth wryly, that added up. It was customary for male children to be given names from the *sperehand* line of descent. That Frith should allow his son to be named after Acha's grandfather demonstrated unmistakably his complete lack of interest in either wife or son.

She glanced sympathetically at Acha. The girl never spoke unless obliged to do so. At first Rhianneth had assumed her to be in a state of shock. Later she had begun to wonder if Acha was lacking mentally. Only to Serena, in a rare moment of shared confidences with another mother to be, had Acha bitterly revealed her love for Brand, her admiration for his powers of sorcery, his influence over her wily father, Aelle. So, as time passed and Acha kept apart at Gefrin with her fiercely loyal Deiran kinswoman Hilde as constant companion, Rhianneth gradually realised how the violent death of Brand and Acha's own violation at the hands of his killer had created in the girl a hatred of them all, so strong not even the emotional torrents of childbirth could move it.

Gods, what a cruel mess, Rhianneth thought now. How many lives have been ended, or changed, because they were touched by the ripples of Elric's affair with Caldis so many years ago? She gripped the tiny curled fingers of Frith's second son, and prayed he might ride high and safe above the last faint stirrings from the past.

Summer slipped away, and the following winter was harsh, with snows drifting deep. By early spring news came that Urien's old friend Aedan of Dal Riada was on the move, and Owain and his brothers were with him. Worse, Mael Uma, wild brother of the Irish High King, had landed from across the sea to join them. They were marching east, combined in one more effort to wipe out Bernicia.

Immediately pleasant thoughts of the summer to come were thrown aside. There would be no hunting or hawking, no wrestling or swimming; no lazy tossing dice while the women sewed and gossiped in the sun.

Now the weapons were sand-cleaned until they glittered, honed sharp on the whetstone. Iron helmets were new-padded inside, leather straps strengthened. The short lived respite won at Catraeth was over.

Once again Bernicia's war-bands gathered beneath Elric's banners to face a great enemy host. So great was the new danger, messages brought break-neck from Mithrasia assured them that Cai was speeding north with his cavalry to join them.

Elric came to Rhianneth as she stood on the ramparts, muffled in her cloak, staring out at the grey wastes of the sea.

'You'll get cold,' he warned her, and his arms slid around, pulling her backwards to lie against him,. She let her head fall back against his chest and closed her eyes.

'Oh, Elric – I'm so tired! So sick of it all. These endless wars! Gods, I crave so for peace . . . the long summers of my childhood. To simply stand and watch the grain ripen and the apples grow fat. That's all I want. Don't you?'

His lips moved against her hair. 'I was born into endless wars, Rhianneth. I've known nothing else. But when we meet Aedan . . . '

She turned swiftly in his arms, her fingers reaching up to close his lips. 'No, don't! Don't boast, Elric. It makes me afraid. It's Baldur . . . after Catraeth, I can't bear him to go! He won't listen to me. But you . . . you could command him to stay here . . . '

He stilled. Then gently, he held her away from him to look into her stormy eyes and wind-whipped face. 'I can't do that, my *deorling*. Baldur would never forgive me – or you.'

'What do I care, as long as he's safe here with me!' She stared back at him, her fingers curling into fists. 'But you – you've never loved Baldur as you love Frith! Is it because you know he'll never turn berserker for you, Elric? That he's too

447

gentle, too kind? Or is it merely that he was born in a Roman city, in Cai's house - '

Abruptly she stopped, even in her distress appalled by what she might have gone on to say. Elric's face was expressionless, his eyes suddenly blank.

'You're wrong, Rhianneth.'

He dropped her wrists, stepped back so that he was no longer touching her. 'My son Baldur is one of the bravest men I know. And unlike Frith, he has to work at it. I cannot, I will not throw it all back in his face and dishonour him by handing his Battle-Riders over to another leader.'

The slow wash of the sea was the only sound that penetrated Rhianneth's mind when he stopped speaking. Inexorable, indestructible as Fate itself, she thought, as her anger died away to be replaced by a deadly weariness. She turned to walk away, but he stopped her.

'Our Battle-Riders attack in two waves,' he said, and hesitated. 'I've already arranged that Reburrus will lead the first. If Cai reaches us in time he'll lead the second. Baldur will merely death-blow an already shattered enemy force. Does that comfort you?'

Nothing will comfort me, she thought bleakly. Not while the *waelrun* sounds for us. Not while that murderous song is heard in the boom of war-horns, the din of conflict.

'I am – somewhat reassured.' she answered him, with cold dignity. And Elric bent, and kissed the lie on her lips.

With Mael Uma's troops and the war-bands of Urien's sons, Aedan's army swelled into a formidable host which despite its size moved eastwards with frightening rapidity.

Cai brought his Mithrasian cavalry eagle-winged, straight up the old military roads to join the Bernicians south-west of Gefrin.

A day later the enemy came within sight.

At a place where stood a tall pillar of stone known as Degsa's Stone, the Bernicians prepared to stop Aedan's eastern march.

*

448

Three riders were fast approaching Bebbanburgh. People crowded near the gateway, anxious for news.

Rhianneth waited in the mead-hall. Beside her, Wermund the priest leaned upon his thick dragon-carved staff, his face impassive. Since the armies left, he had sensed her foreboding and drawn closer. He offered no words of comfort. Yet in some strange way, through his own fatalistic acceptance of whatever might come, he gave her strength.

A man entered through the open doorway. Momentarily he halted, blinking in the soft flare of the daytime torches. Then he walked towards them, the meshed rings of his battle-shirt clinking.

Fear caught wildly in Rhianneth's throat. 'Oh, Gods!' she choked, incredulously. 'Elric?'

His tunic was dark-stained with sweat and blood, and he reeked of battle filth. It was obvious he'd ridden hard, ahead of his troops. Under its coating of grime his face was white with exhaustion. A muscle throbbed high up on one cheek, and his eyes were red-rimmed from the wind.

'The battle's lost?'

Even as the words left her lips Rhianneth realised that if his armies had indeed been defeated, Elric would not be here now.

'No, by Hel!' His voice was hoarse from bellowing orders. 'We've wiped out Aedan's army. Sent Mael Uma scrambling back to his bloody boats!'

She took a quick step towards him, then hesitated. Beside her, Wermund stood as if turned to stone, his face ashen. Fear turned to dread. Colour drained from her face as she whispered: 'Where's Baldur?'

Her whole body began to tremble like a leaf before the fury of winter. A slow shrieking in her head gradually rose until it drowned out thought and rushed away into black silence, bearing her with it. Elric caught her as she fell, swung her up into his arms with an oath.

Rhianneth dressed carefully for the victory feast. Her dress was of deep scarlet edged with gold, and a jewel-studded girdle encircled her waist. Gold flashed defiance from her arms, ears and throat though she was waxen pale and her eyes burned as if with fever.

Dal Riada was finished. Aedan had lost almost all his army, and a son, Domingart. He would never again dare threaten Bernicia. Yet their own losses were grievous. Mourning gave triumph a bitter edge, and they looked towards Rhianneth their folk-queen to set an example of woman-strength.

She did not fail them. She graced the women's table with dry-eyed dignity. When she carried the *maes haeil* cup to Elric the brave fire of her dress and the rich gleam of her ornaments of precious metal illuminated for them all their own pride and enduring courage.

But the days that followed were the blackest she had known. Grief for Baldur was a raw wound inside her.

No one knew what had gone wrong. Reburrus had led his Battle-Riders in the first charge, Cai had followed. Baldur's riders were merely the back-up, the third wave. While they waited behind their cover of trees, Owain's mounted warriors suddenly swept into view, heading for the gap between Baldur and the main battle.

'Baldur must have thought he heard our horn-signal,' Elric told her. 'He reared his horse and charged, far too soon. His whole troop followed him. Owain's cavalry hit them like a storm-wave, broadside on. They never stood a chance.'

'Why would Baldur do that . . . ?' Her voice choked into silence, as a new and secret horror speared into her.

Elric looked away, unable to bear her ashen-faced grief. 'What can I say, Rhianneth?' He shrugged wearily, his expression winter-bleak. ' "Woden needs warriors ready for the last great battle . . . ?" '

For the Grey Wolf is watching the Halls of the Gods . . .

The ancient saying used always upon the death of a hero. Was that Elric's comfort? Ragnarok? The destruction of the world . . . heralded by bitter cold, by strife and the breaking of kinship bonds. Ragnarok. When fettered monsters break loose and the Great Wolf Fenrir springs to attack both men and Gods . . .

450

She gazed at his bowed head, and for a moment glimpsed the alien barbarian she had first thought him. By all the Gods, she thought, Cai has idealism, courage, hope. But Elric . . . Elric is as one with the northland. Ragnarok is bred in his bones. His courage endures, even as hope vanishes. For he knew the end of all things, and accepted it.

Then he looked up, She saw the burnt-out look in his grey eyes, the hard-held tension around his mouth, and the full extent of his misery swept through her. Wordlessly, she held out her arms. As he came into them, she crushed down the fatal knowledge that had come to her, unasked, out of the empty air.

What purpose would it serve now to suggest that Baldur flung himself across the path of the enemy because he was driven by one of the sudden, sight-blinding head pains that were the legacy of his wound at Catraeth? The shadow of a death-marked rune-spear had flown with that Deiran weapon.

Though her own son Brand was dead, his intended bride violated and forced into marriage with his killer, yet Rhianneth knew that at Degsa's Stone Caldis had found her vengeance at last.

She felt the shudder that ran through him, and tightened her arms protectively. Let Elric believe only that Baldur had died a warrior; there was grief enough in that. Dark unprovable knowledge that could only wound was best left unspoken.

Cai came to make his farewell. He took Rhianneth's cold hand in his and dropped a kin-kiss on her upturned pale cheek. She looked forlorn, her brittle dignity for a moment cast aside, and he had to resist the urge to pull her up into his arms, to comfort her with real kisses.

He too, had loved the child Baldur, had come to admire the boy's dogged determination as he grew to manhood, moulding for war a body and character more suited to scholarship. There was no solace he could offer for such a grief.

'I know what you've lost, Rhianneth,' he said after a

moment, 'and I join you in sorrow.' He hesitated. 'The world's grown dark for you, now. But Light will come back, unconquered. You have so much. Have achieved so much, here in Bernicia. All those quiet hours with the wives and daughters of Elric's warriors and thanes, when you read from Marcus's books or told stories of old Rome? That was the sowing time, and those women scattered the seeds. Could any Bernician still think a Roman city was created by Gods? Or like some southern Saxons, call the Great Dyke on Dumnonia's edge "Woden's Dyke" – because they could not believe it was thrown up by men? No! You've let them touch another world, with knowledge more precious than gold.' A smile touched his mouth. 'And they are not a people easily to let slip a prize within reach.'

Her hand tightened on his. 'Must you leave so soon?'

'I have to get my cavalrymen back to the city,' he replied quietly, 'now that the danger up here is over.'

'Is it ever over?' Her slight shrug held a weary resignation that went to his heart.

'Why, the north's all but tamed!' He thrust a strong note of resolution into his voice. 'Deira's safely swallowed. Gododdin and Dal Riada shattered. Rheged in ruin.' He smiled. 'Who dares threaten us now?'

'Ah, someone will.' She forced a smile in response to his. 'Or whatever will Frith find to do?'

Cai's expression altered. 'Frith needs watching, Rhianneth. Something changed in him when he lost Bebba. His bloody massacres of the enemy are no longer sacrifices to her memory. Any natural thirst for vengeance would have been slaked by the victories of these past years. Instead it has . . . become a driving force powered by blood, that will stop at nothing. Not pity, not honour.'

Rhianneth's hand slipped from his. She straightened her shoulders, her faint smile gone. 'What pity would our enemies have shown the women and babes on Metcaud once they had slaughtered Theo's guards? And don't talk to me of honour – not after Aelle and Brand at Catraeth! Frith kills because he must, and will die bravely when he has to, like . . . any Bernician warrior.'

Cai looked at her white, closed face, at the pinched look around her mouth as she held herself in check, and cursed himself for being an insensitive fool. At such a time, when Baldur's death at the hands of Owain filled her mind, how could he have thought to reach her with vague warnings of Frith's savagery?

'Forgive me, cousin fox-cub.' Suddenly he crouched down in front of her, gripped her hands with his own. 'Gods, don't we all ride on the back of some obsession or other? Frith is no different. He'll be all right.'

Her lip trembled. He reached out, placed a finger against its vulnerable softness. 'One smile, before I go?'

'I wish I could go home with you.' Her voice was weary, faint. 'Be with Julia . . . '

'Not just now. You're better here. We have our own troubles, and you don't need any more.'

He released her hand, stood up. 'Before I left home, our spies were already reporting that Aelle's son Edwin is being sheltered by Rhun's new heir Cadfan, whose father we killed at Catraeth. Their fathers' deaths at our hands give them common cause for vengeance, and I dare say Edwin will seize every chance to stir against us not only Gwynned but the other western kingdoms. He lives to regain Deira, avenge his father and sister.'

'Will they listen to him?'

Cai shrugged. 'Who knows? Some of those kingdoms fought alongside Arturius as we did. But . . . ' he hesitated – 'Llywarch's becoming remote from reality, living in the palace like a Christian hermit. We of the Fellowship rule the city – and we are Bernicia's allies. Dumnonia's cut off. With Cadfan and Edwin urging them to unite against us, with Llywarch acting like a Holy Man and Frith like Attila the Hun, what do you think they'll do?' He drew a deep breath, let it out slowly. 'Our alliance with Bernicia may have successfully broken Artur's old enemies in the north. But I sometimes fear that in the end, there will be nothing of Caer Melot, or Rome, left in Britain.'

There was a brief silence.

'I have Frith and Bebba's son here, in my care,' Rhianneth

453

said, 'and Ida's granddaughter Serena is married to your son – whose grandfather died with Artur at Camlann. You spoke of a sowing time? Rome's seeds have already rooted here, and through kinship bonds they'll spread amongst all the north Humbrian peoples . . . '

'That,' Cai answered sombrely, 'would be some flowering! But I doubt I'll live to see it . . . '

CHAPTER 17

That winter the air grew so cold the sea froze along the shore and the earth was like iron. Then snow came, each fall freezing as it lay, until the drifts were mountains of ice.

Around Solmonath, gales lashed out of the north-east, needled with ice that cut hands and faces, and fierce enough to tear away the heavy timbers that topped the old stone ramparts.

Weakened by age and the black grip of frost, the great ash tree fell before the fury of the storm. Immediately, despite Wermund's calm assurances, superstitious fear swept the fortress.

'It was so old.' Rhianneth remarked impatiently to the priest as they walked together into the afternoon warmth of the hall, 'do they imagine it should live forever?'

Wermund indicated a bench comfortably set near the blazing heat of the fire, and they sat down. He took pleasure in the company of Rhianneth, though it never failed to surprise him that he should do so. True, she had never interfered with his healing work, nor had she despised the Gods. On Metcaud he had admired her control when faced with deep grief and fear. But it was with the loss of Baldur at Degsa's Stone that she had, for him, proved herself the undoubted queen of a warrior people.

She had accepted his tentative overtures of friendship even after all the years of distrust, years when he had hated her foreignness, feared her powers. The mutual suspicions of the past were laid aside, without recriminations, and a careful respect gradually warmed into cordial understanding.

'It's not the tree itself, but what it represents.' He straightened his leg towards the fire's warmth, for today his old injury ached with cold and nothing would ease it. 'A shaking of the giant ash Yggdrasil, the Tree of Life. People think of Ragnarok.'

'Ragnarok? An old tree blown down in a storm hardly heralds the end of the world!'

There was scorn in Rhianneth's voice. She was glad to see

the tree go, together with the sinister little offerings on its branches that made her shiver, remembering the night of Ida's funeral.

'We are all tired,' Wermund reminded her quietly. 'Victory demands its toll. Our losses have been great. I felt that in Brand, I lost a son. Only for me,' he hesitated, 'it was in shame. In dishonour,' He fell silent. Then, with an effort, he went on. 'Besides, we've had two unusually bad winters. That always makes people uneasy. Still,' he gave a ghost of a smile, 'Come springtime, we'll be happy to use the wood of the old ash for spear shafts. Its strength comes straight from the gods, after all.'

'And from the many sacrifices made over the years?' Rhianneth slanted a glance at him, her eyes glittering in the firelight. There was a brief silence.

'Lady, that was long ago. At that time, I truly believed you had poisoned Ida.' Wermund's gaunt face was pale. 'And I . . . greatly feared your powers . . . ' His voice cracked, died. After a moment he added beneath his breath, 'I am not a good judge of character.'

Brand's desertion had struck Wermund to the heart, Rhianneth thought. He seemed more than ever old, uncertain. She placed her hand on his arm. It felt stick-thin beneath the warm material of his tunic sleeve.

'Wermund, everything you have ever done has been for the safety of Bernicia. That was plain to me, even then. I never doubted your loyalty to Ida, or to Elric. I value the understanding that is now between us, and I'm honoured that you've given me your trust.'

He made no reply, but kept his gaze on the leaping fire-flames. With Dismay, she realised his eyes were full of tears. Swiftly she loosed his arm, lightened her tone. 'Besides, that power you once feared has long since deserted me! Lost in the bustle of life, the turmoil of these past years.'

Now he dragged his eyes from the fire's glow and surveyed her. The deep-etched lines on his lean craggy face gave him a look older than time, remote, haunted.

'I recognise – and respect – true power,' he said. 'Though I myself have never possessed it.'

Disbelief flashed across her face. He shook his head, lifted his hand in a dismissive gesture. 'I read the runes, perform magical tricks. Yet that – other has never been mine. Brand had it, used it. And you are a child of the serpent, Rhianneth. The power can never leave you. Don't mistake sleep for death. When you are in need it will stir again, for you.'

Rhianneth's hand stole upwards to lie against Glainnader's hardness hidden between her breasts. The Serpent's Egg, whose pictures baffled and terrified her. Child of the Serpent? A disappointing, ungrateful child she had proved, then! Not since her disastrous decision to trust Idwal had she looked into the stone. And had she not been right? So many times of anguish and danger, so many deaths since then . . . she would have lived her griefs twice over, and surely died of them.

Her wild moments of insight were enough, unsteady, unreliable as they were. Even they had waned over the years to little more that a strange feeling of foreboding, or a flash of knowledge. Never again had a great surge of power found and held her, as it had once long ago in Deva's Holy House.

'It will stir for you, lady,' Wermund repeated more strongly, seeing the doubt on her face, 'when you need to call upon it.'

Summer came late, with a fanfare of floods as the snows melted.

There was a brief flare of excitement, when Acha produced another son for Frith, whom they called Oswy.

Then the few weeks of warm weather slid towards a cool wet autumn. Much earlier than usual, wild geese started flocking down from the north with their strange harsh cries, and people gloomily muttered that another bad winter would follow the tail of their flight.

Often Rhianneth lay awake, her thoughts turning to the child so recently born at Gefrin of that cold and loveless union. Acha hated and feared Frith, and he despised her. In their coupling there could have been not even the flare of passion of a wolf for its mate, only the black fire of bitterness in their hearts.

The clear thin calls of redwings pierced the night air as they came in over the sea from the far north. Rhianneth shivered. Ah, Bebba, she cried silently, how different it might have been! At least I have your little Eanfrith safe here in the fortress, away from Gefrin's dark shadows.

Not for anything would she let the child, now seven years old, near Acha. And it was a measure of Frith's dislike and distrust of his wife that he had never once questioned the need for his first-born, his heir, to be brought up at Bebbanburgh.

One morning at first light, while the early rising herring gulls swooped and screeched above the fortress, a hunting party set out seeking the boar. They would not be back until late afternoon. Rhianneth watched them out of sight, half wishing she had decided to follow. But the boar was fast and dangerous. The men would resent the impediment her safety imposed on them, however far back she stayed.

Around mid-morning, bored, restless, she opened her box and let Eanfrith choose a book. Then she took his hand and went to the Queen's Bower.

'I love autumn,' declared Serena, watching her little daughter Rowen's plump fingers delicately picking through an old box piled with bright-coloured threads, 'when all is drawn in snug, ready for winter.'

And Reburrus is safely home from the summer campaign, thought Rhianneth in silent sympathy.

'It's woman's time,' ventured Rowen's nurse Gwynne, who having cared for Serena as a child now claimed the privilege of open speech within the family. 'Now the Lady comes near the earth to light home our harvests and spellbinds the men with her beauty.' A secret smile touched her mouth. 'That's how we get our crop of spring newborns.'

There was a pause. 'Mama . . . ' Serena asked hesitantly, 'perhaps we should ask Acha and the children here to stay for a little while?'

'You imagine she'd come? She really does hate us all.'

Serena shrugged. 'I know. But sometimes I think . . . Gefrin must be lonely. If only for the sake of her two babes, she just might . . . '

'Look!' Eanfrith scrambled to his feet and pulled the door wide. 'Look! Wermund the priest! He's running!'

Silence followed his extraordinary statement. Wermund was lame, and growing old. His slow measured walk was part of his awesome dignity. He never ran, anywhere.

'An accident?' Serena stood up, suddenly pale. 'Oh, Gods!' The hunting party?'

Filled with dismay, her grey eyes met Rhianneth's. With a thudding of feet, one of the stable boys panted up to the door, his face a study of panic.

'L—lady,' he stuttered, 'will you come? It's . . . '

But Rhianneth was already past him. As she ran towards the gates, the scene before her made her throat freeze with fear. Men clustered together, arguing, gesticulating, while with a clatter of hooves the horses were led to the stables. She recognised Elric's great stallion, saw the saddle blanket dark-stained with blood. People moved aside for her, their faces afraid, uncertain.

Elric lay on the ground, his head cushioned by a thick war-cloak and his eyes closed. Wermund, bending over him stony-faced, looked up as Rhianneth knelt beside him, her eyes horrified.

'It's bad, lady,' he stated baldly, breath still rasping from his haste. 'He's lost a lot of blood. But he'll not die of it. Not if I can help it.'

Elric's eyes opened. 'Like Hel I'll die of it! Not of a bloody boar's tusk!' he muttered fiercely, faintly, and slid back into unconsciousness.

Between them, Rhianneth and Wermund nursed Elric through a time of great danger, for the wound became poison-ously inflamed and swollen. Rhianneth remembered the injury that had almost killed Lovan when first they had come to Bernicia, and found herself whispering prayers to all the Gods of heaven while she wiped the sweat from Elric's face as Wermund changed bloodied bandages on the seeping yellow-mattered gaping leg wound.

Elric tossed in recurring fevers, holding her hand so tightly it hurt, as if he grasped the hilt of his war-sword to sweat and curse his way through battles long dead. Each bout of fever left him white and exhausted, scarcely able to lift his head to drink from the cup she held to his lips.

Fear for those close to her was no stranger to Rhianneth. But Elric had always been so strong , never ill. His pain and weakness terrified her as nothing else had ever done. She felt her world trembling. If he died, it would crack apart.

Although overshadowed by the anxieties for their king, the life of the fortress carried on. After such a wet summer the autumn grain arrived late. Cai rode in with the escort, and he brought more sombre news. This time, it appeared his mother really was dying.

To Rhianneth, Julia's fragility had seemed to possess the tensile strength of a spider's thread. She did not want to believe it might at last be about to break.

'Her heart is failing. The slightest effort makes her gasp for breath,' Cai told her. 'She's not left her bed since midsummer.' He shook his head. 'She won't last through winter.'

He hesitated, meeting her gaze. 'Rhianneth, I came to ask you to come back with me. I know Julia would want to see you.'

She stared at him in agonised dismay. 'I can't leave Elric! Cai, you don't know how ill he still is! How could I go, now?'

There was a brief silence. 'No, of course not,' Cai said then.

'Perhaps Reburrus . . . ?' she began, and stopped. For Reburrus was deeply involved at Gefrin, planning war strategems. While Elric lay wounded, men looked to Frith to ensure the safety of the kingdom. Already there had been a flare-up of alarm and suspicion, carefully kept from Elric. A messenger had been discovered bearing greetings from Edwin to his sister Acha. People asked each other how many other innocent-seeming messages, how much information, might Acha have already sent to Edwin plotting in exile? Even the news of Elric's weakness through injury would give comfort to the enemy.

Reburrus would not leave Frith at such a time. Rhianneth

was also uncomfortably aware that because Frith's ruthlessness made Cai increasingly uneasy, he disliked the comradeship that had strengthened between his son and Frith in the years since Hrothgar died at Catraeth.

'Mama, I'd like to go, and take Rowen,' Serena's clear voice broke into the awkward silence that had surrounded Rhianneth's thoughts, 'Eanfrith too, if I can. Aunt Julia will remember me, won't she?'

Cai turned to her. 'Indeed she will.' He smiled suddenly, that quick sweet smile that still made Rhianneth's heart twist. 'And Rowen will bring her much joy. But . . . Eanfrith? Will Frith agree to his son going to Mithrasia?'

Of course he would not. But suddenly Rhianneth made up her mind. 'I wish my grandson to see what his Roman ancestors once built.' Determination hardened her voice. 'Frith is occupied at Gefrin, and won't know until it's too late. You may safely leave Frith to me.'

Then, just for an instant, she hesitated. 'But don't tell your father,' she warned Serena. 'I think he might be angry.'

Serena considered. 'I think you're right,' she answered laconically, in a manner so like Elric's that momentarily Rhianneth suspected mockery. But a sharp glance at her daughter's calm face and clear grey eyes convinced her otherwise.

'I don't want to cause any ill-feeling – ' Cai's glance went from one to the other – 'and neither would Julia. If you think that Elric – '

'I'll choose when to tell Elric,' Rhianneth interrupted him, 'and I'll bear the weight of any displeasure. For the moment I'd . . . prefer him not to be upset, that's all.'

Cai's dark eyes looked straight into hers. An unwilling smile touched the corner of his mouth. 'By the Light, Rhianneth,' he said slowly, 'I believe you enjoy having Elric under your rule.

A month after Samhain, winter came down from the north like a great white wolf, savaging the land.

Besieged, the fortress crouched on its basalt rock while

around it stretched a wasteland, strange, featureless, that vanished at last into an eerie ice-mist which had swallowed the rest of the world.

Now, Rhianneth summoned up courage enough to tell Elric that Eanfrith had gone to Mithrasia with Serena and her baby. 'I envy them,' she kept her voice light, 'in the city, winter never seems to bite as hard!'

For a long moment he looked at her, saying nothing. Determination pinned a faint smile on her lips, though the expression in his eyes made her quail inwardly.

'You should be at Gefrin with Frith and Reburrus, planning our war strategy,' he said tiredly, at last.

Her smile faded. 'What are you talking about?' she queried, her brows slanting upwards.

'You send Eanfrith into the city while I'm too sick to know anything about it. You inform me only when the weather makes it impossible to have him brought back. I'd say that makes you a fair mistress of the snatched opportunity, the well-timed assault?'

'I didn't want to upset you, that's why I . . . '

'Oh, really? You've never shown such concern for my feelings before. No, don't!' His hand clenched into a fist, as she began to protest. 'Don't bother, Rhianneth. I do know when a battle's lost. And since there's nothing I can do, I've no intention of spending the winter trading either lies or insults with the victor.'

He turned his head on the pillow, away from her, his eyes closing wearily. 'I've a notion we're going to need all our strength, just to get through the next months.'

Rhianneth took a deep breath and left, making no further attempt to justify her actions. He was so unrelentingly bloody Saxon, with all that implied, she thought angrily. His people had always lived close to the earth and the sea, their Gods rode the wind and were beside them in battle, and were not worshipped in temples of stone. Elric had no use for the old cities built by Rome, or for the ethos of the Empire. He saw only the plain reality of Mithrasia. He would never understand all that lay behind its crumbling magnificence. Never

462

understand why she wanted Eanfrith to see the city with a child's eye, as an enchanted place, as Frith never had. To see only the grandeur that was, not its present squalor. She wanted to plant a dream in Eanfrith's mind, a dream to grow as he grew. A dream of what had once been and could be, again.

By midwinter it was so cold that birds fell from the skies, frozen in flight. Snow lay thick everywhere, with drifts over twice as deep as a tall man. The land lay bleak and dead, dark-misted in the short hours of daylight and eerie in the strange twilight of the bitter nights.

Meat and bread froze iron-hard. Frost glittered in the mead-hall, menacing even the strength of the great fire.

Though their own fire blazed night and day, cold crept through the walls of the king's house and opened Elric's new-closed wound with icy claws. Towards Solmonath sickness broke out in the fortress, and time became a desperate matter of counting each passing day as one more frozen step towards survival.

Wolf packs hunted close. Their hungry howling echoed across the empty snows and with the sound came renewed fear, more whispers of Fimbulwinter, that great cold that would herald the coming of Ragnarok. Even the oldest people could not recall such another winter as this.

Not until after Eostre's time did the air begin to soften at last. Gradually the snows sank, the icicles dripped away into nothing, and the white wolf of winter slunk northwards. Around the fortress the first signs of returning life thrust greenly into the thin sunlight, and in the mead-hall Elric sat once more in the king's seat as his strength and vitality steadily grew. But as Rhianneth gazed down the length of the hall, at the weary eyes and gaunt faces, the gaps where those who had died once sat, she knew that such a time as they had passed through would never be forgotten, not even if the hawthorn grew thick with blossom and the birds sang sweeter than ever.

The first messenger to get through from Mithrasia brought a letter from Cai.

It appeared that Llywarch had retreated with his priest to

the Holy House at Deva, there to study and contemplate in peace for an indefinite time. The city was left in the guardianship of the Fellowship, under Cai. Edwin of Deira still sheltered in Gwynedd, where many of his dispossessed kinsmen, including his powerful cousin Heric, had joined him. Rumours were that they were inciting the kings of the west to unite once more against the Bernicians and their allies in Mithrasia, but the memory of the defeat at Degsa's Stone was as yet too strong.

Aunt Julia died at midwinter. The stark wording of the brief sentence struck Rhianneth like a blow. It was several moments before she could read on, and when she did her imagination and already jagged nerves wove into the plain letter a hidden cry for help.

Eanfrith and Rowen were well. But Serena was pregnant, and could not travel home. The child would be born around midsummer. Was Rhianneth now able to come to Mithrasia?

It was as if time was repeating itself. Rhianneth's mind flew back to the summer of Baldur's birth, to those strange lost weeks filled with pain and longing . . .

'Serena's so far from home,' she told Elric, with a flutter of alarm, 'I must go to her. You will be all right for a few weeks?'

'Of course.' His smile was weary, sardonic. 'I'm almost back to my usual rough good health. You needn't concern yourself about me. Take care of Serena. I'll expect you all with the autumn grain.'

Exhausted by the emotional strain of Julia's illness and death and by the physical burden of the unborn child she herself was carrying, Serena was pathetically glad to see Rhianneth.

The two children, Eanfrith and Rowen, threw themselves on her with shrieks of delight. As Rhianneth disentangled herself, Torfrida silently held out her arms and she went into them. Julia's old maid seemed to have shrunk, and her golden hair was now entirely grey; only her affectionate warmth towards Rhianneth was undiminished by the passing of the years.

'My poor lady,' she said sadly, later, when Rhianneth stood

in her aunt's bedroom. 'She grew weaker and weaker. Until at last she just faded away. And so quietly. Never a word, after all the years of upsets and tears when she used to work herself into such a state. Sometimes still I imagine I hear her call, and start towards the stairs before I remember; it's so hard to believe she's really gone. I've been glad to have Serena and the little ones about me! What I'd have done without them to keep me busy, I don't know . . . '

Rhianneth moved around the room, unfamiliar in its orderliness. No half-completed sewing lay beside the couch. The table which once had been littered with bottles, jars, combs and ribbons, lay bare and shining.

Torfrida's eyes filled with tears. 'Cai has rented out the house. As soon as the baby is born we shall move into an apartment in the palace. Although what I shall find to do there, I can't imagine!'

Rhianneth stopped short, staring at her in dismay. Julia's beautiful little house – rented to strangers? And yet . . . with Julia gone, with Reburrus and Serena in Bernicia, the house would be empty most of the time, for Cai needed to be immediately available at the centre of affairs, and that meant inside the fortress. So, why should he not rent out the house until he chose to live here again?

But an old familiar sense of panic stirred, such as she'd felt long ago after Marcus died; when they'd left the old house; when Lovan rowed away forever into the sea-mist. As if all the world she knew was inching away from her into darkness.

On a warm day, when Julia's roses were all in bloom and the scent of them hung heavy on the still air, Serena's second daughter was safely born.

'We'll call her Lucina,' Serena announced, as the babe was laid in her arms. Gently, she touched the small crumpled face. 'A Roman name, since she was born in a Roman city. Reburrus will like that. Aunt Julia would have approved – don't you think, Mama?'

'Very suitable,' Rhianneth said gravely. Then she smiled. 'Besides, it has a pretty sound. Julia would certainly have liked that!'.

A month later, they moved into Llywarch's palace. After the elegant simplicity of Julia's home, this part of the fortress seemed a maze of narrow passages, stairs, and countless rooms opening one into the other. Rhianneth helped Torfrida supervise the placing of furniture and precious ornaments. Made sure Serena and the new baby were comfortable. Played with little Rowen.

She was always careful to make time to be with Eanfrith. He was such a dreamy, trusting quiet child, she sometimes found it hard to believe he was born of Frith and Bebba. More and more he reminded her of Baldur. She would watch him gently trace the outline of a word with fingers delicate as a little maid's, her love for him blended with pain. Like Baldur, his joy was to handle books, to run his hand over the covers, feel the texture of the pages.

'That book was given to me by my brother Llywarch, Mithrasia's king,' she told him one day, as he picked up the city annals copied by the Keeper's company of holy men. 'It records a battle won by a great hero.'

Eanfrith looked up, eyes alight with interest. 'Truly a hero? Like Wayland or Sigurd – or Beowulf?'

'To my people, yes.'

At his urging Rhianneth told him of Artur and his battles, of the flowering of Caer Melot and its withering in the black frost of betrayal. Then she translated for him the entry for the year of Badon, the time of high glory. But she was quick to explain that the battle was fought long ago, against a Saxon people far to the south, who were then a savage and terrible enemy. And she was careful to correct, without comment, the error that had once seemed so amusing.

'But there are no dragons!' Eanfrith protested, disappointed. 'And no magic-working at all!'

She drew him close, laying the book aside. 'You don't need magic, to be a hero,' she said. 'And when you're grown, you'll find dragons real enough living in the hearts of men . . . '

When a messenger came from Elric, it was as if a breath of sea-cooled air touched her skin. The world steadied itself.

Home, she thought, with something like relief. Home, with the grain!

But Elric's message was impersonal and disturbing. She must stay in the city. The armies of Bernicia had hosted and were about to move, making the countryside unstable, dangerous.

Edwin and the Deiran nobles plotting in Gwynedd had thrown out such poisoned threads that already Deira was festering like an untended sore. The spiders' nest must be destroyed before its venom infected other potential enemies, such as Raedwald of the Wolf People. While Frith and Hussa, with Reburrus and his Battle-Riders, led the great army towards Deva and the west, Adda and Theo would hold Deira. Elric himself stood ready for a possible attack against the Bernician heartland by Owain, like that once made by his father Urien.

'But Elric can't fight!' Rhianneth cried. 'His wound's not really healed. At the first blow, the first twist, it will break open again!'

'That, I think, is what he's trying to avoid putting into words.' Cai's face was taut, pale. 'The message is clear. You must stay in the city till the fighting's over. Elric is guarding Bernicia itself.' He took a deep breath. 'So it's Frith, Gods help us, who is leading the Bernician host to war.'

At once she caught at his words, her eyes flashing. 'What do you mean? Elric's trusted Frith to command our armies because he's a fine battle-leader . . . '

'Battle-leader? Your little prince of peace has become a symbol of terror! God's Light, Rhianneth, see him as he is! Ruthless, cruel, unstoppable. The Twister, the scourge of the land!'

'Stop it!' she clapped her hands over her ears. 'I don't want to hear – '

But he moved swiftly, pulled away her hands and gripped them within his own. 'This time Frith's not smashing the northern kings. He's coming south, to get at Edwin in Gwynedd! South, through the lands of our own people. Gods help them if they don't give him free passage!' His face

467

tightened. 'I've seen what he did at Catraeth. In Deira. After Degsa's Stone!'

What she read in his eyes, chilled her. 'Edwin must be stopped before he grows stronger!' she insisted, willing strength into her voice. 'Cadfan may seem docile – but remember, his grandsire Rhun once marched over Mithrasia. And his father Gorthyn joined with the Gododdin force to attack us. Now Cadfan befriends Edwin, our sworn enemy. Edwin, son of that treacherous old serpent Aelle! Do you want Elric to wait? While Edwin spreads his poison unhindered? Until he gathers enough support to attack – maybe by first striking here, at Mithrasia?'

Slowly Cai's grip loosened, his hands fell to his sides. Broodingly, he half turned from her. 'I know . . . A Demon's Fork.' He groaned harshly, 'May the Gods help us all!'

Briefly, there was silence. Then he swung back to face her, his eyes glittering. 'Stay and eat with me, cousin fox-cub!' he said. 'Let's drown our doubtings in good Gaulish wine!'

Cai's private rooms were warm and luxurious, as befitted the virtual ruler of Mithrasia. At his insistence they ate in the style of old Rome, reclining on couches in the soft light of lamps. It was like moving back in time, entering a world they had never known. As the wine warmed her blood, Rhianneth was caught up in Cai's mood of reckless gaiety. For a while the outside world retreated from her thoughts, and she could imagine that this was real. That she had indeed found that other place where in dreams she had often walked, and loved, with Cai.

Servants replenished the wine jug and left. Cai lifted his cup in salute. 'To us, Rhianneth!' His dark eyes met hers over the rim. 'And to all that once was, and may not come again!'

Rhianneth sipped the sweet dark wine, ignoring the mockery in his voice just as she shut out the deepening bitter lines about his mouth, the growing hardness in his eyes. They threatened the eggshell fragility of a dream where all the world was young and life was a golden toy to be tossed between them.

The lamplight gleamed, caught for an instant the tiny scar-sign of Mithras on Cai's brow. How well do I really know him? she thought. He has always been to me the last gallant echo of Caer Melot, the vanishing spirit of the Empire. But he is also a dark soldier of the Morning Star, his courage tested by fire and ice, pledged to die in defence of the Light. She shivered, quickly blotting out her thoughts.

'To the unconquered!' she said, and drained her cup. The potent liquid coursed down her throat, warming her blood, numbing her senses.

When Cai began to make love to her, she made no protest. It was all part of the dream. All happening in that other place, outside time. The couch was smooth, silken, and his kisses were sweeter than the wine, draining her strength.

Then came a rapping at the door. Again, more urgently. With an oath, Cai got to his feet. He opened the door, placing his body in the gap to shield the room behind him from view. There was a murmur of voices. With another curse he went through into the room beyond, slamming the door behind him.

When at last he returned, Rhianneth was sitting beside the window. He stood still, looking at her.

'It will never be the right time, the right place, for us, will it? Even an illusion sweet as this – ' his brief smile was bitter as he gestured towards the heart of the lamplit room – 'can be soured by the sound of a fist on wood. That was my messenger from Deva. Cadfan of Gwynedd's call to arms has gone out to all the kings of the west. Already their warriors are flocking to his banners, panting to meet Frith's Saxon host . . . '

CHAPTER 18

While Frith moved steadily south-westwards along the old military roads, in the west a great army gathered and began to stream out of Gwynedd and Powys towards Deva. In haste the Fellowship sent an armed escort to bring Llywarch back from the Holy House to the safety of the city. But the king refused to stir. The days crept by, with mists thickening each night and morning and a gentle sun turning the mid-day air to gold. His impatience with the obstinacy of the king tinged with contempt, Cai turned his whole attention towards the defence of Llywarch's city.

Mithrasia crouched in the autumn warmth like a warrior empress crumbling with age, while her secret messengers darted along the old half-hidden trackways bringing news. Outside the city the winter corn had been sown, and the people could only wait and trust the gods would keep the converging armies from trampling the precious grain hidden in the dark earth.

The wind changed, became thin and sharp. Rhianneth too, felt an inner chill as the year began to close. Soon it would be Samhain. Foreboding fell upon her like a suffocating cloak.

When late one morning Cai at last came to her, she was prepared to receive with dignity and calmness news of Frith's defeat, even of his death. Cai was pale-faced, ice-cold, as he closed the door of her room and turned to face her.

'Victory?' she echoed, in an incredulous whisper. Her heart began a slow pounding. 'We've won?'

He nodded, unsmiling.

'And Frith? Reburrus?'

'Frith's unscathed.' He paused, took a deep breath. 'There's no news of Reburrus. His horse went down in the last charge. I . . . there's still hope. My messengers report chaos for miles around the battlefield. Will you tell Serena? I'm riding to Deva. They say the city's wide open.'

He unpinned his cloak, flung it over a stool. For the first time she noticed he was dressed for travel. 'Gods, my throat's like a sand-pit! Have you got some wine?'

Wordlessly, she crossed the room to the heavy table against the wall. Her hand shook as she poured two cups. By the time she turned and walked back to him she had herself under control.

'Please . . . ' With effort she kept her voice steady, though anxiety for Reburrus, and the sharp remembered agony of Baldur's loss leapt with rekindled flames. 'Please, Cai, don't go! You say there's chaos. What can you hope to achieve? To – find?' She swallowed. 'You know Frith will do everything in his power . . . if Reburrus is wounded, he'll get him home.'

Cai shut his eyes, drank deeply of the wine. Then he looked straight at her. 'It was never my intention to search amongst the battle-dead for Reburrus. I'm going to Deva. To find out whether we still have a king. Then, I shall ride on. To find Frith.'

Llywarch! At once conscience smote her, that she had so easily dismissed her half-brother from her mind. 'But surely Llywarch is safe, within the Holy House?'

'Safe?' he repeated, 'Great Gods, don't you understand – Deva's in flames.'

Cai had just told her of a great victory, the massed armies of the western kings beaten into ignominious flight before the Englisch . . . His apprehension and deep concern for Reburrus, his disquiet over Llywarch, were plain and natural. What puzzled her was the note of anger running beneath his words.

She swallowed. 'Then how can you hope to find the king?'

'If I don't find him in Deva we must assume him dead, the line of Maximus ended.'

'Not quite,' she returned wryly, but he did not hear her, and she went on, 'Llywarch could have fled the city after the battle.'

'He could have done . . . anything.' Cai drew an unsteady breath. 'He's withdrawn so far from reality he scarcely knows summer from winter. He refused to leave Deva when I sent an escort for him. Obviously the influence of the monks there proved stronger than his duty to his people. If it was strong enough it probably killed him.' Cai's mouth twisted, his eyes were dark pools of ice. 'You haven't heard, of course. It seems

471

that before the battle a great number of Christian holy men – my messenger thought well over a thousand – followed a call by a revered old priest called Brocmail. They walked for miles from their scattered monasteries, to join with those from the large house in Deva and welcome with open arms warriors of the western kings, coming to save them from the pagan Englisch.'

She stared at him uncertainly, in silence, while a strange small fear uncurled within her, like a maggot within the flower of her pride and relief at their victory.

'Maybe Llywarch and his priest were amongst them,' Cai went on. 'Who knows? As the opposing armies drew closer, the holy men gathered in what was thought a safe place over-looking the battlefield, and there began ringing bells and chanting their prayers for a British victory.'

He hesitated, for Rhianneth's face had whitened. But there was no way to soften the telling.

'Frith demanded to know what it meant. When told, he shouted in anger: "If these men invoke their god against us, they fight against us, even if they bear no arms!" ' Cai tossed down the rest of his wine, and then stared down into the empty cup, avoiding her eyes. 'He turned his swords on them before the battle began. Just – slaughtered them. It's believed maybe fifty escaped, if that.'

In the silence that followed, Rhianneth's heart-beat was louder in her ears than the muted noise of the palace that came from beyond her doors.

The room around her stilled as if time froze, and she herself turned to ice within it. She remembered the Holy House at Deva and the horror that had rung down the years and found her there, so long ago. How she had crouched, clutching the Druid's Stone while the dark wind howled about her, heralding the power of Elric's gods with sounds of terror then unborn. Battle-clamour filled her ears, and night rushed into her mind. She grasped the edge of a small table with one hand so she might feel reality, solid beneath her fingers. With an effort of will almost beyond her, she raised her cup and drained it. The wine ran like fire down her throat, breaking the ice-spell.

'How could our men go into battle – ' her voice was a hoarse whisper – 'with the spell-weaving of those holy men in their ears? What else could Frith do, but silence them?'

Cai looked at her then. 'God's Light,' her said slowly, 'have I lost you, Rhianneth? Are you truly running with the wolves . . . ? I've no love for Christian priests. But old men? Young boys? Not one of them armed! Doesn't it turn your stomach?'

Not as much as if they had turned the battle-tide against us, she realised with a bleak honesty, and her lashes swept down to hide her thoughts from Cai. Being unarmed, the holy men had thought themselves safe from attack; that Frith would ignore their taunting. But their ill-wishing was a potent force, and their lack of weapons he would see only as an act of contempt towards him.

I can't believe Llywarch was amongst them, she thought, still less the Keeper. However far they have withdrawn from the world, surely they would never pray for an enemy victory? Bernicia was their ally, who had kept Urien from their gates!

'Some of those kings of the west once fought beside Artur,' Cai said after a small silence. 'I won't let Frith plunder their lands, Rhianneth, as I saw him plunder Deira. Because he won't stop with Gwynedd. He'll drive on . . . until he's no longer killing our enemies, but destroying villas, farms, slaughtering those who once supported Caer Melot!'

'And have now joined with Gwynedd,' Rhianneth retorted, with sudden impatience. 'Nothing lasts forever, Cai. Maybe for them Caer Melot truly died at Camlann. Maybe in truth we're seeing the end of a world and the beginning of another.'

Cai went white. Instantly she regretted the words. But it was too late. She placed her empty cup on the small table, unable to bear the expression on his face. She had swallowed too much wine, too quickly. It sang in her veins, wild and fierce and careless.

'When Baldur died, you consoled me, Cai.' Rhianneth cast about in her mind for something, anything, to lift away his look of angry despair. 'You spoke of seeds. Roman seeds, planted in the hearts of the Saxon people. I came to realise then, in what way I could fulfil my vow to the Fellowship. The

473

Empire may never come again to Britain. But Artur's code of honour – and the spirit of Caer Melot – will always find welcome amongst the north-Humbrian peoples. Real victory for us lies in those seeds. In them, Rome will endure when Mithrasia is only a shadow in the grass like Marcus's cities of the past. Gods grant our children see them spring up green!'

'The Alliance has worked well for us all, do you imagine I don't know that?' Cai said heavily. 'Gods, we've survived on it for over twenty years! But it's changed. Frith has changed it. And now with Elric out of action, can't you see . . . '

'No!' she felt herself trembling. 'Can't you see, Cai? It's not our Alliance but our world that has changed. Caer Melot's gone, and Rome's Britannia is dissolving about our ears. We're left with the world that Artur's enemies have made – Owain's world, Pascan's world! There is no other. Except Frith's.'

There was a long silence.

'Bravely put,' Cai said at last. 'But I don't want Frith's bloody world. I can't live in it any more. And I've grown too old to live on dreams. The price is too high.'

She flung up her head. 'Dreams are the only things that last, Cai. And the price is always high for those who would bargain for them with the gods.' A chill slid over her as she heard in her words the echo of her grandmother's voice. 'That was what we really did, all those years ago, wasn't it? Asked the Gods to resurrect the ghosts of Caer Melot, keep Rome alive in Britain? But the Gods are never straight. Their bargains are kept in ways strange to the minds of men . . . and they keep the price hidden.'

'Then your cosmic market is a place of thieves.' Cai's smile was an angry twist of the mouth. 'Murderous thieves, if their true price is the crumbling of our cities, the destruction of Britain.' He thrust his wine-cup into her hand. 'You may scatter your seeds and dream. But I'm a soldier of Mithras. I'll not bow before the demands of your Otherworld rabble! I'm going to Deva. Then I'll find Frith. Before he pursues Cadfan in Gwynedd.'

'You think Frith will listen to you?'

He hesitated. 'We were war-brothers, once,' he replied, evasively.

His face was dark, unreadable. War-brothers or not, Rhianneth thought, Cai's true allegiance lay where it had always lain. It was not altered by ties of blood and love, as was her own. Only for the sake of that old allegiance had he allied with Bernicia against common enemies. A clear-eyed gamble then, for he had always been aware that Elric's ultimate objective was to push the frontiers of Engleland westwards. Why could he not face reality now, and see that nothing could bring back the old peace, the old life of Rome's Britannia?

Something stirred in her mind. Briefly, she closed her eyes. 'There's real darkness coming, Cai. I can feel it. But it's not Frith who will bring it . . . '

'What in Hel are you talking about?'

He was staring at her, a wisp of uncertainty in his eyes.

'I don't know.' Rhianneth raised shaking fingers to her forehead, trying to clear her mind. 'Look, Cai – I'll go with you. Frith will listen to me. At least he'll hold back until Elric . . . '

'He's a wolf, with a bloody pack behind him. He'd brush you aside like a – He saw her wince, and bit off his words. 'Anyway – ' he forced a lighter note into his voice – 'if I let you near the battle area, Elric would kill me!'

Rhianneth raised her chin. 'Let me?' she repeated, with a delicate hauteur that touched the shieldwall of his emotions like a flame. 'If I wish to see my son, I don't need your permission!'

'To leave this city you do, for I command it!' he replied with sudden harshness, his face tightening with the effort of control.

Astonishment and anger struck her silent. The sounds beyond the door faded beneath the thudding of her heart, the slash of rain against the window. He suddenly seemed to her different. Someone she did not know, perhaps had never known.

He turned away. 'I must go. Frith will wait only as long as

it takes to ransack what's left of Deva and re-group his forces.'

At last she found her voice. 'Then I wish you luck. Frith is not easily persuaded.'

'Don't worry,' he replied, 'I'll stop him. One way or another.'

His words hit her with the force of a blow. Words she had heard over and again through many a long grief-filled night. Words that Lovan had spoken before he left Metcaud to murder Urien.

Now their eyes clashed, and in that instant she recognised the look in his. And in that instant she understood his real intent.

'The power will stir again for you . . .´ when you need it . . .'

Wermund's promise echoed, disjointed, through her head. And it's useless, as always! she wanted to scream. Only she knew what lay hidden in Cai's mind, and he must never guess that she understood his true purpose. That would bind her as surely as if he had made her his prisoner. It would prevent her from doing . . . what? Who was there to help her? Mithrasia was ruled by the Fellowship, and Cai ruled the Fellowship. She was alone, only she stood between him and her son's life.

Frith. Images scorched through her brain. She felt again the sweet love that had filled her so long ago, holding him in her arms . . . the terror when she'd thought him dead in the Beacon Tower. She saw him running through the surf with Bebba . . . then wandering along the shore alone, with that hurt, savage look in his eyes that had never again left him. Oh, Gods, Frith?

Fear slid towards panic. She had to stop Cai. In her distress she almost threw herself at his feet weeping, willing to promise anything that would keep him with her and away from Frith. But Cernunnos, Lord of the Wild, remembered all her small sacrifices over the years and awoke in her a deeper instinct. She lowered her eyes and stood still, while reason crept back.

As she watched him, covertly, from beneath her lashes, she saw him pick up his cloak as if to go. Suddenly her whole body turned cold. Her brain cleared, became sharp as splintered ice.

'At least have more wine?' She lifted her eyes to meet his openly. 'It's a long cold road to Deva.'

He gave her a slow, sad smile. 'On that road you first told me your thoughts on war, on the use of cavalry. I knew then you were no ordinary maid. But do you remember how you shied like a wild filly whenever I came near you . . . ?'

I remember only that I felt between us some force, she thought with an inward twist of agony, strong enough for love – or death.

Swiftly she crossed to the wine table. Behind her she heard Cai open a window to look out into the rain-darkened day. 'You are right,' he murmured, 'It's going to be a foul ride.'

A flicker of hope stirred. She stood quite still, the brimming cups in her hands. 'Don't go, Cai. Stay here tonight. With me.'

There was a brief silence. Then he pulled the window shut and latched it. 'That's a tempting offer.' His tone was lightly sardonic. 'But I can't accept. It's too late. Time's short, and my escort's waiting.'

And the whole city is yours to command, she thought. Gods help me, there is no way I can hold you. Nothing I can do. Except . . . this.

She stared into the dark wine, and out of its honied fragrance the scent of cowslips rose up through the vanished years to fill her mind with an aching sweetness.

She clenched her teeth. That was a world away. She was Elric's wife, queen of the two kingdoms he had once promised her; bound to the Englisch people with unbreakable ties of love and loyalty. In their good earth she had left so many beloved dead . . .

Frith was in mortal danger. He would be unguarded, unsuspecting, for Cai was a trusted ally and the father of Reburrus, his friend and brother-in-arms. And Frith was her blood, her bone . . .

'. . . *like the she-wolf you will destroy anything that offers danger to your kin . . . you will spare not a crumb of pity – for anyone . . .* '

Wermund, once more, she thought bitterly, your rune-magic holds more truth that you know.

Turning slowly, she held out the wine-cup. Cai laid down

477

his heavy travelling cloak to take the cup from her. Her mind locked in ice, she watched him drain it.

'That may help me forget the rain.' He replaced the cup on the table. 'But only this will warm that cold road to Deva . . . '

He took her, unresisting, into his arms. His lips were warm on hers, sweet with wine. After a moment as if sensing the numbness within her he drew back uneasily, searching her face. But her eyes were empty of any dark knowledge, and he let out a ragged breath of relief. He had never really known how much of her grandmother was in Rhianneth. Grief for her there would certainly be from this venture, but he did not believe he could have borne at this moment to see the foreshadow of it on her face.

'I have to go,' he whispered, and touched her hair with gentle fingers. 'Alone. Take care, Rhianneth.'

At the door, he looked back. She stood as he had left her beside the table, making no move, no response. He sighed, and raised his hand in a sketchy Roman salute. 'Goodbye, cousin fox-cub.'

Rhianneth stood until the ring of his boots died away and only the occasional splatter of rain on the windows disturbed the quiet of the room. Then she turned in one quick, desperate movement, to lean with clenched fists and bowed head, over the table. Their wine-cups glistened before her, one empty, one brimful. Blindly she thrust out a hand and sent the empty cup spinning away, tiny drops of wine falling as it rolled.

Like a child again, she huddled in the wicker chair; how long, she could not tell. Time meant nothing. She seemed to fall into a trance-like, waking sleep, her mind frozen in chaos.

Only very gradually did she become aware once more of her familiar surroundings, the quiet room; of how cold she was, that her limbs were cramped. Slowly, painfully, she struggled to her feet, crossed to the window and pushed it open, then leant back against the wall to breathe in the wet Samhain wind that lifted her hair and sighed past her into the room beyond.

Time crawled past while the ice within her slowly melted,

running in crystal tears from beneath closed eyes. She felt nothing but a vast emptiness as if life had died within her. A drink . . . not for an enemy, but for a friend . . .

Soon for her, the pain would start. But not for Cai. For him, she had her grandmother's promise that death would seem only the fading of one dream into another. Yet words whispered along the wind; ominous, fearful words, stirring memories of blood sacrifices made to the old Gods to ensure that seeds planted in the dark earth would spring up green, that winter would end and the sun grow stong. '. . . *take care, in the dying of the year . . . when the powers of light and darkness are locked in combat and the world grows dangerous and cries out for blood . . .* '

She heard the opening of the door behind her, and could not stir. She wished whoever it was gone. This time was for her, and for Cai. For the young dreams they had once shared, and for all the haunted years between.

A hand dropped to her shoulder and turned her round, her face still bleak with memories.

'Elric?' she whispered unbelievingly. 'What are you doing . . . here?'

For a moment he did not reply. His grey eyes never left her face. 'I came hoping to find Cai and his cavalry,' he said. 'But it seems I'm too late. He's left to join Frith at Deva.' He touched her tearstained face. 'What a touching farewell that must have been!' he said mockingly. 'How long will you weep for me, Rhianneth?'

'For you?' Her mind stumbled around his words. 'Why should I weep for you?'

His hand fell away from her. He turned, crossed the room to the wine-table.

'Yours?' He indicated the full cup, and without waiting for her answer he righted the fallen one and picked up the jug to pour wine for himself.

'Don't!' She sprang towards him, stumbling in her haste to send the cup ringing to the floor. He caught her in his arms, crushing her against him.

'Hel's Gate! What's wrong with you?'

'Poison-cup . . . ' she whispered.

He froze, staring at her. A slow horror rose in his eyes. 'Rhianneth?' The word seemed to tear, jagged from his throat.

'Not mine. Cai's.'

Silence. She could feel the slow, strong beating of his heart. 'Cai rode out before noon, on the Deva road,' he said blankly.

'He'll never reach Deva. Nor get to Frith. He meant to kill him, you see.'

'*What?*'

'He thinks Frith has become dangerous. To the Fellowship . . . to Mithrasia. A blood-wolf, who must be destroyed – '

'He told you, that? *Cai?*'

Disbelief was plain in his expression, and behind that disbelief was a growing concern. He thinks I'm ill, or mad, she thought without surprise. Perhaps I am. Weariness began to fasten grey fingers around her.

'Ah, no.' She shook her head. 'But I knew. When knowledge flies straight to me – not twisted through fire or stone – it is always certain. As sure as death.'

She eased herself out of his arms and bent to pick up the fallen cup, her face hidden from him by her long dark hair. 'So . . . in this, I put my grandmother's most precious gift. The only power I had, to stop him. To save Frith.' She turned the gleaming thing in her hands, adding forlornly, 'It's quite empty, after all.'

There was a brief silence. Then Elric moved. He took the cup from her hands and crushed it beneath the heel of his boot. He thrust the other wine-cup into her hand.

'Drink it!' he commanded. 'The lot!'

Without a word she obeyed. He refilled the cup. The rich wine ran down her throat and into her blood. Slowly, the cold emptiness within her warmed with returned life and feeling and pain. Naked, raw pain that only the strength of his arms about her contained.

The great battle at Deva. The slaughter of the holy men . . . Reburrus thought lost. Cai's deadly mission. It all came out in a stream of broken, incoherent words.

'Tell me!' she whispered, over and again. 'Tell me there was nothing else I could do!'

'Nothing.' Elric held her close, the grey eyes above her dark head implacable and all doubting gone. 'Hel's snakes, he must have lost his mind! Did he think us like Urien's rabble? That we'd fall apart – or upon each other – if he killed Frith? He knows our battle-law! If the captain's lost – fight on. To the gates of Hel, and through them! By Thunor, if Cai had succeeded I'd have destroyed his city – laid waste this land till twenty years would not have seen it recover!'

He felt her twist of anguish in his arms, and at once his hand pressed against the back of her head, his fingers spreading soothingly into the tumbled hair.

'Don't grieve, *deorling*, for Cai. Only remember you've saved his Alliance, his Mithrasia, and probably his damned Fellowship . . . '

'Fellowship?' she wanted to scream. 'I only thought of our son! Of Frith!' But her throat was choked with salt-tears, and the words came out low and hoarse, muffled against his chest.

When at last she quietened, Elric pushed her into the wicker chair. He smoothed the damp hair back from her forehead, took her hand in his. 'Now I'm going to call for food,' he said. 'All right?'

The room swayed as she tried to drag her thoughts back from the Deva road, to focus her eyes on his face.

'Oh Gods, Elric . . . I'd forgotten how far you've travelled. How is your wound?'

'It's fine,' he replied abruptly. But as he crossed to the door she saw, with a pang, that he was limping badly.

Servants hurried in, bringing cold meats, bread, fruit and wine.

The pale ghost of a smile touched her lips as she watched Elric attack the food with his usual enthusiasm. 'Shall I send for more?'

He shook his head. 'No time. I'm riding to meet an old enemy. Owain is moving south, fast. And Mael Uma is with him.'

Rhianneth's faint smile vanished. 'What?'

'I waited in Bernicia until I was sure which way he intended to jump. Then, we rode breakneck to Mithrasia. Hoped to

481

swell our force with Cai's cavalry.' He shrugged. 'No matter. We'll still give Owain a bloody nose.'

'No, Elric!' Rhianneth gripped the chair arms, her knuckles white. 'You can't go!' Suddenly the air was too thin to breathe. She drew in small shuddering gasps that did not fill her lungs. 'You're injured! How can you fight?'

'There are worse wounds than this.' He looked up suddenly, his eyes bleak.

She slipped from her chair and knelt beside him. 'I can't bear any more,' she said, 'I can't!'

He took one of her hands in his and turning it, dropped a kiss on the palm. 'Oh, the worst is over for you,' he said. 'Isn't it?'

Rhianneth stared at him uncomprehendingly. She lifted his hand, held it against her cheek, and despair rippled in black waves over her. 'Don't go. Please, don't go!'

'And let Owain tear Frith apart?' He shook his head. 'We must hold him back, long enough for our armies at Deva to regroup. Then we'll see the final end of Rheged's power, along with Urien's cubs.'

'But you have only your own war-band with you! How many warriors has Mael Uma brought across from Ireland?'

Again, he shrugged. 'Enough.'

Owain . . . Mael Uma. The names rang with menace through her mind. She thought of Degsa's Stone, and Baldur. Elric? A great wave of terror swept over her, and with it came a revelation of truth so shattering, so devastating, that her throat constricted with shock.

She looked at Elric, at the hard handsome face she knew so well; at the arms that had held her warm while the winter wolves prowled, and her whole body trembled.

Why had she not seen through the mesh of fear and desire, the sharp jealousy, the tenderness that followed the savage birth of their marriage? How could she have been so blind, through all the stormy years? All those years, when Elric had seemed only a disturbing presence who could dissolve her longing for Cai in a scalding cup of passion . . .

Thoughts fluttered through her mind to which her lips

could give no form. Then his grey eyes lifted, looked straight into hers. And all the thoughts twined together to form at last the words so long kept silent and unheeded in her heart.

'I love you, Elric,' she said, hardly above a whisper. 'Don't leave me . . . '

There was a brief silence. Then he trailed a finger down the dry salt paths left along her cheeks by her tears for Cai.

'My *deorling*, you won't stop this pain by using me as your shield. It will have its time, no more, no less. And because Cai must seem to have died naturally, and in honour, you'll have to show on your face only grief for your – cousin. For a gallant ally. The truth, all of it, must be hidden, and will be a thousand times more bitter.' His mouth twisted in a half-smile. 'But you're strong, Rhianneth. You'll fight your way out of this black day into the light again, into life.'

'You are my life!' Her voice cracked with urgency, with the need to reach him. 'Elric, it's you I love, have always loved. Only I . . . don't you understand?'

'No,' he said quietly, 'I don't believe I do. You've never left me in any doubt that Cai held your mind and heart.'

'Oh, I know . . . I know. But – Cai was everything I wanted. He was clever, and gallant, and I shared all his hopes. He was – Rome.' Then she hesitated, amending slowly, 'Marcus's Rome . . . '

Elric said nothing. After a while she went on, desperately searching for the right words. 'At first I – hated you, all those years ago. You were so big, so arrogant. Trampling over – everything . . . ' Her voice trailed, she bowed her head over their joined hands and her loose hair swung forward to hide the sparkle of tears. 'But somehow, sometime, it changed. Perhaps that May morning when you carried me off to Metcaud . . . I never acknowledged it, even to myself. I only know I've been looking at life as once I used to look for pictures in my grandmother's fire; stopping my ears, closing my eyes to anything that prevented me seeing what I wanted to see . . . '

She raised her head once more and looked at him, dreading to find mockery within his silence. It was not there, and his face was white beneath its summer bronze.

'I love you Elric, son of Ida!' she whispered then, casting her pride at his feet. 'I love you with my body, and my heart, and my mind. And if I lose you I shall die.'

He stared at her, without expression. She turned her face away. 'You . . . no longer want me?'

'Want you?' he repeated, after a long moment. 'I've never stopped wanting you since I first saw you at Llywarch's side. But, love?' He paused, then went on with a hesitancy strange to him. 'You . . . knocked love back in my teeth. Each time we seemed to draw closer, it only revealed how little you cared for me. You tested my pride to the limit when you deserted me on our wedding-eve. And Aesc, that wretched minstrel . . . I swear I'll never know for sure why I didn't kill you both. Perhaps because I had a memory, I couldn't lose.' His mouth twisted into a brief, tight smile. 'Or maybe you had bewitched me into love, into holding my honour more cheaply than Ida would ever have done.' He shrugged. 'Whatever it was, I knew that night that I'd lost you. I sealed myself in pride. After a while I came to terms, of a sort, with what we had. But Cai . . . Cai was always a thorn that wounded, Rhianneth. I didn't know, I never knew, what to do. I'm used to situations demanding action. Yet everything I did, or said, drove you further from me.'

She stared up at him, into grey eyes dark with a love so long unnoticed, and recognised beneath his travel-tiredness a deeper weariness than she had ever seen in him before.

'Oh Gods, how I must have hurt you, over the years! If you had only told me, just once, that you loved me . . . '

'You think your dreams of Cai would have vanished?' He shook his head. 'Love's illusions are not so easily dispelled.'

Caldis. The name slithered like ice into Rhianneth's mind. She knew that pain was still buried deep in him. For Caldis's youthful betrayal, and for Brand's calculated treachery.

One wound, at least, I have spared him, she thought. I alone haved borne the weight of that other, darker pain binding Baldur's death within that fatal circle. A rune marked shadow-spear, rising with the power of Caldis's hate and Brand's sorcery, to join the flight of a Deiran weapon at Catraeth . . . She shuddered, and closed off the thought.

'He loves you, any fool can see that . . . ' Lovan's words, that she had once so arrogantly tossed aside. True, for Caldis had been only Elric's boyhood illusion, not his life's love, and Brand had been only the living cord between them when that green passion withered. She knew that, now. Why had it taken her so long to see things straight and clear at last?

'I've been such a blind fool,' she said bleakly, 'And now . . . is it all too late?'

'Too late?' His eyes met hers. 'For what?'

To start again, she wanted to cry, to live together knowing we live with love! But suddenly all her unspoken words seemed worthless, contemptible in their shallowness when seen against the great deeps of anguish that had marked the passing years.

Elric let out his breath on a long sigh, the harsh lines of weariness on his face softened. He cupped her face in his hands and his lips brushed hers, teasing the corners of her mouth.

She felt helpless confusion rise up in her, smothering thought, until only raw longing remained. This, they had always had. But that other, delicate as the violets Lovan used to find for her beneath the snow . . . had that withered and died of cold?

She reached up and let her hands steal around his neck, feeling the tremor that ran through him. At once his hands fell to her shoulders and he stood up, dragging her with him while his mouth claimed hers with a sudden intensity that made the room spin.

Warm joy swooped within her. What is the matter with me? she thought. Elric loved me once. I'll make him love me again. When we're home, it will come to him, as inevitably as the turning of the years. I'll use all the witchery that is still in me, and I'll not need half of it . . .

Elric raised his mouth a hairsbreadth above hers. 'I must go. The light won't hold much longer, and every moment brings Owain nearer.'

His words were like a sword thrust. She had almost forgotten Owain.

'It's all right, Rhianneth!' For just an instant the old

mockery lightly touched his voice. 'We shan't need to hold Owain for long. Just long enough to show him who are the masters of Britain!'

Swiftly her fingers flew up against his lips, muffling the words. 'Ah, take care!' she exclaimed, fearful that his hopes should reach some spiteful God who delighted in thwarting human plans.

He smiled, capturing her hand within his, holding it against his chest. 'I've yet to see Serena's new babe. What will they call her?'

She knew he was talking to distract her, to make light of his dangerous venture against the combined forces of Owain and Mael Uma. To disguise the desperate urgency that was even now making him put her gently from him.

She watched him limp across the room, throw his cloak around his shoulders, and felt a scream of protest rise in her throat.

'Lucina,' she answered, quietly.

He nodded, considering. 'Fine.'

'Elric? Suppose Owain breaks through?'

He paused in the act of fastening the cloak brooch on his shoulder. 'Why then, my *deorling*, I'll show that bloody son of Urien that an Englisch king knows how to die, and with any luck I'll take him with me.' He looked up, and grinned. 'There are worse fates than entering Waelheall with your sword swinging and a battle-song on your lips!'

Her face crumpled. She pressed a fist hard against trembling lips. With two strides he reached her, gathered her into his arms once more, his breath warm against her hair.

'Ah, Rhianneth, don't! Of course I'll be back! We'll hold Owain's pack at bay. You'll see . . . we'll win! Don't we always win, in the end . . . ?'

The day was already darkening, for the time of Samhain was close, the year drawing towards its end. Down the grey hills that shadowed the road north, mist would be rolling, thick, cold, dangerous.

Elric. Her heartbeat faltered, then rallied. Elric would come back to her. He always had, even when the battle-odds were mounted high against him. He must. He was to her the very salt-sting of life itself.

Owain was an old enemy. Elric knew his ways. And the wild fury of Mael Uma's warriors had never been a match for the cool patience of Elric's war-band. Unless . . .

The Gods are strong, but fate is stronger. . .

The fatalistic words of the old saying began to beat remorselessly through her head and she shut her eyes, pressed her hands against her ears, to no avail.

Shivering, she latched the window and turned back into the room. She must go to Serena, tell her about Reburrus. Summon strength enough to comfort her daughter. But not yet. Not yet.

She sat in the wicker chair, laid back her head and closed her eyes. The end of a world, she had told Cai, only half meaning it. Now, it took enormous effort to push away one word, all encompassing and terrible, that threatened to envelope her mind.

Ragnarok.

Already this day was too full of evil. She could bear to stay in it no longer. Escape, she thought. Find comfort out of time, in an old loved place amongst once familiar faces.

She let her mind edge back through the years. Back through the intrigue, the cruelty and the passion of a life in which peace and beauty were interlaced with lies, terror and murderous deeds in a mesh which should make the Gods tremble. Memories stirred, bright and dark, and streaked with sweet fires.

Her fingers closed around the small egg of green crystal which still lay on its slender chain above her heart. Glainnader, source of power for those with the sight and the silent keeper of deeper secrets known only to the Nadredd, the Old Ones. It nestled within her hand, hard in a fading reality and warm with a promise that was old in the centuries before Rome grew great.

The Druid's Glass. Her Serpent's Egg.

She remembered the moment when she first saw it, grasped like a swinging toy by her grandmother in the fierce firelight of a winter night. So long ago. Yet even then the world their fathers had known was, like the legions, the stone cities, the Roman peace, slipping away into the past. The child she had been had felt the threads of fate gathering around her, but the pattern of darkness they would weave she knew she could not have borne, then, to know.

Her grandmother had spoken of sacrifice, of the laws that bounded and honoured it so that the threads of the Universe might not break and the fabric of life crumble back into chaos. Choose a different path, she had pleaded, for the price set by the Gods is always too high . . .

Now Elric had his opening to the western sea, once glimpsed in the enigmatic coils of the Druid's Stone. A road already paid for in blood. Baldur, Lovan, Hrothgar and Bebba, perhaps Reburrus too. And Cai . . .

She had feared the power of the stone, doubted her own capacity to truly see what lay within its symbols. And with reason, for twice she had deceived herself. She had thought Cai carried that flaming torch through darkness – but it was Elric. Terrified by the pictures in the stone she absconded with Idwal and . . . the great legionary city of Eburacum shook, Mithrasia's queen fled into exile, Frith had been born . . . and the tremors of that action were still moving across the years.

Glainnader was a powerful force, dangerous to hold. For the time being it lay hidden and silent, safe above her heart. But almost thirty years had slipped away since that night when crouched at her grandmother's knee she had first held the stone in the palm of her hand. To whom now could she pass it, in the years to come? Serena showed no touch of the old wisdom. Perhaps it always leapt a generation, for her own mother had not had the sight. Her daughter's daughter then, as once her own grandmother had done. To Rowen, or the new-born Lucina . . .

Rhianneth slipped away to wander again through the old house, her feet making no sound on the coloured stones of the picture floor. She bowed her head towards the Lady and her Son on the stone altar. She ran to the kitchen to find Olwen and the men, in from the fields; out to the stables seeking Marcus, and Lovan.

No one was there. Beyond the gate the stream ran clear and untroubled, cowslips grew thick. But in the meadows, no one walked.

Unwilling yet, to let go of the dream that had merged with memory, Rhianneth moaned as Frith's small son Eanfrith touched her wet cheek with a gentle finger.

'Why are you crying . . . ?'

She gasped, caught at his thin little body, holding him against her until the dream dimmed and reality grew strong again.

'For something that has gone,' she managed after a moment, and straightened, brushing away the tears. 'Something I can't reach. Not yet. Perhaps, one day . . . ' She felt something angular and hard between them. 'What's this?'

Eagerly he laid a book in her lap. 'Find it for me!' he pleaded, his face lit with excitement, 'Find the place!'

It was the city annals. Her gift from Llywarch. Rhianneth's faint smile faded. 'Eanfrith? You carried this through the palace? But you know you must never touch a book unless someone is with you.'

He drew back. 'Aunt Serena was reading it to me. When she left the room, I just had to bring it to you. Because you'd never noticed.'

'Noticed what?'

'The magic! It was there all the time. Perhaps you read the wrong words?' He hopped from one leg to the other with impatience. 'Open the book!' he urged her. 'Read about the hero Artur! See how he drew a magic sword from a stone and made himself ruler of Britain! Bretwalda!'

Rhianneth looked at him. 'Oh, Eanfrith.'

But he scarcely heard her. His attention was all on the book in her lap. She sighed opened it, and turned the entry for Badon.

Gently mocking laughter, Llywarch's and her own, trembled across the span of years, trailing sadness. Already, she thought, the true bright memory of Badon is passing away, though we were so sure it would endure forever. Now a sword lies across Artur's heartland, and his fortress Caer Melot has vanished as if ensorcered, behind it.

Where now were those who had fought beside Artur? Had known the fierce blaze of his youth, or the last bitter years that ended at Camlann? Who was left, to bear true witness when memory died? How long before all that great endeavour was quite forgotten?

As Artur's battlemaid she had entered the camp of the Saxons, had sown her seeds, lit her lamps against the long wintertime of the north. But against such a darkness as she felt now approaching, more was needed than was in her power.

The book grew heavy within her hands. Weary despair spilled over, and a tear fell bleakly on the open page. In thick silence she wiped it away with a careful finger.

And in touching the painted words, light came like a swordflash in the sun and her mind opened. Almost it was as if the Keeper himself stood close by with his smile twisted out of an old pain, his clear bright eyes that missed nothing; not the owl's flight nor the trail of the fox, nor things kept hidden in the minds of men.

Lovan's words rang through her mind. '*Some bright scrap of magic . . . to stir their blood . . . bind them close to Britain.*' Within this book was magic, magic deep-dyed and substantial enough to weave a linking legend between the minds of Roman, Celt and Saxon. Sorcery, powerful enough to sweeten the long night though it should last half a thousand years, while the winter shoots grew green.

Once in anger she had accused Cai of being held in thrall by Caer Melot. Of living for a dream of returning Empire. But all men needed a dream to live by. And maybe, to die for.

Ah, Cai, she thought, you drew me into that circle of enchantment after all, even though the way forked and we walked apart. Now here, at last, is my parting gift to you. Lifted from the heart of Caer Melot's ruin and given in love for all we once shared, and with hope for the future.

Eanfrith was leaning against her, waiting. His eyes moved anxiously, uneasily, from the open book to her face, and back again.

She straightened in her chair. 'Bring me the small lamp from the shelf on the wall,' she said, 'and carry it carefully, for it's already lit.'

The child placed the lamp on the table nearby, shielding its flame until it steadied, his face intent. The day's evil crouched back into the shadowed corners of the room. Even Owain began to seem only a hunting bird that screeched in the night.

'Now, let me look again.'

Rhianneth moved the book until the pale light fell across the page. Softly she began to translate the Latin into Englisch. When she reached the vital line she hesitated, glancing up. The child waited, his eyes luminous with trust.

'Why, you're right!' she said slowly. 'How could I have missed that before?'

Eanfrith watched Rhianneth's face, almost holding his breath. 'And it *was* magic,' he ventured, at last, 'Artur's sword?'

Rhianneth drew Frith's son closer, her eyes shining, beautiful in the soft glow of the lamp.

'When Artur held it, it was,' she said. 'And it will be, again. For all the Gods of Britain . . . and for all of us.'

'I knew it! I knew Artur would have magic! How else can a hero fight monsters and giants and demons and dragons?'

'How indeed?'

Rhianneth lowered her eyes once more to the book, thinking of their outnumbered war-band moving north through the gathering darkness towards the enemy, towards the sweat and filth of one more bloody battle. What was it Elric had once told her? Men aimed high, so that their glory-threads might light the way for Gods and heroes on the plain of Vigrid . . .

Then, she had understood nothing. Now into her mind came an image of the ancient ruined cities of which Marcus had spoken so long ago, as they rode together beneath the first evening stars. For those people Ragnarok came, she thought, just as it will come again. And again. Down through the endless spiral of time Empires would fall, cities crumble. Love, and life, be lost.

But now at last she saw that if but one legion stood against the hordes of chaos, one ship dared another Odyssey – or one child stretched tip-toe to hear of Beowulf or Artur – there could be no true darkness of the mind. The monsters, the frost-giants who pulled down Man's best endeavours, who could freeze even thought itself, would not prevail while those frail lights still burned. For only with their extinction could real night fall, and the last battle be lost.

AFTERWORD

The joined kingdoms of Bernicia and Deira rose, as Northumbria, to become a great and powerful kingdom, despite constant wars.

A vivid Latin culture sprang up and a still more remarkable artistic achievement produced fine poetry, both pagan and Christian, as well as magnificent illuminated manuscripts such as the Northumbrian Book of Jarrow and the Lindisfarne Gospels. By the eighth century, Northumbria had become a power house of civilisation, drawing strength from a potent blending of Celtic, Roman and English cultures which was unique amongst the kingdoms of Britain.

It has been said that without this period of comparative stability and achievement in the north, England might not have had strength enough to withstand the first onslaughts of the pagan Vikings.

England survived this longest and darkest period in the Island's history, enabling the Christian Church to preserve into the Middle Ages the great achievements of the past.

DOOM OF THE DARKSWORD
by Margaret Weis & Tracy Hickman

Born without magic, Joram was one of the Dead, denied the throne of Merlion. For years, he lived among outlaws, surviving by wit and sleight-of-hand.

Now, wielding the powerful, magic-absorbing Darksword, Joram returns to the enchanted Kingdom that once was his home to win revenge and claim his birthright. Here he will test Bishop Vanya and his fierce army of Duuktsarith in a battle unlike any their world has known.

Joined by the scholarly catalyst Saryon, the young mage Mosiah, and the trickster Simkin, Joram confronts the shattering secret of his past and discovers the ancient prophecy that puts the fate of the world in his hands—the hands that forged the Darksword.

0 553 17535 1

FORGING THE DARKSWORD
by Margaret Weis & Tracy Hickman

In the enchanted realm of Merlion, magic is life.

Born without magical abilities and denied his birthright, Joram
is left for dead. Yet he grows to manhood in a remote country
village, hiding his lack of powers only through constant
vigilance and ever more skilful sleight-of-hand, until he can
keep his secret no longer, fleeing to the Outlands, Joram joins
the outlawed technologists, who practice the long forbidden
arts of science.

Here he meets the scholarly catalyst Saryon, in the midst of a
battle of wits and power with a renegade warlock of the dark
Duuk-tsarith caste. Together, Joram and Saryon begin their
quest toward a greater destiny – and the forging of the
powerful, magic-absorbing Darksword.

0553 175866

A SELECTION OF
SCIENCE FICTION AND FANTASY TITLES
AVAILABLE FROM BANTAM BOOKS

THE PRICES SHOWN BELOW WERE CORRECT AT THE TIME OF GOING TO PRESS. HOWEVER TRANSWORLD PUBLISHERS RESERVE THE RIGHT TO SHOW NEW RETAIL PRICES ON COVERS WHICH MAY DIFFER FROM THOSE PREVIOUSLY ADVERTISED IN THE TEXT OR ELSEWHERE.

All Corgi/Bantam Books are available at your bookshop or newsagent, or can be ordered from the following address:

Corgi/Bantam Books.
Cash Sales Department
P.O. Box 11, Falmouth, Cornwall TR10 9EN

Please send a cheque or postal order (no currency) and allow 60p for postage and packing for the first book plus 25p for the second book and 15p for each additional book ordered up to a maximum charge of £1.90 in UK.

B.F.P.O. customers please allow 60p for the first book, 25p for the second book plus 15p per copy for the next 7 books, thereafter 9p per book.

Overseas customers, including Eire, please allow £1.25 for postage and packing for the first book, 75p for the second book, and 28p for each subsequent title ordered.